D1108293

Sir Arthur Conan Doyle

THE BEST OF SHERLOCK HOLMES

*This limited edition
is published by
The Franklin Library
exclusively for subscribers to*
THE COLLECTED STORIES OF
THE WORLD'S GREATEST WRITERS

SIR ARTHUR CONAN DOYLE
by Walter Rane

Sir Arthur Conan Doyle

THE BEST OF
SHERLOCK HOLMES

Illustrated by Ben F. Stahl

A LIMITED EDITION

THE FRANKLIN LIBRARY
Franklin Center, Pennsylvania
1977

© Baskervilles Investments Ltd.

© 1977 Franklin Mint Corporation
Printed in the United States of America

Contents

A Scandal in Bohemia

To Sherlock Holmes she is always *the* woman. I have seldom heard him mention her under any other name. In his eyes she eclipses and predominates the whole of her sex. It was not that he felt any emotion akin to love for Irene Adler. All emotions, and that one particularly, were abhorrent to his cold, precise but admirably balanced mind. He was, I take it, the most perfect reasoning and observing machine that the world has seen, but as a lover he would have placed himself in a false position. He never spoke of the softer passions, save with a gibe and a sneer. They were admirable things for the observer—excellent for drawing the veil from men's motives and actions. But for the trained reasoner to admit such intrusions into his own delicate and finely adjusted temperament was to introduce a distracting factor which might throw a doubt upon all his mental results. Grit in a sensitive instrument, or a crack in one of his own high-power lenses, would not be more disturbing than a strong emotion in a nature such as his. And yet there was but one woman to him, and that woman was the late Irene Adler, of dubious and questionable memory.

I had seen little of Holmes lately. My marriage had drifted us away from each other. My own complete happiness, and the home-centred interests which rise up around the man who first finds himself master of his own establishment, were sufficient to absorb all my attention, while Holmes, who loathed every form of society with his whole Bohemian soul, remained in our lodgings in Baker Street, buried among his old books, and alternating from week to week between cocaine and ambition, the drowsiness of the drug and the fierce energy of his own keen nature. He was still, as ever, deeply attracted by the study of crime and occupied his immense faculties and extraordinary powers of observation in following out those clues and clearing up those mysteries which had been abandoned as hopeless by the official police. From time to time I heard some vague account of his doings: of his summons to Odessa in the case of the Trepoff murder, of his clearing up of the singular tragedy of the Atkinson brothers at Trincomalee, and finally of the mission which he had accomplished so delicately and successfully for the reigning family of Holland. Beyond these signs of his activity, however, which I merely shared with all the readers of the daily press, I knew little of my former friend and companion.

One night—it was on the twentieth of March, 1888—I was returning from a journey to a patient (for I had now returned to civil practice) when my way led me through Baker Street. As I passed the well-remembered door, which must always be associated in my mind with my wooing, and with the dark incidents of *A Study in Scarlet*, I was seized with a keen desire to see Holmes again and to know how he was employing his extraordinary powers. His rooms were brilliantly lit, and even as I looked up, I saw his tall, spare figure pass twice in a dark silhouette against the blind. He was pacing the room swiftly, eagerly, with his head sunk upon his chest and his hands clasped behind him. To me, who knew his every mood and habit, his attitude and manner told their own story. He was at work again. He had risen out of his drug-created dreams and was hot upon the scent of some new problem. I rang the bell and was shown up to the chamber which had formerly been in part my own.

His manner was not effusive. It seldom was; but he was glad, I think, to see me. With hardly a word spoken, but with a kindly eye, he waved me to an armchair, threw

across his case of cigars, and indicated a spirit case and a gasogene in the corner. Then he stood before the fire and looked me over in his singular introspective fashion.

"Wedlock suits you," he remarked. "I think, Watson, that you have put on seven and a half pounds since I saw you."

"Seven!" I answered.

"Indeed, I should have thought a little more. Just a trifle more, I fancy, Watson. And in practice again, I observe. You did not tell me that you intended to go into harness."

"Then, how do you know?"

"I see it, I deduce it. How do I know that you have been getting yourself very wet lately and that you have a most clumsy and careless servant girl?"

"My dear Holmes," said I, "this is too much. You would certainly have been burned had you lived a few centuries ago. It is true that I had a country walk on Thursday and came home in a dreadful mess, but as I have changed my clothes I can't imagine how you deduce it. As to Mary Jane, she is incorrigible, and my wife has given her notice; but there, again, I fail to see how you work it out."

He chuckled to himself and rubbed his long, nervous hands together.

"It is simplicity itself," said he; "my eyes tell me that on the inside of your left shoe, just where the firelight strikes it, the leather is scored by six almost parallel cuts. Obviously they have been caused by someone who has very carelessly scraped round the edges of the sole in order to remove crusted mud from it. Hence, you see, my double deduction that you had been out in vile weather and that you had a particularly malignant boot-slitting specimen of the London slavey. As to your practice, if a gentleman walks into my rooms smelling of iodoform, with a black mark of nitrate of silver upon his right forefinger and a bulge on the right side of his top-hat to show where he has secreted his stethoscope, I must be dull, indeed, if I do not pronounce him to be an active member of the medical profession."

I could not help laughing at the ease with which he explained his process of deduction. "When I hear you give your reasons," I remarked, "the thing always appears to me to be so ridiculously simple that I could easily do it myself, though at each successive instance of your reasoning I am baffled until you explain your process. And yet I believe that my eyes are as good as yours."

"Quite so," he answered, lighting a cigarette and throwing himself down into an armchair. "You see, but you do not observe. The distinction is clear. For example, you have frequently seen the steps which lead up from the hall to this room."

"Frequently."

"How often?"

"Well, some hundreds of times."

"Then how many are there?"

"How many? I don't know."

"Quite so! You have not observed. And yet you have seen. That is just my point. Now, I know that there are seventeen steps, because I have both seen and observed. By the way, since you are interested in these little problems, and since you are good enough to chronicle one or two of my trifling experiences, you may be interested in this." He threw over a sheet of thick, pink-tinted note-paper which had been lying open upon the table. "It came by the last post," said he. "Read it aloud."

The note was undated and without either signature or address.

"There will call upon you to-night, at a quarter to eight o'clock," I read, "a gentleman who desires to consult you upon a matter of the very deepest moment. Your recent services to one of the royal houses of Europe have shown that you are one who may safely be trusted with matters which are of an importance which can hardly be exaggerated. This account of you we have from all quarters received. Be in your chamber then at that hour, and do not take it amiss if your visitor wear a mask."

"This is indeed a mystery," I remarked. "What do you imagine that it means?"

"I have no data yet. It is a capital mistake to theorise before one has data. Insensibly one begins to twist facts to suit theories, instead of theories to suit facts. But the note itself. What do you deduce from it?"

I carefully examined the writing and the paper upon which it was written.

"The man who wrote it was presumably well to do," I remarked, endeavouring to imitate my companion's processes. "Such paper could not be bought under half a crown a packet. It is peculiarly strong and stiff."

"Peculiar—that is the very word," said Holmes. "It is not an English paper at all. Hold it up to the light."

I did so and saw a large *E* with a small *g*, a *P,* and a large *G* with a small *t* woven into the texture of the paper.

"What do you make of that?" asked Holmes.

"The name of the maker, no doubt; or his monogram, rather."

"Not at all. The *G* with the small *t* stands for *Gesellschaft,* which is the German for 'Company.' It is a customary contraction like our 'Co.' *P*, of course, stands for *Papier.* Now for the *Eg.* Let us glance at our Continental Gazetteer." He took down a heavy brown volume from his shelves. "Eglow, Eglonitz—here we are, Egria. It is in a German-speaking country—in Bohemia, not far from Carlsbad. 'Remarkable as being the scene of the death of Wallenstein, and for its numerous glass-factories and paper-mills.' Ha, ha, my boy, what do you make of that?" His eyes sparkled, and he sent up a great blue triumphant cloud from his cigarette.

"The paper was made in Bohemia," I said.

"Precisely. And the man who wrote the note is a German. Do you note the peculiar construction of the sentence—'This account of you we have from all quarters received.' A Frenchman or Russian could not have written that. It is the German who is so uncourteous to his verbs. It only remains, therefore, to discover what is wanted by this German who writes upon Bohemian paper and prefers wearing a mask to showing his face. And here he comes, if I am not mistaken, to resolve all our doubts."

As he spoke there was the sharp sound of horses' hoofs and grating wheels against the curb, followed by a sharp pull at the bell. Holmes whistled.

"A pair, by the sound," said he. "Yes," he continued, glancing out of the window. "A nice little brougham and a pair of beauties. A hundred and fifty guineas apiece. There's money in this case, Watson, if there is nothing else."

"I think that I had better go, Holmes."

"Not a bit, Doctor. Stay where you are. I am lost without my Boswell. And this promises to be interesting. It would be a pity to miss it."

"But your client—"

"Never mind him. I may want your help, and so may he. Here he comes. Sit down in that armchair, Doctor, and give us your best attention."

A slow and heavy step, which had been heard upon the stairs and in the passage, paused immediately outside the door. Then there was a loud and authoritative tap.

"Come in!" said Holmes.

A man entered who could hardly have been less than six feet six inches in height, with the chest and limbs of a Hercules. His dress was rich with a richness which would, in England, be looked upon as akin to bad taste. Heavy bands of astrakhan were slashed across the sleeves and fronts of his double-breasted coat, while the deep blue cloak which was thrown over his shoulders was lined with flame-coloured silk and secured at the neck with a brooch which consisted of a single flaming beryl. Boots which extended halfway up his calves, and which were trimmed at the tops with rich brown fur, completed the impression of barbaric opulence which was suggested by his whole appearance. He carried a broad-brimmed hat in his hand, while he wore across the upper part of his face, extending down past the cheekbones, a black vizard mask, which he had apparently adjusted that very moment, for his hand was still raised to it as he entered. From the lower part of the face he appeared to be a man of strong character, with a thick,

7

hanging lip, and a long, straight chin suggestive of resolution pushed to the length of obstinacy.

"You had my note?" he asked with a deep, harsh voice
and a strongly marked German accent. "I told you that I
would call." He looked from one to the other of us, as if
uncertain which to address.

"Pray take a seat," said Holmes. "This is my friend and
colleague, Dr. Watson, who is occasionally good enough
to help me in my cases. Whom have I the honour to
address?"

"You may address me as the Count von Kramm, a
Bohemian nobleman. I understand that this gentleman,
your friend, is a man of honour and discretion, whom I
may trust with a matter of the most extreme importance.
If not, I should much prefer to communicate with you
alone."

I rose to go, but Holmes caught me by the wrist and
pushed me back into my chair. "It is both, or none," said
he. "You may say before this gentleman anything which
you may say to me."

The Count shrugged his broad shoulders. "Then I must
begin," said he, "by binding you both to absolute secrecy
for two years; at the end of that time the matter will be of
no importance. At present it is not too much to say that it is
of such weight it may have an influence upon European
history."

"I promise," said Holmes.

"And I."

"You will excuse this mask," continued our strange visitor. "The august person who employs me wishes his agent
to be unknown to you, and I may confess at once that the
title by which I have just called myself is not exactly
my own."

"I was aware of it," said Holmes drily.

"The circumstances are of great delicacy, and every precaution has to be taken to quench what might grow to be
an immense scandal and seriously compromise one of the
reigning families of Europe. To speak plainly, the matter

implicates the great House of Ormstein, hereditary kings of Bohemia."

"I was also aware of that," murmured Holmes, settling himself down in his armchair and closing his eyes.

Our visitor glanced with some apparent surprise at the languid, lounging figure of the man who had been no doubt depicted to him as the most incisive reasoner and most energetic agent in Europe. Holmes slowly reopened his eyes and looked impatiently at his gigantic client.

"If Your Majesty would condescend to state your case," he remarked, "I should be better able to advise you."

The man sprang from his chair and paced up and down the room in uncontrollable agitation. Then, with a gesture of desperation, he tore the mask from his face and hurled it upon the ground. "You are right," he cried; "I am the King. Why should I attempt to conceal it?"

"Why, indeed?" murmured Holmes. "Your Majesty had not spoken before I was aware that I was addressing Wilhelm Gottsreich Sigismond von Ormstein, Grand Duke of Cassel-Felstein, and hereditary King of Bohemia."

"But you can understand," said our strange visitor, sitting down once more and passing his hand over his high white forehead, "you can understand that I am not accustomed to doing such business in my own person. Yet the matter was so delicate that I could not confide it to an agent without putting myself in his power. I have come incognito from Prague for the purpose of consulting you."

"Then, pray consult," said Holmes, shutting his eyes once more.

"The facts are briefly these: Some five years ago, during a lengthy visit to Warsaw, I made the acquaintance of the well-known adventuress, Irene Adler. The name is no doubt familiar to you."

"Kindly look her up in my index, Doctor," murmured Holmes without opening his eyes. For many years he had adopted a system of docketing all paragraphs concerning men and things, so that it was difficult to name a subject or a person on which he could not at once furnish information. In this case I found her biography sandwiched in between that of a Hebrew rabbi and that of a staff-commander who had written a monograph upon the deep-sea fishes.

"Let me see!" said Holmes. "Hum! Born in New Jersey in the year 1858. Contralto—hum! La Scala, hum! Prima donna Imperial Opera of Warsaw—yes! Retired from operatic stage—ha! Living in London—quite so! Your Majesty, as I understand, became entangled with this young person, wrote her some compromising letters, and is now desirous of getting those letters back."

"Precisely so. But how—"

"Was there a secret marriage?"

"None."

"No legal papers or certificates?"

"None."

"Then I fail to follow Your Majesty. If this young person should produce her letters for blackmailing or other purposes, how is she to prove their authenticity?"

"There is the writing."

"Pooh, pooh! Forgery."

"My private note-paper."

"Stolen."

"My own seal."

"Imitated."

"My photograph."

"Bought."

"We were both in the photograph."

"Oh, dear! This is very bad! Your Majesty has indeed committed an indiscretion."

"I was mad—insane."

"You have compromised yourself seriously."

"I was only Crown Prince then. I was young. I am but thirty now."

"It must be recovered."

"We have tried and failed."

"Your Majesty must pay. It must be bought."

"She will not sell."

"Stolen, then."

"Five attempts have been made. Twice burglars in my pay ransacked her house. Once we diverted her luggage when she travelled. Twice she has been waylaid. There has been no result."

"No sign of it?"

"Absolutely none."

Holmes laughed. "It is quite a pretty little problem," said he.

"But a very serious one to me," returned the King reproachfully.

"Very, indeed. And what does she propose to do with the photograph?"

"To ruin me."

"But how?"

"I am about to be married."

"So I have heard."

"To Clotilde Lothman von Saxe-Meningen, second daughter of the King of Scandinavia. You may know the strict principles of her family. She is herself the very soul of delicacy. A shadow of a doubt as to my conduct would bring the matter to an end."

"And Irene Adler?"

"Threatens to send them the photograph. And she will do it. I know that she will do it. You do not know her, but she has a soul of steel. She has the face of the most beautiful of women, and the mind of the most resolute of men. Rather than I should marry another woman, there are no lengths to which she would not go—none."

"You are sure that she has not sent it yet?"

"I am sure."

"And why?"

"Because she has said that she would send it on the day when the betrothal was publicly proclaimed. That will be next Monday."

"Oh, then we have three days yet," said Holmes with a yawn. "That is very fortunate, as I have one or two matters of importance to look into just at present. Your Majesty will, of course, stay in London for the present?"

"Certainly. You will find me at the Langham under the name of the Count von Kramm."

"Then I shall drop you a line to let you know how we progress."

"Pray do so. I shall be all anxiety."

"Then, as to money?"

"You have carte blanche."

"Absolutely?"

"I tell you that I would give one of the provinces of my kingdom to have that photograph."

"And for present expenses?"

The King took a heavy chamois leather bag from under his cloak and laid it on the table.

"There are three hundred pounds in gold and seven hundred in notes," he said.

Holmes scribbled a receipt upon a sheet of his note-book and handed it to him.

"And Mademoiselle's address?" he asked.

"Is Briony Lodge, Serpentine Avenue, St. John's Wood."

Holmes took a note of it. "One other question," said he. "Was the photograph a cabinet-size?"

"It was."

"Then, good-night, Your Majesty, and I trust that we shall soon have some good news for you. And good-night, Watson," he added, as the wheels of the royal brougham rolled down the street. "If you will be good enough to call to-morrow afternoon at three o'clock, I should like to chat this little matter over with you."

2

At three o'clock precisely I was at Baker Street, but Holmes had not yet returned. The landlady informed me that he had left the house shortly after eight o'clock in the morning. I sat down beside the fire, however, with the intention of awaiting him, however long he might be. I was already deeply interested in his inquiry, for, though it was surrounded by none of the grim and strange features which were associated with the two crimes which I have already recorded, still, the nature of the case and the exalted station of his client gave it a character of its own. Indeed, apart from the nature of the investigation which my friend had on hand, there was something in his masterly grasp of a situation and his keen, incisive reasoning which made it a pleasure to me to study his system of work and to follow the quick, subtle methods by which he disentangled the most inextricable mysteries. So accustomed was I to his invariable success that the very possibility of his failing had ceased to enter into my head.

It was close upon four before the door opened, and a drunken-looking groom, ill-kempt and side-whiskered, with an inflamed face and disreputable clothes, walked into the room. Accustomed as I was to my friend's amazing powers in the use of disguises, I had to look three times before I was certain that it was indeed he. With a nod he vanished into the bedroom, whence he emerged in five minutes tweed-suited and respectable, as of old. Putting his hands into his pockets, he stretched out his legs in front of the fire and laughed heartily for some minutes.

"Well, really!" he cried, and then he choked and laughed again until he was obliged to lie back, limp and helpless, in the chair.

"What is it?"

"It's quite too funny. I am sure you could never guess how I employed my morning, or what I ended by doing."

"I can't imagine. I suppose that you have been watching the habits, and perhaps the house, of Miss Irene Adler."

"Quite so; but the sequel was rather unusual. I will tell you, however. I left the house a little after eight o'clock this morning in the character of a groom out of work. There is a wonderful sympathy and freemasonry among horsy men. Be one of them, and you will know all that there is to know. I soon found Briony Lodge. It is a *bijou* villa, with a garden at the back, but built out in front right up to the road, two stories. Chubb lock to the door. Large sitting-room on the right side, well furnished, with long windows almost to the floor, and those preposterous English window fasteners which a child could open. Behind there was nothing remarkable, save that the passage window could be reached from the top of the coach-house. I walked round it and examined it closely from every point of view, but without noting anything else of interest.

"I then lounged down the street and found, as I expected, that there was a mews in a lane which runs down by one wall of the garden. I lent the ostlers a hand in rubbing down their horses and received in exchange twopence, a glass of half and half, two fills of shag tobacco, and as much information as I could desire about Miss Adler, to say nothing of half a dozen other people in the neighbourhood in whom I was not in the least interested, but whose biographies I was compelled to listen to."

"And what of Irene Adler?" I asked.

"Oh, she has turned all the men's heads down in that part. She is the daintiest thing under a bonnet on this planet. So say the Serpentine-mews, to a man. She lives quietly, sings at concerts, drives out at five every day, and returns at seven sharp for dinner. Seldom goes out at other times, except when she sings. Has only one male visitor, but a good deal of him. He is dark, handsome, and dashing, never calls less than once a day, and often twice. He is a Mr. Godfrey Norton, of the Inner Temple. See the advantages of a cabman as a confidant. They had driven him home a dozen times from Serpentine-mews and knew all about him. When I had listened to all they had to tell, I began to walk up and down near Briony Lodge once more, and to think over my plan of campaign.

"This Godfrey Norton was evidently an important factor in the matter. He was a lawyer. That sounded ominous. What was the relation between them, and what the object of his repeated visits? Was she his client, his friend, or his mistress? If the former, she had probably transferred the photograph to his keeping. If the latter, it was less likely. On the issue of this question depended whether

I should continue my work at Briony Lodge or turn my attention to the gentleman's chambers in the Temple. It was a delicate point, and it widened the field of my inquiry. I fear that I bore you with these details, but I have to let you see my little difficulties if you are to understand the situation."

"I am following you closely," I answered.

"I was still balancing the matter in my mind when a hansom cab drove up to Briony Lodge, and a gentleman sprang out. He was a remarkably handsome man—dark, aquiline, and moustached—evidently the man of whom I had heard. He appeared to be in a great hurry, shouted to the cabman to wait, and brushed past the maid who opened the door, with the air of a man who was thoroughly at home.

"He was in the house about half an hour, and I could catch glimpses of him in the windows of the sitting-room, pacing up and down, talking excitedly, and waving his arms. Of her I could see nothing. Presently he emerged, looking even more flurried than before. As he stepped up to the cab, he pulled a gold watch from his pocket and looked at it earnestly. 'Drive like the devil,' he shouted, 'first to Gross & Hankey's in Regent Street, and then to the Church of St. Monica in the Edgeware Road. Half a guinea if you do it in twenty minutes!'

"Away they went, and I was just wondering whether I should not do well to follow them when up the lane came a neat little landau, the coachman with his coat only half-buttoned, and his tie under his ear, while all the tags of his harness were sticking out of the buckles. It hadn't pulled up before she shot out of the hall door and into it. I only caught a glimpse of her at the moment, but she was a lovely woman, with a face that a man might die for.

"'The Church of St. Monica, John,' she cried, 'and half a sovereign if you reach it in twenty minutes.'

"This was quite too good to lose, Watson. I was just balancing whether I should run for it or whether I should perch behind her landau, when a cab came through the street. The driver looked twice at such a shabby fare, but I jumped in before he could object. 'The Church of St. Monica,' said I, 'and half a sovereign if you reach it in twenty minutes.' It was twenty-five minutes to twelve, and of course it was clear enough what was in the wind.

"My cabby drove fast. I don't think I ever drove faster, but the others were there before us. The cab and the landau with their steaming horses were in front of the door when I arrived. I paid the man and hurried into the church. There was not a soul there save the two whom I had followed and a surpliced clergyman, who seemed to be expostulating with them. They were all three standing in a knot in front of the altar. I lounged up the side aisle like any other idler who has dropped into a church. Suddenly, to my surprise, the three at the altar faced round to me, and Godfrey Norton came running as hard as he could towards me.

"'Thank God,' he cried. 'You'll do. Come! Come!'

"'What then?' I asked.

"'Come, man, come, only three minutes, or it won't be legal.'

"I was half-dragged up to the altar, and before I knew where I was I found myself mumbling responses which were whispered in my ear, and vouching for things of which I knew nothing, and generally assisting in the secure tying up of Irene Adler, spinster, to Godfrey Norton, bachelor. It was all done in an instant, and there was the gentleman thanking me on the one side and the lady on the other, while the clergyman beamed on me in front. It was the most preposterous position in which I ever found myself in my life, and it was the thought of it that started me laughing just now. It seems that there had been some informality about their licence, that the clergyman absolutely refused to marry them without a witness of some sort, and that my lucky appearance saved the bridegroom from having to sally out into the streets in search of a best man. The bride gave me a sovereign, and I mean to wear it on my watch-chain in memory of the occasion."

"This is a very unexpected turn of affairs," said I; "and what then?"

"Well, I found my plans very seriously menanced. It looked as if the pair might take an immediate departure and so necessitate very prompt and energetic measures on my part. At the church door, however, they separated, he driving back to the Temple, and she to her own house. 'I shall drive out in the park at five as usual,' she said as she left him. I heard no more. They drove away in different directions, and I went off to make my own arrangements."

"Which are?"

"Some cold beef and a glass of beer," he answered, ringing the bell. "I have been too busy to think of food, and I am likely to be busier still this evening. By the way, Doctor, I shall want your co-operation."

"I shall be delighted."

"You don't mind breaking the law?"

"Not in the least."

"Nor running a chance of arrest?"

"Not in a good cause."

"Oh, the cause is excellent!"

"Then I am your man."

"I was sure that I might rely on you."

"But what is it you wish?"

"When Mrs. Turner has brought in the tray I will make it clear to you. Now," he said as he turned hungrily on the simple fare that our landlady had provided, "I must discuss it while I eat, for I have not much time. It is nearly five now. In two hours we must be on the scene of action. Miss Irene, or Madame, rather, returns from her drive at seven. We must be at Briony Lodge to meet her."

"And what then?"

"You must leave that to me. I have already arranged what is to occur. There is only one point on which I must insist. You must not interfere, come what may. You understand?"

"I am to be neutral?"

"To do nothing whatever. There will probably be some

small unpleasantness. Do not join in it. It will end in my being conveyed into the house. Four or five minutes afterwards the sitting-room window will open. You are to station yourself close to that open window."

"Yes."

"You are to watch me, for I will be visible to you."

"Yes."

"And when I raise my hand—so—you will throw into the room what I give you to throw, and will, at the same time, raise the cry of 'fire!' You quite follow me?"

"Entirely."

"It is nothing very formidable," he said, taking a long cigar-shaped roll from his pocket. "It is an ordinary plumber's smoke-rocket, fitted with a cap at either end to make it self-lighting. Your task is confined to that. When you raise your cry of fire, it will be taken up by quite a number of people. You may then walk to the end of the street, and I will rejoin you in ten minutes. I hope that I have made myself clear?"

"I am to remain neutral, to get near the window, to watch you, and at the signal to throw in this object, then to raise the cry of 'fire!' and to wait you at the corner of the street."

"Precisely."

"Then you may entirely rely on me."

"That is excellent. I think, perhaps, it is almost time that I prepare for the new rôle I have to play."

He disappeared into his bedroom and returned in a few minutes in the character of an amiable and simple-minded Nonconformist clergyman. His broad black hat, his baggy trousers, his white tie, his sympathetic smile, and general look of peering and benevolent curiosity were such as Mr. John Hare alone could have equalled. It was not merely that Holmes changed his costume. His expression, his manner, his very soul seemed to vary with every fresh part that he assumed. The stage lost a fine actor, even as science lost an acute reasoner, when he became a specialist in crime.

It was a quarter past six when we left Baker Street, and it still wanted ten minutes to the hour when we found ourselves in Serpentine Avenue. It was already dusk, and the lamps were just being lighted as we paced up and down in front of Briony Lodge, waiting for the coming of its occupant. The house was just such as I had pictured it from Sherlock Holmes's succinct description, but the locality appeared to be less private than I expected. On the contrary, for a small street in a quiet neighbourhood, it was remarkably animated. There was a group of shabbily dressed men smoking and laughing in a corner, a scissors-grinder with his wheel, two guardsmen who were flirting with a nurse-girl, and several well-dressed young men who were lounging up and down with cigars in their mouths.

"You see," remarked Holmes, as we paced to and fro in front of the house, "this marriage rather simplifies matters. The photograph becomes a double-edged weapon now. The chances are that she would be as averse to its being seen by Mr. Godfrey Norton as our client is to its coming to the eyes of his Princess. Now the question is, Where are we to find the photograph?"

"Where, indeed?"

"It is most unlikely that she carries it about with her. It is a cabinet-size. Too large for easy concealment about a woman's dress. She knows that the King is capable of having her waylaid and searched. Two attempts of the sort have already been made. We may take it, then, that she does not carry it about with her."

"Where, then?"

"Her banker or her lawyer. There is that double possibility. But I am inclined to think neither. Women are naturally secretive, and they like to do their own secreting. Why should she hand it over to anyone else? She could trust her own guardianship, but she could not tell what indirect or political influence might be brought to bear upon a business man. Besides, remember that she had resolved to use it within a few days. It must be where she can lay her hands upon it. It must be in her own house."

"But it has twice been burgled."

"Pshaw! They did not know how to look."

"But how will you look?"

"I will not look."

"What then?"

"I will get her to show me."

"But she will refuse."

"She will not be able to. But I hear the rumble of wheels. It is her carriage. Now carry out my orders to the letter."

As he spoke the gleam of the side-lights of a carriage came round the curve of the avenue. It was a smart little landau which rattled up to the door of Briony Lodge. As it pulled up, one of the loafing men at the corner dashed forward to open the door in the hope of earning a copper, but was elbowed away by another loafer, who had rushed up with the same intention. A fierce quarrel broke out, which was increased by the two guardsmen, who took sides with one of the loungers, and by the scissors-grinder, who was equally hot upon the other side. A blow was struck, and in an instant the lady, who had stepped from her carriage, was the centre of a little knot of flushed and struggling men, who struck savagely at each other with their fists and sticks. Holmes dashed into the crowd to protect the lady, but just as he reached her he gave a cry and dropped to the ground, with the blood running freely down his face. At his fall the guardsmen took to their heels in one direction and the loungers in the other, while a number of better-dressed people, who had watched the scuffle without taking part in it, crowded in to help the lady and to attend to the injured man. Irene Adler, as I will still call her, had hurried up the steps, but she stood at the top with her superb figure outlined against the lights of the hall, looking back into the street.

"Is the poor gentleman much hurt?" she asked.

"He is dead," cried several voices.

"No, no, there's life in him!" shouted another. "But he'll be gone before you can get him to hospital."

"He's a brave fellow," said a woman. "They would have had the lady's purse and watch if it hadn't been for him.

They were a gang, and a rough one, too. Ah, he's breathing now."

"He can't lie in the street. May we bring him in, marm?"

"Surely. Bring him into the sitting-room. There is a comfortable sofa. This way, please!"

Slowly and solemnly he was borne into Briony Lodge and laid out in the principal room, while I still observed the proceedings from my post by the window. The lamps had been lit, but the blinds had not been drawn, so that I could see Holmes as he lay upon the couch. I do not know whether he was seized with compunction at that moment for the part he was playing, but I know that I never felt more heartily ashamed of myself in my life than when I saw the beautiful creature against whom I was conspiring, and the grace and kindliness with which she waited upon the injured man. And yet it would be the blackest treachery to Holmes to draw back now from the part which he had intrusted to me. I hardened my heart and took the smoke-rocket from under my ulster. After all, I thought, we are not injuring her. We are but preventing her from injuring another.

Holmes had sat up upon the couch, and I saw him motion like a man who is in need of air. A maid rushed across and threw open the window. At the same instant I saw him raise his hand, and at the signal I tossed my rocket into the room with a cry of "fire!" The word was no sooner out of my mouth than the whole crowd of spectators, well dressed and ill—gentlemen, ostlers, and servant-maids—joined in a general shriek of "fire!" Thick clouds of smoke curled through the room and out at the open window. I caught a glimpse of rushing figures, and a moment later the voice of Holmes from within assuring them that it was a false alarm. Slipping through the shouting crowd I made my way to the corner of the street, and in ten minutes was rejoiced to find my friend's arm in mine and to get away from the scene of uproar. He walked swiftly and in silence for some few minutes until we had turned down one of the quiet streets which lead towards the Edgeware Road.

"You did it very nicely, Doctor," he remarked. "Nothing could have been better. It is all right."

"You have the photograph?"

"I know where it is."

"And how did you find out?"

"She showed me, as I told you she would."

"I am still in the dark."

"I do not wish to make a mystery," said he, laughing. "The matter was perfectly simple. You, of course, saw that everyone in the street was an accomplice. They were all engaged for the evening."

"I guessed as much."

"Then, when the row broke out, I had a little moist red paint in the palm of my hand. I rushed forward, fell down, clapped my hand to my face, and became a piteous spectacle. It is an old trick."

"That also I could fathom."

"Then they carried me in. She was bound to have me in. What else could she do? And into her sitting-room, which was the very room which I suspected. It lay between that and her bedroom, and I was determined to see which. They laid me on a couch, I motioned for air, they were compelled to open the window, and you had your chance."

"How did that help you?"

"It was all-important. When a woman thinks that her house is on fire, her instinct is at once to rush to the thing which she values most. It is a perfectly overpowering impulse, and I have more than once taken advantage of it. In the case of the Darlington substitution scandal it was of use to me, and also in the Arnsworth Castle business. A married woman grabs at her baby; an unmarried one reaches for her jewel-box. Now it was clear to me that our lady of to-day had nothing in the house more precious to her than what we are in quest of. She would rush to secure it. The alarm of fire was admirably done. The smoke and shouting were enough to shake nerves of steel. She responded beautifully. The photograph is in a recess behind a sliding panel just above the right bell-pull. She was there in an instant, and I caught a glimpse of it as she half-drew it out. When I cried out that it was a false alarm, she replaced it, glanced at the rocket, rushed from the room, and I have not seen her since. I rose and, making my excuses, escaped from the house. I hesitated whether to attempt to secure the photograph at once, but the coachman had come in, and as he was watching me narrowly it seemed safer to wait. A little over-precipitance may ruin all."

"And now?" I asked.

"Our quest is practically finished. I shall call with the King to-morrow, and with you, if you care to come with us. We will be shown into the sitting-room to wait for the lady, but it is probable that when she comes she may find neither us nor the photograph. It might be a satisfaction to His Majesty to regain it with his own hands."

"And when will you call?"

"At eight in the morning. She will not be up, so that we shall have a clear field. Besides, we must be prompt, for this marriage may mean a complete change in her life and habits. I must wire to the King without delay."

We had reached Baker Street and had stopped at the door. He was searching his pockets for the key when someone passing said:

"Good-night, Mr. Sherlock Holmes."

There were several people on the pavement at the time, but the greeting appeared to come from a slim youth in an ulster who had hurried by.

"I've heard that voice before," said Holmes, staring down the dimly lit street. "Now, I wonder who the deuce that could have been."

3

I slept at Baker Street that night, and we were engaged upon our toast and coffee in the morning when the King of Bohemia rushed into the room.

"You have really got it!" he cried, grasping Sherlock Holmes by either shoulder and looking eagerly into his face.

"Not yet."

"But you have hopes?"

"I have hopes."

"Then, come. I am all impatience to be gone."

"We must have a cab."

"No, my brougham is waiting."

"Then that will simplify matters." We descended and started off once more for Briony Lodge.

"Irene Adler is married," remarked Holmes.

"Married! When?"

"Yesterday."

"But to whom?"

"To an English lawyer named Norton."

"But she could not love him."

"I am in hopes that she does."

"And why in hopes?"

"Because it would spare Your Majesty all fear of future annoyance. If the lady loves her husband, she does not love Your Majesty. If she does not love Your Majesty, there is no reason why she should interfere with Your Majesty's plan."

"It is true. And yet— Well! I wish she had been of my own station! What a queen she would have made!" He relapsed into a moody silence, which was not broken until we drew up in Serpentine Avenue.

The door of Briony Lodge was open, and an elderly woman stood upon the steps. She watched us with a sardonic eye as we stepped from the brougham.

"Mr. Sherlock Holmes, I believe?" said she.

"I am Mr. Holmes," answered my companion, looking at her with a questioning and rather startled gaze.

"Indeed! My mistress told me that you were likely to call. She left this morning with her husband by the 5:15 train from Charing Cross for the Continent."

"What!" Sherlock Holmes staggered back, white with chagrin and surprise. "Do you mean that she has left England?"

"Never to return."

"And the papers?" asked the King hoarsely. "All is lost."

"We shall see." He pushed past the servant and rushed into the drawing-room, followed by the King and myself. The furniture was scattered about in every direction, with dismantled shelves and open drawers, as if the lady had hurriedly ransacked them before her flight. Holmes rushed at the bell-pull, tore back a small sliding shutter, and plunging in his hand, pulled out a photograph and a letter. The photograph was of Irene Adler herself in evening dress; the letter was superscribed to "Sherlock Holmes, Esq. To be left till called for." My friend tore it open, and we all three read it together. It was dated at midnight of the preceding night and ran in this way:

MY DEAR MR. SHERLOCK HOLMES:

You really did it very well. You took me in completely. Until after the alarm of fire, I had not a suspicion. But then, when I found how I had betrayed myself, I began to think. I had been warned against you months ago. I had been told that if the King employed an agent it would certainly be you. And your address had been given me. Yet, with all this, you made me reveal what you wanted to know. Even after I became suspicious, I found it hard to think evil of such a dear, kind old clergyman. But, you know, I have been trained as an actress myself. Male costume is nothing new to me. I often take advantage of the freedom which it gives. I sent John, the coachman, to watch you, ran upstairs, got into my walking-clothes, as I call them, and came down just as you departed.

Well, I followed you to your door and so made sure that I was really an object of interest to the celebrated Mr. Sherlock Holmes. Then I, rather imprudently, wished you good-night, and started for the Temple to see my husband.

We both thought the best resource was flight, when pursued by so formidable an antagonist; so you will find the nest empty when you call to-morrow. As to the photograph, your client may rest in peace. I love and am loved by a better man than he. The King may do what he will without hindrance from one whom he has cruelly wronged. I keep it only to safeguard myself, and to preserve a weapon which will always secure me from any steps which he might take in the future. I leave a photograph which he might care to possess, and I remain, dear Mr. Sherlock Holmes,

Very truly yours,
Irene Norton, *née* Adler

"What a woman—oh, what a woman!" cried the King of Bohemia, when we had all three read this epistle. "Did I not tell you how quick and resolute she was? Would she not have made an admirable queen? Is it not a pity that she was not on my level?"

"From what I have seen of the lady she seems indeed to be on a very different level to Your Majesty," said Holmes coldly. "I am sorry that I have not been able to bring Your Majesty's business to a more successful conclusion."

"On the contrary, my dear sir," cried the King; "nothing could be more successful. I know that her word is inviolate. The photograph is now as safe as if it were in the fire."

"I am glad to hear Your Majesty say so."

"I am immensely indebted to you. Pray tell me in what way I can reward you. This ring—" He slipped an emerald snake ring from his finger and held it out upon the palm of his hand.

"Your Majesty has something which I should value even more highly," said Holmes.

"You have but to name it."

"This photograph!"

The King stared at him in amazement.

"Irene's photograph!" he cried. "Certainly, if you wish it."

"I thank Your Majesty. Then there is no more to be done in the matter. I have the honour to wish you a very good-morning." He bowed, and turning away without observing the hand which the King had stretched out to him, he set off in my company for his chambers.

And that was how a great scandal threatened to affect the kingdom of Bohemia, and how the best plans of Mr. Sherlock Holmes were beaten by a woman's wit. He used to make merry over the cleverness of women, but I have not heard him do it of late. And when he speaks of Irene Adler, or when he refers to her photograph, it is always under the honourable title of *the* woman.

The Red-headed League

I had called upon my friend, Mr. Sherlock Holmes, one day in the autumn of last year and found him in deep conversation with a very stout, florid-faced, elderly gentleman with fiery red hair. With an apology for my intrusion, I was about to withdraw when Holmes pulled me abruptly into the room and closed the door behind me.

"You could not possibly have come at a better time, my dear Watson," he said cordially.

"I was afraid that you were engaged."

"So I am. Very much so."

"Then I can wait in the next room."

"Not at all. This gentleman, Mr. Wilson, has been my partner and helper in many of my most successful cases, and I have no doubt that he will be of the utmost use to me in yours also."

The stout gentleman half rose from his chair and gave a bob of greeting, with a quick little questioning glance from his small, fat-encircled eyes.

"Try the settee," said Holmes, relapsing into his arm-chair and putting his finger-tips together, as was his custom when in judicial moods. "I know, my dear Watson, that you share my love of all that is bizarre and outside the conventions and humdrum routine of everyday life. You have shown your relish for it by the enthusiasm which has prompted you to chronicle, and if you will excuse my saying so, somewhat to embellish so many of my own little adventures."

"Your cases have indeed been of the greatest interest to me," I observed.

"You will remember that I remarked the other day, just before we went into the very simple problem presented by Miss Mary Sutherland, that for strange effects and extraordinary combinations we must go to life itself, which is always far more daring than any effort of the imagination."

"A proposition which I took the liberty of doubting."

"You did, Doctor, but none the less you must come round to my view, for otherwise I shall keep on piling fact upon fact on you until your reason breaks down under them and acknowledges me to be right. Now, Mr. Jabez Wilson here has been good enough to call upon me this morning, and to begin a narrative which promises to be one of the most singular which I have listened to for some time. You have heard me remark that the strangest and most unique things are very often connected not with the larger but with the smaller crimes, and occasionally, indeed, where there is room for doubt whether any positive crime has been committed. As far as I have heard, it is impossible for me to say whether the present case is an instance of crime or not, but the course of events is certainly among the most singular that I have ever listened to. Perhaps, Mr. Wilson, you would have the great kindness to recommence your narrative. I ask you not merely because my friend Dr. Watson has not heard the opening part but also because the peculiar nature of the story makes me anxious to have every possible detail from your lips. As a rule, when I have heard some slight indication of the course of events, I am able to guide myself by the thousands of other similar cases which occur to my memory. In the present instance I am forced to admit that the facts are, to the best of my belief, unique."

The portly client puffed out his chest with an appearance of some little pride and pulled a dirty and wrinkled newspaper from the inside pocket of his greatcoat. As he glanced down the advertisement column, with his head thrust forward and the paper flattened out upon his knee, I took a good look at the man and endeavoured, after the fashion of my companion, to read the indications which might be presented by his dress or appearance.

I did not gain very much, however, by my inspection. Our visitor bore every mark of being an average common-place British tradesman, obese, pompous, and slow. He wore rather baggy grey shepherd's check trousers, a not over-clean black frock-coat, unbuttoned in the front, and a drab waistcoat with a heavy brassy Albert chain, and a square pierced bit of metal dangling down as an orna-ment. A frayed top-hat and a faded brown overcoat with a wrinkled velvet collar lay upon a chair beside him. Al-together, look as I would, there was nothing remarkable about the man save his blazing red head and the expres-sion of extreme chagrin and discontent upon his features.

Sherlock Holmes's quick eye took in my occupation, and he shook his head with a smile as he noticed my ques-tioning glances. "Beyond the obvious facts that he has at some time done manual labour, that he takes snuff, that he is a Freemason, that he has been in China, and that he has done a considerable amount of writing lately, I can de-duce nothing else."

Mr. Jabez Wilson started up in his chair, with his fore-finger upon the paper, but his eyes upon my companion.

"How, in the name of good-fortune, did you know all that, Mr. Holmes?" he asked. "How did you know, for ex-ample, that I did manual labour? It's as true as gospel, for I began as a ship's carpenter."

"Your hands, my dear sir. Your right hand is quite a size larger than your left. You have worked with it, and the muscles are more developed."

"Well, the snuff, then, and the Freemasonry?"

"I won't insult your intelligence by telling you how I read that, especially as, rather against the strict rules of your order, you use an arc-and-compass breastpin."

"Ah, of course, I forgot that. But the writing?"

"What else can be indicated by that right cuff so very

shiny for five inches, and the left one with the smooth patch near the elbow where you rest it upon the desk?"

"Well, but China?"

"The fish that you have tattooed immediately above your wrist could only have been done in China. I have made a small study of tattoo marks and have even contributed to the literature of the subject. That trick of staining the fishes' scales of a delicate pink is quite peculiar to China. When, in addition, I see a Chinese coin hanging from your watch-chain, the matter becomes even more simple."

Mr. Jabez Wilson laughed heavily. "Well, I never!" said he. "I thought at first that you had done something clever, but I see that there was nothing in it, after all."

"I begin to think, Watson," said Holmes, "that I make a mistake in explaining. 'Omne ignotum pro magnifico,' you know, and my poor little reputation, such as it is, will suffer shipwreck if I am so candid. Can you not find the advertisement, Mr. Wilson?"

"Yes, I have got it now," he answered with his thick red finger planted halfway down the column. "Here it is. This is what began it all. You just read it for yourself, sir."

I took the paper from him and read as follows:

To the Red-headed League:

On account of the bequest of the late Ezekiah Hopkins, of Lebanon, Pennsylvania, U.S.A., there is now another vacancy open which entitles a member of the League to a salary of £4 a week for purely nominal services. All red-headed men who are sound in body and mind, and above the age of twenty-one years, are eligible. Apply in person on Monday, at eleven o'clock, to Duncan Ross, at the offices of the League, 7 Pope's Court, Fleet Street.

"What on earth does this mean?" I ejaculated after I had twice read over the extraordinary announcement.

Holmes chuckled and wriggled in his chair, as was his habit when in high spirits. "It is a little off the beaten track, isn't it?" said he. "And now, Mr. Wilson, off you go at scratch and tell us all about yourself, your household, and the effect which this advertisement had upon your fortunes. You will first make a note, Doctor, of the paper and the date."

"It is *The Morning Chronicle* of April 27, 1890. Just two months ago."

"Very good. Now, Mr. Wilson?"

"Well, it is just as I have been telling you, Mr. Sherlock Holmes," said Jabez Wilson, mopping his forehead; "I have a small pawnbroker's business at Saxe-Coburg Square, near the City. It's not a very large affair, and of late years it has not done more than just give me a living. I used to be able to keep two assistants, but now I only keep one; and I would have a job to pay him but that he is willing to come for half wages so as to learn the business."

"What is the name of this obliging youth?" asked Sherlock Holmes.

"His name is Vincent Spaulding, and he's not such a youth, either. It's hard to say his age. I should not wish a smarter assistant, Mr. Holmes; and I know very well that he could better himself and earn twice what I am able to give him. But, after all, if he is satisfied, why should I put ideas in his head?"

"Why, indeed? You seem most fortunate in having an employee who comes under the full market price. It is not a common experience among employers in this age. I don't know that your assistant is not as remarkable as your advertisement."

"Oh, he has his faults, too," said Mr. Wilson. "Never was such a fellow for photography. Snapping away with a camera when he ought to be improving his mind, and then diving down into the cellar like a rabbit into its hole to develop his pictures. That is his main fault, but on the whole he's a good worker. There's no vice in him."

"He is still with you, I presume?"

"Yes, sir. He and a girl of fourteen, who does a bit of simple cooking and keeps the place clean—that's all I have in the house, for I am a widower and never had any family. We live very quietly, sir, the three of us; and we keep a roof over our heads and pay our debts, if we do nothing more.

"The first thing that put us out was that advertisement. Spaulding, he came down into the office just this day eight weeks, with this very paper in his hand, and he says:

"'I wish to the Lord, Mr. Wilson, that I was a red-headed man.'

"'Why that?' I asks.

"'Why,' says he, 'here's another vacancy on the League of the Red-headed Men. It's worth quite a little fortune to any man who gets it, and I understand that there are more vacancies than there are men, so that the trustees are at their wits' end what to do with the money. If my hair would only change colour, here's a nice little crib all ready for me to step into.'

"'Why, what is it, then?' I asked. You see, Mr. Holmes, I am a very stay-at-home man, and as my business came to me instead of my having to go to it, I was often weeks on end without putting my foot over the door-mat. In that way I didn't know much of what was going on outside, and I was always glad of a bit of news.

"'Have you never heard of the League of the Red-headed Men?' he asked with his eyes open.

"'Never.'

"'Why, I wonder at that, for you are eligible yourself for one of the vacancies.'

"'And what are they worth?' I asked.

"'Oh, merely a couple of hundred a year, but the work is slight, and it need not interfere very much with one's other occupations.'

"Well, you can easily think that that made me prick up my ears, for the business has not been over-good for some years, and an extra couple of hundred would have been very handy.

"'Tell me all about it,' said I.

"'Well,' said he, showing me the advertisement, 'you can see for yourself that the League has a vacancy, and there is the address where you should apply for particulars. As far as I can make out, the League was founded by an American millionaire, Ezekiah Hopkins, who was very peculiar in his ways. He was himself red-headed, and he had a great sympathy for all red-headed men; so when he died it was found that he had left his enormous fortune in the hands of trustees, with instructions to apply the interest to the providing of easy berths to men whose hair is of that colour. From all I hear it is splendid pay and very little to do.'

"'But,' said I, 'there would be millions of red-headed men who would apply.'

"'Not so many as you might think,' he answered. 'You see it is really confined to Londoners, and to grown men. This American had started from London when he was young, and he wanted to do the old town a good turn. Then, again, I have heard it is no use your applying if your hair is light red, or dark red, or anything but real bright, blazing, fiery red. Now, if you cared to apply, Mr. Wilson, you would just walk in; but perhaps it would hardly be worth your while to put yourself out of the way for the sake of a few hundred pounds.'

"Now, it is a fact, gentlemen, as you may see for yourselves, that my hair is of a very full and rich tint, so that it seemed to me that if there was to be any competition in the matter I stood as good a chance as any man that I had ever met. Vincent Spaulding seemed to know so much about it that I thought he might prove useful, so I just ordered him to put up the shutters for the day and to come right away with me. He was very willing to have a holiday, so we shut the business up and started off for the address that was given us in the advertisement.

"I never hope to see such a sight as that again, Mr. Holmes. From north, south, east, and west every man who had a shade of red in his hair had tramped into the City to answer the advertisement. Fleet Street was choked with red-headed folk, and Pope's Court looked like a coster's orange barrow. I should not have thought there were so many in the whole country as were brought together by that single advertisement. Every shade of colour they were—straw, lemon, orange, brick, Irish-setter, liver, clay; but, as Spaulding said, there were not many who had the real vivid flame-coloured tint. When I saw how many were waiting, I would have given it up in despair; but Spaulding would not hear of it. How he did it I could not imagine, but he pushed and pulled and butted until he got me through the crowd, and right up to the steps which led to the office. There was a double stream upon the stair, some going up in hope, and some coming back dejected; but we wedged in as well as we could and soon found ourselves in the office."

"Your experience has been a most entertaining one," remarked Holmes as his client paused and refreshed his memory with a huge pinch of snuff. "Pray continue your very interesting statement."

"There was nothing in the office but a couple of wooden chairs and a deal table, behind which sat a small man with a head that was even redder than mine. He said a few words to each candidate as he came up, and then he always managed to find some fault in them which would disqualify them. Getting a vacancy did not seem to be such a very easy matter, after all. However, when our turn came the little man was much more favourable to me than to any of the others, and he closed the door as we entered, so that he might have a private word with us.

"'This is Mr. Jabez Wilson,' said my assistant, 'and he is willing to fill a vacancy in the League.'

"'And he is admirably suited for it,' the other answered. 'He has every requirement. I cannot recall when I have seen anything so fine.' He took a step backwards, cocked his head on one side, and gazed at my hair until I felt quite bashful. Then suddenly he plunged forward, wrung my hand, and congratulated me warmly on my success.

"'It would be injustice to hesitate,' said he. 'You will, however, I am sure, excuse me for taking an obvious precaution.' With that he seized my hair in both his hands and tugged until I yelled with the pain. 'There is water in your eyes,' said he as he released me. 'I perceive that all is as it should be. But we have to be careful, for we have twice been deceived by wigs and once by paint. I could tell you tales of cobbler's wax which would disgust you with human nature.' He stepped over to the window and shouted through it at the top of his voice that the vacancy was filled. A groan of disappointment came up from below, and the folk all trooped away in different directions until there was not a red-head to be seen except my own and that of the manager.

"'My name,' said he, 'is Mr. Duncan Ross, and I am myself one of the pensioners upon the fund left by our noble benefactor. Are you a married man, Mr. Wilson? Have you a family?'

"I answered that I had not.

"His face fell immediately.

"'Dear me!' he said gravely, 'that is very serious indeed! I am sorry to hear you say that. The fund was, of course, for the propagation and spread of the red-heads as well as for their maintenance. It is exceedingly unfortunate that you should be a bachelor.'

"My face lengthened at this, Mr. Holmes, for I thought that I was not to have the vacancy after all; but after thinking it over for a few minutes he said that it would be all right.

"'In the case of another,' said he, 'the objection might be fatal, but we must stretch a point in favour of a man with such a head of hair as yours. When shall you be able to enter upon your new duties?'

"'Well, it is a little awkward, for I have a business already,' said I.

"'Oh, never mind about that, Mr. Wilson!' said Vincent Spaulding. 'I should be able to look after that for you.'

"'What would be the hours?' I asked.

"'Ten to two.'

"Now a pawnbroker's business is mostly done of an evening, Mr. Holmes, especially Thursday and Friday evening, which is just before pay-day; so it would suit me very well to earn a little in the mornings. Besides, I knew that my assistant was a good man, and that he would see to anything that turned up.

"'That would suit me very well,' said I. 'And the pay?'

"'Is four pounds a week.'

"'And the work?'

"'Is purely nominal.'

"'What do you call purely nominal?'

"'Well, you have to be in the office, or at least in the building, the whole time. If you leave, you forfeit your whole position forever. The will is very clear upon that point. You don't comply with the conditions if you budge from the office during that time.'

"'It's only four hours a day, and I should not think of leaving,' said I.

"'No excuse will avail,' said Mr. Duncan Ross; 'neither sickness nor business nor anything else. There you must stay, or you lose your billet.'

"'And the work?'

"'Is to copy out the *Encyclopædia Britannica*. There is the first volume of it in that press. You must find your own ink, pens, and blotting-paper, but we provide this table and chair. Will you be ready to-morrow?'

"'Certainly,' I answered.

"'Then, good-bye, Mr. Jabez Wilson, and let me congratulate you once more on the important position which you have been fortunate enough to gain.' He bowed me out of the room, and I went home with my assistant, hardly knowing what to say or do, I was so pleased at my own good fortune.

"Well, I thought over the matter all day, and by evening I was in low spirits again, for I had quite persuaded myself that the whole affair must be some great hoax or fraud, though what its object might be I could not imagine. It seemed altogether past belief that anyone could make such a will, or that they would pay such a sum for doing anything so simple as copying out the *Encyclopædia Britannica*. Vincent Spaulding did what he could to cheer me up, but by bedtime I had reasoned myself out of the whole thing. However, in the morning I determined to have a look at it anyhow, so I bought a penny bottle of ink, and with a quill-pen and seven sheets of foolscap paper, I started off for Pope's Court.

"Well, to my surprise and delight, everything was as right as possible. The table was set out ready for me, and Mr. Duncan Ross was there to see that I got fairly to work. He started me off on the letter *A*, and then he left me; but he would drop in from time to time to see that all was right with me. At two o'clock he bade me good-day, complimented me upon the amount that I had written, and locked the door of the office after me.

"This went on day after day, Mr. Holmes, and on Saturday the manager came in and planked down four golden sovereigns for my week's work. It was the same next week, and the same the week after. Every morning I was there at ten, and every afternoon I left at two. By degrees Mr. Duncan Ross took to coming in only once of a morning, and then, after a time, he did not come in at all. Still, of course, I never dared to leave the room for an instant, for I was not sure when he might come, and the billet was such a good one and suited me so well, that I would not risk the loss of it.

"Eight weeks passed away like this, and I had written about Abbots and Archery and Armour and Architecture and Attica, and hoped with diligence that I might get on to the *B*'s before very long. It cost me something in foolscap, and I had pretty nearly filled a shelf with my writings. And then suddenly the whole business came to an end."

"To an end?"

"Yes, sir. And no later than this morning. I went to my work as usual at ten o'clock, but the door was shut and locked, with a little square of card-board hammered on to the middle of the panel with a tack. Here it is, and you can read for yourself."

He held up a piece of white card-board about the size of a sheet of note-paper. It read in this fashion:

THE RED-HEADED LEAGUE
Is
DISSOLVED.
October 9, 1890.

Sherlock Holmes and I surveyed this curt announcement and the rueful face behind it, until the comical side of the affair so completely overtopped every other consideration that we both burst out into a roar of laughter.

"I cannot see that there is anything very funny," cried our client, flushing up to the roots of his flaming head. "If you can do nothing better than laugh at me, I can go elsewhere."

"No, no," cried Holmes, shoving him back into the chair from which he had half risen. "I really wouldn't miss your case for the world. It is most refreshingly unusual. But there is, if you will excuse my saying so, something just a little funny about it. Pray what steps did you take when you found the card upon the door?"

"I was staggered, sir. I did not know what to do. Then I called at the offices round, but none of them seemed to know anything about it. Finally, I went to the landlord, who is an accountant living on the ground-floor, and I asked him if he could tell me what had become of the Red-headed League. He said that he had never heard of any such body. Then I asked him who Mr. Duncan Ross was. He answered that the name was new to him.

"'Well,' said I, 'the gentleman at No. 4.'

"'What, the red-headed man?'

"'Yes.'

"'Oh,' said he, 'his name was William Morris. He was a solicitor and was using my room as a temporary convenience until his new premises were ready. He moved out yesterday.'

"'Where could I find him?'

"'Oh, at his new offices. He did tell me the address. Yes, 17 King Edward Street, near St. Paul's.'

"I started off, Mr. Holmes, but when I got to that

address it was a manufactory of artificial knee-caps, and no one in it had ever heard of either Mr. William Morris or Mr. Duncan Ross."

"And what did you do then?" asked Holmes.

"I went home to Saxe-Coburg Square, and I took the advice of my assistant. But he could not help me in any way. He could only say that if I waited, I should hear by post. But that was not quite good enough, Mr. Holmes. I did not wish to lose such a place without a struggle, so, as I had heard that you were good enough to give advice to poor folk who were in need of it, I came right away to you."

"And you did wisely," said Holmes. "Your case is an exceedingly remarkable one, and I shall be happy to look into it. From what you have told me I think that it is possible that graver issues hang from it than might at first sight appear."

"Grave enough!" said Mr. Jabez Wilson. "Why, I have lost four pound a week."

"As far as you are personally concerned," remarked Holmes, "I do not see that you have any grievance against this extraordinary league. On the contrary, you are, as I understand, richer by some thirty pounds, to say nothing of the minute knowledge which you have gained on every subject which comes under the letter *A*. You have lost nothing by them."

"No, sir. But I want to find out about them, and who they are, and what their object was in playing this prank—if it was a prank—upon me. It was a pretty expensive joke for them, for it cost them two and thirty pounds."

"We shall endeavour to clear up these points for you. And first, one or two questions, Mr. Wilson. This assistant of yours who first called your attention to the advertisement—how long had he been with you?"

"About a month then."

"How did he come?"

"In answer to an advertisement."

"Was he the only applicant?"

"No, I had a dozen."

"Why did you pick him?"

"Because he was handy and would come cheap."

"At half-wages, in fact."

"Yes."

"What is he like, this Vincent Spaulding?"

"Small, stout-built, very quick in his ways, no hair on his face, though he's not short of thirty. Has a white splash of acid upon his forehead."

Holmes sat up in his chair with considerable excitement. "I thought as much," said he. "Have you ever observed that his ears are pierced for earrings?"

"Yes, sir. He told me that a gipsy had done it for him when he was a lad."

"Hum!" said Holmes, sinking back in deep thought. "He is still with you?"

"Oh, yes, sir; I have only just left him."

"And has your business been attended to in your absence?"

"Nothing to complain of, sir. There's never very much to do of a morning."

"That will do, Mr. Wilson. I shall be happy to give you an opinion upon the subject in the course of a day or two. To-day is Saturday, and I hope that by Monday we may come to a conclusion."

"Well, Watson," said Holmes when our visitor had left us, "what do you make of it all?"

"I make nothing of it," I answered frankly. "It is a most mysterious business."

"As a rule," said Holmes, "the more bizarre a thing is the less mysterious it proves to be. It is your commonplace, featureless crimes which are really puzzling, just as a commonplace face is the most difficult to identify. But I must be prompt over this matter."

"What are you going to do, then?" I asked.

"To smoke," he answered. "It is quite a three-pipe problem, and I beg that you won't speak to me for fifty minutes." He curled himself up in his chair, with his thin knees drawn up to his hawk-like nose, and there he sat with his eyes closed and his black clay pipe thrusting out like the bill of some strange bird. I had come to the conclusion that he had dropped asleep, and indeed was nodding myself, when he suddenly sprang out of his chair with the gesture of a man who has made up his mind, and put his pipe down upon the mantelpiece.

"Sarasate plays at the St. James's Hall this afternoon," he remarked. "What do you think, Watson? Could your patients spare you for a few hours?"

"I have nothing to do to-day. My practice is never very absorbing."

"Then put on your hat and come. I am going through the City first, and we can have some lunch on the way. I observe that there is a good deal of German music on the programme, which is rather more to my taste than Italian or French. It is introspective, and I want to introspect. Come along!"

We travelled by the Underground as far as Aldersgate, and a short walk took us to Saxe-Coburg Square, the scene of the singular story which we had listened to in the morning. It was a poky, little, shabby-genteel place, where four lines of dingy two-storied brick houses looked out into a small railed-in enclosure, where a lawn of weedy grass and a few clumps of faded laurel-bushes made a hard fight against a smoke-laden and uncongenial atmosphere. Three gilt balls and a brown board with "JABEZ WILSON" in white letters, upon a corner house, announced the place where our red-headed client carried on his business. Sherlock Holmes stopped in front of it with his head on one side and looked it all over, with his eyes shining brightly between puckered lids. Then he walked slowly up the street, and then down again to the corner, still looking keenly at the houses. Finally he returned to the pawn-broker's, and having thumped vigorously upon the pavement with his stick two or three times, he went up to the door and knocked. It was instantly opened by a bright-looking, clean-shaven young fellow, who asked him to step in.

"Thank you," said Holmes, "I only wished to ask you how you would go from here to the Strand."

"Third right, fourth left," answered the assistant promptly, closing the door.

"Smart fellow, that," observed Holmes as we walked away. "He is, in my judgment, the fourth smartest man in London, and for daring I am not sure that he has not a claim to be third. I have known something of him before."

"Evidently," said I, "Mr. Wilson's assistant counts for a good deal in this mystery of the Red-headed League. I am sure that you inquired your way merely in order that you might see him."

"Not him."

"What, then?"

"The knees of his trousers."

"And what did you see?"

"What I expected to see."

"Why did you beat the pavement?"

"My dear Doctor, this is a time for observation, not for talk. We are spies in an enemy's country. We know something of Saxe-Coburg Square. Let us now explore the parts which lie behind it."

The road in which we found ourselves as we turned round the corner from the retired Saxe-Coburg Square presented as great a contrast to it as the front of a picture does to the back. It was one of the main arteries which conveyed the traffic of the City to the north and west. The roadway was blocked with the immense stream of commerce flowing in a double tide inwards and outwards, while the footpaths were black with the hurrying swarm of pedestrians. It was difficult to realise as we looked at the line of fine shops and stately business premises that they really abutted on the other side upon the faded and stagnant square which we had just quitted.

"Let me see," said Holmes, standing at the corner and glancing along the line, "I should like just to remember the order of the houses here. It is a hobby of mine to have an exact knowledge of London. There is Mortimer's, the tobacconist, the little newspaper shop, the Coburg branch of the City and Suburban Bank, the Vegetarian Restaurant, and McFarlane's carriage-building depot. That carries us right on to the other block. And now, Doctor, we've done our work, so it's time we had some play. A sandwich and a cup of coffee, and then off to violin-land, where all is sweetness and delicacy and harmony, and there are no red-headed clients to vex us with their conundrums."

My friend was an enthusiastic musician, being himself not only a very capable performer but a composer of no ordinary merit. All the afternoon he sat in the stalls wrapped in the most perfect happiness, gently waving his long, thin fingers in time to the music, while his gently smiling face and his languid, dreamy eyes were as unlike those of Holmes, the sleuth-hound, Holmes, the relentless, keen-witted, ready-handed criminal agent, as it was possible to conceive. In his singular character the dual nature alternately asserted itself, and his extreme exactness and astuteness represented, as I have often thought, the reaction against the poetic and contemplative mood which occasionally predominated in him. The swing of his nature took him from extreme languor to devouring energy; and as I knew well, he was never so truly formidable as when, for days on end, he had been lounging in his armchair amid his improvisations and his black-letter editions. Then it was that the lust of the chase would suddenly come upon him, and that his brilliant reasoning power would rise to the level of intuition, until those who were unacquainted with his methods would look askance at him as on a man whose knowledge was not that of other mortals. When I saw him that afternoon so enwrapped in the music at St. James's Hall I felt that an evil time might be coming upon those whom he had set himself to hunt down.

"You want to go home, no doubt, Doctor," he remarked as we emerged.

"Yes, it would be as well."

"And I have some business to do which will take some hours. This business at Saxe-Coburg Square is serious."

"Why serious?"

"A considerable crime is in contemplation. I have every reason to believe that we shall be in time to stop it. But to-day being Saturday rather complicates matters. I shall want your help to-night."

"At what time?"

"Ten will be early enough."

"I shall be at Baker Street at ten."

"Very well. And I say, Doctor, there may be some little danger, so kindly put your army revolver in your pocket." He waved his hand, turned on his heel, and disappeared in an instant among the crowd.

I trust that I am not more dense than my neighbours, but I was always oppressed with a sense of my own stupidity in my dealings with Sherlock Holmes. Here I had heard what he had heard, I had seen what he had seen, and yet from his words it was evident that he saw clearly not only what had happened but what was about to happen, while to me the whole business was still confused and grotesque. As I drove home to my house in Kensington I thought over it all, from the extraordinary story of the red-headed copier of the encyclopædia down to the visit to Saxe-Coburg Square and the ominous words with which he had parted from me. What was this nocturnal expedition, and why should I go armed? Where were we going, and what were we to do? I had the hint from Holmes that this smooth-faced pawnbroker's assistant was a formidable man—a man who might play a deep game. I tried to puzzle it out, but gave it up in despair and set the matter aside until night should bring an explanation.

It was a quarter-past nine when I started from home and made my way across the Park, and so through Oxford Street to Baker Street. Two hansoms were standing at the door, and as I entered the passage I heard the sound of voices from above. On entering his room, I found Holmes in animated conversation with two men, one of whom I recognised as Peter Jones, the official police agent, while the other was a long, thin, sad-faced man, with a very shiny hat and oppressively respectable frock-coat.

"Ha, our party is complete!" said Holmes, buttoning up his pea-jacket and taking his heavy hunting crop from the rack. "Watson, I think you know Mr. Jones, of Scotland Yard? Let me introduce you to Mr. Merryweather, who is to be our companion in to-night's adventure."

"We're hunting in couples again, Doctor, you see," said Jones in his consequential way. "Our friend here is a wonderful man for starting a chase. All he wants is an old dog to help him to do the running down."

"I hope a wild goose may not prove to be the end of our chase," observed Mr. Merryweather gloomily.

"You may place considerable confidence in Mr. Holmes, sir," said the police agent loftily. "He has his own little methods, which are, if he won't mind my saying so, just a little too theoretical and fantastic, but he has the makings of a detective in him. It is not too much to say that once or twice, as in that business of the Sholto murder and the Agra treasure, he has been more nearly correct than the official force."

"Oh, if you say so, Mr. Jones, it is all right," said the stranger with deference. "Still, I confess that I miss my rubber. It is the first Saturday night for seven-and-twenty years that I have not had my rubber."

"I think you will find," said Sherlock Holmes, "that you will play for a higher stake to-night than you have ever done yet, and that the play will be more exciting. For you, Mr. Merryweather, the stake will be some thirty thousand pounds; and for you, Jones, it will be the man upon whom you wish to lay your hands."

"John Clay, the murderer, thief, smasher, and forger. He's a young man, Mr. Merryweather, but he is at the head of his profession, and I would rather have my bracelets on him than on any criminal in London. He's a remarkable man, is young John Clay. His grandfather was a royal duke, and he himself has been to Eton and Oxford. His brain is as cunning as his fingers, and though we meet signs of him at every turn, we never know where to find the man himself. He'll crack a crib in Scotland one week

45

and be raising money to build an orphanage in Cornwall the next. I've been on his track for years and have never set eyes on him yet."

"I hope that I may have the pleasure of introducing you to-night. I've had one or two little turns also with Mr. John Clay, and I agree with you that he is at the head of his profession. It is past ten, however, and quite time that we started. If you two will take the first hansom, Watson and I will follow in the second."

Sherlock Holmes was not very communicative during the long drive and lay back in the cab humming the tunes which he had heard in the afternoon. We rattled through an endless labyrinth of gas-lit streets until we emerged into Farrington Street.

"We are close there now," my friend remarked. "This fellow Merryweather is a bank director and personally interested in the matter. I thought it as well to have Jones with us also. He is not a bad fellow, though an absolute imbecile in his profession. He has one positive virtue. He is as brave as a bulldog and as tenacious as a lobster if he gets his claws upon anyone. Here we are, and they are waiting for us."

We had reached the same crowded thoroughfare in which we had found ourselves in the morning. Our cabs were dismissed, and following the guidance of Mr. Merryweather, we passed down a narrow passage and through a side door, which he opened for us. Within there was a small corridor, which ended in a very massive iron gate. This also was opened and led down a flight of winding stone steps, which terminated at another formidable gate. Mr. Merryweather stopped to light a lantern and then conducted us down a dark, earth-smelling passage, and so, after opening a third door, into a huge vault or cellar, which was piled all round with crates and massive boxes.

"You are not very vulnerable from above," Holmes remarked as he held up the lantern and gazed about him.

"Nor from below," said Mr. Merryweather, striking his

stick upon the flags which lined the floor. "Why, dear me, it sounds quite hollow!" he remarked, looking up in surprise.

"I must really ask you to be a little more quiet!" said Holmes severely. "You have already imperilled the whole success of our expedition. Might I beg that you would have the goodness to sit down upon one of those boxes and not to interfere?"

The solemn Mr. Merryweather perched himself upon a crate, with a very injured expression upon his face, while Holmes fell upon his knees upon the floor and, with the lantern and a magnifying lens, began to examine minutely the cracks between the stones. A few seconds sufficed to satisfy him, for he sprang to his feet again and put his glass in his pocket.

"We have at least an hour before us," he remarked, "for they can hardly take any steps until the good pawnbroker is safely in bed. Then they will not lose a minute, for the sooner they do their work the longer time they will have for their escape. We are at present, Doctor—as no doubt you have divined—in the cellar of the City branch of one of the principal London banks. Mr. Merryweather is the chairman of directors, and he will explain to you that there are reasons why the more daring criminals of London should take a considerable interest in this cellar at present."

"It is our French gold," whispered the director. "We have had several warnings that an attempt might be made upon it."

"Your French gold?"

"Yes. We had occasion some months ago to strengthen our resources and borrowed for that purpose thirty thousand napoleons from the Bank of France. It has become known that we have never had occasion to unpack the money, and that it is still lying in our cellar. The crate upon which I sit contains two thousand napoleons packed between layers of lead foil. Our reserve of bullion is much larger at present than is usually kept in a single branch office, and the directors have had misgivings upon the subject."

"Which were very well justified," observed Holmes. "And now it is time that we arranged our little plans. I expect that within an hour matters will come to a head. In the meantime, Mr. Merryweather, we must put the screen over that dark lantern."

"And sit in the dark?"

"I am afraid so. I had brought a pack of cards in my pocket, and I thought that, as we were a *partie carrée,* you might have your rubber after all. But I see that the enemy's preparations have gone so far that we cannot risk the presence of a light. And first of all, we must choose our positions. These are daring men, and though we shall take them at a disadvantage, they may do us some harm unless we are careful. I shall stand behind this crate, and do you conceal yourselves behind those. Then, when I flash a light upon them, close in swiftly. If they fire, Watson, have no compunction about shooting them down."

I placed my revolver, cocked, upon the top of the wooden case behind which I crouched. Holmes shot the slide across the front of his lantern and left us in pitch darkness—such an absolute darkness as I have never before experienced. The smell of hot metal remained to assure us that the light was still there, ready to flash out at a moment's notice. To me, with my nerves worked up to a pitch of expectancy, there was something depressing and subduing in the sudden gloom and in the cold, dank air of the vault.

"They have but one retreat," whispered Holmes. "That is back through the house into Saxe-Coburg Square. I hope that you have done what I asked you, Jones?"

"I have an inspector and two officers waiting at the front door."

"Then we have stopped all the holes. And now we must be silent and wait."

What a wait it seemed! From comparing notes after-

wards it was but an hour and a quarter, yet it appeared to
me that the night must have almost gone and the dawn be
breaking above us. My limbs were weary and stiff, for I
feared to change my position; yet my nerves were worked
up to the highest pitch of tension, and my hearing was so
acute that I could not only hear the gentle breathing of my
companions, but I could distinguish the deeper, heavier
in-breath of the bulky Jones from the thin, sighing note of
the bank director. From my position I could look over the
case in the direction of the floor. Suddenly my eyes caught
the glint of a light.

At first it was but a lurid spark upon the stone pavement. Then it lengthened out until it became a yellow line,
and then, without any warning or sound, a gash seemed to
open and a hand appeared; a white, almost womanly
hand, which felt about in the centre of the little area of
light. For a minute or more the hand, with its writhing
fingers, protruded out of the floor. Then it was withdrawn
as suddenly as it appeared, and all was dark again save the
single lurid spark which marked a chink between the
stones.

Its disappearance, however, was but momentary. With a
rending, tearing sound, one of the broad, white stones
turned over upon its side and left a square, gaping hole,
through which streamed the light of a lantern. Over the
edge there peeped a clean-cut, boyish face, which looked
keenly about it, and then, with a hand on either side of the
aperture, drew itself shoulder-high and waist-high, until
one knee rested upon the edge. In another instant he
stood at the side of the hole and was hauling after him a
companion, lithe and small like himself, with a pale face
and a shock of very red hair.

"It's all clear," he whispered. "Have you the chisel and
the bags? Great Scott! Jump, Archie, jump and I'll swing
for it!"

Sherlock Holmes had sprung out and seized the intruder by the collar. The other dived down the hole, and
I heard the sound of rending cloth as Jones clutched at his

skirts. The light flashed upon the barrel of a revolver, but Holmes's hunting crop came down on the man's wrist, and the pistol clinked upon the stone floor.

"It's no use, John Clay," said Holmes blandly. "You have no chance at all."

"So I see," the other answered with the utmost coolness. "I fancy that my pal is all right, though I see you have got his coat-tails."

"There are three men waiting for him at the door," said Holmes.

"Oh, indeed. You seem to have done the thing very completely. I must compliment you."

"And I you," Holmes answered. "Your red-headed idea was very new and effective."

"You'll see your pal again presently," said Jones. "He's quicker at climbing down holes than I am. Just hold out while I fix the derbies."

"I beg that you will not touch me with your filthy hands," remarked our prisoner as the handcuffs clattered upon his wrists. "You may not be aware that I have royal blood in my veins. Have the goodness, also, when you address me always to say 'sir' and 'please.'"

"All right," said Jones with a stare and a snigger. "Well, would you please, sir, march upstairs, where we can get a cab to carry Your Highness to the police-station?"

"That is better," said John Clay serenely. He made a sweeping bow to the three of us and walked quietly off in the custody of the detective.

"Really, Mr. Holmes," said Mr. Merryweather as we followed them from the cellar, "I do not know how the bank can thank you or repay you. There is no doubt that you have detected and defeated in the most complete manner one of the most determined attempts at bank robbery that have ever come within my experience."

"I have had one or two little scores of my own to settle with Mr. John Clay," said Holmes. "I have been at some small expense over this matter, which I shall expect the bank to refund, but beyond that I am amply repaid by having had an experience which is in many ways unique, and by hearing the very remarkable narrative of the Red-headed League."

"You see, Watson," he explained in the early hours of the morning as we sat over a glass of whisky and soda in Baker Street, "it was perfectly obvious from the first that the only possible object of this rather fantastic business of the advertisement of the League, and the copying of the encyclopædia, must be to get this not over-bright pawnbroker out of the way for a number of hours every day. It was a curious way of managing it, but, really, it would be difficult to suggest a better. The method was no doubt suggested to Clay's ingenious mind by the colour of his accomplice's hair. The four-pounds a week was a lure which must draw him, and what was it to them, who were playing for thousands? They put in the advertisement, one rogue has the temporary office, the other rogue incites the man to apply for it, and together they manage to secure his absence every morning in the week. From the time that I heard of the assistant having come for half-wages, it was obvious to me that he had some strong motive for securing the situation."

"But how could you guess what the motive was?"

"Had there been women in the house, I should have suspected a mere vulgar intrigue. That, however, was out of the question. The man's business was a small one, and there was nothing in his house which could account for such elaborate preparations and such an expenditure as they were at. It must, then, be something out of the house. What could it be? I thought of the assistant's fondness for photography, and his trick of vanishing into the cellar. The cellar! There was the end of this tangled clue. Then I made inquiries as to this mysterious assistant and found that I had to deal with one of the coolest and most daring criminals in London. He was doing something in the cellar—something which took many hours a day for months on end. What could it be, once more? I could think of nothing save that he was running a tunnel to some other building.

"So far I had got when we went to visit the scene of action. I surprised you by beating upon the pavement with my stick. I was ascertaining whether the cellar stretched out in front or behind. It was not in front. Then I rang the bell, and as I hoped, the assistant answered it. We have had some skirmishes, but we had never set eyes upon each other before. I hardly looked at his face. His knees were what I wished to see. You must yourself have remarked how worn, wrinkled, and stained they were. They spoke of those hours of burrowing. The only remaining point was what they were burrowing for. I walked round the corner, saw the City and Suburban Bank abutted on our friend's premises, and felt that I had solved my problem. When you drove home after the concert I called upon Scotland Yard and upon the chairman of the bank directors, with the result that you have seen."

"And how could you tell that they would make their attempt to-night?" I asked.

"Well, when they closed their League offices that was a sign that they cared no longer about Mr. Jabez Wilson's presence—in other words, that they had completed their tunnel. But it was essential that they should use it soon, as it might be discovered, or the bullion might be removed. Saturday would suit them better than any other day, as it would give them two days for their escape. For all these reasons I expected them to come to-night."

"You reasoned it out beautifully," I exclaimed in unfeigned admiration. "It is so long a chain, and yet every link rings true."

"It saved me from ennui," he answered, yawning. "Alas! I already feel it closing in upon me. My life is spent in one long effort to escape from the commonplaces of existence. These little problems help me to do so."

"And you are a benefactor of the race," said I.

He shrugged his shoulders. "Well, perhaps, after all, it is of some little use," he remarked. "'L'homme c'est rien—l'œuvre c'est tout,' as Gustave Flaubert wrote to George Sand."

A Case of Identity

"My dear fellow," said Sherlock Holmes as we sat on either side of the fire in his lodgings at Baker Street, "life is infinitely stranger than anything which the mind of man could invent. We would not dare to conceive the things which are really mere commonplaces of existence. If we could fly out of that window hand in hand, hover over this great city, gently remove the roofs, and peep in at the queer things which are going on, the strange coincidences, the plannings, the cross-purposes, the wonderful chains of events, working through generations and leading to the most *outré* results, it would make all fiction with its conventionalities and foreseen conclusions most stale and unprofitable."

"And yet I am not convinced of it," I answered. "The cases which come to light in the papers are, as a rule, bald enough, and vulgar enough. We have in our police reports realism pushed to its extreme limits, and yet the result is, it must be confessed, neither fascinating nor artistic."

"A certain selection and discretion must be used in producing a realistic effect," remarked Holmes. "This is wanting in the police report, where more stress is laid, perhaps, upon the platitudes of the magistrate than upon the details, which to an observer contain the vital essence of the whole matter. Depend upon it, there is nothing so unnatural as the commonplace."

I smiled and shook my head. "I can quite understand your thinking so," I said. "Of course, in your position of unofficial adviser and helper to everybody who is absolutely puzzled, throughout three continents, you are brought in contact with all that is strange and bizarre. But here"—I picked up the morning paper from the ground—"let us put it to a practical test. Here is the first heading upon which I come. 'A husband's cruelty to his wife.' There is half a column of print, but I know without reading it that it is all perfectly familiar to me. There is, of course, the other woman, the drink, the push, the blow, the bruise, the sympathetic sister or landlady. The crudest of writers could invent nothing more crude."

"Indeed, your example is an unfortunate one for your argument," said Holmes, taking the paper and glancing his eye down it. "This is the Dundas separation case, and as it happens, I was engaged in clearing up some small points in connection with it. The husband was a teetotaller, there was no other woman, and the conduct complained of was that he had drifted into the habit of winding up every meal by taking out his false teeth and hurling them at his wife, which, you will allow, is not an action likely to occur to the imagination of the average story-teller. Take a pinch of snuff, Doctor, and acknowledge that I have scored over you in your example."

He held out his snuffbox of old gold, with a great amethyst in the centre of the lid. Its splendour was in such contrast to his homely ways and simple life that I could not help commenting upon it.

"Ah," said he, "I forgot that I had not seen you for some weeks. It is a little souvenir from the King of Bohemia in return for my assistance in the case of the Irene Adler papers."

"And the ring?" I asked, glancing at a remarkable brilliant which sparkled upon his finger.

"It was from the reigning family of Holland, though the matter in which I served them was of such delicacy that I cannot confide it even to you, who have been good enough to chronicle one or two of my little problems."

"And have you any on hand just now?" I asked with interest.

"Some ten or twelve, but none which present any feature of interest. They are important, you understand, without being interesting. Indeed, I have found that it is usually in unimportant matters that there is a field for the observation, and for the quick analysis of cause and effect which gives the charm to an investigation. The larger crimes are apt to be the simpler, for the bigger the crime the more obvious, as a rule, is the motive. In these cases, save for one rather intricate matter which has been referred to me from Marseilles, there is nothing which presents any features of interest. It is possible, however, that I may have something better before very many minutes are over, for this is one of my clients, or I am much mistaken."

He had risen from his chair and was standing between the parted blinds, gazing down into the dull neutral-tinted London street. Looking over his shoulder, I saw that on the pavement opposite there stood a large woman with a heavy fur boa round her neck, and a large curling red feather in a broad-brimmed hat which was tilted in a coquettish Duchess of Devonshire fashion over her ear. From under this great panoply she peeped up in a nervous, hesitating fashion at our windows, while her body oscillated backward and forward, and her fingers fidgeted with her glove buttons. Suddenly, with a plunge, as of the swimmer who leaves the bank, she hurried across the road, and we heard the sharp clang of the bell.

"I have seen those symptoms before," said Holmes, throwing his cigarette into the fire. "Oscillation upon the pavement always means an *affaire de cœur*. She would like advice, but is not sure that the matter is not too delicate for communication. And yet even here we may discriminate. When a woman has been seriously wronged by a man she no longer oscillates, and the usual symptom is a broken bell wire. Here we may take it that there is a love matter, but that the maiden is not so much angry as perplexed, or grieved. But here she comes in person to resolve our doubts."

As he spoke there was a tap at the door, and the boy in
buttons entered to announce Miss Mary Sutherland, while
the lady herself loomed behind his small black figure like
a full-sailed merchant-man behind a tiny pilot boat.
Sherlock Holmes welcomed her with the easy courtesy for
which he was remarkable, and having closed the door and
bowed her into an armchair, he looked her over in the
minute and yet abstracted fashion which was peculiar
to him.

"Do you not find," he said, "that with your short sight it
is a little trying to do so much typewriting?"

"I did at first," she answered, "but now I know where
the letters are without looking." Then, suddenly realizing
the full purport of his words, she gave a violent start and
looked up, with fear and astonishment upon her broad,
good-humoured face. "You've heard about me, Mr.
Holmes," she cried, "else how could you know all that?"

"Never mind," said Holmes, laughing; "it is my business
to know things. Perhaps I have trained myself to see
what others overlook. If not, why should you come to
consult me?"

"I came to you, sir, because I heard of you from Mrs.
Etherege, whose husband you found so easy when the police and everyone had given him up for dead. Oh, Mr.
Holmes, I wish you would do as much for me. I'm not rich,
but still I have a hundred a year in my own right, besides
the little that I make by the machine, and I would give it all
to know what has become of Mr. Hosmer Angel."

"Why did you come away to consult me in such a hurry?"
asked Sherlock Holmes, with his finger-tips together and
his eyes to the ceiling.

Again a startled look came over the somewhat vacuous
face of Miss Mary Sutherland. "Yes, I did bang out of the
house," she said, "for it made me angry to see the easy way
in which Mr. Windibank—that is, my father—took it all.
He would not go to the police, and he would not go to you,
and so at last, as he would do nothing and kept on saying
that there was no harm done, it made me mad, and I just

57

on with my things and came right away to you."

"Your father," said Holmes, "your stepfather, surely, since the name is different."

"Yes, my stepfather. I call him Father, though it sounds funny, too, for he is only five years and two months older than myself."

"And your mother is alive?"

"Oh, yes, Mother is alive and well. I wasn't best pleased, Mr. Holmes, when she married again so soon after Father's death, and a man who was nearly fifteen years younger than herself. Father was a plumber in the Tottenham Court Road, and he left a tidy business behind him, which Mother carried on with Mr. Hardy, the foreman; but when Mr. Windibank came he made her sell the business, for he was very superior, being a traveller in wines. They got four thousand seven hundred pounds for the good-will and interest, which wasn't near as much as Father could have got if he had been alive."

I had expected to see Sherlock Holmes impatient under this rambling and inconsequential narrative, but, on the contrary, he had listened with the greatest concentration of attention.

"Your own little income," he asked, "does it come out of the business?"

"Oh, no, sir. It is quite separate and was left me by my uncle Ned in Auckland. It is in New Zealand stock, paying four and a half per cent. Two thousand five hundred pounds was the amount, but I can only touch the interest."

"You interest me extremely," said Holmes. "And since you draw so large a sum as a hundred a year, with what you earn into the bargain, you no doubt travel a little and indulge yourself in every way. I believe that a single lady can get on very nicely upon an income of about sixty pounds."

"I could do with much less than that, Mr. Holmes, but you understand that as long as I live at home I don't wish to be a burden to them, and so they have the use of the money just while I am staying with them. Of course, that is only just for the time. Mr. Windibank draws my interest every quarter and pays it over to Mother, and I find that I can do pretty well with what I earn at typewriting. It brings me twopence a sheet, and I can often do from fifteen to twenty sheets in a day."

"You have made your position very clear to me," said Holmes. "This is my friend, Dr. Watson, before whom you can speak as freely as before myself. Kindly tell us now all about your connection with Mr. Hosmer Angel."

A flush stole over Miss Sutherland's face, and she picked nervously at the fringe of her jacket. "I met him first at the gasfitters' ball," she said. "They used to send Father tickets when he was alive, and then afterwards they remembered us and sent them to Mother. Mr. Windibank did not wish us to go. He never did wish us to go anywhere. He would get quite mad if I wanted so much as to join a Sunday-school treat. But this time I was set on going, and I would go, for what right had he to prevent? He said the folk were not fit for us to know, when all Father's friends were to be there. And he said that I had nothing fit to wear, when I had my purple plush that I had never so much as taken out of the drawer. At last, when nothing else would do, he went off to France upon the business of the firm, but we went, Mother and I, with Mr. Hardy, who used to be our foreman, and it was there I met Mr. Hosmer Angel."

"I suppose," said Holmes, "that when Mr. Windibank came back from France he was very annoyed at your having gone to the ball."

"Oh, well, he was very good about it. He laughed, I remember, and shrugged his shoulders, and said there was no use denying anything to a woman, for she would have her way."

"I see. Then at the gasfitters' ball you met, as I understand, a gentleman called Mr. Hosmer Angel."

"Yes, sir. I met him that night, and he called next day to ask if we had got home all safe, and after that we met him—that is to say, Mr. Holmes, I met him twice for walks, but after that Father came back again, and Mr.

Hosmer Angel could not come to the house any more."

"No?"

"Well, you know, Father didn't like anything of the sort. He wouldn't have any visitors if he could help it, and he used to say that a woman should be happy in her own family circle. But then, as I used to say to Mother, a woman wants her own circle to begin with, and I had not got mine yet."

"But how about Mr. Hosmer Angel? Did he make no attempt to see you?"

"Well, Father was going off to France again in a week, and Hosmer wrote and said that it would be safer and better not to see each other until he had gone. We could write in the meantime, and he used to write every day. I took the letters in in the morning, so there was no need for Father to know."

"Were you engaged to the gentleman at this time?"

"Oh, yes, Mr. Holmes. We were engaged after the first walk that we took. Hosmer—Mr. Angel—was a cashier in an office in Leadenhall Street—and—"

"What office?"

"That's the worst of it, Mr. Holmes, I don't know."

"Where did he live, then?"

"He slept on the premises."

"And you don't know his address?"

"No—except that it was Leadenhall Street."

"Where did you address your letters, then?"

"To the Leadenhall Street Post-Office, to be left till called for. He said that if they were sent to the office, he would be chaffed by all the other clerks about having letters from a lady, so I offered to typewrite them, like he did his, but he wouldn't have that, for he said that when I wrote them they seemed to come from me, but when they were typewritten he always felt that the machine had come between us. That will just show you how fond he was of me, Mr. Holmes, and the little things that he would think of."

"It was most suggestive," said Holmes. "It has long been

an axiom of mine that the little things are infinitely the most important. Can you remember any other little things about Mr. Hosmer Angel?"

"He was a very shy man, Mr. Holmes. He would rather walk with me in the evening than in the daylight, for he said that he hated to be conspicuous. Very retiring and gentlemanly he was. Even his voice was gentle. He'd had the quinsy and swollen glands when he was young, he told me, and it had left him with a weak throat and a hesitating, whispering fashion of speech. He was always well dressed, very neat and plain, but his eyes were weak, just as mine are, and he wore tinted glasses against the glare."

"Well, and what happened when Mr. Windibank, your stepfather, returned to France?"

"Mr. Hosmer Angel came to the house again and proposed that we should marry before Father came back. He was in dreadful earnest and made me swear, with my hands on the Testament, that whatever happened I would always be true to him. Mother said he was quite right to make me swear, and that it was a sign of his passion. Mother was all in his favour from the first and was even fonder of him than I was. Then, when they talked of marrying within the week, I began to ask about Father; but they both said never to mind about Father, but just to tell him afterwards, and Mother said she would make it all right with him. I didn't quite like that, Mr. Holmes. It seemed funny that I should ask his leave, as he was only a few years older than me; but I didn't want to do anything on the sly, so I wrote to Father at Bordeaux, where the company has its French offices, but the letter came back to me on the very morning of the wedding."

"It missed him, then?"

"Yes, sir; for he had started to England just before it arrived."

"Ha, that was unfortunate! Your wedding was arranged, then, for the Friday. Was it to be in church?"

"Yes, sir, but very quietly. It was to be at St. Saviour's

near King's Cross, and we were to have breakfast afterwards at the St. Pancras Hotel. Hosmer came for us in a hansom, but as there were two of us he put us both into it and stepped himself into a four-wheeler, which happened to be the only other cab in the street. We got to the church first, and when the four-wheeler drove up we waited for him to step out, but he never did, and when the cabman got down from the box and looked there was no one there! The cabman said that he could not imagine what had become of him, for he had seen him get in with his own eyes. That was last Friday, Mr. Holmes, and I have never seen or heard anything since then to throw any light upon what became of him."

"It seems to me that you have been very shamefully treated," said Holmes.

"Oh, no, sir! He was too good and kind to leave me so. Why, all the morning he was saying to me that, whatever happened, I was to be true; and that even if something quite unforeseen occurred to separate us, I was always to remember that I was pledged to him, and that he would claim his pledge sooner or later. It seemed strange talk for a wedding-morning, but what has happened since gives a meaning to it."

"Most certainly it does. Your own opinion is, then, that some unforeseen catastrophe has occurred to him?"

"Yes, sir. I believe that he foresaw some danger, or else he would not have talked so. And then I think that what he foresaw happened."

"But you have no notion as to what it could have been?"

"None."

"One more question. How did your mother take the matter?"

"She was angry and said I was never to speak of the matter again."

"And your father? Did you tell him?"

"Yes; and he seemed to think, with me, that something had happened, and that I should hear of Hosmer again.

As he said, what interest could anyone have in bringing me to the doors of the church, and then leaving me? Now, if he had borrowed my money, or if he had married me and got my money settled on him, there might be some reason, but Hosmer was very independent about money and never would look at a shilling of mine. And yet, what could have happened? And why could he not write? Oh, it drives me half-mad to think of it, and I can't sleep a wink at night." She pulled a little handkerchief out of her muff and began to sob heavily into it.

"I shall glance into the case for you," said Holmes, rising, "and I have no doubt that we shall reach some definite result. Let the weight of the matter rest upon me now, and do not let your mind dwell upon it further. Above all, try to let Mr. Hosmer Angel vanish from your memory, as he has done from your life."

"Then you don't think I'll see him again?"

"I fear not."

"Then what has happened to him?"

"You will leave that question in my hands. I should like an accurate description of him and any letters of his which you can spare."

"I advertised for him in last Saturday's *Chronicle*," said she. "Here is the slip and here are four letters from him."

"Thank you. And your address?"

"No. 31 Lyon Place, Camberwell."

"Mr. Angel's address you never had, I understand. Where is your father's place of business?"

"He travels for Westhouse & Marbank, the great claret importers of Fenchurch Street."

"Thank you. You have made your statement very clearly. You will leave the papers here, and remember the advice which I have given you. Let the whole incident be a sealed book, and do not allow it to affect your life."

"You are very kind, Mr. Holmes, but I cannot do that. I shall be true to Hosmer. He shall find me ready when he comes back."

For all the preposterous hat and the vacuous face, there

was something noble in the simple faith of our visitor which compelled our respect. She laid her little bundle of papers upon the table and went her way, with a promise to come again whenever she might be summoned.

Sherlock Holmes sat silent for a few minutes with his finger-tips still pressed together, his legs stretched out in front of him, and his gaze directed upwards to the ceiling. Then he took down from the rack the old and oily clay pipe, which was to him as a counsellor, and having lit it, he leaned back in his chair, with the thick blue cloud-wreaths spinning up from him, and a look of infinite languor in his face.

"Quite an interesting study, that maiden," he observed. "I found her more interesting than her little problem, which, by the way, is rather a trite one. You will find parallel cases, if you consult my index, in Andover in '77, and there was something of the sort at The Hague last year. Old as is the idea, however, there were one or two details which were new to me. But the maiden herself was most instructive."

"You appeared to read a good deal upon her which was quite invisible to me," I remarked.

"Not invisible but unnoticed, Watson. You did not know where to look, and so you missed all that was important. I can never bring you to realize the importance of sleeves, the suggestiveness of thumb-nails, or the great issues that may hang from a boot-lace. Now, what did you gather from that woman's appearance? Describe it."

"Well, she had a slate-coloured, broad-brimmed straw hat, with a feather of a brickish red. Her jacket was black, with black beads sewn upon it, and a fringe of little black jet ornaments. Her dress was brown, rather darker than coffee colour, with a little purple plush at the neck and sleeves. Her gloves were greyish and were worn through at the right forefinger. Her boots I didn't observe. She had small, round, hanging gold earrings, and a general air of being fairly well-to-do in a vulgar, comfortable, easy-going way."

Sherlock Holmes clapped his hands softly together and chuckled.

"'Pon my word, Watson, you are coming along wonderfully. You have really done very well indeed. It is true that you have missed everything of importance, but you have hit upon the method, and you have a quick eye for colour. Never trust to general impressions, my boy, but concentrate yourself upon details. My first glance is always at a woman's sleeve. In a man it is perhaps better first to take the knee of the trouser. As you observe, this woman had plush upon her sleeves, which is a most useful material for showing traces. The double line a little above the wrist, where the typewritist presses against the table, was beautifully defined. The sewing-machine, of the hand type, leaves a similar mark, but only on the left arm, and on the side of it farthest from the thumb, instead of being right across the broadest part, as this was. I then glanced at her face, and observing the dint of a pince-nez at either side of her nose, I ventured a remark upon short sight and typewriting, which seemed to surprise her."

"It surprised me."

"But, surely, it was obvious. I was then much surprised and interested on glancing down to observe that, though the boots which she was wearing were not unlike each other, they were really odd ones; the one having a slightly decorated toe-cap, and the other a plain one. One was buttoned only in the two lower buttons out of five, and the other at the first, third, and fifth. Now, when you see that a young lady, otherwise neatly dressed, has come away from home with odd boots, half-buttoned, it is no great deduction to say that she came away in a hurry."

"And what else?" I asked, keenly interested, as I always was, by my friend's incisive reasoning.

"I noted, in passing, that she had written a note before leaving home but after being fully dressed. You observed that her right glove was torn at the forefinger, but you did not apparently see that both glove and finger were stained with violet ink. She had written in a hurry and dipped her

65

pen too deep. It must have been this morning, or the mark would not remain clear upon the finger. All this is amusing, though rather elementary, but I must go back to business, Watson. Would you mind reading me the advertised description of Mr. Hosmer Angel?"

I held the little printed slip to the light.

"Missing," it said, "on the morning of the fourteenth, a gentleman named Hosmer Angel. About five feet seven inches in height; strongly built, sallow complexion, black hair, a little bald in the centre, bushy, black side-whiskers and moustache; tinted glasses, slight infirmity of speech. Was dressed, when last seen, in black frock-coat faced with silk, black waistcoat, gold Albert chain, and grey Harris tweed trousers, with brown gaiters over elastic-sided boots. Known to have been employed in an office in Leadenhall Street. Anybody bringing—"

"That will do," said Holmes. "As to the letters," he continued, glancing over them, "they are very commonplace. Absolutely no clue in them to Mr. Angel, save that he quotes Balzac once. There is one remarkable point, however, which will no doubt strike you."

"They are typewritten," I remarked.

"Not only that, but the signature is typewritten. Look at the neat little 'Hosmer Angel' at the bottom. There is a date, you see, but no superscription except Leadenhall Street, which is rather vague. The point about the signature is very suggestive—in fact, we may call it conclusive."

"Of what?"

"My dear fellow, is it possible you do not see how strongly it bears upon the case?"

"I cannot say that I do unless it were that he wished to be able to deny his signature if an action for breach of promise were instituted."

"No, that was not the point. However, I shall write two letters, which should settle the matter. One is to a firm in the City, the other is to the young lady's stepfather, Mr. Windibank, asking him whether he could meet us here at six o'clock to-morrow evening. It is just as well that we should do business with the male relatives. And now, Doctor, we can do nothing until the answers to those letters come, so we may put our little problem upon the shelf for the interim."

I had had so many reasons to believe in my friend's subtle powers of reasoning and extraordinary energy in action that I felt that he must have some solid grounds for the assured and easy demeanour with which he treated the singular mystery which he had been called upon to fathom. Once only had I known him to fail, in the case of the King of Bohemia and of the Irene Adler photograph; but when I looked back to the weird business of *The Sign of Four,* and the extraordinary circumstances connected with *A Study in Scarlet,* I felt that it would be a strange tangle indeed which he could not unravel.

I left him then, still puffing at his black clay pipe, with the conviction that when I came again on the next evening I would find that he held in his hands all the clues which would lead up to the identity of the disappearing bridegroom of Miss Mary Sutherland.

A professional case of great gravity was engaging my own attention at the time, and the whole of next day I was busy at the bedside of the sufferer. It was not until close upon six o'clock that I found myself free and was able to spring into a hansom and drive to Baker Street, half afraid that I might be too late to assist at the *dénouement* of the little mystery. I found Sherlock Holmes alone, however, half asleep, with his long, thin form curled up in the recesses of his armchair. A formidable array of bottles and test-tubes, with the pungent, cleanly smell of hydrochloric acid, told me that he had spent his day in the chemical work which was so dear to him.

"Well, have you solved it?" I asked as I entered.

"Yes. It was the bisulphate of baryta."

"No, no, the mystery!" I cried.

"Oh, that! I thought of the salt that I have been working upon. There was never any mystery in the matter, though, as I said yesterday, some of the details are of interest. The only drawback is that there is no law, I fear, that can touch the scoundrel."

"Who was he, then, and what was his object in deserting Miss Sutherland?"

The question was hardly out of my mouth, and Holmes had not yet opened his lips to reply, when we heard a heavy footfall in the passage and a tap at the door.

"This is the girl's stepfather, Mr. James Windibank," said Holmes. "He has written to me to say that he would be here at six. Come in!"

The man who entered was a sturdy, middle-sized fellow, some thirty years of age, clean-shaven, and sallow-skinned, with a bland, insinuating manner, and a pair of wonderfully sharp and penetrating grey eyes. He shot a questioning glance at each of us, placed his shiny top-hat upon the sideboard, and with a slight bow sidled down into the nearest chair.

"Good-evening, Mr. James Windibank," said Holmes. "I think that this typewritten letter is from you, in which you made an appointment with me for six o'clock?"

"Yes, sir. I am afraid that I am a little late, but I am not quite my own master, you know. I am sorry that Miss Sutherland has troubled you about this little matter, for I think it is far better not to wash linen of the sort in public. It was quite against my wishes that she came, but she is a very excitable, impulsive girl, as you may have noticed, and she is not easily controlled when she has made up her mind on a point. Of course, I did not mind you so much, as you are not connected with the official police, but it is not pleasant to have a family misfortune like this noised abroad. Besides, it is a useless expense, for how could you possibly find this Hosmer Angel?"

"On the contrary," said Holmes quietly; "I have every reason to believe that I will succeed in discovering Mr. Hosmer Angel."

Mr. Windibank gave a violent start and dropped his gloves. "I am delighted to hear it," he said.

"It is a curious thing," remarked Holmes, "that a typewriter has really quite as much individuality as a man's handwriting. Unless they are quite new, no two of them write exactly alike. Some letters get more worn than others, and some wear only on one side. Now, you remark in this note of yours, Mr. Windibank, that in every case there is some little slurring over of the *e,* and a slight defect in the tail of the *r.* There are fourteen other characteristics, but those are the more obvious."

"We do all our correspondence with this machine at the office, and no doubt it is a little worn," our visitor answered, glancing keenly at Holmes with his bright little eyes.

"And now I will show you what is really a very interesting study, Mr. Windibank," Holmes continued. "I think of writing another little monograph some of these days on the typewriter and its relation to crime. It is a subject to which I have devoted some little attention. I have here four letters which purport to come from the missing man. They are all typewritten. In each case, not only are the *e*'s slurred and the *r*'s tailless, but you will observe, if you care to use my magnifying lens, that the fourteen other characteristics to which I have alluded are there as well."

Mr. Windibank sprang out of his chair and picked up his hat. "I cannot waste time over this sort of fantastic talk, Mr. Holmes," he said. "If you can catch the man, catch him, and let me know when you have done it."

"Certainly," said Holmes, stepping over and turning the key in the door. "I let you know, then, that I have caught him!"

"What! Where?" shouted Mr. Windibank, turning white to his lips and glancing about him like a rat in a trap.

"Oh, it won't do—really it won't," said Holmes suavely. "There is no possible getting out of it, Mr. Windibank. It is quite too transparent, and it was a very bad compliment when you said that it was impossible for me to solve so simple a question. That's right! Sit down and let us talk it over."

Our visitor collapsed into a chair, with a ghastly face and

a glitter of moisture on his brow. "It—it's not actionable," he stammered.

"I am very much afraid that it is not. But between ourselves, Windibank, it was as cruel and selfish and heartless a trick in a petty way as ever came before me. Now, let me just run over the course of events, and you will contradict me if I go wrong."

The man sat huddled up in his chair, with his head sunk upon his breast, like one who is utterly crushed. Holmes stuck his feet up on the corner of the mantelpiece and, leaning back with his hands in his pockets, began talking, rather to himself, as it seemed, than to us.

"The man married a woman very much older than himself for her money," said he, "and he enjoyed the use of the money of the daughter as long as she lived with them. It was a considerable sum, for people in their position, and the loss of it would have made a serious difference. It was worth an effort to preserve it. The daughter was of a good, amiable disposition, but affectionate and warm-hearted in her ways, so that it was evident that with her fair personal advantages, and her little income, she would not be allowed to remain single long. Now her marriage would mean, of course, the loss of a hundred a year, so what does her stepfather do to prevent it? He takes the obvious course of keeping her at home and forbidding her to seek the company of people of her own age. But soon he found that that would not answer forever. She became restive, insisted upon her rights, and finally announced her positive intention of going to a certain ball. What does her clever stepfather do then? He conceives an idea more creditable to his head than to his heart. With the connivance and assistance of his wife he disguised himself, covered those keen eyes with tinted glasses, masked the face with a moustache and a pair of bushy whiskers, sunk that clear voice into an insinuating whisper, and doubly secure on account of the girl's short sight, he appears as Mr. Hosmer Angel and keeps off other lovers by making love himself."

"It was only a joke at first," groaned our visitor. "We never thought that she would have been so carried away."

"Very likely not. However that may be, the young lady was very decidedly carried away, and having quite made up her mind that her stepfather was in France, the suspicion of treachery never for an instant entered her mind. She was flattered by the gentleman's attentions, and the effect was increased by the loudly expressed admiration of her mother. Then Mr. Angel began to call, for it was obvious that the matter should be pushed as far as it would go if a real effect were to be produced. There were meetings, and an engagement, which would finally secure the girl's affections from turning towards anyone else. But the deception could not be kept up forever. These pretended journeys to France were rather cumbrous. The thing to do was clearly to bring the business to an end in such a dramatic manner that it would leave a permanent impression upon the young lady's mind and prevent her from looking upon any other suitor for some time to come. Hence those vows of fidelity exacted upon a Testament, and hence also the allusions to a possibility of something happening on the very morning of the wedding. James Windibank wished Miss Sutherland to be so bound to Hosmer Angel, and so uncertain as to his fate, that for ten years to come, at any rate, she would not listen to another man. As far as the church door he brought her, and then, as he could go no farther, he conveniently vanished away by the old trick of stepping in at one door of a four-wheeler and out at the other. I think that that was the chain of events, Mr. Windibank!"

Our visitor had recovered something of his assurance while Holmes had been talking, and he rose from his chair now with a cold sneer upon his pale face.

"It may be so, or it may not, Mr. Holmes," said he, "but if you are so very sharp, you ought to be sharp enough to know that it is you who are breaking the law now, and not me. I have done nothing actionable from the first, but as long as you keep that door locked you lay yourself open to an action for assault and illegal constraint."

"The law cannot, as you say, touch you," said Holmes, unlocking and throwing open the door, "yet there never was a man who deserved punishment more. If the young lady has a brother or a friend, he ought to lay a whip across your shoulders. By Jove!" he continued, flushing up at the sight of the bitter sneer upon the man's face, "it is not part of my duties to my client, but here's a hunting crop handy, and I think I shall just treat myself to—" He took two swift steps to the whip, but before he could grasp it there was a wild clatter of steps upon the stairs, the heavy hall door banged, and from the window we could see Mr. James Windibank running at the top of his speed down the road.

"There's a cold-blooded scoundrel!" said Holmes, laughing, as he threw himself down into his chair once more. "That fellow will rise from crime to crime until he does something very bad and ends on a gallows. The case has, in some respects, been not entirely devoid of interest."

"I cannot now entirely see all the steps of your reasoning," I remarked.

"Well, of course it was obvious from the first that this Mr. Hosmer Angel must have some strong object for his curious conduct, and it was equally clear that the only man who really profited by the incident, as far as we could see, was the stepfather. Then the fact that the two men were never together, but that the one always appeared when the other was away, was suggestive. So were the tinted spectacles and the curious voice, which both hinted at a disguise, as did the bushy whiskers. My suspicions were all confirmed by his peculiar action in typewriting his signature, which, of course, inferred that his handwriting was so familiar to her that she would recognise even the smallest sample of it. You see, all these isolated facts, together with many minor ones, all pointed in the same direction."

"And how did you verify them?"

"Having once spotted my man, it was easy to get corroboration. I knew the firm for which this man worked. Having taken the printed description, I eliminated everything from it which could be the result of a disguise—the whiskers, the glasses, the voice, and I sent it to the firm, with a request that they would inform me whether it answered to the description of any of their travellers. I had already noticed the peculiarities of the typewriter, and I wrote to the man himself at his business address, asking him if he would come here. As I expected, his reply was typewritten and revealed the same trivial but characteristic defects. The same post brought me a letter from Westhouse & Marbank, of Fenchurch Street, to say that the description tallied in every respect with that of their employee, James Windibank. *Voilà tout!*"

"And Miss Sutherland?"

"If I tell her, she will not believe me. You may remember the old Persian saying, 'There is danger for him who taketh the tiger cub, and danger also for whoso snatches a delusion from a woman.' There is as much sense in Hafiz as in Horace, and as much knowledge of the world."

The Boscombe Valley Mystery

We were seated at breakfast one morning, my wife and I, when the maid brought in a telegram. It was from Sherlock Holmes and ran in this way:

Have you a couple of days to spare? Have just been wired for from the west of England in connection with Boscombe Valley tragedy. Shall be glad if you will come with me. Air and scenery perfect. Leave Paddington by the 11:15.

"What do you say, dear?" said my wife, looking across at me. "Will you go?"

"I really don't know what to say. I have a fairly long list at present."

"Oh, Anstruther would do your work for you. You have been looking a little pale lately. I think that the change would do you good, and you are always so interested in Mr. Sherlock Holmes's cases."

"I should be ungrateful if I were not, seeing what I gained through one of them," I answered. "But if I am to go, I must pack at once, for I have only half an hour."

My experience of camp life in Afghanistan had at least had the effect of making me a prompt and ready traveller. My wants were few and simple, so that in less than the time stated I was in a cab with my valise, rattling away to Paddington Station. Sherlock Holmes was pacing up and down the platform, his tall, gaunt figure made even gaunter and taller by his long grey travelling-cloak and close-fitting cloth cap.

74

"It is really very good of you to come, Watson," said he. "It makes a considerable difference to me, having someone with me on whom I can thoroughly rely. Local aid is always either worthless or else biassed. If you will keep the two corner seats, I shall get the tickets."

We had the carriage to ourselves save for an immense litter of papers which Holmes had brought with him. Among these he rummaged and read, with intervals of note-taking and of meditation, until we were past Reading. Then he suddenly rolled them all into a gigantic ball and tossed them up onto the rack.

"Have you heard anything of the case?" he asked.

"Not a word. I have not seen a paper for some days."

"The London press has not had very full accounts. I have just been looking through all the recent papers in order to master the particulars. It seems, from what I gather, to be one of those simple cases which are so extremely difficult."

"That sounds a little paradoxical."

"But it is profoundly true. Singularity is almost invariably a clue. The more featureless and commonplace a crime is, the more difficult it is to bring it home. In this case, however, they have established a very serious case against the son of the murdered man."

"It is a murder, then?"

"Well, it is conjectured to be so. I shall take nothing for granted until I have the opportunity of looking personally into it. I will explain the state of things to you, as far as I have been able to understand it, in a very few words.

"Boscombe Valley is a country district not very far from Ross, in Herefordshire. The largest landed proprietor in that part is a Mr. John Turner, who made his money in Australia and returned some years ago to the old country. One of the farms which he held, that of Hatherley, was let to Mr. Charles McCarthy, who was also an ex-Australian. The men had known each other in the colonies, so that it was not unnatural that when they came to settle down they should do so as near each other as possible. Turner was apparently the richer man, so McCarthy became his tenant, but still remained, it seems, upon terms of perfect equality, as they were frequently together. McCarthy had one son, a lad of eighteen, and Turner had an only daughter of the same age, but neither of them had wives living. They appear to have avoided the society of the neighbouring English families and to have led retired lives, though both the McCarthys were fond of sport and were frequently seen at the race-meetings of the neighbourhood. McCarthy kept two servants—a man and a girl. Turner had a considerable household, some half-dozen at the least. That is as much as I have been able to gather about the families. Now for the facts.

"On June 3, that is, on Monday last, McCarthy left his house at Hatherley about three in the afternoon and walked down to the Boscombe Pool, which is a small lake formed by the spreading out of the stream which runs down the Boscombe Valley. He had been out with his serving-man in the morning at Ross, and he had told the man that he must hurry, as he had an appointment of importance to keep at three. From that appointment he never came back alive.

"From Hatherley Farmhouse to the Boscombe Pool is a quarter of a mile, and two people saw him as he passed over this ground. One was an old woman, whose name is not mentioned, and the other was William Crowder, a game-keeper in the employ of Mr. Turner. Both these witnesses depose that Mr. McCarthy was walking alone. The game-keeper adds that within a few minutes of his seeing Mr. McCarthy pass he had seen his son, Mr. James McCarthy, going the same way with a gun under his arm. To the best of his belief, the father was actually in sight at the time, and the son was following him. He thought no more of the matter until he heard in the evening of the tragedy that had occurred.

"The two McCarthys were seen after the time when William Crowder, the game-keeper, lost sight of them. The Boscombe Pool is thickly wooded round, with just a fringe of grass and of reeds round the edge. A girl of fourteen, Patience Moran, who is the daughter of the lodge-keeper of the Boscombe Valley estate, was in one of the woods picking flowers. She states that while she was there she saw, at the border of the wood and close by the lake, Mr. McCarthy and his son, and that they appeared to be having a violent quarrel. She heard Mr. McCarthy the elder using very strong language to his son, and she saw the latter raise up his hand as if to strike his father. She was so frightened by their violence that she ran away and told her mother when she reached home that she had left the two McCarthys quarrelling near Boscombe Pool, and that she was afraid that they were going to fight. She had hardly said the words when young McCarthy came running up to the lodge to say he had found his father dead in the wood, and to ask for the help of the lodge-keeper. He was much excited, without either his gun or his hat, and his right hand and sleeve were observed to be stained with fresh blood. On following him, they found the dead body stretched out upon the grass beside the pool. The head had been beaten in by repeated blows of some heavy and blunt weapon. The injuries were such as might very well have been inflicted by the butt-end of his son's gun, which was found lying on the grass within a few paces of the body. Under these circumstances the young man was instantly arrested, and a verdict of 'wilful murder' having been returned at the inquest on Tuesday, he was on Wednesday brought before the magistrates at Ross, who have referred the case to the next Assizes. Those are the main facts of the case as they came out before the coroner and the police-court."

"I could hardly imagine a more damning case," I remarked. "If ever circumstantial evidence pointed to a criminal, it does so here."

"Circumstantial evidence is a very tricky thing," answered Holmes thoughtfully. "It may seem to point very straight to one thing, but if you shift your own point of view a little, you may find it pointing in an equally uncompromising manner to something entirely different. It must be confessed, however, that the case looks exceedingly grave against the young man, and it is very possible that he is indeed the culprit. There are several people in the neighbourhood, however, and among them Miss Turner, the daughter of the neighbouring land-owner, who believe in his innocence and who have retained Lestrade, whom you may recollect in connection with *A Study in Scarlet,* to work out the case in his interest. Lestrade, being rather puzzled, has referred the case to me, and hence it is that two middle-aged gentlemen are flying westward at fifty miles an hour instead of quietly digesting their breakfasts at home."

"I am afraid," said I, "that the facts are so obvious that you will find little credit to be gained out of this case."

"There is nothing more deceptive than an obvious fact," he answered, laughing. "Besides, we may chance to hit upon some other obvious facts which may have been by no means obvious to Mr. Lestrade. You know me too well to think that I am boasting when I say that I shall either confirm or destroy his theory by means which he is quite incapable of employing, or even of understanding. To take the first example to hand, I very clearly perceive that in your bedroom the window is upon the right-hand side, and yet I question whether Mr. Lestrade would have noted even so self-evident a thing as that."

"How on earth——"

"My dear fellow, I know you well. I know the military neatness which characterises you. You shave every morning, and in this season you shave by the sunlight; but since your shaving is less and less complete as we get farther back on the left side, until it becomes positively slovenly as we get round the angle of the jaw, it is surely very clear that that side is less illuminated than the other. I could not imagine a man of your habits looking at himself in an equal light and being satisfied with such a result. I only quote this as a trivial example of observation and inference. Therein lies my *métier,* and it is just possible that it may be of some service in the investigation which lies before us. There are one or two minor points which were brought out in the inquest and which are worth considering."

"What are they?"

"It appears that his arrest did not take place at once, but after the return to Hatherley Farm. On the Inspector of Constabulary informing him that he was a prisoner, he remarked that he was not surprised to hear it, and that it was no more than his deserts. This observation of his had the natural effect of removing any traces of doubt which might have remained in the minds of the Coroner's jury."

"It was a confession," I ejaculated.

"No, for it was followed by a protestation of innocence."

"Coming on the top of such a damning series of events, it was at least a most suspicious remark."

"On the contrary," said Holmes, "it is the brightest rift which I can at present see in the clouds. However innocent he might be, he could not be such an absolute imbecile as not to see that the circumstances were very black against him. Had he appeared surprised at his own arrest, or feigned indignation at it, I should have looked upon it as highly suspicious, because such surprise or anger would not be natural under the circumstances and yet might appear to be the best policy to a scheming man. His frank acceptance of the situation marks him as either an innocent man, or else as a man of considerable self-restraint and firmness. As to his remark about his deserts, it was also not unnatural if you consider that he stood beside the dead body of his father, and that there is no doubt that he had that very day so far forgotten his filial duty as to bandy words with him, and even, according to the little girl whose evidence is so important, to raise his hand as if to strike him. The self-reproach and contrition which are displayed in his remark appear to me to be the signs of a healthy mind rather than of a guilty one."

I shook my head. "Many men have been hanged on far slighter evidence," I remarked.

"So they have. And many men have been wrongfully hanged."

"What is the young man's own account of the matter?"

"It is, I am afraid, not very encouraging to his supporters, though there are one or two points in it which are suggestive. You will find it here and may read it for yourself."

He picked out from his bundle a copy of the local Herefordshire paper, and having turned down the sheet, he pointed out the paragraph in which the unfortunate young man had given his own statement of what had occurred. I settled myself down in the corner of the carriage and read it very carefully. It ran in this way:

Mr. James McCarthy, the only son of the deceased, was then called and gave evidence as follows: I had been away from home for three days at Bristol and had only just returned upon the morning of last Monday, the third. My father was absent from home at the time of my arrival, and I was informed by the maid that he had driven over to Ross with John Cobb, the groom. Shortly after my return I heard the wheels of his trap in the yard, and looking out of my window, I saw him get out and walk rapidly out of the yard, though I was not aware in which direction he was going. I then took my gun and strolled out in the direction of the Boscombe Pool, with the intention of visiting the rabbit-warren which is upon the other side. On my way I saw William Crowder, the game-keeper, as he has stated in his evidence; but he is mistaken in thinking that I was following my father. I had no idea that he was in front of me. When about a hundred yards from the pool I heard a cry of "Cooee!" which was a usual signal between my father and myself. I then hurried forward and found him standing by the pool. He appeared to be much surprised at seeing me and asked me rather roughly what I was doing there. A conversation ensued which led to high words and almost to blows, for my father was a man of a very violent temper. Seeing that his passion was becoming ungovernable, I left him and returned towards Hatherley Farm. I had not gone more than 150 yards, however, when I heard a hideous outcry behind me, which caused me to run back again. I found my father expiring upon the ground, with his head terribly injured. I dropped my gun and held him in my arms, but he almost instantly expired. I knelt beside him for some minutes and then made my way to Mr. Turner's lodge-keeper, his house being the nearest, to ask for assistance. I saw no one near my father when I returned, and I have no idea how he came by his injuries. He was not a popular man, being somewhat cold and forbidding in his manners; but he had, as far as I know, no active enemies. I know nothing further of the matter.

The Coroner: Did your father make any statement to you before he died?

Witness: He mumbled a few words, but I could only catch some allusion to a rat.

The Coroner: What did you understand by that?

Witness: It conveyed no meaning to me. I thought that he was delirious.

The Coroner: What was the point upon which you and your father had this final quarrel?

Witness: I should prefer not to answer.

The Coroner: I am afraid that I must press it.

Witness: It is really impossible for me to tell you. I can assure you that it has nothing to do with the sad tragedy which followed.

The Coroner: That is for the court to decide. I need not point out to you that your refusal to answer will prejudice your case considerably in any future proceedings which may arise.

Witness: I must still refuse.

The Coroner: I understand that the cry of "Cooee" was a common signal between you and your father?

Witness: It was.

The Coroner: How was it, then, that he uttered it before he saw you, and before he even knew that you had returned from Bristol?

Witness (with considerable confusion): I do not know.

A Juryman: Did you see nothing which aroused your suspicions when you returned on hearing the cry and found your father fatally injured?

Witness: Nothing definite.

The Coroner: What do you mean?

Witness: I was so disturbed and excited as I rushed out into the open, that I could think of nothing except of my father. Yet I have a vague impression that as I ran forward something lay upon the ground to the left of me. It seemed to me to be something grey in colour, a coat of some sort, or a plaid perhaps. When I rose from my father I looked round for it, but it was gone.

The Coroner: Do you mean that it disappeared before you went for help?

Witness: Yes, it was gone.

The Coroner: You cannot say what it was?

Witness: No, I had a feeling something was there.

The Coroner: How far from the body?

Witness: A dozen yards or so.

The Coroner: And how far from the edge of the wood?

Witness: About the same.

The Coroner: Then if it was removed, it was while you were within a dozen yards of it?

Witness: Yes, but with my back towards it.

The Coroner: This concluded the examination of the witness.

"I see," said I as I glanced down the column, "that the Coroner in his concluding remarks was rather severe upon young McCarthy. He calls attention, and with reason, to the discrepancy about his father having signalled to him before seeing him, also to his refusal to give details of his conversation with his father, and his singular account of his father's dying words. They are all, as he remarks, very much against the son."

Holmes laughed softly to himself and stretched himself out upon the cushioned seat. "Both you and the Coroner have been at some pains," said he, "to single out the very strongest points in the young man's favour. Don't you see that you alternately give him credit for having too much imagination and too little? Too little, if he could not invent a cause of quarrel which would give him the sympathy of the jury; too much, if he evolved from his own inner consciousness anything so *outré* as a dying reference to a rat, and the incident of the vanishing cloth. No, sir, I shall approach this case from the point of view that what this young man says is true, and we shall see whither that hypothesis will lead us. And now here is my pocket Petrarch, and not another word shall I say of this case until we are on the scene of action. We lunch at Swindon, and I see that we shall be there in twenty minutes."

It was nearly four o'clock when we at last, after passing through the beautiful Stroud Valley and over the broad gleaming Severn, found ourselves at the pretty little country-town of Ross. A lean, ferret-like man, furtive and sly-looking, was waiting for us upon the platform. In spite of the light-brown dustcoat and leather-leggings which he wore in deference to his rustic surroundings, I had no difficulty in recognising Lestrade, of Scotland Yard. With him we drove to the Hereford Arms, where a room had already been engaged for us.

"I have ordered a carriage," said Lestrade as we sat over a cup of tea. "I knew your energetic nature, and that you would not be happy until you had been on the scene of the crime."

"It was very nice and complimentary of you," Holmes answered. "It is entirely a question of barometric pressure."

Lestrade looked startled. "I do not quite follow," he said.

"How is the glass? Twenty-nine, I see. No wind, and not a cloud in the sky. I have a caseful of cigarettes here which need smoking, and the sofa is very much superior to the usual country hotel abomination. I do not think that it is probable that I shall use the carriage to-night."

Lestrade laughed indulgently. "You have, no doubt, already formed your conclusions from the newspapers," he said. "The case is as plain as a pikestaff, and the more one goes into it the plainer it becomes. Still, of course, one can't refuse a lady, and such a very positive one, too. She had heard of you and would have your opinion, though I repeatedly told her that there was nothing which you could do which I had not already done. Why, bless my soul, here is her carriage at the door!"

He had hardly spoken before there rushed into the room one of the most lovely young women that I have ever seen in my life. Her violet eyes were shining, her lips parted, a pink flush upon her cheeks, all thought of her natural reserve lost in her overpowering excitement and concern.

"Oh, Mr. Sherlock Holmes!" she cried, glancing from one to the other of us, and finally, with a woman's quick intuition, fastening upon my companion, "I am so glad that you have come. I have driven down to tell you so. I know that James didn't do it. I know it, and I want you to start upon your work knowing it, too. Never let yourself doubt upon that point. We have known each other since we were little children, and I know his faults as no one else does; but he is too tender-hearted to hurt a fly. Such a charge is absurd to anyone who really knows him."

"I hope we may clear him, Miss Turner," said Sherlock Holmes. "You may rely upon my doing all that I can."

"But you have read the evidence. You have formed some conclusion? Do you not see some loophole, some flaw? Do you not yourself think that he is innocent?"

"I think that it is very probable."

"There, now!" she cried, throwing back her head and looking defiantly at Lestrade. "You hear! He gives me hopes."

Lestrade shrugged his shoulders. "I am afraid that my colleague has been a little quick in forming his conclusions," he said.

"But he is right. Oh! I know that he is right. James never did it. And about his quarrel with his father, I am sure that the reason why he would not speak about it to the Coroner was because I was concerned in it."

"In what way?" asked Holmes.

"It is no time for me to hide anything. James and his father had many disagreements about me. Mr. McCarthy was very anxious that there should be a marriage between us. James and I have always loved each other as brother and sister; but of course he is young and has seen very little of life yet, and—and—well, he naturally did not wish to do anything like that yet. So there were quarrels, and this, I am sure, was one of them."

"And your father?" asked Holmes. "Was he in favour of such a union?"

"No, he was averse to it also. No one but Mr. McCarthy was in favour of it." A quick blush passed over her fresh young face as Holmes shot one of his keen, questioning glances at her.

"Thank you for this information," said he. "May I see your father if I call to-morrow?"

"I am afraid the doctor won't allow it."

"The doctor?"

"Yes, have you not heard? Poor father has never been strong for years back, but this has broken him down completely. He has taken to his bed, and Dr. Willows says that he is a wreck and that his nervous system is shattered. Mr. McCarthy was the only man alive who had known Dad in the old days in Victoria."

"Ha! In Victoria! That is important."

"Yes, at the mines."

"Quite so; at the gold-mines, where, as I understand, Mr. Turner made his money."

"Yes, certainly."

"Thank you, Miss Turner. You have been of material assistance to me."

"You will tell me if you have any news to-morrow. No doubt you will go to the prison to see James. Oh, if you do, Mr. Holmes, do tell him that I know him to be innocent."

"I will, Miss Turner."

"I must go home now, for Dad is very ill, and he misses me so if I leave him. Good-bye, and God help you in your undertaking." She hurried from the room as impulsively as she had entered, and we heard the wheels of her carriage rattle off down the street.

"I am ashamed of you, Holmes," said Lestrade with dignity after a few minutes' silence. "Why should you raise up hopes which you are bound to disappoint? I am not over-tender of heart, but I call it cruel."

"I think that I see my way to clearing James McCarthy," said Holmes. "Have you an order to see him in prison?"

"Yes, but only for you and me."

"Then I shall reconsider my resolution about going out. We have still time to take a train to Hereford and see him to-night?"

"Ample."

"Then let us do so. Watson, I fear that you will find it very slow, but I shall only be away a couple of hours."

I walked down to the station with them, and then wandered through the streets of the little town, finally returning to the hotel, where I lay upon the sofa and tried to interest myself in a yellow-backed novel. The puny plot of the story was so thin, however, when compared to the deep mystery through which we were groping, and I found my attention wander so continually from the fiction to the fact, that I at last flung it across the room and gave myself up entirely to a consideration of the events of the day. Supposing that this unhappy young man's story were absolutely true, then what hellish thing, what absolutely unforeseen and extraordinary calamity could have occurred between the time when he parted from his father and the moment when, drawn back by his screams, he rushed into the glade? It was something terrible and deadly. What could it be? Might not the nature of the injuries reveal something to my medical instincts? I rang the bell and called for the weekly county paper, which contained a verbatim account of the inquest. In the surgeon's deposition it was stated that the posterior third of the left parietal bone and the left half of the occipital bone had been shattered by a heavy blow from a blunt weapon. I marked the spot upon my own head. Clearly such a blow must have been struck from behind. That was to some extent in favour of the accused, as when seen quarrelling he was face to face with his father. Still, it did not go for very much, for the older man might have turned his back before the blow fell. Still, it might be worth while to call Holmes's attention to it. Then there was the peculiar dying reference to a rat. What could that mean? It could not be delirium. A man dying from a sudden blow does not commonly become delirious. No, it was more likely to be an attempt to explain how he met his fate. But what could it indicate? I cudgelled my brains to find some possible explanation. And then the incident of the grey cloth seen by young McCarthy. If that were true, the murderer must have dropped some part of his dress, presumably his overcoat, in his flight and must have had the hardihood to re-

86

turn and to carry it away at the instant when the son was kneeling with his back turned not a dozen paces off. What a tissue of mysteries and improbabilities the whole thing was! I did not wonder at Lestrade's opinion, and yet I had so much faith in Sherlock Holmes's insight that I could not lose hope as long as every fresh fact seemed to strengthen his conviction of young McCarthy's innocence.

It was late before Sherlock Holmes returned. He came back alone, for Lestrade was staying in lodgings in the town.

"The glass still keeps very high," he remarked as he sat down. "It is of importance that it should not rain before we are able to go over the ground. On the other hand, a man should be at his very best and keenest for such nice work as that, and I did not wish to do it when fagged by a long journey. I have seen young McCarthy."

"And what did you learn from him?"

"Nothing."

"Could he throw no light?"

"None at all. I was inclined to think at one time that he knew who had done it and was screening him or her, but I am convinced now that he is as puzzled as everyone else. He is not a very quick-witted youth, though comely to look at and, I should think, sound at heart."

"I cannot admire his taste," I remarked, "if it is indeed a fact that he was averse to a marriage with so charming a young lady as this Miss Turner."

"Ah, thereby hangs a rather painful tale. This fellow is madly, insanely, in love with her, but some two years ago, when he was only a lad, and before he really knew her, for she had been away five years at a boarding-school, what does the idiot do but get into the clutches of a barmaid in Bristol and marry her at a registry office? No one knows a word of the matter, but you can imagine how maddening it must be to him to be upbraided for not doing what he would give his very eyes to do, but what he knows to be absolutely impossible. It was sheer frenzy of this sort which made him throw his hands up into the air when his father,

at their last interview, was goading him on to propose to
Miss Turner. On the other hand, he had no means of sup-
porting himself, and his father, who was by all accounts a
very hard man, would have thrown him over utterly had
he known the truth. It was with his barmaid wife that he
had spent the last three days in Bristol, and his father did
not know where he was. Mark that point. It is of importance. Good has come out of evil, however, for the barmaid, finding from the papers that he is in serious trouble
and likely to be hanged, has thrown him over utterly and
has written to him to say that she has a husband already in
the Bermuda Dockyard, so that there is really no tie
between them. I think that that bit of news has consoled
young McCarthy for all that he has suffered."

"But if he is innocent, who has done it?"

"Ah, who? I would call your attention very particularly
to two points. One is that the murdered man had an appointment with someone at the pool, and that the someone
could not have been his son, for his son was away, and he
did not know when he would return. The second is that
the murdered man was heard to cry 'Cooee!' before he
knew that his son had returned. Those are the crucial
points upon which the case depends. And now let us talk
about George Meredith, if you please, and we shall leave
all minor matters until to-morrow."

There was no rain, as Holmes had foretold, and the
morning broke bright and cloudless. At nine o'clock Lestrade called for us with the carriage, and we set off for
Hatherley Farm and the Boscombe Pool.

"There is serious news this morning," Lestrade observed. "It is said that Mr. Turner, of the Hall, is so ill that
his life is despaired of."

"An elderly man, I presume?" said Holmes.

"About sixty; but his constitution has been shattered by
his life abroad, and he has been in failing health for some
time. This business has had a very bad effect upon him.
He was an old friend of McCarthy's, and I may add, a
great benefactor to him, for I have learned that he gave
him Hatherley Farm rent free."

"Indeed! That is interesting," said Holmes.

"Oh, yes! In a hundred other ways he has helped him. Everybody about here speaks of his kindness to him."

"Really! Does it not strike you as a little singular that this McCarthy, who appears to have had little of his own and to have been under such obligations to Turner, should still talk of marrying his son to Turner's daughter, who is, presumably, heiress to the estate, and that in such a very cocksure manner, as if it were merely a case of a proposal and all else would follow? It is the more strange, since we know that Turner himself was averse to the idea. The daughter told us as much. Do you not deduce something from that?"

"We have got to the deductions and the inferences," said Lestrade, winking at me. "I find it hard enough to tackle facts, Holmes, without flying away after theories and fancies."

"You are right," said Holmes demurely; "you do find it very hard to tackle the facts."

"Anyhow, I have grasped one fact which you seem to find it difficult to get hold of," replied Lestrade with some warmth.

"And that is—"

"That McCarthy senior met his death from McCarthy junior and that all theories to the contrary are the merest moonshine."

"Well, moonshine is a brighter thing than fog," said Holmes, laughing. "But I am very much mistaken if this is not Hatherley Farm upon the left."

"Yes, that is it." It was a widespread, comfortable-looking building, two-storied, slate-roofed, with great yellow blotches of lichen upon the grey walls. The drawn blinds and the smokeless chimneys, however, gave it a stricken look, as though the weight of this horror still lay heavy upon it. We called at the door, when the maid, at Holmes's request, showed us the boots which her master wore at the time of his death, and also a pair of the son's, though not the pair which he had then had. Having measured these very carefully from seven or eight different points, Holmes desired to be led to the court-yard, from which we all followed the winding track which led to Boscombe Pool.

Sherlock Holmes was transformed when he was hot upon such a scent as this. Men who had only known the quiet thinker and logician of Baker Street would have failed to recognise him. His face flushed and darkened. His brows were drawn into two hard black lines, while his eyes shone out from beneath them with a steely glitter. His face was bent downwards, his shoulders bowed, his lips compressed, and the veins stood out like whipcord in his long, sinewy neck. His nostrils seemed to dilate with a purely animal lust for the chase, and his mind was so absolutely concentrated upon the matter before him that a question or remark fell unheeded upon his ears, or, at the most, only provoked a quick, impatient snarl in reply. Swiftly and silently he made his way along the track which ran through the meadows, and so by way of the woods to the Boscombe Pool. It was damp, marshy ground, as is all that district, and there were marks of many feet, both upon the path and amid the short grass which bounded it on either side. Sometimes Holmes would hurry on, sometimes stop dead, and once he made quite a little detour into the meadow. Lestrade and I walked behind him, the detective indifferent and contemptuous, while I watched my friend with the interest which sprang from the conviction that every one of his actions was directed towards a definite end.

The Boscombe Pool, which is a little reed-girt sheet of water some fifty yards across, is situated at the boundary between the Hatherley Farm and the private park of the wealthy Mr. Turner. Above the woods which lined it upon the farther side we could see the red, jutting pinnacles which marked the site of the rich land-owner's dwelling. On the Hatherley side of the pool the woods grew very thick, and there was a narrow belt of sodden grass twenty paces across between the edge of the trees and the reeds which lined the lake. Lestrade showed us the exact spot at which the body had been found, and indeed, so moist was the ground that I could plainly see the traces which had been left by the fall of the stricken man. To Holmes, as I could see by his eager face and peering eyes, very many other things were to be read upon the trampled grass. He ran round, like a dog who is picking up a scent, and then turned upon my companion.

"What did you go into the pool for?" he asked.

"I fished about with a rake. I thought there might be some weapon or other trace. But how on earth—"

"Oh, tut, tut! I have no time! That left foot of yours with its inward twist is all over the place. A mole could trace it and there it vanishes among the reeds. Oh, how simple it would all have been had I been here before they came like a herd of buffalo and wallowed all over it. Here is where the party with the lodge-keeper came, and they have covered all tracks for six or eight feet round the body. But here are three separate tracks of the same feet." He drew out a lens and lay down upon his waterproof to have a better view, talking all the time rather to himself than to us. "These are young McCarthy's feet. Twice he was walking, and once he ran swiftly, so that the soles are deeply marked and the heels hardly visible. That bears out his story. He ran when he saw his father on the ground. Then here are the father's feet as he paced up and down. What is this, then? It is the butt-end of the gun as the son stood listening. And this? Ha, ha! What have we here? Tiptoes, tiptoes! Square, too, quite unusual boots! They come, they go, they come again—of course that was for the cloak. Now where did they come from?" He ran up and down, sometimes losing, sometimes finding the track until we were well within the edge of the wood and under the shadow of a great beech, the largest tree in the neighbourhood. Holmes traced his way to the farther side of this and lay down once more upon his face with a little cry of satisfaction. For a long time he remained there, turning over the leaves and dried sticks, gathering up what seemed to me to be dust into an envelope and examining with his lens not only the ground but even the bark of the tree as far as he could reach. A jagged stone was lying among the moss, and this also he carefully examined and retained. Then he followed a pathway through the wood until he came to the highroad, where all traces were lost.

"It has been a case of considerable interest," he remarked, returning to his natural manner. "I fancy that this grey house on the right must be the lodge. I think that I will go in and have a word with Moran and perhaps write a little note. Having done that, we may drive back to our luncheon. You may walk to the cab, and I shall be with you presently."

It was about ten minutes before we regained our cab and drove back into Ross, Holmes still carrying with him the stone which he had picked up in the wood.

"This may interest you, Lestrade," he remarked, holding it out. "The murder was done with it."

"I see no marks."

"There are none."

"How do you know, then?"

"The grass was growing under it. It had only lain there a few days. There was no sign of a place whence it had been taken. It corresponds with the injuries. There is no sign of any other weapon."

"And the murderer?"

"Is a tall man, left-handed, limps with the right leg, wears thick-soled shooting boots and a grey cloak, smokes Indian cigars, uses a cigar-holder, and carries a blunt penknife in his pocket. There are several other indications, but these may be enough to aid us in our search."

Lestrade laughed. "I am afraid that I am still a sceptic," he said. "Theories are all very well, but we have to deal with a hard-headed British jury."

"*Nous verrons*," answered Holmes calmly. "You work your own method, and I shall work mine. I shall be busy this afternoon and shall probably return to London by the evening train."

"And leave your case unfinished?"

"No, finished."

"But the mystery?"

"It is solved."

"Who was the criminal, then?"

"The gentleman I describe."

"But who is he?"

"Surely it would not be difficult to find out. This is not such a populous neighbourhood."

Lestrade shrugged his shoulders. "I am a practical man," he said, "and I really cannot undertake to go about the country looking for a left-handed gentleman with a game-leg. I should become the laughing-stock of Scotland Yard."

"All right," said Holmes quietly. "I have given you the chance. Here are your lodgings. Good-bye. I shall drop you a line before I leave."

Having left Lestrade at his rooms, we drove to our hotel, where we found lunch upon the table. Holmes was silent and buried in thought with a pained expression upon his face, as one who finds himself in a perplexing position.

"Look here, Watson," he said when the cloth was cleared; "just sit down in this chair and let me preach to you for a little. I don't know quite what to do, and I should value your advice. Light a cigar and let me expound."

"Pray do so."

"Well, now, in considering this case there are two points about young McCarthy's narrative which struck us both instantly, although they impressed me in his favour and you against him. One was the fact that his father should, according to his account, cry 'Cooee!' before seeing him. The other was his singular dying reference to a rat. He mumbled several words, you understand, but that was all that caught the son's ear. Now from this double point our research must commence, and we will begin it by presuming that what the lad says is absolutely true."

"What of this 'Cooee!' then?"

"Well, obviously it could not have been meant for the son. The son, as far as he knew, was in Bristol. It was mere chance that he was within earshot. The 'Cooee!' was meant to attract the attention of whomever it was that he had the appointment with. But 'Cooee' is a distinctly Australian cry, and one which is used between Australians. There is a strong presumption that the person whom McCarthy expected to meet him at Boscombe Pool was someone who had been in Australia."

"What of the rat, then?"

Sherlock Holmes took a folded paper from his pocket and flattened it out on the table. "This is a map of the Colony of Victoria," he said. "I wired to Bristol for it last night." He put his hand over part of the map. "What do you read?"

"ARAT," I read.

"And now?" He raised his hand.

"BALLARAT."

"Quite so. That was the word the man uttered, and of which his son only caught the last two syllables. He was trying to utter the name of his murderer. So and so, of Ballarat."

"It is wonderful!" I exclaimed.

"It is obvious. And now, you see, I had narrowed the field down considerably. The possession of a grey garment was a third point which, granting the son's statement to be correct, was a certainty. We have come now out of mere vagueness to the definite conception of an Australian from Ballarat with a grey cloak."

"Certainly."

"And one who was at home in the district, for the pool can only be approached by the farm or by the estate, where strangers could hardly wander."

"Quite so."

"Then comes our expedition of to-day. By an examination of the ground I gained the trifling details which I gave to that imbecile Lestrade, as to the personality of the criminal."

"But how did you gain them?"

"You know my method. It is founded upon the observation of trifles."

"His height I know that you might roughly judge from the length of his stride. His boots, too, might be told from their traces."

"Yes, they were peculiar boots."

"But his lameness?"

"The impression of his right foot was always less distinct than his left. He put less weight upon it. Why? Because he limped—he was lame."

"But his left-handedness?"

"You were yourself struck by the nature of the injury as recorded by the surgeon at the inquest. The blow was struck from immediately behind, and yet was upon the left side. Now, how can that be unless it were by a left-handed man? He had stood behind that tree during the interview between the father and son. He had even smoked there. I found the ash of a cigar, which my special knowledge of tobacco ashes enables me to pronounce as an Indian cigar. I have, as you know, devoted some attention to this and written a little monograph on the ashes of one hundred forty different varieties of pipe, cigar, and cigarette tobacco. Having found the ash, I then looked round and discovered the stump among the moss where he had tossed it. It was an Indian cigar, of the variety which are rolled in Rotterdam."

"And the cigar-holder?"

"I could see that the end had not been in his mouth. Therefore he used a holder. The tip had been cut off, not bitten off, but the cut was not a clean one, so I deduced a blunt penknife."

"Holmes," I said, "you have drawn a net round this man from which he cannot escape, and you have saved an innocent human life as truly as if you had cut the cord which was hanging him. I see the direction in which all this points. The culprit is—"

"Mr. John Turner," cried the hotel waiter, opening the door of our sitting-room and ushering in a visitor.

The man who entered was a strange and impressive figure. His slow, limping step and bowed shoulders gave the appearance of decrepitude, and yet his hard, deep-lined, craggy features and his enormous limbs showed that he was possessed of unusual strength of body and of character. His tangled beard, grizzled hair, and outstanding, drooping eyebrows combined to give an air of dignity and power to his appearance, but his face was of an ashen white, while his lips and the corners of his nostrils were tinged with a shade of blue. It was clear to me at a glance that he was in the grip of some deadly and chronic disease.

"Pray sit down on the sofa," said Holmes gently. "You had my note?"

"Yes, the lodge-keeper brought it up. You said that you wished to see me here to avoid scandal."

"I thought people would talk if I went to the Hall."

"And why did you wish to see me?" He looked across at my companion with despair in his weary eyes, as though his question was already answered.

"Yes," said Holmes, answering the look rather than the words. "It is so. I know all about McCarthy."

The old man sank his face in his hands. "God help me!" he cried. "But I would not have let the young man come to harm. I give you my word that I would have spoken out if it went against him at the Assizes."

"I am glad to hear you say so," said Holmes gravely.

"I would have spoken now had it not been for my dear girl. It would break her heart—it will break her heart when she hears that I am arrested."

"It may not come to that," said Holmes.

"What?"

"I am no official agent. I understand that it was your daughter who required my presence here, and I am acting in her interests. Young McCarthy must be got off, however."

"I am a dying man," said old Turner. "I have had diabetes for years. My doctor says it is a question whether I shall live a month. Yet I would rather die under my own roof than in a gaol."

Holmes rose and sat down at the table with his pen in his

hand and a bundle of paper before him. "Just tell us the truth," he said. "I shall jot down the facts. You will sign it, and Watson here can witness it. Then I could produce your confession at the last extremity to save young Mc-Carthy. I promise you that I shall not use it unless it is absolutely needed."

"It's as well," said the old man; "it's a question whether I shall live to the Assizes, so it matters little to me, but I should wish to spare Alice the shock. And now I will make the thing clear to you; it has been a long time in the acting, but will not take me long to tell.

"You didn't know this dead man, McCarthy. He was a devil incarnate. I tell you that. God keep you out of the clutches of such a man as he. His grip has been upon me these twenty years, and he has blasted my life. I'll tell you first how I came to be in his power.

"It was in the early sixties at the diggings. I was a young chap then, hot-blooded and reckless, ready to turn my hand at anything; I got among bad companions, took to drink, had no luck with my claim, took to the bush, and in a word became what you would call over here a highway robber. There were six of us, and we had a wild, free life of it, sticking up a station from time to time, or stopping the wagons on the road to the diggings. Black Jack of Ballarat was the name I went under, and our party is still remembered in the colony as the Ballarat Gang.

"One day a gold convoy came down from Ballarat to Melbourne, and we lay in wait for it and attacked it. There were six troopers and six of us, so it was a close thing, but we emptied four of their saddles at the first volley. Three of our boys were killed, however, before we got the swag. I put my pistol to the head of the wagon-driver, who was this very man McCarthy. I wish to the Lord that I had shot him then, but I spared him, though I saw his wicked little eyes fixed on my face, as though to remember every feature. We got away with the gold, became wealthy men, and made our way over to England without being suspected. There I parted from my old pals and determined to settle down to a quiet and respectable life. I bought this estate, which chanced to be in the market, and I set myself to do a little good with my money, to make up for the way in which I had earned it. I married, too, and though my wife died young she left me my dear little Alice. Even when she was just a baby her wee hand seemed to lead me down the right path as nothing else had ever done. In a word, I turned over a new leaf and did my best to make up for the past. All was going well when McCarthy laid his grip upon me.

"I had gone up to town about an investment, and I met him in Regent Street with hardly a coat to his back or a boot to his foot.

"'Here we are, Jack,' says he, touching me on the arm; 'we'll be as good as a family to you. There's two of us, me and my son, and you can have the keeping of us. If you don't—it's a fine, law-abiding country is England, and there's always a policeman within hail.'

"Well, down they came to the west country; there was no shaking them off, and there they have lived rent free on my best land ever since. There was no rest for me, no peace, no forgetfulness; turn where I would, there was his cunning, grinning face at my elbow. It grew worse as Alice grew up, for he soon saw I was more afraid of her knowing my past than of the police. Whatever he wanted he must have, and whatever it was I gave him without question— land, money, houses—until at last he asked a thing which I could not give. He asked for Alice.

"His son, you see, had grown up, and so had my girl, and as I was known to be in weak health, it seemed a fine stroke to him that his lad should step into the whole property. But there I was firm. I would not have his cursed stock mixed with mine; not that I had any dislike to the lad, but his blood was in him, and that was enough. I stood firm. McCarthy threatened. I braved him to do his worst. We were to meet at the pool midway between our houses to talk it over.

"When I went down there I found him talking with his

son, so I smoked a cigar and waited behind a tree until he should be alone. But as I listened to his talk all that was black and bitter in me seemed to come uppermost. He was urging his son to marry my daughter with as little regard for what she might think as if she were a slut from off the streets. It drove me mad to think that I and all that I held most dear should be in the power of such a man as this. Could I not snap the bond? I was already a dying and desperate man. Though clear of mind and fairly strong of limb, I knew that my own fate was sealed. But my memory and my girl! Both could be saved if I could but silence that foul tongue. I did it, Mr. Holmes. I would do it again. Deeply as I have sinned, I have led a life of martyrdom to atone for it. But that my girl should be entangled in the same meshes which held me was more than I could suffer. I struck him down with no more compunction than if he had been some foul and venomous beast. His cry brought back his son; but I had gained the cover of the wood, though I was forced to go back to fetch the cloak which I had dropped in my flint. That is the true story, gentlemen, of all that occurred."

"Well, it is not for me to judge you," said Holmes as the old man signed the statement which had been drawn out. "I pray that we may never be exposed to such a temptation."

"I pray not, sir. And what do you intend to do?"

"In view of your health, nothing. You are yourself aware that you will soon have to answer for your deed at a higher court than the Assizes. I will keep your confession, and if McCarthy is condemned I shall be forced to use it. If not, it shall never be seen by mortal eye; and your secret, whether you be alive or dead, shall be safe with us."

"Farewell, then," said the old man solemnly. "Your own death-beds, when they come, will be the easier for the thought of the peace which you have given to mine." Tottering and shaking in all his giant frame, he stumbled slowly from the room.

"God help us!" said Holmes after a long silence. "Why

does fate play such tricks with poor, helpless worms? I never hear of such a case as this that I do not think of Baxter's words and say, 'There, but for the grace of God, goes Sherlock Holmes.'"

James McCarthy was acquitted at the Assizes on the strength of a number of objections which had been drawn out by Holmes and submitted to the defending counsel. Old Turner lived for seven months after our interview, but he is now dead; and there is every prospect that the son and daughter may come to live happily together in ignorance of the black cloud which rests upon their past.

The Man with the Twisted Lip

Isa Whitney, brother of the late Elias Whitney, D.D., Principal of the Theological College of St. George's, was much addicted to opium. The habit grew upon him, as I understand, from some foolish freak when he was at college; for having read De Quincey's description of his dreams and sensations, he had drenched his tobacco with laudanum in an attempt to produce the same effects. He found, as so many more have done, that the practice is easier to attain than to get rid of, and for many years he continued to be a slave to the drug, an object of mingled horror and pity to his friends and relatives. I can see him now, with yellow, pasty face, drooping lids, and pin-point pupils, all huddled in a chair, the wreck and ruin of a noble man.

One night—it was in June, '89—there came a ring to my bell, about the hour when a man gives his first yawn and glances at the clock. I sat up in my chair, and my wife laid her needle-work down in her lap and made a little face of disappointment.

"A patient!" said she. "You'll have to go out."

I groaned, for I was newly come back from a weary day.

We heard the door open, a few hurried words, and then quick steps upon the linoleum. Our own door flew open, and a lady, clad in some dark-coloured stuff, with a black veil, entered the room.

"You will excuse my calling so late," she began, and then, suddenly losing her self-control, she ran forward, threw her arms about my wife's neck, and sobbed upon her shoulder. "Oh, I'm in such trouble!" she cried; "I do so want a little help."

"Why," said my wife, pulling up her veil, "it is Kate Whitney. How you startled me, Kate! I had not an idea who you were when you came in."

"I didn't know what to do, so I came straight to you." That was always the way. Folk who were in grief came to my wife like birds to a light-house.

"It was very sweet of you to come. Now, you must have some wine and water, and sit here comfortably and tell us all about it. Or should you rather that I sent James off to bed?"

"Oh, no, no! I want the doctor's advice and help, too. It's about Isa. He has not been home for two days. I am so frightened about him!"

It was not the first time that she had spoken to us of her husband's trouble, to me as a doctor, to my wife as an old friend and school companion. We soothed and comforted her by such words as we could find. Did she know where her husband was? Was it possible that we could bring him back to her?

It seems that it was. She had the surest information that of late he had, when the fit was on him, made use of an opium den in the farthest east of the City. Hitherto his orgies had always been confined to one day, and he had come back, twitching and shattered, in the evening. But now the spell had been upon him eight-and-forty hours, and he lay there, doubtless among the dregs of the docks, breathing in the poison or sleeping off the effects. There he was to be found, she was sure of it, at the Bar of Gold, in Upper Swandam Lane. But what was she to do? How could she, a young and timid woman, make her way into such a place and pluck her husband out from among the ruffians who surrounded him?

There was the case, and of course there was but one way out of it. Might I not escort her to this place? And then, as a second thought, why should she come at all? I was Isa Whitney's medical adviser, and as such I had influence

over him. I could manage it better if I were alone. I promised her on my word that I would send him home in a cab within two hours if he were indeed at the address which she had given me. And so in ten minutes I had left my armchair and cheery sitting-room behind me, and was speeding eastwards in a hansom on a strange errand, as it seemed to me at the time, though the future only could show how strange it was to be.

But there was no great difficulty in the first stage of my adventure. Upper Swandam Lane is a vile alley lurking behind the high wharves which line the north side of the river to the east of London Bridge. Between a slop-shop and a gin-shop, approached by a steep flight of steps leading down to a black gap like the mouth of a cave, I found the den of which I was in search. Ordering my cab to wait, I passed down the steps, worn hollow in the centre by the ceaseless tread of drunken feet; and by the light of a flickering oil-lamp above the door I found the latch and made my way into a long, low room, thick and heavy with the brown opium smoke, and terraced with wooden berths, like the forecastle of an emigrant ship.

Through the gloom one could dimly catch a glimpse of bodies lying in strange fantastic poses, bowed shoulders, bent knees, heads thrown back, and chins pointing upwards, with here and there a dark, lack-lustre eye turned upon the newcomer. Out of the black shadows there glimmered little red circles of light, now bright, now faint, as the burning poison waxed or waned in the bowls of the metal pipes. The most lay silent, but some muttered to themselves, and others talked together in a strange, low, monotonous voice, their conversation coming in gushes, and then suddenly tailing off into silence, each mumbling out his own thoughts and paying little heed to the words of his neighbour. At the farther end was a small brazier of burning charcoal, beside which on a three-legged wooden stool there sat a tall, thin old man, with his jaw resting upon his two fists, and his elbows upon his knees, staring into the fire.

As I entered, a sallow Malay attendant had hurried up with a pipe for me and a supply of the drug, beckoning me to an empty berth.

"Thank you. I have not come to stay," said I. "There is a friend of mine here, Mr. Isa Whitney, and I wish to speak with him."

There was a movement and an exclamation from my right, and peering through the gloom I saw Whitney, pale, haggard, and unkempt, staring out at me.

"My God! It's Watson," said he. He was in a pitiable state of reaction, with every nerve in a twitter. "I say, Watson, what o'clock is it?"

"Nearly eleven."

"Of what day?"

"Of Friday, June 19."

"Good heavens! I thought it was Wednesday. It *is* Wednesday. What d'you want to frighten a chap for?" He sank his face onto his arms and began to sob in a high treble key.

"I tell you that it is Friday, man. Your wife has been waiting this two days for you. You should be ashamed of yourself!"

"So I am. But you've got mixed, Watson, for I have only been here a few hours, three pipes, four pipes—I forget how many. But I'll go home with you. I wouldn't frighten Kate—poor little Kate. Give me your hand! Have you a cab?"

"Yes, I have one waiting."

"Then I shall go in it. But I must owe something. Find what I owe, Watson. I am all off colour. I can do nothing for myself."

I walked down the narrow passage between the double row of sleepers, holding my breath to keep out the vile, stupefying fumes of the drug, and looking about for the manager. As I passed the tall man who sat by the brazier I felt a sudden pluck at my skirt, and a low voice whispered, "Walk past me, and then look back at me." The words fell quite distinctly upon my ear. I glanced down. They could only have come from the old man at my side, and yet he sat now as absorbed as ever, very thin, very wrinkled, bent with age, an opium pipe dangling down from between his knees, as though it had dropped in sheer lassitude from his fingers. I took two steps forward and looked back. It took all my self-control to prevent me from breaking out into a cry of astonishment. He had turned his back so that none could see him but I. His form had filled out, his wrinkles were gone, the dull eyes had regained their fire, and there, sitting by the fire and grinning at my surprise, was none other than Sherlock Holmes. He made a slight motion to me to approach him, and instantly, as he turned his face half round to the company once more, subsided into a doddering, loose-lipped senility.

"Holmes!" I whispered, "what on earth are you doing in this den?"

"As low as you can," he answered; "I have excellent ears. If you would have the great kindness to get rid of that sottish friend of yours, I should be exceedingly glad to have a little talk with you."

"I have a cab outside."

"Then pray send him home in it. You may safely trust him, for he appears to be too limp to get into any mischief. I should recommend you also to send a note by the cabman to your wife to say that you have thrown in your lot with me. If you will wait outside, I shall be with you in five minutes."

It was difficult to refuse any of Sherlock Holmes's requests, for they were always so exceedingly definite, and put forward with such a quiet air of mastery. I felt, however, that when Whitney was once confined in the cab my mission was practically accomplished; and for the rest, I could not wish anything better than to be associated with my friend in one of those singular adventures which were the normal condition of his existence. In a few minutes I had written my note, paid Whitney's bill, led him out to the cab, and seen him driven through the darkness. In a very short time a decrepit figure had emerged from the opium den, and I was walking down the street with Sherlock

Holmes. For two streets he shuffled along with a bent back and an uncertain foot. Then, glancing quickly round, he straightened himself out and burst into a hearty fit of laughter.

"I suppose, Watson," said he, "that you imagine that I have added opium-smoking to cocaine injections, and all the other little weaknesses on which you have favoured me with your medical views."

"I was certainly surprised to find you there."

"But not more so than I to find you."

"I came to find a friend."

"And I to find an enemy."

"An enemy?"

"Yes; one of my natural enemies, or, shall I say, my natural prey. Briefly, Watson, I am in the midst of a very remarkable inquiry, and I have hoped to find a clue in the incoherent ramblings of these sots, as I have done before now. Had I been recognised in that den, my life would not have been worth an hour's purchase; for I have used it before now for my own purposes, and the rascally lascar who runs it has sworn to have vengeance upon me. There is a trap-door at the back of that building, near the corner of Paul's Wharf, which could tell some strange tales of what has passed through it upon the moonless nights."

"What! You do not mean bodies?"

"Ay, bodies, Watson. We should be rich men if we had a thousand pounds for every poor devil who has been done to death in that den. It is the vilest murder-trap on the whole riverside, and I fear that Neville St. Clair has entered it never to leave it more. But our trap should be here." He put his two forefingers between his teeth and whistled shrilly—a signal which was answered by a similar whistle from the distance, followed shortly by the rattle of wheels and the clink of horses' hoofs.

"Now, Watson," said Holmes, as a tall dog-cart dashed up through the gloom, throwing out two golden tunnels of yellow light from its side lanterns. "You'll come with me, won't you?"

"If I can be of use."

"Oh, a trusty comrade is always of use; and a chronicler still more so. My room at The Cedars is a double-bedded one."

"The Cedars?"

"Yes; that is Mr. St. Clair's house. I am staying there while I conduct the inquiry."

"Where is it, then?"

"Near Lee, in Kent. We have a seven-mile drive before us."

"But I am all in the dark."

"Of course you are. You'll know all about it presently. Jump up here. All right, John; we shall not need you. Here's half a crown. Look out for me to-morrow, about eleven. Give her her head. So long, then!"

He flicked the horse with his whip, and we dashed away through the endless succession of sombre and deserted streets, which widened gradually, until we were flying across a broad balustraded bridge, with the murky river flowing sluggishly beneath us. Beyond lay another dull wilderness of bricks and mortar, its silence broken only by the heavy, regular footfall of the policeman, or the songs and shouts of some belated party of revellers. A dull wrack was drifting slowly across the sky, and a star or two twinkled dimly here and there through the rifts of the clouds. Holmes drove in silence, with his head sunk upon his breast, and the air of a man who is lost in thought, while I sat beside him, curious to learn what this new quest might be which seemed to tax his powers so sorely, and yet afraid to break in upon the current of his thoughts. We had driven several miles and were beginning to get to the fringe of the belt of suburban villas, when he shook himself, shrugged his shoulders, and lit up his pipe with the air of a man who has satisfied himself that he is acting for the best.

"You have a grand gift of silence, Watson," said he. "It makes you quite invaluable as a companion. 'Pon my word, it is a great thing for me to have someone to talk to, for my own thoughts are not over-pleasant. I was wondering what

I should say to this dear little woman to-night when she meets me at the door."

"You forget that I know nothing about it."

"I shall just have time to tell you the facts of the case before we get to Lee. It seems absurdly simple, and yet, somehow, I can get nothing to go upon. There's plenty of thread, no doubt, but I can't get the end of it into my hand. Now, I'll state the case clearly and concisely to you, Watson, and maybe you can see a spark where all is dark to me."

"Proceed, then."

"Some years ago—to be definite, in May, 1884—there came to Lee a gentleman, Neville St. Clair by name, who appeared to have plenty of money. He took a large villa, laid out the grounds very nicely, and lived generally in good style. By degrees he made friends in the neighbourhood, and in 1887 he married the daughter of a local brewer, by whom he now has two children. He had no occupation, but was interested in several companies and went into town as a rule in the morning, returning by the 5:14 from Cannon Street every night. Mr. St. Clair is now thirty-seven years of age, is a man of temperate habits, a good husband, a very affectionate father, and a man who is popular with all who know him. I may add that his whole debts at the present moment, as far as we have been able to ascertain, amount to eighty-eight pounds, ten shillings, while he has two hundred and twenty pounds standing to his credit in the Capital and Counties Bank. There is no reason, therefore, to think that money troubles have been weighing upon his mind.

"Last Monday Mr. Neville St. Clair went into town rather earlier than usual, remarking before he started that he had two important commissions to perform, and that he would bring his little boy home a box of bricks. Now, by the merest chance, his wife received a telegram upon this same Monday, very shortly after his departure, to the effect that a small parcel of considerable value which she had been expecting was waiting for her at the offices of the

Aberdeen Shipping Company. Now, if you are well up in your London, you will know that the office of the company is in Fresno Street, which branches out of Upper Swandam Lane, where you found me to-night. Mrs. St. Clair had her lunch, started for the City, did some shopping, proceeded to the company's office, got her packet, and found herself at exactly 4:35 walking through Swandam Lane on her way back to the station. Have you followed me so far?"

"It is very clear."

"If you remember, Monday was an exceedingly hot day, and Mrs. St. Clair walked slowly, glancing about in the hope of seeing a cab, as she did not like the neighbourhood in which she found herself. While she was walking in this way down Swandam Lane, she suddenly heard an ejaculation or cry, and was struck cold to see her husband looking down at her and, as it seemed to her, beckoning to her from a second-floor window. The window was open, and she distinctly saw his face, which she describes as being terribly agitated. He waved his hands frantically to her, and then vanished from the window so suddenly that it seemed to her that he had been plucked back by some irresistible force from behind. One singular point which struck her quick feminine eye was that although he wore some dark coat, such as he had started to town in, he had on neither collar nor necktie.

"Convinced that something was amiss with him, she rushed down the steps—for the house was none other than the opium den in which you found me to-night—and running through the front room she attempted to ascend the stairs which led to the first floor. At the foot of the stairs, however, she met this lascar scoundrel of whom I have spoken, who thrust her back and, aided by a Dane, who acts as assistant there, pushed her out into the street. Filled with the most maddening doubts and fears, she rushed down the lane and, by rare good-fortune, met in Fresno Street a number of constables with an Inspector, all on their way to their beat. The Inspector and two men accompanied her back, and in spite of the continued resistance of the proprietor, they made their way to the room in which Mr. St. Clair had last been seen. There was no sign of him there. In fact, in the whole of that floor there was no one to be found save a crippled wretch of hideous aspect, who, it seems, made his home there. Both he and the lascar stoutly swore that no one else had been in the front room during the afternoon. So determined was their denial that the Inspector was staggered and had almost come to believe that Mrs. St. Clair had been deluded when, with a cry, she sprang at a small deal box which lay upon the table and tore the lid from it. Out there fell a cascade of children's bricks. It was the toy which he had promised to bring home.

"This discovery, and the evident confusion which the cripple showed, made the inspector realize that the matter was serious. The rooms were carefully examined, and results all pointed to an abominable crime. The front room was plainly furnished as a sitting-room and led into a small bedroom, which looked out upon the back of one of the wharves. Between the wharf and the bedroom window is a narrow strip, which is dry at low tide but is covered at high tide with at least four and a half feet of water. The bedroom window was a broad one and opened from below. On examination traces of blood were to be seen upon the window-sill, and several scattered drops were visible upon the wooden floor of the bedroom. Thrust away behind a curtain in the front room were all the clothes of Mr. Neville St. Clair, with the exception of his coat. His boots, his socks, his hat, and his watch—all were there. There were no signs of violence upon any of these garments, and there were no other traces of Mr. Neville St. Clair. Out of the window he must apparently have gone, for no other exit could be discovered, and the ominous blood-stains upon the sill gave little promise that he could save himself by swimming, for the tide was at its very highest at the moment of the tragedy.

"And now as to the villains who seemed to be immediately implicated in the matter. The lascar was known to be a man of the vilest antecedents, but as, by Mrs. St. Clair's story, he was known to have been at the foot of the stair within a very few seconds of her husband's appearance at the window, he could hardly have been more than an accessory to the crime. His defence was one of absolute ignorance, and he protested that he had no knowledge as to the doings of Hugh Boone, his lodger, and that he could not account in any way for the presence of the missing gentleman's clothes.

"So much for the lascar manager. Now for the sinister cripple who lives upon the second floor of the opium den, and who was certainly the last human being whose eyes rested upon Neville St. Clair. His name is Hugh Boone, and his hideous face is one which is familiar to every man who goes much to the City. He is a professional beggar, though in order to avoid the police regulations he pretends to a small trade in wax vestas. Some little distance down Threadneedle Street, upon the left-hand side, there is, as you may have remarked, a small angle in the wall. Here it is that this creature takes his daily seat, cross-legged, with his tiny stock of matches on his lap, and as he is a piteous spectacle a small rain of charity descends into the greasy leather cap which lies upon the pavement beside him. I have watched the fellow more than once before ever I thought of making his professional acquaintance, and I have been surprised at the harvest which he has reaped in a short time. His appearance, you see, is so remarkable that no one can pass him without observing him. A shock of orange hair, a pale face disfigured by a horrible scar, which, by its contraction, has turned up the outer edge of his upper lip, a bulldog chin, and a pair of very penetrating dark eyes, which present a singular contrast to the colour of his hair, all mark him out from amid the common crowd of mendicants, and so, too, does his wit, for he is ever ready with a reply to any piece of chaff which may be thrown at him by the passers-by. This is the man whom we now learn to have been the lodger at the opium den, and to have been the last man to see the gentleman of whom we are in quest."

"But a cripple!" said I. "What could he have done single-handed against a man in the prime of life?"

"He is a cripple in the sense that he walks with a limp; but in other respects he appears to be a powerful and well-nurtured man. Surely your medical experience would tell you, Watson, that weakness in one limb is often compensated for by exceptional strength in the others."

"Pray continue your narrative."

"Mrs. St. Clair had fainted at the sight of the blood upon the window, and she was escorted home in a cab by the police, as her presence could be of no help to them in their investigations. Inspector Barton, who had charge of the case, made a very careful examination of the premises, but without finding anything which threw any light upon the matter. One mistake had been made in not arresting Boone instantly, as he was allowed some few minutes during which he might have communicated with his friend the lascar, but this fault was soon remedied, and he was seized and searched, without anything being found which could incriminate him. There were, it is true, some blood-stains upon his right shirt-sleeve, but he pointed to his ring-finger, which had been cut near the nail, and explained that the bleeding came from there, adding that he had been to the window not long before, and that the stains which had been observed there came doubtless from the same source. He denied strenuously having ever seen Mr. Neville St. Clair and swore that the presence of the clothes in his room was as much a mystery to him as to the police. As to Mrs. St. Clair's assertion that she had actually seen her husband at the window, he declared that she must have been either mad or dreaming. He was removed, loudly protesting, to the police-station, while the Inspector remained upon the premises in the hope that the ebbing tide might afford some fresh clue.

"And it did, though they hardly found upon the mud-bank what they had feared to find. It was Neville St. Clair's coat, and not Neville St. Clair, which lay uncovered as the tide receded. And what do you think they found in the pockets?"

"I cannot imagine."

"No, I don't think you would guess. Every pocket stuffed with pennies and half-pennies—four hundred and twenty-one pennies and two hundred and seventy half-pennies. It was no wonder that it had not been swept away by the tide. But a human body is a different matter. There is a fierce eddy between the wharf and the house. It seemed likely enough that the weighted coat had remained when the stripped body had been sucked away into the river."

"But I understand that all the other clothes were found in the room. Would the body be dressed in a coat alone?"

"No, sir, but the facts might be met speciously enough. Suppose that this man Boone had thrust Neville St. Clair through the window, there is no human eye which could have seen the deed. What would he do then? It would of course instantly strike him that he must get rid of the tell-tale garments. He would seize the coat, then, and be in the act of throwing it out, when it would occur to him that it would swim and not sink. He has little time, for he has heard the scuffle downstairs when the wife tried to force her way up, and perhaps he has already heard from his lascar confederate that the police are hurrying up the street. There is not an instant to be lost. He rushes to some secret hoard, where he has accumulated the fruits of his beggary, and he stuffs all the coins upon which he can lay his hands into the pockets to make sure of the coat's sinking. He throws it out and would have done the same with the other garments had not he heard the rush of steps below and only just had time to close the window when the police appeared."

"It certainly sounds feasible."

"Well, we will take it as a working hypothesis for want of a better. Boone, as I have told you, was arrested and taken to the station, but it could not be shown that there had ever before been anything against him. He had for years been known as a professional beggar, but his life appeared to have been a very quiet and innocent one. There the matter stands at present, and the questions which have to be solved—what Neville St. Clair was doing in the opium den, what happened to him when there, where is he now, and what Hugh Boone had to do with his disappearance —are all as far from a solution as ever. I confess that I cannot recall any case within my experience which looked at the first glance so simple and yet which presented such difficulties."

While Sherlock Holmes had been detailing this singular series of events, we had been whirling through the outskirts of the great town until the last straggling houses had been left behind, and we rattled along with a country hedge upon either side of us. Just as he finished, however, we drove through two scattered villages, where a few lights still glimmered in the windows.

"We are on the outskirts of Lee," said my companion. "We have touched on three English counties in our short drive, starting in Middlesex, passing over an angle of Surrey, and ending in Kent. See that light among the trees? That is The Cedars, and beside that lamp sits a woman whose anxious ears have already, I have little doubt, caught the clink of our horse's feet."

"But why are you not conducting the case from Baker Street?" I asked.

"Because there are many inquiries which must be made out here. Mrs. St. Clair has most kindly put two rooms at my disposal, and you may rest assured that she will have nothing but a welcome for my friend and colleague. I hate to meet her, Watson, when I have no news of her husband. Here we are. Whoa, there, whoa!"

We had pulled up in front of a large villa which stood within its own grounds. A stable-boy had run out to the horse's head, and springing down, I followed Holmes up the small, winding gravel-drive which led to the house. As we approached, the door flew open, and a little blonde woman stood in the opening, clad in some sort of light mousseline de soie, with a touch of fluffy pink chiffon at her neck and wrists. She stood with her figure outlined against the flood of light, one hand upon the door, one half-raised in her eagerness, her body slightly bent, her head and face protruded, with eager eyes and parted lips, a standing question.

"Well?" she cried, "well?" And then, seeing that there were two of us, she gave a cry of hope which sank into a groan as she saw that my companion shook his head and shrugged his shoulders.

"No good news?"

"None."

"No bad?"

"No."

"Thank God for that. But come in. You must be weary, for you have had a long day."

"This is my friend, Dr. Watson. He has been of most vital use to me in several of my cases, and a lucky chance has made it possible for me to bring him out and associate him with this investigation."

"I am delighted to see you," said she, pressing my hand warmly. "You will, I am sure, forgive anything that may be wanting in our arrangements, when you consider the blow which has come so suddenly upon us."

"My dear madam," said I, "I am an old campaigner, and if I were not, I can very well see that no apology is needed. If I can be of any assistance, either to you or to my friend here, I shall be indeed happy."

"Now, Mr. Sherlock Holmes," said the lady as we entered a well-lit dining-room, upon the table of which a cold supper had been laid out, "I should very much like to ask you one or two plain questions, to which I beg that you will give a plain answer."

"Certainly, madam."

"Do not trouble about my feelings. I am not hysterical, nor given to fainting. I simply wish to hear your real, real opinion."

"Upon what point?"

"In your heart of hearts, do you think that Neville is alive?"

Sherlock Holmes seemed to be embarrassed by the question. "Frankly, now!" she repeated, standing upon the rug and looking keenly down at him as he leaned back in a basket-chair.

"Frankly, then, madam, I do not."

"You think that he is dead?"

"I do."

"Murdered?"

"I don't say that. Perhaps."

"And on what day did he meet his death?"

"On Monday."

"Then perhaps, Mr. Holmes, you will be good enough to explain how it is that I have received a letter from him to-day."

Sherlock Holmes sprang out of his chair as if he had been galvanised.

"What!" he roared.

"Yes, to-day." She stood smiling, holding up a little slip of paper in the air.

"May I see it?"

"Certainly."

He snatched it from her in his eagerness, and smoothing it out upon the table, he drew over the lamp and examined it intently. I had left my chair and was gazing at it over his shoulder. The envelope was a very coarse one and was stamped with the Gravesend postmark and with the date of that very day, or rather of the day before, for it was considerably after midnight.

"Coarse writing," murmured Holmes. "Surely this is not your husband's writing, madam."

"No, but the enclosure is."

"I perceive also that whoever addressed the envelope had to go and inquire as to the address."

"How can you tell that?"

"The name, you see, is in perfectly black ink, which has dried itself. The rest is of the greyish colour, which shows that blotting-paper has been used. If it had been written straight off, and then blotted, none would be of a deep black shade. This man has written the name, and there has then been a pause before he wrote the address, which can only mean that he was not familiar with it. It is, of course, a trifle, but there is nothing so important as trifles. Let us now see the letter. Ha! There has been an enclosure here!"

"Yes, there was a ring. His signet-ring."

"And you are sure that this is your husband's hand?"

"One of his hands."

"One?"

"His hand when he wrote hurriedly. It is very unlike his usual writing, and yet I know it well."

Dearest do not be frightened. All will come well. There is a huge error which it may take some little time to rectify. Wait in patience.

Neville

"Written in pencil upon the fly-leaf of a book, octavo size, no water-mark. Hum! Posted to-day in Gravesend by a man with a dirty thumb. Ha! And the flap has been gummed, if I am not very much in error, by a person who had been chewing tobacco. And you have no doubt that it is your husband's hand, madam?"

"None. Neville wrote those words."

"And they were posted to-day at Gravesend. Well, Mrs. St. Clair, the clouds lighten, though I should not venture to say that the danger is over."

"But he must be alive, Mr. Holmes."

"Unless this is a clever forgery to put us on the wrong scent. The ring, after all, proves nothing. It may have been taken from him."

"No, no; it is, it is his very own writing!"

"Very well. It may, however, have been written on Monday and only posted to-day."

"That is possible."

"If so, much may have happened between."

"Oh, you must not discourage me, Mr. Holmes. I know that all is well with him. There is so keen a sympathy between us that I should know if evil came upon him. On the very day that I saw him last he cut himself in the bed-room, and yet I in the dining-room rushed upstairs instantly with the utmost certainty that something had happened. Do you think that I would respond to such a trifle and yet be ignorant of his death?"

"I have seen too much not to know that the impression of a woman may be more valuable than the conclusion of an analytical reasoner. And in this letter you certainly have a very strong piece of evidence to corroborate your view. But if your husband is alive and able to write letters, why should he remain away from you?"

"I cannot imagine. It is unthinkable."

"And on Monday he made no remarks before leaving you?"

"No."

"And you were surprised to see him in Swandam Lane?"

"Very much so."

"Was the window open?"

"Yes."

"Then he might have called to you?"

"He might."

"He only, as I understand, gave an inarticulate cry?"

"Yes."

"A call for help, you thought?"

"Yes. He waved his hands."

"But it might have been a cry of surprise. Astonishment at the unexpected sight of you might cause him to throw up his hands?"

"It is possible."

"And you thought he was pulled back?"

"He disappeared so suddenly."

"He might have leaped back. You did not see anyone else in the room?"

"No, but this horrible man confessed to having been there, and the lascar was at the foot of the stairs."

"Quite so. Your husband, as far as you could see, had his ordinary clothes on?"

"But without his collar or tie. I distinctly saw his bare throat."

"Had he ever spoken of Swandam Lane?"

"Never."

"Had he ever showed any signs of having taken opium?"

"Never."

"Thank you, Mrs. St. Clair. Those are the principal points about which I wished to be absolutely clear. We shall now have a little supper and then retire, for we may have a very busy day to-morrow."

A large and comfortable double-bedded room had been placed at our disposal, and I was quickly between the sheets, for I was weary after my night of adventure. Sherlock Holmes was a man, however, who, when he had an unsolved problem upon his mind, would go for days, and even for a week, without rest, turning it over, rear-ranging his facts, looking at it from every point of view until he had either fathomed it or convinced himself that his data were insufficient. It was soon evident to me that he was now preparing for an all-night sitting. He took off his coat and waistcoat, put on a large blue dressing-gown, and then wandered about the room collecting pillows from his bed and cushions from the sofa and armchairs. With these he constructed a sort of Eastern divan, upon which he perched himself cross-legged, with an ounce of shag to-bacco and a box of matches laid out in front of him. In the dim light of the lamp I saw him sitting there, an old briar pipe between his lips, his eyes fixed vacantly upon the corner of the ceiling, the blue smoke curling up from him, silent, motionless, with the light shining upon his strong-set aquiline features. So he sat as I dropped off to sleep, and so he sat when a sudden ejaculation caused me to wake up, and I found the summer sun shining into the apartment. The pipe was still between his lips, the smoke still curled upward, and the room was full of a dense to-bacco haze, but nothing remained of the heap of shag which I had seen upon the previous night.

"Awake, Watson?" he asked.

"Yes."

"Game for a morning drive?"

"Certainly."

"Then dress. No one is stirring yet, but I know where the stable-boy sleeps, and we shall soon have the trap out." He chuckled to himself as he spoke, his eyes twinkled, and he seemed a different man to the sombre thinker of the previous night.

As I dressed I glanced at my watch. It was no wonder that no one was stirring. It was twenty-five minutes past four. I had hardly finished when Holmes returned with the news that the boy was putting in the horse.

"I want to test a little theory of mine," said he, pulling on his boots. "I think, Watson, that you are now standing in the presence of one of the most absolute fools in Europe. I deserve to be kicked from here to Charing Cross. But I think I have the key of the affair now."

"And where is it?" I asked, smiling.

"In the bathroom," he answered. "Oh, yes, I am not joking," he continued, seeing my look of incredulity. "I have just been there, and I have taken it out, and I have got it in this Gladstone bag. Come on, my boy, and we shall see whether it will not fit the lock."

We made our way downstairs as quietly as possible and out into the bright morning sunshine. In the road stood our horse and trap, with the half-clad stable-boy waiting at the head. We both sprang in, and away we dashed down the London Road. A few country carts were stirring, bearing in vegetables to the metropolis, but the lines of villas on either side were as silent and lifeless as some city in a dream.

"It has been in some points a singular case," said Holmes, flicking the horse on into a gallop. "I confess that I have been as blind as a mole, but it is better to learn wisdom late than never to learn it at all."

In town the earliest risers were just beginning to look

sleepily from their windows as we drove through the streets of the Surrey side. Passing down the Waterloo Bridge Road we crossed over the river and, dashing up Wellington Street, wheeled sharply to the right and found ourselves in Bow Street. Sherlock Holmes was well known to the force, and the two constables at the door saluted him. One of them held the horse's head while the other led us in.

"Who is on duty?" asked Holmes.

"Inspector Bradstreet, sir."

"Ah, Bradstreet, how are you?" A tall, stout official had come down the stone-flagged passage, in a peaked cap and frogged jacket. "I wish to have a quiet word with you, Bradstreet."

"Certainly, Mr. Holmes. Step into my room here."

It was a small, office-like room, with a huge ledger upon the table and a telephone projecting from the wall. The Inspector sat down at his desk.

"What can I do for you, Mr. Holmes?"

"I called about that beggarman, Boone—the one who was charged with being concerned in the disappearance of Mr. Neville St. Clair, of Lee."

"Yes. He was brought up and remanded for further inquiries."

"So I heard. You have him here?"

"In the cells."

"Is he quiet?"

"Oh, he gives no trouble. But he is a dirty scoundrel."

"Dirty?"

"Yes, it is all we can do to make him wash his hands, and his face is as black as a tinker's. Well, when once his case has been settled, he will have a regular prison bath; and I think, if you saw him, you would agree with me that he needed it."

"I should like to see him very much."

"Would you? That is easily done. Come this way. You can leave your bag."

"No, I think that I'll take it."

"Very good. Come this way, if you please." He led us down a passage, opened a barred door, passed down a winding stair, and brought us to a whitewashed corridor with a line of doors on each side.

"The third on the right is his," said the Inspector. "Here it is!" He quietly shot back a panel in the upper part of the door and glanced through.

"He is asleep," said he. "You can see him very well."

We both put our eyes to the grating. The prisoner lay with his face towards us, in a very deep sleep, breathing slowly and heavily. He was a middle-sized man, coarsely clad as became his calling, with a coloured shirt protruding through the rent in his tattered coat. He was, as the Inspector had said, extremely dirty, but the grime which covered his face could not conceal its repulsive ugliness. A broad wheal from an old scar ran right across it from eye to chin, and by its contraction had turned up one side of the upper lip, so that three teeth were exposed in a perpetual snarl. A shock of very bright red hair grew low over his eyes and forehead.

"He's a beauty, isn't he?" said the Inspector.

"He certainly needs a wash," remarked Holmes. "I had an idea that he might, and I took the liberty of bringing the tools with me." He opened the Gladstone bag as he spoke, and took out, to my astonishment, a very large bath-sponge.

"He, he! You are a funny one," chuckled the Inspector.

"Now, if you will have the great goodness to open that door very quietly, we will soon make him cut a much more respectable figure."

"Well, I don't know why not," said the Inspector. "He doesn't look a credit to the Bow Street cells, does he?" He slipped his key into the lock, and we all very quietly entered the cell. The sleeper half turned, and then settled down once more into a deep slumber. Holmes stooped to the water-jug, moistened his sponge, and then rubbed it twice vigorously across and down the prisoner's face.

"Let me introduce you," he shouted, "to Mr. Neville St. Clair, of Lee, in the county of Kent."

Never in my life have I seen such a sight. The man's face peeled off under the sponge like the bark from a tree. Gone was the coarse brown tint! Gone, too, was the horrid scar which had seamed it across, and the twisted lip which had given the repulsive sneer to the face! A twitch brought away the tangled red hair, and there, sitting up in his bed, was a pale, sad-faced, refined-looking man, black-haired and smooth-skinned, rubbing his eyes and staring about him with sleepy bewilderment. Then suddenly realizing the exposure, he broke into a scream and threw himself down with his face to the pillow.

"Great Heavens!" cried the Inspector, "it is, indeed, the missing man. I know him from the photograph."

The prisoner turned with the reckless air of a man who abandons himself to his destiny. "Be it so," said he. "And pray, what am I charged with?"

"With making away with Mr. Neville St.—Oh, come, you can't be charged with that unless they make a case of attempted suicide of it," said the Inspector with a grin. "Well, I have been twenty-seven years in the force, but this really takes the cake."

"If I am Mr. Neville St. Clair, then it is obvious that no crime has been committed, and that, therefore, I am illegally detained."

"No crime, but a very great error has been committed," said Holmes. "You would have done better to have trusted your wife."

"It was not the wife; it was the children," groaned the prisoner. "God help me, I would not have them ashamed of their father. My God! What an exposure! What can I do?"

Sherlock Holmes sat down beside him on the couch and patted him kindly on the shoulder.

"If you leave it to a court of law to clear the matter up," said he, "of course you can hardly avoid publicity. On the other hand, if you convince the police authorities that there is no possible case against you, I do not know that there is any reason that the details should find their way into the papers. Inspector Bradstreet would, I am sure, make notes upon anything which you might tell us and submit it to the proper authorities. The case would then never go into court at all."

"God bless you!" cried the prisoner passionately. "I would have endured imprisonment, ay, even execution, rather than have left my miserable secret as a family blot to my children.

"You are the first who have ever heard my story. My father was a school-master in Chesterfield, where I received an excellent education. I travelled in my youth, took to the stage, and finally became a reporter on an evening paper in London. One day my editor wished to have a series of articles upon begging in the metropolis, and I volunteered to supply them. There was the point from which all my adventures started. It was only by trying begging as an amateur that I could get the facts upon which to base my articles. When an actor I had, of course, learned all the secrets of making up, and had been famous in the green-room for my skill. I took advantage now of my attainments. I painted my face, and to make myself as pitiable as possible, I made a good scar and fixed one side of my lip in a twist by the aid of a small slip of flesh-coloured plaster. Then with a red head of hair, and an appropriate dress, I took my station in the business part of the city, ostensibly as a match-seller but really as a beggar. For seven hours I plied my trade, and when I returned home in the evening I found to my surprise that I had received no less than twenty-six shillings, four pence.

"I wrote my articles and thought little more of the matter until, some time later, I backed a bill for a friend and had a writ served upon me for twenty-five pounds. I was at my wit's end where to get the money, but a sudden idea came to me. I begged a fortnight's grace from the creditor, asked for a holiday from my employers, and spent the time in begging in the City under my disguise. In ten days I had the money and had paid the debt.

"Well, you can imagine how hard it was to settle down to arduous work at two pounds a week when I knew that I could earn as much in a day by smearing my face with a little paint, laying my cap on the ground, and sitting still. It was a long fight between my pride and the money, but the dollars won at last, and I threw up reporting and sat day after day in the corner which I had first chosen, inspiring pity by my ghastly face and filling my pockets with coppers. Only one man knew my secret. He was the keeper of a low den in which I used to lodge in Swandam Lane, where I could every morning emerge as a squalid beggar and in the evenings transform myself into a well-dressed man about town. This fellow, a lascar, was well paid by me for his rooms, so that I knew that my secret was safe in his possession.

"Well, very soon I found that I was saving considerable sums of money. I do not mean that any beggar in the streets of London could earn seven hundred pounds a year—which is less than my average takings—but I had exceptional advantages in my power of making up, and also in a facility of repartee, which improved by practice and made me quite a recognised character in the City. All day a stream of pennies, varied by silver, poured in upon me, and it was a very bad day in which I failed to take two pounds.

"As I grew richer I grew more ambitious, took a house in the country, and eventually married, without anyone having a suspicion as to my real occupation. My dear wife knew that I had business in the City. She little knew what.

"Last Monday I had finished for the day and was dressing in my room above the opium den when I looked out of my window and saw, to my horror and astonishment, that my wife was standing in the street, with her eyes fixed full upon me. I gave a cry of surprise, threw up my arms to cover my face, and rushing to my confidant, the lascar, entreated him to prevent anyone from coming up to me. I heard her voice downstairs, but I knew that she could not ascend. Swiftly I threw off my clothes, pulled on those of a beggar, and put on my pigments and wig. Even a wife's eyes could not pierce so complete a disguise. But then it occurred to me that there might be a search in the room, and that the clothes might betray me. I threw open the window, reopening by my violence a small cut which I had inflicted upon myself in the bedroom that morning. Then I seized my coat, which was weighted by the coppers which I had just transferred to it from the leather bag in which I carried my takings. I hurled it out of the window, and it disappeared into the Thames. The other clothes would have followed, but at that moment there was a rush of constables up the stair, and a few minutes after I found, rather, I confess, to my relief, that instead of being identified as Mr. Neville St. Clair, I was arrested as his murderer.

"I do not know that there is anything else for me to explain. I was determined to preserve my disguise as long as possible, and hence my preference for a dirty face. Knowing that my wife would be terribly anxious, I slipped off my ring and confided it to the lascar at a moment when no constable was watching me, together with a hurried scrawl, telling her that she had no cause to fear."

"That note only reached her yesterday," said Holmes.

"Good God! What a week she must have spent!"

"The police have watched this lascar," said Inspector Bradstreet, "and I can quite understand that he might find it difficult to post a letter unobserved. Probably he handed it to some sailor customer of his, who forgot all about it for some days."

"That was it," said Holmes, nodding approvingly; "I have no doubt of it. But have you never been prosecuted for begging?"

"Many times; but what was a fine to me?"

"It must stop here, however," said Bradstreet. "If the police are to hush this thing up, there must be no more of Hugh Boone."

"I have sworn it by the most solemn oaths which a man can take."

"In that case I think that it is probable that no further steps may be taken. But if you are found again, then all must come out, I am sure, Mr. Holmes, that we are very much indebted to you for having cleared the matter up. I wish I knew how you reach your results."

"I reached this one," said my friend, "by sitting upon five pillows and consuming an ounce of shag. I think, Watson, that if we drive to Baker Street we shall just be in time for breakfast."

The Adventure of the
Blue Carbuncle

I had called upon my friend Sherlock Holmes upon the second morning after Christmas, with the intention of wishing him the compliments of the season. He was lounging upon the sofa in a purple dressing-gown, a pipe-rack within his reach upon the right, and a pile of crumpled morning papers, evidently newly studied, near at hand. Beside the couch was a wooden chair, and on the angle of the back hung a very seedy and disreputable hard-felt hat, much the worse for wear, and cracked in several places. A lens and a forceps lying upon the seat of the chair suggested that the hat had been suspended in this manner for the purpose of examination.

"You are engaged," said I; "perhaps I interrupt you."

"Not at all. I am glad to have a friend with whom I can discuss my results. The matter is a perfectly trivial one"—he jerked his thumb in the direction of the old hat—"but there are points in connection with it which are not entirely devoid of interest and even of instruction."

I seated myself in his armchair and warmed my hands before crackling fire, for a sharp frost had set in, and the windows were thick with the ice crystals. "I suppose," I remarked, "that, homely as it looks, this thing has some deadly story linked on to it—that it is the clue which will guide you in the solution of some mystery and the punishment of some crime."

"No, no. No crime," said Sherlock Holmes, laughing. "Only one of those whimsical little incidents which will happen when you have four million human beings all jostling each other within the space of a few square miles. Amid the action and reaction of so dense a swarm of humanity, every possible combination of events may be expected to take place, and many a little problem will be presented which may be striking and bizarre without being criminal. We have already had experience of such."

"So much so," I remarked, "that of the last six cases which I have added to my notes, three have been entirely free of any legal crime."

"Precisely. You allude to my attempt to recover the Irene Adler papers, to the singular case of Miss Mary Sutherland, and to the adventure of the man with the twisted lip. Well, I have no doubt that this small matter will fall into the same innocent category. You know Peterson, the Commissionaire?"

"Yes."

"It is to him that this trophy belongs."

"It is his hat."

"No, no; he found it. Its owner is unknown. I beg that you will look upon it not as a battered billycock but as an intellectual problem. And, first, as to how it came here. It arrived upon Christmas morning, in company with a good fat goose, which is, I have no doubt, roasting at this moment in front of Peterson's fire. The facts are these: about four o'clock on Christmas morning, Peterson, who, as you know, is a very honest fellow, was returning from some small jollification and was making his way homeward down Tottenham Court Road. In front of him he saw, in the gaslight, a tallish man, walking with a slight stagger and carrying a white goose slung over his shoulder. As he reached the corner of Goodge Street, a row broke out between this stranger and a little knot of roughs. One of the latter knocked off the man's hat, on which he raised his stick to defend himself and, swinging it over his head, smashed the shop window behind him. Peterson had rushed forward to protect the stranger from his assailants; but the man, shocked at having broken the window, and seeing an official-looking person in uniform rushing towards him, dropped his goose, took to his heels, and vanished amid the labyrinth of small streets which lie at the back of Tottenham Court Road. The roughs had also fled at the appearance of Peterson, so that he was left in possession of the field of battle, and also of the spoils of victory in the shape of this battered hat and a most unimpeachable Christmas goose."

"Which surely he restored to their owner?"

"My dear fellow, there lies the problem. It is true that 'For Mrs. Henry Baker' was printed upon a small card which was tied to the bird's left leg, and it is also true that the initials H. B. are legible upon the lining of this hat; but as there are some thousands of Bakers, and some hundreds of Henry Bakers in this city of ours, it is not easy to restore lost property to any one of them."

"What, then, did Peterson do?"

"He brought round both hat and goose to me on Christmas morning, knowing that even the smallest problems are of interest to me. The goose we retained until this morning, when there were signs that, in spite of the slight frost, it would be well that it should be eaten without unnecessary delay. Its finder has carried it off, therefore, to fulfil the ultimate destiny of a goose, while I continue to retain the hat of the unknown gentleman who lost his Christmas dinner."

"Did he not advertise?"

"No."

"Then, what clue could you have as to his identity?"

"Only as much as we can deduce."

"From his hat?"

"Precisely."

"But you are joking. What can you gather from this old battered felt?"

"Here is my lens. You know my methods. What can you gather yourself as to the individuality of the man who has worn this article?"

I took the tattered object in my hands and turned it over

rather ruefully. It was a very ordinary black hat of the usual round shape, hard and much the worse for wear. The lining had been of red silk, but was a good deal discoloured. There was no maker's name; but, as Holmes had remarked, the initials H. B. were scrawled upon one side. It was pierced in the brim for a hat-securer, but the elastic was missing. For the rest, it was cracked, exceedingly dusty, and spotted in several places, although there seemed to have been some attempt to hide the discoloured patches by smearing them with ink.

"I can see nothing," said I, handing it back to my friend.

"On the contrary, Watson, you can see everything. You fail, however, to reason from what you see. You are too timid in drawing your inferences."

"Then, pray tell me what it is that you can infer from this hat?"

He picked it up and gazed at it in the peculiar introspective fashion which was characteristic of him. "It is perhaps less suggestive than it might have been," he remarked, "and yet there are a few inferences which are very distinct, and a few others which represent at least a strong balance of probability. That the man was highly intellectual is of course obvious upon the face of it, and also that he was fairly well-to-do within the last three years, although he has now fallen upon evil days. He had foresight, but has less now than formerly, pointing to a moral retrogression, which, when taken with the decline of his fortunes, seems to indicate some evil influence, probably drink, at work upon him. This may account also for the obvious fact that his wife has ceased to love him."

"My dear Holmes!"

"He has, however, retained some degree of self-respect," he continued, disregarding my remonstrance. "He is a man who leads a sedentary life, goes out little, is out of training entirely, is middle-aged, has grizzled hair which he has had cut within the last few days, and which he anoints with lime-cream. These are the more patent facts which are to be deduced from his hat. Also, by the way, that it is extremely improbable that he has gas laid on in his house."

"You are certainly joking, Holmes."

"Not in the least. Is it possible that even now, when I give you these results, you are unable to see how they are attained?"

"I have no doubt that I am very stupid, but I must confess that I am unable to follow you. For example, how did you deduce that this man was intellectual?"

For answer Holmes clapped the hat upon his head. It came right over the forehead and settled upon the bridge of his nose. "It is a question of cubic capacity," said he; "a man with so large a brain must have something in it."

"The decline of his fortunes, then?"

"This hat is three years old. These flat brims curled at the edge came in then. It is a hat of the very best quality. Look at the band of ribbed silk and the excellent lining. If this man could afford to buy so expensive a hat three years ago, and has had no hat since, then he has assuredly gone down in the world."

"Well, that is clear enough, certainly. But how about the foresight and the moral retrogression?"

Sherlock Holmes laughed. "Here is the foresight," said he, putting his finger upon the little disc and loop of the hat-securer. "They are never sold upon hats. If this man ordered one, it is a sign of a certain amount of foresight, since he went out of his way to take this precaution against the wind. But since we see that he has broken the elastic and has not troubled to replace it, it is obvious that he has less foresight now than formerly, which is a distinct proof of a weakening nature. On the other hand, he had endeavoured to conceal some of these stains upon the felt by daubing them with ink, which is a sign that he has not entirely lost his self-respect."

"Your reasoning is certainly plausible."

"The further points, that he is middle-aged, that his hair is grizzled, that it has been recently cut, and that he uses lime-cream, are all to be gathered from a close examination of the lower part of the lining. The lens discloses a large number of hair-ends, clean cut by the scissors of the barber. They all appear to be adhesive, and there is a distinct odour of lime-cream. This dust, you will observe, is not the gritty, gray dust of the street but the fluffy brown dust of the house, showing that it has been hung up indoors most of the time; while the marks of moisture upon the inside are proof positive that the wearer perspired very freely, and could therefore hardly be in the best of training."

"But his wife—you said that she had ceased to love him."

"This hat has not been brushed for weeks. When I see you, my dear Watson, with a week's accumulation of dust upon your hat, and when your wife allows you to go out in such a state, I shall fear that you also have been unfortunate enough to lose your wife's affection."

"But he might be a bachelor."

"Nay, he was bringing home the goose as a peace-offering to his wife. Remember the card upon the bird's leg."

"You have an answer to everything. But how on earth do you deduce that the gas is not laid on in his house?"

"One tallow stain, or even two, might come by chance; but when I see no less than five, I think that there can be little doubt that the individual must be brought into frequent contact with burning tallow—walks upstairs at night probably with his hat in one hand and a guttering candle in the other. Anyhow, he never got tallow-stains from a gas-jet. Are you satisfied?"

"Well, it is very ingenious," said I, laughing; "but since, as you said just now, there has been no crime committed, and no harm done save the loss of a goose, all this seems to be rather a waste of energy."

Sherlock Holmes had opened his mouth to reply, when the door flew open, and Peterson, the Commissionaire, rushed into the apartment with flushed cheeks and the face of a man who is dazed with astonishment.

"The goose, Mr. Holmes! The goose, sir!" he gasped.

"Eh? What of it, then? Has it returned to life and flapped off through the kitchen window?" Holmes twisted himself round upon the sofa to get a fairer view of the man's excited face.

"See here, sir! See what my wife found in its crop!" He held out his hand and displayed upon the centre of the palm a brilliantly scintillating blue stone, rather smaller than a bean in size, but of such purity and radiance that it twinkled like an electric point in the dark hollow of his hand.

Sherlock Holmes sat up with a whistle. "By Jove, Peterson!" said he, "this is treasure trove indeed. I suppose you know what you have got?"

"A diamond, sir? A precious stone. It cuts into glass as though it were putty."

"It's more than a precious stone. It is *the* precious stone."

"Not the Countess of Morcar's blue carbuncle!" I ejaculated.

"Precisely so. I ought to know its size and shape, seeing that I have read the advertisement about it in *The Times* every day lately. It is absolutely unique, and its value can only be conjectured, but the reward offered of a thousand pounds is certainly not within a twentieth part of the market price."

"A thousand pounds! Great Lord of mercy!" The Commissionaire plumped down into a chair and stared from one to the other of us.

"That is the reward, and I have reason to know that there are sentimental considerations in the background which would induce the Countess to part with half her fortune if she could but recover the gem."

"It was lost, if I remember aright, at the Hotel Cosmopolitan," I remarked.

"Precisely so, on December 22, just five days ago. John Horner, a plumber, was accused of having abstracted it from the lady's jewel-case. The evidence against him was so strong that the case has been referred to the Assizes. I have some account of the matter here, I believe." He rummaged amid his newspapers, glancing over the dates, until at last he smoothed one out, doubled it over, and read the following paragraph:

"'Hotel Cosmopolitan Jewel Robbery. John Horner, 26, plumber, was brought up upon the charge of having upon the 22 inst., abstracted from the jewel-case of the Countess of Morcar the valuable gem known as the blue carbuncle. James Ryder, upper-attendant at the hotel, gave his evidence to the effect that he had shown Horner up to the dressing-room of the Countess of Morcar upon the day of the robbery in order that he might solder the second bar of the grate, which was loose. He had remained with Horner some little time, but had finally been called away. On returning, he found that Horner had disappeared, that the bureau had been forced open, and that the small morocco casket in which, as it afterwards transpired, the Countess was accustomed to keep her jewel, was lying empty upon the dressing-table. Ryder instantly gave the alarm, and Horner was arrested the same evening; but the stone could not be found either upon his person or in his rooms. Catherine Cusack, maid to the Countess, deposed to having heard Ryder's cry of dismay on discovering the robbery, and to having rushed into the room, where she found matters as described by the last witness. Inspector Bradstreet, B division, gave evidence as to the arrest of Horner, who struggled frantically and protested his innocence in the strongest terms. Evidence of a previous conviction for robbery having been given against the prisoner, the magistrate refused to deal summarily with the offence, but referred it to the Assizes. Horner, who had shown signs of intense emotion during the proceedings, fainted away at the conclusion and was carried out of court.'

"Hum! So much for the police-court," said Holmes thoughtfully, tossing aside the paper. "The question for us now to solve is the sequence of events leading from a rifled jewel-case at one end to the crop of a goose in Tottenham Court Road at the other. You see, Watson, our little deductions have suddenly assumed a much more important and less innocent aspect. Here is the stone; the stone came from the goose, and the goose came from Mr. Henry Baker, the gentleman with the bad hat and all the other characteristics with which I have bored you. So now we must set ourselves very seriously to finding this gentleman and ascertaining what part he has played in this little mystery. To do this, we must try the simplest means first, and these lie undoubtedly in an advertisement in all the evening papers. If this fail, I shall have recourse to other methods."

"What will you say?"

"Give me a pencil and that slip of paper. Now, then: 'Found at the corner of Goodge Street, a goose and a black felt hat. Mr. Henry Baker can have the same by applying at 6:30 this evening at 221B Baker Street.' That is clear and concise."

"Very. But will he see it?"

"Well, he is sure to keep an eye on the papers, since, to a poor man, the loss was a heavy one. He was clearly so scared by his mischance in breaking the window and by the approach of Peterson that he thought of nothing but flight, but since then he must have bitterly regretted the impulse which caused him to drop his bird. Then, again, the introduction of his name will cause him to see it, for everyone who knows him will direct his attention to it. Here you are, Peterson, run down to the advertising agency and have this put in the evening papers."

"In which, sir?"

"Oh, in the *Globe, Star, Pall Mall, St. James's, Evening News Standard, Echo,* and any others that occur to you."

"Very well, sir. And this stone?"

"Ah, yes, I shall keep the stone. Thank you. And, I say, Peterson, just buy a goose on your way back and leave it here with me, for we must have one to give to this gentleman in place of the one which your family is now devouring."

When the Commissionaire had gone, Holmes took up

the stone and held it against the light. "It's a bonny thing," said he. "Just see how it glints and sparkles. Of course it is a nucleus and focus of crime. Every good stone is. They are the devil's pet baits. In the larger and older jewels every facet may stand for a bloody deed. This stone is not yet twenty years old. It was found on the banks of the Amoy River in southern China and is remarkable in having every characteristic of the carbuncle, save that it is blue in shade instead of ruby red. In spite of its youth, it has already a sinister history. There have been two murders, a vitriol-throwing, a suicide, and several robberies brought about for the sake of this forty-grain weight of crystallized charcoal. Who would think that so pretty a toy would be a purveyor to the gallows and the prison? I'll lock it up in my strong box now and drop a line to the Countess to say that we have it."

"Do you think that this man Horner is innocent?"

"I cannot tell."

"Well, then, do you imagine that this other one, Henry Baker, had anything to do with the matter?"

"It is, I think, much more likely that Henry Baker is an absolutely innocent man, who had no idea that the bird which he was carrying was of considerably more value than if it were made of solid gold. That, however, I shall determine by a very simple test if we have an answer to our advertisement."

"And you can do nothing until then?"

"Nothing."

"In that case I shall continue my professional round. But I shall come back in the evening at the hour you have mentioned, for I should like to see the solution of so tangled a business."

"Very glad to see you. I dine at seven. There is a woodcock, I believe. By the way, in view of recent occurrences, perhaps I ought to ask Mrs. Hudson to examine its crop."

I had been delayed at a case, and it was a little after half-past six when I found myself in Baker Street once more. As I approached the house I saw a tall man in a Scotch bonnet with a coat which was buttoned up to his chin waiting outside in the bright semicircle which was thrown from the fanlight. Just as I arrived the door was opened, and we were shown up together to Holmes's room.

"Mr. Henry Baker, I believe," said he, rising from his armchair and greeting his visitor with the easy air of geniality which he could so readily assume. "Pray take this chair by the fire, Mr. Baker. It is a cold night, and I observe that your circulation is more adapted for summer than for winter. Ah, Watson, you have just come at the right time. Is that your hat, Mr. Baker?"

"Yes, sir, that is undoubtedly my hat."

He was a large man with rounded shoulders, a massive head, and a broad, intelligent face, sloping down to a pointed beard of grizzled brown. A touch of red in nose and cheeks, with a slight tremor of his extended hand, recalled Holmes's surmise as to his habits. His rusty black frock-coat was buttoned right up in front, with the collar turned up, and his lank wrists protruded from his sleeves without a sign of cuff or shirt. He spoke in a slow staccato fashion, choosing his words with care, and gave the impression generally of a man of learning and letters who had had ill-usage at the hands of fortune.

"We have retained these things for some days," said Holmes, "because we expected to see an advertisement from you giving your address. I am at a loss to know now why you did not advertise."

Our visitor gave a rather shamefaced laugh. "Shillings have not been so plentiful with me as they once were," he remarked. "I had no doubt that the gang of roughs who assaulted me had carried off both my hat and the bird. I did not care to spend more money in a hopeless attempt at recovering them."

"Very naturally. By the way, about the bird, we were compelled to eat it."

"To eat it!" Our visitor half rose from his chair in his excitement.

"Yes, it would have been of no use to anyone had we not

done so. But I presume that this other goose upon the sideboard, which is about the same weight and perfectly fresh, will answer your purpose equally well?"

"Oh, certainly, certainly," answered Mr. Baker with a sigh of relief.

"Of course, we still have the feathers, legs, crop, and so on of your own bird, so if you wish—"

The man burst into a hearty laugh. "They might be useful to me as relics of my adventure," said he, "but beyond that I can hardly see what use the *disjecta membra* of my late acquaintance are going to be to me. No, sir, I think that, with your permission, I will confine my attentions to the excellent bird which I perceive upon the sideboard."

Sherlock Holmes glanced sharply across at me with a slight shrug of his shoulders.

"There is your hat, then, and there your bird," said he. "By the way, would it bore you to tell me where you got the other one from? I am somewhat of a fowl fancier, and I have seldom seen a better grown goose."

"Certainly, sir," said Baker, who had risen and tucked his newly gained property under his arm. "There are a few of us who frequent the Alpha Inn, near the Museum—we are to be found in the Museum itself during the day, you understand. This year our good host, Windigate by name, instituted a goose club, by which, on consideration of some few pence every week, we were each to receive a bird at Christmas. My pence were duly paid, and the rest is familiar to you. I am much indebted to you, sir, for a Scotch bonnet is fitted neither to my years nor my gravity." With a comical pomposity of manner he bowed solemnly to both of us and strode off upon his way.

"So much for Mr. Henry Baker," said Holmes when he had closed the door behind him. "It is quite certain that he knows nothing whatever about the matter. Are you hungry, Watson?"

"Not particularly."

"Then I suggest that we turn our dinner into a supper and follow up this clue while it is still hot."

"By all means."

It was a bitter night, so we drew on our ulsters and wrapped cravats about our throats. Outside, the stars were shining coldly in a cloudless sky, and the breath of the passers-by blew out into smoke like so many pistol shots. Our footfalls rang out crisply and loudly as we swung through the doctor's quarter, Wimpole Street, Harley Street, and so through Wigmore Street into Oxford Street. In a quarter of an hour we were in Bloomsbury at the Alpha Inn, which is a small public-house at the corner of one of the streets which runs down into Holborn. Holmes pushed open the door of the private bar and ordered two glasses of beer from the ruddy-faced, white-aproned landlord.

"Your beer should be excellent if it is as good as your geese," said he.

"My geese!" The man seemed surprised.

"Yes. I was speaking only half an hour ago to Mr. Henry Baker, who was a member of your goose club."

"Ah, yes, I see. But you see, sir, them's not *our* geese."

"Indeed! Whose, then?"

"Well, I got the two dozen from a salesman in Covent Garden."

"Indeed? I know some of them. Which was it?"

"Breckinridge is his name."

"Ah! I don't know him. Well, here's your good health, landlord, and prosperity to your house. Good-night.

"Now for Mr. Breckinridge," he continued, buttoning up his coat as we came out into the frosty air. "Remember, Watson, that though we have so homely a thing as a goose at one end of this chain, we have at the other a man who will certainly get seven years' penal servitude unless we can establish his innocence. It is possible that our inquiry may but confirm his guilt; but, in any case, we have a line of investigation which has been missed by the police, and which a singular chance has placed in our hands. Let us follow it out to the bitter end. Faces to the south, then, and quick march!"

We passed across Holborn, down Endell Street, and so through a zigzag of slums to Covent Garden Market. One of the largest stalls bore the name of Breckinridge upon it, and the proprietor, a horsy-looking man, with a sharp face and trim side-whiskers, was helping a boy to put up the shutters.

"Good-evening. It's a cold night," said Holmes.

The salesman nodded and shot a questioning glance at my companion.

"Sold out of geese, I see," continued Holmes, pointing at the bare slabs of marble.

"Let you have five hundred to-morrow morning."

"That's no good."

"Well, there are some on the stall with the gas-flare."

"Ah, but I was recommended to you."

"Who by?"

"The landlord of the Alpha."

"Oh, yes; I sent him a couple of dozen."

"Fine birds they were, too. Now where did you get them from?"

To my surprise the question provoked a burst of anger from the salesman.

"Now, then, mister," said he, with his head cocked and his arms akimbo, "what are you driving at? Let's have it straight, now."

"It is straight enough. I should like to know who sold you the geese which you supplied to the Alpha."

"Well, then, I shan't tell you. So now!"

"Oh, it is a matter of no importance; but I don't know why you should be so warm over such a trifle."

"Warm! You'd be as warm, maybe, if you were as pestered as I am. When I pay good money for a good article there should be an end of the business; but it's 'Where are the geese?' and 'Who did you sell the geese to?' and 'What will you take for the geese?' One would think they were the only geese in the world, to hear the fuss that is made over them."

"Well, I have no connection with any other people who have been making inquiries," said Holmes carelessly. "If you won't tell us the bet is off, that is all. But I'm always ready to back my opinion on a matter of fowls, and I have a fiver on it that the bird I ate is country bred."

"Well, then, you've lost your fiver, for it's town bred," snapped the salesman.

"It's nothing of the kind."

"I say it is."

"I don't believe it."

"D'you think you know more about fowls than I, who have handled them ever since I was a nipper? I tell you, all those birds that went to the Alpha were town bred."

"You'll never persuade me to believe that."

"Will you bet, then?"

"It's merely taking your money, for I know that I am right. But I'll have a sovereign on with you, just to teach you not to be obstinate."

The salesman chuckled grimly. "Bring me the books, Bill," said he.

The small boy brought round a small thin volume and a great greasy-backed one, laying them out together beneath the hanging lamp.

"Now then, Mr. Cocksure," said the salesman, "I thought that I was out of geese, but before I finish you'll find that there is still one left in my shop. You see this little book?"

"Well?"

"That's the list of the folk from whom I buy. D'you see? Well, then, here on this page are the country folk, and the numbers after their names are where their accounts are in the big ledger. Now, then! You see this other page in red ink? Well, that is a list of my town suppliers. Now, look at that third name. Just read it out to me."

"Mrs. Oakshott, 117 Brixton Road number 249," read Holmes.

"Quite so. Now turn that up in the ledger."

Holmes turned to the page indicated. "Here you are, 'Mrs. Oakshott, 117 Brixton Road, egg and poultry supplier.'"

"Now, then, what's the last entry?"

"'December 22. Twenty-four geese at seven shillings, six pence.'"

"Quite so. There you are. And underneath?"

"'Sold to Mr. Windigate of the Alpha, at twelve shillings.'"

"What have you to say now?"

Sherlock Holmes looked deeply chagrined. He drew a sovereign from his pocket and threw it down upon the slab, turning away with the air of a man whose disgust is too deep for words. A few yards off he stopped under a lamp-post and laughed in the hearty, noiseless fashion which was peculiar to him.

"When you see a man with whiskers of that cut and the 'Pink 'un' protruding out of his pocket, you can always draw him by a bet," said he. "I daresay that if I had put a hundred pounds down in front of him, that man would not have given me such complete information as was drawn from him by the idea that he was doing me on a wager. Well, Watson, we are, I fancy, nearing the end of our quest, and the only point which remains to be determined is whether we should go on to this Mrs. Oakshott to-night, or whether we should reserve it for to-morrow. It is clear from what that surly fellow said that there are others besides ourselves who are anxious about the matter, and I should—"

His remarks were suddenly cut short by a loud hubbub which broke out from the stall which we had just left. Turning round we saw a little rat-faced fellow standing in the centre of the circle of yellow light which was thrown by the swinging lamp, while Breckinridge, the salesman, framed in the door of his stall, was shaking his fists fiercely at the cringing figure.

"I've had enough of you and your geese," he shouted. "I wish you were all at the devil together. If you come pestering me any more with your silly talk I'll set the dog at you. You bring Mrs. Oakshott here and I'll answer her, but what have you to do with it? Did I buy the geese off you?"

"No; but one of them was mine all the same," whined the little man.

"Well, then, ask Mrs. Oakshott for it."

"She told me to ask you."

"Well, you can ask the King of Proosia, for all I care. I've had enough of it. Get out of this!" He rushed fiercely forward, and the inquirer flitted away into the darkness.

"Ha! This may save us a visit to Brixton Road," whispered Holmes. "Come with me, and we will see what is to be made of this fellow." Striding through the scattered knots of people who lounged round the flaring stalls, my companion speedily overtook the little man and touched him upon the shoulder. He sprang round, and I could see in the gas-light that every vestige of colour had been driven from his face.

"Who are you, then? What do you want?" he asked in a quavering voice.

"You will excuse me," said Holmes blandly, "but I could not help overhearing the questions which you put to the salesman just now. I think that I could be of assistance to you."

"You? Who are you? How could you know anything of the matter?"

"My name is Sherlock Holmes. It is my business to know what other people don't know."

"But you can know nothing of this?"

"Excuse me, I know everything of it. You are endeavouring to trace some geese which were sold by Mrs. Oakshott, of Brixton Road, to a salesman named Breckinridge, by him in turn to Mr. Windigate, of the Alpha, and by him to his club, of which Mr. Henry Baker is a member."

"Oh, sir, you are the very man whom I have longed to meet," cried the little fellow with outstretched hands and quivering fingers. "I can hardly explain to you how interested I am in this matter."

Sherlock Holmes hailed a four-wheeler which was passing. "In that case we had better discuss it in a cosy room rather than in this wind-swept market-place," said he. "But pray tell me, before we go farther, who it is that I have the pleasure of assisting."

The man hesitated for an instant. "My name is John

Robinson," he answered with a sidelong glance.

"No, no; the real name," said Holmes sweetly. "It is always awkward doing business with an alias."

A flush sprang to the white cheeks of the stranger. "Well, then," said he, "my real name is James Ryder."

"Precisely so. Head attendant at the Hotel Cosmopolitan. Pray step into the cab, and I shall soon be able to tell you everything which you would wish to know."

The little man stood glancing from one to the other of us with half-frightened, half-hopeful eyes, as one who is not sure whether he is on the verge of a windfall or of a catastrophe. Then he stepped into the cab, and in half an hour we were back in the sitting-room at Baker Street. Nothing had been said during our drive, but the high, thin breathing of our new companion, and the claspings and unclaspings of his hands, spoke of the nervous tension within him.

"Here we are!" said Holmes cheerily as we filed into the room. "The fire looks very seasonable in this weather. You look cold, Mr. Ryder. Pray take the basket-chair. I will just put on my slippers before we settle this little matter of yours. Now, then! You want to know what became of those geese?"

"Yes, sir."

"Or rather, I fancy, of that goose. It was one bird, I imagine, in which you were interested—white, with a black bar across the tail."

Ryder quivered with emotion. "Oh, sir," he cried, "can you tell me where it went to?"

"It came here."

"Here?"

"Yes, and a most remarkable bird it proved. I don't wonder that you should take an interest in it. It laid an egg after it was dead—the bonniest, brightest little blue egg that ever was seen. I have it here in my museum."

Our visitor staggered to his feet and clutched the mantelpiece with his right hand. Holmes unlocked his strongbox and held up the blue carbuncle, which shone out like a star, with a cold, brilliant, many-pointed radiance. Ryder stood glaring with a drawn face, uncertain whether to claim or to disown it.

"The game's up, Ryder," said Holmes quietly. "Hold up, man, or you'll be into the fire! Give him an arm back into his chair, Watson. He's not got blood enough to go in for felony with impunity. Give him a dash of brandy. So! Now he looks a little more human. What a shrimp it is, to be sure!"

For a moment he had staggered and nearly fallen, but the brandy brought a tinge of colour into his cheeks, and he sat staring with frightened eyes at his accuser.

"I have almost every link in my hands, and all the proofs which I could possibly need, so there is little which you need tell me. Still, that little may as well be cleared up to make the case complete. You had heard, Ryder, of this blue stone of the Countess of Morcar's?"

"It was Catherine Cusack who told me of it," said he in a crackling voice.

"I see—her ladyship's waiting-maid. Well, the temptation of sudden wealth so easily acquired was too much for you, as it has been for better men before you; but you were not very scrupulous in the means you used. It seems to me, Ryder, that there is the making of a very pretty villain in you. You knew that this man Horner, the plumber, had been concerned in some such matter before, and that suspicion would rest the more readily upon him. What did you do, then? You made some small job in my lady's room—you and your confederate Cusack—and you managed that he should be the man sent for. Then, when he had left, you rifled the jewel-case, raised the alarm, and had this unfortunate man arrested. You then—"

Ryder threw himself down suddenly upon the rug and clutched at my companion's knees. "For God's sake, have mercy!" he shrieked. "Think of my father, of my mother! It would break their hearts. I never went wrong before! I never will again. I swear it. I'll swear it on a Bible. Oh, don't bring it into court! For Christ's sake, don't!"

"Get back into your chair!" said Holmes sternly. "It is very well to cringe and crawl now, but you thought little enough of this poor Horner in the dock for a crime of which he knew nothing."

"I will fly, Mr. Holmes. I will leave the country, sir. Then the charge against him will break down."

"Hum! We will talk about that. And now let us hear a true account of the next act. How came the stone into the goose, and how came the goose into the open market? Tell us the truth, for there lies your only hope of safety."

Ryder passed his tongue over his parched lips. "I will tell you it just as it happened, sir," said he. "When Horner had been arrested, it seemed to me that it would be best for me to get away with the stone at once, for I did not know at what moment the police might not take it into their heads to search me and my room. There was no place about the hotel where it would be safe. I went out, as if on some commission, and I made for my sister's house. She had married a man named Oakshott, and lived in Brixton Road, where she fattened fowls for the market. All the way there every man I met seemed to me to be a policeman or a detective; and, for all that it was a cold night, the sweat was pouring down my face before I came to the Brixton Road. My sister asked me what was the matter, and why I was so pale; but I told her that I had been upset by the jewel robbery at the hotel. Then I went into the back yard and smoked a pipe and wondered what it would be best to do.

"I had a friend once called Maudsley, who went to the bad and has just been serving his time in Pentonville. One day he had met me, and fell into talk about the ways of thieves, and how they could get rid of what they stole. I knew that he would be true to me, for I knew one or two things about him; so I made up my mind to go right on to Kilburn, where he lived, and take him into my confidence. He would show me how to turn the stone into money. But how to get to him in safety? I thought of the agonies I had gone through in coming from the hotel. I might at any moment be seized and searched, and there would be the stone in my waistcoat pocket. I was leaning against the wall at the time and looking at the geese which were waddling about round my feet, and suddenly an idea came into my head which showed me how I could beat the best detective that ever lived.

"My sister had told me some weeks before that I might have the pick of her geese for a Christmas present, and I knew that she was always as good as her word. I would take my goose now, and in it I would carry my stone to Kilburn. There was a little shed in the yard, and behind this I drove one of the birds—a fine big one, white, with a barred tail. I caught it, and prying its bill open, I thrust the stone down its throat as far as my finger could reach. The bird gave a gulp, and I felt the stone pass along its gullet and down into its crop. But the creature flapped and struggled, and out came my sister to know what was the matter. As I turned to speak to her the brute broke loose and fluttered off among the others.

"'Whatever were you doing with that bird, Jem?' says she.

"'Well,' said I, 'you said you'd give me one for Christmas, and I was feeling which was the fattest.'

"'Oh,' says she, 'we've set yours aside for you—Jem's bird, we call it. It's the big white one over yonder. There's twenty-six of them, which makes one for you, and one for us, and two dozen for the market.'

"'Thank you, Maggie,' says I; 'but if it is all the same to you, I'd rather have that one I was handling just now.'

"'The other is a good three pound heavier,' said she, 'and we fattened it expressly for you.'

"'Never mind. I'll have the other, and I'll take it now,' said I.

"'Oh, just as you like,' said she, a little huffed. 'Which is it you want, then?'

"'That white one with the barred tail, right in the middle of the flock.'

"'Oh, very well. Kill it and take it with you.'

"Well, I did what she said, Mr. Holmes, and I carried the

bird all the way to Kilburn. I told my pal what I had done, for he was a man that it was easy to tell a thing like that to. He laughed until he choked, and we got a knife and opened the goose. My heart turned to water, for there was no sign of the stone, and I knew that some terrible mistake had occurred. I left the bird, rushed back to my sister's, and hurried into the back yard. There was not a bird to be seen there.

"'Where are they all, Maggie?' I cried.

"'Gone to the dealer's, Jem.'

"'Which dealer's?'

"'Breckinridge, of Covent Garden.'

"'But was there another with a barred tail?' I asked, 'the same as the one I chose?'

"'Yes, Jem; there were two barred-tailed ones, and I could never tell them apart.'

"Well, then, of course I saw it all, and I ran off as hard as my feet would carry me to this man Breckinridge; but he had sold the lot at once, and not one word would he tell me as to where they had gone. You heard him yourselves to-night. Well, he has always answered me like that. My sister thinks that I am going mad. Sometimes I think that I am myself. And now—and now I am myself a branded thief, without ever having touched the wealth for which I sold my character. God help me! God help me!" He burst into convulsive sobbing, with his face buried in his hands.

There was a long silence, broken only by his heavy breathing, and by the measured tapping of Sherlock Holmes's finger-tips upon the edge of the table. Then my friend rose and threw open the door.

"Get out!" said he.

"What, sir! Oh, Heaven bless you!"

"No more words. Get out!"

And no more words were needed. There was a rush, a clatter upon the stairs, the bang of a door, and the crisp rattle of running footfalls from the street.

"After all, Watson," said Holmes, reaching up his hand for his clay pipe, "I am not retained by the police to supply their deficiencies. If Horner were in danger, it would be another thing; but this fellow will not appear against him, and the case must collapse. I suppose that I am commuting a felony, but it is just possible that I am saving a soul. This fellow will not go wrong again; he is too terribly frightened. Send him to jail now, and you make him a gaol-bird for life. Besides, it is the season of forgiveness. Chance has put in our way a most singular and whimsical problem, and its solution is its own reward. If you will have the goodness to touch the bell, Doctor, we will begin another investigation, in which, also, a bird will be the chief feature."

The Adventure of the
Speckled Band

On glancing over my notes of the seventy odd cases in which I have during the last eight years studied the methods of my friend Sherlock Holmes, I find many tragic, some comic, a large number merely strange, but none commonplace; for working as he did rather for the love of his art than for the acquirement of wealth, he refused to associate himself with any investigation which did not tend towards the unusual, and even the fantastic. Of all these varied cases, however, I cannot recall any which presented more singular features than that which was associated with the well-known Surrey family of the Roylotts of Stoke Moran. The events in question occurred in the early days of my association with Holmes, when we were sharing rooms as bachelors in Baker Street. It is possible that I might have placed them upon record before, but a promise of secrecy was made at the time, from which I have only been freed during the last month by the untimely death of the lady to whom the pledge was given. It is perhaps as well that the facts should now come to light, for I have reasons to know that there are widespread rumours as to the death of Dr. Grimesby Roylott which tend to make the matter even more terrible than the truth.

It was early in April in the year '83 that I woke one morning to find Sherlock Holmes standing, fully dressed, by the side of my bed. He was a late riser, as a rule, and as the clock on the mantelpiece showed me that it was only a quarter-past seven, I blinked up at him in some surprise, and perhaps just a little resentment, for I was myself regular in my habits.

"Very sorry to knock you up, Watson," said he, "but it's the common lot this morning. Mrs. Hudson has been knocked up, she retorted upon me, and I on you."

"What is it, then—a fire?"

"No; a client. It seems that a young lady has arrived in a considerable state of excitement, who insists upon seeing me. She is waiting now in the sitting-room. Now, when young ladies wander about the metropolis at this hour of the morning and knock sleepy people up out of their beds, I presume that it is something very pressing which they have to communicate. Should it prove to be an interesting case, you would, I am sure, wish to follow it from the outset. I thought, at any rate, that I should call you and give you the chance."

"My dear fellow, I would not miss it for anything."

I had no keener pleasure than in following Holmes in his professional investigations, and in admiring the rapid deductions, as swift as intuitions, and yet always founded on a logical basis, with which he unravelled the problems which were submitted to him. I rapidly threw on my clothes and was ready in a few minutes to accompany my friend down to the sitting-room. A lady dressed in black and heavily veiled, who had been sitting in the window, rose as we entered.

"Good-morning, madam," said Holmes cheerily. "My name is Sherlock Holmes. This is my intimate friend and associate, Dr. Watson, before whom you can speak as freely as before myself. Ha! I am glad to see that Mrs. Hudson has had the good sense to light the fire. Pray draw up to it, and I shall order you a cup of hot coffee, for I observe that you are shivering."

"It is not cold which makes me shiver," said the woman in a low voice, changing her seat as requested.

"What, then?"

"It is fear, Mr. Holmes. It is terror." She raised her veil as she spoke, and we could see that she was indeed in a pitiable state of agitation, her face all drawn and grey, with restless, frightened eyes, like those of some hunted animal. Her features and figure were those of a woman of thirty, but her hair was shot with premature grey, and her expression was weary and haggard. Sherlock Holmes ran her over with one of his quick, all-comprehensive glances.

"You must not fear," said he soothingly, bending forward and patting her forearm. "We shall soon set matters right, I have no doubt. You have come in by train this morning, I see."

"You know me, then?"

"No, but I observe the second half of a return ticket in the palm of your left glove. You must have started early, and yet you had a good drive in a dog-cart, along heavy roads, before you reached the station."

The lady gave a violent start and stared in bewilderment at my companion.

"There is no mystery, my dear madam," said he, smiling. "The left arm of your jacket is spattered with mud in no less than seven places. The marks are perfectly fresh. There is no vehicle save a dog-cart which throws up mud in that way, and then only when you sit on the left-hand side of the driver."

"Whatever your reasons may be, you are perfectly correct," said she. "I started from home before six, reached Leatherhead at twenty past, and came in by the first train to Waterloo. Sir, I can stand this strain no longer; I shall go mad if it continues. I have no one to turn to—none, save only one, who cares for me, and he, poor fellow, can be of little aid. I have heard of you, Mr. Holmes; I have heard of you from Mrs. Farintosh, whom you helped in the hour of her sore need. It was from her that I had your address. Oh, sir, do you not think that you could help me, too, and at least throw a little light through the dense darkness which surrounds me? At present it is out of my power to reward you for your services, but in a month or six weeks I shall be married, with the control of my own income, and then at least you shall not find me ungrateful."

Holmes turned to his desk and, unlocking it, drew out a small case-book, which he consulted.

"Farintosh," said he. "Ah yes, I recall the case; it was concerned with an opal tiara. I think it was before your time, Watson. I can only say, madam, that I shall be happy to devote the same care to your case as I did to that of your friend. As to reward, my profession is its own reward; but you are at liberty to defray whatever expenses I may be put to, at the time which suits you best. And now I beg that you will lay before us everything that may help us in forming an opinion upon the matter."

"Alas!" replied our visitor, "the very horror of my situation lies in the fact that my fears are so vague, and my suspicions depend so entirely upon small points, which might seem trivial to another, that even he to whom of all others I have a right to look for help and advice looks upon all that I tell him about it as the fancies of a nervous woman. He does not say so, but I can read it from his soothing answers and averted eyes. But I have heard, Mr. Holmes, that you can see deeply into the manifold wickedness of the human heart. You may advise me how to walk amid the dangers which encompass me."

"I am all attention, madam."

"My name is Helen Stoner, and I am living with my stepfather, who is the last survivor of one of the oldest Saxon families in England, the Roylotts of Stoke Moran, on the western border of Surrey."

Holmes nodded his head. "The name is familiar to me," said he.

"The family was at one time among the richest in England, and the estates extended over the borders into Berkshire in the north and Hampshire in the west. In the last century, however, four successive heirs were of a dissolute and wasteful disposition, and the family ruin was eventually completed by a gambler in the days of the Regency. Nothing was left save a few acres of ground, and the two-hundred-year-old house, which is itself crushed under a heavy mortgage. The last squire dragged out his existence there, living the horrible life of an aristocratic pauper; but his only son, my stepfather, seeing that he must adapt himself to the new conditions, obtained an advance from a relative, which enabled him to take a medical degree, and went out to Calcutta, where, by his professional skill and his force of character, he established a large practice. In a fit of anger, however, caused by some robberies which had been perpetrated in the house, he beat his native butler to death and narrowly escaped a capital sentence. As it was, he suffered a long term of imprisonment and afterwards returned to England a morose and disappointed man.

"When Dr. Roylott was in India he married my mother, Mrs. Stoner, the young widow of Major-General Stoner, of the Bengal Artillery. My sister, Julia, and I were twins, and we were only two years old at the time of my mother's re-marriage. She had a considerable sum of money—not less than one thousand pounds a year—and this she bequeathed to Dr. Roylott entirely while we resided with him, with a provision that a certain annual sum should be allowed to each of us in the event of our marriage. Shortly after our return to England my mother died—she was killed eight years ago in a railway accident near Crewe. Dr. Roylott then abandoned his attempts to establish himself in practice in London and took us to live with him in the old ancestral house at Stoke Moran. The money which my mother had left was enough for our wants, and there seemed to be no obstacle to our happiness.

"But a terrible change came over our stepfather about this time. Instead of making friends and exchanging visits with our neighbours, who had at first been overjoyed to see a Roylott of Stoke Moran back in the old family seat, he shut himself up in his house and seldom came out save to indulge in ferocious quarrels with whoever might cross his path. Violence of temper approaching to mania has been hereditary in the men of the family, and in my stepfather's case it had, I believe, been intensified by his long residence in the tropics. A series of disgraceful brawls took place, two of which ended in the police-court, until at last he became the terror of the village, and the folks would fly at his approach, for he is a man of immense strength, and absolutely uncontrollable in his anger.

"Last week he hurled the local blacksmith over a parapet into a stream, and it was only by paying over all the money which I could gather together that I was able to avert another public exposure. He had no friends at all save the wandering gipsies, and he would give these vagabonds leave to encamp upon the few acres of bramble-covered land which represent the family estate and would accept in return the hospitality of their tents, wandering away with them sometimes for weeks on end. He has a passion also for Indian animals, which are sent over to him by a correspondent, and he has at this moment a cheetah and a baboon, which wander freely over his grounds and are feared by the villagers almost as much as their master.

"You can imagine from what I say that my poor sister, Julia, and I had no great pleasure in our lives. No servant would stay with us, and for a long time we did all the work of the house. She was but thirty at the time of her death, and yet her hair had already begun to whiten, even as mine has."

"Your sister is dead, then?"

"She died just two years ago, and it is of her death that I wish to speak to you. You can understand that, living the life which I have described, we were little likely to see anyone of our own age and position. We had, however, an aunt, my mother's maiden sister, Miss Honoria Westphail, who lives near Harrow, and we were occasionally allowed to pay short visits at this lady's house. Julia went there at Christmas two years ago and met there a half-pay major of marines, to whom she became engaged. My stepfather learned of the engagement when my sister returned and offered no objection to the marriage; but within a fortnight of the day which had been fixed for the wedding, the terrible event occurred which has deprived me of my only companion."

Sherlock Holmes had been leaning back in his chair with

his eyes closed and his head sunk in a cushion, but he half opened his lids now and glanced across at his visitor.

"Pray be precise as to details," said he.

"It is easy for me to be so, for every event of that dreadful time is seared into my memory. The manor-house is, as I have already said, very old, and only one wing is now inhabited. The bedrooms in this wing are on the ground floor, the sitting-rooms being in the central block of the buildings. Of these bedrooms the first is Dr. Roylott's, the second my sister's, and the third my own. There is no communication between them, but they all open out into the same corridor. Do I make myself plain?"

"Perfectly so."

"The windows of the three rooms open out upon the lawn. That fatal night Dr. Roylott had gone to his room early, though we knew that he had not retired to rest, for my sister was troubled by the smell of the strong Indian cigars which it was his custom to smoke. She left her room, therefore, and came into mine, where she sat for some time, chatting about her approaching wedding. At eleven o'clock she rose to leave me, but she paused at the door and looked back.

"'Tell me, Helen,' said she, 'have you ever heard any-one whistle in the dead of the night?'

"'Never,' said I.

"'I suppose that you could not possibly whistle, yourself, in your sleep?'

"'Certainly not. But why?'

"'Because during the last few nights I have always, about three in the morning, heard a low, clear whistle. I am a light sleeper, and it has awakened me. I cannot tell where it came from—perhaps from the next room, perhaps from the lawn. I thought that I would just ask you whether you had heard it.'

"'No, I have not. It must be those wretched gipsies in the plantation.'

"'Very likely. And yet if it were on the lawn, I wonder that you did not hear it also.'

"'Ah, but I sleep more heavily than you.'

"'Well, it is of no great consequence, at any rate.' She smiled back at me, closed my door, and a few moments later I heard her key turn in the lock."

"Indeed," said Holmes. "Was it your custom always to lock yourselves in at night?"

"Always."

"And why?"

"I think that I mentioned to you that the doctor kept a cheetah and a baboon. We had no feeling of security unless our doors were locked."

"Quite so. Pray proceed with your statement."

"I could not sleep that night. A vague feeling of impending misfortune impressed me. My sister and I, you will recollect, were twins, and you know how subtle are the links which bind two souls which are so closely allied. It was a wild night. The wind was howling outside, and the rain was beating and splashing against the windows. Suddenly, amid all the hubbub of the gale, there burst forth the wild scream of a terrified woman. I knew that it was my sister's voice. I sprang from my bed, wrapped a shawl round me, and rushed into the corridor. As I opened my door I seemed to hear a low whistle, such as my sister described, and a few moments later a clanging sound, as if a mass of metal had fallen. As I ran down the passage, my sister's door was unlocked and revolved slowly upon its hinges. I stared at it horror-stricken, not knowing what was about to issue from it. By the light of the corridor-lamp I saw my sister appear at the opening, her face blanched with terror, her hands groping for help, her whole figure swaying to and fro like that of a drunkard. I ran to her and threw my arms round her, but at that moment her knees seemed to give way and she fell to the ground. She writhed as one who is in terrible pain, and her limbs were dreadfully convulsed. At first I thought that she had not recognised me, but as I bent over her she suddenly shrieked out in a voice which I shall never forget, 'Oh, my God! Helen! It was the band! The speckled band!' There was something else which she would fain have said, and she stabbed with her finger into the air in the direction of the doctor's room, but a fresh convulsion seized her and choked her words. I rushed out, calling loudly for my stepfather, and I met him hastening from his room in his dressing-gown. When he reached my sister's side she was unconscious, and though he poured brandy down her throat and sent for medical aid from the village, all efforts were in vain, for she slowly sank and died without having recovered her consciousness. Such was the dreadful end of my beloved sister."

"One moment," said Holmes; "are you sure about this whistle and metallic sound? Could you swear to it?"

"That was what the county Coroner asked me at the inquiry. It is my strong impression that I heard it, and yet, among the crash of the gale and the creaking of an old house, I may possibly have been deceived."

"Was your sister dressed?"

"No, she was in her night-dress. In her right hand was found the charred stump of a match, and in her left a match-box."

"Showing that she had struck a light and looked about her when the alarm took place. That is important. And what conclusions did the Coroner come to?"

"He investigated the case with great care, for Dr. Roylott's conduct had long been notorious in the county, but he was unable to find any satisfactory cause of death. My evidence showed that the door had been fastened upon the inner side, and the windows were blocked by old-fashioned shutters with broad iron bars, which were se-cured every night. The walls were carefully sounded and were shown to be quite solid all round, and the flooring was also thoroughly examined, with the same result. The chimney is wide, but is barred up by four large staples. It is certain, therefore, that my sister was quite alone when she met her end. Besides, there were no marks of any violence upon her."

"How about poison?"

"The doctors examined her for it, but without success."

"What do you think that this unfortunate lady died of, then?"

"It is my belief that she died of pure fear and nervous shock, though what it was that frightened her I cannot imagine."

"Were there gipsies in the plantation at the time?"

"Yes, there are nearly always some there."

"Ah, and what did you gather from this allusion to a band—a speckled band?"

"Sometimes I have thought that it was merely the wild talk of delirium, sometimes that it may have referred to some band of people, perhaps to these very gipsies in the plantation. I do not know whether the spotted handkerchiefs which so many of them wear over their heads might have suggested the strange adjective which she used."

Holmes shook his head like a man who is far from being satisfied.

"These are very deep waters," said he; "pray go on with your narrative."

"Two years have passed since then, and my life has been until lately lonelier than ever. A month ago, however, a dear friend, whom I have known for many years, has done me the honour to ask my hand in marriage. His name is Armitage—Percy Armitage—the second son of Mr. Armitage, of Crane Water, near Reading. My stepfather has offered no opposition to the match, and we are to be married in the course of the spring. Two days ago some repairs were started in the west wing of the building, and my bedroom wall has been pierced, so that I have had to move into the chamber in which my sister died, and to sleep in the very bed in which she slept. Imagine, then, my thrill of terror when last night, as I lay awake, thinking over her terrible fate, I suddenly heard in the silence of the night the low whistle which had been the herald of her own death. I sprang up and lit the lamp, but nothing was to be seen in the room. I was too shaken to go to bed again, however, so I dressed, and as soon as it was daylight I slipped down, got a dog-cart at the Crown Inn, which is opposite, and drove to Leatherhead, from whence I have come on this morning with the one object of seeing you and asking your advice."

"You have done wisely," said my friend. "But have you told me all?"

"Yes, all."

"Miss Roylott, you have not. You are screening your stepfather."

"Why, what do you mean?"

For answer Holmes pushed back the frill of black lace which fringed the hand that lay upon our visitor's knee. Five little livid spots, the marks of four fingers and a thumb, were printed upon the white wrist.

"You have been cruelly used," said Holmes.

The lady coloured deeply and covered over her injured wrist. "He is a hard man," she said, "and perhaps he hardly knows his own strength."

There was a long silence, during which Holmes leaned his chin upon his hands and stared into the crackling fire.

"This is a very deep business," he said at last. "There are a thousand details which I should desire to know before I decide upon our course of action. Yet we have not a moment to lose. If we were to come to Stoke Moran to-day, would it be possible for us to see over these rooms without the knowledge of your stepfather?"

"As it happens, he spoke of coming into town to-day upon some most important business. It is probable that he will be away all day, and that there would be nothing to disturb you. We have a housekeeper now, but she is old and foolish, and I could easily get her out of the way."

"Excellent. You are not averse to this trip, Watson?"

"By no means."

"Then we shall both come. What are you going to do yourself?"

"I have one or two things which I would wish to do now that I am in town. But I shall return by the twelve o'clock train, so as to be there in time for your coming."

"And you may expect us early in the afternoon. I have

myself some small business matters to attend to. Will you not wait and breakfast?"

"No, I must go. My heart is lightened already since I have confided my trouble to you. I shall look forward to seeing you again this afternoon." She dropped her thick black veil over her face and glided from the room.

"And what do you think of it all, Watson?" asked Sherlock Holmes, leaning back in his chair.

"It seems to me to be a most dark and sinister business."

"Dark enough and sinister enough."

"Yet if the lady is correct in saying that the flooring and walls are sound, and that the door, window, and chimney are impassable, then her sister must have been undoubtedly alone when she met her mysterious end."

"What becomes, then, of these nocturnal whistles, and what of the very peculiar words of the dying woman?"

"I cannot think."

"When you combine the ideas of whistles at night, the presence of a band of gipsies who are on intimate terms with this old doctor, the fact that we have every reason to believe that the doctor has an interest in preventing his stepdaughter's marriage, the dying allusion to a band, and finally, the fact that Miss Helen Stoner heard a metallic clang, which might have been caused by one of those metal bars that secured the shutters falling back into its place, I think that there is good ground to think that the mystery may be cleared along those lines."

"But what, then, did the gipsies do?"

"I cannot imagine."

"I see many objections to any such theory."

"And so do I. It is precisely for that reason that we are going to Stoke Moran this day. I want to see whether the objections are fatal, or if they may be explained away. But what in the name of the devil!"

The ejaculation had been drawn from my companion by the fact that our door had been suddenly dashed open, and that a huge man had framed himself in the aperture. His costume was a peculiar mixture of the professional

and of the agricultural, having a black top-hat, a long
frock-coat, and a pair of high gaiters, with a hunting crop
swinging in his hand. So tall was he that his hat actually
brushed the cross bar of the doorway, and his breadth
seemed to span it across from side to side. A large face,
seared with a thousand wrinkles, burned yellow with the
sun, and marked with every evil passion, was turned from
one to the other of us, while his deep-set, bile-shot eyes,
and his high, thin, fleshless nose, gave him somewhat the
resemblance of a fierce old bird of prey.

"Which of you is Holmes?" asked the apparition.

"My name, sir; but you have the advantage of me," said
my companion quietly.

"I am Dr. Grimesby Roylott, of Stoke Moran."

"Indeed, Doctor," said Holmes blandly. "Pray take a
seat."

"I will do nothing of the kind. My stepdaughter has
been here. I have traced her. What has she been saying to
you?"

"It is a little cold for the time of the year," said Holmes.

"What has she been saying to you?" screamed the old
man furiously.

"But I have heard that the crocuses promise well," continued my companion imperturbably.

"Ha! You put me off, do you?" said our new visitor,
taking a step forward and shaking his hunting crop. "I
know you, you scoundrel! I have heard of you before. You
are Holmes, the meddler."

My friend smiled.

"Holmes, the busybody!"

His smile broadened.

"Holmes, the Scotland Yard Jack-in-office!"

Holmes chuckled heartily. "Your conversation is most
entertaining," said he. "When you go out close the door,
for there is a decided draught."

"I will go when I have said my say. Don't you dare
meddle with my affairs. I know that Miss Stoner has been
here. I traced her! I am a dangerous man to fall foul of!

See here." He stepped swiftly forward, seized the poker, and bent it into a curve with his huge brown hands.

"See that you keep yourself out of my grip," he snarled, and hurling the twisted poker into the fireplace, he strode out of the room.

"He seems a very amiable person," said Holmes, laughing. "I am not quite so bulky, but if he had remained, I might have shown him that my grip was not much more feeble than his own." As he spoke he picked up the steel poker and, with a sudden effort, straightened it out again.

"Fancy his having the insolence to confound me with the official detective force! This incident gives zest to our investigation, however, and I only trust that our little friend will not suffer from her imprudence in allowing this brute to trace her. And now, Watson, we shall order breakfast, and afterwards I shall walk down to Doctors' Commons, where I hope to get some data which may help us in this matter."

It was nearly one o'clock when Sherlock Holmes returned from his excursion. He held in his hand a sheet of blue paper, scrawled over with notes and figures.

"I have seen the will of the deceased wife," said he. "To determine its exact meaning I have been obliged to work out the present prices of the investments with which it is concerned. The total income, which at the time of the wife's death was little short of £1,100, is now, through the fall in agricultural prices, not more than £750. Each daughter can claim an income of £250, in case of marriage. It is evident, therefore, that if both girls had married, this beauty would have had a mere pittance, while even one of them would cripple him to a very serious extent. My morning's work has not been wasted, since it has proved that he has the very strongest motives for standing in the way of anything of the sort. And now, Watson, this is too serious for dawdling, especially as the old man is aware that we are interesting ourselves in his affairs; so if you are ready, we shall call a cab and drive to Waterloo. I should be very much obliged if you would slip your revolver in your pocket. An Eley's No. 2 is an excellent argument with gentlemen who can twist steel pokers into knots. That and a tooth-brush are, I think, all that we need."

At Waterloo we were fortunate in catching a train for Leatherhead, where we hired a trap at the station inn and drove for four or five miles through the lovely Surrey lanes. It was a perfect day, with a bright sun and a few fleecy clouds in the heavens. The trees and wayside hedges were just throwing out their first green shoots, and the air was full of the pleasant smell of the moist earth. To me at least there was a strange contrast between the sweet promise of the spring and this sinister quest upon which we were engaged. My companion sat in the front of the trap, his arms folded, his hat pulled down over his eyes, and his chin sunk upon his breast, buried in the deepest thought. Suddenly, however, he started, tapped me on the shoulder, and pointed over the meadows.

"Look there!" said he.

A heavily timbered park stretched up in a gentle slope, thickening into a grove at the highest point. From amid the branches there jutted out the grey gables and high roof-tree of a very old mansion.

"Stoke Moran?" said he.

"Yes, sir, that be the house of Dr. Grimesby Roylott," remarked the driver.

"There is some building going on there," said Holmes; "that is where we are going."

"There's the village," said the driver, pointing to a cluster of roofs some distance to the left; "but if you want to get to the house, you'll find it shorter to get over this stile, and so by the foot-path over the fields. There it is, where the lady is walking."

"And the lady, I fancy, is Miss Stoner," observed Holmes, shading his eyes. "Yes, I think we had better do as you suggest."

We got off, paid our fare, and the trap rattled back on its way to Leatherhead.

"I thought it as well," said Holmes as we climbed the

stile, "that this fellow should think we had come here as architects, or on some definite business. It may stop his gossip. Good-afternoon, Miss Stoner. You see that we have been as good as our word."

Our client of the morning had hurried forward to meet us with a face which spoke her joy, "I have been waiting so eagerly for you," she cried, shaking hands with us warmly. "All has turned out splendidly. Dr. Roylett has gone to town, and it is unlikely that he will be back before evening."

"We have had the pleasure of making the Doctor's acquaintance," said Holmes, and in a few words he sketched out what had occurred. Miss Stoner turned white to the lips as she listened.

"Good Heavens!" she cried, "he has followed me, then."

"So it appears."

"He is so cunning that I never know when I am safe from him. What will he say when he returns?"

"He must guard himself, for he may find that there is someone more cunning than himself upon his track. You must lock yourself up from him to-night. If he is violent, we shall take you away to your aunt's at Harrow. Now, we must make the best use of our time, so kindly take us at once to the rooms which we are to examine."

The building was of grey, lichen-blotched stone, with a high central portion and two curving wings, like the claws of a crab, thrown out on each side. In one of these wings the windows were broken and blocked with wooden boards, while the roof was partly caved in, a picture of ruin. The central portion was in little better repair, but the right-hand block was comparatively modern, and the blinds in the windows, with the blue smoke curling up from the chimneys, showed that this was where the family resided. Some scaffolding had been erected against the end wall, and the stone-work had been broken into, but there were no signs of any workmen at the moment of our visit. Holmes walked slowly up and down the ill-trimmed lawn and examined with deep attention the outsides of the windows.

"This, I take it, belongs to the room in which you used to sleep, the centre one to your sister's, and the one next to the main building to Dr. Roylott's chamber?"

"Exactly so. But I am now sleeping in the middle one."

"Pending the alterations, as I understand. By the way, there does not seem to be any very pressing need for repairs at that end wall."

"There were none. I believe that it was an excuse to move me from my room."

"Ah, that is suggestive! Now, on the other side of this narrow wing runs the corridor from which these three rooms open. There are windows in it, of course?"

"Yes, but very small ones. Too narrow for anyone to pass through."

"As you both locked your doors at night, your rooms were unapproachable from that side. Now, would you have the kindness to go into your room and bar your shutters?"

Miss Stoner did so, and Holmes, after a careful examination through the open window, endeavoured in every way to force the shutter open, but without success. There was no slit through which a knife could be passed to raise the bar. Then with his lens he tested the hinges, but they were of solid iron, built firmly into the massive masonry. "Hum!" said he, scratching his chin in some perplexity, "my theory certainly presents some difficulties. No one could pass these shutters if they were bolted. Well, we shall see if the inside throws any light upon the matter."

A small side door led into the whitewashed corridor from which the three bedrooms opened. Holmes refused to examine the third chamber, so we passed at once to the second, that in which Miss Stoner was now sleeping, and in which her sister had met with her fate. It was a homely little room, with a low ceiling and a gaping fireplace, after the fashion of old country-houses. A brown chest of drawers stood in one corner, a narrow white-counterpaned bed in another, and a dressing-table on the left-hand side of the window. These articles, with two small wickerwork chairs, made up all the furniture in the room save for a square of Wilton carpet in the centre. The boards round and the panelling of the walls were of brown, worm-eaten oak, so old and discoloured that it may have dated from the original building of the house. Holmes drew one of the chairs into a corner and sat silent, while his eyes travelled round and round and up and down, taking in every detail of the apartment.

"Where does the bell communicate with?" he asked at last, pointing to a thick bell-rope which hung down beside the bed, the tassel actually lying upon the pillow.

"It goes to the housekeeper's room."

"It looks newer than the other things?"

"Yes, it was only put there a couple of years ago."

"Your sister asked for it, I suppose?"

"No, I never heard of her using it. We used always to get what we wanted for ourselves."

"Indeed, it seemed unnecessary to put so nice a bell-pull there. You will excuse me for a few minutes while I satisfy myself as to this floor." He threw himself down upon his face with his lens in his hand and crawled swiftly backward and forward, examining minutely the cracks between the boards. Then he did the same with the wood-work with which the chamber was panelled. Finally he walked over to the bed and spent some time in staring at it and in running his eye up and down the wall. Finally he took the bell-rope in his hand and gave it a brisk tug.

"Why, it's a dummy," said he.

"Won't it ring?"

"No, it is not even attached to a wire. This is very interesting. You can see now that it is fastened to a hook just above where the little opening for the ventilator is."

"How very absurd! I never noticed that before."

"Very strange!" muttered Holmes, pulling at the rope. "There are one or two very singular points about this room. For example, what a fool a builder must be to open a ventilator into another room, when, with the same trouble, he might have communicated with the outside air!"

"That is also quite modern," said the lady.

"Done about the same time as the bell-rope?" remarked Holmes.

"Yes, there were several little changes carried out about that time."

"They seem to have been of a most interesting character—dummy bell-ropes and ventilators which do not ventilate. With your permission, Miss Stoner, we shall now carry our researches into the inner apartment."

Dr. Grimesby Roylott's chamber was larger than that of his stepdaughter, but was as plainly furnished. A camp-bed, a small wooden shelf full of books, mostly of a technical character, an armchair beside the bed, a plain wooden chair against the wall, a round table, and a large iron safe were the principal things which met the eye. Holmes walked slowly round and examined each and all of them with the keenest interest.

"What's in here?" he asked, tapping the safe.

"My stepfather's business papers."

"Oh, you have seen inside, then?"

"Only once, some years ago. I remember that it was full of papers."

"There isn't a cat in it, for example?"

"No. What a strange idea!"

"Well, look at this!" He took up a small saucer of milk which stood on the top of it.

"No; we don't keep a cat. But there is a cheetah and a baboon."

"Ah, yes, of course! Well, a cheetah is just a big cat, and yet a saucer of milk does not go very far in satisfying its wants, I daresay. There is one point which I should wish to determine." He squatted down in front of the wooden chair and examined the seat of it with the greatest attention.

"Thank you. That is quite settled," said he, rising and putting his lens in his pocket. "Hello! Here is something interesting!"

The object which had caught his eye was a small dog

lash hung on one corner of the bed. The lash, however, was curled upon itself and tied so as to make a loop of whipcord.

"What do you make of that, Watson?"

"It's a common enough lash. But I don't know why it should be tied."

"That is not quite so common, is it? Ah, me! It's a wicked world, and when a clever man turns his brains to crime it is the worst of all. I think that I have seen enough now, Miss Stoner, and with your permission we shall walk out upon the lawn."

I had never seen my friend's face so grim or his brow so dark as it was when we turned from the scene of this investigation. We had walked several times up and down the lawn, neither Miss Stoner nor myself liking to break in upon his thoughts before he roused himself from his reverie.

"It is very essential, Miss Stoner," said he, "that you should absolutely follow my advice in every respect."

"I shall most certainly do so."

"The matter is too serious for any hesitation. Your life may depend upon your compliance."

"I assure you that I am in your hands."

"In the first place, both my friend and I must spend the night in your room."

Both Miss Stoner and I gazed at him in astonishment.

"Yes, it must be so. Let me explain. I believe that that is the village inn over there?"

"Yes, that is the Crown."

"Very good. Your windows would be visible from there?"

"Certainly."

"You must confine yourself to your room, on pretence of a headache, when your stepfather comes back. Then when you hear him retire for the night, you must open the shutters of your window, undo the hasp, put your lamp there as a signal to us, and then withdraw quietly with everything which you are likely to want into the room which you used to occupy. I have no doubt that, in spite of the repairs, you could manage there for one night."

"Oh, yes, easily."

"The rest you will leave in our hands."

"But what will you do?"

"We shall spend the night in your room, and we shall investigate the cause of this noise which has disturbed you."

"I believe, Mr. Holmes, that you have already made up your mind," said Miss Stoner, laying her hand upon my companion's sleeve.

"Perhaps I have."

"Then, for pity's sake, tell me what was the cause of my sister's death."

"I should prefer to have clearer proofs before I speak."

"You can at least tell me whether my own thought is correct, and if she died from some sudden fright."

"No, I do not think so. I think that there was probably some more tangible cause. And now, Miss Stoner, we must leave you, for if Dr. Roylott returned and saw us our journey would be in vain. Good-bye, and be brave, for if you will do what I have told you, you may rest assured that we shall soon drive away the dangers that threaten you."

Sherlock Holmes and I had no difficulty in engaging a bedroom and sitting-room at the Crown Inn. They were on the upper floor and from our window we could command a view of the avenue gate, and of the inhabited wing of Stoke Moran Manor House. At dusk we saw Dr. Grimesby Roylott drive past, his huge form looming up beside the little figure of the lad who drove him. The boy had some slight difficulty in undoing the heavy iron gates, and we heard the hoarse roar of the Doctor's voice and saw the fury with which he shook his clinched fists at him. The trap drove on, and a few minutes later we saw a sudden light spring up among the trees as the lamp was lit in one of the sitting-rooms.

"Do you know, Watson," said Holmes as we sat together

in the gathering darkness, "I have really some scruples as to taking you to-night. There is a distinct element of danger."

"Can I be of assistance?"

"Your presence might be invaluable."

"Then I shall certainly come."

"It is very kind of you."

"You speak of danger. You have evidently seen more in these rooms than was visible to me."

"No, but I fancy that I may have deduced a little more. I imagine that you saw all that I did."

"I saw nothing remarkable save the bell-rope, and what purpose that could answer I confess is more than I can imagine."

"You saw the ventilator, too?"

"Yes, but I do not think that it is such a very unusual thing to have a small opening between two rooms. It was so small that a rat could hardly pass through."

"I knew that we should find a ventilator before ever we came to Stoke Moran."

"My dear Holmes!"

"Oh, yes, I did. You remember in her statement she said that her sister could smell Dr. Roylott's cigar. Now, of course that suggested at once that there must be a communication between the two rooms. It could only be a small one, or it would have been remarked upon at the Coroner's inquiry. I deduced a ventilator."

"But what harm can there be in that?"

"Well, there is at least a curious coincidence of dates. A ventilator is made, a cord is hung, and a lady who sleeps in the bed dies. Does not that strike you?"

"I cannot as yet see any connection."

"Did you observe anything very peculiar about that bed?"

"No."

"It was clamped to the floor. Did you ever see a bed fastened like that before?"

"I cannot say that I have."

"The lady could not move her bed. It must always be in

the same relative position to the ventilator and to the rope—or so we may call it, since it was clearly never meant for a bell-pull."

"Holmes," I cried, "I seem to see dimly what you are hinting at. We are only just in time to prevent some subtle and horrible crime."

"Subtle enough and horrible enough. When a doctor does go wrong he is the first of criminals. He has nerve and he has knowledge. Palmer and Pritchard were among the heads of their profession. This man strikes even deeper, but I think, Watson, that we shall be able to strike deeper still. But we shall have horrors enough before the night is over; for goodness' sake let us have a quiet pipe and turn our minds for a few hours to something more cheerful."

About nine o'clock the light among the trees was extinguished, and all was dark in the direction of the Manor House. Two hours passed slowly away, and then, suddenly, just at the stroke of eleven, a single bright light shone out right in front of us.

"That is our signal," said Holmes, springing to his feet; "it comes from the middle window."

As we passed out he exchanged a few words with the landlord, explaining that we were going on a late visit to an acquaintance, and that it was possible that we might spend the night there. A moment later we were out on the dark road, a chill wind blowing in our faces, and one yellow light twinkling in front of us through the gloom to guide us on our sombre errand.

There was little difficulty in entering the grounds, for unrepaired breaches gaped in the old park wall. Making our way among the trees, we reached the lawn, crossed it, and were about to enter through the window when out from a clump of laurel bushes there darted what seemed to be a hideous and distorted child, who threw itself upon the grass with writhing limbs and then ran swiftly across the lawn into the darkness.

"My God!" I whispered; "did you see it?"

Holmes was for the moment as startled as I. His hand closed like a vise upon my wrist in his agitation. Then he broke into a low laugh and put his lips to my ear.

"It is a nice household," he murmured. "That is the baboon."

I had forgotten the strange pets which the Doctor affected. There was a cheetah, too; perhaps we might find it upon our shoulders at any moment. I confess that I felt easier in my mind when, after following Holmes's example and slipping off my shoes, I found myself inside the bedroom. My companion noiselessly closed the shutters, moved the lamp onto the table, and cast his eyes round the room. All was as we had seen it in the daytime. Then creeping up to me and making a trumpet of his hand, he whispered into my ear again so gently that it was all that I could do to distinguish the words:

"The least sound would be fatal to our plans."

I nodded to show that I had heard.

"We must sit without light. He would see it through the ventilator."

I nodded again.

"Do not go asleep; your very life may depend upon it. Have your pistol ready in case we should need it. I will sit on the side of the bed, and you in that chair."

I took out my revolver and laid it on the corner of the table.

Holmes had brought up a long, thin cane, and this he placed upon the bed beside him. By it he laid the box of matches and the stump of a candle. Then he turned down the lamp, and we were left in darkness.

How shall I ever forget that dreadful vigil? I could not hear a sound, not even the drawing of a breath, and yet I knew that my companion sat open-eyed, within a few feet of me, in the same state of nervous tension in which I was myself. The shutters cut off the least ray of light, and we waited in absolute darkness. From outside came the occasional cry of a night-bird, and once at our very window a long drawn cat-like whine, which told us that the cheetah was indeed at liberty. Far away we could hear the deep tones of the parish clock, which boomed out every quarter of an hour. How long they seemed, those quarters! Twelve struck, and one and two and three, and still we sat waiting silently for whatever might befall.

Suddenly there was the momentary gleam of a light up in the direction of the ventilator, which vanished immediately, but was succeeded by a strong smell of burning oil and heated metal. Someone in the next room had lit a dark-lantern. I heard a gentle sound of movement, and then all was silent once more, though the smell grew stronger. For half an hour I sat with straining ears. Then suddenly another sound became audible—a very gentle, soothing sound, like that of a small jet of steam escaping continually from a kettle. The instant that we heard it, Holmes sprang from the bed, struck a match, and lashed furiously with his cane at the bell-pull.

"You see it, Watson?" he yelled. "You see it?"

But I saw nothing. At the moment when Holmes struck the light I heard a low, clear whistle, but the sudden glare flashing into my weary eyes made it impossible for me to tell what it was at which my friend lashed so savagely. I could, however, see that his face was deadly pale and filled with horror and loathing.

He had ceased to strike and was gazing up at the ventilator when suddenly there broke from the silence of the night the most horrible cry to which I have ever listened. It swelled up louder and louder, a hoarse yell of pain and fear and anger all mingled in the one dreadful shriek. They say that away down in the village, and even in the distant parsonage, that cry raised the sleepers from their beds. It struck cold to our hearts, and I stood gazing at Holmes, and he at me, until the last echoes of it had died away into the silence from which it rose.

"What can it mean?" I gasped.

"It means that it is all over," Holmes answered. "And perhaps, after all, it is for the best. Take your pistol, and we will enter Dr. Roylott's room."

With a grave face he lit the lamp and led the way down the corridor. Twice he struck at the chamber door without any reply from within. Then he turned the handle and entered, I at his heels, with the cocked pistol in my hand.

It was a singular sight which met our eyes. On the table stood a dark-lantern with the shutter half open, throwing a brilliant beam of light upon the iron safe, the door of which was ajar. Beside this table, on the wooden chair, sat Dr. Grimesby Roylott, clad in a long, grey dressing-gown, his bare ankles protruding beneath, and his feet thrust into red heelless Turkish slippers. Across his lap lay the short stock with the long lash which we had noticed during the day. His chin was cocked upwards and his eyes were fixed in a dreadful, rigid stare at the corner of the ceiling. Round his brow he had a peculiar yellow band, with brownish speckles, which seemed to be bound tightly round his head. As we entered he made neither sound nor motion.

"The band, the speckled band!" whispered Holmes.

I took a step forward. In an instant his strange head-gear began to move, and there reared itself from among his hair the squat diamond-shaped head and puffed neck of a loathsome serpent.

"It is a swamp adder!" cried Holmes; "the deadliest snake in India. He has died within ten seconds of being bitten. Violence does, in truth, recoil upon the violent, and the schemer falls into the pit which he digs for another. Let us thrust this creature back into its den, and we can then remove Miss Stoner to some place of shelter and let the county police know what has happened."

As he spoke he drew the dog-whip swiftly from the dead man's lap, and throwing the noose round the reptile's neck, he drew it from its horrid perch and, carrying it at arm's length, threw it into the iron safe, which he closed upon it.

Such are the true facts of the death of Dr. Grimesby Roylott, of Stoke Moran. It is not necessary that I should

prolong a narrative which has already run to too great a
length by telling how we broke the sad news to the terrified girl, how we conveyed her by the morning train to the
care of her good aunt at Harrow, of how the slow process
of official inquiry came to the conclusion that the Doctor
met his fate while indiscreetly playing with a dangerous
pet. The little which I had yet to learn of the case was told
me by Sherlock Holmes as we travelled back next day.

"I had," said he, "come to an entirely erroneous conclusion, which shows, my dear Watson, how dangerous it
always is to reason from insufficient data. The presence of
the gipsies, and the use of the word 'band,' which was used
by the poor girl, no doubt to explain the appearance which
she had caught a hurried glimpse of by the light of her
match, were sufficient to put me upon an entirely wrong
scent. I can only claim the merit that I instantly reconsid-
ered my position when, however, it became clear to me
that whatever danger threatened an occupant of the room
could not come either from the window or the door. My
attention was speedily drawn, as I have already remarked
to you, to this ventilator, and to the bell-rope which hung
down to the bed. The discovery that this was a dummy,
and that the bed was clamped to the floor, instantly gave
rise to the suspicion that the rope was there as a bridge for
something passing through the hole and coming to the
bed. The idea of a snake instantly occurred to me, and
when I coupled it with my knowledge that the Doctor was
furnished with a supply of creatures from India, I felt that
I was probably on the right track. The idea of using a form
of poison which could not possibly be discovered by any
chemical test was just such a one as would occur to a clever
and ruthless man who had had an Eastern training. The
rapidity with which such a poison would take effect would
also, from his point of view, be an advantage. It would be a
sharp-eyed coroner, indeed, who could distinguish the two
little dark punctures which would show where the poison
fangs had done their work. Then I thought of the whistle.
Of course he must recall the snake before the morning

light revealed it to the victim. He had trained it, probably by the use of the milk which we saw, to return to him when summoned. He would put it through this ventilator at the hour that he thought best, with the certainty that it would crawl down the rope and land on the bed. It might or might not bite the occupant; perhaps she might escape every night for a week, but sooner or later she must fall a victim.

"I had come to these conclusions before ever I had entered his room. An inspection of his chair showed me that he had been in the habit of standing on it, which of course would be necessary in order that he should reach the ventilator. The sight of the safe, the saucer of milk, and the loop of whipcord were enough to finally dispel any doubts which may have remained. The metallic clang heard by Miss Stoner was obviously caused by her stepfather hastily closing the door of his safe upon its terrible occupant. Having once made up my mind, you know the steps which I took in order to put the matter to the proof. I heard the creature hiss as I have no doubt that you did also, and I instantly lit the light and attacked it."

"With the result of driving it through the ventilator."

"And also with the result of causing it to turn upon its master at the other side. Some of the blows of my cane came home and roused its snakish temper, so that it flew upon the first person it saw. In this way I am no doubt indirectly responsible for Dr. Grimesby Roylott's death, and I cannot say that it is likely to weigh very heavily upon my conscience."

The Adventure of the
Noble Bachelor

The Lord St. Simon marriage, and its curious termination, have long ceased to be a subject of interest in those exalted circles in which the unfortunate bridegroom moves. Fresh scandals have eclipsed it, and their more piquant details have drawn the gossips away from this four-year-old drama. As I have reason to believe, however, that the full facts have never been revealed to the general public, and as my friend Sherlock Holmes had a considerable share in clearing the matter up, I feel that no memoir of him would be complete without some little sketch of this remarkable episode.

It was a few weeks before my own marriage, during the days when I was still sharing rooms with Holmes in Baker Street, that he came home from an afternoon stroll to find a letter on the table waiting for him. I had remained in-doors all day, for the weather had taken a sudden turn to rain, with high autumnal winds, and the Jezail bullet which I had brought back in one of my limbs as a relic of my Afghan campaign throbbed with dull persistence. With my body in one easy-chair and my legs upon another, I had surrounded myself with a cloud of newspapers until at last, saturated with the news of the day, I tossed them all aside and lay listless, watching the huge crest and mono-gram upon the envelope upon the table and wondering la-zily who my friend's noble correspondent could be.

"Here is a very fashionable epistle," I remarked as he entered. "Your morning letters, if I remember right, were from a fish-monger and a tide-waiter."

"Yes, my correspondence has certainly the charm of variety," he answered, smiling, "and the humbler are usually the more interesting. This looks like one of those unwelcome social summonses which call upon a man either to be bored or to lie."

He broke the seal and glanced over the contents.

"Oh, come, it may prove to be something of interest, after all."

"Not social, then?"

"No, distinctly professional."

"And from a noble client?"

"One of the highest in England."

"My dear fellow, I congratulate you."

"I assure you, Watson, without affectation, that the status of my client is a matter of less moment to me than the interest of his case. It is just possible, however, that that also may not be wanting in this new investigation. You have been reading the papers diligently of late, have you not?"

"It looks like it," said I ruefully, pointing to a huge bundle in the corner. "I have had nothing else to do."

"It is fortunate, for you will perhaps be able to post me up. I read nothing except the criminal news and the agony column. The latter is always instructive. But if you have followed recent events so closely, you must have read about Lord St. Simon and his wedding?"

"Oh, yes, with the deepest interest."

"That is well. The letter which I hold in my hand is from Lord St. Simon. I will read it to you, and in return you must turn over these papers and let me have whatever bears upon the matter. This is what he says:

MY DEAR MR. SHERLOCK HOLMES:

Lord Backwater tells me that I may place implicit reliance upon your judgment and discretion. I have determined, therefore, to call upon you and to consult you in reference to the very painful event which has occurred in connection with my wedding. Mr. Lestrade, of Scotland Yard, is acting already in the matter, but he assures me that he sees no objection to your co-operation, and that he even thinks that it might be of some assistance. I will call at four o'clock in the afternoon, and should you have any other engagement at that time, I hope that you will postpone it, as this matter is of paramount importance.

Yours faithfully,

St. Simon

"It is dated from Grosvenor Mansions, written with a quill pen, and the noble lord has had the misfortune to get a smear of ink upon the outer side of his right little finger," remarked Holmes as he folded up the epistle.

"He says four o'clock. It is three now. He will be here in an hour."

"Then I have just time, with your assistance, to get clear upon the subject. Turn over those papers and arrange the extracts in their order of time, while I take a glance as to who our client is." He picked a red-covered volume from a line of books of reference beside the mantelpiece. "Here he is," said he, sitting down and flattening it out upon his knee. "Lord Robert Walsingham de Vere St. Simon, second son of the Duke of Balmoral. Hum! Arms: Azure, three caltrops in chief over a fess sable. Born in 1846. He's forty-one years of age, which is mature for marriage. Was Under-Secretary for the colonies in a late administration. The Duke, his father, was at one time Secretary for Foreign Affairs. They inherit Plantagenet blood by direct descent, and Tudor on the distaff side. Ha! Well, there is nothing very instructive in all this. I think that I must turn to you, Watson, for something more solid."

"I have very little difficulty in finding what I want," said I, "for the facts are quite recent, and the matter struck me as remarkable. I feared to refer them to you, however, as I knew that you had an inquiry on hand and that you disliked the intrusion of other matters."

"Oh, you mean the little problem of the Grosvenor Square furniture van. That is quite cleared up now —though, indeed, it was obvious from the first. Pray give me the results of your newspaper selections."

"Here is the first notice which I can find. It is in the personal column of the *Morning Post* and dates, as you see, some weeks back: 'A marriage has been arranged,' it says, 'and will, if rumour is correct, very shortly take place, between Lord Robert St. Simon, second son of the Duke of Balmoral, and Miss Hatty Doran, the only daughter of Aloysius Doran, Esq., of San Francisco, Cal., U.S.A.' That is all."

"Terse and to the point," remarked Holmes, stretching his long, thin legs towards the fire.

"There was a paragraph amplifying this in one of the society papers of the same week. Ah, here it is: 'There will soon be a call for protection in the marriage market, for the present free-trade principle appears to tell heavily against our home product. One by one the management of the noble houses of Great Britain is passing into the hands of our fair cousins from across the Atlantic. An important addition has been made during the last week to the list of the prizes which have been borne away by these charming invaders. Lord St. Simon, who has shown himself for over twenty years proof against the little god's arrows, has now definitely announced his approaching marriage with Miss Hatty Doran, the fascinating daughter of a California millionaire. Miss Doran, whose graceful figure and striking face attracted much attention at the Westbury House festivities, is an only child, and it is currently reported that her dowry will run to considerably over the six figures, with expectancies for the future. As it is an open secret that the Duke of Balmoral has been compelled to sell his pictures within the last few years, and as Lord St. Simon has no property of his own save the small estate of Birchmoor, it is obvious that the Californian heiress is not the only gainer by an alliance which will enable her to make the easy and common transition from a Republican lady to a British peeress.' "Anything else?" asked Holmes, yawning.

"Oh, yes; plenty. Then there is another note in the *Morning Post* to say that the marriage would be an absolutely quiet one, that it would be at St. George's, Hanover Square, that only half a dozen intimate friends would be invited, and that the party would return to the furnished house at Lancaster Gate which has been taken by Mr. Aloysius Doran. Two days later—that is, on Wednesday last—there is a curt announcement that the wedding had taken place, and that the honeymoon would be passed at Lord Backwater's place, near Petersfield. Those are all the notices which appeared before the disappearance of the bride."

"Before the what?" asked Holmes with a start.

"The vanishing of the lady."

"When did she vanish, then?"

"At the wedding breakfast."

"Indeed. This is more interesting than it promised to be; quite dramatic, in fact."

"Yes; it struck me as being a little out of the common."

"They often vanish before the ceremony, and occasionally during the honeymoon; but I cannot call to mind anything quite so prompt as this. Pray let me have the details."

"I warn you that they are very incomplete."

"Perhaps we may make them less so."

"Such as they are, they are set forth in a single article of a morning paper of yesterday, which I will read to you. It is headed, 'Singular Occurrence at a Fashionable Wedding': 'The family of Lord Robert St. Simon has been thrown into the greatest consternation by the strange and painful episodes which have taken place in connection with his wedding. The ceremony, as shortly announced in the papers of yesterday, occurred on the previous morning; but it is only now that it has been possible to confirm the strange rumours which have been so persistently floating about. In spite of the attempts of the friends to hush the matter up, so much public attention has now been drawn to it that no good purpose can be served by affecting to disregard what is a common subject for conversation.

"'The ceremony, which was performed at St. George's, Hanover Square, was a very quiet one, no one being present save the father of the bride, Mr. Aloysius Doran, the Duchess of Balmoral, Lord Backwater, Lord Eustace, and Lady Clara St. Simon (the younger brother and sister of the bridegroom), and Lady Alicia Whittington. The whole party proceeded afterwards to the house of Mr. Aloysius Doran, at Lancaster Gate, where breakfast had been prepared. It appears that some little trouble was caused by a woman, whose name has not been ascertained, who endeavoured to force her way into the house after the bridal party, alleging that she had some claim upon Lord St. Simon. It was only after a painful and prolonged scene that she was ejected by the butler and the footman. The bride, who had fortunately entered the house before this unpleasant interruption, had sat down to breakfast with the rest, when she complained of a sudden indisposition and retired to her room. Her prolonged absence having caused some comment, her father followed her, but learned from her maid that she had only come up to her chamber for an instant, caught up an ulster and bonnet, and hurried down to the passage. One of the footmen declared that he had seen a lady leave the house thus apparelled, but had refused to credit that it was his mistress, believing her to be with the company. On ascertaining that his daughter had disappeared, Mr. Aloysius Doran, in conjunction with the bridegroom, instantly put themselves in communication with the police, and very energetic inquiries are being made, which will probably result in a speedy clearing up of this very singular business. Up to a late hour last night, however, nothing had transpired as to the whereabouts of the missing lady. There are rumours of foul play in the matter, and it is said that the police have caused the arrest of the woman who had caused the original disturbance, in the belief that, from jealousy or some other motive, she may have been concerned in the strange disappearance of the bride.'"

"And is that all?"

"Only one little item in another of the morning papers, but it is a suggestive one."

"And it is—"

"That Miss Flora Millar, the lady who had caused the disturbance, has actually been arrested. It appears that she was formerly a *danseuse* at the Allegro, and that she has known the bridegroom for some years. There are no further particulars, and the whole case is in your hands now—so far as it has been set forth in the public press."

"And an exceedingly interesting case it appears to be. I would not have missed it for worlds. But there is a ring at the bell, Watson, and as the clock makes it a few minutes after four, I have no doubt that this will prove to be our nobel client. Do not dream of going, Watson, for I very much prefer having a witness, if only as a check to my own memory."

"Lord Robert St. Simon," announced our page-boy, throwing open the door. A gentleman entered, with a pleasant, cultured face, high-nosed and pale, with something perhaps of petulance about the mouth, and with the steady, well-opened eye of a man whose pleasant lot it had ever been to command and to be obeyed. His manner was brisk, and yet his general appearance gave an undue impression of age, for he had a slight forward stoop and a little bend of the knees as he walked. His hair, too, as he swept off his very curly-brimmed hat, was grizzled round the edges and thin upon the top. As to his dress, it was careful to the verge of foppishness, with high collar, black frock-coat, white waistcoat, yellow gloves, patent-leather shoes, and light-coloured gaiters. He advanced slowly into the room, turning his head from left to right, and swinging in his right hand the cord which held his golden eyeglasses.

"Good-day, Lord St. Simon," said Holmes, rising and bowing. "Pray take the basket-chair. This is my friend and colleague, Dr. Watson. Draw up a little to the fire, and we will talk this matter over."

"A most painful matter to me, as you can most readily

imagine, Mr. Holmes. I have been cut to the quick. I understand that you have already managed several delicate cases of this sort, sir, though I presume that they were hardly from the same class of society."

"No, I am descending."

"I beg pardon."

"My last client of the sort was a king."

"Oh, really! I had no idea. And which king?"

"The King of Scandinavia."

"What! Had he lost his wife?"

"You can understand," said Holmes suavely, "that I extend to the affairs of my clients the same secrecy which I promise to you in yours."

"Of course! Very right! Very right! I'm sure I beg pardon. As to my own case, I am ready to give you any information which may assist you in forming an opinion."

"Thank you. I have already learned all that is in the public prints, nothing more. I presume that I may take it as correct—this article, for example, as to the disappearance of the bride."

Lord St. Simon glanced over it. "Yes, it is correct, as far as it goes."

"But it needs a great deal of supplementing before anyone could offer an opinion. I think that I may arrive at my facts most directly by questioning you."

"Pray do so."

"When did you first meet Miss Hatty Doran?"

"In San Francisco, a year ago."

"You were travelling in the States?"

"Yes."

"Did you become engaged then?"

"No."

"But you were on a friendly footing?"

"I was amused by her society, and she could see that I was amused."

"Her father is very rich?"

"He is said to be the richest man on the Pacific slope."

"And how did he make his money?"

"In mining. He had nothing a few years ago. Then he struck gold, invested it, and came up by leaps and bounds."

"Now, what is your own impression as to the young lady's—your wife's character?"

The nobleman swung his glasses a little faster and stared down into the fire. "You see, Mr. Holmes," said he, "my wife was twenty before her father became a rich man. During that time she ran free in a mining camp and wandered through woods or mountains, so that her education has come from Nature rather than from the schoolmaster. She is what we call in England a tomboy, with a strong nature, wild and free, unfettered by any sort of traditions. She is impetuous—volcanic, I was about to say. She is swift in making up her mind and fearless in carrying out her resolutions. On the other hand, I would not have given her the name which I have the honour to bear"—he gave a little stately cough—"had not I thought her to be at bottom a noble woman. I believe that she is capable of heroic self-sacrifice and that anything dishonourable would be repugnant to her."

"Have you her photograph?"

"I brought this with me." He opened a locket and showed us the full face of a very lovely woman. It was not a photograph but an ivory miniature, and the artist had brought out the full effect of the lustrous black hair, the large dark eyes, and the exquisite mouth. Holmes gazed long and earnestly at it. Then he closed the locket and handed it back to Lord St. Simon.

"The young lady came to London, then, and you renewed your acquaintance?"

"Yes, her father brought her over for this last London season. I met her several times, became engaged to her, and have now married her."

"She brought, I understand, a considerable dowry?"

"A fair dowry. Not more than is usual in my family."

"And this, of course, remains to you, since the marriage is a *fait accompli?*"

"I really have made no inquiries on the subject."

"Very naturally not. Did you see Miss Doran on the day before the wedding?"

"Yes."

"Was she in good spirits?"

"Never better. She kept talking of what we should do in our future lives."

"Indeed! That is very interesting. And on the morning of the wedding?"

"She was as bright as possible—at least until after the ceremony."

"And did you observe any change in her then?"

"Well, to tell the truth, I saw then the first signs that I had ever seen that her temper was just a little sharp. The incident, however, was too trivial to relate and can have no possible bearing upon the case."

"Pray let us have it, for all that."

"Oh, it is childish. She dropped her bouquet as we went towards the vestry. She was passing the front pew at the time, and it fell over into the pew. There was a moment's delay, but the gentleman in the pew handed it up to her again, and it did not appear to be the worse for the fall. Yet when I spoke to her of the matter, she answered me abruptly; and in the carriage, on our way home, she seemed absurdly agitated over this trifling cause."

"Indeed! You say that there was a gentleman in the pew. Some of the general public were present, then?"

"Oh, yes. It is impossible to exclude them when the church is open."

"This gentleman was not one of your wife's friends?"

"No, no; I call him a gentleman by courtesy, but he was quite a common-looking person. I hardly noticed his appearance. But really I think that we are wandering rather far from the point."

"Lady St. Simon, then, returned from the wedding in a less cheerful frame of mind than she had gone to it. What did she do on re-entering her father's house?"

"I saw her in conversation with her maid."

"And who is her maid?"

"Alice is her name. She is an American and came from California with her."

"A confidential servant?"

"A little too much so. It seemed to me that her mistress allowed her to take great liberties. Still, of course, in America they look upon these things in a different way."

"How long did she speak to this Alice?"

"Oh, a few minutes. I had something else to think of."

"You did not overhear what they said?"

"Lady St. Simon said something about 'jumping a claim.' She was accustomed to use slang of the kind. I have no idea what she meant."

"American slang is very expressive sometimes. And what did your wife do when she finished speaking to her maid?"

"She walked into the breakfast-room."

"On your arm?"

"No, alone. She was very independent in little matters like that. Then, after we had sat down for ten minutes or so, she rose hurriedly, muttered some words of apology, and left the room. She never came back."

"But this maid, Alice, as I understand, deposes that she went to her room, covered her bride's dress with a long ulster, put on a bonnet, and went out."

"Quite so. And she was afterwards seen walking into Hyde Park in company with Flora Millar, a woman who is now in custody, and who had already made a disturbance at Mr. Doran's house that morning."

"Ah, yes. I should like a few particulars as to this young lady, and your relations to her."

Lord St. Simon shrugged his shoulders and raised his eyebrows. "We have been on a friendly footing for some years—I may say on a *very* friendly footing. She used to be at the Allegro. I have not treated her ungenerously, and she had no just cause of complaint against me, but you know what women are, Mr. Holmes. Flora was a dear little thing, but exceedingly hot-headed and devotedly attached

191

to me. She wrote me dreadful letters when she heard that I
was about to be married, and to tell the truth, the reason
why I had the marriage celebrated so quietly was that I
feared lest there might be a scandal in the church. She
came to Mr. Doran's door just after we returned, and she
endeavoured to push her way in, uttering very abusive ex-
pressions towards my wife, and even threatening her, but I
had foreseen the possibility of something of the sort, and I
had two police fellows there in private clothes, who soon
pushed her out again. She was quiet when she saw that
there was no good in making a row."

"Did your wife hear all this?"

"No, thank goodness, she did not."

"And she was seen walking with this very woman
afterwards?"

"Yes. That is what Mr. Lestrade, of Scotland Yard, looks
upon as so serious. It is thought that Flora decoyed my
wife out and laid some terrible trap for her."

"Well, it is a possible supposition."

"You think so, too?"

"I did not say a probable one. But you do not yourself
look upon this as likely?"

"I do not think Flora would hurt a fly."

"Still, jealousy is a strange transformer of characters.
Pray what is your own theory as to what took place?"

"Well, really, I came to seek a theory, not to propound
one. I have given you all the facts. Since you ask me, however, I may say that it has occurred to me as possible that
the excitement of this affair, the consciousness that she
had made so immense a social stride, had the effect of
causing some little nervous disturbance in my wife."

"In short, that she had become suddenly deranged?"

"Well, really, when I consider that she has turned her
back—I will not say upon me, but upon so much that
many have aspired to without success—I can hardly explain it in any other fashion."

"Well, certainly that is also a conceivable hypothesis,"
said Holmes, smiling. "And now, Lord St. Simon, I think

that I have nearly all my data. May I ask whether you were seated at the breakfast-table so that you could see out of the window?"

"We could see the other side of the road and the Park."

"Quite so. Then I do not think that I need to detain you longer. I shall communicate with you."

"Should you be fortunate enough to solve this problem," said our client, rising.

"I have solved it."

"Eh? What was that?"

"I say that I have solved it."

"Where, then, is my wife?"

"That is a detail which I shall speedily supply."

Lord St. Simon shook his head. "I am afraid that it will take wiser heads than yours or mine," he remarked, and bowing in a stately, old-fashioned manner, he departed.

"It is very good of Lord St. Simon to honour my head by putting it on a level with his own," said Sherlock Holmes, laughing. "I think that I shall have a whisky and soda and a cigar after all this cross-questioning. I had formed my conclusions as to the case before our client came into the room."

"My dear Holmes!"

"I have notes of several similar cases, though none, as I remarked before, which were quite as prompt. My whole examination served to turn my conjecture into a certainty. Circumstantial evidence is occasionally very convincing, as when you find a trout in the milk, to quote Thoreau's example."

"But I have heard all that you have heard."

"Without, however, the knowledge of pre-existing cases which serves me so well. There was a parallel instance in Aberdeen some years back, and something on very much the same lines at Munich the year after the Franco-Prussian War. It is one of these cases—but, hello, here is Lestrade! Good-afternoon, Lestrade! You will find an extra tumbler upon the sideboard, and there are cigars in the box."

The official detective was attired in a pea-jacket and cravat, which gave him a decidedly nautical appearance, and he carried a black canvas bag in his hand. With a short greeting he seated himself and lit the cigar which had been offered to him.

"What's up, then?" asked Holmes with a twinkle in his eye. "You look dissatisfied."

"And I feel dissatisfied. It is this infernal St. Simon marriage case. I can make neither head nor tail of the business."

"Really! You surprise me."

"Who ever heard of such a mixed affair? Every clue seems to slip through my fingers. I have been at work upon it all day."

"And very wet it seems to have made you," said Holmes, laying his hand upon the arm of the pea-jacket.

"Yes, I have been dragging the Serpentine."

"In heaven's name, what for?"

"In search of the body of Lady St. Simon."

Sherlock Holmes leaned back in his chair and laughed heartily.

"Have you dragged the basin of Trafalgar Square fountain?" he asked.

"Why? What do you mean?"

"Because you have just as good a chance of finding this lady in the one as in the other."

Lestrade shot an angry glance at my companion. "I suppose you know all about it," he snarled.

"Well, I have only just heard the facts, but my mind is made up."

"Oh, indeed! Then you think that the Serpentine plays no part in the matter?"

"I think it very unlikely."

"Then perhaps you will kindly explain how it is that we found this in it?" He opened his bag as he spoke and tumbled onto the floor a wedding-dress of watered silk, a pair of white satin shoes, and a bride's wreath and veil, all discoloured and soaked in water. "There," said he, putting a new wedding-ring upon the top of the pile. "There is a little nut for you to crack, Master Holmes."

"Oh, indeed!" said my friend, blowing blue rings into the air. "You dragged them from the Serpentine?"

"No. They were found floating near the margin by a park-keeper. They have been identified as her clothes, and it seemed to me that if the clothes were there, the body would not be far off."

"By the same brilliant reasoning, every man's body is to be found in the neighbourhood of his wardrobe. And pray what did you hope to arrive at through this?"

"At some evidence implicating Flora Millar in the disappearance."

"I am afraid that you will find it difficult."

"Are you, indeed, now?" cried Lestrade with some bitterness. "I am afraid, Holmes, that you are not very practical with your deductions and your inferences. You have made two blunders in as many minutes. This dress does implicate Miss Flora Millar."

"And how?"

"In the dress is a pocket. In the pocket is a card-case. In the card-case is a note. And here is the very note." He slapped it down upon the table in front of him. "Listen to this: 'You will see me when all is ready. Come at once. F.H.M.' Now my theory all along has been that Lady St. Simon was decoyed away by Flora Millar, and that she, with confederates, no doubt, was responsible for her disappearance. Here, signed with her initials, is the very note which was no doubt quietly slipped into her hand at the door and which lured her within their reach."

"Very good, Lestrade," said Holmes, laughing. "You really are very fine indeed. Let me see it." He took up the paper in a listless way, but his attention instantly became riveted, and he gave a little cry of satisfaction. "This is indeed important," said he.

"Ha, you find it so?"

"Extremely so. I congratulate you warmly."

Lestrade rose in his triumph and bent his head to look.

"Why," he shrieked, "you're looking at the wrong side!"

"On the contrary, this is the right side."

"The right side? You're mad! Here is the note written in pencil over here."

"And over here is what appears to be the fragment of a hotel bill, which interests me deeply."

"There's nothing in it. I looked at it before," said Lestrade. "'Oct. 4th, room 8s., breakfast 2s. 6d., cocktail 1s., lunch 2s. 6d., glass sherry, 8d.' I see nothing in that."

"Very likely not. It is most important, all the same. As to the note, it is important also, or at least the initials are, so I congratulate you again."

"I've wasted time enough," said Lestrade, rising. "I believe in hard work and not in sitting by the fire spinning fine theories. Good-day, Mr. Holmes, and we shall see which gets to the bottom of the matter first." He gathered up the garments, thrust them into the bag, and made for the door.

"Just one hint to you, Lestrade," drawled Holmes before his rival vanished; "I will tell you the true solution of the matter. Lady St. Simon is a myth. There is not, and there never has been, any such person."

Lestrade looked sadly at my companion. Then he turned to me, tapped his forehead three times, shook his head solemnly, and hurried away.

He had hardly shut the door behind him when Holmes rose to put on his overcoat. "There is something in what the fellow says about outdoor work," he remarked, "so I think, Watson, that I must leave you to your papers for a little."

It was after five o'clock when Sherlock Holmes left me, but I had no time to be lonely, for within an hour there arrived a confectioner's man with a very large flat box. This he unpacked with the help of a youth whom he had brought with him, and presently, to my very great astonishment, a quite epicurean little cold supper began to be laid out upon our humble lodging-house mahogany. There were a couple of brace of cold woodcock, a pheasant, a *pâté de foie gras* pie, with a group of ancient and cob-webby bottles. Having laid out all these luxuries, my two visitors vanished away, like the genii of the Arabian Nights, with no explanation save that the things had been paid for and were ordered to this address.

Just before nine o'clock Sherlock Holmes stepped briskly into the room. His features were gravely set, but there was a light in his eye which made me think that he had not been disappointed in his conclusions.

"They have laid the supper, then," he said, rubbing his hands.

"You seem to expect company. They have laid for five."

"Yes, I fancy we may have some company dropping in," said he. "I am surprised that Lord St. Simon has not already arrived. Ha! I fancy that I hear his step now upon the stairs."

It was indeed our visitor of the afternoon who came bustling in, dangling his glasses more vigorously than ever, and with a very perturbed expression upon his aristocratic features.

"My messenger reached you, then?" asked Holmes.

"Yes, and I confess that the contents startled me beyond measure. Have you good authority for what you say?"

"The best possible."

Lord St. Simon sank into a chair and passed his hand over his forehead.

"What will the Duke say," he murmured, "when he hears that one of the family has been subjected to such humiliation?"

"It is the purest accident. I cannot allow that there is any humiliation."

"Ah, you look on these things from another standpoint."

"I fail to see that anyone is to blame. I can hardly see how the lady could have acted otherwise, though her abrupt method of doing it was undoubtedly to be regretted. Having no mother, she had no one to advise her at such a crisis."

"It was a slight, sir, a public slight," said Lord St.

Simon, tapping his fingers upon the table.

"You must make allowance for this poor girl, placed in so unprecedented a position."

"I will make no allowance. I am very angry indeed, and I have been shamefully used."

"I think that I heard a ring," said Holmes. "Yes, there are steps on the landing. If I cannot persuade you to take a lenient view of the matter, Lord St. Simon, I have brought an advocate here who may be more successful." He opened the door and ushered in a lady and gentleman. "Lord St. Simon," said he, "allow me to introduce you to Mr. and Mrs. Francis Hay Moulton. The lady, I think, you have already met."

At the sight of these new-comers our client had sprung from his seat and stood very erect, with his eyes cast down and his hand thrust into the breast of his frock-coat, a picture of offended dignity. The lady had taken a quick step forward and had held out her hand to him, but he still refused to raise his eyes. It was as well for his resolution, perhaps, for her pleading face was one which it was hard to resist.

"You're angry, Robert," said she. "Well, I guess you have every cause to be."

"Pray make no apology to me," said Lord St. Simon bitterly.

"Oh, yes, I know that I have treated you real bad and that I should have spoken to you before I went; but I was kind of rattled, and from the time when I saw Frank here again I just didn't know what I was doing or saying. I only wonder I didn't fall down and do a faint right there before the altar."

"Perhaps, Mrs. Moulton, you would like my friend and me to to leave the room while you explain this matter?"

"If I may give an opinion," remarked the strange gentleman, "we've had just a little too much secrecy over this business already. For my part, I should like all Europe and America to hear the rights of it." He was a small, wiry, sunburnt man, clean-shaven, with a sharp face and alert manner.

"Then I'll tell our story right away," said the lady. "Frank here and I met in '84, in McQuire's camp, near the Rockies, where Pa was working a claim. We were engaged to each other, Frank and I; but then one day Father struck a rich pocket and made a pile, while poor Frank here had a claim that petered out and came to nothing. The richer Pa grew the poorer was Frank; so at last Pa wouldn't hear of our engagement lasting any longer, and he took me away to 'Frisco. Frank wouldn't throw up his hand, though; so he followed me there, and he saw me without Pa knowing anything about it. It would only have made him mad to know, so we just fixed it all up for ourselves. Frank said that he would go and make his pile, too, and never come back to claim me until he had as much as Pa. So then I promised to wait for him to the end of time and pledged myself not to marry anyone else while he lived. 'Why shouldn't we be married right away, then,' said he, 'and then I will feel sure of you; and I won't claim to be your husband until I come back?' Well, we talked it over, and he had fixed it all up so nicely, with a clergyman all ready in waiting, that we just did it right there; and then Frank went off to seek his fortune, and I went back to Pa.

"The next I heard of Frank was that he was in Montana, and then he went prospecting in Arizona, and then I heard of him from New Mexico. After that came a long newspaper story about how a miners' camp had been attacked by Apache Indians, and there was my Frank's name among the killed. I fainted dead away, and I was very sick for months after. Pa thought I had a decline and took me to half the doctors in 'Frisco. Not a word of news came for a year and more, so that I never doubted that Frank was really dead. Then Lord St. Simon came to 'Frisco, and we came to London, and a marriage was arranged, and Pa was very pleased, but I felt all the time that no man on this earth would ever take the place in my heart that had been given to my poor Frank.

"Still, if I had married Lord St. Simon, of course I'd have done my duty by him. We can't command our love, but we can our actions. I went to the altar with him with the intention to make him just as good a wife as it was in me to be. But you may imagine what I felt when, just as I came to the altar rails, I glanced back and saw Frank standing and looking at me out of the first pew. I thought it was his ghost at first; but when I looked again there he was still, with a kind of question in his eyes, as if to ask me whether I were glad or sorry to see him. I wonder I didn't drop. I know that everything was turning round, and the words of the clergyman were just like the buzz of a bee in my ear. I didn't know what to do. Should I stop the service and make a scene in the church? I glanced at him again, and he seemed to know what I was thinking, for he raised his finger to his lips to tell me to be still. Then I saw him scribble on a piece of paper, and I knew that he was writing me a note. As I passed his pew on the way out I dropped my bouquet over to him, and he slipped the note into my hand when he returned me the flowers. It was only a line asking me to join him when he made the sign to me to do so. Of course I never doubted for a moment that my first duty was now to him, and I determined to do just whatever he might direct.

"When I got back I told my maid, who had known him in California and had always been his friend. I ordered her to say nothing, but to get a few things packed and my ulster ready. I know I ought to have spoken to Lord St. Simon, but it was dreadful hard before his mother and all those great people. I just made up my mind to run away and explain afterwards. I hadn't been at the table ten minutes before I saw Frank out of the window at the other side of the road. He beckoned to me and then began walking into the Park. I slipped out, put on my things, and followed him. Some woman came talking something or other about Lord St. Simon to me—seemed to me from the little I heard as if he had a little secret of his own before marriage also—but I managed to get away from her and soon overtook Frank. We got into a cab together, and away we drove to some lodgings he had taken in Gordon Square, and that was my true wedding after all those years of waiting. Frank had been a prisoner among the Apaches, had escaped, came on to 'Frisco, found that I had given him up for dead and had gone to England, followed me there, and had come upon me at last on the very morning of my second wedding."

"I saw it in a paper," explained the American. "It gave the name and the church but not where the lady lived."

"Then we had a talk as to what we should do, and Frank was all for openness, but I was so ashamed of it all that I felt as if I should like to vanish away and never see any of them again—just sending a line to Pa, perhaps, to show him that I was alive. It was awful to me to think of all those lords and ladies sitting round that breakfast-table and waiting for me to come back. So Frank took my wedding-clothes and things and made a bundle of them, so that I should not be traced, and dropped them away somewhere where no one could find them. It is likely that we should have gone on to Paris to-morrow, only that this good gentleman, Mr. Holmes, came round to us this evening, though how he found us is more than I can think, and he showed us very clearly and kindly that I was wrong and that Frank was right, and that we should be putting ourselves in the wrong if we were so secret. Then he offered to give us a chance of talking to Lord St. Simon alone, and so we came right away round to his rooms at once. Now, Robert, you have heard it all, and I am very sorry if I have given you pain, and I hope that you do not think very meanly of me."

Lord St. Simon had by no means relaxed his rigid attitude, but had listened with a frowning brow and a compressed lip to this long narrative.

"Excuse me," he said, "but it is not my custom to discuss my most intimate personal affairs in this public manner."

"Then you won't forgive me? You won't shake hands before I go?"

"Oh, certainly, if it would give you any pleasure." He put out his hand and coldly grasped that which she extended to him.

"I had hoped," suggested Holmes, "that you would have joined us in a friendly supper."

"I think that there you ask a little too much," responded his Lordship. "I may be forced to acquiesce in these recent developments, but I can hardly be expected to make merry over them. I think that with your permission I will now wish you all a very good night." He included us all in a sweeping bow and stalked out of the room.

"Then I trust that you at least will honour me with your company," said Sherlock Holmes. "It is always a joy to meet an American, Mr. Moulton, for I am one of those who believe that the folly of a monarch and the blundering of a minister in far-gone years will not prevent our children from being some day citizens of the same world-wide country under a flag which shall be a quartering of the Union Jack with the Stars and Stripes."

"The case has been an interesting one," remarked Holmes when our visitors had left us, "because it serves to show very clearly how simple the explanation may be of an affair which at first sight seems to be almost inexplicable. Nothing could be more natural than the sequence of events as narrated by this lady, and nothing stranger than the result when viewed, for instance, by Mr. Lestrade, of Scotland Yard."

"You were not yourself at fault at all, then?"

"From the first, two facts were very obvious to me, the one that the lady had been quite willing to undergo the wedding ceremony, the other that she had repented of it within a few minutes of returning home. Obviously something had occurred during the morning, then, to cause her to change her mind. What could that something be? She could not have spoken to anyone when she was out, for she had been in the company of the bridegroom. Had she seen someone, then? If she had, it must be someone from America because she had spent so short a time in this country that she could hardly have allowed anyone to acquire so deep an influence over her that the mere sight of him would induce her to change her plans so completely. You see we have already arrived, by a process of exclusion, at the idea that she might have seen an American. Then who could this American be, and why should he possess so much influence over her? It might be a lover; it might be a husband. Her young womanhood had, I knew, been spent in rough scenes and under strange conditions. So far I had got before I ever heard Lord St. Simon's narrative. When he told us of a man in a pew, of the change in the bride's manner, of so transparent a device for obtaining a note as the dropping of a bouquet, of her resort to her confidential maid, and of her very significant allusion to claim-jumping—which in miners' parlance means taking possession of that which another person has a prior claim to—the whole situation became absolutely clear. She had gone off with a man, and the man was either a lover or was a previous husband—the chances being in favour of the latter."

"And how in the world did you find them?"

"It might have been difficult, but friend Lestrade held information in his hands the value of which he did not himself know. The initials were, of course, of the highest importance, but more valuable still was it to know that within a week he had settled his bill at one of the most select London hotels."

"How did you deduce the select?"

"By the select prices. Eight shillings for a bed and eightpence for a glass of sherry pointed to one of the most expensive hotels. There are not many in London which charge at that rate. In the second one which I visited in Northumberland Avenue, I learned by an inspection of the book that Francis H. Moulton, an American gentleman, had left only the day before, and on looking over the entries against him, I came upon the very items which I had seen in the duplicate bill. His letters were to be forwarded to 226 Gordon Square; so thither I travelled, and being fortunate enough to find the loving couple at home, I ventured to give them some paternal advice and to point out to them that it would be better in every way that they should make their position a little clearer both to the general public and to Lord St. Simon in particular. I invited them to meet him here, and as you see, I made him keep the appointment."

"But with no very good result," I remarked. "His conduct was certainly not very gracious."

"Ah, Watson," said Holmes, smiling, "perhaps you would not be very gracious either, if, after all the trouble of wooing and wedding, you found yourself deprived in an instant of wife and of fortune. I think that we may judge Lord St. Simon very mercifully and thank our stars that we are never likely to find ourselves in the same position. Draw your chair up and hand me my violin, for the only problem we have still to solve is how to while away these bleak autumnal evenings."

The Adventure of the
Copper Beeches

"To the man who loves art for its own sake," remarked Sherlock Holmes, tossing aside the advertisement sheet of the *Daily Telegraph*, "it is frequently in its least important and lowliest manifestations that the keenest pleasure is to be derived. It is pleasant to me to observe, Watson, that you have so far grasped this truth that in these little records of our cases which you have been good enough to draw up, and, I am bound to say, occasionally to embellish, you have given prominence not so much to the many *causes célèbres* and sensational trials in which I have figured but rather to those incidents which may have been trivial in themselves, but which have given room for those faculties of deduction and of logical synthesis which I have made my special province."

"And yet," said I, smiling, "I cannot quite hold myself absolved from the charge of sensationalism which has been urged against my records."

"You have erred, perhaps," he observed, taking up a glowing cinder with the tongs and lighting with it the long cherry-wood pipe which was wont to replace his clay when he was in a disputatious rather than a meditative mood—"you have erred perhaps in attempting to put colour and life into each of your statements instead of confining yourself to the task of placing upon record that severe reasoning from cause to effect which is really the only notable feature about the thing."

"It seems to me that I have done you full justice in the

matter," I remarked with some coldness, for I was repelled by the egotism which I had more than once observed to be a strong factor in my friend's singular character.

"No, it is not selfishness or conceit," said he, answering, as was his wont, my thoughts rather than my words. "If I claim full justice for my art, it is because it is an impersonal thing—a thing beyond myself. Crime is common. Logic is rare. Therefore it is upon the logic rather than upon the crime that you should dwell. You have degraded what should have been a course of lectures into a series of tales."

It was a cold morning of the early spring, and we sat after breakfast on either side of a cheery fire in the old room at Baker Street. A thick fog rolled down between the lines of dun-coloured houses, and the opposing windows loomed like dark, shapeless blurs through the heavy yellow wreaths. Our gas was lit and shone on the white cloth and glimmer of china and metal, for the table had not been cleared yet. Sherlock Holmes had been silent all the morning, dipping continuously into the advertisement columns of a succession of papers until at last, having apparently given up his search, he had emerged in no very sweet temper to lecture me upon my literary shortcomings.

"At the same time," he remarked after a pause, during which he had sat puffing at his long pipe and gazing down into the fire, "you can hardly be open to a charge of sensationalism, for out of these cases which you have been so kind as to interest yourself in, a fair proportion do not treat of crime, in its legal sense, at all. The small matter in which I endeavoured to help the King of Bohemia, the singular experience of Miss Mary Sutherland, the problem connected with the man with the twisted lip, and the incident of the noble bachelor, were all matters which are outside the pale of the law. But in avoiding the sensational, I fear that you may have bordered on the trivial."

"The end may have been so," I answered, "but the methods I hold to have been novel and of interest."

"Pshaw, my dear fellow, what do the public, the great

unobservant public, who could hardly tell a weaver by his tooth or a compositor by his left thumb, care about the finer shades of analysis and deduction! But, indeed, if you are trivial, I cannot blame you, for the days of the great cases are past. Man, or at least criminal man, has lost all enterprise and originality. As to my own little practice, it seems to be degenerating into an agency for recovering lost lead pencils and giving advice to young ladies from boarding-schools. I think that I have touched bottom at last, however. This note I had this morning marks my zero-point, I fancy. Read it!" He tossed a crumpled letter across to me.

It was dated from Montague Place upon the preceding evening, and ran thus:

DEAR MR. HOLMES:

I am very anxious to consult you as to whether I should or should not accept a situation which has been offered to me as governess. I shall call at half-past ten to-morrow if I do not inconvenience you.

Yours faithfully,
VIOLET HUNTER

"Do you know the young lady?" I asked.

"Not I."

"It is half-past ten now."

"Yes, and I have no doubt that is her ring."

"It may turn out to be of more interest than you think. You remember that the affair of the blue carbuncle, which appeared to be a mere whim at first, developed into a serious investigation. It may be so in this case, also."

"Well, let us hope so. But our doubts will very soon be solved, for here, unless I am much mistaken, is the person in question."

As he spoke the door opened and a young lady entered the room. She was plainly but neatly dressed, with a bright, quick face, freckled like a plover's egg, and with the brisk manner of a woman who has had her own way to make in the world.

"You will excuse my troubling you, I am sure," said she,

as my companion rose to greet her, "but I have had a very strange experience, and as I have no parents or relations of any sort from whom I could ask advice, I thought that perhaps you would be kind enough to tell me what I should do."

"Pray take a seat, Miss Hunter. I shall be happy to do anything that I can to serve you."

I could see that Holmes was favourably impressed by the manner and speech of his new client. He looked her over in his searching fashion, and then composed himself, with his lids drooping and his finger-tips together, to listen to her story.

"I have been a governess for five years," said she, "in the family of Colonel Spence Munro, but two months ago the Colonel received an appointment at Halifax, in Nova Scotia, and took his children over to America with him, so that I found myself without a situation. I advertised, and I answered advertisements, but without success. At last the little money which I had saved began to run short, and I was at my wit's end as to what I should do.

"There is a well-known agency for governesses in the West End called Westaway's, and there I used to call about once a week in order to see whether anything had turned up which might suit me. Westaway was the name of the founder of the business, but it is really managed by Miss Stoper. She sits in her own little office, and the ladies who are seeking employment wait in an anteroom and are then shown in one by one, when she consults her ledgers and sees whether she has anything which would suit them.

"Well, when I called last week I was shown into the little office as usual, but I found that Miss Stoper was not alone. A prodigiously stout man with a very smiling face and a great heavy chin which rolled down in fold upon fold over his throat sat at her elbow with a pair of glasses on his nose, looking very earnestly at the ladies who entered. As I came in he gave quite a jump in his chair and turned quickly to Miss Stoper.

" 'That will do,' said he; 'I could not ask for anything better. Capital! Capital!' He seemed quite enthusiastic and rubbed his hands together in the most genial fashion. He was such a comfortable-looking man that it was quite a pleasure to look at him.

" 'You are looking for a situation, miss?' he asked.

" 'Yes, sir.'

" 'As governess?'

" 'Yes, sir.'

" 'And what salary do you ask?'

" 'I had four pounds a month in my last place with Colonel Spence Munro.'

" 'Oh, tut, tut! Sweating—rank sweating!' he cried, throwing his fat hands out into the air like a man who is in a boiling passion. 'How could anyone offer so pitiful a sum to a lady with such attractions and accomplishments?'

" 'My accomplishments, sir, may be less than you imagine,' said I. 'A little French, a little German, music, and drawing—'

" 'Tut, tut!' he cried. 'This is all quite beside the question. The point is, have you or have you not the bearing and deportment of a lady? There it is in a nutshell. If you have not, you are not fitted for the rearing of a child who may some day play a considerable part in the history of the country. But if you have, why, then, how could any gentleman ask you to condescend to accept anything under the three figures? Your salary with me, madam, would commence at a hundred pounds a year.'

"You may imagine, Mr. Holmes, that to me, destitute as I was, such an offer seemed almost too good to be true. The gentleman, however, seeing perhaps the look of incredulity upon my face, opened a pocket-book and took out a note.

" 'It is also my custom,' said he, smiling in the most pleasant fashion until his eyes were just two little shining slits amid the white creases of his face, 'to advance to my young ladies half their salary beforehand, so that they may meet any little expenses of their journey and their wardrobe.'

"It seemed to me that I had never met so fascinating and

so thoughtful a man. As I was already in debt to my trades-
men, the advance was a great convenience, and yet there
was something unnatural about the whole transaction
which made me wish to know a little more before I quite
committed myself.

"'May I ask where you live, sir?' said I.

"'Hampshire. Charming rural place. The Copper
Beeches, five miles on the far side of Winchester. It is the
most lovely country, my dear young lady, and the dearest
old country-house.'

"'And my duties, sir? I should be glad to know what they
would be.'

"'One child—one dear little romper just six years old.
Oh, if you could see him killing cockroaches with a
slipper! Smack! Smack! Smack! Three gone before you
could wink!' He leaned back in his chair and laughed his
eyes into his head again.

"I was a little startled at the nature of the child's amusement, but the father's laughter made me think that
perhaps he was joking.

"'My sole duties, then,' I asked, 'are to take charge of a
single child?'

"'No, no, not the sole, not the sole, my dear young lady,'
he cried. 'Your duty would be, as I am sure your good
sense would suggest, to obey any little commands my wife
might give, provided always that they were such commands
as a lady might with propriety obey. You see no difficulty,
heh?'

"'I should be happy to make myself useful.'

"'Quite so. In dress now, for example, We are faddy
people, you know—faddy but kind-hearted. If you were
asked to wear any dress which we might give you, you
would not object to our little whim. Heh?'

"'No,' said I, considerably astonished at his words.

"'Or to sit here, or sit there, that would not be offensive
to you?'

"'Oh, no.'

"'Or to cut your hair quite short before you come to us?'

"I could hardly believe my ears. As you may observe,

Mr. Holmes, my hair is somewhat luxuriant, and of a rather peculiar tint of chestnut. It has been considered artistic. I could not dream of sacrificing it in this offhand fashion.

"'I am afraid that that is quite impossible,' said I. He had been watching me eagerly out of his small eyes, and I could see a shadow pass over his face as I spoke.

"'I am afraid that it is quite essential,' said he. 'It is a little fancy of my wife's, and ladies' fancies, you know, madam, ladies' fancies must be consulted. And so you won't cut your hair?'

"'No, sir, I really could not,' I answered firmly.

"'Ah, very well; then that quite settles the matter. It is a pity, because in other respects you would really have done very nicely. In that case, Miss Stoper, I had best inspect a few more of your young ladies.'

"The manageress had sat all this while busy with her papers without a word to either of us, but she glanced at me now with so much annoyance upon her face that I could not help suspecting that she had lost a handsome commission through my refusal.

"'Do you desire your name to be kept upon the books?' she asked.

"'If you please, Miss Stoper.'

"'Well, really, it seems rather useless since you refuse the most excellent offers in this fashion,' said she sharply. 'You can hardly expect us to exert ourselves to find another such opening for you. Good-day to you, Miss Hunter.' She struck a gong upon the table, and I was shown out by the page.

"Well, Mr. Holmes, when I got back to my lodgings and found little enough in the cupboard, and two or three bills upon the table, I began to ask myself whether I had not done a very foolish thing. After all, if these people had strange fads and expected obedience on the most extraordinary matters, they were at least ready to pay for their eccentricity. Very few governesses in England are getting a hundred pounds a year. Besides, what use was my hair to me? Many people are improved by wearing it short, and perhaps I should be among the number. Next day I was inclined to think that I had made a mistake, and by the day after I was sure of it. I had almost overcome my pride so far as to go back to the agency and inquire whether the place was still open when I received this letter from the gentleman himself. I have it here, and I will read it to you:

> The Copper Beeches, near Winchester
>
> DEAR MISS HUNTER:
>
> Miss Stoper has very kindly given me your address, and I write from here to ask you whether you have reconsidered your decision. My wife is very anxious that you should come, for she has been much attracted by my description of you. We are willing to give £30 a quarter, or £120 a year, so as to recompense you for any little inconvenience which our fads may cause you. They are not very exacting, after all. My wife is fond of a particular shade of electric blue, and would like you to wear such a dress indoors in the morning. You need not, however, go to the expense of purchasing one, as we have one belonging to my dear daughter Alice (now in Philadelphia), which would, I should think, fit you very well. Then, as to sitting here or there, or amusing yourself in any manner indicated, that need cause you no inconvenience. As regards your hair, it is no doubt a pity, especially as I could not help remarking its beauty during our short interview, but I am afraid that I must remain firm upon this point, and I only hope that the increased salary may recompense you for the loss. Your duties, as far as the child is concerned, are very light. Now do try to come, and I shall meet you with the dog-cart at Winchester. Let me know your train.
>
> Yours faithfully,
> JEPHRO RUCASTLE

"That is the letter which I have just received, Mr. Holmes, and my mind is made up that I will accept it. I thought, however, that before taking the final step I should like to submit the whole matter to your consideration."

"Well, Miss Hunter, if your mind is made up, that settles the question," said Holmes, smiling.

"But you would not advise me to refuse?"

"I confess that it is not the situation which I should like to see a sister of mine apply for."

"What is the meaning of it all, Mr. Holmes?"

"Ah, I have no data. I cannot tell. Perhaps you have yourself formed some opinion?"

"Well, there seems to me to be only one possible solution. Mr. Rucastle seemed to be a very kind, good-natured man. Is it not possible that his wife is a lunatic, that he desires to keep the matter quiet for fear she should be taken to an asylum, and that he humours her fancies in every way in order to prevent an outbreak?"

"That is a possible solution—in fact, as matters stand, it is the most probable one. But in any case it does not seem to be a nice household for a young lady."

"But the money, Mr. Holmes, the money!"

"Well, yes, of course the pay is good—too good. That is what makes me uneasy. Why should they give you a hundred and twenty pounds a year, when they could have their pick for forty pounds? There must be some strong reason behind."

"I thought that if I told you the circumstances you would understand afterwards if I wanted your help. I should feel so much stronger if I felt that you were at the back of me."

"Oh, you may carry that feeling away with you. I assure you that your little problem promises to be the most interesting which has come my way for some months. There is something distinctly novel about some of the features. If you should find yourself in doubt or in danger—"

"Danger! What danger do you foresee?"

Holmes shook his head gravely. "It would cease to be a danger if we could define it," said he. "But at any time, day or night, a telegram would bring me down to your help."

"That is enough." She rose briskly from her chair with the anxiety all swept from her face. "I shall go down to Hampshire quite easy in my mind now. I shall write to Mr. Rucastle at once, sacrifice my poor hair to-night, and start for Winchester to-morrow." With a few grateful words to Holmes she bade us both good-night and bustled off upon her way.

"At least," said I as we heard her quick, firm steps

descending the stairs, "she seems to be a young lady who is very well able to take care of herself."

"And she would need to be," said Holmes gravely. "I am much mistaken if we do not hear from her before many days are past."

It was not very long before my friend's prediction was fulfilled. A fortnight went by, during which I frequently found my thoughts turning in her direction and wondering what strange side-alley of human experience this lonely woman had strayed into. The unusual salary, the curious conditions, the light duties, all pointed to something abnormal, though whether a fad or a plot, or whether the man were a philanthropist or a villain, it was quite beyond my powers to determine. As to Holmes, I observed that he sat frequently for half an hour on end, with knitted brows and an abstracted air, but he swept the matter away with a wave of his hand when I mentioned it. "Data! Data! Data!" he cried impatiently. "I can't make bricks without clay." And yet he would always wind up by muttering that no sister of his should ever have accepted such a situation.

The telegram which we eventually received came late one night just as I was thinking of turning in and Holmes was settling down to one of those all-night chemical researches which he frequently indulged in, when I would leave him stooping over a retort and a test-tube at night and find him in the same position when I came down to breakfast in the morning. He opened the yellow envelope, and then, glancing at the message, threw it across to me.

"Just look up the trains in Bradshaw," said he, and turned back to his chemical studies.

The summons was a brief and urgent one.

Please be at the Black Swan Hotel at Winchester at midday tomorrow. Do come! I am at my wit's end.

HUNTER

"Will you come with me?" asked Holmes, glancing up.

214

"I should wish to."

"Just look it up, then."

"There is a train at half-past nine," said I, glancing over my Bradshaw. "It is due at Winchester at 11:30."

"That will do very nicely. Then perhaps I had better postpone my analysis of the acetones, as we may need to be at our best in the morning."

By eleven o'clock the next day we were well upon our way to the old English capital. Holmes had been buried in the morning papers all the way down, but after we had passed the Hampshire border he threw them down and began to admire the scenery. It was an ideal spring day, a light blue sky, flecked with little fleecy white clouds drifting across from west to east. The sun was shining very brightly, and yet there was an exhilarating nip in the air, which set an edge to a man's energy. All over the countryside, away to the rolling hills around Aldershot, the little red and grey roofs of the farm-steadings peeped out from amid the light green of the new foliage.

"Are they not fresh and beautiful?" I cried with all the enthusiasm of a man fresh from the fogs of Baker Street.

But Holmes shook his head gravely.

"Do you know, Watson," said he, "that it is one of the curses of a mind with a turn like mine that I must look at everything with reference to my own special subject. You look at these scattered houses, and you are impressed by their beauty. I look at them, and the only thought which comes to me is a feeling of their isolation and of the impunity with which crime may be committed there."

"Good Heavens!" I cried. "Who would associate crime with these dear old homesteads?"

"They always fill me with a certain horror. It is my belief, Watson, founded upon my experience, that the lowest and vilest alleys in London do not present a more dreadful record of sin than does the smiling and beautiful countryside."

"You horrify me!"

"But the reason is very obvious. The pressure of public opinion can do in the town what the law cannot accomplish. There is no lane so vile that the scream of a tortured child, or the thud of a drunkard's blow, does not beget sympathy and indignation among the neighbours, and then the whole machinery of justice is ever so close that a word of complaint can set it going, and there is but a step between the crime and the dock. But look at these lonely houses, each in its own fields, filled for the most part with poor ignorant folk who know little of the law. Think of the deeds of hellish cruelty, the hidden wickedness which may go on, year in, year out, in such places, and none the wiser. Had this lady who appeals to us for help gone to live in Winchester, I should never have had a fear for her. It is the five miles of country which makes the danger. Still, it is clear that she is not personally threatened."

"No. If she can come to Winchester to meet us she can get away."

"Quite so. She has her freedom."

"What *can* be the matter, then? Can you suggest no explanation?"

"I have devised seven separate explanations, each of which would cover the facts as far as we know them. But which of these is correct can only be determined by the fresh information which we shall no doubt find waiting for us. Well, there is the tower of the cathedral, and we shall soon learn all that Miss Hunter has to tell."

The Black Swan is an inn of repute in the High Street, at no distance from the station, and there we found the young lady waiting for us. She had engaged a sitting-room, and our lunch awaited us upon the table.

"I am so delighted that you have come," she said earnestly. "It is so very kind of you both; but indeed I do not know what I should do. Your advice will be altogether invaluable to me."

"Pray tell us what has happened to you."

"I will do so, and I must be quick, for I have promised Mr. Rucastle to be back before three. I got his leave to come into town this morning, though he little knew for what purpose."

"Let us have everything in its due order." Holmes thrust his long thin legs out towards the fire and composed himself to listen.

"In the first place, I may say that I have met, on the whole, with no actual ill-treatment from Mr. and Mrs. Rucastle. It is only fair to them to say that. But I cannot understand them, and I am not easy in my mind about them."

"What can you not understand?"

"Their reasons for their conduct. But you shall have it all just as it occurred. When I came down, Mr. Rucastle met me here and drove me in his dog-cart to the Copper Beeches. It is, as he said, beautifully situated, but it is not beautiful in itself, for it is a large square block of a house, whitewashed, but all stained and streaked with damp and bad weather. There are gounds round it, woods on three sides, and on the fourth a field which slopes down to the Southampton highroad, which curves past about a hundred yards from the front door. This ground in front belongs to the house, but the woods all round are part of Lord Southerton's preserves. A clump of copper beeches immediately in front of the hall door has given its name to the place.

"I was driven over by my employer, who was as amiable as ever, and was introduced by him that evening to his wife and the child. There was no truth, Mr. Holmes, in the conjecture which seemed to us to be probable in your rooms at Baker Street. Mrs. Rucastle is not mad. I found her to be a silent, pale-faced woman, much younger than her husband, not more than thirty, I should think, while he can hardly be less than forty-five. From their conversation I have gathered that they have been married about seven years, that he was a widower, and that his only child by the first wife was the daughter who had gone to Philadelphia. Mr. Rucastle told me in private that the reason why she had left them was that she had an unreasoning aversion to her stepmother. As the daughter could not have been less than twenty, I can quite imagine that her position must have been uncomfortable with her father's young wife.

"Mrs. Rucastle seemed to me to be colourless in mind as well as in feature. She impressed me neither favourably nor the reverse. She was a nonentity. It was easy to see that she was passionately devoted both to her husband and to her little son. Her light grey eyes wandered continually from one to the other, noting every little want and forestalling it if possible. He was kind to her also in his bluff, boisterous fashion, and on the whole they seemed to be a happy couple. And yet she had some secret sorrow, this woman. She would often be lost in deep thought, with the saddest look upon her face. More than once I have surprised her in tears. I have thought sometimes that it was the disposition of her child which weighed upon her mind, for I have never met so utterly spoiled and so ill-natured a little creature. He is small for his age, with a head which is quite disproportionately large. His whole life appears to be spent in an alternation between savage fits of passion and gloomy intervals of sulking. Giving pain to any creature weaker than himself seems to be his one idea of amusement, and he shows quite remarkable talent in planning the capture of mice, little birds, and insects. But I would rather not talk about the creature, Mr. Holmes, and, indeed, he has little to do with my story."

"I am glad of all details," remarked my friend, "whether they seem to you to be relevant or not."

"I shall try not to miss anything of importance. The one unpleasant thing about the house, which struck me at once, was the appearance and conduct of the servants. There are only two, a man and his wife. Toller, for that is his name, is a rough, uncouth man, with grizzled hair and whiskers, and a perpetual smell of drink. Twice since I have been with them he has been quite drunk, and yet Mr. Rucastle seemed to take no notice of it. His wife is a very tall and strong woman with a sour face, as silent as Mrs. Rucastle and much less amiable. They are a most unpleasant couple, but fortunately I spend most of my time in the nursery and my own room, which are next to each other in one corner of the building.

"For two days after my arrival at the Copper Beeches my life was very quiet; on the third, Mrs. Rucastle came down just after breakfast and whispered something to her husband.

"'Oh, yes,' said he, turning to me, 'we are very much obliged to you, Miss Hunter, for falling in with our whims so far as to cut your hair. I assure you that it has not detracted in the tiniest iota from your appearance. We shall now see how the electric-blue dress will become you. You will find it laid out upon the bed in your room, and if you would be so good as to put it on we should both be extremely obliged.'

"The dress which I found waiting for me was of a peculiar shade of blue. It was of excellent material, a sort of beige, but it bore unmistakable signs of having been worn before. It could not have been a better fit if I had been measured for it. Both Mr. and Mrs. Rucastle expressed a delight at the look of it, which seemed quite exaggerated in its vehemence. They were waiting for me in the drawing-room, which is a very large room, stretching along the entire front of the house, with three long windows reaching down to the floor. A chair had been placed close to the central window, with its back turned towards it. In this I was asked to sit, and then Mr. Rucastle, walking up and down on the other side of the room, began to tell me a series of the funniest stories that I have ever listened to. You cannot imagine how comical he was, and I laughed until I was quite weary. Mrs. Rucastle, however, who has evidently no sense of humour, never so much as smiled, but sat with her hands in her lap, and a sad, anxious look upon her face. After an hour or so, Mr. Rucastle suddenly remarked that it was time to commence the duties of the day, and that I might change my dress and go to little Edward in the nursery.

"Two days later this same performance was gone

through under exactly similar circumstances. Again I changed my dress, again I sat in the window, and again I laughed very heartily at the funny stories of which my employer had an immense repertoire, and which he told inimitably. Then he handed me a yellow-backed novel, and moving my chair a little sideways, that my own shadow might not fall upon the page, he begged me to read aloud to him. I read for about ten minutes, beginning in the heart of a chapter, and then suddenly, in the middle of a sentence, he ordered me to cease and to change my dress.

"You can easily imagine, Mr. Holmes, how curious I became as to what the meaning of this extraordinary performance could possibly be. They were always very careful, I observed, to turn my face away from the window, so that I became consumed with the desire to see what was going on behind my back. At first it seemed to be impossible, but I soon devised a means. My hand-mirror had been broken, so a happy thought seized me, and I concealed a piece of the glass in my handkerchief. On the next occasion, in the midst of my laughter, I put my handkerchief up to my eyes, and was able with a little management to see all that there was behind me. I confess that I was disappointed. There was nothing. At least that was my first impression. At the second glance, however, I perceived that there was a man standing in the Southampton Road, a small bearded man in a grey suit, who seemed to be looking in my direction. The road is an important highway, and there are usually people there. This man, however, was leaning against the railings which bordered our field and was looking earnestly up. I lowered my handkerchief and glanced at Mrs. Rucastle to find her eyes fixed upon me with a most searching gaze. She said nothing, but I am convinced that she had divined that I had a mirror in my hand and had seen what was behind me. She rose at once.

"'Jephro,' said she, 'there is an impertinent fellow upon the road there who stares up at Miss Hunter.'

"'No friend of yours, Miss Hunter?' he asked.

"'No, I know no one in these parts.'

"'Dear me! How very impertinent! Kindly turn round and motion to him to go away.'

"'Surely it would be better to take no notice.'

"'No, no, we should have him loitering here always. Kindly turn round and wave him away like that.'

"I did as I was told, and at the same instant Mrs. Rucastle drew down the blind. That was a week ago, and from that time I have not sat again in the window, nor have I worn the blue dress, nor seen the man in the road."

"Pray continue," said Holmes. "Your narrative promises to be a most interesting one."

"You will find it rather disconnected, I fear, and there may prove to be little relation between the different incidents of which I speak. On the very first day that I was at the Copper Beeches, Mr. Rucastle took me to a small outhouse which stands near the kitchen door. As we approached it I heard the sharp rattling of a chain, and the sound as of a large animal moving about.

"'Look in here!' said Mr. Rucastle, showing me a slit between two planks. 'Is he not a beauty?'

"I looked through and was conscious of two glowing eyes, and of a vague figure huddled up in the darkness.

"'Don't be frightened,' said my employer, laughing at the start which I had given. 'It's only Carlo, my mastiff. I call him mine, but really old Toller, my groom, is the only man who can do anything with him. We feed him once a day, and not too much then, so that he is always as keen as mustard. Toller lets him loose every night, and God help the trespasser whom he lays his fangs upon. For goodness' sake don't you ever on any pretext set your foot over the threshold at night, for it's as much as your life is worth.'

"The warning was no idle one, for two nights later I happened to look out of my bedroom window about two o'clock in the morning. It was a beautiful moonlight night, and the lawn in front of the house was silvered over and almost as bright as day. I was standing, rapt in the peaceful beauty of the scene, when I was aware that something was moving under the shadow of the copper beeches. As it emerged into the moonshine I saw what it was. It was a giant dog, as large as a calf, tawny tinted, with hanging jowl, black muzzle, and huge projecting bones. It walked slowly across the lawn and vanished into the shadow upon the other side. That dreadful sentinel sent a chill to my heart which I do not think that any burglar could have done.

"And now I have a very strange experience to tell you. I had, as you know, cut off my hair in London, and I had placed it in a great coil at the bottom of my trunk. One evening, after the child was in bed, I began to amuse myself by examining the furniture of my room and by rearranging my own little things. There was an old chest of drawers in the room, the two upper ones empty and open, the lower one locked. I had filled the first two with my linen, and as I had still much to pack away I was naturally annoyed at not having the use of the third drawer. It struck me that it might have been fastened by a mere oversight, so I took out my bunch of keys and tried to open it. The very first key fitted to perfection, and I drew the drawer open. There was only one thing in it, but I am sure that you would never guess what it was. It was my coil of hair.

"I took it up and examined it. It was of the same peculiar tint, and the same thickness. But then the impossibility of the thing obtruded itself upon me. How *could* my hair have been locked in the drawer? With trembling hands I undid my trunk, turned out the contents, and drew from the bottom my own hair. I laid the two tresses together, and I assure you that they were identical. Was it not extraordinary? Puzzle as I would, I could make nothing at all of what it meant. I returned the strange hair to the drawer, and I said nothing of the matter to the Rucastles as I felt that I had put myself in the wrong by opening a drawer which they had locked.

"I am naturally observant, as you may have remarked, Mr. Holmes, and I soon had a pretty good plan of the whole house in my head. There was one wing, however, which appeared not to be inhabited at all. A door which faced that which led into the quarters of the Tollers opened into this suite, but it was invariably locked. One day, however, as I ascended the stair, I met Mr. Rucastle coming out through this door, his keys in his hand, and a look on his face which made him a very different person to the round, jovial man to whom I was accustomed. His cheeks were red, his brow was all crinkled with anger, and the veins stood out at his temples with passion. He locked the door and hurried past me without a word or a look.

"This aroused my curiosity; so when I went out for a walk in the grounds with my charge, I strolled round to the side from which I could see the windows of this part of the house. There were four of them in a row, three of which were simply dirty, while the fourth was shuttered up. They were evidently all deserted. As I strolled up and down, glancing at them occasionally, Mr. Rucastle came out to me, looking as merry and jovial as ever.

"'Ah!' said he, 'you must not think me rude if I passed you without a word, my dear young lady. I was preoccupied with business matters.'

"I assured him that I was not offended. 'By the way,' said I, 'you seem to have quite a suite of spare rooms up there, and one of them has the shutters up.'

"He looked surprised and, as it seemed to me, a little startled at my remark.

"'Photography is one of my hobbies,' said he. 'I have made my dark room up there. But, dear me! What an observant young lady we have come upon. Who would have believed it? Who would have ever believed it?' He spoke in a jesting tone, but there was no jest in his eyes as he looked at me. I read suspicion there and annoyance, but no jest.

"Well, Mr. Holmes, from the moment that I understood that there was something about that suite of rooms which I was not to know, I was all on fire to go over them. It was not mere curiosity, though I have my share of that. It was more a feeling of duty—a feeling that some good might

223

come from my penetrating to this place. They talk of woman's instinct; perhaps it was woman's instinct which gave me that feeling. At any rate, it was there, and I was keenly on the lookout for any chance to pass the forbidden door.

"It was only yesterday that the chance came. I may tell you that, besides Mr. Rucastle, both Toller and his wife find something to do in these deserted rooms, and I once saw him carrying a large black linen bag with him through the door. Recently he has been drinking hard, and yesterday evening he was very drunk; and when I came upstairs there was the key in the door. I have no doubt at all that he had left it there. Mr. and Mrs. Rucastle were both downstairs, and the child was with them, so that I had an admirable opportunity. I turned the key gently in the lock, opened the door, and slipped through.

"There was a little passage in front of me, unpapered and uncarpeted, which turned at a right angle at the farther end. Round this corner were three doors in a line, the first and third of which were open. They each led into an empty room, dusty and cheerless, with two windows in the one and one in the other, so thick with dirt that the evening light glimmered dimly through them. The centre door was closed, and across the outside of it had been fastened one of the broad bars of an iron bed, padlocked at one end to a ring in the wall, and fastened at the other with stout cord. The door itself was locked as well, and the key was not there. This barricaded door corresponded clearly with the shuttered window outside, and yet I could see by the glimmer from beneath it that the room was not in darkness. Evidently there was a skylight which let in light from above. As I stood in the passage gazing at the sinister door and wondering what secret it might veil, I suddenly heard the sound of steps within the room and saw a shadow pass backward and forward against the little slit of dim light which shone out from under the door. A mad, unreasoning terror rose up in me at the sight, Mr. Holmes. My overstrung nerves failed me suddenly, and I turned and ran—ran as though some dreadful hand were behind me clutching at the skirt of my dress. I rushed down the passage, through the door, and straight into the arms of Mr. Rucastle, who was waiting outside.

"'So,' said he, smiling, 'it was you, then. I thought that it must be when I saw the door open.'

"'Oh, I am so frightened!' I panted.

"'My dear young lady! My dear young lady!'—you cannot think how caressing and soothing his manner was—'and what has frightened you, my dear young lady?'

"But his voice was just a little too coaxing. He overdid it. I was keenly on my guard against him.

"'I was foolish enough to go into the empty wing,' I answered. 'But it is so lonely and eerie in this dim light that I was frightened and ran out again. Oh, it is so dreadfully still in there!'

"'Only that?' said he, looking at me keenly.

"'Why, what did you think?' I asked.

"'Why do you think that I lock this door?'

"'I am sure that I do not know.'"

"'It is to keep people out who have no business there. Do you see?' He was still smiling in the most amiable manner.

"'I am sure if I had known—'

"'Well, then, you know now. And if you ever put your foot over that threshold again'—here in an instant the smile hardened into a grin of rage, and he glared down at me with the face of a demon—'I'll throw you to the mastiff.'

"I was so terrified that I do not know what I did. I suppose that I must have rushed past him into my room. I remember nothing until I found myself lying on my bed trembling all over. Then I thought of you, Mr. Holmes. I could not live there longer without some advice. I was frightened of the house, of the man, of the woman, of the servants, even of the child. They were all horrible to me. If I could only bring you down all would be well. Of course I might have fled from the house, but my curiosity was almost as strong as my fears. My mind was soon made up. I would send you a wire. I put on my hat and cloak, went down to the office, which is about half a mile from the house, and then returned, feeling very much easier. A horrible doubt came into my mind as I appproached the door lest the dog might be loose, but I remembered that Toller had drunk himself into a state of insensibility that evening, and I knew that he was the only one in the household who had any influence with the savage creature, or who would venture to set him free. I slipped in in safety and lay awake half the night in my joy at the thought of seeing you. I had no difficulty in getting leave to come into Winchester this morning, but I must be back before three o'clock, for Mr. and Mrs. Rucastle are going on a visit and will be away all the evening, so that I must look after the child. Now I have told you all my adventures, Mr. Holmes, and I should be very glad if you could tell me what it all means, and above all, what I should do."

Holmes and I had listened spellbound to this extraordinary story. My friend rose now and paced up and down the room, his hands in his pockets, and an expression of the most profound gravity upon his face.

"Is Toller still drunk?" he asked.

"Yes. I heard his wife tell Mrs. Rucastle that she could do nothing with him."

"That is well. And the Rucastles go out to-night?"

"Yes."

"Is there a cellar with a good strong lock?"

"Yes, the wine-cellar."

"You seem to me to have acted all through this matter like a very brave and sensible girl, Miss Hunter. Do you think that you could perform one more feat? I should not ask it of you if I did not think you a quite exceptional woman."

"I will try. What is it?"

"We shall be at the Copper Beeches by seven o'clock, my friend and I. The Rucastles will be gone by that time, and Toller will, we hope, be incapable. There only remains Mrs. Toller, who might give the alarm. If you could send her into the cellar on some errand, and then turn the key upon her, you would facilitate matters immensely."

"I will do it."

"Excellent! We shall then look thoroughly into the affair. Of course there is only one feasible explanation. You have been brought there to personate someone, and the real person is imprisoned in this chamber. That is obvious. As to who this prisoner is, I have no doubt that it is the daughter, Miss Alice Rucastle, if I remember right, who was said to have gone to America. You were chosen, doubtless, as resembling her in height, figure, and the colour of your hair. Hers had been cut off, very possibly in some illness through which she has passed, and so, of course, yours had to be sacrificed also. By a curious chance you came upon her tresses. The man in the road was undoubtedly some friend of hers—possibly her fiancé—and no doubt, as you wore the girl's dress and were so like her, he was convinced from your laughter, whenever he saw you, and afterwards from your gesture, that Miss Rucastle was perfectly happy, and that she no longer desired his attentions. The dog is let loose at night to prevent him from endeavouring to communicate with her. So much is fairly clear. The most serious point in the case is the disposition of the child."

"What on earth has that to do with it?" I ejaculated.

"My dear Watson, you as a medical man are continually gaining light as to the tendencies of a child by the study of the parents. Don't you see that the converse is equally valid? I have frequently gained my first real insight into the character of parents by studying their children. This child's disposition is abnormally cruel, merely for cruelty's sake, and whether he derives this from his smiling father, as I should suspect, or from his mother, it bodes evil for the poor girl who is in their power."

"I am sure that you are right, Mr. Holmes," cried our client. "A thousand things come back to me which make me certain that you have hit it. Oh, let us lose not an instant in bringing help to this poor creature."

"We must be circumspect, for we are dealing with a very cunning man. We can do nothing until seven o'clock. At that hour we shall be with you, and it will not be long before we solve the mystery."

We were as good as our word, for it was just seven when we reached the Copper Beeches, having put up our trap at a wayside public-house. The group of trees, with their dark leaves shining like burnished metal in the light of the setting sun, were sufficient to mark the house even had Miss Hunter not been standing smiling on the door-step.

"Have you managed it?" asked Holmes.

A loud thudding noise came from somewhere downstairs. "That is Mrs. Toller in the cellar," said she. "Her husband lies snoring on the kitchen rug. Here are his keys, which are the duplicates of Mr. Rucastle's."

"You have done well indeed!" cried Holmes with enthusiasm. "Now lead the way, and we shall soon see the end of this black business."

We passed up the stair, unlocked the door, followed on down a passage, and found ourselves in front of the barricade which Miss Hunter had described. Holmes cut the cord and removed the transverse bar. Then he tried the various keys in the lock, but without successs. No sound came from within, and at the silence Holmes's face clouded over.

"I trust that we are not too late," said he. "I think, Miss Hunter, that we had better go in without you. Now, Watson, put your shoulder to it, and we shall see whether we cannot make our way in."

It was an old rickety door and gave at once before our united strength. Together we rushed into the room. It was empty. There was no furniture save a little pallet bed, a small table, and a basketful of linen. The skylight above was open, and the prisoner gone.

"There has been some villainy here," said Holmes; "this beauty has guessed Miss Hunter's intentions and has carried his victim off."

"But how?"

"Through the skylight. We shall soon see how he managed it." He swung himself up onto the roof. "Ah, yes," he cried, "here's the end of a long light ladder against the eaves. That is how he did it."

"But it is impossible," said Miss Hunter; "the ladder was not there when the Rucastles went away."

"He has come back and done it. I tell you that he is a clever and dangerous man. I should not be very much surprised if this were he whose step I hear now upon the stair. I think, Watson, that it would be as well for you to have your pistol ready."

The words were hardly out of his mouth before a man appeared at the door of the room, a very fat and burly man, with a heavy stick in his hand. Miss Hunter screamed and shrunk against the wall at the sight of him, but Sherlock Holmes sprang forward and confronted him.

"You villain!" said he, "where's your daughter?"

The fat man cast his eyes round, and then up at the open skylight.

"It is for me to ask you that," he shrieked, "you thieves! Spies and thieves! I have caught you, have I? You are in my power. I'll serve you!" He turned and clattered down the stairs as hard as he could go.

"He's gone for the dog!" cried Miss Hunter.

"I have my revolver," said I.

"Better close the front door," cried Holmes, and we all rushed down the stairs together. We had hardly reached the hall when we heard the baying of a hound, and then a scream of agony, with a horrible worrying sound which it was dreadful to listen to. An elderly man with a red face and shaking limbs came staggering out at a side door.

"My God!" he cried. "Someone has loosed the dog. It's not been fed for two days. Quick, quick, or it'll be too late!"

Holmes and I rushed out and round the angle of the house, with Toller hurrying behind us. There was the huge famished brute, its black muzzle buried in Rucastle's throat, while he writhed and screamed upon the ground.

Running up, I blew its brains out, and it fell over with its keen white teeth still meeting in the great creases of his neck. With much labour we separated them and carried him, living but horribly mangled, into the house. We laid him upon the drawing-room sofa, and having dispatched the sobered Toller to bear the news to his wife, I did what I could to relieve his pain. We were all assembled round him when the door opened, and a tall, gaunt woman entered the room.

"Mrs. Toller!" cried Miss Hunter.

"Yes, miss. Mr. Rucastle let me out when he came back before he went up to you. Ah, miss, it is a pity you didn't let me know what you were planning, for I would have told you that your pains were wasted."

"Ha!" said Holmes, looking keenly at her. "It is clear that Mrs. Toller knows more about this matter than anyone else."

"Yes, sir, I do, and I am ready enough to tell what I know."

"Then, pray, sit down, and let us hear it, for there are several points on which I must confess that I am still in the dark."

"I will soon make it clear to you," said she; "and I'd have done so before now if I could ha' got out from the cellar. If there's police-court business over this, you'll remember that I was the one that stood your friend, and that I was Miss Alice's friend too.

"She was never happy at home, Miss Alice wasn't, from the time that her father married again. She was slighted like and had no say in anything, but it never really became bad for her until after she met Mr. Fowler at a friend's house. As well as I could learn, Miss Alice had rights of her own by will, but she was so quiet and patient, she was, that she never said a word about them, but just left everything in Mr. Rucastle's hands. He knew he was safe with her; but when there was a chance of a husband coming forward, who would ask for all that the law would give him, then her father thought it time to put a stop on it. He wanted

230

her to sign a paper, so that whether she married or not, he could use her money. When she wouldn't do it, he kept on worrying her until she got brain-fever, and for six weeks was at death's door. Then she got better at last, all worn to a shadow, and with her beautiful hair cut off; but that didn't make no change in her young man, and he stuck to her as true as man could be."

"Ah," said Holmes, "I think that what you have been good enough to tell us makes the matter fairly clear, and that I can deduce all that remains. Mr. Rucastle then, I presume, took to this system of imprisonment?"

"Yes, sir."

"And brought Miss Hunter down from London in order to get rid of the disagreeable persistence of Mr. Fowler."

"That was it, sir."

"But Mr. Fowler being a persevering man, as a good seaman should be, blockaded the house, and having met you succeeded by certain arguments, metallic or otherwise, in convincing you that your interests were the same as his."

"Mr. Fowler was a very kind-spoken, free-handed gentleman," said Mrs. Toller serenely.

"And in this way he managed that your good man should have no want of drink, and that a ladder should be ready at the moment when your master had gone out."

"You have it, sir, just as it happened."

"I am sure we owe you an apology, Mrs. Toller," said Holmes, "for you have certainly cleared up everything which puzzled us. And here comes the country surgeon and Mrs. Rucastle, so I think, Watson, that we had best escort Miss Hunter back to Winchester, as it seems to me that our *locus standi* now is rather a questionable one."

And thus was solved the mystery of the sinister house with the copper beeches in front of the door. Mr. Rucastle survived, but was always a broken man, kept alive solely through the care of his devoted wife. They still live with their old servants, who probably know so much of Rucastle's past life that he finds it difficult to part from them. Mr. Fowler and Miss Rucastle were married, by special license, in Southampton the day after their flight, and he is now the holder of a government appointment in the island of Mauritius. As to Miss Violet Hunter, my friend Holmes, rather to my disappointment, manifested no further interest in her when once she had ceased to be the centre of one of his problems, and she is now the head of a private school at Walsall, where I believe that she has met with considerable success.

Silver Blaze

"I am afraid, Watson, that I shall have to go," said Holmes as we sat down together to our breakfast one morning.

"Go! Where to?"

"To Dartmoor; to King's Pyland."

I was not surprised. Indeed, my only wonder was that he had not already been mixed up in this extraordinary case, which was the one topic of conversation through the length and breadth of England. For a whole day my companion had rambled about the room with his chin upon his chest and his brows knitted, charging and recharging his pipe with the strongest black tobacco, and absolutely deaf to any of my questions or remarks. Fresh editions of every paper had been sent up by our news agent, only to be glanced over and tossed down into a corner. Yet, silent as he was, I knew perfectly well what it was over which he was brooding. There was but one problem before the public which could challenge his powers of analysis, and that was the singular disappearance of the favourite for the Wessex Cup, and the tragic murder of its trainer. When, therefore, he suddenly announced his intention of setting out for the scene of the drama, it was only what I had both expected and hoped for.

"I should be most happy to go down with you if I should not be in the way," said I.

"My dear Watson, you would confer a great favour upon me by coming. And I think that your time will not be misspent, for there are points about the case which promise to make it an absolutely unique one. We have, I think, just time to catch our train at Paddington, and I will go further into the matter upon our journey. You would oblige me by bringing with you your very excellent field-glass."

And so it happened that an hour or so later I found myself in the corner of a first-class carriage flying along en route for Exeter, while Sherlock Holmes, with his sharp, eager face framed in his ear-flapped travelling-cap, dipped rapidly into the bundle of fresh papers which he had procured at Paddington. We had left Reading far behind us before he thrust the last one of them under the seat and offered me his cigar-case.

"We are going well," said he, looking out of the window and glancing at his watch. "Our rate at present is fifty-three and a half miles an hour."

"I have not observed the quarter-mile posts," said I.

"Nor have I. But the telegraph posts upon this line are sixty yards apart, and the calculation is a simple one. I presume that you have looked into this matter of the murder of John Straker and the disappearance of Silver Blaze?"

"I have seen what the *Telegraph* and the *Chronicle* have to say."

"It is one of those cases where the art of the reasoner should be used rather for the sifting of details than for the acquiring of fresh evidence. The tragedy has been so uncommon, so complete, and of such personal importance to so many people that we are suffering from a plethora of surmise, conjecture, and hypothesis. The difficulty is to detach the framework of fact—of absolute undeniable fact—from the embellishments of theorists and reporters. Then, having established ourselves upon this sound basis, it is our duty to see what inferences may be drawn and what are the special points upon which the whole mystery turns. On Tuesday evening I received telegrams from both Colonel Ross, the owner of the horse, and from Inspector Gregory, who is looking after the case, inviting my co-operation."

"Tuesday evening!" I exclaimed. "And this is Thursday morning. Why didn't you go down yesterday?"

"Because I made a blunder, my dear Watson—which is, I am afraid, a more common occurrence than anyone would think who only knew me through your memoirs. The fact is that I could not believe it possible that the most remarkable horse in England could long remain concealed, especially in so sparsely inhabited a place as the north of Dartmoor. From hour to hour yesterday I expected to hear that he had been found, and that his abductor was the murderer of John Straker. When, however, another morning had come and I found that beyond the arrest of young Fitzroy Simpson nothing had been done, I felt that it was time for me to take action. Yet in some ways I feel that yesterday has not been wasted."

"You have formed a theory, then?"

"At least I have got a grip of the essential facts of the case. I shall enumerate them to you, for nothing clears up a case so much as stating it to another person, and I can hardly expect your co-operation if I do not show you the position from which we start."

I lay back against the cushions, puffing at my cigar, while Holmes, leaning forward, with his long, thin forefinger checking off the points upon the palm of his left hand, gave me a sketch of the events which had led to our journey.

"Silver Blaze," said he, "is from the Somomy stock and holds as brilliant a record as his famous ancestor. He is now in his fifth year and has brought in turn each of the prizes of the turf to Colonel Ross, his fortunate owner. Up to the time of the catastrophe he was the first favourite for the Wessex Cup, the betting being three to one on him. He has always, however, been a prime favourite with the racing public and has never yet disappointed them, so that even at those odds enormous sums of money have been laid upon him. It is obvious, therefore, that there were many people who had the strongest interest in preventing Silver Blaze from being there at the fall of the flag next Tuesday.

"The fact was, of course, appreciated at King's Pyland, where the Colonel's training-stable is situated. Every precaution was taken to guard the favourite. The trainer, John Straker, is a retired jockey who rode in Colonel Ross's colours before he became too heavy for the weighing-chair. He has served the Colonel for five years as jockey and for seven as trainer and has always shown himself to be a zealous and honest servant. Under him were three lads, for the establishment was a small one, containing only four horses in all. One of these lads sat up each night in the stable, while the others slept in the loft. All three bore excellent characters. John Straker, who is a married man, lived in a small villa about two hundred yards from the stables. He has no children, keeps one maidservant, and is comfortably off. The country round is very lonely, but about a half a mile to the north there is a small cluster of villas which have been built by a Tavistock contractor for the use of invalids and others who may wish to enjoy the pure Dartmoor air. Tavistock itself lies two miles to the west, while across the moor, also about two miles distant, is the larger establishment of Mapleton, which belongs to Lord Backwater and is managed by Silas Brown. In every other direction the moor is a complete wilderness, inhabited only by a few roaming gipsies. Such was the general situation last Monday night when the catastrophe occurred.

"On that evening the horses had been exercised and watered as usual, and the stables were locked up at nine o'clock. Two of the lads walked up to the trainer's house, where they had supper in the kitchen, while the third, Ned Hunter, remained on guard. At a few minutes after nine the maid, Edith Baxter, carried down to the stables his supper, which consisted of a dish of curried mutton. She took no liquid, as there was a water-tap in the stables, and it was the rule that the lad on duty should drink nothing else. The maid carried a lantern with her, as it was very dark and the path ran across the open moor.

"Edith Baxter was within thirty yards of the stables when a man appeared out of the darkness and called to her to stop. As she stepped into the circle of yellow light thrown by the lantern she saw that he was a person of gentlemanly bearing, dressed in a grey suit of tweeds, with a cloth cap. He wore gaiters and carried a heavy stick with a knob to it. She was most impressed, however, by the extreme pallor of his face and by the nervousness of his manner. His age, she thought, would be rather over thirty than under it.

"'Can you tell me where I am?' he asked. 'I had almost made up my mind to sleep on the moor when I saw the light of your lantern.'

"'You are close to the King's Pyland training-stables,' said she.

"'Oh, indeed! What a stroke of luck!' he cried. 'I understand that a stable-boy sleeps there alone every night. Perhaps that is his supper which you are carrying to him. Now I am sure that you would not be too proud to earn the price of a new dress, would you?' He took a piece of white paper folded up out of his waistcoat pocket. 'See that the boy has this to-night, and you shall have the prettiest frock that money can buy.'

"She was frightened by the earnestness of his manner and ran past him to the window through which she was accustomed to hand the meals. It was already opened, and Hunter was seated at the small table inside. She had begun to tell him of what had happened when the stranger came up again.

"'Good-evening,' said he, looking through the window. 'I wanted to have a word with you.' The girl has sworn that as he spoke she noticed the corner of the little paper packet protruding from his closed hand.

"'What business have you here?' asked the lad.

"'It's business that may put something into your pocket,' said the other. 'You've two horses in for the Wessex Cup—Silver Blaze and Bayard. Let me have the straight tip and you won't be a loser. Is it a fact that at the weights Bayard could give the other a hundred yards in five furlongs, and that the stable have put their money on him?'

"'So, you're one of those damned touts!' cried the lad. 'I'll show you how we serve them in King's Pyland.' He sprang up and rushed across the stable to unloose the dog. The girl fled away to the house, but as she ran she looked back and saw that the stranger was leaning though the window. A minute later, however, when Hunter rushed out with the hound he was gone, and though he ran all round the buildings he failed to find any trace of him."

"One moment," I asked. "Did the stable-boy, when he ran out with the dog, leave the door unlocked behind him?"

"Excellent, Watson, excellent!" murmured my companion. "The importance of the point struck me so forcibly that I sent a special wire to Dartmoor yesterday to clear the matter up. The boy locked the door before he left it. The window, I may add, was not large enough for a man to get through.

"Hunter waited until his fellow-grooms had returned, when he sent a message to the trainer and told him what had occurred. Straker was excited at hearing the account, although he does not seem to have quite realized its true significance. It left him, however, vaguely uneasy, and Mrs. Straker, waking at one in the morning, found that he was dressing. In reply to her inquiries, he said that he could not sleep on account of his anxiety about the horses, and that he intended to walk down to the stables to see that all was well. She begged him to remain at home, as she could hear the pattering against the window, but in spite of her entreaties he pulled on his large mackintosh and left the house.

"Mrs. Straker awoke at seven in the morning to find that her husband had not yet returned. She dressed herself hastily, called the maid, and set off for the stables. The door was open; inside, huddled together upon a chair, Hunter was sunk in a state of absolute stupor, the favourite's stall was empty, and there were no signs of his trainer.

"The two lads who slept in the chaff-cutting loft above the harness-room were quickly aroused. They had heard nothing during the night, for they are both sound sleepers. Hunter was obviously under the influence of some powerful drug, and as no sense could be got out of him, he was left to sleep it off while the two lads and the two women ran out in search of the absentees. They still had hopes that the trainer had for some reason taken out the horse for early exercise, but on ascending the knoll near the house, from which all the neighbouring moors were visible, they not only could see no signs of the missing favourite, but they perceived something which warned them that they were in the presence of a tragedy.

"About a quarter of a mile from the stables John Straker's overcoat was flapping from a furze-bush. Immediately beyond there was a bowl-shaped depression in the moor, and at the bottom of this was found the dead body of the unfortunate trainer. His head had been shattered by a savage blow from some heavy weapon, and he was wounded on the thigh, where there was a long, clean cut, inflicted evidently by some very sharp instrument. It was clear, however, that Straker had defended himself vigorously against his assailants, for in his right hand he held a small knife, which was clotted with blood up to the handle, while in his left he clasped a red and black silk cravat, which was recognised by the maid as having been worn on the preceding evening by the stranger who had visited the stables. Hunter, on recovering from his stupor, was also quite positive as to the ownership of the cravat. He was equally certain that the same stranger had, while standing at the window, drugged his curried mutton and so deprived the stables of their watchman. As to the missing horse, there were abundant proofs in the mud which lay at the bottom of the fatal hollow that he had been there at the time of the struggle. But from that morning he has disappeared, and although a large reward has been offered, and all the gipsies of Dartmoor are on the alert, no news has come of him. Finally, an analysis has shown that the remains of his supper left by the stable-lad contained an appreciable quantity of powdered opium, while the people at the house partook of the same dish on the same night without any ill effect.

"Those are the main facts of the case, stripped of all surmise, and stated as baldly as possible. I shall now recapitulate what the police have done in the matter.

"Inspector Gregory, to whom the case has been committed, is an extremely competent officer. Were he but gifted with imagination he might rise to great heights in his profession. On his arrival he promptly found and arrested the man upon whom suspicion naturally rested. There was little difficulty in finding him, for he inhabited one of those villas which I have mentioned. His name, it appears, was Fitzroy Simpson. He was a man of excellent birth and education, who had squandered a fortune upon the turf, and who lived now by doing a little quiet and genteel book-making in the sporting clubs of London. An examination of his betting-book shows that bets to the amount of five thousand pounds had been registered by him against the favourite. On being arrested he volunteered the statement that he had come down to Dartmoor in the hope of getting some information about the King's Pyland horses, and also about Desborough, the second favourite, which was in charge of Silas Brown at the Mapleton stables. He did not attempt to deny that he had acted as described upon the evening before, but declared that he had no sinister designs and had simply wished to obtain firsthand information. When confronted with his cravat he turned very pale and was utterly unable to account for its presence in the hand of the murdered man. His wet clothing showed that he had been out in the storm of the night before, and his stick, which was a penang-lawyer weighted with lead, was just such a weapon as might, by repeated blows, have inflicted the terrible injuries to which the trainer had succumbed. On the other hand, there was no wound upon his person, while the state of Straker's knife would show that one at least of his assailants must bear his mark upon him. There you have it all in a nutshell, Watson, and if you can give me any light I shall be infinitely obliged to you."

I had listened with the greatest interest to the statement

which Holmes, with characteristic clearness, had laid before me. Though most of the facts were familiar to me, I had not sufficiently appreciated their relative importance, nor their connection to each other.

"Is it not possible," I suggested, "that the incised wound upon Straker may have been caused by his own knife in the convulsive struggles which follow any brain injury?"

"It is more than possible; it is probable," said Holmes. "In that case one of the main points in favour of the accused disappears."

"And yet," said I, "even now I fail to understand what the theory of the police can be."

"I am afraid that whatever theory we state has very grave objections to it," returned my companion. "The police imagine, I take it, that this Fitzroy Simpson, having drugged the lad, and having in some way obtained a duplicate key, opened the stable door and took out the horse, with the intention, apparently, of kidnapping him altogether. His bridle is missing, so that Simpson must have put this on. Then, having left the door open behind him, he was leading the horse away over the moor when he was either met or overtaken by the trainer. A row naturally ensued. Simpson beat out the trainer's brains with his heavy stick without receiving any injury from the small knife which Straker used in self-defence, and then the thief either led the horse on to some secret hiding-place, or else it may have bolted during the struggle and be now wandering out on the moors. That is the case as it appears to the police, and improbable as it is, all other explanations are more improbable still. However, I shall very quickly test the matter when I am once upon the spot, and until then I cannot really see how we can get much further than our present position."

It was evening before we reached the little town of Tavistock, which lies, like the boss of a shield, in the middle of the huge circle of Dartmoor. Two gentlemen were awaiting us in the station—the one a tall, fair man with lion-like hair and beard and curiously penetrating light blue eyes; the other a small, alert person, very neat and dapper, in a frock-coat and gaiters, with trim little side-whiskers and an eyeglass. The latter was Colonel Ross, the well-known sportsman; the other, Inspector Gregory; a man who was rapidly making his name in the English detective service.

"I am delighted that you have come down, Mr. Holmes," said the Colonel. "The Inspector here has done all that could possibly be suggested, but I wish to leave no stone unturned in trying to avenge poor Straker and in recovering my horse."

"Have there been any fresh developments?" asked Holmes.

"I am sorry to say that we have made very little progress," said the Inspector. "We have an open carriage outside, and as you would no doubt like to see the place before the light fails, we might talk it over as we drive."

A minute later we were all seated in a comfortable landau and were rattling through the quaint old Devonshire city. Inspector Gregory was full of his case and poured out a stream of remarks, while Holmes threw in an occasional question or interjection. Colonel Ross leaned back with his arms folded and his hat tilted over his eyes, while I listened with interest to the dialogue of the two detectives. Gregory was formulating his theory, which was almost exactly what Holmes had foretold in the train.

"The net is drawn pretty close round Fitzroy Simpson," he remarked, "and I believe myself that he is our man. At the same time I recognise that the evidence is purely circumstantial, and that some new development may upset it."

"How about Straker's knife?"

"We have quite come to the conclusion that he wounded himself in his fall."

"My friend Dr. Watson made that suggestion to me as we came down. If so, it would tell against this man Simpson."

"Undoubtedly. He has neither a knife or any sign of a

wound. The evidence against him is certainly very strong. He had a great interest in the disappearance of the favourite. He lies under suspicion of having poisoned the stable-boy; he was undoubtedly out in the storm; he was armed with a heavy stick, and his cravat was found in the dead man's hand. I really think we have enough to go before a jury."

Holmes shook his head. "A clever counsel would tear it all to rags," said he "Why should he take the horse out of the stable? If he wished to injure it, why could he not do it there? Has a duplicate key been found in his possession? What chemist sold him the powdered opium? Above all, where could he, a stranger to the district, hide a horse, and such a horse as this? What is his own explanation as to the paper which he wished the maid to give to the stable-boy?"

"He says that it was a ten-pound note. One was found in his purse. But your other difficulties are not so formidable as they seem. He is not a stranger to the district. He has twice lodged at Tavistock in the summer. The opium was probably brought from London. The key, having served its purpose, would be hurled away. The horse may be at the bottom of one of the pits or old mines upon the moor."

"What does he say about the cravat?"

"He acknowledges that it is his and declares that he had lost it. But a new element has been introduced into the case which may account for his leading the horse from the stable."

Holmes pricked up his ears.

"We have found traces which show that a party of gipsies encamped on Monday night within a mile of the spot where the murder took place. On Tuesday they were gone. Now, presuming that there was some understanding between Simpson and these gipsies, might he not have been leading the horse to them when he was overtaken, and may they not have him now?"

"It is certainly possible."

"The moor is being scoured for these gipsies. I have also examined every stable and outhouse in Tavistock, and for a radius of ten miles."

"There is another training-stable quite close, I understand?"

"Yes, and that is a factor which we must certainly not neglect. As Desborough, their horse, was second in the betting, they had an interest in the disappearance of the favourite. Silas Brown, the trainer, is known to have had large bets upon the event, and he was no friend to poor Straker. We have, however, examined the stables, and there is nothing to connect him with the affair."

"And nothing to connect this man Simpson with the interests of the Mapleton stables?"

"Nothing at all."

Holmes leaned back in the carriage, and the conversation ceased. A few minutes later our driver pulled up at a neat little red-brick villa with overhanging eaves which stood by the road. Some distance off, across a paddock, lay a long grey-tiled outbuilding. In every other direction the low curves of the moor, bronze-coloured from the fading ferns, stretched away to the sky-line, broken only by the steeples of Tavistock, and by a cluster of houses away to the westward which marked the Mapleton stables. We all sprang out with the exception of Holmes, who continued to lean back with his eyes fixed upon the sky in front of him, entirely absorbed in his own thoughts. It was only when I touched his arm that he roused himself with a violent start and stepped out of the carriage.

"Excuse me," said he, turning to Colonel Ross, who had looked at him in some surprise. "I was day-dreaming." There was a gleam in his eyes and a suppressed excitement in his manner which convinced me, used as I was to his ways, that his hand was upon a clue, though I could not imagine where he had found it.

"Perhaps you would prefer at once to go on to the scene of the crime, Mr. Holmes?" said Gregory.

"I think that I should prefer to stay here a little and go into one or two questions of detail. Straker was brought back here, I presume?"

"Yes, he lies upstairs. The inquest is to-morrow."

"He has been in your service some years, Colonel Ross?"

"I have always found him an excellent servant."

"I presume that you made an inventory of what he had in his pockets at the time of his death, Inspector?"

"I have the things themselves in the sitting-room if you would care to see them."

"I should be very glad." We all filed into the front room and sat round the central table while the Inspector unlocked a square tin box and laid a small heap of things before us. There was a box of vestas, two inches of tallow candle, an A D P briarroot pipe, a pouch of sealskin with half an ounce of long-cut Cavendish, a silver watch with a gold chain, five sovereigns in gold, an aluminum pencil-case, a few papers, and an ivory-handled knife with a very delicate, inflexible blade marked Weiss & Co., London.

"This is a very singular knife," said Holmes, lifting it up and examining it minutely. "I presume, as I see blood-stains upon it, that it is the one which was found in the dead man's grasp. Watson, this knife is surely in your line?"

"It is what we call a cataract knife," said I.

"I thought so. A very delicate blade devised for very delicate work. A strange thing for a man to carry with him upon a rough expedition, especially as it would not shut in his pocket."

"The tip was guarded by a disc of cork which we found beside his body," said the Inspector. "His wife tells us that the knife had lain upon the dressing-table, and that he had picked it up as he left the room. It was a poor weapon, but perhaps the best that he could lay his hands on at the moment."

"Very possibly. How about these papers?"

"Three of them are receipted hay-dealers' accounts. One of them is a letter of instructions from Colonel Ross. This other is a milliner's account for thirty-seven pounds fifteen made out by Madame Lesurier, of Bond Street, to William Derbyshire. Mrs. Straker tells us that Derbyshire was a friend of her husband's, and that occasionally his letters were addressed here."

"Madame Derbyshire had somewhat expensive tastes," remarked Holmes, glancing down the account. "Twenty-two guineas is rather heavy for a single costume. However, there appears to be nothing more to learn, and we may now go down to the scene of the crime."

As we emerged from the sitting-room a woman, who had been waiting in the passage, took a step forward and laid her hand upon the Inspector's sleeve. Her face was haggard and thin and eager, stamped with the print of a recent horror.

"Have you got them? Have you found them?" she panted.

"No, Mrs. Straker. But Mr. Holmes here has come from London to help us, and we shall do all that is possible."

"Surely I met you in Plymouth at a garden-party some little time ago, Mrs. Straker?" said Holmes.

"No, sir; you are mistaken."

"Dear me! Why I could have sworn to it. You wore a costume of dove-coloured silk with ostrich-feather trimming."

"I never had such a dress, sir," answered the lady.

"Ah, that quite settles it," said Holmes. And with an apology he followed the Inspector outside. A short walk across the moor took us to the hollow in which the body had been found. At the brink of it was the furze-bush upon which the coat had been hung.

"There was no wind that night, I understand," said Holmes.

"None, but very heavy rain."

"In that case the overcoat was not blown against the furze-bush, but placed there."

"Yes, it was laid across the bush."

"You fill me with interest. I perceive that the ground has been trampled up a good deal. No doubt many feet have been here since Monday night."

"A piece of matting has been laid here at the side, and we have all stood upon that."

"Excellent."

"In this bag I have one of the boots which Straker wore,

one of Fitzroy Simpson's shoes, and a cast horseshoe of Silver Blaze."

"My dear Inspector, you surpass yourself!" Holmes took the bag, and, descending into the hollow, he pushed the matting into a more central position. Then stretching himself upon his face and leaning his chin upon his hands, he made a careful study of the trampled mud in front of him. "Hullo!" said he suddenly. "What's this?" It was a wax vesta, half burned, which was so coated with mud that it looked at first like a little chip of wood.

"I cannot think how I came to overlook it," said the Inspector with an expression of annoyance.

"It was invisible, buried in the mud. I only saw it because I was looking for it."

"What! you expected to find it?"

"I thought it not unlikely."

He took the boots from the bag and compared the impressions of each of them with marks upon the ground. Then he clambered up to the rim of the hollow and crawled about among the ferns and bushes.

"I am afraid that there are no more tracks," said the Inspector. "I have examined the ground very carefully for a hundred yards in each direction."

"Indeed!" said Holmes, rising. "I should not have the impertinence to do it again after what you say. But I should like to take a little walk over the moor before it grows dark that I may know my ground to-morrow, and I think that I shall put this horseshoe into my pocket for luck."

Colonel Ross, who had shown some signs of impatience at my companion's quiet and systematic method of work, glanced at his watch. "I wish you would come back with me, Inspector," said he. "There are several points on which I should like your advice, and especially as to whether we do not owe it to the public to remove our horse's name from the entries for the cup."

"Certainly not," cried Holmes with decision. "I should let the name stand."

The Colonel bowed. "I am very glad to have had your opinion, sir," said he. "You will find us at poor Straker's house when you have finished your walk, and we can drive together into Tavistock."

He turned back with the Inspector, while Holmes and I walked slowly across the moor. The sun was beginning to sink behind the stable of Mapleton, and the long, sloping plain in front of us was tinged with gold, deepening into rich, ruddy browns where the faded ferns and brambles caught the evening light. But the glories of the landscape were all wasted upon my companion, who was sunk in the deepest thought.

"It's this way, Watson," said he at last. "We may leave the question of who killed John Straker for the instant and confine ourselves to finding out what has become of the horse. Now, supposing that he broke away during or after the tragedy, where could he have gone to? The horse is a very gregarious creature. If left to himself his instincts would have been either to return to King's Pyland or go over to Mapleton. Why should he run wild upon the moor? He would surely have been seen by now. And why should gipsies kidnap him? These people always clear out when they hear of trouble, for they do not wish to be pestered by the police. They could not hope to sell such a horse. They would run a great risk and gain nothing by taking him. Surely that is clear."

"Where is he, then?"

"I have already said that he must have gone to King's Pyland or to Mapleton. He is not at King's Pyland. Therefore he is at Mapleton. Let us take that as a working hypothesis and see what it leads us to. This part of the moor, as the Inspector remarked, is very hard and dry. But it falls away towards Mapleton, and you can see from here that there is a long hollow over yonder, which must have been very wet on Monday night. If our supposition is correct, then the horse must have crossed that, and there is the point where we should look for his tracks."

We had been walking briskly during this conversation,

and a few more minutes brought us to the hollow in question. At Holmes's request I walked down the bank to the right, and he to the left, but I had not taken fifty paces before I heard him give a shout and saw him waving his hand to me. The track of a horse was plainly outlined in the soft earth in front of him, and the shoe which he took from his pocket exactly fitted the impression.

"See the value of imagination," said Holmes. "It is the one quality which Gregory lacks. We imagined what might have happened, acted upon the supposition, and find ourselves justified. Let us proceed."

We crossed the marshy bottom and passed over a quarter of a mile of dry, hard turf. Again the ground sloped, and again we came on the tracks. Then we lost them for half a mile, but only to pick them up once more quite close to Mapleton. It was Holmes who saw them first, and he stood pointing with a look of triumph upon his face. A man's track was visible beside the horse's.

"The horse was alone before," I cried.

"Quite so. It was alone before. Hullo, what is this?"

The double track turned sharp off and took the direction of King's Pyland. Holmes whistled, and we both followed along after it. His eyes were on the trail, but I happened to look a little to one side and saw to my surprise the same tracks coming back again in the opposite direction.

"One for you, Watson," said Holmes when I pointed it out. "You have saved us a long walk, which would have brought us back on our own traces. Let us follow the return track."

We had not to go far. It ended at the paving of asphalt which led up to the gates of the Mapleton stables. As we approached, a groom ran out from them.

"We don't want any loiterers about here," said he.

"I only wished to ask a question," said Holmes, with his finger and thumb in his waistcoat pocket. "Should I be too early to see your master, Mr. Silas Brown, if I were to call at five o'clock to-morrow morning?"

"Bless you, sir, if anyone is about he will be, for he is always the first stirring. But here he is, sir, to answer your questions for himself. No, sir, no, it is as much as my place is worth to let him see me touch your money. Afterwards, if you like."

As Sherlock Holmes replaced the half-crown which he had drawn from his pocket, a fierce-looking elderly man strode out from the gate with a hunting-crop swinging in his hand.

"What's this, Dawson!" he cried. "No gossiping! Go about your business! And you, what the devil do you want here?"

"Ten minutes' talk with you, my good sir," said Holmes in the sweetest of voices.

"I've no time to talk to every gadabout. We want no strangers here. Be off, or you may find a dog at your heels."

Holmes leaned forward and whispered something in the trainer's ear. He started violently and flushed to the temples.

"It's a lie!" he shouted. "An infernal lie!"

"Very good. Shall we argue about it here in public or talk it over in your parlour?"

"Oh, come in if you wish to."

Holmes smiled. "I shall not keep you more than a few minutes, Watson," said he. "Now, Mr. Brown, I am quite at your disposal."

It was twenty minutes, and the reds had all faded into greys before Holmes and the trainer reappeared. Never have I seen such a change as had been brought about in Silas Brown in that short time. His face was ashy pale, beads of perspiration shone upon his brow, and his hands shook until the hunting-crop wagged like a branch in the wind. His bullying, overbearing manner was all gone too, and he cringed along at my companion's side like a dog with its master.

"Your instructions will be done. It shall all be done," said he.

"There must be no mistake," said Holmes, looking round at him. The other winced as he read the menace in his eyes.

"Oh, no, there shall be no mistake. It shall be there. Should I change it first or not?"

Holmes thought a little and then burst out laughing. "No, don't" said he, "I shall write to you about it. No tricks, now, or—"

"Oh, you can trust me, you can trust me!"

"Yes, I think I can. Well, you shall hear from me tomorrow." He turned upon his heel, disregarding the trembling hand which the other held out to him, and we set off for King's Pyland.

"A more perfect compound of the bully, coward, and sneak than Master Silas Brown I have seldom met with," remarked Holmes as we trudged along together.

"He has the horse, then?"

"He tried to bluster out of it, but I described to him so exactly what his actions had been upon that morning that he is convinced that I was watching him. Of course you observed the peculiarly square toes in the impressions, and that his own boots exactly corresponded to them. Again, of course no subordinate would have dared to do such a thing. I described to him how, when according to his custom he was the first down, he perceived a strange horse wandering over the moor. How he went out to it, and his astonishment at recognising, from the white forehead which has given the favourite its name, that chance had put in his power the only horse which could beat the one upon which he had put his money. Then I described how his first impulse had been to lead him back to King's Pyland, and how the devil had shown him how he could hide the horse until the race was over, and how he had led it back and concealed it at Mapleton. When I told him every detail he gave it up and thought only of saving his own skin."

"But his stables had been searched?"

"Oh, an old horse-faker like him has many a dodge."

"But are you not afraid to leave the horse in his power now, since he has every interest in injuring it?"

"My dear fellow, he will guard it as the apple of his eye.

He knows that his only hope of mercy is to produce it safe."

"Colonel Ross did not impress me as a man who would be likely to show much mercy in any case."

"The matter does not rest with Colonel Ross. I follow my own methods and tell as much or as little as I choose. That is the advantage of being unofficial. I don't know whether you observed it, Watson, but the Colonel's manner has been just a trifle cavalier to me. I am inclined now to have a little amusement at his expense. Say nothing to him about the horse."

"Certainly not without your permission."

"And of course this is all quite a minor point compared to the question of who killed John Straker."

"And you will devote yourself to that?"

"On the contrary, we both go back to London by the night train."

I was thunderstruck by my friend's words. We had only been a few hours in Devonshire, and that he should give up an investigation which he had begun so brilliantly was quite incomprehensible to me. Not a word more could I draw from him until we were back at the trainer's house. The Colonel and the Inspector were awaiting us in the parlour.

"My friend and I return to town by the night-express," said Holmes. "We have had a charming little breath of your beautiful Dartmoor air."

The Inspector opened his eyes, and the Colonel's lip curled in a sneer.

"So you despair of arresting the murderer of poor Straker," said he.

Holmes shrugged his shoulders. "There are certainly grave difficulties in the way," said he. "I have every hope, however, that your horse will start upon Tuesday, and I beg that you will have your jockey in readiness. Might I ask for a photograph of Mr. John Straker?"

The Inspector took one from an envelope and handed it to him.

"My dear Gregory, you anticipate all my wants. If I might ask you to wait here for an instant, I have a question which I should like to put to the maid."

"I must say that I am rather disappointed in our London consultant," said Colonel Ross bluntly as my friend left the room. "I do not see that we are any further than when he came."

"At least you have his assurance that your horse will run," said I.

"Yes, I have his assurance," said the Colonel with a shrug of his shoulders. "I should prefer to have the horse."

I was about to make some reply in defence of my friend when he entered the room again.

"Now, gentlemen," said he, "I am quite ready for Tavistock."

As we stepped into the carriage one of the stable-lads held the door open for us. A sudden idea seemed to occur to Holmes, for he leaned forward and touched the lad upon the sleeve.

"You have a few sheep in the paddock," he said. "Who attends to them?"

"I do, sir."

"Have you noticed anything amiss with them of late?"

"Well, sir, not of much account, but three of them have gone lame, sir."

I could see that Holmes was extremely pleased, for he chuckled and rubbed his hands together.

"A long shot, Watson, a very long shot," said he, pinching my arm. "Gregory, let me recommend to your attention this singular epidemic among the sheep. Drive on, Coachman!"

Colonel Ross still wore an expression which showed the poor opinion which he had formed of my companion's ability, but I saw by the Inspector's face that his attention had been keenly aroused.

"You consider that to be important?" he asked.

"Exceedingly so."

"Is there any point to which you would wish to draw my attention?"

"To the curious incident of the dog in the night-time."

"The dog did nothing in the night-time."

"That was the curious incident," remarked Sherlock Holmes.

Four days later Holmes and I were again in the train, bound for Winchester to see the race for the Wessex Cup. Colonel Ross met us by appointment outside the station, and we drove in his drag to the course beyond the town. His face was grave, and his manner was cold in the extreme.

"I have seen nothing of my horse," said he.

"I suppose that you would know him when you saw him?" asked Holmes.

The Colonel was very angry. "I have been on the turf for twenty years and never was asked such a question as that before," said he. "A child would know Silver Blaze with his white forehead and his mottled off-foreleg."

"How is the betting?"

"Well, that is the curious part of it. You could have got fifteen to one yesterday, but now the price has become shorter and shorter, until you can hardly get three to one now."

"Hum!" said Holmes. "Somebody knows something, that is clear."

As the drag drew up in the enclosure near the grandstand I glanced at the card to see the entries.

Wessex Plate [it ran] 50 sovs. each h ft with 1000 sovs. added, for four and five year olds. Second, £300. Third, £200. New course (one mile and five furlongs).
1. Mr. Heath Newton's The Negro. Red cap. Cinnamon jacket.
2. Colonel Wardlaw's Pugilist. Pink cap. Blue and black jacket.
3. Lord Backwater's Desborough. Yellow cap and sleeves.
4. Colonel Ross's Silver Blaze. Black cap. Red jacket.
5. Duke of Balmoral's Iris. Yellow and black stripes.
6. Lord Singleford's Rasper. Purple cap. Black sleeves.

"We scratched our other one and put all hopes on your word," said the Colonel. "Why, what is that? Silver Blaze favourite?"

"Five to four against Silver Blaze!" roared the ring. "Five to four against Silver Blaze! Five to fifteen against Desborough! Five to four on the field!"

"There are the numbers up," I cried. "They are all six there."

"All six there? Then my horse is running," cried the Colonel in great agitation. "But I don't see him. My colours have not passed."

"Only five have passed. This must be he."

As I spoke a powerful bay horse swept out from the weighing enclosure and cantered past us, bearing on its back the well-known black and red of the Colonel.

"That's not my horse," cried the owner. "That beast has not a white hair upon its body. What is this that you have done, Mr. Holmes?"

"Well, well, let us see how he gets on," said my friend imperturbably. For a few minutes he gazed through my field-glass. "Capital! An excellent start!" he cried suddenly. "There they are, coming round the curve!"

From our drag we had a superb view as they came up the straight. The six horses were so close together that a carpet could have covered them, but halfway up the yellow of the Mapleton stable showed to the front. Before they reached us, however, Desborough's bolt was shot, and the Colonel's horse, coming away with a rush, passed the post a good six lengths before its rival, the Duke of Balmoral's Iris making a bad third.

"It's my race, anyhow," gasped the Colonel, passing his hand over his eyes. "I confess that I can make neither head nor tail of it. Don't you think that you have kept up your mystery long enough, Mr. Holmes?"

"Certainly, Colonel, you shall know everything. Let us all go round and have a look at the horse together. Here he is," he continued as we made our way into the weighing enclosure, where only owners and their friends find admittance. "You have only to wash his face and his leg in spirits of wine, and you will find that he is the same old Silver Blaze as ever."

"You take my breath away!"

"I found him in the hands of a faker and took the liberty of running him just as he was sent over."

"My dear sir, you have done wonders. The horse looks very fit and well. It never went better in its life. I owe you a thousand apologies for having doubted your ability. You have done me a great service by recovering my horse. You would do me a greater still if you could lay your hands on the murderer of John Straker."

"I have done so," said Holmes quietly.

The Colonel and I stared at him in amazement. "You have got him! Where is he, then?"

"He is here."

"Here! Where?"

"In my company at the present moment."

The Colonel flushed angrily. "I quite recognise that I am under obligations to you, Mr. Holmes," said he, "but I must regard what you have just said as either a very bad joke or an insult."

Sherlock Holmes laughed. "I assure you that I have not associated you with the crime, Colonel," said he. "The real murderer is standing immediately behind you." He stepped past and laid his hand upon the glossy neck of the thoroughbred.

"The horse!" cried both the Colonel and myself.

"Yes, the horse. And it may lessen his guilt if I say that it was done in self-defence, and that John Straker was a man who was entirely unworthy of your confidence. But there goes the bell, and as I stand to win a little on this next race, I shall defer a lengthy explanation until a more fitting time."

We had the corner of a Pullman car to ourselves that evening as we whirled back to London, and I fancy that the journey was a short one to Colonel Ross as well as to myself as we listened to our companion's narrative of the events which had occurred at the Dartmoor training-stables upon that Monday night, and the means by which he had unravelled them.

"I confess," said he, "that any theories which I had

formed from the newspaper reports were entirely erroneous. And yet there were indications there, had they not
been overlaid by other details which concealed their true
import. I went to Devonshire with the conviction that
Fitzroy Simpson was the true culprit, although, of course,
I saw that the evidence against him was by no means complete. It was while I was in the carriage, just as we reached
the trainer's house, that the immense significance of the
curried mutton occurred to me. You may remember that I
was distrait and remained sitting after you had alighted. I
was marvelling in my own mind how I could possibly have
overlooked so obvious a clue."

"I confess," said the Colonel, "that even now I cannot
see how it helps us."

"It was the first link in my chain of reasoning. Powdered
opium is by no means tasteless. The flavour is not disagreeable, but it is perceptible. Were it mixed with any
ordinary dish the eater would undoubtedly detect it and
would probably eat no more. A curry was exactly the
medium which would disguise this taste. By no possible
supposition could this stranger, Fitzroy Simpson, have
caused curry to be served in the trainer's family that night,
and it is surely too monstrous a coincidence to suppose
that he happened to come along with powdered opium
upon the very night when a dish happened to be served
which would disguise the flavour. That is unthinkable.
Therefore Simpson becomes eliminated from the case,
and our attention centres upon Straker and his wife, the
only two people who could have chosen curried mutton
for supper that night. The opium was added after the dish
was set aside for the stable-boy, for the others had the
same for supper with no ill effects. Which of them, then,
had access to the dish without the maid seeing them?

"Before deciding that question I had grasped the significance of the silence of the dog, for one true inference invariably suggests others. The Simpson incident had shown
me that a dog was kept in the stables, and yet, though
someone had been in and had fetched out a horse, he had

not barked enough to arouse the two lads in the loft. Obviously the midnight visitor was someone whom the dog knew well.

"I was already convinced, or almost convinced, that John Straker went down to the stables in the dead of the night and took out Silver Blaze. For what purpose? For a dishonest one, obviously, or why should he drug his own stable-boy? And yet I was at a loss to know why. There have been cases before now where trainers have made sure of great sums of money by laying against their own horses through agents and then preventing them from winning by fraud. Sometimes it is a pulling jockey. Sometimes it is some surer and subtler means. What was it here? I hoped that the contents of his pockets might help me to form a conclusion.

"And they did so. You cannot have forgotten the singular knife which was found in the dead man's hand, a knife which certainly no sane man would choose for a weapon. It was, as Dr. Watson told us, a form of knife which is used for the most delicate operations known in surgery. And it was to be used for a delicate operation that night. You must know, with your wide experience of turf matters, Colonel Ross, that it is possible to make a slight nick upon the tendons of a horse's ham, and to do it subcutaneously, so as to leave absolutely no trace. A horse so treated would develop a slight lameness, which would be put down to a strain in exercise or a touch of rheumatism, but never to foul play."

"Villain! Scoundrel!" cried the Colonel.

"We have here the explanation of why John Straker wished to take the horse out on the moor. So spirited a creature would have certainly roused the soundest of sleepers when it felt the prick of the knife. It was absolutely necessary to do it in the open air."

"I have been blind!" cried the Colonel. "Of course that was why he needed the candle and struck the match."

"Undoubtedly. But in examining his belongings I was fortunate enough to discover not only the method of the crime but even its motives. As a man of the world, Colonel, you know that men do not carry other people's bills about in their pockets. We have most of us quite enough to do to settle our own. I at once concluded that Straker was leading a double life and keeping a second establishment. The nature of the bill showed that there was a lady in the case, and one who had expensive tastes. Liberal as you are with your servants, one can hardly expect that they can buy twenty-guinea walking dresses for their ladies. I questioned Mrs. Straker as to the dress without her knowing it, and, having satisfied myself that it had never reached her, I made a note of the milliner's address and felt that by calling there with Straker's photograph I could easily dispose of the mythical Derbyshire.

"From that time on all was plain. Straker had led out the horse to a hollow where his light would be invisible. Simpson in his flight had dropped his cravat, and Straker had picked it up—with some idea, perhaps, that he might use it in securing the horse's leg. Once in the hollow, he had got behind the horse and had struck a light; but the creature, frightened at the sudden glare, and with the strange instinct of animals feeling that some mischief was intended, had lashed out, and the steel shoe had struck Straker full on the forehead. He had already, in spite of the rain, taken off his overcoat in order to do his delicate task, and so, as he fell, his knife gashed his thigh. Do I make it clear?"

"Wonderful!" cried the Colonel. "Wonderful! You might have been there!"

"My final shot was, I confess, a very long one. It struck me that so astute a man as Straker would not undertake this delicate tendon-nicking without a little practise. What could he practise on? My eyes fell upon the sheep, and I asked a question which, rather to my surprise, showed that my surmise was correct.

"When I returned to London I called upon the milliner, who had recognised Straker as an excellent customer of the name of Derbyshire, who had a very dashing wife, with a strong partiality for expensive dresses. I have no doubt that this woman had plunged him over head and ears in debt, and so led him into this miserable plot."

"You have explained all but one thing," cried the Colonel. "Where was the horse?"

"Ah, it bolted and was cared for by one of your neighbours. We must have an amnesty in that direction, I think. This is Clapham Junction, if I am not mistaken, and we shall be in Victoria in less than ten minutes. If you care to smoke a cigar in our rooms, Colonel, I shall be happy to give you any other details which might interest you."

The Musgrave Ritual

An anomaly which often struck me in the character of my friend Sherlock Holmes was that, although in his methods of thought he was the neatest and most methodical of mankind, and although also he affected a certain quiet primness of dress, he was none the less in his personal habits one of the most untidy men that ever drove a fellow-lodger to distraction. Not that I am in the least conventional in that respect myself. The rough-and-tumble work in Afghanistan, coming on the top of natural Bohemianism of disposition, has made me rather more lax than befits a medical man. But with me there is a limit, and when I find a man who keeps his cigars in the coal-scuttle, his tobacco in the toe end of a Persian slipper, and his unanswered correspondence transfixed by a jack-knife into the very centre of his wooden mantelpiece, then I begin to give myself virtuous airs. I have always held, too, that pistol practice should be distinctly an open-air pastime; and when Holmes, in one of his queer humours, would sit in an arm-chair with his hair-trigger and a hundred Boxer cartridges and proceed to adorn the opposite wall with a patriotic V. R. done in bullet-pocks, I felt strongly that neither the atmosphere nor the appearance of our room was improved by it.

Our chambers were always full of chemicals and of criminal relics which had a way of wandering into unlikely positions, and of turning up in the butter-dish or in even less desirable places. But his papers were my great crux. He had a horror of destroying documents, especially those which were connected with his past cases, and yet it was only once in every year or two that he would muster energy to docket and arrange them; for, as I have mentioned somewhere in these incoherent memoirs, the outbursts of passionate energy when he performed the remarkable feats with which his name is associated were followed by reactions of lethargy during which he would lie about with his violin and his books, hardly moving save from the sofa to the table. Thus month after month his papers accumulated until every corner of the room was stacked with bundles of manuscript which were on no account to be burned, and which could not be put away save by their owner. One winter's night, as we sat together by the fire, I ventured to suggest to him that, as he had finished pasting extracts into his commonplace book, he might employ the next two hours in making our room a little more habitable. He could not deny the justice of my request, so with a rather rueful face he went off to his bedroom, from which he returned presently pulling a large tin box behind him. This he placed in the middle of the floor, and squatting down upon a stool in front of it, he threw back the lid. I could see that it was already a third full of bundles of paper tied up with red tape into separate packages.

"There are cases enough here, Watson," said he, looking at me with mischievous eyes. "I think that if you knew all that I had in this box you would ask me to pull some out instead of putting others in."

"These are the records of your early work, then?" I asked. "I have often wished that I had notes of those cases."

"Yes, my boy, these are all done prematurely before my biographer had come to glorify me." He lifted bundle after bundle in a tender, caressing sort of way. "They are not all successes, Watson," said he. "But there are some pretty little problems among them. Here's the record of the Tarleton murders, and the case of Vamberry, the wine merchant, and the adventure of the old Russian woman, and the singular affair of the aluminum crutch, as well as a full account of Ricoletti of the club-foot and his abominable wife. And here—ah, now, this really is something a little *recherché*."

He dived his arm down to the bottom of the chest and brought up a small wooden box with a sliding lid such as children's toys are kept in. From within he produced a crumpled piece of paper, an old-fashioned brass key, a peg of wood with a ball of string attached to it, and three rusty old discs of metal.

"Well, my boy, what do you make of this lot?" he asked, smiling at my expression.

"It is a curious collection."

"Very curious, and the story that hangs round it will strike you as being more curious still."

"These relics have a history, then?"

"So much so that they *are* history."

"What do you mean by that?"

Sherlock Holmes picked them up one by one and laid them along the edge of the table. Then he reseated himself in his chair and looked them over with a gleam of satisfaction in his eyes.

"These," said he, "are all that I have left to remind me of the adventure of the Musgrave Ritual."

I had heard him mention the case more than once, though I had never been able to gather the details. "I should be so glad," said I, "if you would give me an account of it."

"And leave the litter as it is?" he cried mischievously. "Your tidiness won't bear much strain, after all, Watson. But I should be glad that you should add this case to your annals, for there are points in it which make it quite unique in the criminal records of this or, I believe, any other country. A collection of my trifling achievements would certainly be incomplete which contained no account of this very singular business.

"You may remember how the affair of the *Gloria Scott,* and my conversation with the unhappy man whose fate I told you of, first turned my attention in the direction of the profession which has become my life's work. You see me now when my name has become known far and wide, and when I am generally recognised both by the public and by the official force as being a final court of appeal in doubtful cases. Even when you knew me first, at the time of the affair which you have commemorated in *A Study in Scarlet,* I had already established a considerable, though not a very lucrative, connection. You can hardly realize, then, how difficult I found it at first, and how long I had to wait before I succeeded in making any headway.

"When I first came up to London I had rooms in Montague Street, just round the corner from the British Museum, and there I waited, filling in my too abundant leisure time by studying all those branches of science which might make me more efficient. Now and again cases came in my way, principally through the introduction of old fellow-students, for during my last years at the university there was a good deal of talk there about myself and my methods. The third of these cases was that of the Musgrave Ritual, and it is to the interest which was aroused by that singular chain of events, and the large issues which proved to be at stake, that I trace my first stride towards the position which I now hold.

"Reginald Musgrave had been in the same college as myself, and I had some slight acquaintance with him. He was generally popular among the undergraduates, though it always seemed to me that what was set down as pride was really an attempt to cover extreme natural diffidence. In appearance he was a man of an exceedingly aristocratic type, thin, high-nosed, and large-eyed, with languid and yet courtly manners. He was indeed a scion of one of the very oldest families in the kingdom, though his branch was a cadet one which had separated from the northern Musgraves some time in the sixteenth century and had established itself in western Sussex, where the manor-house of Hurlstone is perhaps the oldest inhabited building in the county. Something of his birth-place seemed to cling to the man, and I never looked at his pale, keen face or the poise of his head without associating him with grey archways and mullioned windows and all the venerable wreckage of a feudal keep. Once or twice we drifted into talk, and I can remember that more than once he expressed a keen interest in my methods of observation and inference.

"For four years I had seen nothing of him until one morning he walked into my room in Montague Street. He had changed little, was dressed like a young man of fashion—he was always a bit of a dandy—and preserved the same quiet, suave manner which had formerly distinguished him.

"'How has all gone with you, Musgrave?' I asked after we had cordially shaken hands.

"'You probably heard of my poor father's death,' said he; 'he was carried off about two years ago. Since then I have of course had the Hurlstone estate to manage, and as I am member for my district as well, my life has been a busy one. But I understand, Holmes, that you are turning to practical ends those powers with which you used to amaze us?'

"'Yes,' said I, 'I have taken to living by my wits.'

"'I am delighted to hear it, for your advice at present would be exceedingly valuable to me. We have had some very strange doings at Hurlstone, and the police have been able to throw no light upon the matter. It is really the most extraordinary and inexplicable business.'

"You can imagine with what eagerness I listened to him, Watson, for the very chance for which I had been panting during all those months of inaction seemed to have come within my reach. In my inmost heart I believed that I could succeed where others failed, and now I had the opportunity to test myself.

"'Pray let me have the details,' I cried.

"Reginald Musgrave sat down opposite to me and lit the cigarette which I pushed towards him.

"'You must know,' said he, 'that though I am a bachelor, I have to keep up a considerable staff of servants at Hurlstone, for it is a rambling old place and takes a good deal of looking after. I preserve, too, and in the pheasant months I usually have a house-party, so that it would not do to be short-handed. Altogether there are eight maids, the cook, the butler, two footmen, and a boy. The garden and the stables of course have a separate staff.

"'Of these servants the one who has been longest in our service was Brunton, the butler. He was a young school-master out of place when he was first taken up by my father, but he was a man of great energy and character, and he soon became quite invaluable in the household. He was a well-grown, handsome man, with a splendid fore-head, and though he has been with us for twenty years he cannot be more than forty now. With his personal advantages and his extraordinary gifts—for he can speak several languages and play nearly every musical instrument—it is wonderful that he should have been satisfied so long in such a position, but I suppose that he was comfortable and lacked energy to make any change. The butler of Hurlstone is always a thing that is remembered by all who visit us.

"'But this paragon has one fault. He is a bit of a Don Juan, and you can imagine that for a man like him it is not a very difficult part to play in a quiet country district. When he was married it was all right, but since he has been a widower we have had no end of trouble with him. A few months ago we were in hopes that he was about to settle down again, for he became engaged to Rachel Howells, our second housemaid; but he has thrown her over since then and taken up with Janet Tregellis, the daughter of the head game-keeper. Rachel—who is a very good girl, but of an excitable Welsh temperament—had a sharp touch of brain-fever and goes about the house now—or did until yesterday—like a black-eyed shadow of her former self. That was our first drama at Hurlstone; but a second one came to drive it from our minds, and it was prefaced by the disgrace and dismissal of butler Brunton.

"'This was how it came about. I have said that the man

was intelligent, and this very intelligence has caused his ruin, for it seems to have led to an insatiable curiosity about things which did not in the least concern him. I had no idea of the lengths to which this would carry him until the merest accident opened my eyes to it.

"'I have said that the house is a rambling one. One day last week—on Thursday night, to be more exact—I found that I could not sleep, having foolishly taken a cup of strong *café noir* after my dinner. After struggling against it until two in the morning, I felt that it was quite hopeless, so I rose and lit the candle with the intention of continuing a novel which I was reading. The book, however, had been left in the billiard-room, so I pulled on my dressing-gown and started off to get it.

"'In order to reach the billiard-room I had to descend a flight of stairs and then to cross the head of a passage which led to the library and the gun-room. You can imagine my surprise when, as I looked down this corridor, I saw a glimmer of light coming from the open door of the library. I had myself extinguished the lamp and closed the door before coming to bed. Naturally my first thought was of burglars. The corridors at Hurlstone have their walls largely decorated with trophies of old weapons. From one of these I picked a battle-axe, and then, leaving my candle behind me, I crept on tip-toe down the passage and peeped in at the open door.

"'Brunton, the butler, was in the library. He was sitting, fully dressed, in an easy-chair, with a slip of paper which looked like a map upon his knee, and his forehead sunk forward upon his hand in deep thought. I stood dumb with astonishment, watching him from the darkness. A small taper on the edge of the table shed a feeble light which sufficed to show me that he was fully dressed. Suddenly, as I looked, he rose from his chair, and walking over to a bureau at the side, he unlocked it and drew out one of the drawers. From this he took a paper, and returning to his seat, he flattened it out beside the taper on the edge of the table and began to study it with minute attention. My indignation at this calm examination of our family documents overcame me so far that I took a step forward, and Brunton, looking up, saw me standing in the doorway. He sprang to his feet, his face turned livid with fear, and he thrust into his breast the chart-like paper which he had been originally studying.

"'"So!" said I. "This is how you repay the trust which we have reposed in you. You will leave my service to-morrow."

"'He bowed with the look of a man who is utterly crushed and slunk past me without a word. The taper was still on the table, and by its light I glanced to see what the paper was which Brunton had taken from the bureau. To my surprise it was nothing of any importance at all, but simply a copy of the questions and answers in the singular old observance called the Musgrave Ritual. It is a sort of ceremony peculiar to our family, which each Musgrave for centuries past has gone through on his coming of age—a thing of private interest and perhaps of some little importance to the archæologist, like our own blazonings and charges, but of no practical use whatever.'

"'We had better come back to the paper afterwards,' said I.

"'If you think it really necessary,' he answered with some hesitation. "To continue my statement, however: I relocked the bureau, using the key which Brunton had left, and I turned to go when I was surprised to find that the butler had returned and was standing before me.

"'"Mr. Musgrave, sir," he cried in a voice which was hoarse with emotion, "I can't bear disgrace, sir. I've always been proud above my station in life, and disgrace would kill me. My blood will be on your head, sir—it will, indeed—if you drive me to despair. If you cannot keep me after what has passed, then for God's sake let me give you notice and leave in a month, as if of my own free will. I could stand that, Mr. Musgrave, but not to be cast out before all the folk that I know so well."

"'"You don't deserve much consideration, Brunton," I

269

answered. "Your conduct has been most infamous. However, as you have been a long time in the family, I have no
wish to bring public disgrace upon you. A month, however, is too long. Take yourself away in a week and give
what reason you like for going."

" ' "Only a week, sir?" he cried in a despairing voice. "A
fortnight—say at least a fortnight!"

" ' "A week," I repeated, "and you may consider yourself
to have been very leniently dealt with."

" 'He crept away, his face sunk upon his breast, like a
broken man, while I put out the light and returned to
my room.

" 'For two days after this Brunton was most assiduous in
his attention to his duties. I made no allusion to what had
passed and waited with some curiosity to see how he would
cover his disgrace. On the third morning, however, he did
not appear, as was his custom, after breakfast to receive
my instructions for the day. As I left the dining-room I
happened to meet Rachel Howells, the maid. I have told
you that she had only recently recovered from an illness
and was looking so wretchedly pale and wan that I remon-
strated with her for being at work.

" ' "You should be in bed," I said. "Come back to your
duties when you are stronger."

" 'She looked at me with so strange an expression that I
began to suspect that her brain was affected.

" ' "I am strong enough, Mr. Musgrave," said she.

" ' "We will see what the doctor says," I answered. "You
must stop work now, and when you go downstairs just say
that I wish to see Brunton."

" ' "The butler is gone," said she.

" ' "Gone! Gone where?"

" ' "He is gone. No one has seen him. He is not in his
room. Oh, yes, he is gone, he is gone!" She fell back
against the wall with shriek after shriek of laughter, while
I, horrified at this sudden hysterical attack, rushed to the
bell to summon help. The girl was taken to her room, still
screaming and sobbing, while I made inquiries about
Brunton. There was no doubt about it that he had disap-

peared. His bed had not been slept in, he had been seen by no one since he had retired to his room the night before, and yet it was difficult to see how he could have left the house, as both windows and doors were found to be fastened in the morning. His clothes, his watch, and even his money were in his room, but the black suit which he usually wore was missing. His slippers, too, were gone, but his boots were left behind. Where then could butler Brunton have gone in the night, and what could have become of him now?

"'Of course we searched the house from cellar to garret, but there was no trace of him. It is, as I have said, a labyrinth of an old house, especially the original wing, which is now practically uninhabited; but we ransacked every room and cellar without discovering the least sign of the missing man. It was incredible to me that he could have gone away leaving all his property behind him, and yet where could he be? I called in the local police, but without success. Rain had fallen on the night before, and we examined the lawn and the paths all round the house, but in vain. Matters were in this state, when a new development quite drew our attention away from the original mystery.

"'For two days Rachel Howells had been so ill, sometimes delirious sometimes hysterical, that a nurse had been employed to sit up with her at night. On the third night after Brunton's disappearance, the nurse, finding her patient sleeping nicely, had dropped into a nap in the armchair, when she woke in the early morning to find the bed empty, the window open, and no signs of the invalid. I was instantly aroused, and with the two footmen, started off at once in search of the missing girl. It was not difficult to tell the direction which she had taken, for starting from under her window, we could follow her footmarks easily across the lawn to the edge of the mere, where they vanished close to the gravel path which leads out of the grounds. The lake there is eight feet deep, and you can imagine our feelings when we saw that the trail of the poor demented girl came to an end at the edge of it.

"'Of course, we had the drags at once and set to work to

recover the remains, but no trace of the body could we find. On the other hand, we brought to the surface an object of a most unexpected kind. It was a linen bag which contained within it a mass of old rusted and discoloured metal and several dull-coloured pieces of pebble or glass. This strange find was all that we could get from the mere, and although we made every possible search and inquiry yesterday, we know nothing of the fate either of Rachel Howells or of Richard Brunton. The county police are at their wit's end, and I have come up to you as a last resource.'

"You can imagine, Watson, with what eagerness I listened to this extraordinary sequence of events and endeavoured to piece them together, and to devise some common thread upon which they might all hang. The butler was gone. The maid was gone. The maid had loved the butler, but had afterwards had cause to hate him. She was of Welsh blood, fiery and passionate. She had been terribly excited immediately after his disappearance. She had flung into the lake a bag containing some curious contents. These were all factors which had to be taken into consideration, and yet none of them got quite to the heart of the matter. What was the starting-point of this chain of events? There lay the end of this tangled line.

"'I must see that paper, Musgrave,' said I, 'which this butler of yours thought it worth his while to consult, even at the risk of the loss of his place.'

"'It is rather an absurd business, this ritual of ours,' he answered. 'But it has at least the saving grace of antiquity to excuse it. I have a copy of the questions and answers here if you care to run your eye over them.'

"He handed me the very paper which I have here, Watson, and this is the strange catechism to which each Musgrave had to submit when he came to man's estate. I will read you the questions and answers as they stand.

"'Whose was it?'

"'His who is gone.'

"'Who shall have it?'

"'He who will come.'

" 'Where was the sun?'

" 'Over the oak.'

" 'Where was the shadow?'

" 'Under the elm.'

" 'How was it stepped?'

" 'North by ten and by ten, east by five and by five, south by two and by two, west by one and by one, and so under.'

" 'What shall we give for it?'

" 'All that is ours.'

" 'For the sake of the trust.'

" 'The original has no date, but is in the spelling of the middle of the seventeenth century' remarked Musgrave. 'I am afraid, however, that it can be of little help to you in solving this mystery.'

" 'At least,' said I, 'it gives us another mystery, and one which is even more interesting than the first. It may be that the solution of the one may prove to be the solution of the other. You will excuse me, Musgrave, if I say that your butler appears to me to have been a very clever man and to have had a clearer insight than ten generations of his masters.'

" 'I hardly follow you,' said Musgrave. 'The paper seems to me to be of no practical importance.'

" 'But to me it seems immensely practical, and I fancy that Brunton took the same view. He had probably seen it before that night on which you caught him.'

" 'It is very possible. We took no pains to hide it.'

" 'He simply wished, I should imagine, to refresh his memory upon that last occasion. He had, as I understand, some sort of map or chart which he was comparing with the manuscript, and which he thrust into his pocket when you appeared.'

" 'That is true. But what could he have to do with this old family custom of ours, and what does this rigmarole mean?'

" 'I don't think that we should have much difficulty in determining that,' said I; 'with your permission we will take the first train down to Sussex and go a little more deeply into the matter upon the spot.'

"The same afternoon saw us both at Hurlstone. Possibly you have seen pictures and read descriptions of the famous old building, so I will confine my account of it to saying that it is built in the shape of an L, the long arm being the more modern portion, and the shorter the ancient nucleus from which the other has developed. Over the low, heavy-lintelled door, in the centre of this old part, is chiselled the date, 1607, but experts are agreed that the beams and stonework are really much older than this. The enormously thick walls and tiny windows of this part had in the last century driven the family into building the new wing, and the old one was used now as a storehouse and a cellar, when it was used at all. A splendid park with fine old timber surrounds the house, and the lake, to which my client had referred, lay close to the avenue, about two hundred yards from the building.

"I was already firmly convinced, Watson, that there were not three separate mysteries here, but one only, and that if I could read the Musgrave Ritual aright I should hold in my hand the clue which would lead me to the truth concerning both the butler Brunton and the maid Howells. To that then I turned all my energies. Why should this servant be so anxious to master this old formula? Evidently because he saw something in it which had escaped all those generations of country squires, and from which he expected some personal advantage. What was it then, and how had it affected his fate?

"It was perfectly obvious to me, on reading the Ritual, that the measurements must refer to some spot to which the rest of the document alluded, and that if we could find that spot we should be in a fair way towards finding what the secret was which the old Musgraves had thought it necessary to embalm in so curious a fashion. There were two guides given us to start with, an oak and an elm. As to the oak there could be no question at all. Right in front of the house, upon the left-hand side of the drive, there stood a patriarch among oaks, one of the most magnificent trees I have ever seen.

" 'That was there when your Ritual was drawn up,' said I as we drove past it.

" 'It was there at the Norman Conquest in all probability,' he answered. 'It has a girth of twenty-three feet.'

"Here was one of my fixed points secured.

" 'Have you any old elms?' I asked.

" 'There used to be a very old one over yonder, but it was struck by lightning ten years ago, and we cut down the stump.'

" 'You can see where it used to be?'

" 'Oh, yes.'

" 'There are no other elms?'

" 'No old ones, but plenty of beeches.'

" 'I should like to see where it grew.'

"We had driven up in a dog-cart, and my client led me away at once, without our entering the house, to the scar on the lawn where the elm had stood. It was nearly midway between the oak and the house. My investigation seemed to be progressing.

" 'I suppose it is impossible to find out how high the elm was?' I asked.

" 'I can give you it at once. It was sixty-four feet.'

" 'How do you come to know it?' I asked in surprise.

" 'When my old tutor used to give me an exercise in trigonometry, it always took the shape of measuring heights. When I was a lad I worked out every tree and building in the estate.'

"This was an unexpected piece of luck. My data were coming more quickly than I could have reasonably hoped.

" 'Tell me,' I asked, 'did your butler ever ask you such a question?'

"Reginald Musgrave looked at me in astonishment. 'Now that you call it to my mind,' he answered, 'Brunton *did* ask me about the height of the tree some months ago in connection with some little argument with the groom.'

"This was excellent news, Watson, for it showed me that I was on the right road. I looked up at the sun. It was low in the heavens, and I calculated that in less than an hour it would lie just above the topmost branches of the old oak. One condition mentioned in the Ritual would then be fulfilled. And the shadow of the elm must mean the farther end of the shadow, otherwise the trunk would have been chosen as the guide. I had, then, to find where the far end of the shadow would fall when the sun was just clear of the oak."

"That must have been difficult, Holmes, when the elm was no longer there."

"Well, at least I knew that if Brunton could do it, I could also. Besides, there was no real difficulty. I went with Musgrave to his study and whittled myself this peg, to which I tied this long string with a knot at each yard. Then I took two lengths of a fishing-rod, which came to just six feet, and I went back with my client to where the elm had been. The sun was just grazing the top of the oak. I fastened the rod on end, marked out the direction of the shadow, and measured it. It was nine feet in length.

"Of course the calculation now was a simple one. If a rod of six feet threw a shadow of nine, a tree of sixty-four feet would throw one of ninety-six, and the line of the one would of course be the line of the other. I measured out the distance, which brought me almost to the wall of the house, and I thrust a peg into the spot. You can imagine my exultation, Watson, when within two inches of my peg I saw a conical depression in the ground. I knew that it was the mark made by Brunton in his measurements, and that I was still upon his trail.

"From this starting-point I proceeded to step, having first taken the cardinal points by my pocket-compass. Ten steps with each foot took me along parallel with the wall of the house, and again I marked my spot with a peg. Then I carefully paced off five to the east and two to the south. It brought me to the very threshold of the old door. Two steps to the west meant now that I was to go two paces down the stone-flagged passage, and this was the place indicated by the Ritual.

"Never have I felt such a cold chill of disappointment, Watson. For a moment it seemed to me that there must be some radical mistake in my calculations. The setting sun shone full upon the passage floor, and I could see that the old, foot-worn grey stones with which it was paved were firmly cemented together, and had certainly not been moved for many a long year. Brunton had not been at work here. I tapped upon the floor, but it sounded the same all over, and there was no sign of any crack or crevice. But, fortunately, Musgrave, who had begun to appreciate the meaning of my proceedings, and who was now as excited as myself, took out his manuscript to check my calculations.

"'And under,' he cried. 'You have omitted the "and under."'

"I had thought that it meant that we were to dig, but now, of course, I saw at once that I was wrong. 'There is a cellar under this then?' I cried.

"'Yes, and as old as the house. Down here, through this door.'

"We went down a winding stone stair, and my companion, striking a match, lit a large lantern which stood on a barrel in the corner. In an instant it was obvious that we had at last come upon the true place, and that we had not been the only people to visit the spot recently.

"It had been used for the storage of wood, but the billets, which had evidently been littered over the floor, were now piled at the sides, so as to leave a clear space in the middle. In this space lay a large and heavy flagstone with a rusted iron ring in the centre to which a thick shepherd's-check muffler was attached.

"'By Jove!' cried my client. "That's Brunton's muffler. I have seen it on him and could swear to it. What has the villain been doing here?'

"At my suggestion a couple of the county police were summoned to be present, and I then endeavoured to raise the stone by pulling on the cravat. I could only move it slightly, and it was with the aid of one of the constables that I succeeded at last in carrying it to one side. A black hole yawned beneath into which we all peered, while Musgrave, kneeling at the side, pushed down the lantern.

"A small chamber about seven feet deep and four feet square lay open to us. At one side of this was a squat, brass-bound wooden box, the lid of which was hinged upward, with this curious old-fashioned key projecting from the lock. It was furred outside by a thick layer of dust, and damp and worms had eaten through the wood, so that a crop of livid fungi was growing on the inside of it. Several discs of metal, old coins apparently, such as I hold here, were scattered over the bottom of the box, but it contained nothing else.

"At the moment, however, we had no thought for the old chest, for our eyes were riveted upon that which crouched beside it. It was the figure of a man, clad in a suit of black, who squatted down upon his hams with his forehead sunk upon the edge of the box and his two arms thrown out on each side of it. The attitude had drawn all the stagnant blood to the face, and no man could have recognised that distorted liver-coloured countenance; but his height, his dress, and his hair were all sufficient to show my client, when we had drawn the body up, that it was indeed his missing butler. He had been dead some days, but there was no wound or bruise upon his person to show how he had met his dreadful end. When his body had been carried from the cellar we found ourselves still confronted with a problem which was almost as formidable as that with which we had started.

"I confess that so far, Watson, I had been disappointed in my investigation. I had reckoned upon solving the matter when once I had found the place referred to in the Ritual; but now I was there and was apparently as far as ever from knowing what it was which the family had concealed with such elaborate precautions. It is true that I had thrown a light upon the fate of Brunton, but now I had to ascertain how that fate had come upon him, and what part had been played in the matter by the woman who had disappeared. I sat down upon a keg in the corner and thought the whole matter carefully over.

"You know my methods in such cases, Watson. I put myself in the man's place, and having first gauged his intelligence, I try to imagine how I should myself have proceeded under the same circumstances. In this case the matter was simplified by Brunton's intelligence being quite first-rate, so that it was unnecessary to make any allowance for the personal equation, as the astronomers have dubbed it. He knew that something valuable was concealed. He had spotted the place. He found that the stone which covered it was just too heavy for a man to move unaided. What would he do next? He could not get help from outside, even if he had someone whom he could trust, without the unbarring of doors and considerable risk of detection. It was better, if he could, to have his helpmate inside the house. But whom could he ask? This girl had been devoted to him. A man always finds it hard to realize that he may have finally lost a woman's love, however badly he may have treated her. He would try by a few attentions to make his peace with the girl Howells, and then would engage her as his accomplice. Together they would come at night to the cellar, and their united force would suffice to raise the stone. So far I could follow their actions as if I had actually seen them.

"But for two of them, and one a woman, it must have been heavy work, the raising of that stone. A burly Sussex policeman and I had found it no light job. What would they do to assist them? Probably what I should have done myself. I rose and examined carefully the different billets of wood which were scattered around the floor. Almost at once I came upon what I expected. One piece, about three feet in length, had a very marked indentation at one end, while several were flattened at the sides as if they had been compressed by some considerable weight. Evidently, as they had dragged the stone up, they had thrust the chunks of wood into the chink until at last when the opening was large enough to crawl through, they would hold it open by a billet placed lengthwise, which might very well become indented at the lower end, since the whole weight of the stone would press it down on to the edge of this other slab. So far I was still on safe ground.

"And now how was I to proceed to reconstruct this midnight drama? Clearly, only one could fit into the hole, and that one was Brunton. The girl must have waited above. Brunton then unlocked the box, handed up the contents presumably—since they were not to be found—and then—and then what happened?

"What smouldering fire of vengeance had suddenly sprung into flame in this passionate Celtic woman's soul when she saw the man who had wronged her—wronged her, perhaps, far more than we suspected—in her power? Was it a chance that the wood had slipped and that the stone had shut Brunton into what had become his sepulchre? Had she only been guilty of silence as to his fate? Or had some sudden blow from her hand dashed the support away and sent the slab crashing down into its place? Be that as it might, I seemed to see that woman's figure still clutching at her treasure trove and flying wildly up the winding stair, with her ears ringing perhaps with the muffled screams from behind her and with the drumming of frenzied hands against the slab of stone which was choking her faithless lover's life out.

"Here was the secret of her blanched face, her shaken nerves, her peals of hysterical laughter on the next morning. But what had been in the box? What had she done with that? Of course, it must have been the old metal and pebbles which my client had dragged from the mere. She had thrown them in there at the first opportunity to remove the last trace of her crime.

"For twenty minutes I had sat motionless, thinking the matter out. Musgrave still stood with a very pale face, swinging his lantern and peering down into the hole.

"'These are coins of Charles the First,' said he, holding out the few which had been in the box; 'you see we were right in fixing our date for the Ritual.'

"'We may find something else of Charles the First,' I cried, as the probable meaning of the first two questions of the Ritual broke suddenly upon me. 'Let me see the contents of the bag which you fished from the mere.'

"We ascended to his study, and he laid the débris before

me. I could understand his regarding it as of small importance when I looked at it, for the metal was almost black
and the stones lustreless and dull. I rubbed one of them on
my sleeve, however, and it glowed afterwards like a spark
in the dark hollow of my hand. The metal work was in the
form of a double ring, but it had been bent and twisted out
of its original shape.

"'You must bear in mind,' said I, 'that the royal party
made head in England even after the death of the king,
and that when they at last fled they probably left many of
their most precious possessions buried behind them, with
the intention of returning for them in more peaceful
times.'

"'My ancestor, Sir Ralph Musgrave, was a prominent
cavalier and the right-hand man of Charles the Second in
his wanderings,' said my friend.

"'Ah, indeed!' I answered. 'Well now, I think that really
should give us the last link that we wanted. I must congratulate you on coming into the possession, though in
rather a tragic manner, of a relic which is of great intrinsic
value, but of even greater importance as a historical
curiosity.'

"'What is it, then?' he gasped in astonishment.

"'It is nothing less than the ancient crown of the kings of
England.'

"'The crown!'

"'Precisely. Consider what the Ritual says. How does it
run? "Whose was it?" "His who is gone." That was after the
execution of Charles. Then, "Who shall have it?" "He who
will come." That was Charles the Second, whose advent
was already foreseen. There can, I think, be no doubt that
this battered and shapeless diadem once encircled the
brows of the royal Stuarts.'

"'And how came it in the pond?'

"'Ah, that is a question that will take some time to
answer.' And with that I sketched out to him the whole
long chain of surmise and of proof which I had constructed. The twilight had closed in and the moon was

281

shining brightly in the sky before my narrative was finished.

"'And how was it then that Charles did not get his crown when he returned?' asked Musgrave, pushing back the relic into its linen bag.

"'Ah, there you lay your finger upon the one point which we shall probably never be able to clear up. It is likely that the Musgrave who held the secret died in the interval and by some oversight left this guide to his descendant without explaining the meaning of it. From that day to this it has been handed down from father to son, until at last it came within reach of a man who tore its secret out of it and lost his life in the venture.'

"And that's the story of the Musgrave Ritual, Watson. They have the crown down at Hurlstone—though they had some legal bother and a considerable sum to pay before they were allowed to retain it. I am sure that if you mentioned my name they would be happy to show it to you. Of the woman nothing was ever heard, and the probability is that she got away out of England and carried herself and the memory of her crime to some land beyond the seas."

The Naval Treaty

The July which immediately succeeded my marriage was made memorable by three cases of interest, in which I had the privilege of being associated with Sherlock Holmes and of studying his methods. I find them recorded in my notes under the headings of "The Adventure of the Second Stain," "The Adventure of the Naval Treaty," and "The Adventure of the Tired Captain." The first of these, however, deals with interests of such importance and implicates so many of the first families in the kingdom that for many years it will be impossible to make it public. No case, however, in which Holmes was engaged has ever illustrated the value of his analytical methods so clearly or has impressed those who were associated with him so deeply. I still retain an almost *verbatim* report of the interview in which he demonstrated the true facts of the case to Monsieur Dubugue of the Paris police, and Fritz von Waldbaum, the well-known specialist of Dantzig, both of whom had wasted their energies upon what proved to be side-issues. The new century will have come, however, before the story can be safely told. Meanwhile I pass on to the second on my list, which promised also at one time to be of national importance and was marked by several incidents which give it a quite unique character.

During my school-days I had been intimately associated with a lad named Percy Phelps, who was of much the same age as myself, though he was two classes ahead of me. He was a very brilliant boy and carried away every prize which the school had to offer, finishing his exploits by winning a scholarship which sent him on to continue his triumphant career at Cambridge. He was, I remember, extremely well connected, and even when we were all little boys together we knew that his mother's brother was Lord Holdhurst, the great conservative politician. This gaudy relationship did him little good at school. On the contrary, it seemed rather a piquant thing to us to chevy him about the playground and hit him over the shins with a wicket. But it was another thing when he came out into the world. I heard vaguely that his abilities and the influences which he commanded had won him a good position at the Foreign Office, and then he passed completely out of my mind until the following letter recalled his existence:

Briarbrae, Woking

My dear Watson:

I have no doubt that you can remember "Tadpole" Phelps, who was in the fifth form when you were in the third. It is possible even that you may have heard that through my uncle's influence I obtained a good appointment at the Foreign Office, and that I was in a situation of trust and honour until a horrible misfortune came suddenly to blast my career.

There is no use writing the details of that dreadful event. In the event of your acceding to my request it is probable that I shall have to narrate them to you. I have only just recovered from nine weeks of brain-fever and am still exceedingly weak. Do you think that you could bring your friend Mr. Holmes down to see me? I should like to have his opinion of the case, though the authorities assure me that nothing more can be done. Do try to bring him down, and as soon as possible. Every minute seems an hour while I live in this state of horrible suspense. Assure him that if I have not asked his advice sooner it was not because I did not appreciate his talents, but because I have been off my head ever since the blow fell. Now I am clear again, though I dare not think of it too much for fear of a relapse. I am still so weak that I have to write, as you see, by dictating. Do try to bring him.

Your old school-fellow,
Percy Phelps

There was something that touched me as I read this letter,

something pitiable in the reiterated appeals to bring Holmes. So moved was I that even had it been a difficult matter I should have tried it, but of course I knew well that Holmes loved his art, so that he was ever as ready to bring his aid as his client could be to receive it. My wife agreed with me that not a moment should be lost in laying the matter before him, and so within an hour of breakfast-time I found myself back once more in the old rooms in Baker Street.

Holmes was seated at his side-table clad in his dressing-gown and working hard over a chemical investigation. A large curved retort was boiling furiously in the bluish flame of a Bunsen burner, and the distilled drops were condensing into a two-litre measure. My friend hardly glanced up as I entered, and I, seeing that his investigation must be of importance, seated myself in an armchair and waited. He dipped into this bottle or that, drawing out a few drops of each with his glass pipette, and finally brought a test-tube containing a solution over to the table. In his right hand he held a slip of litmus-paper.

"You come at a crisis, Watson," said he. "If this paper remains blue, all is well. If it turns red, it means a man's life." He dipped it into the test-tube and it flushed at once into a dull, dirty crimson. "Hum! I thought as much!" he cried. "I will be at your service in an instant, Watson. You will find tobacco in the Persian slipper." He turned to his desk and scribbled off several telegrams, which were handed over to the page-boy. Then he threw himself down into the chair opposite and drew up his knees until his fingers clasped round his long, thin shins.

"A very commonplace little murder," said he. "You've got something better, I fancy. You are the stormy petrel of crime, Watson. What is it?"

I handed him the letter, which he read with the most concentrated attention.

"It does not tell us very much, does it?" he remarked as he handed it back to me.

"Hardly anything."

"And yet the writing is of interest."

"But the writing is not his own."

"Precisely. It is a woman's."

"A man's surely," I cried.

"No, a woman's, and a woman of rare character. You see, at the commencement of an investigation it is something to know that your client is in close contact with someone who, for good or evil, has an exceptional nature. My interest is already awakened in the case. If you are ready we will start at once for Woking and see this diplomatist who is in such evil case and the lady to whom he dictates his letters."

We were fortunate enough to catch an early train at Waterloo, and in a little under an hour we found ourselves among the fir-woods and the heather of Woking. Briarbrae proved to be a large detached house standing in extensive grounds within a few minutes' walk of the station. On sending in our cards we were shown into an elegantly appointed drawing-room, where we were joined in a few minutes by a rather stout man who received us with much hospitality. His age may have been nearer forty than thirty, but his cheeks were so ruddy and his eyes so merry that he still conveyed the impression of a plump and mischievous boy.

"I am so glad that you have come," said he, shaking our hands with effusion. "Percy has been inquiring for you all morning. Ah, poor old chap, he clings to any straw! His father and his mother asked me to see you, for the mere mention of the subject is very painful to them."

"We have had no details yet," observed Holmes. "I perceive that you are not yourself a member of the family."

Our acquaintance looked surprised, and then, glancing down, he began to laugh.

"Of course you saw the J H monogram on my locket," said he. "For a moment I thought you had done something clever. Joseph Harrison is my name, and as Percy is to marry my sister Annie I shall at least be a relation by marriage. You will find my sister in his room, for she has nursed him hand and foot this two months back. Perhaps we'd better go in at once, for I know how impatient he is."

The chamber into which we were shown was on the same floor as the drawing-room. It was furnished partly as a sitting and partly as a bedroom, with flowers arranged daintily in every nook and corner. A young man, very pale and worn, was lying upon a sofa near the open window, through which came the rich scent of the garden and the balmy summer air. A woman was sitting beside him, who rose as we entered.

"Shall I leave, Percy?" she asked.

He clutched her hand to detain her. "How are you, Watson?" said he cordially. "I should never have known you under that moustache, and I daresay you would not be prepared to swear to me. This I presume is your celebrated friend, Mr. Sherlock Holmes?"

I introduced him in a few words, and we both sat down. The stout young man had left us, but his sister still remained with her hand in that of the invalid. She was a striking-looking woman, a little short and thick for symmetry, but with a beautiful olive complexion, large, dark, Italian eyes, and a wealth of deep black hair. Her rich tints made the white face of her companion the more worn and haggard by the contrast.

"I won't waste your time," said he, raising himself upon the sofa. "I'll plunge into the matter without further preamble. I was a happy and successful man, Mr. Holmes, and on the eve of being married, when a sudden and dreadful misfortune wrecked all my prospects in life.

"I was, as Watson may have told you, in the Foreign Office, and through the influence of my uncle, Lord Holdhurst, I rose rapidly to a responsible position. When my uncle became Foreign Minister in this administration he gave me several missions of trust, and as I always brought them to a successful conclusion, he came at last to have the utmost confidence in my ability and tact.

"Nearly ten weeks ago—to be more accurate, on the twenty-third of May—he called me into his private room, and after complimenting me on the good work which I had done, he informed me that he had a new commission of trust for me to execute.

" 'This,' said he, taking a grey roll of paper from his bureau, 'is the original of that secret treaty between England and Italy of which, I regret to say, some rumours have already got into the public press. It is of enormous importance that nothing further should leak out. The French or the Russian Embassy would pay an immense sum to learn the contents of these papers. They should not leave my bureau were it not that it is absolutely necessary to have them copied. You have a desk in your office?'

" 'Yes, sir.'

" 'Then take the treaty and lock it up there. I shall give directions that you may remain behind when the others go, so that you may copy it at your leisure without fear of being overlooked. When you have finished, relock both the original and the draft in the desk and hand them over to me personally to-morrow morning.'

"I took the papers and—"

"Excuse me an instant," said Holmes. "Were you alone during this conversation?"

"Absolutely."

"In a large room?"

"Thirty feet each way."

"In the centre?"

"Yes, about it."

"And speaking low?"

"My uncle's voice is always remarkably low. I hardly spoke at all."

"Thank you," said Holmes, shutting his eyes; "pray go on."

"I did exactly what he indicated and waited until the other clerks had departed. One of them in my room, Charles Gorot, had some arrears of work to make up, so I left him there and went out to dine. When I returned he was gone. I was anxious to hurry my work, for I knew that Joseph—the Mr. Harrison whom you saw just now—was in town, and that he would travel down to Woking by the eleven-o'clock train, and I wanted if possible to catch it.

"When I came to examine the treaty I saw at once that it was of such importance that my uncle had been guilty of no exaggeration in what he said. Without going into details, I may say that it defined the position of Great Britain towards the Triple Alliance, and foreshadowed the policy which this country would pursue in the event of the French fleet gaining a complete ascendency over that of Italy in the Mediterranean. The questions treated in it were purely naval. At the end were the signatures of the high dignitaries who had signed it. I glanced my eyes over it and then settled down to my task of copying.

"It was a long document, written in the French language and containing twenty-six separate articles. I copied as quickly as I could, but at nine o'clock I had only done nine articles, and it seemed hopeless for me to attempt to catch my train. I was feeling drowsy and stupid, partly from my dinner and also from the effects of a long day's work. A cup of coffee would clear my brain. A Commissionaire remains all night in a little lodge at the foot of the stairs and is in the habit of making coffee at his spirit-lamp for any of the officials who may be working overtime. I rang the bell, therefore, to summon him.

"To my surprise, it was a woman who answered the summons, a large, coarse-faced, elderly woman, in an apron. She explained that she was the Commissionaire's wife, who did the charing, and I gave her the order for the coffee.

"I wrote two more articles, and then, feeling more drowsy than ever, I rose and walked up and down the room to stretch my legs. My coffee had not yet come, and I wondered what the cause of the delay could be. Opening the door, I started down the corridor to find out. There was a straight passage, dimly lighted, which led from the room in which I had been working, and was the only exit from it. It ended in a curving staircase, with the Commissionaire's lodge in the passage at the bottom. Halfway down this staircase is a small landing, with another passage running into it at right angles. This second one leads by means of a second small stair to a side door, used by servants, and also as a short cut by clerks when coming from Charles Street. Here is a rough chart of the place."

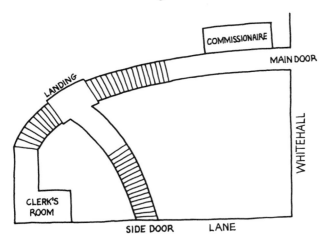

"Thank you. I think that I quite follow you," said Sherlock Holmes.

"It is of the utmost importance that you should notice this point. I went down the stairs and into the hall, where I found the Commissionaire fast asleep in his box, with the kettle boiling furiously upon the spirit-lamp. I took off the kettle and blew out the lamp, for the water was spurting over the floor. Then I put out my hand and was about to shake the man, who was still sleeping soundly, when a bell over his head rang loudly, and he woke with a start.

"'Mr. Phelps, sir!' said he, looking at me in bewilderment.

"'I came down to see if my coffee was ready.'

"'I was boiling the kettle when I fell asleep, sir.' He looked at me and then up at the still quivering bell with an ever-growing astonishment upon his face.

"'If you was here, sir, then who rang the bell?' he asked.

"'The bell!' I cried. 'What bell is it?'

"'It's the bell of the room you were working in.'

"A cold hand seemed to close round my heart. Someone, then, was in that room where my precious treaty lay upon the table. I ran frantically up the stair and along the passage. There was no one in the corridors, Mr. Holmes. There was no one in the room. All was exactly as I left it, save only that the papers which had been committed to my care had been taken from the desk on which they lay. The copy was there, and the original was gone."

Holmes sat up in his chair and rubbed his hands. I could see that the problem was entirely to his heart. "Pray, what did you do then?" he murmured.

"I recognised in an instant that the thief must have come up the stairs from the side door. Of course I must have met him if he had come the other way."

"You were satisfied that he could not have been concealed in the room all the time, or in the corridor which you have just described as dimly lighted?"

"It is absolutely impossible. A rat could not conceal himself either in the room or the corridor. There is no cover at all."

"Thank you. Pray proceed."

"The Commissionaire, seeing by my pale face that something was to be feared, had followed me upstairs. Now we both rushed along the corridor and down the steep steps which led to Charles Street. The door at the bottom was closed but unlocked. We flung it open and rushed out. I can distinctly remember that as we did so there came three chimes from a neighbouring clock. It was a quarter to ten."

"That is of enormous importance," said Holmes, making a note upon his shirt-cuff.

"The night was very dark, and a thin, warm rain was falling. There was no one in Charles Street, but a great traffic was going on, as usual, in Whitehall, at the extremity. We rushed along the pavement, bare-headed as we were, and at the far corner we found a policeman standing.

"'A robbery has been committed,' I gasped. 'A document of immense value has been stolen from the Foreign Office. Has anyone passed this way?'

"'I have been standing here for a quarter of an hour, sir,' said he, 'only one person has passed during that time—a woman, tall and elderly, with a Paisley shawl.'

"'Ah, that is only my wife,' cried the Commissionaire; 'has no one else passed?'

" 'No one.'

" 'Then it must be the other way that the thief took,' cried the fellow, tugging at my sleeve.

"But I was not satisfied, and the attempts which he made to draw me away increased my suspicions.

" 'Which way did the woman go?' I cried.

" 'I don't know, sir. I noticed her pass, but I had no special reason for watching her. She seemed to be in a hurry.'

" 'How long ago was it?'

" 'Oh, not very many minutes.'

" 'Within the last five?'

" 'Well, it could not be more than five.'

" 'You're only wasting your time, sir, and every minute now is of importance,' cried the Commissionaire; 'take my word for it that my old woman has nothing to do with it and come down to the other end of the street. Well, if you won't, I will.' And with that he rushed off in the other direction.

"But I was after him in an instant and caught him by the sleeve.

" 'Where do you live?' said I.

" '16 Ivy Lane, Brixton,' he answered. 'But don't let yourself be drawn away upon a false scent, Mr. Phelps. Come to the other end of the street and let us see if we can hear of anything.'

"Nothing was to be lost by following his advice. With the policeman we both hurried down, but only to find the street full of traffic, many people coming and going, but all only too eager to get to a place of safety upon so wet a night. There was no lounger who could tell us who had passed.

"Then we returned to the office and searched the stairs and the passage without result. The corridor which led to the room was laid down with a kind of creamy linoleum which shows an impression very easily. We examined it very carefully, but found no outline of any footmark."

"Had it been raining all evening?"

"Since about seven."

"How is it, then, that the woman who came into the

room about nine left no traces with her muddy boots?"

"I am glad you raised the point. It occurred to me at the time. The charwomen are in the habit of taking off their boots at the Commissionaire's office and putting on list slippers."

"That is very clear. There were no marks, then, though the night was a wet one? The chain of events is certainly one of extraordinary interest. What did you do next?"

"We examined the room also. There is no possibility of a secret door, and the windows are quite thirty feet from the ground. Both of them were fastened on the inside. The carpet prevents any possibility of a trap-door, and the ceiling is of the ordinary whitewashed kind. I will pledge my life that whoever stole my papers could only have come through the door."

"How about the fireplace?"

"They use none. There is a stove. The bell-rope hangs from the wire just to the right of my desk. Whoever rang it must have come right up to the desk to do it. But why should any criminal wish to ring the bell? It is a most insoluble mystery."

"Certainly the incident was unusual. What were your next steps? You examined the room, I presume, to see if the intruder had left any traces—any cigar-end or dropped glove or hairpin or other trifle?"

"There was nothing of the sort."

"No smell?"

"Well, we never thought of that."

"Ah, a scent of tobacco would have been worth a great deal to us in such an investigation."

"I never smoke myself, so I think I should have observed it if there had been any smell of tobacco. There was absolutely no clue of any kind. The only tangible fact was that the Commissionaire's wife—Mrs. Tangey was the name—had hurried out of the place. He could give no explanation save that it was about the time when the woman always went home. The policeman and I agreed that our best plan would be to seize the woman before she could get rid of the papers, presuming that she had them.

"The alarm had reached Scotland Yard by this time, and Mr. Forbes, the detective, came round at once and took up the case with a great deal of energy. We hired a hansom, and in half an hour we were at the address which had been given to us. A young woman opened the door, who proved to be Mrs. Tangey's eldest daughter. Her mother had not come back yet, and we were shown into the front room to wait.

"About ten minutes later a knock came at the door, and here we made the one serious mistake for which I blame myself. Instead of opening the door ourselves, we allowed the girl to do so. We heard her say, 'Mother, there are two men in the house waiting to see you,' and an instant afterwards we heard the patter of feet rushing down the passage. Forbes flung open the door, and we both ran into the back room or kitchen, but the woman had got there before us. She stared at us with defiant eyes, and then, suddenly recognising me, an expression of absolute astonishment came over her face.

"'Why, if it isn't Mr. Phelps, of the office!' she cried.

"'Come, come, who did you think we were when you ran away from us?' asked my companion.

"'I thought you were the brokers,' said she; 'we have had some trouble with a tradesman.'

"'That's not quite good enough,' answered Forbes. 'We have reason to believe that you have taken a paper of importance from the Foreign Office, and that you ran in here to dispose of it. You must come back with us to Scotland Yard to be searched.'

"It was in vain that she protested and resisted. A four-wheeler was brought, and we all three drove back in it. We had first made an examination of the kitchen, and especially of the kitchen fire, to see whether she might have made away with the papers during the instant that she was alone. There were no signs, however, of any ashes or scraps. When we reached Scotland Yard she was handed over at once to the female searcher. I waited in an agony of suspense until she came back with her report. There were no signs of the papers.

"Then for the first time the horror of my situation came in its full force. Hitherto I had been acting, and action had numbed thought. I had been so confident of regaining the treaty at once that I had not dared to think of what would be the consequence if I failed to do so. But now there was nothing more to be done, and I had leisure to realize my position. It was horrible. Watson there would tell you that I was a nervous, sensitive boy at school. It is my nature. I thought of my uncle and of his colleagues in the Cabinet, of the shame which I had brought upon him, upon myself, upon everyone connected with me. What though I was the victim of an extraordinary accident? No allowance is made for accidents where diplomatic interests are at stake. I was ruined, shamefully, hopelessly ruined. I don't know what I did. I fancy I must have made a scene. I have a dim recollection of a group of officials who crowded round me, endeavouring to soothe me. One of them drove down with me to Waterloo and saw me into the Woking train. I believe that he would have come all the way had it not been that Dr. Ferrier, who lives near me, was going down by that very train. The Doctor most kindly took charge of me, and it was well he did so, for I had a fit in the station, and before we reached home I was practically a raving maniac.

"You can imagine the state of things here when they were roused from their beds by the Doctor's ringing and found me in this condition. Poor Annie here and my mother were broken-hearted. Dr. Ferrier had just heard enough from the detective at the station to be able to give an idea of what had happened, and his story did not mend matters. It was evident to all that I was in for a long illness, so Joseph was bundled out of this cheery bedroom, and it was turned into a sick-room for me. Here I have lain, Mr. Holmes, for over nine weeks, unconscious and raving with brain-fever. If it had not been for Miss Harrison here and for the Doctor's care, I should not be speaking to you now. She has nursed me by day and a hired nurse has looked after me by night, for in my mad fits I was capable of anything. Slowly my reason has cleared, but it is only during the last three days that my memory has quite returned. Sometimes I wish that it never had. The first thing that I did was to wire to Mr. Forbes, who had the case in hand. He came out, and assures me that, though everything has been done, no trace of a clue has been discovered. The Commissionaire and his wife have been examined in every way without any light being thrown upon the matter. The suspicions of the police then rested upon young Gorot, who, as you may remember, stayed overtime in the office that night. His remaining behind and his French name were really the only two points which could suggest suspicion; but, as a matter of fact, I did not begin work until he had gone, and his people are of Huguenot extraction, but as English in sympathy and tradition as you and I are. Nothing was found to implicate him in any way, and there the matter dropped. I turn to you, Mr. Holmes, as absolutely my last hope. If you fail me, then my honour as well as my position are forever forfeited."

The invalid sank back upon his cushions, tired out by this long recital, while his nurse poured him out a glass of some stimulating medicine. Holmes sat silently, with his head thrown back and his eyes closed, in an attitude which might seem listless to a stranger, but which I knew betokened the most intense self-absorption.

"Your statement has been so explicit," said he at last, "that you have really left me very few questions to ask. There is one of the very utmost importance, however. Did you tell anyone that you had this special task to perform?"

"No one."

"Not Miss Harrison here, for example?"

"No. I had not been back to Woking between getting the order and executing the commission."

"And none of your people had by chance been to see you?"

"None."

"Did any of them know their way about in the office?"

"Oh, yes, all of them had been shown over it."

"Still, of course, if you said nothing to anyone about the treaty these inquiries are irrelevant."

"I said nothing."

"Do you know anything of the Commissionaire?"

"Nothing except that he is an old soldier."

"What regiment?"

"Oh, I have heard—Coldstream Guards."

"Thank you. I have no doubt I can get details from Forbes. The authorities are excellent at amassing facts, though they do not always use them to advantage. What a lovely thing a rose is!"

He walked past the couch to the open window and held up the drooping stalk of a moss-rose, looking down at the dainty blend of crimson and green. It was a new phase of his character to me, for I had never before seen him show any keen interest in natural objects.

"There is nothing in which deduction is so necessary as in religion," said he, leaning with his back against the shutters. "It can be built up as an exact science by the reasoner. Our highest assurance of the goodness of Providence seems to me to rest in the flowers. All other things, our powers, our desires, our food, are all really necessary for our existence in the first instance. But this rose is an extra. Its smell and its colour are an embellishment of life, not a condition of it. It is only goodness which gives extras, and so I say again that we have much to hope from the flowers."

Percy Phelps and his nurse looked at Holmes during this demonstration with surprise and a good deal of disappointment written upon their faces. He had fallen into a reverie, with the moss-rose between his fingers. It had lasted some minutes before the young lady broke in upon it.

"Do you see any prospect of solving this mystery, Mr. Holmes?" she asked with a touch of asperity in her voice.

"Oh, the mystery!" he answered, coming back with a start to the realities of life. "Well, it would be absurd to deny that the case is a very abstruse and complicated one, but I can promise you that I will look into the matter and let you know any points which may strike me."

"Do you see any clue?"

"You have furnished me with seven, but of course I must test them before I can pronounce upon their value."

"You suspect someone?"

"I suspect myself."

"What!"

"Of coming to conclusions too rapidly."

"Then go to London and test your conclusions."

"Your advice is very excellent, Miss Harrison," said Holmes, rising. "I think, Watson, we cannot do better. Do not allow yourself to indulge in false hopes, Mr. Phelps. The affair is a very tangled one."

"I shall be in a fever until I see you again," cried the diplomatist.

"Well, I'll come out by the same train to-morrow, though it's more than likely that my report will be a negative one."

"God bless you for promising to come," cried our client. "It gives me fresh life to know that something is being done. By the way, I have had a letter from Lord Holdhurst."

"Ha! What did he say?"

"He was cold, but not harsh. I dare say my severe illness prevented him from being that. He repeated that the matter was of the utmost importance and added that no steps would be taken about my future—by which he means, of course, my dismissal—until my health was restored and I had an opportunity of repairing my misfortune."

"Well, that was reasonable and considerate," said Holmes. "Come, Watson, for we have a good day's work before us in town."

Mr. Joseph Harrison drove us down to the station, and we were soon whirling up in a Portsmouth train. Holmes was sunk in profound thought and hardly opened his mouth until we had passed Clapham Junction.

"It's a very cheery thing to come into London by any of

these lines which run high and allow you to look down upon the houses like this."

I thought he was joking, for the view was sordid enough, but he soon explained himself.

"Look at those big, isolated clumps of buildings rising up above the slates, like brick islands in a lead-coloured sea."

"The board-schools."

"Light-houses, my boy! Beacons of the future! Capsules with hundreds of bright little seeds in each, out of which will spring the wiser, better England of the future. I suppose that man Phelps does not drink?"

"I should not think so."

"Nor should I, but we are bound to take every possibility into account. The poor devil has certainly got himself into very deep water, and it's a question whether we shall ever be able to get him ashore. What do you think of Miss Harrison?"

"A girl of strong character."

"Yes, but she is a good sort, or I am mistaken. She and her brother are the only children of an iron-master somewhere up Northumberland way. He got engaged to her when travelling last winter, and she came down to be introduced to his people, with her brother as escort. Then came the smash, and she stayed on to nurse her lover, while brother Joseph, finding himself pretty snug, stayed on, too. I've been making a few independent inquiries, you see. But to-day must be a day of inquiries."

"My practice—" I began.

"Oh, if you find your own cases more interesting than mine—" said Holmes with some asperity.

"I was going to say that my practice could get along very well for a day or two, since it is the slackest time in the year."

"Excellent," said he, recovering his good-humour. "Then we'll look into this matter together. I think that we should begin by seeing Forbes. He can probably tell us all the details we want until we know from what side the case is to be approached."

"You said you had a clue?"

"Well, we have several, but we can only test their value by further inquiry. The most difficult crime to track is the one which is purposeless. Now this is not purposeless. Who is it who profits by it? There is the French Ambassador, there is the Russian, there is whoever might sell it to either of these, and there is Lord Holdhurst."

"Lord Holdhurst!"

"Well, it is just conceivable that a statesman might find himself in a position where he was not sorry to have such a document accidentally destroyed."

"Not a statesman with the honourable record of Lord Holdhurst?"

"It is a possibility and we cannot afford to disregard it. We shall see the noble lord to-day and find out if he can tell us anything. Meanwhile I have already set inquiries on foot."

"Already?"

"Yes, I sent wires from Woking station to every evening paper in London. This advertisement will appear in each of them."

He handed over a sheet torn from a note-book. On it was scribbled in pencil:

£10 reward, The number of the cab which dropped a fare at or about the door of the Foreign Office in Charles Street at quarter to ten in the evening of May 23d. Apply 221B, Baker Street.

"You are confident that the thief came in a cab?"

"If not, there is no harm done. But if Mr. Phelps is correct in stating that there is no hiding-place either in the room or the corridors, then the person must have come from outside. If he came from outside on so wet a night, and yet left no trace of damp upon the linoleum, which was examined within a few minutes of his passing, then it is exceedingly probable that he came in a cab. Yes, I think that we may safely deduce a cab."

"It sounds plausible."

"That is one of the clues of which I spoke. It may lead

us to something. And then, of course, there is the bell—which is the most distinctive feature of the case. Why should the bell ring? Was it the thief who did it out of bravado? Or was it someone who was with the thief who did it in order to prevent the crime? Or was it an accident? Or was it—?" He sank back into the state of intense and silent thought from which he had emerged; but it seemed to me, accustomed as I was to his every mood, that some new possibility had dawned suddenly upon him.

It was twenty past three when we reached our terminus, and after a hasty luncheon at the buffet we pushed on at once to Scotland Yard. Holmes had already wired to Forbes, and we found him waiting to receive us—a small, foxy man with a sharp but by no means amiable expression. He was decidedly frigid in his manner to us, especially when he heard the errand upon which we had come.

"I've heard of your methods before now, Mr. Holmes," said he tartly. "You are ready enough to use all the information that the police can lay at your disposal, and then you try to finish the case yourself and bring discredit on them."

"On the contrary," said Holmes, "out of my last fifty-three cases my name has only appeared in four, and the police have had all the credit in forty-nine. I don't blame you for not knowing this, for you are young and inexperienced, but if you wish to get on in your new duties you will work with me and not against me."

"I'd be very glad of a hint or two," said the detective, changing his manner. "I've certainly had no credit from the case so far."

"What steps have you taken?"

"Tangey, the Commissionaire, has been shadowed. He left the Guards with a good character, and we can find nothing against him. His wife is a bad lot, though. I fancy she knows more about this than appears."

"Have you shadowed her?"

"We have set one of our women on to her. Mrs. Tangey drinks, and our woman has been with her twice when she was well on, but she could get nothing out of her."

"I understand that they have had brokers in the house?"

"Yes, but they were paid off."

"Where did the money come from?"

"That was all right. His pension was due. They have not shown any sign of being in funds."

"What explanation did she give of having answered the bell when Mr. Phelps rang for the coffee?"

"She said that her husband was very tired and she wished to relieve him."

"Well, certainly that would agree with his being found a little later asleep in his chair. There is nothing against them then but the woman's character. Did you ask her why she hurried away that night? Her haste attracted the attention of the police constable."

"She was later than usual and wanted to get home."

"Did you point out to her that you and Mr. Phelps, who started at least twenty minutes after her, got home before her?"

"She explains that by the difference between a 'bus and a hansom."

"Did she make it clear why, on reaching her house, she ran into the back kitchen?"

"Because she had the money there with which to pay off the brokers."

"She has at least an answer for everything. Did you ask her whether in leaving she met anyone or saw anyone loitering about Charles Street?"

"She saw no one but the constable."

"Well, you seem to have cross-examined her pretty thoroughly. What else have you done?"

"The clerk Gorot has been shadowed all these nine weeks, but without result. We can show nothing against him."

"Anything else?"

"Well, we have nothing else to go upon—no evidence of any kind."

"Have you formed any theory about how that bell rang?"

"Well, I must confess that it beats me. It was a cool hand, whoever it was, to go and give the alarm like that."

"Yes, it was a queer thing to do. Many thanks to you for what you have told me. If I can put the man into your hands you shall hear from me. Come along, Watson."

"Where are we going to now?" I asked as we left the office.

"We are now going to interview Lord Holdhurst, the Cabinet Minister and future Premier of England."

We were fortunate in finding that Lord Holdhurst was still in his chambers in Downing Street, and on Holmes sending in his card we were instantly shown up. The statesman received us with that old-fashioned courtesy for which he is remarkable and seated us on the two luxuriant lounges on either side of the fireplace. Standing on the rug between us, with his slight, tall figure, his sharp features, thoughtful face, and curling hair prematurely tinged with grey, he seemed to represent that not too common type, a nobleman who is in truth noble.

"Your name is very familiar to me, Mr. Holmes," said he, smiling. "And of course I cannot pretend to be ignorant of the object of your visit. There has only been one occurrence in these offices which could call for your attention. In whose interest are you acting, may I ask?"

"In that of Mr. Percy Phelps," answered Holmes.

"Ah, my unfortunate nephew! You can understand that our kinship makes it the more impossible for me to screen him in any way. I fear that the incident must have a very prejudicial effect upon his career."

"But if the document is found?"

"Ah, that, of course, would be different."

"I had one or two questions which I wished to ask you, Lord Holdhurst."

"I shall be happy to give you any information in my power."

"Was it in this room that you gave your instructions as to the copying of the document?"

"It was."

"Then you could hardly have been overheard?"

"It is out of the question."

"Did you ever mention to anyone that it was your intention to give anyone the treaty to be copied?"

"Never."

"You are certain of that?"

"Absolutely."

"Well, since you never said so, and Mr. Phelps never said so, and nobody else knew anything of the matter, then the thief's presence in the room was purely accidental. He saw his chance and he took it."

The statesman smiled. "You take me out of my province there," said he.

Holmes considered for a moment. "There is another very important point which I wish to discuss with you," said he. "You feared, as I understand, that very grave results might follow from the details of this treaty becoming known."

A shadow passed over the expressive face of the statesman. "Very grave results indeed."

"And have they occurred?"

"Not yet."

"If the treaty had reached, let us say, the French or Russian Foreign Office, you would expect to hear of it?"

"I should," said Lord Holdhurst with a wry face.

"Since nearly ten weeks have elapsed, then, and nothing has been heard, it is not unfair to suppose that for some reason the treaty has not reached them."

Lord Holdhurst shrugged his shoulders.

"We can hardly suppose, Mr. Holmes, that the thief took the treaty in order to frame it and hang it up."

"Perhaps he is waiting for a better price."

"If he waits a little longer he will get no price at all. The treaty will cease to be secret in a few months."

"That is most important," said Holmes. "Of course, it is a possible supposition that the thief has had a sudden illness—"

"An attack of brain-fever, for example?" asked the statesman, flashing a swift glance at him.

"I did not say so," said Holmes imperturbably. "And

now, Lord Holdhurst, we have already taken up too much of your valuable time, and we shall wish you good-day."

"Every success to your investigation, be the criminal who it may," answered the nobleman as he bowed us out at the door.

"He's a fine fellow," said Holmes as we came out into Whitehall. "But he has a struggle to keep up his position. He is far from rich and has many calls. You noticed, of course, that his boots had been resoled. Now, Watson, I won't detain you from your legitimate work any longer. I shall do nothing more to-day unless I have an answer to my cab advertisement. But I should be extremely obliged to you if you would come down with me to Woking to-morrow by the same train which we took yesterday."

I met him accordingly next morning and we travelled down to Woking together. He had had no answer to his advertisement, he said, and no fresh light had been thrown upon the case. He had, when he so willed it, the utter immobility of countenance of a red Indian, and I could not gather from his appearance whether he was satisfied or not with the position of the case. His conversation, I remember, was about the Bertillon system of measurements, and he expressed his enthusiastic admiration of the French savant.

We found our client still under the charge of his devoted nurse, but looking considerably better than before. He rose from the sofa and greeted us without difficulty when we entered.

"Any news?" he asked eagerly.

"My report, as I expected, is a negative one," said Holmes. "I have seen Forbes, and I have seen your uncle, and I have set one or two trains of inquiry upon foot which may lead to something."

"You have not lost heart, then?"

"By no means."

"God bless you for saying that!" cried Miss Harrison. "If we keep our courage and our patience the truth must come out."

"We have more to tell you than you have for us," said Phelps, reseating himself upon the couch.

"I hoped you might have something."

"Yes, we have had an adventure during the night, and one which might have proved to be a serious one." His expression grew very grave as he spoke, and a look of something akin to fear sprang up in his eyes. "Do you know," said he, "that I begin to believe that I am the unconscious centre of some monstrous conspiracy, and that my life is aimed at as well as my honour?"

"Ah!" cried Holmes.

"It sounds incredible, for I have not, as far as I know, an enemy in the world. Yet from last night's experience I can come to no other conclusion."

"Pray let me hear it."

"You must know that last night was the very first night that I have ever slept without a nurse in the room. I was so much better that I thought I could dispense with one. I had a night-light burning, however. Well, about two in the morning I had sunk into a light sleep when I was suddenly aroused by a slight noise. It was like the sound which a mouse makes when it is gnawing a plank, and I lay listening to it for some time under the impression that it must come from that cause. Then it grew louder, and suddenly there came from the window a sharp metallic snick. I sat up in amazement. There could be no doubt what the sounds were now. The first ones had been caused by someone forcing an instrument through the slit between the sashes, and the second by the catch being pressed back.

"There was a pause then for about ten minutes, as if the person were waiting to see whether the noise had awakened me. Then I heard a gentle creaking as the window was very slowly opened. I could stand it no longer, for my nerves are not what they used to be. I sprang out of bed and flung open the shutters. A man was crouching at the window. I could see little of him, for he was gone like a flash. He was wrapped in some sort of cloak which came across the lower part of his face. One thing only I am sure

307

of, and that is that he had some weapon in his hand. It looked to me like a long knife. I distinctly saw the gleam of it as he turned to run."

"This is most interesting," said Holmes. "Pray what did you do then?"

"I should have followed him through the open window if I had been stronger. As it was, I rang the bell and roused the house. It took some little time, for the bell rings in the kitchen and the servants all sleep upstairs. I shouted, however, and that brought Joseph down, and he roused the others. Joseph and the groom found marks on the bed outside the window, but the weather has been so dry lately that they found it hopeless to follow the trail across the grass. There's a place, however, on the wooden fence which skirts the road which shows signs, they tell me, as if someone had got over and had snapped the top of the rail in doing so. I have said nothing to the local police yet, for I thought I had best have your opinion first."

This tale of our client's appeared to have an extraordinary effect upon Sherlock Holmes. He rose from his chair and paced about the room in uncontrollable excitement.

"Misfortunes never come single," said Phelps, smiling, though it was evident that his adventure had somewhat shaken him.

"You have certainly had your share," said Holmes. "Do you think you could walk round the house with me?"

"Oh, yes, I should like a little sunshine. Joseph will come, too."

"And I also," said Miss Harrison.

"I am afraid not," said Holmes, shaking his head. "I think I must ask you to remain sitting exactly where you are."

The young lady resumed her seat with an air of displeasure. Her brother, however, had joined us and we set off all four together. We passed round the lawn to the outside of the young diplomatist's window. There were, as he had said, marks upon the bed, but they were hopelessly blurred and vague. Holmes stooped over them for an instant and then rose shrugging his shoulders.

"I don't think anyone could make much of this," said he. "Let us go round the house and see why this particular room was chosen by the burglar. I should have thought those larger windows of the drawing-room and dining-room would have had more attractions for him."

"They are more visible from the road," suggested Mr. Joseph Harrison.

"Ah, yes, of course. There is a door here which he might have attempted. What is it for?"

"It is the side entrance for trades-people. Of course it is locked at night."

"Have you ever had an alarm like this before?"

"Never," said our client.

"Do you keep plate in the house, or anything to attract burglars?"

"Nothing of value."

Holmes strolled round the house with his hands in his pockets and a negligent air which was unusual with him.

"By the way," said he to Joseph Harrison, "you found some place, I understand, where the fellow scaled the fence. Let us have a look at that!"

The plump young man led us to a spot where the top of one of the wooden rails had been cracked. A small fragment of the wood was hanging down. Holmes pulled it off and examined it critically.

"Do you think that was done last night? It looks rather old, does it not?"

"Well, possibly so."

"There are no marks of anyone jumping down upon the other side. No, I fancy we shall get no help here. Let us go back to the bedroom and talk the matter over."

Percy Phelps was walking very slowly, leaning upon the arm of his future brother-in-law. Holmes walked swiftly across the lawn, and we were at the open window of the bedroom long before the others came up.

"Miss Harrison," said Holmes, speaking with the utmost intensity of manner. "you must stay where you are all day. Let nothing prevent you from staying where you are all day. It is of the utmost importance."

"Certainly, if you wish it, Mr. Holmes," said the girl in astonishment.

"When you go to bed lock the door of this room on the outside and keep the key. Promise to do this."

"But Percy?"

"He will come to London with us."

"And am I to remain here?"

"It is for his sake. You can serve him. Quick! Promise!"

She gave a quick nod of assent just as the other two came up.

"Why do you sit moping there, Annie?" cried her brother. "Come out into the sunshine!"

"No, thank you, Joseph. I have a slight headache and this room is deliciously cool and soothing."

"What do you propose now, Mr. Holmes?" asked our client.

"Well, in investigating this minor affair we must not lose sight of our main inquiry. It would be a very great help to me if you would come up to London with us."

"At once?"

"Well, as soon as you conveniently can. Say in an hour."

"I feel quite strong enough, if I can really be of any help."

"The greatest possible."

"Perhaps you would like me to stay there to-night?"

"I was just going to propose it."

"Then, if my friend of the night comes to revisit me, he will find the bird flown. We are all in your hands, Mr. Holmes, and you must tell us exactly what you would like done. Perhaps you would prefer that Joseph came with us so as to look after me?"

"Oh, no, my friend Watson is a medical man, you know, and he'll look after you. We'll have our lunch here, if you will permit us, and then we shall all three set off for town together."

It was arranged as he suggested, though Miss Harrison excused herself from leaving the bedroom, in accordance with Holmes's suggestion. What the object of my friend's manœuvres was I could not conceive, unless it were to keep the lady away from Phelps, who, rejoiced by his returning health and by the prospect of action, lunched with us in the dining-room. Holmes had a still more startling surprise for us, however, for after accompanying us down to the station and seeing us into our carriage, he calmly announced that he had no intention of leaving Woking.

"There are one or two small points which I should desire to clear up before I go," said he. "Your absence, Mr. Phelps, will in some ways rather assist me. Watson, when you reach London you would oblige me by driving at once to Baker Street with our friend here and remaining with him until I see you again. It is fortunate that you are old school-fellows, as you must have much to talk over. Mr. Phelps can have the spare bedroom to-night, and I will be with you in time for breakfast, for there is a train which will take me into Waterloo at eight."

"But how about our investigation in London?" asked Phelps ruefully.

"We can do that to-morrow. I think that just at present I can be of more immediate use here."

"You might tell them at Briarbrae that I hope to be back to-morrow night," cried Phelps, as we began to move from the platform.

"I hardly expect to go back to Briarbrae," answered Holmes, and waved his hand to us cheerily as we shot out from the station.

Phelps and I talked it over on our journey, but neither of us could devise a satisfactory reason for this new development.

"I suppose he wants to find out some clues as to the burglary last night, if a burglar it was. For myself, I don't believe it was an ordinary thief."

"What is your own idea, then?"

"Upon my word, you may put it down to my weak nerves or not, but I believe there is some deep political intrigue going on around me, and that for some reason that passes my understanding my life is aimed at by the conspirators. It sounds high-flown and absurd, but consider the facts! Why should a thief try to break in at a bedroom window where there could be no hope of any plunder, and why should he come with a long knife in his hand?"

"You are sure it was not a house-breaker's jemmy?"

"Oh, no, it was a knife. I saw the flash of the blade quite distinctly."

"But why on earth should you be pursued with such animosity?"

"Ah, that is the question."

"Well, if Holmes takes the same view, that would account for his action, would it not? Presuming that your theory is correct, if he can lay his hands upon the man who threatened you last night he will have gone a long way towards finding who took the naval treaty. It is absurd to suppose that you have two enemies, one of whom robs you, while the other threatens your life."

"But Holmes said that he was not going to Briarbrae."

"I have known him for some time," said I, "but I never knew him do anything yet without a very good reason," and with that our conversation drifted off on to other topics.

But it was a weary day for me. Phelps was still weak after his long illness, and his misfortunes made him querulous and nervous. In vain I endeavoured to interest him in Afghanistan, in India, in social questions, in anything which might take his mind out of the groove. He would always come back to his lost treaty, wondering, guessing, speculating as to what Holmes was doing, what steps Lord Holdhurst was taking, what news we should have in the morning. As the evening wore on his excitement became quite painful.

"You have implicit faith in Holmes?" he asked.

"I have seen him do some remarkable things."

"But he never brought light into anything quite so dark as this?"

"Oh, yes, I have known him solve questions which presented fewer clues than yours."

"But not where such large interests are at stake?"

"I don't know that. To my certain knowledge he has acted on behalf of three of the reigning houses of Europe in very vital matters."

"But you know him well, Watson. He is such an inscrutable fellow that I never quite know what to make of him. Do you think he is hopeful? Do you think he expects to make a success of it?"

"He has said nothing."

"That is a bad sign."

"On the contrary. I have noticed that when he is off the trail he generally says so. It is when he is on a scent and is not quite absolutely sure yet that it is the right one that he is most taciturn. Now, my dear fellow, we can't help matters by making ourselves nervous about them, so let me implore you to go to bed and so be fresh for whatever may await us to-morrow."

I was able at last to persuade my companion to take my advice, though I knew from his excited manner that there was not much hope of sleep for him. Indeed, his mood was infectious, for I lay tossing half the night myself, brooding over this strange problem and inventing a hundred theories, each of which was more impossible than the last. Why had Holmes remained at Woking? Why had he asked Miss Harrison to remain in the sick-room all day? Why had he been so careful not to inform the people at Briarbrae that he intended to remain near them? I cudgelled my brains until I fell asleep in the endeavour to find some explanation which would cover all these facts.

It was seven o'clock when I awoke, and I set off at once for Phelps's room to find him haggard and spent after a sleepless night. His first question was whether Holmes had arrived yet.

"He'll be here when he promised," said I, "and not an instant sooner or later."

And my words were true, for shortly after eight a hansom dashed up to the door and our friend got out of it. Standing in the window we saw that his left hand was swathed in a bandage and that his face was very grim and pale. He entered the house, but it was some little time before he came upstairs.

"He looks like a beaten man," cried Phelps.

I was forced to confess that he was right. "After all," said I, "the clue of the matter lies probably here in town."

Phelps gave a groan.

"I don't know how it is," said he, "but I had hoped for so much from his return. But surely his hand was not tied up like that yesterday. What can be the matter?"

"You are not wounded, Holmes?" I asked as my friend entered the room.

"Tut, it is only a scratch through my own clumsiness," he answered, nodding his good-morning to us. "This case of yours, Mr. Phelps, is certainly one of the darkest which I have ever investigated."

"I feared that you would find it beyond you."

"It has been a most remarkable experience."

"That bandage tells of adventures," said I. "Won't you tell us what has happened?"

"After breakfast, my dear Watson. Remember that I have breathed thirty miles of Surrey air this morning. I suppose that there has been no answer from my cabman advertisement? Well, well, we cannot expect to score every time."

The table was all laid, and just as I was about to ring Mrs. Hudson entered with the tea and coffee. A few minutes later she brought in three covers, and we all drew up to the table, Holmes ravenous, I curious, and Phelps in the gloomiest state of depression.

"Mrs. Hudson has risen to the occasion," said Holmes, uncovering a dish of curried chicken. "Her cuisine is a little limited, but she has as good an idea of breakfast as a Scotchwoman. What have you there, Watson?"

"Ham and eggs," I answered.

"Good! What are you going to take, Mr. Phelps—curried fowl or eggs, or will you help yourself?"

"Thank you. I can eat nothing," said Phelps.

"Oh, come! Try the dish before you."

"Thank you, I would really rather not."

"Well, then," said Holmes with a mischievous twinkle, "I suppose that you have no objection to helping me?"

Phelps raised the cover, and as he did so he uttered a scream and sat there staring with a face as white as the plate upon which he looked. Across the centre of it was lying a little cylinder of blue-grey paper. He caught it up, devoured it with his eyes, and then danced madly about the room, pressing it to his bosom and shrieking out in his delight. Then he fell back into an armchair, so limp and exhausted with his own emotions that we had to pour brandy down his throat to keep him from fainting.

"There! There!" said Holmes soothingly, patting him upon the shoulder. "It was too bad to spring it on you like this, but Watson here will tell you that I never can resist a touch of the dramatic."

Phelps seized his hand and kissed it. "God bless you!" he cried. "You have saved my honour."

"Well, my own was at stake, you know," said Holmes. "I assure you it is just as hateful to me to fail in a case as it can be to you to blunder over a commission."

Phelps thrust away the precious document into the innermost pocket of his coat.

"I have not the heart to interrupt your breakfast any further, and yet I am dying to know how you got it and where it was."

Sherlock Holmes swallowed a cup of coffee and turned his attention to the ham and eggs. Then he rose, lit his pipe, and settled himself down into his chair.

"I'll tell you what I did first, and how I came to do it afterwards," said he. "After leaving you at the station I went for a charming walk through some admirable Surrey scenery to a pretty little village called Ripley, where I had my tea at an inn and took the precaution of filling my flask and of putting a paper of sandwiches in my pocket. There I remained until evening, when I set off for Woking again and found myself in the highroad outside Briarbrae just after sunset.

"Well, I waited until the road was clear—it is never a very frequented one at any time, I fancy—and then I clambered over the fence into the grounds."

"Surely the gate was open!" ejaculated Phelps.

"Yes, but I have a peculiar taste in these matters. I chose the place where the three fir-trees stand, and behind their screen I got over without the least chance of anyone in the house being able to see me. I crouched down among the bushes on the other side and crawled from one to the other—witness the disreputable state of my trouser knees—until I had reached the clump of rhododendrons just opposite to your bedroom window. There I squatted down and awaited developments.

"The blind was not down in your room, and I could see Miss Harrison sitting there reading by the table. It was a quarter-past ten when she closed her book, fastened the shutters, and retired.

"I heard her shut the door and felt quite sure that she had turned the key in the lock."

"The key!" ejaculated Phelps.

"Yes, I had given Miss Harrison instructions to lock the door on the outside and take the key with her when she went to bed. She carried out every one of my injunctions to the letter, and certainly without her co-operation you would not have that paper in your coat-pocket. She departed then and the lights went out, and I was left squatting in the rhododendron-bush.

"The night was fine, but still it was a very weary vigil. Of course it has the sort of excitement about it that the sportsman feels when he lies beside the watercourse and waits for the big game. It was very long, though—almost as long, Watson, as when you and I waited in that deadly room when we looked into the little problem of the Speckled Band. There was a church-clock down at Woking which struck the quarters, and I thought more than once that it had stopped. At last, however, about two in the morning, I suddenly heard the gentle sound of a bolt being pushed back and the creaking of a key. A moment later the servants' door was opened, and Mr. Joseph Harrison stepped out into the moonlight."

"Joseph!" ejaculated Phelps.

"He was bare-headed, but he had a black cloak thrown over his shoulder, so that he could conceal his face in an instant if there were any alarm. He walked on tip-toe under the shadow of the wall, and when he reached the window he worked a long-bladed knife through the sash and pushed back the catch. Then he flung open the window, and putting his knife through the crack in the shutters, he thrust the bar up and swung them open.

"From where I lay I had a perfect view of the inside of the room and of every one of his movements. He lit the two candles which stood upon the mantelpiece, and then he proceeded to turn back the corner of the carpet in the neighbourhood of the door. Presently he stooped and picked out a square piece of board, such as is usually left to enable plumbers to get at the joints of the gas-pipes. This one covered, as a matter of fact, the T joint which gives off the pipe which supplies the kitchen underneath. Out of this hiding-place he drew that little cylinder of paper, pushed down the board, rearranged the carpet, blew out the candles, and walked straight into my arms as I stood waiting for him outside the window.

"Well, he has rather more viciousness than I gave him credit for, has Master Joseph. He flew at me with his knife, and I had to grasp him twice and got a cut over the knuckles, before I had the upper hand of him. He looked murder out of the only eye he could see with when we had finished, but he listened to reason and gave up the papers. Having got them I let my man go, but I wired full particulars to Forbes this morning. If he is quick enough to catch his bird, well and good. But if, as I shrewdly suspect, he finds the nest empty before he gets there, why, all the better for the government. I fancy that Lord Holdhurst, for one, and Mr. Percy Phelps for another, would very much rather that the affair never got as far as a police-court."

"My God!" gasped our client. "Do you tell me that during these long ten weeks of agony the stolen papers were within the very room with me all the time?"

"So it was."

"And Joseph! Joseph a villain and a thief!"

"Hum! I am afraid Joseph's character is a rather deeper and more dangerous one than one might judge from his appearance. From what I have heard from him this morning, I gather that he has lost heavily in dabbling with stocks, and that he is ready to do anything on earth to better his fortunes. Being an absolutely selfish man, when a chance presents itself he did not allow either his sister's happiness or your reputation to hold his hand."

Percy Phelps sank back in his chair. "My head whirls," said he. "Your words have dazed me."

"The principal difficulty in your case," remarked Holmes in his didactic fashion, "lay in the fact of there being too much evidence. What was vital was overlaid and hidden by what was irrelevant. Of all the facts which were presented to us we had to pick just those which we deemed to be essential, and then piece them together in their order, so as to reconstruct this very remarkable chain of events. I had already begun to suspect Joseph from the fact that you had intended to travel home with him that night, and that therefore it was a likely enough thing that he should call for you, knowing the Foreign Office well, upon his way. When I heard that someone had been so anxious to get into the bedroom, in which no one but Joseph could have concealed anything—you told us in your narrative how you had turned Joseph out when you arrived with the doctor—my suspicions all changed to certainties, especially as the attempt was made on the first night upon which the nurse was absent, showing that the intruder was well acquainted with the ways of the house."

"How blind I have been!"

"The facts of the case, as far as I have worked them out, are these: This Joseph Harrison entered the office through the Charles Street door, and knowing his way he walked straight into your room the instant after you left it. Finding no one there he promptly rang the bell, and at the instant that he did so his eyes caught the paper upon the table. A glance showed him that chance had put in his way a State document of immense value, and in an instant he had thrust it into his pocket and was gone. A few minutes elapsed, as you remember, before the sleepy Commissionaire drew your attention to the bell, and those were just enough to give the thief time to make his escape.

"He made his way to Woking by the first train, and having examined his booty and assured himself that it really was of immense value, he had concealed it in what he thought was a very safe place, with the intention of taking it out again in a day or two and carrying it to the French Embassy, or wherever he thought that a long price was to be had. Then came your sudden return. He, without a moment's warning, was bundled out of his room, and from that time onward there were always at least two of you there to prevent him from regaining his treasure. The situation to him must have been a maddening one. But at last he thought he saw his chance. He tried to steal in, but was baffled by your wakefulness. You may remember that you did not take your usual draught that night."

"I remember."

"I fancy that he had taken steps to make that draught efficacious, and that he quite relied upon your being unconscious. Of course, I understood that he would repeat the attempt whenever it could be done with safety. Your leaving the room gave him the chance he wanted. I kept Miss Harrison in it all day so that he might not anticipate us. Then, having given him the idea that the coast was clear, I kept guard as I have described. I already knew that the papers were probably in the room, but I had no desire to rip up all the planking and skirting in search of them. I let him take them, therefore, from the hiding-place, and so saved myself an infinity of trouble. Is there any other point which I can make clear?"

"Why did he try the window on the first occasion," I asked, "when he might have entered by the door?"

"In reaching the door he would have to pass seven bedrooms. On the other hand, he could get out on to the lawn with ease. Anything else?"

"You do not think," asked Phelps, "that he had any murderous intention? The knife was only meant as a tool."

"It may be so," answered Holmes, shrugging his shoulders. "I can only say for certain that Mr. Joseph Harrison is a gentleman to whose mercy I should be extremely unwilling to trust."

The Final Problem

It is with a heavy heart that I take up my pen to write these
the last words in which I shall ever record the singular gifts
by which my friend Mr. Sherlock Holmes was distinguished. In an incoherent and, as I deeply feel, an entirely
inadequate fashion, I have endeavoured to give some account of my strange experiences in his company from the
chance which first brought us together at the period of the
Study in Scarlet, up to the time of his interference in
the matter of the "Naval Treaty"—an interference which
had the unquestionable effect of preventing a serious international complication. It was my intention to have stopped
there, and to have said nothing of that event which has
created a void in my life which the lapse of two years has
done little to fill. My hand has been forced, however, by
the recent letters in which Colonel James Moriarty de-
fends the memory of his brother, and I have no choice but
to lay the facts before the public exactly as they occurred. I
alone know the absolute truth of the matter, and I am satisfied that the time has come when no good purpose is to
be served by its suppression. As far as I know, there have
been only three accounts in the public press: that in the
Journal de Genève on May 6th, 1891, the Reuter's dispatch
in the English papers on May 7th, and finally the recent
letters to which I have alluded. Of these the first and second were extremely condensed, while the last is, as I shall
now show, an absolute perversion of the facts. It lies with
me to tell for the first time what really took place between
Professor Moriarty and Mr. Sherlock Holmes.

It may be remembered that after my marriage, and my subsequent start in private practice, the very intimate relations which had existed between Holmes and myself became to some extent modified. He still came to me from time to time when he desired a companion in his investigations, but these occasions grew more and more seldom, until I find that in the year 1890 there were only three cases of which I retain any record. During the winter of that year and the early spring of 1891, I saw in the papers that he had been engaged by the French government upon a matter of supreme importance, and I received two notes from Holmes, dated from Narbonne and from Nîmes, from which I gathered that his stay in France was likely to be a long one. It was with some surprise, therefore, that I saw him walk into my consulting-room upon the evening of April 24th. It struck me that he was looking even paler and thinner than usual.

"Yes, I have been using myself up rather too freely," he remarked, in answer to my look rather than to my words; "I have been a little pressed of late. Have you any objection to my closing your shutters?"

The only light in the room came from the lamp upon the table at which I had been reading. Holmes edged his way round the wall, and flinging the shutters together, he bolted them securely.

"You are afraid of something?" I asked.

"Well, I am."

"Of what?"

"Of air-guns."

"My dear Holmes, what do you mean?"

"I think that you know me well enough, Watson, to understand that I am by no means a nervous man. At the same time, it is stupidity rather than courage to refuse to recognise danger when it is close upon you. Might I trouble you for a match?" He drew in the smoke of his cigarette as if the soothing influence was grateful to him.

"I must apologize for calling so late," said he, "and I must further beg you to be so unconventional as to allow me to leave your house presently by scrambling over your back garden wall."

"But what does it all mean?" I asked.

He held out his hand, and I saw in the light of the lamp that two of his knuckles were burst and bleeding.

"It's not an airy nothing, you see," said he, smiling. "On the contrary, it is solid enough for a man to break his hand over. Is Mrs. Watson in?"

"She is away upon a visit."

"Indeed! You are alone?"

"Quite."

"Then it makes it the easier for me to propose that you should come away with me for a week to the Continent."

"Where?"

"Oh, anywhere. It's all the same to me."

There was something very strange in all this. It was not Holmes's nature to take an aimless holiday, and something about his pale, worn face told me that his nerves were at their highest tension. He saw the question in my eyes, and, putting his finger-tips together and his elbows upon his knees, he explained the situation.

"You have probably never heard of Professor Moriarty?" said he.

"Never."

"Ay, there's the genius and the wonder of the thing!" he cried. "The man pervades London, and no one has heard of him. That's what puts him on a pinnacle in the records of crime. I tell you Watson, in all seriousness, that if I could beat that man, if I could free society of him, I should feel that my own career had reached its summit, and I should be prepared to turn to some more placid line in life. Between ourselves, the recent cases in which I have been of assistance to the royal family of Scandinavia, and to the French republic, have left me in such a position that I could continue to live in the quiet fashion which is most congenial to me, and to concentrate my attention upon my chemical researches. But I could not rest, Watson, I could not sit quiet in my chair, if I thought that such a man as

Professor Moriarty were walking the streets of London un-
challenged."

"What has he done, then?"

"His career has been an extraordinary one. He is a man
of good birth and excellent education, endowed by nature
with a phenomenal mathematical faculty. At the age of
twenty-one he wrote a treatise upon the Binomial
Theorem, which has had a European vogue. On the
strength of it he won the mathematical chair at one of our
smaller universities and had, to all appearances, a most
brilliant career before him. But the man had hereditary
tendencies of the most diabolical kind. A criminal strain
ran in his blood, which, instead of being modified, was increased and rendered infinitely more dangerous by his
extraordinary mental powers. Dark rumours gathered
round him in the university town, and eventually he was
compelled to resign his chair and to come down to
London, where he set up as an army coach. So much is
known to the world, but what I am telling you now is what
I have myself discovered.

"As you are aware, Watson, there is no one who knows
the higher criminal world of London so well as I do. For
years past I have continually been conscious of some
power behind the malefactor, some deep organizing
power which forever stands in the way of the law and
throws its shield over the wrong-doer. Again and again in
cases of the most varying sorts—forgery cases, robberies,
murders—I have felt the presence of this force, and I
have deduced its action in many of those undiscovered
crimes in which I have not been personally consulted. For
years I have endeavoured to break through the veil which
shrouded it, and at last the time came when I seized my
thread and followed it, until it led me, after a thousand
cunning windings, to ex-Professor Moriarty, of mathematical celebrity.

"He is the Napoleon of crime, Watson. He is the orga-
nizer of half that is evil and of nearly all that is undetected
in this great city. He is a genius, a philosopher, an abstract

thinker. He has a brain of the first order. He sits motionless, like a spider in the centre of its web, but that web has a thousand radiations, and he knows well every quiver of each of them. He does little himself. He only plans. But his agents are numerous and splendidly organized. Is there a crime to be done, a paper to be abstracted, we will say, a house to be rifled, a man to be removed—the word is passed to the Professor, the matter is organized and carried out. The agent may be caught. In that case money is found for his bail or his defence. But the central power which uses the agent is never caught—never so much as suspected. This was the organization which I deduced, Watson, and which I devoted my whole energy to exposing and breaking up.

"But the Professor was fenced round with safeguards so cunningly devised that, do what I would, it seemed impossible to get evidence which would convict in a court of law. You know my powers, my dear Watson, and yet at the end of three months I was forced to confess that I had at last met an antagonist who was my intellectual equal. My horror at his crimes was lost in my admiration at his skill. But at last he made a trip—only a little, little trip—but it was more than he could afford, when I was so close upon him. I had my chance, and, starting from that point, I have woven my net round him until now it is all ready to close. In three days—that is to say, on Monday next—matters will be ripe, and the Professor, with all the principal members of his gang, will be in the hands of the police. Then will come the greatest criminal trial of the century, the clearing up of over forty mysteries, and the rope for all of them; but if we move at all prematurely, you understand, they may slip out of our hands even at the last moment.

"Now, if I could have done this without the knowledge of Professor Moriarty, all would have been well. But he was too wily for that. He saw every step which I took to draw my toils round him. Again and again he strove to break away, but I as often headed him off. I tell you, my friend, that if a detailed account of that silent contest could be written, it would take its place as the most brilliant bit of thrust-and-parry work in the history of detection. Never have I risen to such a height, and never have I been so hard pressed by an opponent. He cut deep, and yet I just undercut him. This morning the last steps were taken, and three days only were wanted to complete the business. I was sitting in my room thinking the matter over when the door opened and Professor Moriarty stood before me.

"My nerves are fairly proof, Watson, but I must confess to a start when I saw the very man who had been so much in my thoughts standing there on my threshold. His appearance was quite familiar to me. He is extremely tall and thin, his forehead domes out in a white curve, and his two eyes are deeply sunken in his head. He is clean-shaven, pale, and ascetic-looking, retaining something of the professor in his features. His shoulders are rounded from much study, and his face protrudes forward and is forever slowly oscillating from side to side in a curiously reptilian fashion. He peered at me with great curiosity in his puckered eyes.

"'You have less frontal development than I should have expected,' said he at last. 'It is a dangerous habit to finger loaded firearms in the pocket of one's dressing-gown.'

"The fact is that upon his entrance I had instantly recognised the extreme personal danger in which I lay. The only conceivable escape for him lay in silencing my tongue. In an instant I had slipped the revolver from the drawer into my pocket and was covering him through the cloth. At his remark I drew the weapon out and laid it cocked upon the table. He still smiled and blinked, but there was something about his eyes which made me feel very glad that I had it there.

"'You evidently don't know me,' said he.

"'On the contrary,' I answered, 'I think it is fairly evident that I do. Pray take a chair. I can spare you five minutes if you have anything to say.'

"'All that I have to say has already crossed your mind,' said he.

" 'Then possibly my answer has crossed yours,' I replied.

" 'You stand fast?'

" 'Absolutely.'

"He clapped his hand into his pocket, and I raised the pistol from the table. But he merely drew out a memorandum-book in which he had scribbled some dates.

" 'You crossed my path on the fourth of January,' said he. 'On the twenty-third you incommoded me; by the middle of February I was seriously inconvenienced by you; at the end of March I was absolutely hampered in my plans; and now, at the close of April, I find myself placed in such a position through your continual persecution that I am in positive danger of losing my liberty. The situation is becoming an impossible one.'

" 'Have you any suggestion to make?' I asked.

" 'You must drop it, Mr. Holmes,' said he, swaying his face about. 'You really must, you know.'

" 'After Monday,' said I.

" 'Tut, tut!' said he. 'I am quite sure that a man of your intelligence will see that can be but one outcome to this affair. It is necessary that you should withdraw. You have worked things in such a fashion that we have only one resource left. It has been an intellectual treat to me to see the way in which you have grappled with this affair, and I say, unaffectedly, that it would be a grief to me to be forced to take any extreme measure. You smile, sir, but I assure you that it really would.'

" 'Danger is part of my trade,' I remarked.

" 'This is not danger,' said he. 'It is inevitable destruction. You stand in the way not merely of an individual but of a mighty organization, the full extent of which you, with all your cleverness, have been unable to realize. You must stand clear, Mr. Holmes, or be trodden under foot.'

" 'I am afraid,' said I, rising, 'that in the pleasure of this conversation I am neglecting business of importance which awaits me elsewhere.'

"He rose also and looked at me in silence, shaking his head sadly.

" 'Well, well,' said he at last. 'It seems a pity, but I have done what I could. I know every move of your game. You can do nothing before Monday. It has been a duel between you and me, Mr. Holmes. You hope to place me in the dock. I tell you that I will never stand in the dock. You hope to beat me. I tell you that you will never beat me. If you are clever enough to bring destruction upon me, rest assured that I shall do as much to you.'

" 'You have paid me several compliments, Mr. Moriarty,' said I. 'Let me pay you one in return when I say that if I were assured of the former eventuality I would, in the interests of the public, cheerfully accept the latter.'

" 'I can promise you the one, but not the other,' he snarled, and so turned his rounded back upon me and went peering and blinking out of the room.

"That was my singular interview with Professor Moriarty. I confess that it left an unpleasant effect upon my mind. His soft, precise fashion of speech leaves a conviction of sincerity which a mere bully could not produce. Of course, you will say: 'Why not take police precautions against him?' The reason is that I am well convinced that it is from his agents the blow would fall. I have the best of proofs that it would be so."

"You have already been assaulted?"

"My dear Watson, Professor Moriarty is not a man who lets the grass grow under his feet. I went out about midday to transact some business in Oxford Street. As I passed the corner which leads from Bentinck Street on to the Welbeck Street crossing a two-horse van furiously driven whizzed round and was on me like a flash. I sprang for the foot-path and saved myself by the fraction of a second. The van dashed around by Marylebone Lane and was gone in an instant. I kept to the pavement after that, Watson, but as I walked down Vere Street a brick came down from the roof of one of the houses and was shattered to fragments at my feet. I called the police and had the place examined. There were slates and bricks piled up on the roof preparatory to some repairs, and they would have me believe that the wind had toppled over one of these. Of course I knew better, but I could prove nothing. I took a cab after that and reached my brother's rooms in Pall Mall, where I spent the day. Now I have come round to you, and on my way I was attacked by a rough with a bludgeon. I knocked him down, and the police have him in custody; but I can tell you with the most absolute confidence that no possible connection will ever be traced between the gentleman upon whose front teeth I have barked my knuckles and the retiring mathematical coach, who is, I daresay, working out problems upon a blackboard ten miles away. You will not wonder, Watson, that my first act on entering your rooms was to close your shutters, and that I have been compelled to ask your permission to leave the house by some less conspicuous exit than the front door."

I had often admired my friend's courage, but never more than now, as he sat quietly checking off a series of incidents which must have combined to make up a day of horror.

"You will spend the night here?" I said.

"No, my friend, you might find me a dangerous guest. I have my plans laid, and all will be well. Matters have gone so far now that they can move without my help as far as the arrest goes, though my presence is necessary for a conviction. It is obvious, therefore, that I cannot do better than get away for the few days which remain before the police are at liberty to act. It would be a great pleasure to me, therefore, if you could come on to the Continent with me."

"The practice is quiet," said I, "and I have an accommodating neighbour. I should be glad to come."

"And to start to-morrow morning?"

"If necessary."

"Oh, yes, it is most necessary. Then these are your instructions, and I beg, my dear Watson, that you will obey them to the letter, for you are now playing a double-handed game with me against the cleverest rogue and the most powerful syndicate of criminals in Europe. Now listen! You will dispatch whatever luggage you intend to take by a trusty messenger unaddressed to Victoria to-night. In the morning you will send for a hansom, desiring your man to take neither the first nor the second which may present itself. Into this hansom you will jump, and you will drive to the Strand end of the Lowther Arcade, handing the address to the cabman upon a slip of paper, with a request that he will not throw it away. Have your fare ready, and the instant that your cab stops, dash through the Arcade, timing yourself to reach the other side at a quarter-past nine. You will find a small brougham waiting close to the curb, driven by a fellow with a heavy black cloak tipped at the collar with red. Into this you will step, and you will reach Victoria in time for the Continental express."

"Where shall I meet you?"

"At the station. The second first-class carriage from the front will be reserved for us."

"The carriage is our rendezvous, then?"

"Yes."

It was in vain that I asked Holmes to remain for the evening. It was evident to me that he thought he might bring trouble to the roof he was under, and that that was the motive which impelled him to go. With a few hurried words as to our plans for the morrow he rose and came out with me into the garden, clambering over the wall which leads into Mortimer Street, and immediately whistling for a hansom, in which I heard him drive away.

In the morning I obeyed Holmes's injunctions to the letter. A hansom was procured with such precautions as would prevent its being one which was placed ready for us, and I drove immediately after breakfast to the Lowther Arcade, through which I hurried at the top of my speed. A brougham was waiting with a very massive driver wrapped in a dark cloak, who, the instant that I had stepped in, whipped up the horse and rattled off to Victoria Station. On my alighting there he turned the carriage and dashed away again without so much as a look in my direction.

So far all had gone admirably. My luggage was waiting

for me, and I had no difficulty in finding the carriage which Holmes had indicated, the less so as it was the only one in the train which was marked "Engaged." My only source of anxiety now was the non-appearance of Holmes. The station clock marked only seven minutes from the time when we were due to start. In vain I searched among the groups of travellers and leave-takers for the lithe figure of my friend. There was no sign of him. I spent a few minutes in assisting a venerable Italian priest, who was endeavouring to make a porter understand, in his broken English, that his luggage was to be booked through to Paris. Then, having taken another look round, I returned to my carriage, where I found that the porter, in spite of the ticket, had given me my decrepit Italian friend as a travelling companion. It was useless for me to explain to him that his presence was an intrusion, for my Italian was even more limited than his English, so I shrugged my shoulders resignedly and continued to look out anxiously for my friend. A chill of fear had come over me, as I thought that his absence might mean that some blow had fallen during the night. Already the doors had all been shut and the whistle blown, when—

"My dear Watson," said a voice, "you have not even condescended to say good-morning."

I turned in uncontrollable astonishment. The aged ecclesiastic had turned his face towards me. For an instant the wrinkles were smoothed away, the nose drew away from the chin, the lower lip ceased to protrude and the mouth to mumble, the dull eyes regained their fire, the drooping figure expanded. The next the whole frame collapsed again, and Holmes had gone as quickly as he had come.

"Good Heavens!" I cried. "How you startled me!"

"Every precaution is still necessary," he whispered. "I have reason to think that they are hot upon our trail. Ah, there is Moriarty himself."

The train had already begun to move as Holmes spoke. Glancing back, I saw a tall man pushing his way furiously through the crowd and waving his hand as if he desired to have the train stopped. It was too late, however, for we were rapidly gathering momentum, and an instant later had shot clear of the station.

"With all our precautions, you see that we have cut it rather fine," said Holmes, laughing. He rose, and throwing off the black cassock and hat which had formed his disguise, he packed them away in a hand-bag.

"Have you seen the morning paper, Watson?"

"No."

"You haven't seen about Baker Street, then?"

"Baker Street?"

"They set fire to our rooms last night. No great harm was done."

"Good Heavens, Holmes, this is intolerable!"

"They must have lost my track completely after their bludgeonman was arrested. Otherwise they could not have imagined that I had returned to my rooms. They have evidently taken the precaution of watching you, however, and that is what has brought Moriarty to Victoria. You could not have made any slip in coming?"

"I did exactly what you advised."

"Did you find your brougham?"

"Yes, it was waiting."

"Did you recognise your coachman?"

"No."

"It was my brother Mycroft. It is an advantage to get about in such a case without taking a mercenary into your confidence. But we must plan what we are to do about Moriarty now."

"As this is an express, and as the boat runs in connection with it, I should think we have shaken him off very effectively."

"My dear Watson, you evidently did not realize my meaning when I said that this man may be taken as being quite on the same intellectual plane as myself. You do not imagine that if I were the pursuer I should allow myself to be baffled by so slight an obstacle. Why, then, should you think so meanly of him?"

"What will he do?"

"What I should do."

"What would you do, then?"

"Engage a special."

"But it must be late."

"By no means. This train stops at Canterbury; and there is always at least a quarter of an hour's delay at the boat. He will catch us there."

"One would think that we were the criminals. Let us have him arrested on his arrival."

"It would be to ruin the work of three months. We should get the big fish, but the smaller would dart right and left out of the net. On Monday we should have them all. No, an arrest is inadmissible."

"What then?"

"We shall get out at Canterbury."

"And then?"

"Well, then we must make a cross-country journey to Newhaven, and so over to Dieppe. Moriarty will again do what I should do. He will get on to Paris, mark down our luggage, and wait for two days at the depot. In the meantime we shall treat ourselves to a couple of carpet-bags, encourage the manufactures of the countries through which we travel, and make our way at our leisure into Switzerland, via Luxembourg and Basle."

At Canterbury, therefore, we alighted only to find that we should have to wait an hour before we could get a train to Newhaven.

I was still looking rather ruefully after the rapidly disappearing luggage-van which contained my wardrobe, when Holmes pulled my sleeve and pointed up the line.

"Already, you see," said he.

Far away, from among the Kentish woods there rose a thin spray of smoke. A minute later a carriage and engine could be seen flying along the open curve which leads to the station. We had hardly time to take our place behind a pile of luggage when it passed with a rattle and a roar, beating a blast of hot air into our faces.

"There he goes," said Holmes, as we watched the carriage swing and rock over the points. "There are limits, you see, to our friend's intelligence. It would have been a *coup-de-maître* had he deduced what I would deduce and acted accordingly."

"And what would he have done had he overtaken us?"

"There cannot be the least doubt that he would have made a murderous attack upon me. It is, however, a game at which two may play. The question now is whether we should take a premature lunch here, or run our chance of starving before we reach the buffet at Newhaven."

We made our way to Brussels that night and spent two days there, moving on upon the third day as far as Strasbourg. On the Monday morning Holmes had telegraphed to the London police, and in the evening we found a reply waiting for us at our hotel. Holmes tore it open, and then with a bitter curse hurled it into the grate.

"I might have known it!" he groaned. "He has escaped!"

"Moriarty?"

"They have secured the whole gang with the exception of him. He has given them the slip. Of course, when I had left the country there was no one to cope with him. But I did think that I had put the game in their hands. I think that you had better return to England, Watson."

"Why?"

"Because you will find me a dangerous companion now. This man's occupation is gone. He is lost if he returns to London. If I read his character right he will devote his whole energies to revenging himself upon me. He said as much in our short interview, and I fancy that he meant it. I should certainly recommend you to return to your practice."

It was hardly an appeal to be successful with one who was an old campaigner as well as an old friend. We sat in the Strasbourg *salle-à-manger* arguing the question for half an hour, but the same night we had resumed our journey and were well on our way to Geneva.

For a charming week we wandered up the valley of the Rhone, and then, branching off at Leuk, we made our way over the Gemmi Pass, still deep in snow, and so, by way of Interlaken, to Meiringen. It was a lovely trip, the dainty green of the spring below, the virgin white of the winter above; but it was clear to me that never for one instant did Holmes forget the shadow which lay across him. In the homely Alpine villages or in the lonely mountain passes, I could still tell by his quick glancing eyes and his sharp scrutiny of every face that passed us, that he was well convinced that, walk where we would, we could not walk ourselves clear of the danger which was dogging our footsteps.

Once, I remember, as we passed over the Gemmi and walked along the border of the melancholy Daubensee, a large rock which had been dislodged from the ridge upon our right clattered down and roared into the lake behind us. In an instant Holmes had raced up on to the ridge, and, standing upon a lofty pinnacle, craned his neck in every direction. It was in vain that our guide assured him that a fall of stones was a common chance in the springtime at that spot. He said nothing, but he smiled at me with the air of a man who sees the fulfillment of that which he expected.

And yet for all his watchfulness he was never depressed. On the contrary, I can never recollect having seen him in such exuberant spirits. Again and again he recurred to the fact that if he could be assured that society was freed from Professor Moriarty he would cheerfully bring his own career to a conclusion.

"I think that I may go so far as to say, Watson, that I have not lived wholly in vain," he remarked. "If my record were closed to-night I could still survey it with equanimity. The air of London is the sweeter for my presence. In over a thousand cases I am not aware that I have ever used my powers upon the wrong side. Of late I have been tempted to look into the problems furnished by nature rather than those more superficial ones for which our artificial state of society is responsible. Your memoirs will draw to an end, Watson, upon the day that I crown my career by the capture or extinction of the most dangerous and capable criminal in Europe."

I shall be brief, and yet exact, in the little which remains for me to tell. It is not a subject on which I would willingly dwell, and yet I am conscious that a duty devolves upon me to omit no detail.

It was on the third of May that we reached the little village of Meiringen, where we put up at the Englischer Hof, then kept by Peter Steiler the elder. Our landlord was an intelligent man and spoke excellent English, having served for three years as waiter at the Grosvenor Hotel in London. At his advice, on the afternoon of the fourth we set off together, with the intention of crossing the hills and spending the night at the hamlet of Rosenlaui. We had strict injunctions, however, on no account to pass the falls of Reichenbach, which are about halfway up the hills, without making a small detour to see them.

It is, indeed, a fearful place. The torrent, swollen by the melting snow, plunges into a tremendous abyss, from which the spray rolls up like the smoke from a burning house. The shaft into which the river hurls itself is an immense chasm, lined by glistening coal-black rock, and narrowing into a creaming, boiling pit of incalculable depth, which brims over and shoots the stream onward over its jagged lip. The long sweep of green water roaring forever down, and the thick flickering curtain of spray hissing forever upward, turn a man giddy with their constant whirl and clamour. We stood near the edge peering down at the gleam of the breaking water far below us against the black rocks, and listening to the half-human shout which came booming up with the spray out of the abyss.

The path has been cut halfway round the fall to afford a complete view, but it ends abruptly, and the traveller has to return as he came. We had turned to do so, when we saw a Swiss lad come running along it with a letter in his hand. It bore the mark of the hotel which we had just left and was addressed to me by the landlord. It appeared that within a very few minutes of our leaving, an English lady had arrived who was in the last stage of consumption. She had wintered at Davos Platz and was journeying now to join her friends at Lucerne, when a sudden hemorrhage had overtaken her. It was thought that she could hardly live a few hours, but it would be a great consolation to her to see an English doctor, and, if I would only return, etc. The good Steiler assured me in a postscript that he would himself look upon my compliance as a very great favour, since the lady absolutely refused to see a Swiss physician, and he could not but feel that he was incurring a great responsibility.

The appeal was one which could not be ignored. It was impossible to refuse the request of a fellow-countrywoman dying in a strange land. Yet I had my scruples about leaving Holmes. It was finally agreed, however, that he should retain the young Swiss messenger with him as guide and companion while I returned to Meiringen. My friend would stay some little time at the fall, he said, and would then walk slowly over the hill to Rosenlaui, where I was to rejoin him in the evening. As I turned away I saw Holmes, with his back against a rock and his arms folded, gazing down at the rush of waters. It was the last that I was ever destined to see of him in this world.

When I was near the bottom of the descent I looked back. It was impossible, from that position, to see the fall, but I could see the curving path which winds over the shoulder of the hills and leads to it. Along this a man was, I remember, walking very rapidly.

I could see his black figure clearly outlined against the green behind him. I noted him, and the energy with which he walked, but he passed from my mind again as I hurried on upon my errand.

It may have been a little over an hour before I reached Meiringen. Old Steiler was standing at the porch of his hotel.

"Well," said I, as I came hurrying up, "I trust that she is no worse?"

A look of surprise passed over his face, and at the first

quiver of his eyebrows my heart turned to lead in my breast.

"You did not write this?" I said, pulling the letter from my pocket. "There is no sick Englishwoman in the hotel?"

"Certainly not!" he cried. "But it has the hotel mark upon it! Ha, it must have been written by that tall Englishman who came in after you had gone. He said—"

But I waited for none of the landlord's explanation. In a tingle of fear I was already running down the village street, and making for the path which I had so lately descended. It had taken me an hour to come down. For all my efforts two more had passed before I found myself at the fall of Reichenbach once more. There was Holmes's Alpine-stock still leaning against the rock by which I had left him. But there was no sign of him, and it was in vain that I shouted. My only answer was my own voice reverberating in a rolling echo from the cliffs around me.

It was the sight of that Alpine-stock which turned me cold and sick. He had not gone to Rosenlaui, then. He had remained on that three-foot path, with sheer wall on one side and sheer drop on the other, until his enemy had overtaken him. The young Swiss had gone too. He had probably been in the pay of Moriarty and had left the two men together. And then what had happened? Who was to tell us what had happened then?

I stood for a minute or two to collect myself, for I was dazed with the horror of the thing. Then I began to think of Holmes's own methods and to try to practise them in reading this tragedy. It was, alas, only too easy to do. During our conversation we had not gone to the end of the path, and the Alpine-stock marked the place where we had stood. The blackish soil is kept forever soft by the incessant drift of spray, and a bird would leave its tread upon it. Two lines of footmarks were clearly marked along the farther end of the path, both leading away from me. There were none returning. A few yards from the end the soil was all ploughed up into a patch of mud, and the brambles and ferns which fringed the chasm were torn and bedraggled. I lay upon my face and peered over with the spray spouting up all around me. It had darkened since I left, and now I could only see here and there the glistening of moisture upon the black walls, and far away down at the end of the shaft the gleam of the broken water. I shouted; but only that same half-human cry of the fall was borne back to my ears.

But it was destined that I should, after all, have a last word of greeting from my friend and comrade. I have said that his Alpine-stock had been left leaning against a rock which jutted on to the path. From the top of this bowlder the gleam of something bright caught my eye, and raising my hand I found that it came from the silver cigarette-case which he used to carry. As I took it up a small square of paper upon which it had lain fluttered down on to the ground. Unfolding it, I found that it consisted of three pages torn from his note-book and addressed to me. It was characteristic of the man that the direction was as precise, and the writing as firm and clear, as though it had been written in his study.

MY DEAR WATSON [it said]:
I write these few lines through the courtesy of Mr. Moriarty, who awaits my convenience for the final discussion of those questions which lie between us. He has been giving me a sketch of the methods by which he avoided the English police and kept himself informed of our movements. They certainly confirm the very high opinion which I had formed of his abilities. I am pleased to think that I shall be able to free society from any further effects of his presence, though I fear that it is at a cost which will give pain to my friends, and especially, my dear Watson, to you. I have already explained to you, however, that my career had in any case reached its crisis, and that no possible conclusion to it could be more congenial to me than this. Indeed, if I may make a full confession to you, I was quite convinced that the letter from Meiringen was a hoax, and I allowed you to depart on that errand under the persuasion that some development of this sort would follow. Tell Inspector Patterson that the papers which he needs to convict the gang are in pigeonhole M., done up in a blue envelope and inscribed "Moriarty." I made every disposition of my property before leaving England and handed

it to my brother Mycroft. Pray give my greetings to Mrs. Watson, and believe me to be, my dear fellow,

Very sincerely yours,
SHERLOCK HOLMES

A few words may suffice to tell the little that remains. An examination by experts leaves little doubt that a personal contest between the two men ended, as it could hardly fail to end in such a situation, in their reeling over, locked in each other's arms. Any attempt at recovering the bodies was absolutely hopeless, and there, deep down in that dreadful cauldron of swirling water and seething foam, will lie for all time the most dangerous criminal and the foremost champion of the law of their generation. The Swiss youth was never found again, and there can be no doubt that he was one of the numerous agents whom Moriarty kept in his employ. As to the gang, it will be within the memory of the public how completely the evidence which Holmes had accumulated exposed their organization, and how heavily the hand of the dead man weighed upon them. Of their terrible chief few details came out during the proceedings, and if I have now been compelled to make a clear statement of his career, it is due to those injudicious champions who have endeavoured to clear his memory by attacks upon him whom I shall ever regard as the best and the wisest man whom I have ever known.

The Adventure of the
Empty House

It was in the spring of the year 1894 that all London was interested, and the fashionable world dismayed, by the murder of the Honourable Ronald Adair under most unusual and inexplicable circumstances. The public has already learned those particulars of the crime which came out in the police investigation, but a good deal was suppressed upon that occasion, since the case for the prosecution was so overwhelmingly strong that it was not necessary to bring forward all the facts. Only now, at the end of nearly ten years, am I allowed to supply those missing links which make up the whole of that remarkable chain. The crime was of interest in itself, but that interest was as nothing to me compared to the inconceivable sequel, which afforded me the greatest shock and surprise of any event in my adventurous life. Even now, after this long interval, I find myself thrilling as I think of it and feeling once more that sudden flood of joy, amazement, and incredulity which utterly submerged my mind. Let me say to that public, which has shown some interest in those glimpses which I have occasionally given them of the thoughts and actions of a very remarkable man, that they are not to blame me if I have not shared my knowledge with them, for I should have considered it my first duty to do so, had I not been barred by a positive prohibition from his own lips, which was only withdrawn upon the third of last month.

It can be imagined that my close intimacy with Sherlock

Holmes had interested me deeply in crime, and that after his disappearance I never failed to read with care the various problems which came before the public. And I even attempted, more than once, for my own private satisfaction, to employ his methods in their solution, though with indifferent success. There was none, however, which appealed to me like this tragedy of Ronald Adair. As I read the evidence at the inquest, which led up to a verdict of wilful murder against some person or persons unknown, I realized more clearly than I had ever done the loss which the community had sustained by the death of Sherlock Holmes. There were points about this strange business which would, I was sure, have specially appealed to him, and the efforts of the police would have been supplemented, or more probably anticipated, by the trained observation and the alert mind of the first criminal agent in Europe. All day, as I drove upon my round, I turned over the case in my mind and found no explanation which appeared to me to be adequate. At the risk of telling a twice-told tale, I will recapitulate the facts as they were known to the public at the conclusion of the inquest.

The Honourable Ronald Adair was the second son of the Earl of Maynooth, at that time Governor of one of the Australian colonies. Adair's mother had returned from Australia to undergo the operation for cataract, and she, her son Ronald, and her daughter Hilda were living together at 427 Park Lane. The youth moved in the best society—had, so far as was known, no enemies and no particular vices. He had been engaged to Miss Edith Woodley, of Carstairs, but the engagement had been broken off by mutual consent some months before, and there was no sign that it had left any very profound feeling behind it. For the rest of the man's life moved in a narrow and conventional circle, for his habits were quiet and his nature unemotional. Yet it was upon this easy-going young aristocrat that death came, in most strange and unexpected form, between the hours of ten and eleven-twenty on the night of March 30, 1894.

Ronald Adair was fond of cards—playing continually, but never for such stakes as would hurt him. He was a member of the Baldwin, the Cavendish, and the Bagatelle card clubs. It was shown that, after dinner on the day of his death, he had played a rubber of whist at the latter club. He had also played there in the afternoon. The evidence of those who had played with him—Mr. Murray, Sir John Hardy, and Colonel Moran—showed that the game was whist, and that there was a fairly equal fall of the cards. Adair might have lost five pounds, but not more. His fortune was a considerable one, and such a loss could not in any way affect him. He had played nearly every day at one club or other, but he was a cautious player and usually rose a winner. It came out in evidence that, in partnership with Colonel Moran, he had actually won as much as four hundred and twenty pounds in a sitting, some weeks before, from Godfrey Milner and Lord Balmoral. So much for his recent history as it came out at the inquest.

On the evening of the crime, he returned from the club exactly at ten. His mother and sister were out spending the evening with a relation. The servant deposed that she heard him enter the front room on the second floor, generally used as his sitting-room. She had lit a fire there, and as it smoked she had opened the window. No sound was heard from the room until eleven-twenty, the hour of the return of Lady Maynooth and her daughter. Desiring to say good-night, she attempted to enter her son's room. The door was locked on the inside, and no answer could be got to their cries and knocking. Help was obtained, and the door forced. The unfortunate young man was found lying near the table. His head had been horribly mutilated by an expanding revolver bullet, but no weapon of any sort was to be found in the room. On the table lay two banknotes for ten pounds each and seventeen pounds ten in silver and gold, the money arranged in little piles of varying amount. There were some figures also upon a sheet of paper, with the names of some club friends opposite to them, from which it was conjectured that before his death he was endeavouring to make out his losses or winnings at cards.

A minute examination of the circumstances served only to make the case more complex. In the first place, no reason could be given why the young man should have fastened the door upon the inside. There was the possibility that the murderer had done this and had afterwards escaped by the window. The drop was at least twenty feet, however, and a bed of crocuses in full bloom lay beneath. Neither the flowers nor the earth showed any sign of having been disturbed, nor were there any marks upon the narrow strip of grass which separated the house from the road. Apparently, therefore, it was the young man himself who had fastened the door. But how did he come by his death? No one could have climbed up to the window without leaving traces. Suppose a man had fired through the window, he would indeed be a remarkable shot who could with a revolver inflict so deadly a wound. Again, Park Lane is a frequented thoroughfare; there is a cab stand within a hundred yards of the house. No one had heard a shot. And yet there was the dead man, and there the revolver bullet, which had mushroomed out, as softnosed bullets will, and so inflicted a wound which must have caused instantaneous death. Such were the circumstances of the Park Lane Mystery, which were further complicated by entire absence of motive, since, as I have said, young Adair was not known to have any enemy, and no attempt had been made to remove the money or valuables in the room.

All day I turned these facts over in my mind, endeavouring to hit upon some theory which could reconcile them all, and to find that line of least resistance which my poor friend had declared to be the starting-point of every investigation. I confess that I made little progress. In the evening I strolled across the Park and found myself about six o'clock at the Oxford Street end of Park Lane. A group of loafers upon the pavements, all staring up at a particular window, directed me to the house which I had come to see. A tall, thin man with coloured glasses, whom I strongly suspected of being a plain-clothes detective, was pointing out some theory of his own, while the others crowded round to listen to what he said. I got as near him as I could, but his observations seemed to me to be absurd, so I withdrew again in some disgust. As I did so I struck against an elderly, deformed man, who had been behind me, and I knocked down several books which he was carrying. I remember that as I picked them up, I observed the title of one of them, *The Origin of Tree Worship*, and it struck me that the fellow must be some poor bibliophile, who, either as a trade or as a hobby, was a collector of obscure volumes. I endeavoured to apologize for the accident, but it was evident that these books which I had so unfortunately maltreated were very precious objects in the eyes of their owner. With a snarl of contempt he turned upon his heel, and I saw his curved back and white side-whiskers disappear among the throng.

My observations of No. 427 Park Lane did little to clear up the problem in which I was interested. The house was separated from the street by a low wall and railing, the whole not more than five feet high. It was perfectly easy, therefore, for anyone to get into the garden, but the window was entirely inaccessible, since there was no water-pipe or anything which could help the most active man to climb it. More puzzled than ever, I retraced my steps to Kensington. I had not been in my study five minutes when the maid entered to say that a person desired to see me. To my astonishment it was none other than my strange old book collector, his sharp, wizened face peering out from a frame of white hair, and his precious volumes, a dozen of them at least, wedged under his right arm.

"You're surprised to see me, sir," said he, in a strange, croaking voice.

I acknowledged that I was.

"Well, I've a conscience, sir, and when I chanced to see you go into this house, as I came hobbling after you, I thought to myself, I'll just step in and see that kind gentleman and tell him that if I was a bit gruff in my manner there was not any harm meant, and that I am much obliged to him for picking up my books."

"You make too much of a trifle," said I. "May I ask how you knew who I was?"

"Well, sir, if it isn't too great a liberty, I am a neighbour of yours, for you'll find my little bookshop at the corner of Church Street, and very happy to see you, I am sure. Maybe you collect yourself, sir. Here's *British Birds,* and *Catullus,* and *The Holy War*—a bargain, every one of them. With five volumes you could just fill that gap on that second shelf. It looks untidy, does it not, sir?"

I moved my head to look at the cabinet behind me. When I turned again, Sherlock Holmes was standing smiling at me across my study table. I rose to my feet, stared at him for some seconds in utter amazement, and then it appears that I must have fainted for the first and the last time in my life. Certainly a grey mist swirled before my eyes, and when it cleared I found my collar-ends undone and the tingling after-taste of brandy upon my lips. Holmes was bending over my chair, his flask in his hand.

"My dear Watson," said the well-remembered voice, "I owe you a thousand apologies. I had no idea that you would be so affected."

I gripped him by the arms.

"Holmes!" I cried. "Is it really you? Can it indeed be that you are alive? Is it possible that you succeeded in climbing out of that awful abyss?"

"Wait a moment," said he. "Are you sure that you are really fit to discuss things? I have given you a serious shock by my unnecessarily dramatic reappearance."

"I am all right, but indeed, Holmes, I can hardly believe my eyes. Good Heavens! To think that you—you of all men—should be standing in my study." Again I gripped him by the sleeve and felt the thin, sinewy arm beneath it. "Well, you're not a spirit, anyhow," said I. "My dear chap, I'm overjoyed to see you. Sit down and tell me how you came alive out of that dreadful chasm."

He sat opposite to me and lit a cigarette in his old, nonchalant manner. He was dressed in the seedy frock-coat of the book merchant, but the rest of that individual lay in a pile of white hair and old books upon the table. Holmes looked even thinner and keener than of old, but there was a dead-white tinge in his aquiline face which told me that his life recently had not been a healthy one.

"I am glad to stretch myself, Watson," said he. "It is no joke when a tall man has to take a foot off his stature for several hours on end. Now, my dear fellow, in the matter of these explanations, we have, if I may ask for your co-operation, a hard and dangerous night's work in front of us. Perhaps it would be better if I gave you an account of the whole situation when that work is finished."

"I am full of curiosity. I should much prefer to hear now."

"You'll come with me to-night?"

"When you like and where you like."

"This is, indeed, like the old days. We shall have time for a mouthful of dinner before we need go. Well, then, about that chasm. I had no serious difficulty in getting out of it, for the very simple reason that I never was in it."

"You never were in it?"

"No, Watson, I never was in it. My note to you was absolutely genuine. I had little doubt that I had come to the end of my career when I perceived the somewhat sinister figure of the late Professor Moriarty standing upon the narrow pathway which led to safety. I read an inexorable purpose in his grey eyes. I exchanged some remarks with him, therefore, and obtained his courteous permission to write the short note which you afterwards received. I left it with my cigarette-box and my stick, and I walked along the pathway, Moriarty still at my heels. When I reached the end I stood at bay. He drew no weapon, but he rushed at me and threw his long arms around me. He knew that his own game was up and was only anxious to revenge himself upon me. We tottered together upon the brink of the fall. I have some knowledge, however, of baritsu, or the Japanese system of wrestling, which has more than once been very useful to me. I slipped through his grip, and he with a horrible scream kicked madly for a few seconds and clawed the air with both his hands. But for all his efforts he could not get his balance, and over he went. With my face over the brink, I saw him fall for a long way. Then he struck a rock, bounded off, and splashed into the water."

I listened with amazement to this explanation, which Holmes delivered between the puffs of his cigarette.

"But the tracks!" I cried. "I saw, with my own eyes, that two went down the path and none returned."

"It came about in this way. The instant that the Professor had disappeared, it struck me what a really extraordinarily lucky chance Fate had placed in my way. I knew that Moriarty was not the only man who had sworn my death. There were at least three others whose desire for vengeance upon me would only be increased by the death of their leader. They were all most dangerous men. One or other would certainly get me. On the other hand, if all the world was convinced that I was dead they would take liberties, these men, they would soon lay themselves open, and sooner or later I could destroy them. Then it would be time for me to announce that I was still in the land of the living. So rapidly does the brain act that I believe I had thought this all out before Professor Moriarty had reached the bottom of the Reichenbach Fall.

"I stood up and examined the rocky wall behind me. In your picturesque account of the matter, which I read with great interest some months later, you assert that the wall was sheer. That was not literally true. A few small footholds presented themselves, and there was some indication of a ledge. The cliff is so high that to climb it all was an obvious impossibility, and it was equally impossible to make my way along the wet path without leaving some tracks. I might, it is true, have reversed my boots, as I have done on similar occasions, but the sight of three sets of tracks in one direction would certainly have suggested a deception. On the whole, then, it was best that I should risk the climb. It was not a pleasant business, Watson. The fall roared beneath me. I am not a fanciful person, but I give you my word that I seemed to hear Moriarty's voice screaming at me out of the abyss. A mistake would have been fatal. More than once, as tufts of grass came out in my hand or my foot slipped in the wet notches of the rock, I thought that I was gone. But I struggled upward, and at last I reached a ledge several feet deep and covered with soft green moss, where I could lie unseen, in the most perfect comfort. There I was stretched, when you, my dear Watson, and all your following were investigating in the most sympathetic and inefficient manner the circumstances of my death.

"At last, when you had all formed your inevitable and totally erroneous conclusions, you departed for the hotel, and I was left alone. I had imagined that I had reached the end of my adventures, but a very unexpected occurrence showed me that there were surprises still in store for me. A huge rock, falling from above, boomed past me, struck the path, and bounded over into the chasm. For an instant I thought that it was an accident, but a moment later, looking up, I saw a man's head against the darkening sky, and another stone struck the very ledge upon which I was stretched, within a foot of my head. Of course, the meaning of this was obvious. Moriarty had not been alone. A confederate—and even that one glance had told me how dangerous a man that confederate was—had kept guard while the Professor had attacked me. From a distance, unseen by me, he had been a witness of his friend's death and of my escape. He had waited, and then making his way round to the top of the cliff, he had endeavoured to succeed where his comrade had failed.

"I did not take long to think about it, Watson. Again I saw that grim face look over the cliff, and I knew that it was the precursor of another stone. I scrambled down on to the path. I don't think I could have done it in cold blood. It was a hundred times more difficult than getting up. But I had no time to think of the danger, for another stone sang past me as I hung by my hands from the edge of the ledge. Halfway down I slipped, but, by the blessing

349

of God, I landed, torn and bleeding, upon the path. I took
to my heels, did ten miles over the mountains in the darkness, and a week later I found myself in Florence, with the
certainty that no one in the world knew what had become
of me.

"I had only one confidant—my brother Mycroft. I owe
you many apologies, my dear Watson, but it was all-
important that it should be thought I was dead, and it is
quite certain that you would not have written so convincing an account of my unhappy end had you not yourself
thought that it was true. Several times during the last three
years I have taken up my pen to write to you, but always I
feared lest your affectionate regard for me should tempt
you to some indiscretion which would betray my secret.
For that reason I turned away from you this evening when
you upset my books, for I was in danger at the time, and
any show of surprise and emotion upon your part might
have drawn attention to my identity and led to the most
deplorable and irreparable results. As to Mycroft, I had to
confide in him in order to obtain the money which I
needed. The course of events in London did not run so
well as I had hoped, for the trial of the Moriarty gang left
two of its most dangerous members, my own most vindictive enemies, at liberty. I travelled for two years in Tibet,
therefore, and amused myself by visiting Lhassa and
spending some days with the head lama. You may have
read of the remarkable explorations of a Norwegian
named Sigerson, but I am sure that it never occurred to
you that you were receiving news of your friend. I then
passed through Persia, looked in at Mecca, and paid a
short but interesting visit to the Khalifa at Khartoum, the
results of which I have communicated to the Foreign
Office. Returning to France, I spent some months in a research into the coal-tar derivatives, which I conducted in a
laboratory at Montpellier, in the south of France. Having
concluded this to my satisfaction and learning that only
one of my enemies was now left in London, I was about to
return when my movements were hastened by the news of
this very remarkable Park Lane Mystery, which not only

appealed to me by its own merits, but which seemed to offer some most peculiar personal opportunities. I came over at once to London, called in my own person at Baker Street, threw Mrs. Hudson into violent hysterics, and found that Mycroft had preserved my rooms and my papers exactly as they had always been. So it was, my dear Watson, that at two o'clock to-day I found myself in my old armchair in my own old room and only wishing that I could have seen my old friend Watson in the other chair which he has so often adorned."

Such was the remarkable narrative to which I listened on that April evening—a narrative which would have been utterly incredible to me had it not been confirmed by the actual sight of the tall, spare figure and the keen, eager face, which I had never thought to see again. In some manner he had learned of my own sad bereavement, and his sympathy was shown in his manner rather than in his words. "Work is the best antidote to sorrow, my dear Watson," said he; "and I have a piece of work for us both to-night which, if we can bring it to a successful conclusion, will in itself justify a man's life on this planet." In vain I begged him to tell me more. "You will hear and see enough before morning," he answered. "We have three years of the past to discuss. Let that suffice until half-past nine, when we start upon the notable adventure of the empty house."

It was indeed like old times when, at that hour, I found myself seated beside him in a hansom, my revolver in my pocket, and the thrill of adventure in my heart. Holmes was cold and stern and silent. As the gleam of the street-lamps flashed upon his austere features, I saw that his brows were drawn down in thought and his thin lips compressed. I knew not what wild beast we were about to hunt down in the dark jungle of criminal London, but I was well assured, from the bearing of this master huntsman, that the adventure was a most grave one—while the sardonic smile which occasionally broke through his ascetic gloom boded little good for the object of our quest.

I had imagined that we were bound for Baker Street,

SIR ARTHUR CONAN DOYLE

but Holmes stopped the cab at the corner of Cavendish Square. I observed that as he stepped out he gave a most searching glance to right and left, and at every subsequent street corner he took the utmost pains to assure that he was not followed. Our route was certainly a singular one. Holmes's knowledge of the byways of London was extraordinary, and on this occasion he passed rapidly and with an assured step through a network of mews and stables, the very existence of which I had never known. We emerged at last into a small road, lined with old, gloomy houses, which led us into Manchester Street, and so to Blandford Street. Here he turned swiftly down a narrow passage, passed through a wooden gate into a deserted yard, and then opened with a key the back door of a house. We entered together, and he closed it behind us.

The place was pitch dark, but it was evident to me that it was an empty house. Our feet creaked and crackled over the bare planking, and my outstretched hand touched a wall from which the paper was hanging in ribbons. Holmes's cold, thin fingers closed round my wrist and led me forward down a long hall, until I dimly saw the murky fanlight over the door. Here Holmes turned suddenly to the right, and we found ourselves in a large, square, empty room, heavily shadowed in the corners, but faintly lit in the centre from the lights of the street beyond. There was no lamp near, and the window was thick with dust, so that we could only just discern each other's figures within. My companion put his hand upon my shoulder and his lips close to my ear.

"Do you know where we are?" he whispered.

"Surely that is Baker Street," I answered, staring through the dim window.

"Exactly. We are in Camden House, which stands opposite to our own old quarters."

"But why are we here?"

"Because it commands so excellent a view of that picturesque pile. Might I trouble you, my dear Watson, to draw a little nearer to the window, taking every precaution not to show yourself, and then to look up at our old rooms—the starting-point of so many of your little fairy-tales? We will see if my three years of absence have entirely taken away my power to surprise you."

I crept forward and looked across at the familiar window. As my eyes fell upon it, I gave a gasp and a cry of amazement. The blind was down, and a strong light was burning in the room. The shadow of a man who was seated in a chair within was thrown in hard, black outline upon the luminous screen of the window. There was no mistaking the poise of the head, the squareness of the shoulders, the sharpness of the features. The face was turned half-round, and the effect was that of one of those black silhouettes which our grandparents loved to frame. It was a perfect reproduction of Holmes. So amazed was I that I threw out my hand to make sure that the man himself was standing beside me. He was quivering with silent laughter.

"Well?" said he.

"Good Heavens!" I cried. "It is marvellous."

"I trust that age doth not wither nor custom stale my infinite variety," said he, and I recognised in his voice the joy and pride which the artist takes in his own creation. "It really is rather like me, is it not?"

"I should be prepared to swear that it was you."

"The credit of the execution is due to Monsieur Oscar Meunier, of Grenoble, who spent some days in doing the moulding. It is a bust in wax. The rest I arranged myself during my visit to Baker Street this afternoon."

"But why?"

"Because, my dear Watson, I had the strongest possible reason for wishing certain people to think that I was there when I was really elsewhere."

"And you thought the rooms were watched?"

"I *knew* that they were watched."

"By whom?"

"By my old enemies, Watson. By the charming society whose leader lies in the Reichenbach Fall. You must remember that they knew, and only they knew, that I was still alive. Sooner or later they believed that I should come back to my rooms. They watched them continuously, and this morning they saw me arrive."

"How do you know?"

"Because I recognised their sentinel when I glanced out of my window. He is a harmless enough fellow, Parker by name, a garroter by trade, and a remarkable performer upon the jew's-harp. I cared nothing for him. But I cared a great deal for the much more formidable person who was behind him, the bosom friend of Moriarty, the man who dropped the rocks over the cliff, the most cunning and dangerous criminal in London. That is the man who is after me to-night, Watson, and that is the man who is quite unaware that we are after *him*."

My friend's plans were gradually revealing themselves. From this convenient retreat, the watchers were being watched and the trackers tracked. That angular shadow up yonder was the bait, and we were the hunters. In silence we stood together in the darkness and watched the hurrying figures who passed and repassed in front of us. Holmes was silent and motionless; but I could tell that he was keenly alert, and that his eyes were fixed intently upon the stream of passers-by. It was a bleak and boisterous night, and the wind whistled shrilly down the long street. Many people were moving to and fro, most of them muffled in their coats and cravats. Once or twice it seemed to me that I had seen the same figure before, and I especially noticed two men who appeared to be sheltering themselves from the wind in the doorway of a house some distance up the street. I tried to draw my companion's attention to them; but he gave a little ejaculation of impatience and continued to stare into the street. More than once he fidgeted with his feet and tapped rapidly with his fingers upon the wall. It was evident to me that he was becoming uneasy, and that his plans were not working out altogether as he had hoped. At last, as midnight approached and the street gradually cleared, he paced up and down the room

in uncontrollable agitation. I was about to make some remark to him, when I raised my eyes to the lighted window
and again experienced almost as great a surprise as before.
I clutched Holmes's arm and pointed upward.

"The shadow has moved!" I cried.

It was indeed no longer the profile, but the back, which
was turned towards us.

Three years had certainly not smoothed the asperities of
his temper or his impatience with a less active intelligence
than his own.

"Of course it has moved," said he. "Am I such a farcical
bungler, Watson, that I should erect an obvious dummy
and expect that some of the sharpest men in Europe
would be deceived by it? We have been in this room two
hours, and Mrs. Hudson has made some change in that
figure eight times, or once in every quarter of an hour.
She works it from the front, so that her shadow may never
be seen. Ah!" He drew in his breath with a shrill, excited
intake. In the dim light I saw his head thrown forward, his
whole attitude rigid with attention. Outside the street was
absolutely deserted. Those two men might still be
crouching in the doorway, but I could no longer see them.
All was still and dark, save only that brilliant yellow screen
in front of us with the black figure outlined upon its
centre. Again in the utter silence I heard that thin, sibilant
note which spoke of intense suppressed excitement. An instant later he pulled me back into the blackest corner of
the room, and I felt his warning hand upon my lips. The
fingers which clutched me were quivering. Never had I
known my friend more moved, and yet the dark street still
stretched lonely and motionless before us.

But suddenly I was aware of that which his keener
senses had already distinguished. A low, stealthy sound
came to my ears, not from the direction of Baker Street,
but from the back of the very house in which we lay concealed. A door opened and shut. An instant later steps
crept down the passage—steps which were meant to be silent, but which reverberated harshly through the empty

355

house. Holmes crouched back against the wall, and I did the same, my hand closing upon the handle of my revolver. Peering through the gloom, I saw the vague outline of a man, a shade blacker than the blackness of the open door. He stood for an instant, and then he crept forward, crouching, menacing, into the room. He was within three yards of us, this sinister figure, and I had braced myself to meet his spring, before I realized that he had no idea of our presence. He passed close beside us, stole over to the window, and very softly and noiselessly raised it for half a foot. As he sank to the level of this opening, the light of the street, no longer dimmed by the dusty glass, fell full upon his face. The man seemed to be beside himself with excitement. His two eyes shone like stars, and his features were working convulsively. He was an elderly man, with a thin, projecting nose, a high, bald forehead, and a huge grizzled moustache. An opera hat was pushed to the back of his head, and an evening-dress shirt-front gleamed out through his open overcoat. His face was gaunt and swarthy, scored with deep, savage lines. In his hand he carried what appeared to be a stick, but as he laid it down upon the floor it gave a metallic clang. Then from the pocket of his overcoat he drew a bulky object, and he busied himself in some task which ended with a loud, sharp click, as if a spring or bolt had fallen into its place. Still kneeling upon the floor he bent forward and threw all his weight and strength upon some lever, with the result that there came a long, whirling, grinding noise, ending once more in a powerful click. He straightened himself then, and I saw that what he held in his hand was a sort of gun, with a curiously misshapen butt. He opened it at the breech, put something in, and snapped the breech-lock. Then, crouching down, he rested the end of the barrel upon the ledge of the open window, and I saw his long moustache droop over the stock and his eye gleam as it peered along the sights. I heard a little sigh of satisfaction as he cuddled the butt into his shoulder, and saw that amazing target, the black man on the yellow ground, standing clear at the end of his foresight. For an instant he was rigid and motionless. Then his finger tightened on the trigger. There was a strange, loud whiz and a long, silvery tinkle of broken glass. At that instant Holmes sprang like a tiger on to the marksman's back and hurled him flat upon his face. He was up again in a moment, and with convulsive strength he seized Holmes by the throat, but I struck him on the head with the butt of my revolver, and he dropped again upon the floor. I fell upon him, and as I held him my comrade blew a shrill call upon a whistle. There was the clatter of running feet upon the pavement, and two policemen in uniform, with one plain-clothes detective, rushed through the front entrance and into the room.

"That you, Lestrade?" said Holmes.

"Yes, Mr. Holmes. I took the job myself. It's good to see you back in London, sir."

"I think you want a little unofficial help. Three undetected murders in one year won't do, Lestrade. But you handled the Molesey Mystery with less than your usual—that's to say, you handled it fairly well."

We had all risen to our feet, our prisoner breathing hard, with a stalwart constable on each side of him. Already a few loiterers had begun to collect in the street. Holmes stepped up to the window, closed it, and dropped the blinds. Lestrade had produced two candles, and the policemen had uncovered their lanterns. I was able at last to have a good look at our prisoner.

It was a tremendously virile and yet sinister face which was turned towards us. With the brow of a philosopher above and the jaw of a sensualist below, the man must have started with great capacities for good or for evil. But one could not look upon his cruel blue eyes, with their drooping, cynical lids, or upon the fierce, aggressive nose and the threatening, deep-lined brow, without reading Nature's plainest danger-signals. He took no heed of any of us, but his eyes were fixed upon Holmes's face with an expression in which hatred and amazement were equally blended. "You fiend!" he kept on muttering. "You clever, clever fiend!"

"Ah, Colonel!" said Holmes, arranging his rumpled collar. "'Journeys end in lovers' meetings,' as the old play says. I don't think I have had the pleasure of seeing you since you favoured me with those attentions as I lay on the ledge above the Reichenbach Fall."

The Colonel still stared at my friend like a man in a trance. "You cunning, cunning fiend!" was all that he could say.

"I have not introduced you yet," said Holmes. "This, gentlemen, is Colonel Sebastian Moran, once of Her Majesty's Indian Army, and the best heavy-game shot that our Eastern Empire has ever produced. I believe I am correct, Colonel, in saying that your bag of tigers still remains unrivalled?"

The fierce old man said nothing, but still glared at my companion. With his savage eyes and bristling moustache he was wonderfully like a tiger himself.

"I wonder that my very simple stratagem could deceive so old a *shikari*," said Holmes. "It must be very familiar to you. Have you not tethered a young kid under a tree, lain above it with your rifle, and waited for the bait to bring up your tiger? This empty house is my tree, and you are my tiger. You have possibly had other guns in reserve in case there should be several tigers, or in the unlikely supposition of your own aim failing you. These," he pointed around, "are my other guns. The parallel is exact."

Colonel Moran sprang forward with a snarl of rage, but the constables dragged him back. The fury upon his face was terrible to look at.

"I confess that you had one small surprise for me," said Holmes. "I did not anticipate that you would yourself make use of this empty house and this convenient front window. I had imagined you as operating from the street, where my friend Lestrade and his merry men were awaiting you. With that exception, all has gone as I expected."

Colonel Moran turned to the official detective.

"You may or may not have just cause for arresting me," said he, "but at least there can be no reason why I should submit to the gibes of this person. If I am in the hands of the law, let things be done in a legal way."

"Well, that's reasonable enough," said Lestrade. "Nothing further you have to say, Mr. Holmes, before we go?"

Holmes had picked up the powerful air-gun from the floor and was examining its mechanism.

"An admirable and unique weapon," said he, "noiseless and of tremendous power: I knew Von Herder, the blind German mechanic, who constructed it to the order of the late Professor Moriarty. For years I have been aware of its existence, though I have never before had the opportunity of handling it. I commend it very specially to your attention, Lestrade, and also the bullets which fit it."

"You can trust us to look after that, Mr. Holmes," said Lestrade, as the whole party moved towards the door.

"Anything further to say?"

"Only to ask what charge you intend to prefer?"

"What charge, sir? Why, of course, the attempted murder of Mr. Sherlock Holmes."

"Not so, Lestrade. I do not propose to appear in the matter at all. To you, and to you only, belongs the credit of the remarkable arrest which you have effected. Yes, Lestrade, I congratulate you! With your usual happy mixture of cunning and audacity, you have got him."

"Got him! Got whom, Mr. Holmes?"

"The man that the whole force has been seeking in vain—Colonel Sebastian Moran, who shot the Honourable Ronald Adair with an expanding bullet from an air-gun through the open window of the second-floor front of No. 427 Park Lane, upon the thirtieth of last month. That's the charge, Lestrade. And now, Watson, if you can endure the draught from a broken window, I think that half an hour in my study over a cigar may afford you some profitable amusement."

359

Our old chambers had been left unchanged through the supervision of Mycroft Holmes and the immediate care of Mrs. Hudson. As I entered I saw, it is true, an unwonted tidiness, but the old landmarks were all in their place. There were the chemical corner and the acid-stained, deal-topped table. There upon a shelf was the row of formidable scrap-books and books of reference which many of our fellow-citizens would have been so glad to burn. The diagrams, the violin-case, and the pipe-rack—even the Persian slipper which contained the tobacco—all met my eyes as I glanced round me. There were two occupants of the room—one, Mrs. Hudson, who beamed upon us both as we entered—the other, the strange dummy which had played so important a part in the evening's adventures. It was a wax-coloured model of my friend, so admirably done that it was a perfect facsimile. It stood on a small pedestal table with an old dressing-gown of Holmes's so draped round it that the illusion from the street was absolutely perfect.

"I hold you observed all precautions, Mrs. Hudson?" said Holmes.

"I went to it on my knees, sir, just as you told me."

"Excellent. You carried the thing out very well. Did you observe where the bullet went?"

"Yes, sir. I'm afraid it has spoilt your beautiful bust, for it passed right through the head and flattened itself on the wall. I picked it up from the carpet. Here it is!"

Holmes held it out to me. "A soft revolver bullet, as you perceive, Watson. There's genius in that, for who would expect to find such a thing fired from an air-gun? All right, Mrs. Hudson. I am much obliged for your assistance. And now, Watson, let me see you in your old seat once more, for there are several points which I should like to discuss with you."

He had thrown off the seedy frock-coat, and now he was the Holmes of old in the mouse-coloured dressing-gown which he took from his effigy.

"The old *shikari's* nerves have not lost their steadiness,

nor his eyes their keenness," said he, with a laugh, as he inspected the shattered forehead of his bust.

"Plumb in the middle of the back of the head and smack through the brain. He was the best shot in India, and I expect that there are few better in London. Have you heard the name?"

"No, I have not."

"Well, well, such is fame! But, then, if I remember right, you had not heard the name of Professor James Moriarty, who had one of the great brains of the century. Just give me down my index of biographies from the shelf."

He turned over the pages lazily, leaning back in his chair and blowing great clouds from his cigar.

"My collection of M's is a fine one," said he. "Moriarty himself is enough to make any letter illustrious, and here is Morgan the poisoner, and Merridew of abominable memory, and Mathews, who knocked out my left canine in the waiting-room at Charing Cross, and, finally, here is our friend of to-night."

He handed over the book, and I read:

Moran, Sebastian, Colonel. Unemployed. Formerly 1st Bangalore Pioneers. Born London, 1840. Son of Sir Augustus Moran, C. B., once British Minister to Persia. Educated Eton and Oxford. Served in Jowaki Campaign, Afghan Campaign, Charasiab (despatches), Sherpur, and Cabul. Author of *Heavy Game of the Western Himalayas* (1881); *Three Months in the Jungle* (1884). Address: Conduit Street. Clubs: The Anglo-Indian, the Tankerville, the Bagatelle Card Club.

On the margin was written, in Holmes's precise hand:

The second most dangerous man in London.

"This is astonishing," said I, as I handed back the volume. "The man's career is that of an honourable soldier."

"It is true," Holmes answered. "Up to a certain point he did well. He was always a man of iron nerve, and the story is still told in India how he crawled down a drain after a wounded man-eating tiger. There are some trees, Watson, which grow to a certain height and then suddenly develop some unsightly eccentricity. You will see it often in humans. I have a theory that the individual represents in his development the whole procession of his ancestors, and that such a sudden turn to good or evil stands for some strong influence which came into the line of his pedigree. The person becomes, as it were, the epitome of the history of his own family."

"It is surely rather fanciful."

"Well, I don't insist upon it. Whatever the cause, Colonel Moran began to go wrong. Without any open scandal, he still made India too hot to hold him. He retired, came to London, and again acquired an evil name. It was at this time that he was sought out by Professor Moriarty, to whom for a time he was chief of the staff. Moriarty supplied him liberally with money and used him only in one or two very high-class jobs, which no ordinary criminal could have undertaken. You may have some recollection of the death of Mrs. Stewart, of Lauder, in 1887. Not? Well, I am sure Moran was at the bottom of it, but nothing could be proved. So cleverly was the Colonel concealed that, even when the Moriarty gang was broken up, we could not incriminate him. You remember at that date, when I called upon you in your rooms, how I put up the shutters for fear of air-guns? No doubt you thought me fanciful. I knew exactly what I was doing, for I knew of the existence of this remarkable gun, and I knew also that one of the best shots in the world would be behind it. When we were in Switzerland he followed us with Moriarty, and it was undoubtedly he who gave me that evil five minutes on the Reichenbach ledge.

"You may think that I read the papers with some attention during my sojourn in France, on the look-out for any chance of laying him by the heels. So long as he was free in London, my life would really not have been worth living. Night and day the shadow would have been over me, and sooner or later his chance must have come. What could I do? I could not shoot him at sight, or I should myself be in the dock. There was no use appealing to a magistrate. They cannot interfere on the strength of what would appear to them to be a wild suspicion. So I could do nothing. But I watched the criminal news, knowing that sooner or later I should get him. Then came the death of this Ronald Adair. My chance had come at last. Knowing what I did, was it not certain that Colonel Moran had done it? He had played cards with the lad, he had followed him home from the club, he had shot him through the open window. There was not a doubt of it. The bullets alone are enough to put his head in a noose. I came over at once. I was seen by the sentinel, who would, I knew, direct the Colonel's attention to my presence. He could not fail to connect my sudden return with his crime and to be terribly alarmed. I was sure that he would make an attempt to get me out of the way *at once* and would bring round his murderous weapon for that purpose. I left him an excellent mark in the window, and, having warned the police that they might be needed—by the way, Watson, you spotted their presence in that doorway with unerring accuracy—I took up what seemed to me to be a judicious post for observation, never dreaming that he would choose the same spot for his attack. Now, my dear Watson, does anything remain for me to explain?"

"Yes," said I. "You have not made it clear what was Colonel Moran's motive in murdering the Honourable Ronald Adair?"

"Ah! My dear Watson, there we come into those realms of conjecture, where the most logical mind may be at fault. Each may form his own hypothesis upon the present evidence, and yours is as likely to be correct as mine."

"You have formed one, then?"

"I think that it is not difficult to explain the facts. It came out in evidence that Colonel Moran and young Adair had, between them, won a considerable amount of money. Now, Moran undoubtedly played foul—of that I have long been aware. I believe that on the day of the murder

Adair had discovered that Moran was cheating. Very likely he had spoken to him privately and had threatened to expose him unless he voluntarily resigned his membership of the club and promised not to play cards again. It is unlikely that a youngster like Adair would at once make a hideous scandal by exposing a well-known man so much older than himself. Probably he acted as I suggest. The exclusion from his clubs would mean ruin to Moran, who lived by his ill-gotten card-gains. He therefore murdered Adair, who at the time was endeavouring to work out how much money he should himself return, since he could not profit by his partner's foul play. He locked the door lest the ladies should surprise him and insist upon knowing what he was doing with these names and coins. Will it pass?"

"I have no doubt that you have hit upon the truth."

"It will be verified or disproved at the trial. Meanwhile, come what may, Colonel Moran will trouble us no more. The famous air-gun of Von Herder will embellish the Scotland Yard Museum, and once again Mr. Sherlock Holmes is free to devote his life to examining those interesting little problems which the complex life of London so plentifully presents."

The Adventure of the
Norwood Builder

"From the point of view of the criminal expert," said Mr. Sherlock Holmes, "London has become a singularly uninteresting city since the death of the late lamented Professor Moriarty."

"I can hardly think that you would find many decent citizens to agree with you," I answered.

"Well, well, I must not be selfish," said he, with a smile, as he pushed back his chair from the breakfast-table. "The community is certainly the gainer, and no one the loser, save the poor out-of-work specialist, whose occupation has gone. With that man in the field, one's morning paper presented infinite possibilities. Often it was only the smallest trace, Watson, the faintest indication, and yet it was enough to tell me that the great malignant brain was there, as the gentlest tremors of the edges of the web remind one of the foul spider which lurks in the centre. Petty thefts, wanton assaults, purposeless outrage—to the man who held the clue all could be worked into one connected whole. To the scientific student of the higher criminal world, no capital in Europe offered the advantages which London then possessed. But now—" He shrugged his shoulders in humorous deprecation of the state of things which he had himself done so much to produce.

At the time of which I speak, Holmes had been back for some months, and I at his request had sold my practice and returned to share the old quarters in Baker Street. A young doctor named Verner had purchased my small Kensington practice and given with astonishingly little demur the highest price that I ventured to ask—an incident which only explained itself some years later, when I found that Verner was a distant relation of Holmes, and that it was my friend who had really found the money.

Our months of partnership had not been so uneventful as he had stated, for I find, on looking over my notes, that this period includes the case of the papers of ex-President Murillo, and also the shocking affair of the Dutch steamship *Friesland*, which so nearly cost us both our lives. His cold and proud nature was always averse, however, from anything in the shape of public applause, and he bound me in the most stringent terms to say no further word of himself, his methods, or his successes—a prohibition which, as I have explained, has only now been removed.

Mr. Sherlock Holmes was leaning back in his chair after his whimsical protest and was unfolding his morning paper in a leisurely fashion, when our attention was arrested by a tremendous ring at the bell, followed immediately by a hollow drumming sound, as if someone were beating on the outer door with his fist. As it opened there came a tumultuous rush into the hall, rapid feet clattered up the stair, and an instant later a wild-eyed and frantic young man, pale, dishevelled, and palpitating, burst into the room. He looked from one to the other of us, and under our gaze of inquiry he became conscious that some apology was needed for this unceremonious entry.

"I'm sorry, Mr. Holmes," he cried. "You mustn't blame me. I am nearly mad. Mr. Holmes, I am the unhappy John Hector McFarlane."

He made the announcement as if the name alone would explain both his visit and its manner, but I could see, by my companion's unresponsive face, that it meant no more to him than to me.

"Have a cigarette, Mr. McFarlane," said he, pushing his case across. "I am sure that, with your symptoms, my friend Dr. Watson here would prescribe a sedative. The

weather has been so very warm these last few days. Now, if
you feel a little more composed, I should be glad if you
would sit down in that chair and tell us very slowly and
quietly who you are, and what it is that you want. You
mentioned your name, as if I should recognise it, but I assure you that, beyond the obvious facts that you are a
bachelor, a solicitor, a Freemason, and an asthmatic, I
know nothing whatever about you."

Familiar as I was with my friend's methods, it was not
difficult for me to follow his deductions, and to observe
the untidiness of attire, the sheaf of legal papers, the
watch-charm, and the breathing which had prompted
them. Our client, however, stared in amazement.

"Yes, I am all that, Mr. Holmes; and, in addition, I am
the most unfortunate man at this moment in London. For
Heaven's sake, don't abandon me, Mr. Holmes! If they
come to arrest me before I have finished my story, make
them give me time, so that I may tell you the whole truth. I
could go to gaol happy if I knew that you were working for
me outside."

"Arrest you!" said Holmes. "This is really most
grati—most interesting. On what charge do you expect to
be arrested?"

"Upon the charge of murdering Mr. Jonas Oldacre, of
Lower Norwood."

My companion's expressive face showed a sympathy which was not, I am afraid, entirely unmixed with
satisfaction.

"Dear me," said he, "it was only this moment at breakfast
that I was saying to my friend, Dr. Watson, that sensational
cases had disappeared out of our papers."

Our visitor stretched forward a quivering hand and
picked up the *Daily Telegraph,* which still lay upon Holmes's
knee.

"If you had looked at it, sir, you would have seen at a
glance what the errand is on which I have come to you this
morning. I feel as if my name and my misfortune must be
in every man's mouth." He turned it over to expose the

central page. "Here it is, and with your permission I will read it to you. Listen to this, Mr. Holmes. The headlines are: 'Mysterious Affair at Lower Norwood. Disappearance of a Well-Known Builder. Suspicion of Murder and Arson. A Clue to the Criminal.' That is the clue which they are already following, Mr. Holmes, and I know that it leads infallibly to me. I have been followed from London Bridge Station, and I am sure that they are only waiting for the warrant to arrest me. It will break my mother's heart—it will break her heart!" He wrung his hands in an agony of apprehension and swayed backward and forward in his chair.

I looked with interest upon this man, who was accused of being the perpetrator of a crime of violence. He was flaxen-haired and handsome, in a washed-out negative fashion, with frightened blue eyes, and a clean-shaven face, with a weak, sensitive mouth. His age may have been about twenty-seven, his dress and bearing that of a gentleman. From the pocket of his light summer overcoat protruded the bundle of indorsed papers which proclaimed his profession.

"We must use what time we have," said Holmes. "Watson, would you have the kindness to take the paper and to read the paragraph in question?"

Underneath the vigorous headlines which our client had quoted, I read the following suggestive narrative:

"Late last night, or early this morning, an incident occurred at Lower Norwood which points, it is feared, to a serious crime. Mr. Jonas Oldacre is a well-known resident of that suburb, where he has carried on his business as a builder for many years. Mr. Oldacre is a bachelor, fifty-two years of age, and lives in Deep Dene House, at the Sydenham end of the road of that name. He has had the reputation of being a man of eccentric habits, secretive and retiring. For some years he has practically withdrawn from the business, in which he is said to have massed considerable wealth. A small timber-yard still exists, however, at the back of the house, and last night, about twelve o'clock, an alarm was given that one of the stacks was on fire. The engines were soon upon the spot, but the dry wood burned with great fury, and it was impossible to arrest the conflagration until the stack had been entirely consumed. Up to this point the incident bore the appearance of an ordinary accident, but fresh indications seem to point to serious crime. Surprise was expressed at the absence of the master of the establishment from the scene of the fire, and an inquiry followed, which showed that he had disappeared from the house. An examination of his room revealed that the bed had not been slept in, that a safe which stood in it was open, that a number of important papers were scattered about the room, and finally, that there were signs of a murderous struggle, slight traces of blood being found within the room, and an oaken walking-stick, which also showed stains of blood upon the handle. It is known that Mr. Jonas Oldacre had received a late visitor in his bedroom upon that night, and the stick found has been identified as the property of this person, who is a young London solicitor named John Hector McFarlane, junior partner of Graham and McFarlane, of 426 Gresham Buildings, E. C. The police believe that they have evidence in their possession which supplies a very convincing motive for the crime, and altogether it cannot be doubted that sensational developments will follow.

"LATER.—It is rumoured as we go to press that Mr. John Hector McFarlane has actually been arrested on the charge of the murder of Mr. Jonas Oldacre. It is at least certain that a warrant has been issued. There have been further and sinister developments in the investigation at Norwood. Besides the signs of a struggle in the room of the unfortunate builder it is now known that the French windows of his bedroom (which is on the ground floor) were found to be open, that there were marks as if some bulky object had been dragged across to the wood-pile, and, finally, it is asserted that charred remains have been found among the charcoal ashes of the fire. The police theory is that a most sensational crime has been committed, that the victim was clubbed to death in his own bedroom, his papers rifled, and his dead body dragged across to the wood-stack, which was then ignited so as to hide all traces of the crime. The conduct of the criminal investigation has been left in the experienced hands of Inspector Lestrade, of Scotland Yard, who is following up the clues with his accustomed energy and sagacity."

Sherlock Holmes listened with closed eyes and finger-tips together to this remarkable account.

"The case has certainly some points of interest," said he,

in his languid fashion. "May I ask, in the first place, Mr. McFarlane, how it is that you are still at liberty, since there appears to be enough evidence to justify your arrest?"

"I live at Torrington Lodge, Blackheath, with my parents, Mr. Holmes, but last night, having to do business very late with Mr. Jonas Oldacre, I stayed at an hotel in Norwood and came to my business from there. I knew nothing of this affair until I was in the train, when I read what you have just heard. I at once saw the horrible danger of my position, and I hurried to put the case into your hands. I have no doubt that I should have been arrested either at my city office or at my home. A man followed me from London Bridge Station, and I have no doubt— Great Heaven! What is that?"

It was a clang of the bell, followed instantly by heavy steps upon the stair. A moment later, our old friend Lestrade appeared in the doorway. Over his shoulder I caught a glimpse of one or two uniformed policemen outside.

"Mr. John Hector McFarlane?" said Lestrade.

Our unfortunate client rose with a ghastly face.

"I arrest you for the wilful murder of Mr. Jonas Oldacre, of Lower Norwood."

McFarlane turned to us with a gesture of despair and sank into his chair once more like one who is crushed.

"One moment, Lestrade," said Holmes. "Half an hour more or less can make no difference to you, and the gentleman was about to give us an account of this very interesting affair, which might aid us in clearing it up."

"I think there will be no difficulty in clearing it up," said Lestrade, grimly.

"None the less, with your permission, I should be much interested to hear his account."

"Well, Mr. Holmes, it is difficult for me to refuse you anything, for you have been of use to the force once or twice in the past, and we owe you a good turn at Scotland Yard," said Lestrade. "At the same time I must remain with my prisoner, and I am bound to warn him that anything he may say will appear in evidence against him."

"I wish nothing better," said our client. "All I ask is that you should hear and recognise the absolute truth."

Lestrade looked at his watch. "I'll give you half an hour," said he.

"I must explain first," said McFarlane, "that I knew nothing of Mr. Jonas Oldacre. His name was familiar to me, for many years ago my parents were acquainted with him, but they drifted apart. I was very much surprised, therefore, when yesterday, about three o'clock in the afternoon, he walked into my office in the city. But I was still more astonished when he told me the object of his visit. He had in his hand several sheets of a note-book, covered with scribbled writing—here they are—and he laid them on my table.

"'Here is my will,' said he. 'I want you, Mr. McFarlane, to cast it into proper legal shape. I will sit here while you do so.'

"I set myself to copy it, and you can imagine my astonishment when I found that, with some reservations, he had left all his property to me. He was a strange little ferret-like man, with white eyelashes, and when I looked up at him I found his keen grey eyes fixed upon me with an amused expression. I could hardly believe my own senses as I read the terms of the will; but he explained that he was a bachelor with hardly any living relation, that he had known my parents in his youth, and that he had always heard of me as a very deserving young man and was assured that his money would be in worthy hands. Of course, I could only stammer out my thanks. The will was duly finished, signed, and witnessed by my clerk. This is it on the blue paper, and these slips, as I have explained, are the rough draft. Mr. Jonas Oldacre then informed me that there were a number of documents—building leases, title-deeds, mortgages, scrip, and so forth—which it was necessary that I should see and understand. He said that his mind would not be easy until the whole thing was settled, and he begged me to come out to his house at Norwood that night, bringing the will with me, and to arrange matters. 'Remember, my boy, not one word to your parents about the affair until everything is settled. We will keep it as a little surprise for them.' He was very insistent upon this point and made me promise it faithfully.

"You can imagine, Mr. Holmes, that I was not in a humour to refuse him anything that he might ask. He was my benefactor, and all my desire was to carry out his wishes in every particular. I sent a telegram home, therefore, to say that I had important business on hand, and that it was impossible for me to say how late I might be. Mr. Oldacre had told me that he would like me to have supper with him at nine, as he might not be home before that hour. I had some difficulty in finding his house, however, and it was nearly half-past before I reached it. I found him—"

"One moment!" said Holmes. "Who opened the door?"

"A middle-aged woman, who was, I suppose, his housekeeper."

"And it was she, I presume, who mentioned your name?"

"Exactly," said McFarlane.

"Pray proceed."

McFarlane wiped his damp brow and then continued his narrative:

"I was shown by this woman into a sitting-room, where a frugal supper was laid out. Afterwards, Mr. Jonas Oldacre led me into his bedroom, in which there stood a heavy safe. This he opened and took out a mass of documents, which we went over together. It was between eleven and twelve when we finished. He remarked that we must not disturb the housekeeper. He showed me out through his own French window, which had been open all this time."

"Was the blind down?" asked Holmes.

"I will not be sure, but I believe that it was only half down. Yes, I remember how he pulled it up in order to swing open the window. I could not find my stick, and he said, 'Never mind, my boy, I shall see a good deal of you now, I hope, and I will keep your stick until you come back to claim it.' I left him there, the safe open, and the papers made up in packets upon the table. It was so late that I could not get back to Blackheath, so I spent the night at the Anerley Arms, and I knew nothing more until I read of this horrible affair in the morning."

"Anything more that you would like to ask, Mr. Holmes?" said Lestrade, whose eyebrows had gone up once or twice during this remarkable explanation.

"Not until I have been to Blackheath."

"You mean to Norwood," said Lestrade.

"Oh, yes, no doubt that is what I must have meant," said Holmes, with his enigmatical smile. Lestrade had learned by more experiences than he would care to acknowledge that that razor-like brain could cut through that which was impenetrable to him. I saw him look curiously at my companion.

"I think I should like to have a word with you presently, Mr. Sherlock Holmes," said he. "Now, Mr. McFarlane, two of my constables are at the door, and there is a four-wheeler waiting." The wretched young man arose and, with a last beseeching glance at us, walked from the room. The officers conducted him to the cab, but Lestrade remained.

Holmes had picked up the pages which formed the rough draft of the will and was looking at them with the keenest interest upon his face.

"There are some points about that document, Lestrade, are there not?" said he, pushing them over.

The official looked at them with a puzzled expression.

"I can read the first few lines, and these in the middle of the second page, and one or two at the end. Those are as clear as print," said he, "but the writing in between is very bad, and there are three places where I cannot read it at all."

"What do you make of that?" said Holmes.

"Well, what do *you* make of it?"

"That it was written in a train. The good writing represents stations, the bad writing movement, and the very bad writing passing over points. A scientific expert would pronounce at once that this was drawn up on a suburban line, since nowhere save in the immediate vicinity of a great city could there be so quick a succession of points. Granting that his whole journey was occupied in drawing up the will, then the train was an express, only stopping once between Norwood and London Bridge."

Lestrade began to laugh.

"You are too many for me when you begin to get on your theories, Mr. Holmes," said he. "How does this bear on the case?"

"Well, it corroborates the young man's story to the extent that the will was drawn up by Jonas Oldacre in his journey yesterday. It is curious—is it not?—that a man should draw up so important a document in so haphazard a fashion. It suggests that he did not think it was going to be of much practical importance. If a man drew up a will which he did not intend ever to be effective, he might do it so."

"Well, he drew up his own death warrant at the same time," said Lestrade.

"Oh, you think so?"

"Don't you?"

"Well, it is quite possible, but the case is not clear to me yet."

"Not clear? Well, if that isn't clear, what *could* be clear? Here is a young man who learns suddenly that, if a certain older man dies, he will succeed to a fortune. What does he do? He says nothing to anyone, but he arranges that he shall go out on some pretext to see his client that night. He waits until the only other person in the house is in bed, and then in the solitude of a man's room he murders him, burns his body in the wood-pile, and departs to a neighbouring hotel. The blood-stains in the room and also on the stick are very slight. It is probable that he imagined his crime to be a bloodless one, and hoped that if the body were consumed it would hide all traces of the method of his death—traces which, for some reason, must have pointed to him. Is not all this obvious?"

"It strikes me, my good Lestrade, as being just a trifle

too obvious," said Holmes. "You do not add imagination to your other great qualities, but if you could for one moment put yourself in the place of this young man, would you choose the very night after the will had been made to commit your crime? Would it not seem dangerous to you to make so very close a relation between the two incidents? Again, would you choose an occasion when you are known to be in the house, when a servant has let you in? And, finally, would you take the great pains to conceal the body, and yet leave your own stick as a sign that you were the criminal? Confess, Lestrade, that all this is very unlikely."

"As to the stick, Mr. Holmes, you know as well as I do that a criminal is often flurried and does such things, which a cool man would avoid. He was very likely afraid to go back to the room. Give me another theory that would fit the facts."

"I could very easily give you half a dozen," said Holmes. "Here, for example, is a very possible and even probable one. I make you a free present of it. The older man is showing documents which are of evident value. A passing tramp sees them through the window, the blind of which is only half down. Exit the solicitor. Enter the tramp! He seizes a stick, which he observes there, kills Oldacre, and departs after burning the body."

"Why should the tramp burn the body?"

"For the matter of that, why should McFarlane?"

"To hide some evidence."

"Possibly the tramp wanted to hide that any murder at all had been committed."

"And why did the tramp take nothing?"

"Because they were papers that he could not negotiate."

Lestrade shook his head, though it seemed to me that his manner was less absolutely assured than before.

"Well, Mr. Sherlock Holmes, you may look for your tramp, and while you are finding him we will hold on to our man. The future will show which is right. Just notice this point, Mr. Holmes: that so far as we know, none of the papers were removed, and that the prisoner is the one man in the world who had no reason for removing them, since he was heir-at-law and would come into them in any case."

My friend seemed struck by this remark.

"I don't mean to deny that the evidence is in some ways very strongly in favour of your theory," said he. "I only wish to point out that there are other theories possible. As you say, the future will decide. Good-morning! I dare say that in the course of the day I shall drop in at Norwood and see how you are getting on."

When the detective departed, my friend rose and made his preparations for the day's work with the alert air of a man who has a congenial task before him.

"My first movement, Watson," said he, as he bustled into his frock-coat, "must, as I said, be in the direction of Blackheath."

"And why not Norwood?"

"Because we have in this case one singular incident coming close to the heels of another singular incident. The police are making the mistake of concentrating their attention upon the second, because it happens to be the one which is actually criminal. But it is evident to me that the logical way to approach the case is to begin by trying to throw some light upon the first incident—the curious will, so suddenly made, and to so unexpected an heir. It may do something to simplify what followed. No, my dear fellow, I don't think you can help me. There is no prospect of danger, or I should not dream of stirring out without you. I trust that when I see you in the evening, I will be able to report that I have been able to do something for this unfortunate youngster, who has thrown himself upon my protection."

It was late when my friend returned, and I could see, by a glance at his haggard and anxious face, that the high hopes with which he had started had not been fulfilled. For an hour he droned away upon his violin, endeavouring to soothe his own ruffled spirits. At last he flung down the instrument and plunged into a detailed account of his misadventures.

"It's all going wrong, Watson—all as wrong as it can go.

I kept a bold face before Lestrade, but, upon my soul, I believe that for once the fellow is on the right track and we are on the wrong. All my instincts are one way, and all the facts are the other, and I much fear that British juries have not yet attained that pitch of intelligence when they will give the preference to my theories over Lestrade's facts."

"Did you go to Blackheath?"

"Yes, Watson, I went there, and I found very quickly that the late lamented Oldacre was a pretty considerable blackguard. The father was away in search of his son. The mother was at home—a little, fluffy, blue-eyed person, in a tremor of fear and indignation. Of course, she would not admit even the possibility of his guilt. But she would not express either surprise or regret over the fate of Oldacre. On the contrary, she spoke of him with such bitterness that she was unconsciously considerably strengthening the case of the police for, of course, if her son had heard her speak of the man in this fashion, it would predispose him towards hatred and violence. 'He was more like a malignant and cunning ape than a human being,' said she, 'and he always was, ever since he was a young man.'

"'You knew him at that time?' said I.

"'Yes, I knew him well; in fact, he was an old suitor of mine. Thank Heaven that I had the sense to turn away from him and to marry a better, if poorer, man. I was engaged to him, Mr. Holmes, when I heard a shocking story of how he had turned a cat loose in an aviary, and I was so horrified at his brutal cruelty that I would have nothing more to do with him.' She rummaged in a bureau, and presently she produced a photograph of a woman, shamefully defaced and mutilated with a knife. 'That is my own photograph,' she said. 'He sent it to me in that state, with his curse, upon my wedding morning.'

"'Well,' said I, 'at least he has forgiven you now, since he has left all his property to your son.'

"'Neither my son nor I want anything from Jonas Oldacre, dead or alive!' she cried, with a proper spirit. 'There is a God in Heaven, Mr. Holmes, and that same

God who has punished that wicked man will show, in His own good time, that my son's hands are guiltless of his blood.'

"Well, I tried one or two leads, but could get at nothing which would help our hypothesis, and several points which would make against it. I gave it up at last, and off I went to Norwood.

"This place, Deep Dene House, is a big modern villa of staring brick, standing back in its own grounds, with a laurel-clumped lawn in front of it. To the right and some distance back from the road was the timber-yard which had been the scene of the fire. Here's a rough plan on a leaf of my note-book. This window on the left is the one which opens into Oldacre's room. You can look into it from the road, you see. That is about the only bit of consolation I have had to-day. Lestrade was not there, but his head constable did the honours. They had just found a great treasure-trove. They had spent the morning raking among the ashes of the burned wood-pile, and besides the charred organic remains they had secured several discoloured metal discs. I examined them with care, and there was no doubt that they were trouser buttons. I even distinguished that one of them was marked with the name of 'Hyams,' who was Oldacre's tailor. I then worked the lawn very carefully for signs and traces, but this drought has made everything as hard as iron. Nothing was to be seen save that some body or bundle had been dragged through a low privet hedge which is in a line with the wood-pile. All that, of course, fits in with the official theory. I crawled about the lawn with an August sun on my back, but I got up at the end of an hour no wiser than before.

"Well, after this fiasco I went into the bedroom and examined that also. The blood-stains were very slight, mere smears and discolourations, but undoubtedly fresh. The stick had been removed, but there also the marks were slight. There is no doubt about the stick belonging to our client. He admits it. Footmarks of both men could be made out on the carpet, but none of any third person, which again is a trick for the other side. They were piling up their score all the time and we were at a standstill.

"Only one little gleam of hope did I get—and yet it amounted to nothing. I examined the contents of the safe, most of which had been taken out and left on the table. The papers had been made up into sealed envelopes, one or two of which had been opened by the police. They were not, so far as I could judge, of any great value, nor did the bank-book show that Mr. Oldacre was in such very affluent circumstances. But it seemed to me that all the papers were not there. There were allusions to some deeds—possibly the more valuable—which I could not find. This, of course, if we could definitely prove it, would turn Lestrade's argument against himself; for who would steal a thing if he knew that he would shortly inherit it?

"Finally, having drawn every other cover and picked up no scent, I tried my luck with the housekeeper. Mrs. Lexington is her name—a little, dark, silent person, with suspicious and sidelong eyes. She could tell us something if she would—I am convinced of it. But she was as close as wax. Yes, she had let Mr. McFarlane in at half-past nine. She wished her hand had withered before she had done so. She had gone to bed at half-past ten. Her room was at the other end of the house, and she could hear nothing of what passed. Mr. McFarlane had left his hat, and to the best of her belief his stick, in the hall. She had been awakened by the alarm of fire. Her poor, dear master had certainly been murdered. Had he any enemies? Well, every man had enemies, but Mr. Oldacre kept himself very much to himself and only met people in the way of business. She had seen the buttons and was sure that they belonged to the clothes which he had worn last night. The wood-pile was very dry, for it had not rained for a month. It burned like tinder, and by the time she reached the spot, nothing could be seen but flames. She and all the firemen smelled the burned flesh from inside it. She knew nothing of the papers, nor of Mr. Oldacre's private affairs.

"So, my dear Watson, there's my report of a failure. And

yet—and yet—" he clenched his thin hands in a paroxysm of conviction—"I *know* it's all wrong. I feel it in my bones. There is something that has not come out, and that house-keeper knows it. There was a sort of sulky defiance in her eyes, which only goes with guilty knowledge. However, there's no good talking any more about it, Watson; but unless some lucky chance comes our way I fear that the Norwood Disappearance Case will not figure in that chronicle of our successes which I foresee that a patient public will sooner or later have to endure."

"Surely," said I, "the man's appearance would go far with any jury?"

"That is a dangerous argument, my dear Watson. You remember that terrible murderer, Bert Stevens, who wanted us to get him off in '87? Was there ever a more mild-mannered, Sunday-school young man?"

"It is true."

"Unless we succeed in establishing an alternative theory, this man is lost. You can hardly find a flaw in the case which can now be presented against him, and all further investigation has served to strengthen it. By the way, there is one curious little point about those papers which may serve us as the starting-point for an inquiry. On looking over the bank-book I found that the low state of the balance was principally due to large checks which have been made out during the last year to Mr. Cornelius. I confess that I should be interested to know who this Mr. Cornelius may be with whom a retired builder has had such very large transactions. Is it possible that he has had a hand in the affair? Cornelius might be a broker, but we have found no scrip to correspond with these large payments. Failing any other indication, my researches must now take the direction of an inquiry at the bank for the gentleman who has cashed these checks. But I fear, my dear fellow, that our case will end ingloriously by Lestrade hanging our client, which will certainly be a triumph for Scotland Yard."

I do not know how far Sherlock Holmes took any sleep

that night, but when I came down to breakfast I found him pale and harassed, his bright eyes the brighter for the dark shadows round them. The carpet round his chair was littered with cigarette-ends and with the early editions of the morning papers. An open telegram lay upon the table.

"What do you think of this, Watson?" he asked, tossing it across.

It was from Norwood and ran as follows:

Important fresh evidence to hand. McFarlane's guilt definitely established. Advise you to abandon case.

LESTRADE

"This sounds serious," said I.

"It is Lestrade's little cock-a-doodle of victory," Holmes answered, with a bitter smile. "And yet it may be premature to abandon the case. After all, important fresh evidence is a two-edged thing and may possibly cut in a very different direction to that which Lestrade imagines. Take your breakfast, Watson, and we will go out together and see what we can do. I feel as if I shall need your company and your moral support to-day."

My friend had no breakfast himself, for it was one of his peculiarities that in his more intense moments he would permit himself no food, and I have known him presume upon his iron strength until he has fainted from pure inanition. "At present I cannot spare energy and nerve force for digestion," he would say in answer to my medical remonstrances. I was not surprised, therefore, when this morning he left his untouched meal behind him and started with me for Norwood. A crowd of morbid sightseers were still gathered round Deep Dene House, which was just such a suburban villa as I had pictured. Within the gates Lestrade met us, his face flushed with victory, his manner grossly triumphant.

"Well, Mr. Holmes, have you proved us to be wrong yet? Have you found your tramp?" he cried.

"I have formed no conclusion whatever," my companion answered.

"But we formed ours yesterday, and now it proves to be

correct, so you must acknowledge that we have been a little in front of you this time, Mr. Holmes."

"You certainly have the air of something unusual having occurred," said Holmes.

Lestrade laughed loudly.

"You don't like being beaten any more than the rest of us do," said he. "A man can't expect always to have it his own way, can he, Dr. Watson? Step this way, if you please, gentlemen, and I think I can convince you once for all that it was John McFarlane who did this crime."

He led us through the passage and out into a dark hall beyond.

"This is where young McFarlane must have come out to get his hat after the crime was done," said he. "Now look at this." With dramatic suddenness he struck a match and by its light exposed a stain of blood upon the whitewashed wall. As he held the match nearer, I saw that it was more than a stain. It was the well-marked print of a thumb.

"Look at that with your magnifying glass, Mr. Holmes."

"Yes, I am doing so."

"You are aware that no two thumb-marks are alike?"

"I have heard something of the kind."

"Well, then, will you please compare that print with this wax impression of young McFarlane's right thumb, taken by my orders this morning?"

As he held the waxen print close to the blood-stain, it did not take a magnifying glass to see that the two were undoubtedly from the same thumb. It was evident to me that our unfortunate client was lost.

"That is final," said Lestrade.

"Yes, that is final," I involuntarily echoed.

"It is final," said Holmes.

Something in his tone caught my ear, and I turned to look at him. An extraordinary change had come over his face. It was writhing with inward merriment. His two eyes were shining like stars. It seemed to me that he was making desperate efforts to restrain a convulsive attack of laughter.

"Dear me! Dear me!" he said at last. "Well, now, who

SIR ARTHUR CONAN DOYLE

would have thought it? And how deceptive appearances may be, to be sure! Such a nice young man to look at! It is a lesson to us not to trust our own judgment, is it not, Lestrade?"

"Yes, some of us are a little too much inclined to be cocksure, Mr. Holmes," said Lestrade. The man's insolence was maddening, but we could not resent it.

"What a providential thing that this young man should press his right thumb against the wall in taking his hat from the peg! Such a very natural action, too, if you come to think of it." Holmes was outwardly calm, but his whole body gave a wriggle of suppressed excitement as he spoke.

"By the way, Lestrade, who made this remarkable discovery?"

"It was the housekeeper, Mrs. Lexington, who drew the night constable's attention to it."

"Where was the night constable?"

"He remained on guard in the bedroom where the crime was committed, so as to see that nothing was touched."

"But why didn't the police see this mark yesterday?"

"Well, we had no particular reason to make a careful examination of the hall. Besides, it's not in a very prominent place, as you see."

"No, no—of course not. I suppose there is no doubt that the mark was there yesterday?"

Lestrade looked at Holmes as if he thought he was going out of his mind. I confess that I was myself surprised both at his hilarious manner and at his rather wild observation.

"I don't know whether you think that McFarlane came out of gaol in the dead of the night in order to strengthen the evidence against himself," said Lestrade. "I leave it to any expert in the world whether that is not the mark of his thumb."

"It is unquestionably the mark of his thumb."

"There, that's enough," said Lestrade. "I am a practical man, Mr. Holmes, and when I have got my evidence I come to my conclusions. If you have anything to say, you will find me writing my report in the sitting-room."

384

Holmes had recovered his equanimity, though I still seemed to detect gleams of amusement in his expression.

"Dear me, this is a very sad development, Watson, is it not?" said he. "And yet there are singular points about it which hold out some hopes for our client."

"I am delighted to hear it," said I, heartily. "I was afraid it was all up with him."

"I would hardly go so far as to say that, my dear Watson. The fact is that there is one really serious flaw in this evidence to which our friend attaches so much importance."

"Indeed, Holmes! What is it?"

"Only this: that I *know* that that mark was not there when I examined the hall yesterday. And now, Watson, let us have a little stroll round in the sunshine."

With a confused brain, but with a heart into which some warmth of hope was returning, I accompanied my friend in a walk round the garden. Holmes took each face of the house in turn and examined it with great interest. He then led the way inside and went over the whole building from basement to attic. Most of the rooms were unfurnished, but none the less Holmes inspected them all minutely. Finally, on the top corridor, which ran outside three untenanted bedrooms, he again was seized with a spasm of merriment.

"There are really some very unique features about this case, Watson," said he. "I think it is time now that we took our friend Lestrade into our confidence. He has had his little smile at our expense, and perhaps we may do as much by him, if my reading of this problem proves to be correct. Yes, yes, I think I see how we should approach it."

The Scotland Yard inspector was still writing in the parlour when Holmes interrupted him.

"I understood that you were writing a report of this case," said he.

"So I am."

"Don't you think it may be a little premature? I can't help thinking that your evidence is not complete."

Lestrade knew my friend too well to disregard his words. He laid down his pen and looked curiously at him.

"What do you mean, Mr. Holmes?"

"Only that there is an important witness whom you have not seen."

"Can you produce him?"

"I think I can."

"Then do so."

"I will do my best. How many constables have you?"

"There are three within call."

"Excellent!" said Holmes. "May I ask if they are all large, able-bodied men with powerful voices?"

"I have no doubt they are, though I fail to see what their voices have to do with it."

"Perhaps I can help you to see that and one or two other things as well," said Holmes. "Kindly summon your men, and I will try."

Five minutes later, three policemen had assembled in the hall.

"In the outhouse you will find a considerable quantity of straw," said Holmes. "I will ask you to carry in two bundles of it. I think it will be of the greatest assistance in producing the witness whom I require. Thank you very much. I believe you have some matches in your pocket, Watson. Now, Mr. Lestrade, I will ask you all to accompany me to the top landing."

As I have said, there was a broad corridor there, which ran outside three empty bedrooms. At one end of the corridor we were all marshalled by Sherlock Holmes, the constables grinning and Lestrade staring at my friend with amazement, expectation, and derision chasing each other across his features. Holmes stood before us with the air of a conjurer who is performing a trick.

"Would you kindly send one of your constables for two buckets of water? Put the straw on the floor here, free from the wall on either side. Now I think that we are all ready."

Lestrade's face had begun to grow red and angry.

"I don't know whether you are playing a game with us, Mr. Sherlock Holmes," said he. "If you know anything, you can surely say it without all this tomfoolery."

"I assure you, my good Lestrade, that I have an excellent reason for everything that I do. You may possibly remember that you chaffed me a little, some hours ago, when the sun seemed on your side of the hedge, so you must not grudge me a little pomp and ceremony now. Might I ask you, Watson, to open that window, and then to put a match to the edge of the straw?"

I did so, and driven by the draught, a coil of grey smoke swirled down the corridor, while the dry straw crackled and flamed.

"Now we must see if we can find this witness for you, Lestrade. Might I ask you all to join in the cry of 'Fire!'? Now then; one, two, three—"

"Fire!" we all yelled.

"Thank you. I will trouble you once again."

"Fire!"

"Just once more, gentlemen, and all together."

"Fire!" The shout must have rung over Norwood.

It had hardly died away when an amazing thing happened. A door suddenly flew open out of what appeared to be solid wall at the end of the corridor, and a little, wizened man darted out of it, like a rabbit out of its burrow.

"Capital!" said Holmes, calmly. "Watson, a bucket of water over the straw. That will do! Lestrade, allow me to present you with your principal missing witness, Mr. Jonas Oldacre."

The detective stared at the newcomer with blank amazement. The latter was blinking in the bright light of the corridor, and peering at us and at the smouldering fire. It was an odious face—crafty, vicious, malignant, with shifty, light-grey eyes and white lashes.

"What's this, then?" said Lestrade, at last. "What have you been doing all this time, eh?"

Oldacre gave an uneasy laugh, shrinking back from the furious red face of the angry detective.

"I have done no harm."

"No harm? You have done your best to get an innocent man hanged. If it wasn't for this gentleman here, I am not sure that you would not have succeeded."

The wretched creature began to whimper.

"I am sure, sir, it was only my practical joke."

"Oh, a joke, was it? You won't find the laugh on your side, I promise you. Take him down, and keep him in the sitting-room until I come. Mr. Holmes," he continued, when they had gone, "I could not speak before the constables, but I don't mind saying, in the presence of Dr. Watson, that this is the brightest thing that you have done yet, though it is a mystery to me how you did it. You have saved an innocent man's life, and you have prevented a very grave scandal which would have ruined my reputation in the Force."

Holmes smiled and clapped Lestrade upon the shoulder.

"Instead of being ruined, my good sir, you will find that your reputation has been enormously enhanced. Just make a few alterations in that report which you were writing, and they will understand how hard it is to throw dust in the eyes of Inspector Lestrade."

"And you don't want your name to appear?"

"Not at all. The work is its own reward. Perhaps I shall get the credit also at some distant day, when I permit my zealous historian to lay out his foolscap once more—eh, Watson? Well, now, let us see where this rat has been lurking."

A lath-and-plaster partition had been run across the passage six feet from the end, with a door cunningly concealed in it. It was lit within by slits under the eaves. A few articles of furniture and a supply of food and water were within, together with a number of books and papers.

"There's the advantage of being a builder," said Holmes, as we came out. "He was able to fix up his own little hiding-place without any confederate—save, of course, that precious housekeeper of his, whom I should lose no time in adding to your bag, Lestrade."

"I'll take your advice. But how did you know of this place, Mr. Holmes?"

"I made up my mind that the fellow was in hiding in the

house. When I paced one corridor and found it six feet shorter than the corresponding one below, it was pretty clear where he was. I thought he had not the nerve to lie quiet before an alarm of fire. We could, of course, have gone in and taken him, but it amused me to make him reveal himself. Besides, I owed you a little mystification, Lestrade, for your chaff in the morning."

"Well, sir, you certainly got equal with me on that. But how in the world did you know that he was in the house at all?"

"The thumb-mark, Lestrade. You said it was final; and so it was, in a very different sense. I knew it had not been there the day before. I pay a good deal of attention to matters of detail, as you may have observed, and I had examined the hall and was sure that the wall was clear. Therefore, it had been put on during the night."

"But how?"

"Very simply. When those packets were sealed up, Jonas Oldacre got McFarlane to secure one of the seals by putting his thumb upon the soft wax. It would be done so quickly and so naturally, that I daresay the young man himself has no recollection of it. Very likely it just so happened, and Oldacre had himself no notion of the use he would put it to. Brooding over the case in that den of his, it suddenly struck him what absolutely damning evidence he could make against McFarlane by using that thumb-mark. It was the simplest thing in the world for him to take a wax impression from the seal, to moisten it in as much blood as he could get from a pin-prick, and to put the mark upon the wall during the night, either with his own hand or with that of his housekeeper. If you examine among those documents which he took with him into his retreat, I will lay you a wager that you find the seal with the thumb-mark upon it."

"Wonderful!" said Lestrade. "Wonderful! It's all as clear as crystal, as you put it. But what is the object of this deep deception, Mr. Holmes?"

It was amusing to me to see how the detective's overbearing manner had changed suddenly to that of a child asking questions of its teacher.

"Well, I don't think that is very hard to explain. A very deep, malicious, vindictive person is the gentleman who is now awaiting us downstairs. You know that he was once refused by McFarlane's mother? You don't! I told you that you should go to Blackheath first and Norwood afterwards. Well, this injury, as he would consider it, has rankled in his wicked, scheming brain, and all his life he has longed for vengeance, but never seen his chance. During the last year or two, things have gone against him—secret speculation, I think—and he finds himself in a bad way. He determines to swindle his creditors, and for this purpose he pays large checks to a certain Mr. Cornelius, who is, I imagine, himself under another name. I have not traced these checks yet, but I have no doubt that they were banked under that name at some provincial town where Oldacre from time to time led a double existence. He intended to change his name altogether, draw this money, and vanish, starting life again elsewhere."

"Well, that's likely enough."

"It would strike him that in disappearing he might throw all pursuit off his track, and at the same time have an ample and crushing revenge upon his old sweetheart, if he could give the impression that he had been murdered by her only child. It was a masterpiece of villainy, and he carried it out like a master. The idea of the will, which would give an obvious motive for the crime, the secret visit unknown to his own parents, the retention of the stick, the blood, and the animal remains and buttons in the woodpile, all were admirable. It was a net from which it seemed to me, a few hours ago, that there was no possible escape. But he had not that supreme gift of the artist, the knowledge of when to stop. He wished to improve that which was already perfect—to draw the rope tighter yet round the neck of his unfortunate victim—and so he ruined all. Let us descend, Lestrade. There are just one or two questions that I would ask him."

The malignant creature was seated in his own parlour, with a policeman upon each side of him.

"It was a joke, my good sir—a practical joke, nothing more," he whined incessantly. "I assure you, sir, that I simply concealed myself in order to see the effect of my disappearance, and I am sure that you would not be so unjust as to imagine that I would have allowed any harm to befall poor young Mr. McFarlane."

"That's for a jury to decide," said Lestrade. "Anyhow, we shall have you on a charge of conspiracy, if not for attempted murder."

"And you'll probably find that your creditors will impound the banking account of Mr. Cornelius," said Holmes.

The little man started and turned his malignant eyes upon my friend.

"I have to thank you for a good deal," said he. "Perhaps I'll pay my debt some day."

Holmes smiled indulgently.

"I fancy that, for some few years, you will find your time very fully occupied," said he. 'By the way, what was it you put into the wood-pile besides your old trousers? A dead dog, or rabbits, or what? You won't tell? Dear me, how very unkind of you! Well, well, I daresay that a couple of rabbits would account both for the blood and for the charred ashes. If ever you write an account, Watson, you can make rabbits serve your turn."

The Adventure of the
Dancing Men

Holmes had been seated for some hours in silence with his long, thin back curved over a chemical vessel in which he was brewing a particularly malodorous product. His head was sunk upon his breast, and he looked from my point of view like a strange, lank bird, with dull grey plumage and a black top-knot.

"So, Watson," said he, suddenly, "you do not propose to invest in South African securities?"

I gave a start of astonishment. Accustomed as I was to Holmes's curious faculties, this sudden intrusion into my most intimate thoughts was utterly inexplicable.

"How on earth do you know that?" I asked.

He wheeled round upon his stool, with a steaming test-tube in his hand, and a gleam of amusement in his deep-set eyes.

"Now, Watson, confess yourself utterly taken aback," said he.

"I am."

"I ought to make you sign a paper to that effect."

"Why?"

"Because in five minutes you will say that it is all so absurdly simple."

"I am sure that I shall say nothing of the kind."

"You see, my dear Watson"—he propped his test-tube in the rack, and began to lecture with the air of a professor addressing his class—"it is not really difficult to construct a series of inferences, each dependent upon its predecessor and each simple in itself. If, after doing so, one simply knocks out all the central inferences and presents one's audience with the starting-point and the conclusion, one may produce a startling, though possibly a meretricious, effect. Now, it was not really difficult, by an inspection of the groove between your left forefinger and thumb, to feel sure that you did *not* propose to invest your small capital in the gold fields."

"I see no connection."

"Very likely not; but I can quickly show you a close connection. Here are the missing links of the very simple chain: 1. You had chalk between your left finger and thumb when you returned from the club last night. 2. You put chalk there when you play billiards, to steady the cue. 3. You never play billiards except with Thurston. 4. You told me, four weeks ago, that Thurston had an option on some South African property which would expire in a month, and which he desired you to share with him. 5. Your check book is locked in my drawer, and you have not asked for the key. 6. You do not propose to invest your money in this manner."

"How absurdly simple!" I cried.

"Quite so!" said he, a little nettled. "Every problem becomes very childish when once it is explained to you. Here is an unexplained one. See what you can make of that, friend Watson." He tossed a sheet of paper upon the table and turned once more to his chemical analysis.

I looked with amazement at the absurd hieroglyphics upon the paper.

"Why, Holmes, it is a child's drawing," I cried.

"Oh, that's your idea!"

"What else should it be?"

"That is what Mr. Hilton Cubitt, of Riding Thorpe Manor, Norfolk, is very anxious to know. This little conundrum came by the first post, and he was to follow by the next train. There's a ring at the bell, Watson. I should not be very much surprised if this were he."

A heavy step was heard upon the stairs, and an instant later there entered a tall, ruddy, clean-shaven gentleman, whose clear eyes and florid cheeks told of a life led far from the fogs of Baker Street. He seemed to bring a whiff of his strong, fresh, bracing, east-coast air with him as he entered. Having shaken hands with each of us, he was about to sit down, when his eye rested upon the paper with the curious markings, which I had just examined and left upon the table.

"Well, Mr. Holmes, what do you make of these?" he cried. "They told me that you were fond of queer mysteries, and I don't think you can find a queerer one than that. I sent the paper on ahead, so that you might have time to study it before I came."

"It is certainly rather a curious production," said Holmes. "At first sight it would appear to be some childish prank. It consists of a number of absurd little figures dancing across the paper upon which they are drawn. Why should you attribute any importance to so grotesque an object?"

"I never should, Mr. Holmes. But my wife does. It is frightening her to death. She says nothing, but I can see terror in her eyes. That's why I want to sift the matter to the bottom."

Holmes held up the paper so that the sunlight shone full upon it. It was a page torn from a note-book. The markings were done in pencil and ran in this way:

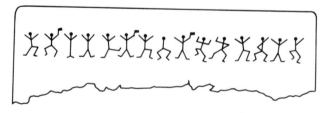

Holmes examined it for some time, and then, folding it carefully up, he placed it in his pocket-book.

"This promises to be a most interesting and unusual case," said he. "You gave me a few particulars in your letter, Mr. Hilton Cubitt, but I should be very much obliged if you would kindly go over it all again for the benefit of my friend, Dr. Watson."

"I'm not much of a story-teller," said our visitor, nervously clasping and unclasping his great, strong hands. "You'll just ask me anything that I don't make clear. I'll begin at the time of my marriage last year, but I want to say first of all that, though I'm not a rich man, my people have been at Riding Thorpe for a matter of five centuries, and there is no better known family in the County of Norfolk. Last year I came up to London for the Jubilee, and I stopped at a boarding-house in Russell Square, because Parker, the vicar of our parish, was staying in it. There was an American young lady there—Patrick was the name—Elsie Patrick. In some way we became friends, until before my month was up I was as much in love as man could be. We were quietly married at a registry office, and we returned to Norfolk a wedded couple. You'll think it very mad, Mr. Holmes, that a man of a good old family should marry a wife in this fashion, knowing nothing of her past or of her people, but if you saw her and knew her, it would help you to understand.

"She was very straight about it, was Elsie. I can't say that she did not give me every chance of getting out of it if I wished to do so. 'I have had some very disagreeable associations in my life,' said she, 'I wish to forget all about them. I would rather never allude to the past, for it is very painful to me. If you take me, Hilton, you will take a woman who has nothing that she need be personally ashamed of; but you will have to be content with my word for it, and to allow me to be silent as to all that passed up to the time when I became yours. If these conditions are too hard, then go back to Norfolk and leave me to the lonely life in which you found me.' It was only the day before our wedding that she said those very words to me. I told her that I was content to take her on her own terms, and I have been as good as my word.

"Well, we have been married now for a year, and very happy we have been. But about a month ago, at the end of June, I saw for the first time signs of trouble. One day my wife received a letter from America. I saw the American stamp. She turned deadly white, read the letter, and threw it into the fire. She made no allusion to it afterwards, and I made none, for a promise is a promise, but she has never known an easy hour from that moment. There is always a look of fear upon her face—a look as if she were waiting and expecting. She would do better to trust me. She would find that I was her best friend. But until she speaks, I can say nothing. Mind you, she is a truthful woman, Mr. Holmes, and whatever trouble there may have been in her past life it has been no fault of hers. I am only a simple Norfolk squire, but there is not a man in England who ranks his family honour more highly than I do. She knows it well, and she knew it well before she married me. She would never bring any stain upon it—of that I am sure.

"Well, now I come to the queer part of my story. About a week ago—it was the Tuesday of last week—I found on one of the window-sills a number of absurd little dancing figures like these upon the paper. They were scrawled with chalk. I thought that it was the stable-boy who had drawn them, but the lad swore he knew nothing about it. Anyhow, they had come there during the night. I had them washed out, and I only mentioned the matter to my wife afterwards. To my surprise, she took it very seriously and begged me if any more came to let her see them. None did come for a week, and then yesterday morning I found this paper lying on the sun-dial in the garden. I showed it to Elsie, and down she dropped in a dead faint. Since then she has looked like a woman in a dream, half dazed, and with terror always lurking in her eyes. It was then that I wrote and sent the paper to you, Mr. Holmes. It was not a thing that I could take to the police, for they would have laughed at me, but you will tell me what to do. I am not a rich man, but if there is any danger threatening my little woman, I would spend my last copper to shield her."

He was a fine creature, this man of the old English soil—simple, straight, and gentle, with his great, earnest blue eyes and broad, comely face. His love for his wife and his trust in her shone in his features. Holmes had listened to his story with the utmost attention, and now he sat for some time in silent thought.

"Don't you think, Mr. Cubitt," said he, at last, "that your best plan would be to make a direct appeal to your wife, and to ask her to share her secret with you?"

Hilton Cubitt shook his massive head.

"A promise is a promise, Mr. Holmes. If Elsie wished to tell me she would. If not, it is not for me to force her confidence. But I am justified in taking my own line—and I will."

"Then I will help you with all my heart. In the first place, have you heard of any strangers being seen in your neighbourhood?"

"No."

"I presume that it is a very quiet place. Any fresh face would cause comment?"

"In the immediate neighbourhood, yes. But we have several small watering-places not very far away. And the farmers take in lodgers."

"These hieroglyphics have evidently a meaning. If it is a purely arbitrary one, it may be impossible for us to solve it. If, on the other hand, it is systematic, I have no doubt that we shall get to the bottom of it. But this particular sample is so short that I can do nothing, and the facts which you have brought me are so indefinite that we have no basis for an investigation. I would suggest that you return to Norfolk, that you keep a keen lookout, and that you take an exact copy of any fresh dancing men which may appear. It is a thousand pities that we have not a reproduction of those which were done in chalk upon the window-sill. Make a discreet inquiry also as to any strangers in the neighbourhood. When you have collected some fresh evidence, come to me again. That is the best advice which I can give you, Mr. Hilton Cubitt. If there are any pressing fresh developments, I shall be always ready to run down and see you in your Norfolk home."

The interview left Sherlock Holmes very thoughtful, and several times in the next few days I saw him take his slip of paper from his note-book and look long and earnestly at the curious figures inscribed upon it. He made no allusion to the affair, however, until one afternoon a fortnight or so later. I was going out when he called me back.

"You had better stay here, Watson."

"Why?"

"Because I had a wire from Hilton Cubitt this morning. You remember Hilton Cubitt, of the dancing men? He was to reach Liverpool Street at one-twenty. He may be here at any moment. I gather from his wire that there have been some new incidents of importance."

We had not long to wait, for our Norfolk squire came straight from the station as fast as a hansom could bring him. He was looking worried and depressed, with tired eyes and a lined forehead.

"It's getting on my nerves, this business, Mr. Holmes," said he, as he sank, like a wearied man, into an armchair. "It's bad enough to feel that you are surrounded by unseen, unknown folk, who have some kind of design upon you, but when, in addition to that, you know that it is just killing your wife by inches, then it becomes as much as flesh and blood can endure. She's wearing away under it—just wearing away before my eyes."

"Has she said anything yet?"

"No, Mr. Holmes, she has not. And yet there have been times when the poor girl has wanted to speak and yet could not quite bring herself to take the plunge. I have tried to help her, but I daresay I did it clumsily and scared her from it. She has spoken about my old family, and our reputation in the county, and our pride in our unsullied honour, and I always felt it was leading to the point, but somehow it turned off before we got there."

"But you have found out something for yourself?"

"A good deal, Mr. Holmes. I have several fresh dancing-men pictures for you to examine, and, what is more important, I have seen the fellow."

"What, the man who draws them?"

"Yes, I saw him at his work. But I will tell you everything in order. When I got back after my visit to you, the very first thing I saw next morning was a fresh crop of dancing men. They had been drawn in chalk upon the black wooden door of the tool-house, which stands beside the lawn in full view of the front windows. I took an exact copy, and here it is." He unfolded a paper and laid it upon the table. Here is a copy of the hieroglyphics:

"Excellent!" said Holmes. "Excellent! Pray continue."

"When I had taken the copy, I rubbed out the marks, but, two mornings later, a fresh inscription had appeared. I have a copy of it here":

Holmes rubbed his hands and chuckled with delight.

"Our material is rapidly accumulating," said he.

"Three days later a message was left scrawled upon paper and placed under a pebble upon the sun-dial. Here it is. The characters are, as you see, exactly the same as the last one. After that I determined to lie in wait, so I got out my revolver and I sat up in my study, which overlooks the lawn and garden. About two in the morning I was seated by the window, all being dark save for the moonlight outside, when I heard steps behind me, and there was my wife in her dressing-gown. She implored me to come to bed. I told her frankly that I wished to see who it was who played such absurd tricks upon us. She answered that it was some senseless practical joke, and that I should not take any notice of it.

"'If it really annoys you, Hilton, we might go and travel, you and I, and so avoid this nuisance.'

"'What, be driven out of our own house by a practical joker?' said I. 'Why, we should have the whole county laughing at us.'

"'Well, come to bed,' she said, 'and we can discuss it in the morning.'

"Suddenly, as she spoke, I saw her white face grow whiter yet in the moonlight, and her hand tightened upon my shoulder. Something was moving in the shadow of the tool-house. I saw a dark, creeping figure which crawled round the corner and squatted in front of the door. Seizing my pistol, I was rushing out, when my wife threw her arms round me and held me with convulsive strength. I tried to throw her off, but she clung to me most desperately. At last I got clear, but by the time I had opened the door and reached the house the creature was gone. He had left a trace of his presence, however, for there on the door was the very same arrangement of dancing men which had already twice appeared, and which I have copied on that paper. There was no other sign of the fellow anywhere, though I ran all over the grounds. And yet the amazing thing is that he must have been there all the time, for when I examined the door again in the morning, he had scrawled some more of his pictures under the line which I had already seen."

"Have you that fresh drawing?"

"Yes, it is very short, but I made a copy of it, and here it is."

Again he produced a paper. The new dance was in this form:

"Tell me," said Holmes—and I could see by his eyes that he was much excited—"was this a mere addition to the first or did it appear to be entirely separate?"

"It was on a different panel of the door."

"Excellent! This is far the most important of all for our purpose. It fills me with hopes. Now, Mr. Hilton Cubitt, please continue your most interesting statement."

"I have nothing more to say, Mr. Holmes, except that I was angry with my wife that night for having held me back when I might have caught the skulking rascal. She said that she feared that I might come to harm. For an instant it had crossed my mind that perhaps what she really feared was that *he* might come to harm, for I could not doubt that she knew who this man was, and what he meant by these strange signals. But there is a tone in my wife's voice, Mr. Holmes, and a look in her eyes which forbid doubt, and I am sure that it was indeed my own safety that was in her mind. There's the whole case, and now I want your advice as to what I ought to do. My own inclination is to put half a dozen of my farm lads in the shrubbery, and when this fellow comes again to give him such a hiding that he will leave us in peace for the future."

"I fear it is too deep a case for such simple remedies," said Holmes. "How long can you stay in London?"

"I must go back to-day. I would not leave my wife alone all night for anything. She is very nervous and begged me to come back."

"I daresay you are right. But if you could have stopped, I might possibly have been able to return with you in a day or two. Meanwhile you will leave me these papers, and I think that it is very likely that I shall be able to pay you a visit shortly and to throw some light upon your case."

Sherlock Holmes preserved his calm professional manner until our visitor had left us, although it was easy for me, who knew him so well, to see that he was profoundly excited. The moment that Hilton Cubitt's broad back had disappeared through the door my comrade rushed to the table, laid out all the slips of paper containing dancing men in front of him, and threw himself into an intricate and elaborate calculation. For two hours I watched him as he covered sheet after sheet of paper with figures and letters, so completely absorbed in his task that he had evidently forgotten my presence. Sometimes he was making progress and whistled and sang at his work; sometimes he was puzzled and would sit for long spells with a furrowed brow and a vacant eye. Finally he sprang from his chair with a cry of satisfaction and walked up and down the room rubbing his hands together. Then he wrote a long telegram upon a cable form. "If my answer to this is as I hope, you will have a very pretty case to add to your collection, Watson," said he. "I expect that we shall be able to go down to Norfolk to-morrow, and to take our friend some very definite news as to the secret of his annoyance."

I confess that I was filled with curiosity, but I was aware that Holmes liked to make his disclosures at his own time and in his own way, so I waited until it should suit him to take me into his confidence.

But there was a delay in that answering telegram, and two days of impatience followed, during which Holmes pricked up his ears at every ring of the bell. On the evening of the second there came a letter from Hilton Cubitt. All was quiet with him, save that a long inscription had appeared that morning upon the pedestal of the sun-dial. He inclosed a copy of it, which is here reproduced:

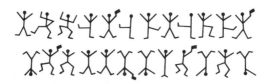

Holmes bent over this grotesque frieze for some minutes and then suddenly sprang to his feet with an exclamation of surprise and dismay. His face was haggard with anxiety.

"We have let this affair go far enough," said he. "Is there a train to North Walsham to-night?"

I turned up the time-table. The last had just gone.

"Then we shall breakfast early and take the very first in the morning," said Holmes. "Our presence is most urgently needed. Ah! Here is our expected cablegram. One moment, Mrs. Hudson, there may be an answer. No, that is quite as I expected. This message makes it even more essential that we should not lose an hour in letting Hilton Cubitt know how matters stand, for it is a singular and a dangerous web in which our simple Norfolk squire is entangled."

So, indeed, it proved, and as I come to the dark conclusion of a story which had seemed to me to be only childish and bizarre, I experience once again the dismay and horror with which I was filled. Would that I had some brighter ending to communicate to my readers, but these are the chronicles of fact, and I must follow to their dark crisis the strange chain of events which for some days made Riding Thorpe Manor a household word through the length and breadth of England.

We had hardly alighted at North Walsham and mentioned the name of our destination, when the station-master hurried towards us. "I suppose that you are the detectives from London?" said he.

A look of annoyance passed over Holmes's face.

"What makes you think such a thing?"

"Because Inspector Martin from Norwich has just passed through. But maybe you are the surgeons. She's not dead—or wasn't by last accounts. You may be in time to save her yet—though it be for the gallows."

Holmes's brow was dark with anxiety.

"We are going to Riding Thorpe Manor," said he, "but we have heard nothing of what has passed there."

"It's a terrible business," said the station-master. "They are shot, both Mr. Hilton Cubitt and his wife. She shot him and then herself—so the servants say. He's dead and her life is despaired of. Dear, dear, one of the oldest families in the county of Norfolk, and one of the most honoured."

Without a word Holmes hurried to a carriage, and during the long seven miles' drive he never opened his mouth. Seldom have I seen him so utterly despondent. He had been uneasy during all our journey from town, and I had observed that he had turned over the morning papers with anxious attention, but now this sudden realization of his worst fears left him in a blank melancholy. He leaned back in his seat, lost in gloomy speculation. Yet there was much around to interest us, for we were passing through as singular a countryside as any in England, where a few scattered cottages represented the population of to-day, while on every hand enormous square-towered churches bristled up from the flat green landscape and told of the glory and prosperity of old East Anglia. At last the violet rim of the German Ocean appeared over the green edge of the Norfolk coast, and the driver pointed with his whip to two old brick and timber gables which projected from a grove of trees. "That's Riding Thorpe Manor," said he.

As we drove up to the porticoed front door, I observed in front of it, beside the tennis lawn, the black tool-house and the pedestalled sun-dial with which we had such strange associations. A dapper little man, with a quick, alert manner and a waxed moustache, had just descended from a high dog-cart. He introduced himself as Inspector Martin, of the Norfolk Constabulary, and he was considerably astonished when he heard the name of my companion.

"Why, Mr. Holmes, the crime was only committed at three this morning. How could you hear of it in London and get to the spot as soon as I?"

"I anticipated it. I came in the hope of preventing it."

"Then you must have important evidence, of which we are ignorant, for they were said to be a most united couple."

"I have only the evidence of the dancing men," said Holmes. "I will explain the matter to you later. Meanwhile, since it is too late to prevent this tragedy, I am very anxious that I should use the knowledge which I possess in order to insure that justice be done. Will you associate me in your investigation, or will you prefer that I should act independently?"

"I should be proud to feel that we were acting together, Mr. Holmes," said the Inspector, earnestly.

"In that case I should be glad to hear the evidence and to examine the premises without an instant of unnecessary delay."

Inspector Martin had the good sense to allow my friend

to do things in his own fashion and contented himself with carefully noting the results. The local surgeon, an old, white-haired man, had just come down from Mrs. Hilton Cubitt's room, and he reported that her injuries were serious, but not necessarily fatal. The bullet had passed through the front of her brain, and it would probably be some time before she could regain consciousness. On the question of whether she had been shot or had shot herself, he would not venture to express any decided opinion. Certainly the bullet had been discharged at very close quarters. There was only the one pistol found in the room, two barrels of which had been emptied. Mr. Hilton Cubitt had been shot through the heart. It was equally conceivable that he had shot her and then himself, or that she had been the criminal, for the revolver lay upon the floor midway between them.

"Has he been moved?" asked Holmes.

"We have moved nothing except the lady. We could not leave her lying wounded upon the floor."

"How long have you been here, Doctor?"

"Since four o'clock."

"Anyone else?"

"Yes, the constable here."

"And you have touched nothing?"

"Nothing."

"You have acted with great discretion. Who sent for you?"

"The housemaid, Saunders."

"Was it she who gave the alarm?"

"She and Mrs. King, the cook."

"Where are they now?"

"In the kitchen, I believe."

"Then I think we had better hear their story at once."

The old hall, oak-panelled and high-windowed, had been turned into a court of investigation. Holmes sat in a great, old-fashioned chair, his inexorable eyes gleaming out of his haggard face. I could read in them a set purpose to devote his life to this quest until the client whom he had failed to save should at last be avenged. The trim Inspector Martin, the old, grey-headed country doctor, myself, and a stolid village policeman made up the rest of that strange company.

The two women told their story clearly enough. They had been aroused from their sleep by the sound of an explosion, which had been followed a minute later by a second one. They slept in adjoining rooms, and Mrs. King had rushed in to Saunders. Together they had descended the stairs. The door of the study was open, and a candle was burning upon the table. Their master lay upon his face in the centre of the room. He was quite dead. Near the window his wife was crouching, her head leaning against the wall. She was horribly wounded, and the side of her face was red with blood. She breathed heavily, but was incapable of saying anything. The passage, as well as the room, was full of smoke and the smell of powder. The window was certainly shut and fastened upon the inside. Both women were positive upon the point. They had at once sent for the doctor and for the constable. Then, with the aid of the groom and the stable-boy, they had conveyed their injured mistress to her room. Both she and her husband had occupied the bed. She was clad in her dress—he in his dressing-gown, over his night-clothes. Nothing had been moved in the study. So far as they knew, there had never been any quarrel between husband and wife. They had always looked upon them as a very united couple.

These were the main points of the servants' evidence. In answer to Inspector Martin, they were clear that every door was fastened upon the inside, and that no one could have escaped from the house. In answer to Holmes, they both remembered that they were conscious of the smell of powder from the moment that they ran out of their rooms upon the top floor. "I commend that fact very carefully to your attention," said Holmes to his professional colleague. "And now I think that we are in a position to undertake a thorough examination of the room."

The study proved to be a small chamber, lined on three sides with books, and with a writing-table facing an ordinary window, which looked out upon the garden. Our first attention was given to the body of the unfortunate squire, whose huge frame lay stretched across the room. His disordered dress showed that he had been hastily aroused from sleep. The bullet had been fired at him from the front and had remained in his body, after penetrating the heart. His death had certainly been instantaneous and painless. There was no powder-marking either upon his dressing-gown or on his hands. According to the country surgeon, the lady had stains upon her face, but none upon her hand.

"The absence of the latter means nothing, though its presence may mean everything," said Holmes. "Unless the powder from a badly fitting cartridge happens to spurt backward, one may fire many shots without leaving a sign. I would suggest that Mr. Cubitt's body may now be removed. I suppose, Doctor, you have not recovered the bullet which wounded the lady?"

"A serious operation will be necessary before that can be done. But there are still four cartridges in the revolver. Two have been fired and two wounds inflicted, so that each bullet can be accounted for."

"So it would seem," said Holmes. "Perhaps you can account also for the bullet which has so obviously struck the edge of the window?"

He had turned suddenly, and his long, thin finger was pointing to a hole which had been drilled right through the lower window-sash, about an inch above the bottom.

"By George!" cried the Inspector. "How ever did you see that?"

"Because I looked for it."

"Wonderful!" said the country doctor. "You are certainly right, sir. Then a third shot has been fired, and therefore a third person must have been present. But who could that have been, and how could he have got away?"

"That is the problem which we are now about to solve,"

said Sherlock Holmes. "You remember, Inspector Martin, when the servants said that on leaving their room they were at once conscious of a smell of powder, I remarked that the point was an extremely important one?"

"Yes, sir; but I confess I did not quite follow you."

"It suggested that at the time of the firing, the window as well as the door of the room had been open. Otherwise the fumes of powder could not have been blown so rapidly through the house. A draught in the room was necessary for that. Both door and window were only open for a very short time, however."

"How do you prove that?"

"Because the candle was not guttered."

"Capital!" cried the Inspector. "Capital!"

"Feeling sure that the window had been open at the time of the tragedy, I conceived that there might have been a third person in the affair, who stood outside this opening and fired through it. Any shot directed at this person might hit the sash. I looked, and there, sure enough, was the bullet mark!"

"But how came the window to be shut and fastened?"

"The woman's first instinct would be to shut and fasten the window. But, halloa! What is this?"

It was a lady's hand-bag which stood upon the study table—a trim little hand-bag of crocodile-skin and silver. Holmes opened it and turned the contents out. There were twenty fifty-pound notes of the Bank of England, held together by an india-rubber band—nothing else.

"This must be preserved, for it will figure in the trial," said Holmes, as he handed the bag with its contents to the Inspector. "It is now necessary that we should try to throw some light upon this third bullet, which has clearly, from the splintering of the wood, been fired from inside the room. I should like to see Mrs. King, the cook, again. You said, Mrs. King, that you were awakened by a *loud* explosion. When you said that, did you mean that it seemed to you to be louder than the second one?"

"Well, sir, it wakened me from my sleep, so it is hard to judge. But it did seem very loud."

"You don't think that it might have been two shots fired almost at the same instant?"

"I am sure I couldn't say, sir."

"I believe that it was undoubtedly so. I rather think, Inspector Martin, that we have now exhausted all that this room can teach us. If you will kindly step round with me, we shall see what fresh evidence the garden has to offer."

A flower-bed extended up to the study window, and we all broke into an exclamation as we approached it. The flowers were trampled down, and the soft soil was imprinted all over with footmarks. Large, masculine feet they were, with peculiarly long, sharp toes. Holmes hunted about among the grass and leaves like a retriever after a wounded bird. Then, with a cry of satisfaction, he bent forward and picked up a little brazen cylinder.

"I thought so," said he; "the revolver had an ejector, and here is the third cartridge. I really think, Inspector Martin, that our case is almost complete."

The country inspector's face had shown his intense amazement at the rapid and masterful progress of Holmes's investigation. At first he had shown some disposition to assert his own position, but now he was overcome with admiration and ready to follow without question wherever Holmes led.

"Whom do you suspect?" he asked.

"I'll go into that later. There are several points in this problem which I have not been able to explain to you yet. Now that I have got so far, I had best proceed on my own lines and then clear the whole matter up once and for all."

"Just as you wish, Mr. Holmes, so long as we get our man."

"I have no desire to make mysteries, but it is impossible at the moment of action to enter into long and complex explanations. I have the threads of this affair all in my hand. Even if this lady should never recover consciousness, we can still reconstruct the events of last night and insure that justice be done. First of all, I wish to know whether there is any inn in this neighbourhood known as Elrige's?"

The servants were cross-questioned, but none of them had heard of such a place. The stable-boy threw a light upon the matter by remembering that a farmer of that name lived some miles off, in the direction of East Ruston.

"Is it a lonely farm?"

"Very lonely, sir."

"Perhaps they have not heard yet of all that happened here during the night?"

"Maybe not, sir."

Holmes thought for a little, and then a curious smile played over his face.

"Saddle a horse, my lad," said he. "I shall wish you to take a note to Elrige's Farm."

He took from his pocket the various slips of the dancing men. With these in front of him, he worked for some time at the study-table. Finally he handed a note to the boy, with directions to put it into the hands of the person to whom it was addressed, and especially to answer no questions of any sort which might be put to him. I saw the outside of the note, addressed in straggling, irregular characters, very unlike Holmes's precise hand. It was consigned to Mr. Abe Slaney, Elrige's Farm, East Ruston, Norfolk.

"I think, Inspector," Holmes remarked, "that you would do well to telegraph for an escort, as, if my calculations prove to be correct, you may have a particularly dangerous prisoner to convey to the county jail. The boy who takes this note could no doubt forward your telegram. If there is an afternoon train to town, Watson, I think we should do well to take it, as I have a chemical analysis of some interest to finish, and this investigation draws rapidly to a close."

When the youth had been dispatched with the note, Sherlock Holmes gave his instructions to the servants. If any visitor were to call asking for Mrs. Hilton Cubitt, no information should be given as to her condition, but he was to be shown at once into the drawing-room. He impressed these points upon them with the utmost earnestness. Finally he led the way into the drawing-room, with the remark that the business was now out of our hands, and that we must while away the time as best we might until we could see what was in store for us. The doctor had departed to his patients, and only the Inspector and myself remained.

"I think that I can help you to pass an hour in an interesting and profitable manner," said Holmes, drawing his chair up to the table and spreading out in front of him the various papers upon which were recorded the antics of the dancing men. "As to you, friend Watson, I owe you every atonement for having allowed your natural curiosity to remain so long unsatisfied. To you, Inspector, the whole incident may appeal as a remarkable professional study. I must tell you, first of all, the interesting circumstances connected with the previous consultations which Mr. Hilton Cubitt has had with me in Baker Street." He then shortly recapitulated the facts which have already been recorded. "I have here in front of me these singular productions, at which one might smile, had they not proved themselves to be the forerunners of so terrible a tragedy. I am fairly familiar with all forms of secret writings, and am myself the author of a trifling monograph upon the subject, in which I analyse one hundred and sixty separate ciphers, but I confess that this is entirely new to me. The object of those who invented the system has apparently been to conceal that these characters convey a message, and to give the idea that they are the mere random sketches of children.

"Having once recognised, however, that the symbols stood for letters, and having applied the rules which guide us in all forms of secret writings, the solution was easy enough. The first message submitted to me was so short that it was impossible for me to do more than to say, with some confidence, that the symbol 𝍑 stood for E. As you are aware, E is the most common letter in the English alphabet, and it predominates to so marked an extent that even in a short sentence one would expect to find it most often. Out of fifteen symbols in the first message, four were the same, so it was reasonable to set this down as E. It is true that in some cases the figure was bearing a flag, and in some cases not, but it was probable, from the way in which the flags were distributed, that they were used to break the sentence up into words. I accepted this as a hypothesis and noted that E was represented by 𝙓.

"But now came the real difficulty of the inquiry. The order of the English letters after E is by no means well marked, and any preponderance which may be shown in an average of a printed sheet may be reversed in a single short sentence. Speaking roughly, T, A, O, I, N, S, H, R, D, and L are the numerical order in which letters occur; but T, A, O, and I are very nearly abreast of each other, and it would be an endless task to try each combination until a meaning was arrived at. I therefore waited for fresh material. In my second interview with Mr. Hilton Cubitt he was able to give me two other short sentences and one message, which appeared—since there was no flag—to be a single word. Here are the symbols. Now, in the single word I have already got the two E's coming second and fourth in a word of five letters. It might be 'sever,' or 'lever,' or 'never.' There can be no question that the latter as a reply to an appeal is far the most probable, and the circumstances pointed to its being a reply written by the lady. Accepting it as correct, we are now able to say that the symbols stand respectively for N, V, and R.

"Even now I was in considerable difficulty, but a happy thought put me in possession of several other letters. It occurred to me that if these appeals came, as I expected, from someone who had been intimate with the lady in her early life, a combination which contained two E's with three letters between might very well stand for the name 'ELSIE.' On examination I found that such a combination formed the termination of the message which was three times repeated. It was certainly some appeal to 'Elsie.' In this way I had got my L, S, and I. But what appeal could it be? There were only four letters in the word which pre-

412

ceded 'Elsie,' and it ended in E. Surely the word must be 'COME.' I tried all other four letters ending in E, but could find none to fit the case. So now I was in possession of C, O, and M, and I was in a position to attack the first message once more, dividing it into words and putting dots for each symbol which was still unknown. So treated, it worked out in this fashion:

. M . ERE . . E SL . NE.

"Now the first letter *can* only be A, which is a most useful discovery, since it occurs no fewer than three times in this short sentence, and the H is also apparent in the second word. Now it becomes:

AM HERE A.E SLANE.

Or, filling in the obvious vacancies in the name:

AM HERE ABE SLANEY.

I had so many letters now that I could proceed with considerable confidence to the second message, which worked out in this fashion:

A . ELRI . ES.

Here I could only make sense by putting T and G for the missing letters, and supposing that the name was that of some house or inn at which the writer was staying."

Inspector Martin and I had listened with the utmost interest to the full and clear account of how my friend had produced results which had led to so complete a command over our difficulties.

"What did you do then, sir?" asked the Inspector.

"I had every reason to suppose that this Abe Slaney was an American, since Abe is an American contraction, and since a letter from America had been the starting-point of all the trouble. I had also every cause to think that there was some criminal secret in the matter. The lady's allusions to her past, and her refusal to take her husband into her confidence, both pointed in that direction. I therefore cabled to my friend, Wilson Hargreave, of the New York Po-

lice Bureau, who has more than once made use of my
knowledge of London crime. I asked him whether the
name of Abe Slaney was known to him. Here is his reply:
'The most dangerous crook in Chicago.' On the very
evening upon which I had his answer, Hilton Cubitt sent
me the last message from Slaney. Working with known letters, it took this form:

ELSIE . RE . ARE TO MEET THY GO.

The addition of a P and a D completed a message which
showed me that the rascal was proceeding from persuasion to threats, and my knowledge of the crooks of Chicago prepared me to find that he might very rapidly put
his words into action. I at once came to Norfolk with my
friend and colleague, Dr. Watson, but, unhappily, only in
time to find that the worst had already occurred."

"It is a privilege to be associated with you in the handling of a case," said the Inspector, warmly. "You will excuse me, however, if I speak frankly to you. You are only
answerable to yourself, but I have to answer to my superi-
ors. If this Abe Slaney, living at Elrige's, is indeed the murderer, and if he has made his escape while I am seated
here, I should certainly get into serious trouble."

"You need not be uneasy. He will not try to escape."

"How do you know?"

"To fly would be a confession of guilt."

"Then let us go to arrest him."

"I expect him here every instant."

"But why should he come?"

"Because I have written and asked him."

"But this is incredible, Mr. Holmes! Why should he
come because you have asked him? Would not such a request rather rouse his suspicions and cause him to fly?"

"I think I have known how to frame the letter," said
Sherlock Holmes. "In fact, if I am not very much mistaken, here is the gentleman himself coming up the
drive."

A man was striding up the path which led to the door.
He was a tall, handsome, swarthy fellow, clad in a suit of

grey flannel, with a Panama hat, a bristling black beard, and a great, aggressive hooked nose, and flourishing a cane as he walked. He swaggered up the path as if the place belonged to him, and we heard his loud, confident peal at the bell.

"I think, gentlemen," said Holmes, quietly, "that we had best take up our position behind the door. Every precaution is necessary when dealing with such a fellow. You will need your handcuffs, Inspector. You can leave the talking to me."

We waited in silence for a minute—one of those minutes which one can never forget. Then the door opened and the man stepped in. In an instant Holmes clapped a pistol to his head, and Martin slipped the handcuffs over his wrists. It was all done so swiftly and deftly that the fellow was helpless before he knew that he was attacked. He glared from one to the other of us with a pair of blazing black eyes. Then he burst into a bitter laugh.

"Well, gentlemen, you have the drop on me this time. I seem to have knocked up against something hard. But I came here in answer to a letter from Mrs. Hilton Cubitt. Don't tell me that she is in this? Don't tell me that she helped to set a trap for me?"

"Mrs. Hilton Cubitt was seriously injured and is at death's door."

The man gave a hoarse cry of grief, which rang through the house.

"You're crazy!" he cried, fiercely. "It was he that was hurt, not she. Who would have hurt little Elsie? I may have threatened her—God forgive me!—but I would not have touched a hair of her pretty head. Take it back—you! Say that she is not hurt!"

"She was found, badly wounded, by the side of her dead husband."

He sank with a deep groan on to the settee and buried his face in his manacled hands. For five minutes he was silent. Then he raised his face once more and spoke with the cold composure of despair.

"I have nothing to hide from you, gentlemen," said he.

415

"If I shot the man he had his shot at me, and there's no
murder in that. But if you think I could have hurt that
woman, then you don't know either me or her. I tell you,
there was never a man in this world loved a woman more
than I loved her. I had a right to her. She was pledged to
me years ago. Who was this Englishman that he should
come between us? I tell you that I had the first right to her,
and that I was only claiming my own."

"She broke away from your influence when she found
the man that you are," said Holmes, sternly. "She fled
from America to avoid you, and she married an honourable gentleman in England. You dogged her and followed her and made her life a misery to her, in order to
induce her to abandon the husband whom she loved and
respected in order to fly with you, whom she feared
and hated. You have ended by bringing about the death
of a noble man and driving his wife to suicide. That is
your record in this business, Mr. Abe Slaney, and you
will answer for it to the law."

"If Elsie dies, I care nothing what becomes of me," said
the American. He opened one of his hands and looked at
a note crumpled up in his palm. "See here, mister," he
cried, with a gleam of suspicion in his eyes, "you're not
trying to scare me over this, are you? If the lady is hurt as
bad as you say, who was it that wrote this note?" He tossed it
forward on to the table.

"I wrote it, to bring you here."

"You wrote it? There was no one on earth outside the
Joint who knew the secret of the dancing men. How came
you to write it?"

"What one man can invent another can discover," said
Holmes. "There is a cab coming to convey you to Norwich,
Mr. Slaney. But, meanwhile, you have time to make some
small reparation for the injury you have wrought. Are you
aware that Mrs. Hilton Cubitt has herself lain under grave
suspicion of the murder of her husband, and that it was
only my presence here, and the knowledge which I happened to possess, which has saved her from the accusation?

The least that you owe her is to make it clear to the whole world that she was in no way, directly or indirectly, responsible for his tragic end."

"I ask nothing better," said the American. "I guess the very best case I can make for myself is the absolute naked truth."

"It is my duty to warn you that it will be used against you," cried the Inspector, with the magnificent fair play of the British criminal law.

Slaney shrugged his shoulders.

"I'll chance that," said he. "First of all, I want you gentlemen to understand that I have known this lady since she was a child. There were seven of us in a gang in Chicago, and Elsie's father was the boss of the Joint. He was a clever man, was old Patrick. It was he who invented that writing, which would pass as a child's scrawl unless you just happened to have the key to it. Well, Elsie learned some of our ways, but she couldn't stand the business, and she had a bit of honest money of her own, so she gave us all the slip and got away to London. She had been engaged to me, and she would have married me, I believe, if I had taken over another profession, but she would have nothing to do with anything on the cross. It was only after her marriage to this Englishman that I was able to find out where she was. I wrote to her, but got no answer. After that I came over, and, as letters were no use, I put my messages where she could read them.

"Well, I have been here a month now. I lived in that farm, where I had a room down below, and could get in and out every night, and no one the wiser. I tried all I could to coax Elsie away. I knew that she read the messages, for once she wrote an answer under one of them. Then my temper got the better of me, and I began to threaten her. She sent me a letter then, imploring me to go away, and saying that it would break her heart if any scandal should come upon her husband. She said that she would come down when her husband was asleep at three in the morning and speak with me through the end

window, if I would go away afterwards and leave her in
peace. She came down and brought money with her,
trying to bribe me to go. This made me mad, and I caught
her arm and tried to pull her through the window. At that
moment in rushed the husband with his revolver in his
hand. Elsie had sunk down upon the floor, and we were
face to face. I was heeled also, and I held up my gun to
scare him off and let me get away. He fired and missed
me. I pulled off almost at the same instant, and down he
dropped. I made away across the garden, and as I went I
heard the window shut behind me. That's God's truth,
gentlemen, every word of it; and I heard no more about it
until that lad came riding up with a note which made me
walk in here, like a jay, and give myself into your hands."

A cab had driven up whilst the American had been
talking. Two uniformed policeman sat inside. Inspector
Martin rose and touched his prisoner on the shoulder.

"It is time for us to go."

"Can I see her first?"

"No, she is not conscious. Mr. Sherlock Holmes, I only
hope that, if ever again I have an important case, I shall
have the good fortune to have you by my side."

We stood at the window and watched the cab drive away.
As I turned back, my eye caught the pellet of paper which
the prisoner had tossed upon the table. It was the note
with which Holmes had decoyed him.

"See if you can read it, Watson," said he, with a smile.

It contained no word, but this little line of dancing men:

"If you use the code which I have explained," said
Holmes, "you will find that it simply means 'Come here at
once.' I was convinced that it was an invitation which he
would not refuse, since he could never imagine that it
could come from anyone but the lady. And so, my dear
Watson, we have ended by turning the dancing men to

good when they have so often been the agents of evil, and I think that I have fulfilled my promise of giving you something unusual for your note-book. Three-forty is our train, and I fancy we should be back in Baker Street for dinner."

Only one word of epilogue. The American, Abe Slaney, was condemned to death at the winter Assizes at Norwich, but his penalty was changed to penal servitude in consideration of mitigating circumstances, and the certainty that Hilton Cubitt had fired the first shot. Of Mrs. Hilton Cubitt I only know that I have heard she recovered entirely, and that she still remains a widow, devoting her whole life to the care of the poor and to the administration of her husband's estate.

The Adventure of the
Solitary Cyclist

From the years 1894 to 1901 inclusive, Mr. Sherlock Holmes was a very busy man. It is safe to say that there was no public case of any difficulty in which he was not consulted during those eight years, and there were hundreds of private cases, some of them of the most intricate and extraordinary character, in which he played a prominent part. Many startling successes and a few unavoidable failures were the outcome of this long period of continuous work. As I have preserved very full notes of all these cases and was myself personally engaged in many of them, it may be imagined that it is no easy task to know which I should select to lay before the public. I shall, however, preserve my former rule and give the preference to those cases which derive their interest not so much from the brutality of the crime as from the ingenuity and dramatic quality of the solution. For this reason I will now lay before the reader the facts connected with Miss Violet Smith, the solitary cyclist of Charlington, and the curious sequel of our investigation, which culminated in unexpected tragedy. It is true that the circumstance did not admit of any striking illustration of those powers for which my friend was famous, but there were some points about the case which made it stand out in those long records of crime from which I gather the material for these little narratives.

On referring to my note-book for the year 1895, I find that it was upon Saturday, the 23d of April, that we first heard of Miss Violet Smith. Her visit was, I remember, extremely unwelcome to Holmes, for he was immersed at the moment in a very abstruse and complicated problem concerning the peculiar persecution to which John Vincent Harden, the well-known tobacco millionaire, had been subjected. My friend, who loved above all things precision and concentration of thought, resented anything which distracted his attention from the matter in hand. And yet, without a harshness which was foreign to his nature, it was impossible to refuse to listen to the story of the young and beautiful woman, tall, graceful, and queenly, who presented herself at Baker Street late in the evening and implored his assistance and advice. It was vain to urge that his time was already fully occupied, for the young lady had come with the determination to tell her story, and it was evident that nothing short of force could get her out of the room until she had done so. With a resigned air and a somewhat weary smile, Holmes begged the beautiful intruder to take a seat, and to inform us what it was that was troubling her.

"At least it cannot be your health," said he, as his keen eyes darted over her; "so ardent a bicyclist must be full of energy."

She glanced down in surprise at her own feet, and I observed the slight roughening of the side of the sole caused by the friction of the edge of the pedal.

"Yes, I bicycle a good deal, Mr. Holmes, and that has something to do with my visit to you to-day."

My friend took the lady's ungloved hand and examined it with as close an attention and as little sentiment as a scientist would show to a specimen.

"You will excuse me, I am sure. It is my business," said he, as he dropped it. "I nearly fell into the error of supposing that you were typewriting. Of course, it is obvious that it is music. You observe the spatulate finger-ends, Watson, which is common to both professions? There is a spirituality about the face, however"—she gently turned it towards the light—"which the typewriter does not generate. This lady is a musician."

"Yes, Mr. Holmes, I teach music."

"In the country, I presume, from your complexion."

"Yes, sir, near Farnham, on the borders of Surrey."

"A beautiful neighbourhood, and full of the most interesting associations. You remember, Watson, that it was near there that we took Archie Stamford, the forger. Now, Miss Violet, what has happened to you, near Farnham, on the borders of Surrey?"

The young lady, with great clearness and composure, made the following curious statement:

"My father is dead, Mr. Holmes. He was James Smith, who conducted the orchestra at the old Imperial Theatre. My mother and I were left without a relation in the world except one uncle, Ralph Smith, who went to Africa twenty-five years ago, and we have never had a word from him since. When Father died, we were left very poor, but one day we were told that there was an advertisement in the *Times*, inquiring for our whereabouts. You can imagine how excited we were, for we thought that someone had left us a fortune. We went at once to the lawyer whose name was given in the paper. There we met two gentlemen, Mr. Carruthers and Mr. Woodley, who were home on a visit from South Africa. They said that my uncle was a friend of theirs, that he had died some months before in great poverty in Johannesburg, and that he had asked them with his last breath to hunt up his relations and see that they were in no want. It seemed strange to us that Uncle Ralph, who took no notice of us when he was alive, should be so careful to look after us when he was dead, but Mr. Carruthers explained that the reason was that my uncle had just heard of the death of his brother, and so felt responsible for our fate."

"Excuse me," said Holmes. "When was this interview?"

"Last December—four months ago."

"Pray proceed."

"Mr. Woodley seemed to me to be a most odious person. He was forever making eyes at me—a coarse, puffy-faced, red-moustached young man, with his hair plastered down on each side of his forehead. I thought that he was

perfectly hateful—and I was sure that Cyril would not wish me to know such a person."

"Oh, Cyril is his name!" said Holmes, smiling.

The young lady blushed and laughed.

"Yes, Mr. Holmes, Cyril Morton, an electrical engineer, and we hope to be married at the end of the summer. Dear me, how *did* I get talking about him? What I wished to say was that Mr. Woodley was perfectly odious, but that Mr. Carruthers, who was a much older man, was more agreeable. He was a dark, sallow, clean-shaven, silent person, but he had polite manners and a pleasant smile. He inquired how we were left, and on finding that we were very poor, he suggested that I should come and teach music to his only daughter, aged ten. I said that I did not like to leave my mother, on which he suggested that I should go home to her every week-end, and he offered me a hundred a year, which was certainly splendid pay. So it ended by my accepting, and I went down to Chiltern Grange, about six miles from Farnham. Mr. Carruthers was a widower, but he had engaged a lady housekeeper, a very respectable, elderly person, called Mrs. Dixon, to look after his establishment. The child was a dear, and everything promised well. Mr. Carruthers was very kind and very musical, and we had most pleasant evenings together. Every week-end I went home to my mother in town.

"The first flaw in my happiness was the arrival of the red-moustached Mr. Woodley. He came for a visit of a week, and oh, it seemed three months to me. He was a dreadful person—a bully to everyone else, but to me something infinitely worse. He made odious love to me, boasted of his wealth, said that if I married him I could have the finest diamonds in London, and finally, when I would have nothing to do with him, he seized me in his arms one day after dinner—he was hideously strong—and swore that he would not let me go until I had kissed him. Mr. Carruthers came in and tore him from me, on which he turned upon his own host, knocking him down and cutting his face open. That was the end of his visit, as you can imagine. Mr. Carruthers apologized to me next day and assured me that I should never be exposed to such an insult again. I have not seen Mr. Woodley since.

"And now, Mr. Holmes, I come at last to the special thing which has caused me to ask your advice to-day. You must know that every Saturday forenoon I ride on my bicycle to Farnham Station, in order to get the twelve-twenty-two to town. The road from Chiltern Grange is a lonely one, and at one spot it is particularly so, for it lies for over a mile between Charlington Heath upon one side and the woods which lie round Charlington Hall upon the other. You could not find a more lonely tract of road anywhere, and it is quite rare to meet so much as a cart, or a peasant, until you reach the high road near Crooksbury Hill. Two weeks ago I was passing this place, when I chanced to look back over my shoulder, and about two hundred yards behind me I saw a man, also on a bicycle. He seemed to be a middle-aged man, with a short, dark beard. I looked back before I reached Farnham, but the man was gone, so I thought no more about it. But you can imagine how surprised I was, Mr. Holmes, when, on my return on the Monday, I saw the same man on the same stretch of road. My astonishment was increased when the incident occurred again, exactly as before, on the following Saturday and Monday. He always kept his distance and did not molest me in any way, but still it certainly was very odd. I mentioned it to Mr. Carruthers, who seemed interested in what I said and told me that he had ordered a horse and trap, so that in future I should not pass over these lonely roads without some companion.

"The horse and trap were to have come this week, but for some reason they were not delivered, and again I had to cycle to the station. That was this morning. You can think that I looked out when I came to Charlington Heath, and there, sure enough, was the man, exactly as he had been the two weeks before. He always kept so far from me that I could not clearly see his face, but it was certainly someone whom I did not know. He was dressed in a dark

425

suit with a cloth cap. The only thing about his face that I could clearly see was his dark beard. To-day I was not alarmed, but I was filled with curiosity, and I determined to find out who he was and what he wanted. I slowed down my machine, but he slowed down his. Then I stopped altogether, but he stopped also. Then I laid a trap for him. There is a sharp turning of the road, and I pedalled very quickly round this, and then I stopped and waited. I expected him to shoot round and pass me before he could stop. But he never appeared. Then I went back and looked round the corner. I could see a mile of road, but he was not on it. To make it the more extraordinary, there was no side road at this point down which he could have gone."

Holmes chuckled and rubbed his hands. "This case certainly presents some features of its own," said he. "How much time elapsed between your turning the corner and your discovery that the road was clear?"

"Two or three minutes."

"Then he could not have retreated down the road, and you say that there are no side roads?"

"None."

"Then he certainly took a footpath on one side or the other."

"It could not have been on the side of the heath, or I should have seen him."

"So, by the process of exclusion, we arrive at the fact that he made his way towards Charlington Hall, which, as I understand, is situated in its own ground on one side of the road. Anything else?"

"Nothing, Mr. Holmes, save that I was so perplexed that I felt I should not be happy until I had seen you and had your advice."

Holmes sat in silence for some little time.

"Where is the gentleman to whom you are engaged?" he asked at last.

"He is in the Midland Electrical Company, at Coventry."

"He would not pay you a surprise visit?"

"Oh, Mr. Holmes! As if I should not know him!"

"Have you had any other admirers?"

"Several before I knew Cyril."

"And since?"

"There was this dreadful man, Woodley, if you can call him an admirer."

"No one else?"

Our fair client seemed a little confused.

"Who was he?" asked Holmes.

"Oh, it may be a mere fancy of mine; but it had seemed to me sometimes that my employer, Mr. Carruthers, takes a great deal of interest in me. We are thrown rather together. I play his accompaniments in the evening. He has never said anything. He is a perfect gentleman. But a girl always knows."

"Ha!" Holmes looked grave. "What does he do for a living?"

"He is a rich man."

"No carriages or horses?"

"Well, at least he is fairly well-to-do. But he goes into the city two or three times a week. He is deeply interested in South African gold shares."

"You will let me know any fresh development, Miss Smith. I am very busy just now, but I will find time to make some inquiries into your case. In the meantime, take no step without letting me know. Good-bye, and I trust that we shall have nothing but good news from you."

"It is part of the settled order of Nature that such a girl should have followers," said Holmes, as he pulled at his meditative pipe, "but for choice not on bicycles in lonely country roads. Some secretive lover, beyond all doubt. But there are curious and suggestive details about the case, Watson."

"That he should appear only at that point?"

"Exactly. Our first effort must be to find who are the tenants of Charlington Hall. Then, again, how about the connection between Carruthers and Woodley, since they appear to be men of such a different type? How came they *both* to be so keen upon looking up Ralph Smith's relations? One more point. What sort of a ménage is it which pays double the market price for a governess but does not keep a horse, although six miles from the station? Odd, Watson—very odd!"

"You will go down?"

"No, my dear fellow, *you* will go down. This may be some trifling intrigue, and I cannot break my other important research for the sake of it. On Monday you will arrive early at Farnham; you will conceal yourself near Charlington Heath; you will observe these facts for yourself and act as your own judgment advises. Then, having inquired as to the occupants of the Hall, you will come back to me and report. And now, Watson, not another word of the matter until we have a few solid stepping-stones on which we may hope to get across to our solution."

We had ascertained from the lady that she went down upon the Monday by the train which leaves Waterloo at nine-fifty, so I started early and caught the nine-thirteen. At Farnham Station I had no difficulty in being directed to Charlington Heath. It was impossible to mistake the scene of the young lady's adventure, for the road runs between the open heath on one side and an old yew hedge upon the other, surrounding a park which is studded with magnificent trees. There was a main gateway of lichen-studded stone, each side pillar surmounted by mouldering heraldic emblems, but besides this central carriage drive I observed several points where there were gaps in the hedge and paths leading through them. The house was invisible from the road, but the surroundings all spoke of gloom and decay.

The heath was covered with golden patches of flowering gorse, gleaming magnificently in the light of the bright spring sunshine. Behind one of these clumps I took up my position, so as to command both the gateway of the Hall and a long stretch of the road upon either side. It had been deserted when I left it, but now I saw a cyclist riding down it from the opposite direction to that in which I had come. He was clad in a dark suit, and I saw that he had a black beard. On reaching the end of the Charlington grounds, he sprang from his machine and led it through a gap in the hedge, disappearing from my view.

A quarter of an hour passed, and then a second cyclist appeared. This time it was the young lady coming from the station. I saw her look about her as she came to the Charlington hedge. An instant later the man emerged from his hiding-place, sprang upon his cycle, and followed her. In all the broad landscape those were the only moving figures, the graceful girl sitting very straight upon her machine, and the man behind her bending low over his handle-bar with a curiously furtive suggestion in every movement. She looked back at him and slowed her pace. He slowed also. She stopped. He at once stopped, too, keeping two hundred yards behind her. Her next movement was as unexpected as it was spirited. She suddenly whisked her wheels round and dashed straight at him. He was as quick as she, however, and darted off in desperate flight. Presently she came back up the road again, her head haughtily in the air, not deigning to take any further notice of her silent attendant. He had turned also and still kept his distance until the curve of the road hid them from my sight.

I remained in my hiding-place, and it was well that I did so, for presently the man reappeared, cycling slowly back. He turned in at the Hall gates and dismounted from his machine. For some minutes I could see him standing among the trees. His hands were raised, and he seemed to be settling his necktie. Then he mounted his cycle and rode away from me down the drive towards the Hall. I ran across the heath and peered through the trees. Far away I could catch glimpses of the old grey building with its bristling Tudor chimneys, but the drive ran through a dense shrubbery, and I saw no more of my man.

However, it seemed to me that I had done a fairly good morning's work, and I walked back in high spirits to

Farnham. The local house agent could tell me nothing about Charlington Hall and referred me to a well-known firm in Pall Mall. There I halted on my way home and met with courtesy from the representative. No, I could not have Charlington Hall for the summer. I was just too late. It had been let about a month ago. Mr. Williamson was the name of the tenant. He was a respectable, elderly gentleman. The polite agent was afraid he could say no more, as the affairs of his clients were not matters which he could discuss.

Mr. Sherlock Holmes listened with attention to the long report which I was able to present to him that evening, but it did not elicit that word of curt praise which I had hoped for and should have valued. On the contrary, his austere face was even more severe than usual as he commented upon the things that I had done and the things that I had not.

"Your hiding-place, my dear Watson, was very faulty. You should have been behind the hedge, then you would have had a close view of this interesting person. As it is, you were some hundreds of yards away and can tell me even less than Miss Smith. She thinks she does not know the man; I am convinced she does. Why, otherwise, should he be so desperately anxious that she should not get so near him as to see his features? You describe him as bending over the handle-bar. Concealment again, you see. You really have done remarkably badly. He returns to the house, and you want to find out who he is. You come to a London house agent!"

"What should I have done?" I cried, with some heat.

"Gone to the nearest public-house. That is the centre of country gossip. They would have told you every name, from the master to the scullery-maid. Williamson? It conveys nothing to my mind. If he is an elderly man he is not this active cyclist who sprints away from that young lady's athletic pursuit. What have we gained by your expedition? The knowledge that the girl's story is true. I never doubted it. That there is a connection between the cyclist and the Hall. I never doubted that either. That the Hall is tenanted by Williamson. Who's the better for that? Well, well, my dear sir, don't look so depressed. We can do little more until next Saturday, and in the meantime I may make one or two inquiries myself."

Next morning, we had a note from Miss Smith, recounting shortly and accurately the very incidents which I had seen, but the pith of the letter lay in the postscript:

I am sure that you will respect my confidence, Mr. Holmes, when I tell you that my place here has become difficult, owing to the fact that my employer has proposed marriage to me. I am convinced that his feelings are most deep and most honourable. At the same time, my promise is of course given. He took my refusal very seriously, but also very gently. You can understand, however, that the situation is a little strained.

"Our young friend seems to be getting into deep waters," said Holmes, thoughtfully, as he finished the letter. "The case certainly presents more features of interest and more possibility of development than I had originally thought. I should be none the worse for a quiet, peaceful day in the country, and I am inclined to run down this afternoon and test one or two theories which I have formed."

Holmes's quiet day in the country had a singular termination, for he arrived at Baker Street late in the evening, with a cut lip and a discoloured lump upon his forehead, besides a general air of dissipation which would have made his own person the fitting object of a Scotland Yard investigation. He was immensely tickled by his own adventures and laughed heartily as he recounted them.

"I get so little active exercise that it is always a treat," said he. "You are aware that I have some proficiency in the good old British sport of boxing. Occasionally, it is of service; to-day, for example, I should have come to very ignominious grief without it."

I begged him to tell me what had occurred.

"I found that country pub which I had already recommended to your notice, and there I made my discreet inquiries. I was in the bar, and a garrulous landlord was giving me all that I wanted. Williamson is a white-bearded man, and he lives alone with a small staff of servants at the Hall. There is some rumour that he is or has been a clergyman, but one or two incidents of his short residence at the Hall struck me as peculiarly unecclesiastical. I have already made some inquiries at a clerical agency, and they tell me that there *was* a man of that name in orders, whose career has been a singularly dark one. The landlord further informed me that there are usually weekend visitors—'a warm lot, sir'—at the Hall, and especially one gentleman with a red moustache, Mr. Woodley by name, who was always there. We had got as far as this, when who should walk in but the gentleman himself, who had been drinking his beer in the tap-room and had heard the whole conversation. Who was I? What did I want? What did I mean by asking questions? He had a fine flow of language, and his adjectives were very vigorous. He ended a string of abuse by a vicious backhander, which I failed to entirely avoid. The next few minutes were delicious. It was a straight left against a slogging ruffian. I emerged as you see me. Mr. Woodley went home in a cart. So ended my country trip, and it must be confessed that, however enjoyable, my day on the Surrey border has not been much more profitable than your own."

The Thursday brought us another letter from our client.

You will not be surprised, Mr. Holmes [said she] to hear that I am leaving Mr. Carruthers's employment. Even the high pay cannot reconcile me to the discomforts of my situation. On Saturday I come up to town, and I do not intend to return. Mr. Carruthers has got a trap, and so the dangers of the lonely road, if there ever were any dangers, are now over.

As to the special cause of my leaving, it is not merely the strained situation with Mr. Carruthers, but it is the reappearance of that odious man, Mr. Woodley. He was always hideous, but he looks more awful than ever now, for he appears to have had an accident, and he is much disfigured. I saw him out of the window, but I am glad to say I did not meet him. He had a long talk with Mr. Carruthers, who seemed much excited afterwards. Woodley must be staying in the neighbourhood, for he did not sleep here, and yet I caught a glimpse of him again this morning, slinking about in the shrubbery. I would sooner have a savage wild animal loose about the place. I loathe and fear him more than I can say. How *can* Mr. Carruthers endure such a creature for a moment? However, all my troubles will be over on Saturday.

"So I trust, Watson, so I trust," said Holmes, gravely. "There is some deep intrigue going on round that little woman, and it is our duty to see that no one molests her upon that last journey. I think, Watson, that we must spare time to run down together on Saturday morning and make sure that this curious and inclusive investigation has no untoward ending."

I confess that I had not up to now taken a very serious view of the case, which had seemed to me rather grotesque and bizarre than dangerous. That a man should lie in wait for and follow a very handsome woman is no unheard-of thing, and if he has so little audacity that he not only dared not address her, but even fled from her approach, he was not a very formidable assailant. The ruffian Woodley was a very different person, but, except on one occasion, he had not molested our client, and now he visited the house of Carruthers without intruding upon her presence. The man on the bicycle was doubtless a member of those week-end parties at the Hall of which the publican had spoken, but who he was, or what he wanted, was as obscure as ever. It was the severity of Holmes's manner and the fact that he slipped a revolver into his pocket before leaving our rooms which impressed me with the feeling that tragedy might prove to lurk behind this curious train of events.

A rainy night had been followed by a glorious morning, and the heath-covered countryside, with the glowing clumps of flowering gorse, seemed all the more beautiful

433

to eyes which were weary of the duns and drabs and slate-greys of London. Holmes and I walked along the broad, sandy road inhaling the fresh morning air and rejoicing in the music of the birds and the fresh breath of the spring. From a rise of the road on the shoulder of Crooksbury Hill, we could see the grim Hall bristling out from amidst the ancient oaks, which, old as they were, were still younger than the building which they surrounded. Holmes pointed down the long tract of road which wound, a reddish yellow band, between the brown of the heath and the budding green of the woods. Far away, a black dot, we could see a vehicle moving in our direction. Holmes gave an exclamation of impatience.

"I have given a margin of half an hour," said he. "If that is her trap, she must be making for the earlier train. I fear, Watson, that she will be past Charlington before we can possibly meet her."

From the instant that we passed the rise, we could no longer see the vehicle, but we hastened onward at such a pace that my sedentary life began to tell upon me, and I was compelled to fall behind. Holmes, however, was always in training, for he had inexhaustible stores of nervous energy upon which to draw. His springy step never slowed until suddenly, when he was a hundred yards in front me, he halted, and I saw him throw up his hand with a gesture of grief and despair. At the same instant an empty dog-cart, the horse cantering, the reins trailing, appeared round the curve of the road and rattled swiftly towards us.

"Too late, Watson, too late!" cried Holmes, as I ran panting to his side. "Fool that I was not to allow for that earlier train! It's abduction, Watson—abduction! Murder! Heaven knows what! Block the road! Stop the horse! That's right. Now, jump in, and let us see if I can repair the consequences of my own blunder."

We had sprung into the dog-cart, and Holmes, after turning the horse, gave it a sharp cut with the whip, and we flew back along the road. As we turned the curve, the

434

whole stretch of road between the Hall and the heath was opened up. I grasped Holmes's arm.

"That's the man!" I gasped.

A solitary cyclist was coming towards us. His head was down and his shoulders rounded, as he put every ounce of energy that he possessed on to the pedals. He was flying like a racer. Suddenly he raised his bearded face, saw us close to him, and pulled up, springing from his machine. That coal-black beard was in singular contrast to the pallor of his face, and his eyes were as bright as if he had a fever. He stared at us and at the dog-cart. Then a look of amazement came over his face.

"Halloa! Stop there!" he shouted, holding his bicycle to block our road. "Where did you get that dog-cart? Pull up, man!" he yelled, drawing a pistol from his side pocket. "Pull up, I say, or, by George, I'll put a bullet into your horse."

Holmes threw the reins into my lap and sprang down from the cart.

"You're the man we want to see. Where is Miss Violet Smith?" he said, in his quick, clear way.

"That's what I'm asking you. You're in her dog-cart. You ought to know where she is."

"We met the dog-cart on the road. There was no one in it. We drove back to help the young lady."

"Good Lord! Good Lord! What shall I do?" cried the stranger, in an ecstasy of despair. "They've got her, that hell-hound Woodley and the blackguard parson. Come, man, come, if you really are her friend. Stand by me and we'll save her, if I have to leave my carcass in Charlington Wood."

He ran distractedly, his pistol in his hand, towards a gap in the hedge. Holmes followed him, and I, leaving the horse grazing beside the road, followed Holmes.

"This is where they came through," said he, pointing to the marks of several feet upon the muddy path. "Halloa! Stop a minute! Who's this in the bush?"

It was a young fellow about seventeen, dressed like an

ostler, with leather cords and gaiters. He lay upon his back, his knees drawn up, a terrible cut upon his head. He was insensible, but alive. A glance at his wound told me that it had not penetrated the bone.

"That's Peter, the groom," cried the stranger. "He drove her. The beasts have pulled him off and clubbed him. Let him lie; we can't do him any good, but we may save her from the worst fate that can befall a woman."

We ran frantically down the path, which wound among the trees. We had reached the shrubbery which surrounded the house when Holmes pulled up.

"They didn't go to the house. Here are their marks on the left—here, beside the laurel bushes. Ah! I said so."

As he spoke, a woman's shrill scream—a scream which vibrated with a frenzy of horror—burst from the thick, green clump of bushes in front of us. It ended suddenly on its highest note with a choke and a gurgle.

"This way! This way! They are in the bowling-alley," cried the stranger, darting through the bushes. "Ah, the cowardly dogs! Follow me, gentlemen! Too late! Too late! By the living Jingo!"

We had broken suddenly into a lovely glade of greensward surrounded by ancient trees. On the farther side of it, under the shadow of a mighty oak, there stood a singular group of three people. One was a woman, our client, drooping and faint, a handkerchief round her mouth. Opposite her stood a brutal, heavy-faced, red-moustached young man, his gaitered legs parted wide, one arm akimbo, the other waving a riding crop, his whole attitude suggestive of triumphant bravado. Between them an elderly, grey-bearded man, wearing a short surplice over a light tweed suit, had evidently just completed the wedding service, for he pocketed his prayer-book as we appeared and slapped the sinister bridegroom upon the back in jovial congratulation.

"They're married?" I gasped.

"Come on!" cried our guide; "Come on!" He rushed across the glade, Holmes and I at his heels. As we approached, the lady staggered against the trunk of the tree for support. Williamson, the ex-clergyman, bowed to us with mock politeness, and the bully, Woodley, advanced with a shout of brutal and exultant laughter.

"You can take your beard off, Bob," said he. "I know you, right enough. Well, you and your pals have just come in time for me to be able to introduce you to Mrs. Woodley."

Our guide's answer was a singular one. He snatched off the dark beard which had disguised him and threw it on the ground, disclosing a long, sallow, clean-shaven face below it. Then he raised his revolver and covered the young ruffian, who was advancing upon him with his dangerous riding crop swinging in his hand.

"Yes," said our ally, "I *am* Bob Carruthers, and I'll see this woman righted, if I have to swing for it. I told you what I'd do if you molested her, and, by the Lord! I'll be as good as my word."

"You're too late. She's my wife."

"No, she's your widow."

His revolver cracked, and I saw the blood spurt from the front of Woodley's waistcoat. He spun round with a scream and fell upon his back, his hideous red face turning suddenly to a dreadful mottled pallor. The old man, still clad in his surplice, burst into such a string of foul oaths as I have never heard and pulled out a revolver of his own, but, before he could raise it, he was looking down the barrel of Holmes's weapon.

"Enough of this," said my friend, coldly. "Drop that pistol! Watson, pick it up! Hold it to his head! Thank you. You, Carruthers, give me that revolver. We'll have no more violence. Come, hand it over!"

"Who are you, then?"

"My name is Sherlock Holmes."

"Good Lord!"

"You have heard of me, I see. I will represent the official police until their arrival. Here, you!" he shouted to a frightened groom, who had appeared at the edge of the glade. "Come here. Take this note as hard as you can ride to Farnham." He scribbled a few words upon a leaf from his note-book. "Give it to the superintendent at the police-station. Until he comes, I must detain you all under my personal custody."

The strong, masterful personality of Holmes dominated the tragic scene, and all were equally puppets in his hands. Williamson and Carruthers found themselves carrying the wounded Woodley into the house, and I gave my arm to the frightened girl. The injured man was laid on his bed, and at Holmes's request I examined him. I carried my report to where he sat in the old tapestry-hung dining-room with his two prisoners before him.

"He will live," said I.

"What!" cried Carruthers, springing out of his chair. "I'll go upstairs and finish him first. Do you tell me that that girl, that angel, is to be tied to Roaring Jack Woodley for life?"

"You need not concern yourself about that," said Holmes. "There are two very good reasons why she should under no circumstances be his wife. In the first place, we are very safe in questioning Mr. Williamson's right to solemnize a marriage."

"I have been ordained," cried the old rascal.

"And also unfrocked."

"Once a clergyman, always a clergyman."

"I think not. How about the licence?"

"We had a licence for the marriage. I have it here in my pocket."

"Then you got it by a trick. But, in any case, a forced marriage is no marriage, but it is a very serious felony, as you will discover before you have finished. You'll have time to think the point out during the next ten years or so, unless I am mistaken. As to you, Carruthers, you would have done better to keep your pistol in your pocket."

"I begin to think so, Mr. Holmes, but when I thought of all the precaution I had taken to shield this girl—for I loved her, Mr. Holmes, and it is the only time that ever I knew what love was—it fairly drove me mad to think that she was in the power of the greatest brute and bully in South Africa—a man whose name is a holy terror from Kimberley to Johannesburg. Why, Mr. Holmes, you'll hardly believe it, but ever since that girl has been in my employment I never once let her go past this house, where I knew the rascals were lurking, without following her on my bicycle, just to see that she came to no harm. I kept my distance from her, and I wore a beard, so that she should not recognise me, for she is a good and high-spirited girl, and she wouldn't have stayed in my employment long if she had thought that I was following her about the country roads."

"Why didn't you tell her of her danger?"

"Because then, again, she would have left me, and I couldn't bear to face that. Even if she couldn't love me, it was a great deal to me just to see her dainty form about the house, and to hear the sound of her voice."

"Well," said I, "you call that love, Mr. Carruthers, but I should call it selfishness."

"Maybe the two things go together. Anyhow, I couldn't let her go. Besides, with this crowd about, it was well that she should have someone near to look after her. Then, when the cable came, I knew they were bound to make a move."

"What cable?"

Carruthers took a telegram from his pocket.

"That's it," said he.

It was short and concise:

THE OLD MAN IS DEAD.

"Hum!" said Holmes. "I think I see how things worked, and I can understand how this message would, as you say, bring them to a head. But while you wait, you might tell me what you can."

The old reprobate with the surplice burst into a volley of bad language.

"By Heaven!" said he, "if you squeal on us, Bob

439

Carruthers, I'll serve you as you served Jack Woodley. You can bleat about the girl to your heart's content, for that's your own affair, but if you round on your pals to this plain-clothes copper, it will be the worst day's work that ever you did."

"Your Reverence need not be excited," said Holmes, lighting a cigarette. "The case is clear enough against you, and all I ask is a few details for my private curiosity. However, if there's any difficulty in your telling me, I'll do the talking, and then you will see how far you have a chance of holding back your secrets. In the first place, three of you came from South Africa on this game—you Williamson, you Carruthers, and Woodley."

"Lie number one," said the old man; "I never saw either of them until two months ago, and I have never been in Africa in my life, so you can put that in your pipe and smoke it, Mr. Busybody Holmes!"

"What he says is true," said Carruthers.

"Well, well, two of you came over. His Reverence is our own homemade article. You had known Ralph Smith in South Africa. You had reason to believe he would not live long. You found out that his niece would inherit his fortune. How's that—eh?"

Carruthers nodded and Williamson swore.

"She was next of kin, no doubt, and you were aware that the old fellow would make no will."

"Couldn't read or write," said Carruthers.

"So you came over, the two of you, and hunted up the girl. The idea was that one of you was to marry her, and the other have a share of the plunder. For some reason, Woodley was chosen as the husband. Why was that?"

"We played cards for her on the voyage. He won."

"I see. You got the young lady into your service, and there Woodley was to do the courting. She recognised the drunken brute that he was and would have nothing to do with him. Meanwhile, your arrangement was rather upset by the fact that you had yourself fallen in love with the lady. You could no longer bear the idea of this ruffian owning her?"

"No, by George, I couldn't!"

"There was a quarrel between you. He left you in a rage and began to make his own plans independently of you."

"It strikes me, Williamson, there isn't very much that we can tell this gentleman," cried Carruthers, with a bitter laugh. "Yes, we quarreled, and he knocked me down. I am level with him on that, anyhow. Then I lost sight of him. That was when he picked up with this outcast padre here. I found that they had set up housekeeping together at this place on the line that she had to pass for the station. I kept my eye on her after that, for I knew there was some devilry in the wind. I saw them from time to time, for I was anxious to know what they were after. Two days ago Woodley came up to my house with this cable, which showed that Ralph Smith was dead. He asked me if I would stand by the bargain. I said I would not. He asked me if I would marry the girl myself and give him a share. I said I would willingly do so, but that she would not have me. He said, 'Let us get her married first, and after a week or two she may see things a bit different.' I said I would have nothing to do with violence. So he went off cursing, like the foul-mouthed blackguard that he was, and swearing that he would have her yet. She was leaving me this week-end, and I had got a trap to take her to the station, but I was so uneasy in my mind that I followed her on my bicycle. She had got a start, however, and before I could catch her, the mischief was done. The first thing I knew about it was when I saw you two gentlemen driving back in the dog-cart."

Holmes rose and tossed the end of his cigarette into the grate. "I have been very obtuse, Watson," said he. "When in your report you said that you had seen the cyclist as you thought arrange his necktie in the shrubbery, that alone should have told me all. However, we may congratulate ourselves upon a curious and, in some respects, a unique case. I perceive three of the county constabulary in the drive, and I am glad to see that the little ostler is able to keep pace with them, so it is likely that neither he nor the interesting bridegroom will be permanently damaged by their morning's adventures. I think, Watson, that in your medical capacity, you might wait upon Miss Smith and tell her that if she is sufficiently recovered, we shall be happy to escort her to her mother's home. If she is not quite convalescent, you will find that a hint that we were about to telegraph to a young electrician in the Midlands would probably complete the cure. As to you, Mr. Carruthers, I think that you have done what you could to make amends for your share in an evil plot. There is my card, sir, and if my evidence can be of help in your trial, it shall be at your disposal."

In the whirl of our incessant activity, it has often been difficult for me, as the reader has probably observed, to round off my narratives, and to give those final details which the curious might expect. Each case has been the prelude to another, and the crisis once over, the actors have passed for ever out of our busy lives. I find, however, a short note at the end of my manuscript dealing with this case, in which I have put it upon record that Miss Violet Smith did indeed inherit a large fortune, and that she is now the wife of Cyril Morton, the senior partner of Morton & Kennedy, the famous Westminster electricians. Williamson and Woodley were both tried for abduction and assault, the former getting seven years and the latter ten. Of the fate of Carruthers, I have no record, but I am sure that his assault was not viewed very gravely by the court, since Woodley had the reputation of being a most dangerous ruffian, and I think that a few months were sufficient to satisfy the demands of justice.

The Adventure of
Black Peter

I have never known my friend to be in better form, both mental and physical, than in the year '95. His increasing fame had brought with it an immense practice, and I should be guilty of an indiscretion if I were even to hint at the identity of some of the illustrious clients who crossed our humble threshold in Baker Street. Holmes, however, like all great artists, lived for his art's sake, and save in the case of the Duke of Holdernesse, I have seldom known him claim any large reward for his inestimable services. So unworldly was he—or so capricious—that he frequently refused his help to the powerful and wealthy where the problem made no appeal to his sympathies, while he would devote weeks of most intense application to the affairs of some humble client whose case presented those strange and dramatic qualities which appealed to his imagination and challenged his ingenuity.

In this memorable year '95, a curious and incongruous succession of cases had engaged his attention, ranging from his famous investigation of the sudden death of Cardinal Tosca—an inquiry which was carried out by him at the express desire of His Holiness the Pope—down to his arrest of Wilson, the notorious canary-trainer, which removed a plague-spot from the East End of London. Close on the heels of these two famous cases came the tragedy of Woodman's Lee, and the very obscure circumstances which surrounded the death of Captain Peter Carey. No record of the doings of Mr. Sherlock Holmes would be complete which did not include some account of this very unusual affair.

During the first week of July, my friend had been absent so often and so long from our lodgings that I knew he had something on hand. The fact that several rough-looking men called during that time and inquired for Captain Basil made me understand that Holmes was working somewhere under one of the numerous disguises and names with which he concealed his own formidable identity. He had at least five small refuges in different parts of London, in which he was able to change his personality. He said nothing of his business to me, and it was not my habit to force a confidence. The first positive sign which he gave me of the direction which his investigation was taking was an extraordinary one. He had gone out before breakfast, and I had sat down to mine when he strode into the room, his hat upon his head and a huge barbed-headed spear tucked like an umbrella under his arm.

"Good gracious, Holmes!" I cried. "You don't mean to say that you have been walking about London with that thing?"

"I drove to the butcher's and back."

"The butcher's?"

"And I return with an excellent appetite. There can be no question, my dear Watson, of the value of exercise before breakfast. But I am prepared to bet that you will not guess the form that my exercise has taken."

"I will not attempt it."

He chuckled as he poured out the coffee.

"If you could have looked into Allardyce's back shop, you would have seen a dead pig swung from a hook in the ceiling, and a gentleman in his shirt sleeves furiously stabbing at it with this weapon. I was that energetic person, and I have satisfied myself that by no exertion of my strength can I transfix the pig with a single blow. Perhaps you would care to try?"

"Not for worlds. But why were you doing this?"

444

"Because it seemed to me to have an indirect bearing upon the mystery of Woodman's Lee. Ah, Hopkins, I got your wire last night, and I have been expecting you. Come and join us."

Our visitor was an exceedingly alert man, thirty years of age, dressed in a quiet tweed suit, but retaining the erect bearing of one who was accustomed to official uniform. I recognised him at once as Stanley Hopkins, a young Police Inspector, for whose future Holmes had high hopes, while he in turn professed the admiration and respect of a pupil for the scientific methods of the famous amateur. Hopkins's brow was clouded, and he sat down with an air of deep dejection.

"No, thank you, sir. I breakfasted before I came round. I spent the night in town, for I came up yesterday to report."

"And what had you to report?"

"Failure, sir, absolute failure."

"You have made no progress?"

"None."

"Dear me! I must have a look at the matter."

"I wish to Heavens that you would, Mr. Holmes. It's my first big chance, and I am at my wit's end. For goodness' sake, come down and lend me a hand."

"Well, well, it just happens that I have already read all the available evidence, including the report of the inquest, with some care. By the way, what do you make of that to-bacco pouch, found on the scene of the crime? Is there no clue there?"

Hopkins looked surprised.

"It was the man's own pouch, sir. His initials were inside it. And it was of sealskin—and he was an old sealer."

"But he had no pipe."

"No, sir, we could find no pipe. Indeed, he smoked very little, and yet he might have kept some tobacco for his friends."

"No doubt. I only mention it because, if I had been han-dling the case, I should have been inclined to make that the starting-point of my investigation. However, my friend, Dr. Watson, knows nothing of this matter, and I should be none the worse for hearing the sequence of events once more. Just give us some short sketches of the essentials."

Stanley Hopkins drew a slip of paper from his pocket.

"I have a few dates here which will give you the career of the dead man, Captain Peter Carey. He was born in '45—fifty years of age. He was a most daring and successful seal and whale fisher. In 1883 he commanded the steam sealer *Sea Unicorn,* of Dundee. He had then had several successful voyages in succession, and in the following year, 1884, he retired. After that he travelled for some years, and finally he bought a small place called Woodman's Lee, near Forest Row, in Sussex. There he has lived for six years, and there he died just a week ago to-day.

"There were some most singular points about the man. In ordinary life, he was a strict Puritan—a silent, gloomy fellow. His household consisted of his wife, his daughter, aged twenty, and two female servants. These last were continually changing, for it was never a very cheery situation, and sometimes it became past all bearing. The man was an intermittent drunkard, and when he had the fit on him he was a perfect fiend. He has been known to drive his wife and daughter out of doors in the middle of the night and flog them through the park until the whole village outside the gates was aroused by their screams.

"He was summoned once for a savage assault upon the old vicar, who had called upon him to remonstrate with him upon his conduct. In short, Mr. Holmes, you would go far before you found a more dangerous man than Peter Carey, and I have heard that he bore the same character when he commanded his ship. He was known in the trade as Black Peter, and the name was given him, not only on account of his swarthy features and the colour of his huge beard, but for the humours which were the terror of all around him. I need not say that he was loathed and avoided by every one of his neighbours, and that I have

446

not heard one single word of sorrow about his terrible end.

"You must have read in the account of the inquest about the man's cabin, Mr. Holmes, but perhaps your friend here has not heard of it. He had built himself a wooden outhouse—he always called it the 'cabin'—a few hundred yards from his house, and it was here that he slept every night. It was a little, single-roomed hut, sixteen feet by ten. He kept the key in his pocket, made his own bed, cleaned it himself, and allowed no other foot to cross the threshold. There are small windows on each side, which were covered by curtains and never opened. One of these windows was turned towards the high road, and when the light burned in it at night the folk used to point it out to each other and wonder what Black Peter was doing in there. That's the window, Mr. Holmes, which gave us one of the few bits of positive evidence that came out at the inquest.

"You remember that a stonemason, named Slater, walking from Forest Row about one o'clock in the morning—two days before the murder—stopped as he passed the grounds and looked at the square of light still shining among the trees. He swears that the shadow of a man's head turned sideways was clearly visible on the blind, and that this shadow was certainly not that of Peter Carey, whom he knew well. It was that of a bearded man, but the beard was short and bristled forward in a way very different from that of the Captain. So he says, but he had been two hours in the public-house, and it is some distance from the road to the window. Besides, this refers to the Monday, and the crime was done upon the Wednesday.

"On the Tuesday, Peter Carey was in one of his blackest moods, flushed with drink and as savage as a dangerous wild beast. He roamed about the house, and the women ran for it when they heard him coming. Late in the evening, he went down to his own hut. About two o'clock the following morning, his daughter, who slept with her window open, heard a most fearful yell from that direction, but it was no unusual thing for him to bawl and shout

447

when he was in drink, so no notice was taken. On rising at seven, one of the maids noticed that the door of the hut was open, but so great was the terror which the man caused that it was midday before anyone would venture down to see what had become of him. Peeping into the open door, they saw a sight which sent them flying, with white faces, into the village. Within an hour, I was on the spot and had taken over the case.

"Well, I have fairly steady nerves, as you know, Mr. Holmes, but I give you my word, that I got a shake when I put my head into that little house. It was droning like a harmonium with the flies and bluebottles, and the floor and walls were like a slaughter-house. He had called it a cabin, and a cabin it was, sure enough, for you would have thought that you were in a ship. There was a bunk at one end, a sea-chest, maps and charts, a picture of the *Sea Unicorn*, a line of log-books on a shelf, all exactly as one would expect to find it in a captain's room. And there, in the middle of it, was the man himself—his face twisted like a lost soul in torment, and his great brindled beard stuck upward in his agony. Right through his broad breast a steel harpoon had been driven, and it had sunk deep into the wood of the wall behind him. He was pinned like a beetle on a card. Of course, he was quite dead and had been so from the instant that he had uttered that last yell of agony.

"I know your methods, sir, and I applied them. Before I permitted anything to be moved, I examined most carefully the ground outside, and also the floor of the room. There were no footmarks."

"Meaning that you saw none?"

"I assure you, sir, that there were none."

"My good Hopkins, I have investigated many crimes, but I have never yet seen one which was committed by a flying creature. As long as the criminal remains upon two legs so long must there be some indentation, some abrasion, some trifling displacement which can be detected by the scientific searcher. It is incredible that this blood-bespattered room contained no trace which could have

448

aided us. I understand, however, from the inquest that there were some objects which you failed to overlook?"

The young Inspector winced at my companion's ironical comments.

"I was a fool not to call you in at the time, Mr. Holmes. However, that's past praying for now. Yes, there were several objects in the room which called for special attention. One was the harpoon with which the deed was committed. It had been snatched down from a rack on the wall. Two others remained there, and there was a vacant place for the third. On the stock was engraved 'SS. *Sea Unicorn, Dundee.*' This seemed to establish that the crime had been done in a moment of fury, and that the murderer had seized the first weapon which came in his way. The fact that the crime was committed at two in the morning, and yet Peter Carey was fully dressed, suggested that he had an appointment with the murderer, which is borne out by the fact that a bottle of rum and two dirty glasses stood upon the table."

"Yes," said Holmes; "I think that both inferences are permissible. Was there any other spirit but rum in the room?"

"Yes, there was a tantalus containing brandy and whisky on the sea-chest. It is of no importance to us, however, since the decanters were full, and it had therefore not been used."

"For all that, its presence has some significance," said Holmes. "However, let us hear some more about the objects which do seem to you to bear upon the case."

"There was this tobacco-pouch upon the table."

"What part of the table?"

"It lay in the middle. It was of coarse sealskin—the straight-haired skin, with a leather thong to bind it. Inside was 'P. C.' on the flap. There was half an ounce of strong ship's tobacco in it."

"Excellent! What more?"

Stanley Hopkins drew from his pocket a drab-covered note-book. The outside was rough and worn, the leaves discoloured. On the first page were written the initials "J. H. N." and the date "1883." Holmes laid it on the table and examined it in his minute way, while Hopkins and I gazed over each shoulder. On the second page were printed letters "C. P. R.," and then came several sheets of numbers. Another heading was "Argentine," another "Costa Rica," and another "San Paulo," each with pages of signs and figures after it.

"What do you make of these?" asked Holmes.

"They appear to be lists of Stock Exchange securities. I thought that 'J. H. N.' were the initials of a broker, and that 'C. P. R.' may have been his client."

"Try Canadian Pacific Railway," said Holmes.

Stanley Hopkins swore between his teeth and struck his thigh with his clenched hand.

"What a fool I have been!" he cried. "Of course, it is as you say. Then 'J. H. N.' are the only initials we have to solve. I have already examined the old Stock Exchange lists, and I can find no one in 1883, either in the house or among the outside brokers, whose initials correspond with these. Yet I feel that the clue is the most important one that I hold. You will admit, Mr. Holmes, that there is a possibility that these initials are those of the second person who was present—in other words, of the murderer. I would also urge that the introduction into the case of a document relating to large masses of valuable securities gives us for the first time some indication of a motive for the crime."

Sherlock Holmes's face showed that he was thoroughly taken aback by this new development.

"I must admit both your points," said he. "I confess that this note-book, which did not appear at the inquest, modifies any views which I may have formed. I had come to a theory of the crime in which I can find no place for this. Have you endeavoured to trace any of the securities here mentioned?"

"Inquiries are now being made at the offices, but I fear that the complete register of the stockholders of these South American concerns is in South America, and that some weeks must elapse before we can trace the shares."

Holmes had been examining the cover of the note-book with his magnifying lens.

"Surely there is some discolouration here," said he.

"Yes, sir, it is a blood-stain. I told you that I picked the book off the floor."

"Was the blood-stain above or below?"

"On the side next the boards."

"Which proves, of course, that the book was dropped after the crime was committed."

"Exactly, Mr. Holmes. I appreciated that point, and I conjectured that it was dropped by the murderer in his hurried flight. It lay near the door."

"I suppose that none of these securities have been found among the property of the dead man?"

"No, sir."

"Have you any reason to suspect robbery?"

"No, sir. Nothing seemed to have been touched."

"Dear me, it is certainly a very interesting case. Then there was a knife, was there not?"

"A sheath-knife, still in its sheath. It lay at the feet of the dead man. Mrs. Carey has identified it as being her husband's property."

Holmes was lost in thought for some time.

"Well," said he, at last, "I suppose I shall have to come out and have a look at it."

Stanley Hopkins gave a cry of joy.

"Thank you, sir. That will, indeed, be a weight off my mind."

"Holmes shook his finger at the Inspector.

"It would have been an easier task a week ago," said he. "But even now my visit may not be entirely fruitless. Watson, if you can spare the time, I should be very glad of your company. If you will call a four-wheeler, Hopkins, we shall be ready to start for the Forest Row in a quarter of an hour."

Alighting at the small wayside station, we drove for some miles through the remains of widespread woods, which were once part of that great forest which for so long held the Saxon invaders at bay—the impenetrable "weald," for sixty years the bulwark of Britain. Vast sections of it have been cleared, for this is the seat of the first iron-works of the country, and the trees have been felled to smelt the ore. Now the richer fields of the North have absorbed the trade, and nothing save these ravaged groves and great scars in the earth show the work of the past. Here, in a clearing upon the green slope of a hill, stood a long, low, stone house, approached by a curving drive running through the fields. Nearer the road and surrounded on three sides by bushes, was a small outhouse, one window and the door facing in our direction. It was the scene of the murder.

Stanley Hopkins led us first to the house, where he introduced us to a haggard, grey-haired woman, the widow of the murdered man, whose gaunt and deep-lined face, with the furtive look of terror in the depths of her red-rimmed eyes, told of the years of hardship and ill-usage which she had endured. With her was her daughter, a pale, fair-haired girl, whose eyes blazed defiantly at us as she told us that she was glad that her father was dead, and that she blessed the hand which had struck him down. It was a terrible household that Black Peter Carey had made for himself, and it was with a sense of relief that we found ourselves in the sunlight again and making our way along a path which had been worn across the fields by the feet of the dead man.

The outhouse was the simplest of dwellings, wooden-walled, shingle-roofed, one window beside the door and one on the farther side. Stanley Hopkins drew the key from his pocket and had stooped to the lock, when he paused with a look of attention and surprise upon his face.

"Someone has been tampering with it," he said.

There could be no doubt of the fact. The woodwork was cut, and the scratches showed white through the paint, as if they had been that instant done. Holmes had been examining the window.

"Someone has tried to force this also. Whoever it was has failed to make his way in. He must have been a very poor burglar."

"This is a most extraordinary thing," said the Inspector, "I could swear that these marks were not here yesterday evening."

"Some curious person from the village, perhaps," I suggested.

"Very unlikely. Few of them would dare to set foot in the grounds, far less try to force their way into the cabin. What do you think of it, Mr. Holmes?"

"I think that fortune is very kind to us."

"You mean that the person will come again?"

"It is very probable. He came expecting to find the door open. He tried to get in with the blade of a very small penknife. He could not manage it. What would he do?"

"Come again next night with a more useful tool."

"So I should say. It will be our fault if we are not there to receive him. Meanwhile, let me see the inside of the cabin."

The traces of the tragedy had been removed, but the furniture within the little room still stood as it had been on the night of the crime. For two hours, with most intense concentration, Holmes examined every object in turn, but his face showed that his quest was not a successful one. Once only he paused in his patient investigation.

"Have you taken anything off this shelf, Hopkins?"

"No, I have moved nothing."

"Something has been taken. There is less dust in this corner of the shelf than elsewhere. It may have been a book lying on its side. It may have been a box. Well, well, I can do nothing more. Let us walk in these beautiful woods, Watson, and give a few hours to the birds and the flowers. We shall meet you here later, Hopkins, and see if we can come to closer quarters with the gentleman who has paid this visit in the night."

It was past eleven o'clock when we formed our little ambuscade. Hopkins was for leaving the door of the hut open, but Holmes was of the opinion that this would rouse the suspicions of the stranger. The lock was a perfectly simple one, and only a strong blade was needed to push it back. Holmes also suggested that we should wait, not inside the hut, but outside it, among the bushes which grew round the farther window. In this way we should be able to watch our man if he struck a light and see what his object was in this stealthy nocturnal visit.

It was a long and melancholy vigil, and yet brought with it something of the thrill which the hunter feels when he lies beside the water-pool and waits for the coming of the thirsty beast of prey. What savage creature was it which might steal upon us out of the darkness? Was it a fierce tiger of crime, which could only be taken fighting hard with flashing fang and claw, or would it prove to be some skulking jackal, dangerous only to the weak and unguarded?

In absolute silence we crouched amongst the bushes, waiting for whatever might come. At first the steps of a few belated villagers, or the sound of voices from the village lightened our vigil, but one by one these interruptions died away, and an absolute stillness fell upon us, save for the chimes of the distant church, which told us of the progress of the night, and for the rustle and whisper of a fine rain falling amid the foliage which roofed us in.

Half-past two had chimed, and it was the darkest hour which precedes the dawn, when we all started as a low but sharp click came from the direction of the gate. Someone had entered the drive. Again there was a long silence, and I had begun to fear that it was a false alarm, when a stealthy step was heard upon the other side of the hut, and a moment later a metallic scraping and clinking. The man was trying to force the lock. This time his skill was greater or his tool was better, for there was a sudden snap and the creak of the hinges. Then a match was struck, and the next instant the steady light from a candle filled the interior of the hut. Through the gauze curtain our eyes were all riveted upon the scene within.

The nocturnal visitor was a young man, frail and thin, with a black moustache, which intensified the deadly pallor of his face. He could not have been much above twenty years of age. I have never seen any human being who appeared to be in such a pitiable fright, for his teeth were visibly chattering, and he was shaking in every limb. He was dressed like a gentleman, in Norfolk jacket and knickerbockers, with a cloth cap upon his head. We watched him staring round with frightened eyes. Then he laid the candle-end upon the table and disappeared from our view into one of the corners. He returned with a large book, one of the log-books which formed a line upon the shelves. Leaning on the table, he rapidly turned over the leaves of this volume until he came to the entry which he sought. Then, with an angry gesture of his clenched hand, he closed the book, replaced it in the corner, and put out the light. He had hardly turned to leave the hut when Hopkins's hand was on the fellow's collar, and I heard his loud gasp of terror as he understood that he was taken. The candle was relit, and there was our wretched captive, shivering and cowering in the grasp of the detective. He sank down upon the sea-chest and looked helplessly from one of us to the other.

"Now, my fine fellow," said Stanley Hopkins, "who are you, and what do you want here?"

The man pulled himself together and faced us with an effort at self-composure.

"You are detectives, I suppose?" said he. "You imagine I am connected with the death of Captain Peter Carey. I assure you that I am innocent."

"We'll see about that," said Hopkins. "First of all, what is your name?"

"It is John Hopley Neligan."

I saw Holmes and Hopkins exchange a quick glance.

"What are you doing here?"

"Can I speak confidentially?"

"No, certainly not."

"Why should I tell you?"

"If you have no answer, it may go badly with you at the trial."

The young man winced.

"Well, I will tell you," he said. "Why should I not? And yet I hate to think of this old scandal gaining a new lease of life. Did you ever hear of Dawson and Neligan?"

I could see, from Hopkins's face, that he never had, but Holmes was keenly interested.

"You mean the West Country bankers," said he. "They failed for a million, ruined half the county families of Cornwall, and Neligan disappeared."

"Exactly. Neligan was my father."

At last we were getting something positive, and yet it seemed a long gap between an absconding banker and Captain Peter Carey pinned against the wall with one of his own harpoons. We all listened intently to the young man's words.

"It was my father who was really concerned. Dawson had retired. I was only ten years of age at the time, but I was old enough to feel the shame and horror of it all. It has always been said that my father stole all the securities and fled. It is not true. It was his belief that if he were given time in which to realize them, all would be well and every creditor paid in full. He started in his little yacht for Norway just before the warrant was issued for his arrest. I can remember that last night, when he bade farewell to my mother. He left us a list of the securities he was taking, and he swore that he would come back with his honour cleared, and that none who had trusted him would suffer. Well, no word was ever heard from him again. Both the yacht and he vanished utterly. We believed, my mother and I, that he and it, with the securities that he had taken with him, were at the bottom of the sea. We had a faithful friend, however, who is a business man, and it was he who discovered some time ago that some of the securities which my father had with him had reappeared on the London market. You can imagine our amazement. I spent months in trying to trace them, and at last, after many doubtings and difficulties, I discovered that the original seller had been Captain Peter Carey, the owner of this hut.

"Naturally, I made some inquiries about the man. I

456

found that he had been in command of a whaler which was due to return from the Arctic seas at the very time when my father was crossing to Norway. The autumn of that year was a stormy one, and there was a long succession of southerly gales. My father's yacht may well have been blown to the north and there met by Captain Peter Carey's ship. If that were so, what had become of my father? In any case, if I could prove from Peter Carey's evidence how these securities came on the market it would be a proof that my father had not sold them, and that he had no view to personal profit when he took them.

"I came down to Sussex with the intention of seeing the Captain, but it was at this moment that his terrible death occurred. I read at the inquest a description of his cabin, in which it stated that the old log-books of his vessel were preserved in it. It struck me that if I could see what occurred in the month of August, 1883, on board the *Sea Unicorn*, I might settle the mystery of my father's fate. I tried last night to get at these log-books, but was unable to open the door. To-night I tried again and succeeded, but I find that the pages which deal with that month have been torn from the book. It was at that moment I found myself a prisoner in your hands."

"Is that all?" asked Hopkins.

"Yes, that is all." His eyes shifted as he said it.

"You have nothing else to tell us?"

He hesitated.

"No, there is nothing."

"You have not been here before last night?"

"No."

"Then how do you account for *that?*" cried Hopkins, as he held up the damning note-book, with the initials of our prisoner on the first leaf and the blood-stain on the cover.

The wretched man collapsed. He sank his face in his hands and trembled all over.

"Where did you get it?" he groaned. "I did not know. I thought I had lost it at the hotel."

"That is enough," said Hopkins, sternly. "Whatever else

457

you have to say, you must say in court. You will walk down with me now to the police-station. Well, Mr. Holmes, I am very much obliged to you and to your friend for coming down to help me. As it turns out your presence was unnecessary, and I would have brought the case to this successful issue without you, but none the less, I am grateful. Rooms have been reserved for you at the Brambletye Hotel, so we can all walk down to the village together."

"Well, Watson, what do you think of it?" asked Holmes, as we travelled back next morning.

"I can see that you are not satisfied."

"Oh, yes, my dear Watson, I am perfectly satisfied. At the same time, Stanley Hopkins's methods do not commend themselves to me. I am disappointed in Stanley Hopkins. I had hoped for better things from him. One should always look for a possible alternative and provide against it. It is the first rule of criminal investigation."

"What, then, is the alternative?"

"The line of investigation which I have myself been pursuing. It may give us nothing. I cannot tell. But at least I shall follow it to the end."

Several letters were waiting for Holmes at Baker Street. He snatched one of them up, opened it, and burst out into a triumphant chuckle of laughter.

"Excellent, Watson! The alternative develops. Have you telegraph forms? Just write a couple of messages for me: 'Sumner, Shipping Agent, Ratcliff Highway. Send three men on, to arrive ten to-morrow morning.—Basil' That's my name in those parts. The other is: 'Inspector Stanley Hopkins, 46 Lord Street, Brixton. Come breakfast to-morrow at nine-thirty. Important. Wire if unable to come.—Sherlock Holmes.' There, Watson, this infernal case has haunted me for ten days. I hereby banish it completely from my presence. To-morrow, I trust that we shall hear the last of it forever."

Sharp at the hour named Inspector Stanley Hopkins appeared, and we sat down together to the excellent breakfast which Mrs. Hudson had prepared. The young detective was in high spirits at his success.

"You really think that your solution must be correct?" asked Holmes.

"I could not imagine a more complete case."

"It did not seem to me conclusive."

"You astonish me, Mr. Holmes. What more could one ask for?"

"Does your explanation cover every point?"

"Undoubtedly. I find that young Neligan arrived at the Brambletye Hotel on the very day of the crime. He came on the pretence of playing golf. His room was on the ground-floor, and he could get out when he liked. That very night he went down to Woodman's Lee, saw Peter Carey at the hut, quarrelled with him, and killed him with the harpoon. Then, horrified by what he had done, he fled out of the hut, dropping the note-book which he had brought with him in order to question Peter Carey about these different securities. You may have observed that some of them were marked with ticks, and the others—the great majority—were not. Those which are ticked have been traced on the London market, but the others, presumably, were still in the possession of Carey, and young Neligan, according to his own account, was anxious to recover them in order to do the right thing by his father's creditors. After his flight he did not dare to approach the hut again for some time, but at last he forced himself to do so in order to obtain the information which he needed. Surely that is all simple and obvious?"

Holmes smiled and shook his head.

"It seems to me to have only one drawback, Hopkins, and that is that it is intrinsically impossible. Have you tried to drive a harpoon through a body? No? Tut, tut, my dear sir, you must really pay attention to these details. My friend Watson could tell you that I spent a whole morning in that exercise. It is no easy matter and requires a strong and practised arm. But this blow was delivered with such violence that the head of the weapon sank deep into the wall. Do you imagine that this anæmic youth was capable of so frightful an assault? Is he the man who hobnobbed in rum and water with Black Peter in the dead of the night? Was it his profile that was seen on the blind two nights before? No, no, Hopkins, it is another and more formidable person for whom we must seek."

The detective's face had grown longer and longer during Holmes's speech. His hopes and his ambitions were all crumbling about him. But he would not abandon his position without a struggle.

"You can't deny that Neligan was present that night, Mr. Holmes. The book will prove that. I fancy that I have evidence enough to satisfy a jury, even if you are able to pick a hole in it. Besides, Mr. Holmes, I have laid my hand upon *my* man. As to this terrible person of yours, where is he?"

"I rather fancy that he is on the stair," said Holmes, serenely. "I think, Watson, that you would do well to put that revolver where you can reach it." He rose and laid a written paper upon a side-table. "Now we are ready," said he.

There had been some talking in gruff voices outside, and now Mrs. Hudson opened the door to say that there were three men inquiring for Captain Basil.

"Show them in one by one," said Holmes.

The first who entered was a little Ribston pippin of a man, with ruddy cheeks and fluffy white side-whiskers. Holmes had drawn a letter from his pocket.

"What name?" he asked.

"James Lancaster."

"I am sorry, Lancaster, but the berth is full. Here is half a sovereign for your trouble. Just step into this room and wait there for a few minutes."

The second man was a long, dried-up creature, with lank hair and sallow cheeks. His name was Hugh Pattins. He also received his dismissal, his half-sovereign, and the order to wait.

The third applicant was a man of remarkable appearance. A fierce bull-dog face was framed in a tangle of hair and beard, and two bold, dark eyes gleamed behind the cover of thick, tufted, overhung eyebrows. He saluted and

460

stood sailor-fashion, turning his cap round in his hands.

"Your name?" asked Holmes.

"Patrick Cairns."

"Harpooner?"

"Yes, sir. Twenty-six voyages."

"Dundee, I suppose?"

"Yes, sir."

"And ready to start with an exploring ship?"

"Yes, sir."

"What wages?"

"Eight pounds a month."

"Could you start at once?"

"As soon as I get my kit."

"Have you your papers?"

"Yes, sir." He took a sheaf of worn and greasy forms from his pocket. Holmes glanced over them and returned them.

"You are just the man I want," said he. "Here's the agreement on the side-table. If you sign it the whole matter will be settled."

The seaman lurched across the room and took up the pen.

"Shall I sign here?" he asked, stooping over the table.

Holmes leaned over his shoulder and passed both hands over his neck.

"This will do," said he.

I heard a click of steel and a bellow like an enraged bull. The next instant Holmes and the seaman were rolling on the ground together. He was a man of such gigantic strength that, even with the handcuffs which Holmes had so deftly fastened upon his wrists, he would have very quickly overpowered my friend had Hopkins and I not rushed to his rescue. Only when I pressed the cold muzzle of the revolver to his temple did he at last understand that resistance was vain. We lashed his ankles with cord and rose breathless from the struggle.

"I must really apologize, Hopkins," said Sherlock Holmes. "I fear that the scrambled eggs are cold. How-

461

ever, you will enjoy the rest of your breakfast all the better, will you not, for the thought that you have brought your case to a triumphant conclusion."

Stanley Hopkins was speechless with amazement.

"I don't know what to say, Mr. Holmes," he blurted out at last, with a very red face. "It seems to me that I have been making a fool of myself from the beginning. I understand now, what I should never have forgotten, that I am the pupil and you are the master. Even now I see what you have done, but I don't know how you did it or what it signifies."

"Well, well," said Holmes, good-humouredly. "We all learn by experience, and your lesson this time is that you should never lose sight of the alternative. You were so absorbed in young Neligan that you could not spare a thought to Patrick Cairns, the true murderer of Peter Carey."

The hoarse voice of the seaman broke in on our conversation.

"See here, mister," said he, "I make no complaint of being man-handled in this fashion, but I would have you call things by their right names. You say I murdered Peter Carey, I say I *killed* Peter Carey, and there's all the difference. Maybe you don't believe what I say. Maybe you think I am just slinging you a yarn."

"Not at all," said Holmes. "Let us hear what you have to say."

"It's soon told, and by the Lord, every word of it is truth. I knew Black Peter, and when he pulled out his knife I whipped a harpoon through him sharp, for I knew that it was him or me. That's how he died. You can call it murder. Anyhow, I'd as soon die with a rope around my neck as with Black Peter's knife in my heart."

"How came you there?" asked Holmes.

"I'll tell it you from the beginning. Just sit me up a little, so as I can speak easy. It was in '83 that it happened—August of that year. Peter Carey was master of the *Sea Unicorn*, and I was spare harpooner. We were coming out of the ice-pack on our way home, with head winds and a week's southerly gale, when we picked up a little craft that had been blown north. There was one man on her—a landsman. The crew had thought she would founder and had made for the Norwegian coast in the dinghy. I guess they were all drowned. Well, we took him on board, this man, and he and the Skipper had some long talks in the cabin. All the baggage we took off with him was one tin box. So far as I know, the man's name was never mentioned, and on the second night he disappeared as if he had never been. It was given out that he had either thrown himself overboard or fallen overboard in the heavy weather that we were having. Only one man knew what had happened to him, and that was me, for with my own eyes, I saw the Skipper tip up his heels and put him over the rail in the middle watch of a dark night, two days before we sighted the Shetland Lights.

"Well, I kept my knowledge to myself and waited to see what would come of it. When we got back to Scotland it was easily hushed up, and nobody asked any questions. A stranger died by accident, and it was nobody's business to inquire. Shortly after Peter Carey gave up the sea, and it was long years before I could find where he was. I guessed that he had done the deed for the sake of what was in that tin box, and that he could afford now to pay me well for keeping my mouth shut.

"I found out where he was through a sailor man that had met him in London, and down I went to squeeze him. The first night he was reasonable enough and was ready to give me what would make me free of the sea for life. We were to fix it all two nights later. When I came, I found him three parts drunk and in a vile temper. We sat down and we drank and we yarned about old times, but the more he drank the less I liked the look on his face. I spotted that harpoon upon the wall, and I thought I might need it before I was through. Then at last he broke out at me, spitting and cursing, with murder in his eyes and a great clasp-knife in his hand. He had not time to get it from the sheath before I had the harpoon through him. Heavens, what a yell he gave! And his face gets between me and my sleep. I stood there, with his blood splashing round me, and I waited for a bit, but all was quiet, so I took heart once more. I looked round, and there was the tin box on the shelf. I had as much right to it as Peter Carey, anyhow, so I took it with me and left the hut. Like a fool I left my baccy-pouch upon the table.

"Now I'll tell you the queerest part of the whole story. I had hardly got outside the hut when I heard someone coming, and I hid among the bushes. A man came slinking along, went into the hut, gave a cry as if he had seen a ghost, and legged it as hard as he could run until he was out of sight. Who he was or what he wanted is more than I can tell. For my part I walked ten miles, got a train at Tunbridge Wells, and so reached London, and no one the wiser.

"Well, when I came to examine the box I found there was no money in it, and nothing but papers that I would not dare to sell. I had lost my hold on Black Peter and was stranded in London without a shilling. There was only my trade left. I saw these advertisements about harpooners and high wages, so I went to the shipping agents, and they sent me here. That's all I know, and I say again that if I killed Black Peter, the law should give me thanks, for I saved them the price of a hempen rope."

"A very clear statement," said Holmes, rising and lighting his pipe. "I think, Hopkins, that you should lose no time in conveying your prisoner to a place of safety. This room is not well adapted for a cell, and Mr. Patrick Cairns occupies too large a proportion of our carpet."

"Mr. Holmes," said Hopkins, "I do not know how to express my gratitude. Even now I do not understand how you attained this result."

"Simply by having the good fortune to get the right clue from the beginning. It is very possible if I had known about this note-book it might have led away my thoughts, as it did yours. But all I heard pointed in the one direction.

The amazing strength, the skill in the use of the harpoon, the rum and water, the sealskin tobacco-pouch with the coarse tobacco—all these pointed to a seaman, and one who had been a whaler. I was convinced that the initials 'P. C.' upon the pouch were a coincidence, and not those of Peter Carey, since he seldom smoked, and no pipe was found in his cabin. You remember that I asked whether whisky and brandy were in the cabin. You said they were. How many landsmen are there who would drink rum when they could get these other spirits? Yes, I was certain it was a seaman."

"And how did you find him?"

"My dear sir, the problem had become a very simple one. If it were a seaman, it could only be a seaman who had been with him on the *Sea Unicorn*. So far as I could learn he had sailed in no other ship. I spent three days in wiring to Dundee, and at the end of that time I ascertained the names of the crew of the *Sea Unicorn* in 1883. When I found Patrick Cairns among the harpooners, my research was nearing its end. I argued that the man was probably in London, and that he would desire to leave the country for a time. I therefore spent some days in the East End, devised an Arctic expedition, put forth tempting terms for harpooners who would serve under Captain Basil—and behold the result!"

"Wonderful!" cried Hopkins. "Wonderful!"

"You must obtain the release of young Neligan as soon as possible," said Holmes. "I confess that I think you owe him some apology. The tin box must be returned to him, but, of course, the securities which Peter Carey has sold are lost forever. There's the cab, Hopkins, and you can remove your man. If you want me for the trial, my address and that of Watson will be somewhere in Norway—I'll send particulars later."

The Adventure of
Charles Augustus Milverton

It is years since the incidents of which I speak took place, and yet it is with diffidence that I allude to them. For a long time, even with the utmost discretion and reticence, it would have been impossible to make the facts public, but now the principal person concerned is beyond the reach of human law, and with due suppression the story may be told in such fashion as to injure no one. It records an absolutely unique experience in the career both of Mr. Sherlock Holmes and of myself. The reader will excuse me if I conceal the date or any other fact by which he might trace the actual occurrence.

We had been out for one of our evening rambles, Holmes and I, and had returned about six o'clock on a cold, frosty winter's evening. As Holmes turned up the lamp the light fell upon a card on the table. He glanced at it, and then, with an ejaculation of disgust, threw it on the floor. I picked it up and read:

CHARLES AUGUSTUS MILVERTON,
Appledore Towers,
Hampstead

Agent

"Who is he?" I asked.

"The worst man in London," Holmes answered, as he sat down and stretched his legs before the fire. "Is anything on the back of the card?"

I turned it over.

"Will call at 6:30—C. A. M.," I read.

"Hum! He's about due. Do you feel a creeping, shrinking sensation, Watson, when you stand before the serpents in the Zoo and see the slithery, gliding, venomous creatures, with their deadly eyes and wicked, flattened faces? Well, that's how Milverton impresses me. I've had to do with fifty murderers in my career, but the worst of them never gave me the repulsion which I have for this fellow. And yet I can't get out of doing business with him—indeed, he is here at my invitation."

"But who is he?"

"I'll tell you, Watson. He is the king of all the blackmailers. Heaven help the man, and still more the woman, whose secret and reputation come into the power of Milverton! With a smiling face and a heart of marble, he will squeeze and squeeze until he has drained them dry. The fellow is a genius in his way and would have made his mark in some more savoury trade. His method is as follows: He allows it to be known that he is prepared to pay very high sums for letters which compromise people of wealth and position. He receives these wares not only from treacherous valets or maids, but frequently from genteel ruffians, who have gained the confidence and affection of trusting women. He deals with no niggard hand. I happen to know that he paid seven hundred pounds to a footman for a note two lines in length, and that the ruin of a noble family was the result. Everything which is in the market goes to Milverton, and there are hundreds in this great city who turn white at his name. No one knows where his grip may fall, for he is far too rich and far too cunning to work from hand to mouth. He will hold a card back for years in order to play it at the moment when the stake is best worth winning. I have said that he is the worst man in London, and I would ask you how could one compare the ruffian, who in hot blood bludgeons his mate, with this man, who methodically and at his leisure tortures the soul and wrings the nerves in order to add to his already swollen money-bags?"

I had seldom heard my friend speak with such intensity of feeling.

"But surely," said I, "the fellow must be within the grasp of the law?"

"Technically, no doubt, but practically not. What would it profit a woman, for example, to get him a few months' imprisonment if her own ruin must immediately follow? His victims dare not hit back. If ever he blackmailed an innocent person, then indeed we should have him, but he is as cunning as the Evil One. No, no, we must find other ways to fight him."

"And why is he here?"

"Because an illustrious client has placed her piteous case in my hands. It is the Lady Eva Blackwell, the most beautiful débutante of last season. She is to be married in a fortnight to the Earl of Dovercourt. This fiend has several imprudent letters—imprudent, Watson, nothing worse— which were written to an impecunious young squire in the country. They would suffice to break off the match. Milverton will send the letters to the Earl unless a large sum of money is paid him. I have been commissioned to meet him and—to make the best terms I can."

At that instant there was a clatter and a rattle in the street below. Looking down I saw a stately carriage and pair, the brilliant lamps gleaming on the glossy haunches of the noble chestnuts. A footman opened the door, and a small, stout man in a shaggy astrakhan overcoat descended. A minute later he was in the room.

Charles Augustus Milverton was a man of fifty, with a large, intellectual head, a round, plump, hairless face, a perpetual frozen smile, and two keen grey eyes, which gleamed brightly from behind broad, gold-rimmed glasses. There was something of Mr. Pickwick's benevolence in his appearance, marred only by the insincerity of the fixed smile and by the hard glitter of those restless and penetrating eyes. His voice was as smooth and suave as his countenance, as he advanced with a plump little hand extended, murmuring his regret for having missed us at his first visit. Holmes disregarded the outstretched hand and looked at him with a face of granite. Milverton's smile broadened, he shrugged his shoulders, removed his overcoat, folded it with great deliberation over the back of a chair, and then took a seat.

"This gentleman?" said he, with a wave in my direction. "Is it discreet? Is it right?"

"Dr. Watson is my friend and partner."

"Very good, Mr. Holmes. It is only in your client's interests that I protested. The matter is so very delicate—"

"Dr. Watson has already heard of it."

"Then we can proceed to business. You say that you are acting for Lady Eva. Has she empowered you to accept my terms?"

"What are your terms?"

"Seven thousand pounds."

"And the alternative?"

"My dear sir, it is painful for me to discuss it, but if the money is not paid on the 14th, there certainly will be no marriage on the 18th." His insufferable smile was more complacent than ever.

Holmes thought for a little.

"You appear to me," he said, at last, "to be taking matters too much for granted. I am, of course, familiar with the contents of these letters. My client will certainly do what I may advise. I shall counsel her to tell her future husband the whole story and to trust to his generosity."

Milverton chuckled.

"You evidently do not know the Earl," said he.

From the baffled look upon Holmes's face, I could see clearly that he did.

"What harm is there in the letters?" he asked.

"They are sprightly—very sprightly," Milverton answered. "The lady was a charming correspondent. But I can assure you that the Earl of Dovercourt would fail to appreciate them. However, since you think otherwise, we will let it rest at that. It is purely a matter of business. If you think that it is in the best interests of your client that these letters should be placed in the hands of the Earl, then you would indeed be foolish to pay so large a sum of money to regain them." He rose and seized his astrakhan coat.

Holmes was grey with anger and mortification.

"Wait a little," he said. "You go too fast. We should certainly make every effort to avoid scandal in so delicate a matter."

Milverton relapsed into his chair.

"I was sure that you would see it in that light," he purred.

"At the same time," Holmes continued, "Lady Eva is not a wealthy woman. I assure you that two thousand pounds would be a drain upon her resources, and that the sum you name is utterly beyond her power. I beg, therefore, that you will moderate your demands, and that you will return the letters at the price I indicate, which is, I assure you, the highest that you can get."

Milverton's smile broadened and his eyes twinkled humorously.

"I am aware that what you say is true about the lady's resources," said he. "At the same time you must admit that the occasion of a lady's marriage is a very suitable time for her friends and relatives to make some little effort upon her behalf. They may hesitate as to an acceptable wedding present. Let me assure them that this little bundle of letters would give more joy than all the candelabra and butter-dishes in London."

"It is impossible," said Holmes.

"Dear me, dear me, how unfortunate!" cried Milverton, taking out a bulky pocket-book. "I cannot help thinking that ladies are ill-advised in not making an effort. Look at this!" He held up a little note with a coat-of-arms upon the envelope. "That belongs to—well, perhaps it is hardly fair to tell the name until to-morrow morning. But at that time it will be in the hands of the lady's husband. And all because she will not find a beggarly sum which she could get by turning her diamonds into paste. It *is* such a pity! Now, you remember the sudden end of the engagement between the Honourable Miss Miles and Colonel Dorking? Only two days before the wedding, there was a paragraph in the *Morning Post* to say that it was all off. And why? It is almost incredible, but the absurd sum of twelve hundred pounds would have settled the whole question. Is it not pitiful? And here I find you, a man of sense, boggling about terms, when your client's future and honour are at stake. You surprise me, Mr. Holmes."

"What I say is true," Holmes answered. "The money cannot be found. Surely it is better for you to take the substantial sum which I offer than to ruin this woman's career, which can profit you in no way?"

"There you make a mistake, Mr. Holmes. An exposure would profit me indirectly to a considerable extent. I have eight or ten similar cases maturing. If it was circulated among them that I had made a severe example of the Lady Eva, I should find all of them much more open to reason. You see my point?"

Holmes sprang from his chair.

"Get behind him, Watson! Don't let him out! Now, sir, let us see the contents of that note-book."

Milverton had glided as quick as a rat to the side of the room and stood with his back against the wall.

"Mr. Holmes, Mr. Holmes," he said, turning the front of his coat and exhibiting the butt of a large revolver, which projected from the inside pocket. "I have been expecting you to do something original. This has been done so often, and what good has ever come from it? I assure you that I am armed to the teeth, and I am perfectly prepared to use my weapons, knowing that the law will support me. Besides, your supposition that I would bring the letters here in a note-book is entirely mistaken. I would do nothing so foolish. And now, gentlemen, I have one or two little interviews this evening, and it is a long drive to Hampstead." He stepped forward, took up his coat, laid his hand on his revolver, and turned to the door. I picked up a chair, but Holmes shook his head, and I laid it down again. With a bow, a smile, and a twinkle, Milverton was out of the room, and a few moments after we heard the slam of the carriage door and the rattle of the wheels as he drove away.

Holmes sat motionless by the fire, his hands buried deep in his trouser pockets, his chin sunk upon his breast, his eyes fixed upon the glowing embers. For half an hour he was silent and still. Then, with the gesture of a man who has taken his decision, he sprang to his feet and passed into his bedroom. A little later a rakish young workman, with a goatee beard and a swagger, lit his clay pipe at the lamp before descending into the street. "I'll be back some time, Watson," said he, and vanished into the night. I understood that he had opened his campaign against Charles Augustus Milverton, but I little dreamed the strange shape which that campaign was destined to take.

For some days Holmes came and went at all hours in this attire, but beyond a remark that his time was spent at Hampstead, and that it was not wasted, I knew nothing of what he was doing. At last, however, on a wild, tempestuous evening, when the wind screamed and rattled against the windows, he returned from his last expedition, and having removed his disguise he sat before the fire and laughed heartily in his silent inward fashion.

"You would not call me a marrying man, Watson?"

"No, indeed!"

"You'll be interested to hear that I'm engaged."

"My dear fellow! I congrat—"

"To Milverton's housemaid."

"Good Heavens, Holmes!"

"I wanted information, Watson."

"Surely you have gone too far?"

"It was a most necessary step. I am a plumber with a rising business, Escott, by name. I have walked out with her each evening, and I have talked with her. Good Heavens, those talks! However, I have got all I wanted. I know Milverton's house as I know the palm of my hand."

"But the girl, Holmes?"

He shrugged his shoulders.

"You can't help it, my dear Watson. You must play your cards as best you can when such a stake is on the table. However, I rejoice to say that I have a hated rival, who will certainly cut me out the instant that my back is turned. What a splendid night it is!"

"You like this weather?"

"It suits my purpose. Watson, I mean to burgle Milverton's house to-night."

I had a catching of the breath, and my skin went cold at the words, which were slowly uttered in a tone of concentrated resolution. As a flash of lightning in the night shows up in an instant every detail of a wild landscape, so at one glance I seemed to see every possible result of such an action—the detection, the capture, the honoured career ending in irreparable failure and disgrace, my friend himself lying at the mercy of the odious Milverton.

"For Heaven's sake, Holmes, think what you are doing," I cried.

"My dear fellow, I have given it every consideration. I am never precipitate in my actions, nor would I adopt so energetic and, indeed, so dangerous a course, if any other were possible. Let us look at the matter clearly and fairly. I suppose that you will admit that the action is morally justifiable, though technically criminal. To burgle his house is no more than to forcibly take his pocket-book—an action in which you were prepared to aid me."

I turned it over in my mind.

"Yes," I said, "it is morally justifiable so long as our object is to take no articles save those which are used for an illegal purpose."

"Exactly. Since it is morally justifiable, I have only to consider the question of personal risk. Surely a gentleman should not lay much stress upon this, when a lady is in most desperate need of his help?"

"You will be in such a false position."

"Well, that is part of the risk. There is no other possible way of regaining these letters. The unfortunate lady has not the money, and there are none of her people in whom

473

she could confide. To-morrow is the last day of grace, and unless we can get the letters to-night, this villain will be as good as his word and will bring about her ruin. I must, therefore, abandon my client to her fate or I must play this last card. Between ourselves, Watson, it's a sporting duel between this fellow Milverton and me. He had, as you saw, the best of the first exchanges, but my self-respect and my reputation are concerned to fight it to a finish."

"Well, I don't like it, but I suppose it must be," said I. "When do we start?"

"You are not coming."

"Then you are not going," said I. "I give you my word of honour—and I never broke it in my life—that I will take a cab straight to the police-station and give you away, unless you let me share this adventure with you."

"You can't help me."

"How do you know that? You can't tell what may happen. Anyway, my resolution is taken. Other people besides you have self-respect, and even reputations."

Holmes had looked annoyed, but his brow cleared, and he clapped me on the shoulder.

"Well, well, my dear fellow, be it so. We have shared this same room for some years, and it would be amusing if we ended by sharing the same cell. You know, Watson, I don't mind confessing to you that I have always had an idea that I would have made a highly efficient criminal. This is the chance of my lifetime in that direction. See here!" He took a neat little leather case out of a drawer, and opening it he exhibited a number of shining instruments. "This is a first-class, up-to-date burgling kit, with nickel-plated jemmy, diamond-tipped glass-cutter, adaptable keys, and every modern improvement which the march of civilization demands, Here, too, is my dark lantern. Everything is in order. Have you a pair of silent shoes?"

"I have rubber-soled tennis shoes."

"Excellent! And a mask?"

"I can make a couple out of black silk."

"I can see that you have a strong, natural turn for this

sort of thing. Very good, do you make the masks. We shall have some cold supper before we start. It is now nine-thirty. At eleven we shall drive as far as Church Row. It is a quarter of an hour's walk from there to Appledore Towers. We shall be at work before midnight. Milverton is a heavy sleeper and retires punctually at ten-thirty. With any luck we should be back here by two, with the Lady Eva's letters in my pocket."

Holmes and I put on our dress-clothes, so that we might appear to be two theatre-goers homeward bound. In Oxford Street we picked up a hansom and drove to an address in Hampstead. Here we paid off our cab, and with our great-coats buttoned up, for it was bitterly cold, and the wind seemed to blow through us, we walked along the edge of the heath.

"It's a business that needs delicate treatment," said Holmes. "These documents are contained in a safe in the fellow's study, and the study is the ante-room of his bed-chamber. On the other hand, like all these stout, little men who do themselves well, he is a plethoric sleeper. Agatha—that's my fiancée—says it is a joke in the serv-ants' hall that it's impossible to wake the master. He has a secretary who is devoted to his interests and never budges from the study all day. That's why we are going at night. Then he has a beast of a dog which roams the garden. I met Agatha late the last two evenings, and she locks the brute up so as to give me a clear run. This is the house, this big one in its own grounds. Through the gate—now to the right among the laurels. We might put on our masks here, I think. You see, there is not a glimmer of light in any of the windows, and everything is working splendidly."

With our black silk face-coverings, which turned us into two of the most truculent figures in London, we stole up to the silent, gloomy house. A sort of tiled veranda extended along one side of it, lined by several windows and two doors.

"That's his bedroom," Holmes whispered. "This door opens straight into the study. It would suit us best, but it is bolted as well as locked, and we should make too much noise getting in. Come round here. There's a greenhouse which opens into the drawing-room."

The place was locked, but Holmes removed a circle of glass and turned the key from the inside. An instant afterwards he had closed the door behind us, and we had become felons in the eyes of the law. The thick, warm air of the conservatory and the rich, choking fragrance of exotic plants took us by the throat. He seized my hand in the darkness and led me swiftly past banks of shrubs which brushed against our faces. Holmes had remarkable powers, carefully cultivated, of seeing in the dark. Still holding my hand in one of his, he opened a door, and I was vaguely conscious that we had entered a large room in which a cigar had been smoked not long before. He felt his way among the furniture, opened another door, and closed it behind us. Putting out my hand I felt several coats hanging from the wall, and I understood that I was in a passage. We passed along it, and Holmes very gently opened a door upon the right-hand side. Something rushed out at us and my heart sprang into my mouth, but I could have laughed when I realized that it was the cat. A fire was burning in this new room, and again the air was heavy with tobacco smoke. Holmes entered on tip-toe, waited for me to follow, and then very gently closed the door. We were in Milverton's study, and a portière at the farther side showed the entrance to his bedroom.

It was a good fire, and the room was illuminated by it. Near the door I saw the gleam of an electric switch, but it was unnecessary, even if it had been safe, to turn it on. At one side of the fireplace was a heavy curtain which covered the bay window we had seen from outside. On the other side was the door which communicated with the veranda. A desk stood in the centre, with a turning-chair of shining red leather. Opposite was a large bookcase, with a marble bust of Athene on the top. In the corner, between the bookcase and the wall, there stood a tall, green safe, the firelight flashing back from the polished brass knobs upon its face. Holmes stole across and looked at it. Then he crept to the door of the bedroom and stood with slanting head listening intently. No sound came from within. Meanwhile it had struck me that it would be wise to secure our retreat through the outer door, so I examined it. To my amazement, it was neither locked nor bolted. I touched Holmes on the arm, and he turned his masked face in that direction. I saw him start, and he was evidently as surprised as I.

"I don't like it," he whispered, putting his lips to my very ear. "I can't quite make it out. Anyhow, we have no time to lose."

"Can I do anything?"

"Yes, stand by the door. If you hear anyone come, bolt it on the inside, and we can get away as we came. If they come the other way, we can get through the door if our job is done, or hide behind these window curtains if it is not. Do you understand?"

I nodded and stood by the door. My first feeling of fear had passed away, and I thrilled now with a keener zest than I had ever enjoyed when we were the defenders of the law instead of its defiers. The high object of our mission, the consciousness that it was unselfish and chivalrous, the villainous character of our opponent, all added to the sporting interest of the adventure. Far from feeling guilty, I rejoiced and exulted in our dangers. With a glow of admiration I watched Holmes unrolling his case of instruments and choosing his tool with the calm, scientific accuracy of a surgeon who performs a delicate operation. I knew that the opening of safes was a particular hobby with him, and I understood the joy which it gave him to be confronted with this green and gold monster, the dragon which held in its maw the reputations of many fair ladies. Turning up the cuffs of his dress-coat—he had placed his overcoat on a chair—Holmes laid out two drills, a jemmy, and several skeleton keys. I stood at the centre door with my eyes glancing at each of the others, ready for any emergency, though, indeed, my plans were somewhat

477

vague as to what I should do if we were interrupted. For half an hour, Holmes worked with concentrated energy, laying down one tool, picking up another, handling each with the strength and delicacy of the trained mechanic. Finally I heard a click, the broad green door swung open, and inside I had a glimpse of a number of paper packets, each tied, sealed, and inscribed. Holmes picked one out, but it was hard to read by the flickering fire, and he drew out his little dark lantern, for it was too dangerous, with Milverton in the next room, to switch on the electric light. Suddenly I saw him halt, listen intently, and then in an instant he had swung the door of the safe to, picked up his coat, stuffed his tools into the pockets, and darted behind the window curtain, motioning me to do the same.

It was only when I had joined him there that I heard what had alarmed his quicker senses. There was a noise somewhere within the house. A door slammed in the distance. Then a confused, dull murmur broke itself into the measured thud of heavy footsteps rapidly approaching. They were in the passage outside the room. They paused at the door. The door opened. There was a sharp snick as the electric light was turned on. The door closed once more, and the pungent reek of a strong cigar was borne to our nostrils. Then the footsteps continued backward and forward, backward and forward, within a few yards of us. Finally there was a creak from a chair, and the footsteps ceased. Then a key clicked in a lock, and I heard the rustle of papers.

So far I had not dared to look out, but now I gently parted the division of the curtains in front of me and peeped through. From the pressure of Holmes's shoulder against mine, I knew that he was sharing my observations. Right in front of us, and almost within our reach, was the broad, rounded back of Milverton. It was evident that we had entirely miscalculated his movements, that he had never been to his bedroom, but that he had been sitting up in some smoking or billiard room in the farther wing of the house, the windows of which we had not seen. His broad, grizzled head, with its shining patch of baldness, was in the immediate foreground of our vision. He was leaning far back in the red leather chair, his legs outstretched, a long, black cigar projecting at an angle from his mouth. He wore a semi-military smoking jacket, claret-coloured, with a black velvet collar. In his hand he held a long, legal document which he was reading in an indolent fashion, blowing rings of tobacco smoke from his lips as he did so. There was no promise of a speedy departure in his composed bearing and his comfortable attitude.

I felt Holmes's hand steal into mine and give me a re-assuring shake, as if to say that the situation was within his powers, and that he was easy in his mind. I was not sure whether he had seen what was only too obvious from my position, that the door of the safe was imper-fectly closed, and that Milverton might at any moment ob-serve it. In my own mind I had determined that if I were sure, from the rigidity of his gaze, that it had caught his eye, I would at once spring out, throw my great-coat over his head, pinion him, and leave the rest to Holmes. But Milverton never looked up. He was languidly interested by the papers in his hand, and page after page was turned as he followed the argument of the lawyer. At least, I thought, when he has finished the document and the cigar he will go to his room, but before he had reached the end of either, there came a remarkable devel-opment, which turned our thoughts into quite another channel.

Several times I had observed that Milverton looked at his watch, and once he had risen and sat down again, with a gesture of impatience. The idea, however, that he might have an appointment at so strange an hour never occurred to me until a faint sound reached my ears from the veranda outside. Milverton dropped his papers and sat rigid in his chair. The sound was repeated, and then there came a gentle tap at the door. Milverton rose and opened it.

"Well," said he, curtly, "you are nearly half an hour late."

So this was the explanation of the unlocked door and of

the nocturnal vigil of Milverton. There was the gentle rustle of a woman's dress. I had closed the slit between the curtains as Milverton's face had turned in our direction, but now I ventured very carefully to open it once more. He had resumed his seat, the cigar still projecting at an insolent angle from the corner of his mouth. In front of him, in the full glare of the electric light, there stood a tall, slim, dark woman, a veil over her face, a mantle drawn round her chin. Her breath came quick and fast, and every inch of the lithe figure was quivering with strong emotion.

"Well," said Milverton, "you made me lose a good night's rest, my dear. I hope you'll prove worth it. You couldn't come any other time—eh?"

The woman shook her head.

"Well, if you couldn't you couldn't. If the Countess is a hard mistress, you have your chance to get level with her now. Bless the girl, what are you shivering about? That's right. Pull yourself together. Now, let us get down to business." He took a note-book from the drawer of his desk. "You say that you have five letters which compromise the Countess d'Albert. You want to sell them. I want to buy them. So far so good. It only remains to fix a price. I should want to inspect the letters, of course. If they are really good specimens—Great Heavens, is it you?"

The woman, without a word, had raised her veil and dropped the mantle from her chin. It was a dark, handsome, clear-cut face which confronted Milverton—a face with a curved nose, strong, dark eyebrows shading hard, glittering eyes, and a straight, thin-lipped mouth set in a dangerous smile.

"It is I," she said, "the woman whose life you have ruined."

Milverton laughed, but fear vibrated in his voice. "You were so very obstinate," said he. "Why did you drive me to such extremities? I assure you I wouldn't hurt a fly of my own accord, but every man has his business, and what was I to do? I put the price well within your means. You would not pay."

"So you sent the letters to my husband, and he—the noblest gentleman that ever lived, a man whose boots I was never worthy to lace—he broke his gallant heart and died. You remember that last night, when I came through that door, I begged and prayed you for mercy, and you laughed in my face as you are trying to laugh now, only your coward heart cannot keep your lips from twitching. Yes, you never thought to see me here again, but it was that night which taught me how I could meet you face to face, and alone. Well, Charles Milverton, what have you to say?"

"Don't imagine that you can bully me," said he, rising to his feet. "I have only to raise my voice, and I could call my servants and have you arrested. But I will make allowance for your natural anger. Leave the room at once as you came, and I will say no more."

The woman stood with her hand buried in her bosom, and the same deadly smile on her thin lips.

"You will ruin no more lives as you have ruined mine. You will wring no more hearts as you wrung mine. I will free the world of a poisonous thing. Take that, you hound—and that!—and that!—and that!—and that!"

She had drawn a little gleaming revolver and emptied barrel after barrel into Milverton's body, the muzzle within two feet of his shirt front. He shrank away and then fell forward upon the table, coughing furiously and clawing among the papers. Then he staggered to his feet, received another shot, and rolled upon the floor. "You've done me," he cried, and lay still. The woman looked at him intently and ground her heel into his upturned face. She looked again, but there was no sound or movement. I heard a sharp rustle, the night air blew into the heated room, and the avenger was gone.

No interference upon our part could have saved the man from his fate, but, as the woman poured bullet after bullet into Milverton's shrinking body I was about to spring out, when I felt Holmes's cold, strong grasp upon my wrist. I understood the whole argument of that firm,

481

restraining grip—that it was no affair of ours, that justice had overtaken a villain, that we had our own duties and our own objects, which were not to be lost sight of. But hardly had the woman rushed from the room when Holmes, with swift, silent steps, was over at the other door. He turned the key in the lock. At the same instant we heard voices in the house and the sound of hurrying feet. The revolver shots had roused the household. With perfect coolness Holmes slipped across to the safe, filled his two arms with bundles of letters, and poured them all into the fire. Again and again he did it, until the safe was empty. Someone turned the handle and beat upon the outside of the door. Holmes looked swiftly round. The letter which had been the messenger of death for Milverton lay, all mottled with his blood, upon the table. Holmes tossed it in among the blazing papers. Then he drew the key from the outer door, passed through after me, and locked it on the outside. "This way, Watson," said he, "we can scale the garden wall in this direction."

I could not have believed that an alarm could have spread so swiftly. Looking back, the huge house was one blaze of light. The front door was open, and figures were rushing down the drive. The whole garden was alive with people, and one fellow raised a view-halloa as we emerged from the veranda and followed hard at our heels. Holmes seemed to know the grounds perfectly, and he threaded his way swiftly among a plantation of small trees, I close at his heels, and our foremost pursuer panting behind us. It was a six-foot wall which barred our path, but he sprang to the top and over. As I did the same I felt the hand of the man behind me grab at my ankle, but I kicked myself free and scrambled over a grass-strewn coping. I fell upon my face among some bushes, but Holmes had me on my feet in an instant, and together we dashed away across the huge expanse of Hampstead Heath. We had run two miles, I suppose, before Holmes at last halted and listened intently. All was absolute silence behind us. We had shaken off our pursuers and were safe.

We had breakfasted and were smoking our morning pipe on the day after the remarkable experience which I have recorded, when Mr. Lestrade, of Scotland Yard, very solemn and impressive, was ushered into our modest sitting-room.

"Good-morning, Mr. Holmes," said he; "good-morning. May I ask if you are very busy just now?"

"Not too busy to listen to you."

"I thought that, perhaps, if you had nothing particular on hand, you might care to assist us in a most remarkable case, which occurred only last night at Hampstead."

"Dear me!" said Holmes. "What was that?"

"A murder—a most dramatic and remarkable murder. I know how keen you are upon these things, and I would take it as a great favour if you would step down to Appledore Towers and give us the benefit of your advice. It is no ordinary crime. We have had our eyes upon this Mr. Milverton for some time, and between ourselves, he was a bit of a villain. He is known to have held papers which he used for blackmailing purposes. These papers have all been burned by the murderers. No article of value was taken, as it is probable that the criminals were men of good position, whose sole object was to prevent social exposure."

"Criminals?" said Holmes. "Plural?"

"Yes, there were two of them. They were as nearly as possible captured red-handed. We have their footmarks, we have their description, it's ten to one that we trace them. The first fellow was a bit too active, but the second was caught by the under-gardener and only got away after a struggle. He was a middle-sized, strongly built man—square jaw, thick neck, moustache, a mask over his eyes."

"That's rather vague," said Sherlock Holmes. "Why, it might be a description of Watson!"

"It's true," said the Inspector, with amusement. "It might be a description of Watson."

"Well, I'm afraid I can't help you, Lestrade," said

Holmes. "The fact is that I knew this fellow Milverton, that I considered him one of the most dangerous men in London, and that I think there are certain crimes which the law cannot touch, and which therefore, to some extent, justify private revenge. No, it's no use arguing. I have made up my mind. My sympathies are with the criminals rather than with the victim, and I will not handle this case."

Holmes had not said one word to me about the tragedy which we had witnessed, but I observed all the morning that he was in his most thoughtful mood, and he gave me the impression, from his vacant eyes and his abstracted manner, of a man who is striving to recall something to his memory. We were in the middle of our lunch, when he suddenly sprang to his feet. "By Jove, Watson, I've got it!" he cried. "Take your hat! Come with me!" He hurried at his top speed down Baker Street and along Oxford Street, until we had almost reached Regent Circus. Here, on the left hand, there stands a shop window filled with photographs of the celebrities and beauties of the day. Holmes's eyes fixed themselves upon one of them, and following his gaze I saw the picture of a regal and stately lady in Court dress, with a high diamond tiara upon her noble head. I looked at that delicately curved nose, at the marked eyebrows, at the straight mouth, and the strong little chin beneath it. Then I caught my breath as I read the time-honoured title of the great nobleman and statesman whose wife she had been. My eyes met those of Holmes, and he put his finger to his lips as we turned away from the window.

The Adventure of the

Bruce-Partington Plans

In the third week of November, in the year 1895, a dense yellow fog settled down upon London. From the Monday to the Thursday I doubt whether it was ever possible from our windows in Baker Street to see the loom of the opposite houses. The first day Holmes had spent in cross-indexing his huge book of references. The second and third had been patiently occupied upon a subject which he had recently made his hobby—the music of the Middle Ages. But when, for the fourth time, after pushing back our chairs from breakfast we saw the greasy, heavy brown swirl still drifting past us and condensing in oily drops upon the window-panes, my comrade's impatient and active nature could endure this drab existence no longer. He paced restlessly about our sitting-room in a fever of suppressed energy, biting his nails, tapping the furniture, and chafing against inaction.

"Nothing of interest in the paper, Watson?" he said.

I was aware that by anything of interest, Holmes meant anything of criminal interest. There was the news of a revolution, of a possible war, and of an impending change of government; but these did not come within the horizon of my companion. I could see nothing recorded in the shape of crime which was not commonplace and futile. Holmes groaned and resumed his restless meanderings.

"The London criminal is certainly a dull fellow," said he in the querulous voice of the sportsman whose game has failed him. "Look out of this window, Watson. See how the figures loom up, are dimly seen, and then blend once more into the cloud-bank. The thief or the murderer could roam London on such a day as the tiger does the jungle, unseen until he pounces, and then evident only to his victim."

"There have," said I, "been numerous petty thefts."

Holmes snorted his contempt.

"This great and sombre stage is set for something more worthy than that," said he. "It is fortunate for this community that I am not a criminal."

"It is, indeed!" said I heartily.

"Suppose that I were Brooks or Woodhouse, or any of the fifty men who have good reason for taking my life, how long could I survive against my own pursuit? A summons, a bogus appointment, and all would be over. It is well they don't have days of fog in the Latin countries—the countries of assassination. By Jove! Here comes something at last to break our dead monotony."

It was the maid with a telegram. Holmes tore it open and burst out laughing.

"Well, well! What next?" said he. "Brother Mycroft is coming round."

"Why not?" I asked.

"Why not? It is as if you met a tram-car coming down a country lane. Mycroft has his rails and he runs on them. His Pall Mall lodgings, the Diogenes Club, Whitehall—that is his cycle. Once, and only once, he has been here. What upheaval can possibly have derailed him?"

"Does he not explain?"

Holmes handed me his brother's telegram.

Must see you over Cadogan West. Coming at once.

MYCROFT

"Cadogan West? I have heard the name."

"It recalls nothing to my mind. But that Mycroft should break out in this erratic fashion! A planet might as well leave its orbit. By the way, do you know what Mycroft is?"

I had some vague recollection of an explanation at the time of the adventure of the Greek interpreter.

"You told me that he had some small office under the British government."

Holmes chuckled.

"I did not know you quite so well in those days. One has to be discreet when one talks of high matters of state. You are right in thinking that he is under the British government. You would also be right in a sense if you said that occasionally he *is* the British government."

"My dear Holmes!"

"I thought I might surprise you. Mycroft draws four hundred and fifty pounds a year, remains a subordinate, has no ambitions of any kind, will receive neither honour nor title, but remains the most indispensable man in the country."

"But how?"

"Well, his position is unique. He has made it for himself. There has never been anything like it before, nor will be again. He has the tidiest and most orderly brain, with the greatest capacity for storing facts, of any man living. The same great powers which I have turned to the detection of crime he has used for this particular business. The conclusions of every department are passed to him, and he is the central exchange, the clearing-house, which makes out the balance. All other men are specialists, but his specialism is omniscience. We will suppose that a minister needs information as to a point which involves the Navy, India, Canada and the bimetallic question; he could get his separate advices from various departments upon each, but only Mycroft can focus them all and say offhand how each factor would affect the other. They began by using him as a short-cut, a convenience; now he has made himself an essential. In that great brain of his everything is pigeon-holed and can be handed out in an instant. Again and again his word has decided the national policy. He lives in it. He thinks of nothing else save when, as an intellectual exercise, he unbends if I call upon him and ask him to advise me on one of my little problems. But Jupiter is descending to-day. What on earth can it mean? Who is Cadogan West, and what is he to Mycroft?"

"I have it," I cried, and plunged among the litter of papers upon the sofa. "Yes, yes, here he is, sure enough! Cadogan West was the young man who was found dead on the Underground on Tuesday morning."

Holmes sat up at attention, his pipe halfway to his lips.

"This must be serious, Watson. A death which has caused my brother to alter his habits can be no ordinary one. What in the world can he have to do with it? The case was featureless as I remember it. The young man had apparently fallen out of the train and killed himself. He had not been robbed, and there was no particular reason to suspect violence. Is that not so?"

"There has been an inquest," said I, "and a good many fresh facts have come out. Looked at more closely, I should certainly say that it was a curious case."

"Judging by its effect upon my brother, I should think it must be a most extraordinary one." He snuggled down in his armchair. "Now, Watson, let us have the facts."

"The man's name was Arthur Cadogan West. He was twenty-seven years of age, unmarried, and a clerk at Woolwich Arsenal."

"Government employ. Behold the link with Brother Mycroft!"

"He left Woolwich suddenly on Monday night. Was last seen by his fiancée, Miss Violet Westbury, whom he left abruptly in the fog about seven-thirty that evening. There was no quarrel between them and she can give no motive for his action. The next thing heard of him was when his dead body was discovered by a plate-layer named Mason, just outside Aldgate Station on the Underground system in London."

"When?"

"The body was found at six on the Tuesday morning. It was lying wide of the metals upon the left hand of the track as one goes eastward, at a point close to the station, where the line emerges from the tunnel in which it runs. The head was badly crushed—an injury which might well have been caused by a fall from the train. The body could only have come on the line in that way. Had it been carried down from any neighbouring street, it must have passed the station barriers, where a collector is always standing. This point seems absolutely certain."

"Very good. The case is definite enough. The man, dead or alive, either fell or was precipitated from a train. So much is clear to me. Continue."

"The trains which traverse the lines of rail beside which the body was found are those which run from west to east, some being purely Metropolitan, and some from Willesden and outlying junctions. It can be stated for certain that this young man, when he met his death, was travelling in this direction at some late hour of the night, but at what point he entered the train it is impossible to state."

"His ticket, of course, would show that."

"There was no ticket in his pockets."

"No ticket! Dear me, Watson, this is really very singular. According to my experience it is not possible to reach the platform of a Metropolitan train without exhibiting one's ticket. Presumably, then, the young man had one. Was it taken from him in order to conceal the station from which he came? It is possible. Or did he drop it in the carriage? That also is possible. But the point is of curious interest. I understand that there was no sign of robbery?"

"Apparently not. There is a list here of his possessions. His purse contained two pounds fifteen. He had also a check-book on the Woolwich branch of the Capital and Counties Bank. Through this his identity was established. There were also two dress-circle tickets for the Woolwich Theatre, dated for that very evening. Also a small packet of technical papers."

Holmes gave an exclamation of satisfaction.

"There we have it at last, Watson! British government—Woolwich. Arsenal—technical papers—Brother Mycroft, the chain is complete. But here he comes, if I am not mistaken, to speak for himself."

A moment later the tall and portly form of Mycroft Holmes was ushered into the room. Heavily built and massive, there was a suggestion of uncouth physical inertia in the figure, but above this unwieldy frame there was perched a head so masterful in its brow, so alert in its steel-grey, deep-set eyes, so firm in its lips, and so subtle in its play of expression, that after the first glance one forgot the gross body and remembered only the dominant mind.

At his heels came our old friend Lestrade, of Scotland Yard—thin and austere. The gravity of both their faces foretold some weighty quest. The detective shook hands without a word. Mycroft Holmes struggled out of his overcoat and subsided into an armchair.

"A most annoying business, Sherlock," said he. "I extremely dislike altering my habits, but the powers that be would take no denial. In the present state of Siam it is most awkward that I should be away from the office. But it is a real crisis. I have never seen the Prime Minister so upset. As to the Admiralty—it is buzzing like an overturned bee-hive. Have you read up the case?"

"We have just done so. What were the technical papers?"

"Ah, there's the point! Fortunately, it has not come out. The press would be furious if it did. The papers which this wretched youth had in his pocket were the plans of the Bruce-Partington submarine."

Mycroft Holmes spoke with a solemnity which showed his sense of the importance of the subject. His brother and I sat expectant.

"Surely you have heard of it? I thought everyone had heard of it."

"Only as a name."

"Its importance can hardly be exaggerated. It has been the most jealously guarded of all government secrets. You may take it from me that naval warfare becomes impossible within the radius of a Bruce-Partington's operation. Two years ago a very large sum was smuggled through the Estimates and was expended in acquiring a monopoly of the invention. Every effort has been made to keep the secret. The plans, which are exceedingly intricate, comprising some thirty separate patents, each essential to the working of the whole, are kept in an elaborate safe in a confidential office adjoining the arsenal, with burglar-proof doors and windows. Under no conceivable circumstances were the plans to be taken from the office. If the chief constructor of the Navy desired to consult them, even he was forced to go to the Woolwich office for the purpose. And yet here we find them in the pocket of a dead junior clerk in the heart of London. From an official point of view it's simply awful."

"But you have recovered them?"

"No, Sherlock, no! That's the pinch. We have not. Ten papers were taken from Woolwich. There were seven in the pocket of Cadogan West. The three most essential are gone—stolen, vanished. You must drop everything, Sherlock. Never mind your usual petty puzzles of the police-court. It's a vital international problem that you have to solve. Why did Cadogan West take the papers, where are the missing ones, how did he die, how came his body where it was found, how can the evil be set right? Find an answer to all these questions, and you will have done good service for your country."

"Why do you not solve it yourself, Mycroft? You can see as far as I."

"Possibly, Sherlock. But it is a question of getting details. Give me your details, and from an armchair I will return you an excellent expert opinion. But to run here and run there, to cross-question railway guards, and lie on my face with a lens to my eye—it is not my *métier*. No, you are the one man who can clear the matter up. If you have a fancy to see your name in the next honours list—"

My friend smiled and shook his head.

"I play the game for the game's own sake," said he. "But the problem certainly presents some points of interest, and I shall be very pleased to look into it. Some more facts, please."

"I have jotted down the more essential ones upon this sheet of paper, together with a few addresses which you will find of service. The actual official guardian of the papers is the famous government expert, Sir James

Walter, whose decorations and sub-titles fill two lines of a book of reference. He has grown grey in the service, is a gentleman, a favoured guest in the most exalted houses, and above all, a man whose patriotism is beyond suspicion. He is one of two who have a key of the safe. I may add that the papers were undoubtedly in the office during working hours on Monday, and that Sir James left for London about three o'clock taking his key with him. He was at the house of Admiral Sinclair at Barclay Square during the whole of the evening when this incident occurred."

"Has the fact been verified?"

"Yes; his brother, Colonel Valentine Walter, has testified to his departure from Woolwich, and Admiral Sinclair to his arrival in London; so Sir James is no longer a direct factor in the problem."

"Who was the other man with a key?"

"The senior clerk and draughtsman, Mr. Sidney Johnson. He is a man of forty, married, with five children. He is a silent, morose man, but he has, on the whole, an excellent record in the public service. He is unpopular with his colleagues, but a hard worker. According to his own account, corroborated only by the word of his wife, he was at home the whole of Monday evening after office hours, and his key has never left the watch-chain upon which it hangs."

"Tell us about Cadogan West."

"He has been ten years in the service and has done good work. He has the reputation of being hot-headed and impetuous, but a straight, honest man. We have nothing against him. He was next to Sidney Johnson in the office. His duties brought him into daily, personal contact with the plans. No one else had the handling of them."

"Who locked the plans up that night?"

"Mr. Sidney Johnson, the senior clerk."

"Well, it is surely perfectly clear who took them away. They are actually found upon the person of this junior clerk, Cadogan West. That seems final, does it not?"

"It does, Sherlock, and yet it leaves so much unexplained. In the first place, why did he take them?"

"I presume they were of value?"

"He could have got several thousands for them very easily."

"Can you suggest any possible motive for taking the papers to London except to sell them?"

"No, I cannot."

"Then we must take that as our working hypothesis. Young West took the papers. Now this could only be done by having a false key—"

"Several false keys. He had to open the building and the room."

"He had, then, several false keys. He took the papers to London to sell the secret, intending, no doubt, to have the plans themselves back in the safe next morning before they were missed. While in London on this treasonable mission he met his end."

"How?"

"We will suppose that he was travelling back to Woolwich when he was killed and thrown out of the compartment."

"Aldgate, where the body was found, is considerably past the station for London Bridge, which would be his route to Woolwich."

"Many circumstances could be imagined under which he would pass London Bridge. There was someone in the carriage, for example, with whom he was having an absorbing interview. This interview led to a violent scene in which he lost his life. Possibly he tried to leave the carriage, fell out on the line, and so met his end. The other closed the door. There was a thick fog, and nothing could be seen."

"No better explanation can be given with our present knowledge; and yet consider, Sherlock, how much you leave untouched. We will suppose, for argument's sake, that young Cadogan West *had* determined to convey these papers to London. He would naturally have made an appointment with the foreign agent and kept his evening clear. Instead of that he took two tickets for the theatre, es-

494

corted his fiancée halfway there, and then suddenly disappeared."

"A blind," said Lestrade, who had sat listening with some impatience to the conversation.

"A very singular one. That is objection No. 1. Objection No. 2: We will suppose that he reaches London and sees the foreign agent. He must bring back the papers before morning or the loss will be discovered. He took away ten. Only seven were in his pocket. What had become of the other three? He certainly would not leave them of his own free will. Then, again, where is the price of his treason? One would have expected to find a large sum of money in his pocket."

"It seems to me perfectly clear," said Lestrade. "I have no doubt at all as to what occurred. He took the papers to sell them. He saw the agent. They could not agree as to price. He started home again, but the agent went with him. In the train the agent murdered him, took the more essential papers, and threw his body from the carriage. That would account for everything, would it not?"

"Why had he no ticket?"

"The ticket would have shown which station was nearest the agent's house. Therefore he took it from the murdered man's pocket."

"Good, Lestrade, very good," said Holmes. "Your theory holds together. But if this is true, then the case is at an end. On the one hand, the traitor is dead. On the other, the plans of the Bruce-Partington submarine are presumably already on the Continent. What is there for us to do?"

"To act, Sherlock—to act!" cried Mycroft, springing to his feet. "All my instincts are against this explanation. Use your powers! Go to the scene of the crime! See the people concerned! Leave no stone unturned! In all your career you have never had so great a chance of serving your country."

"Well, well!" said Holmes, shrugging his shoulders. "Come, Watson! And you, Lestrade, could you favour us with your company for an hour or two? We will begin our investigation by a visit to Aldgate Station. Good-bye, Mycroft. I shall let you have a report before evening, but I warn you in advance that you have little to expect."

An hour later Holmes, Lestrade, and I stood upon the Underground railroad at the point where it emerges from the tunnel immediately before Aldgate Station. A courteous red-faced old gentleman represented the railway company.

"This is where the young man's body lay," said he, indicating a spot about three feet from the metals. "It could not have fallen from above, for these, as you see, are all blank walls. Therefore, it could only have come from a train, and that train, so far as we can trace it, must have passed about midnight on Monday."

"Have the carriages been examined for any sign of violence?"

"There are no such signs, and no ticket has been found."

"No record of a door being found open?"

"None."

"We have had some fresh evidence this morning," said Lestrade. "A passenger who passed Aldgate in an ordinary Metropolitan train about 11:40 on Monday night declares that he heard a heavy thud, as of a body striking the line, just before the train reached the station. There was dense fog, however, and nothing could be seen. He made no report of it at the time. Why, whatever is the matter with Mr. Holmes?"

My friend was standing with an expression of strained intensity upon his face, staring at the railway metals where they curved out of the tunnel. Aldgate is a junction, and there was a network of points. On these his eager, questioning eyes were fixed, and I saw on his keen, alert face that tightening of the lips, that quiver of the nostrils, and concentration of the heavy, tufted brows which I knew so well.

"Points," he muttered; "the points."

"What of it? What do you mean?"

"I suppose there are no great number of points on a system such as this?"

496

"No; there are very few."

"And a curve, too. Points, and a curve. By Jove! If it were only so."

"What is it, Mr. Holmes? Have you a clue?"

"An idea—an indication, no more. But the case certainly grows in interest. Unique, perfectly unique, and yet why not? I do not see any indications of bleeding on the line."

"There were hardly any."

"But I understand that there was a considerable wound."

"The bone was crushed, but there was no great external injury."

"And yet one would have expected some bleeding. Would it be possible for me to inspect the train which contained the passenger who heard the thud of a fall in the fog?"

"I fear not, Mr. Holmes. The train has been broken up before now, and the carriages redistributed."

"I can assure you, Mr. Holmes," said Lestrade, "that every carriage has been carefully examined. I saw to it myself."

It was one of my friend's most obvious weaknesses that he was impatient with less alert intelligences than his own.

"Very likely," said he, turning away. "As it happens, it was not the carriages which I desired to examine. Watson, we have done all we can here. We need not trouble you any further, Mr. Lestrade. I think our investigations must now carry us to Woolwich."

At London Bridge, Holmes wrote a telegram to his brother, which he handed to me before dispatching it. It ran thus:

See some light in the darkness, but it may possibly flicker out. Meanwhile, please send by messenger, to await return at Baker Street, a complete list of all foreign spies or international agents known to be in England, with full address.

SHERLOCK

"That should be helpful, Watson," he remarked as we took our seats in the Woolwich train. "We certainly owe Brother Mycroft a debt for having introduced us to what promises to be a really very remarkable case."

His eager face still wore that expression of intense and high-strung energy, which showed me that some novel and suggestive circumstance had opened up a stimulating line of thought. See the foxhound with hanging ears and drooping tail as it lolls about the kennels, and compare it with the same hound as, with gleaming eyes and straining muscles, it runs upon a breast-high scent—such was the change in Holmes since the morning. He was a different man from the limp and lounging figure in the mouse-coloured dressing-gown who had prowled so restlessly only a few hours before round the fog-girt room.

"There is material here. There is scope," said he. "I am dull indeed not to have understood its possibilities."

"Even now they are dark to me."

"The end is dark to me also, but I have hold of one idea which may lead us far. The man met his death elsewhere, and his body was on the *roof* of a carriage."

"On the roof!"

"Remarkable, is it not? But consider the facts. Is it a coincidence that it is found at the very point where the train pitches and sways as it comes round on the points? Is not that the place where an object upon the roof might be expected to fall off? The points would affect no object inside the train. Either the body fell from the roof, or a very curious coincidence has occurred. But now consider the question of the blood. Of course, there was no bleeding on the line if the body had bled elsewhere. Each fact is suggestive in itself. Together they have a cumulative force."

"And the ticket, too!" I cried.

"Exactly. We could not explain the absence of a ticket. This would explain it. Everything fits together."

"But suppose it were so, we are still as far as ever from unravelling the mystery of his death. Indeed, it becomes not simpler but stranger."

"Perhaps," said Holmes thoughtfully, "perhaps." He relapsed into a silent reverie, which lasted until the slow train
drew up at last in Woolwich Station. There he called a cab
and drew Mycroft's paper from his pocket.

"We have quite a little round of afternoon calls to
make," said he. "I think that Sir James Walter claims our
first attention."

The house of the famous official was a fine villa with
green lawns stretching down to the Thames. As we
reached it the fog was lifting, and a thin, watery sunshine
was breaking through. A butler answered our ring.

"Sir James, sir!" said he with solemn face. "Sir James
died this morning."

"Good Heavens!" cried Holmes in amazement. "How
did he die?"

"Perhaps you would care to step in, sir, and see his
brother, Colonel Valentine?"

"Yes, we had best do so."

We were ushered into a dim-lit drawing-room, where an
instant later we were joined by a very tall, handsome, light-
bearded man of fifty, the younger brother of the dead scientist. His wild eyes, stained cheeks, and unkempt hair all
spoke of the sudden blow which had fallen upon the
household. He was hardly articulate as he spoke of it.

"It was this horrible scandal," said he. "My brother, Sir
James, was a man of very sensitive honour, and he could
not survive such an affair. It broke his heart. He was
always so proud of the efficiency of his department, and
this was a crushing blow."

"We had hoped that he might have given us some indications which would have helped us to clear the matter up."

"I assure you that it was all a mystery to him as it is to
you and to all of us. He had already put all his knowledge
at the disposal of the police. Naturally he had no doubt
that Cadogan West was guilty. But all the rest was inconceivable."

"You cannot throw any new light upon the affair?"

"I know nothing myself save what I have read or heard.

I have no desire to be discourteous, but you can understand, Mr. Holmes, that we are much disturbed at present,
and I must ask you to hasten this interview to an end."

"This is indeed an unexpected development," said my
friend when we had regained the cab. "I wonder if the
death was natural, or whether the poor old fellow killed
himself! If the latter, may it be taken as some sign of self-
reproach for duty neglected? We must leave that question
to the future. Now we shall turn to the Cadogan Wests."

A small but well-kept house in the outskirts of the town
sheltered the bereaved mother. The old lady was too
dazed with grief to be of any use to us, but at her side was a
white-faced young lady, who introduced herself as Miss
Violet Westbury, the fiancée of the dead man and the last
to see him upon that fatal night.

"I cannot explain it, Mr. Holmes," she said. "I have not
shut an eye since the tragedy, thinking, thinking, thinking,
night and day, what the true meaning of it can be. Arthur
was the most single-minded, chivalrous, patriotic man
upon earth. He would have cut his right hand off before
he would sell a State secret confided to his keeping. It is
absurd, impossible, preposterous to anyone who knew
him."

"But the facts, Miss Westbury?"

"Yes, yes; I admit I cannot explain them."

"Was he in any want of money?"

"No; his needs were very simple and his salary ample.
He had saved a few hundreds, and we were to marry at the
New Year."

"No signs of any mental excitement? Come, Miss Westbury, be absolutely frank with us."

The quick eye of my companion had noted some change
in her manner. She coloured and hesitated.

"Yes," she said at last, "I had a feeling that there was
something on his mind."

"For long?"

"Only for the last week or so. He was thoughtful and
worried. Once I pressed him about it. He admitted that
there was something, and that it was concerned with his of-

ficial life. 'It is too serious for me to speak about, even to you,' said he. I could get nothing more."

Holmes looked grave.

"Go on, Miss Westbury. Even if it seems to tell against him, go on. We cannot say what it may lead to."

"Indeed, I have nothing more to tell. Once or twice it seemed to me that he was on the point of telling me something. He spoke one evening of the importance of the secret, and I have some recollection that he said that no doubt foreign spies would pay a great deal to have it."

My friend's face grew graver still.

"Anything else?"

"He said that we were slack about such matters—that it would be easy for a traitor to get the plans."

"Was it only recently that he made such remarks?"

"Yes, quite recently."

"Now tell us of that last evening."

"We were to go to the theatre. The fog was so thick that a cab was useless. We walked, and our way took us close to the office. Suddenly he darted away into the fog."

"Without a word?"

"He gave an exclamation; that was all. I waited but he never returned. Then I walked home. Next morning, after the office opened, they came to inquire. About twelve o'clock we heard the terrible news. Oh, Mr. Holmes, if you could only, only save his honour! It was so much to him."

Holmes shook his head sadly.

"Come, Watson," said he, "our ways lie elsewhere. Our next station must be the office from which the papers were taken.

"It was black enough before against this young man, but our inquiries make it blacker," he remarked as the cab lumbered off. "His coming marriage gives a motive for the crime. He naturally wanted money. The idea was in his head, since he spoke about it. He nearly made the girl an accomplice in the treason by telling her his plans. It is all very bad."

"But surely, Holmes, character goes for something?

Then, again, why should he leave the girl in the street and dart away to commit a felony?"

"Exactly! There are certainly objections. But it is a formidable case which they have to meet."

Mr. Sidney Johnson, the senior clerk, met us at the office and received us with that respect which my companion's card always commanded. He was a thin, gruff, bespectacled man of middle age, his cheeks haggard, and his hands twitching from the nervous strain to which he had been subjected.

"It is bad, Mr. Holmes, very bad! Have you heard of the death of the chief?"

"We have just come from his house."

"The place is disorganized. The chief dead, Cadogan West dead, our papers stolen. And yet, when we closed our door on Monday evening, we were as efficient an office as any in the government service. Good God, it's dreadful to think of! That West, of all men, should have done such a thing!"

"You are sure of his guilt, then?"

"I can see no other way out of it. And yet I would have trusted him as I trust myself."

"At what hour was the office closed on Monday?"

"At five."

"Did you close it?"

"I am always the last man out."

"Where were the plans?"

"In that safe. I put them there myself."

"Is there no watchman to the building?"

"There is, but he has other departments to look after as well. He is an old soldier and a most trustworthy man. He saw nothing that evening. Of course the fog was very thick."

"Suppose that Cadogan West wished to make his way into the building after hours; he would need three keys, would he not, before he could reach the papers?"

"Yes, he would. The key of the outer door, the key of the office, and the key of the safe."

"Only Sir James Walter and you had those keys?"

"I had no keys of the doors—only of the safe."

"Was Sir James a man who was orderly in his habits?"

"Yes, I think he was. I know that so far as those three keys are concerned he kept them on the same ring. I have often seen them there."

"And that ring went with him to London?"

"He said so."

"And your key never left your possession?"

"Never."

"Then West, if he is the culprit, must have had a duplicate. And yet none was found upon his body. One other point: if a clerk in this office desired to sell the plans, would it not be simpler to copy the plans for himself than to take the originals, as was actually done?"

"It would take considerable technical knowledge to copy the plans in an effective way."

"But I suppose either Sir James, or you, or West had that technical knowledge?"

"No doubt we had, but I beg you won't try to drag me into the matter, Mr. Holmes. What is the use of our speculating in this way when the original plans were actually found on West?"

"Well, it is certainly singular that he should run the risk of taking originals if he could safely have taken copies, which would have equally served his turn."

"Singular, no doubt—and yet he did so."

"Every inquiry in this case reveals something inexplicable. Now there are three papers still missing. They are, as I understand, the vital ones."

"Yes, that is so."

"Do you mean to say that anyone holding these three papers, and without the seven others, could construct a Bruce-Partington submarine?"

"I reported to that effect to the Admiralty. But to-day I have been over the drawings again, and I am not so sure of it. The double valves with the automatic self-adjusting slots are drawn in one of the papers which have been re-

turned. Until the foreigners had invented that for themselves they could not make the boat. Of course they might
soon get over the difficulty."

"But the three missing drawings are the most important?"

"Undoubtedly."

"I think, with your permission, I will now take a stroll
round the premises. I do not recall any other question
which I desired to ask."

He examined the lock of the safe, the door of the room,
and finally the iron shutters of the window. It was only
when we were on the lawn outside that his interest was
strongly excited. There was a laurel bush outside the
window, and several of the branches bore signs of having
been twisted or snapped. He examined them carefully
with his lens, and then some dim and vague marks upon
the earth beneath. Finally he asked the chief clerk to close
the iron shutters, and he pointed out to me that they
hardly met in the centre, and that it would be possible for
anyone outside to see what was going on within the room.

"The indications are ruined by the three days' delay.
They may mean something or nothing. Well, Watson, I do
not think that Woolwich can help us further. It is a small
crop which we have gathered. Let us see if we can do
better in London."

Yet we added one more sheaf to our harvest before
we left Woolwich Station. The clerk in the ticket office
was able to say with confidence that he saw Cadogan
West—whom he knew well by sight—upon the Monday
night, and that he went to London by the eight-fifteen to
London Bridge. He was alone and took a single third-class
ticket. The clerk was struck at the time by his excited and
nervous manner. So shaky was he that he could hardly
pick up his change, and the clerk had helped him with it. A
reference to the timetable showed that the eight-fifteen
was the first train which it was possible for West to take
after he had left the lady about seven-thirty.

"Let us reconstruct, Watson," said Holmes after half an

hour of silence. "I am not aware that in all our joint researches we have ever had a case which was more difficult to get at. Every fresh advance which we make only reveals a fresh ridge beyond. And yet we have surely made
some appreciable progress.

"The effect of our inquiries at Woolwich has in the main
been against young Cadogan West; but the indications at
the window would lend themselves to a more favourable
hypothesis. Let us suppose, for example, that he had been
approached by some foreign agent. It might have been
done under such pledges as would have prevented him
from speaking of it, and yet would have affected his
thoughts in the direction indicated by his remarks to his
fiancée. Very good. We will now suppose that as he went to
the theatre with the young lady he suddenly, in the fog,
caught a glimpse of this same agent going in the direction
of the office. He was an impetuous man, quick in his deci-
sions. Everything gave way to his duty. He followed the
man, reached the window, saw the abstraction of the documents, and pursued the thief. In this way we get over the
objection that no one would take originals when he could
make copies. This outsider had to take originals. So far it
holds together."

"What is the next step?"

"Then we come into difficulties. One would imagine
that under such circumstances the first act of young Cadogan West would be to seize the villain and raise the
alarm. Why did he not do so? Could it have been an official
superior who took the papers? That would explain West's
conduct. Or could the thief have given West the slip in the
fog, and West started at once to London to head him off
from his own rooms, presuming that he knew where the
rooms were? The call must have been very pressing, since
he left his girl standing in the fog and made no effort to
communicate with her. Our scent runs cold here, and
there is a vast gap between either hypothesis and the
laying of West's body, with seven papers in his pocket, on
the roof of a Metropolitan train. My instinct now is to work

from the other end. If Mycroft has given us the list of addresses we may be able to pick our man and follow two tracks instead of one."

Surely enough, a note awaited us at Baker Street. A government messenger had brought it post-haste. Holmes glanced at it and threw it over to me.

There are numerous small fry, but few who would handle so big an affair. The only men worth considering are Adolph Meyer, of 13 Great George Street, Westminster; Louis La Rothière, of Campden Mansions, Notting Hill; and Hugo Oberstein, 13 Caulfield Gardens, Kensington. The latter was known to be in town on Monday and is now reported as having left. Glad to hear you have seen some light. The Cabinet awaits your final report with the utmost anxiety. Urgent representations have arrived from the very highest quarter. The whole force of the State is at your back if you should need it.

MYCROFT

"I'm afraid," said Holmes, smiling, "that all the Queen's horses and all the Queen's men cannot avail in this matter." He had spread out his big map of London and leaned eagerly over it. "Well, well," said he presently with an exclamation of satisfaction, "things are turning a little in our direction at last. Why, Watson, I do honestly believe that we are going to pull it off, after all." He slapped me on the shoulder with a sudden burst of hilarity. "I am going out now. It is only a reconnaissance. I will do nothing serious without my trusted comrade and biographer at my elbow. Do you stay here, and the odds are that you will see me again in an hour or two. If time hangs heavy get foolscap and a pen, and begin your narrative of how we saved the State."

I felt some reflection of his elation in my own mind, for I knew well that he would not depart so far from his usual austerity of demeanour unless there was good cause for exultation. All the long November evening I waited, filled with impatience for his return. At last, shortly after nine o'clock, there arrived a messenger with a note:

Am dining at Goldini's Restaurant, Gloucester Road, Kensington. Please come at once and join me there. Bring with you a jemmy, a dark lantern, a chisel, and a revolver.

S. H.

It was a nice equipment for a respectable citizen to carry through the dim, fog-draped streets. I stowed them all discreetly away in my overcoat and drove straight to the address given. There sat my friend at a little round table near the door of the garish Italian restaurant.

"Have you had something to eat? Then join me in a coffee and curaçao. Try one of the proprietor's cigars. They are less poisonous than one would expect. Have you the tools?"

"They are here, in my overcoat."

"Excellent. Let me give you a short sketch of what I have done, with some indication of what we are about to do. Now it must be evident to you, Watson, that this young man's body was *placed* on the roof of the train. That was clear from the instant that I determined the fact that it was from the roof, and not from a carriage, that he had fallen."

"Could it not have been dropped from a bridge?"

"I should say it was impossible. If you examine the roofs you will find that they are slightly rounded, and there is no railing round them. Therefore, we can say for certain that young Cadogan West was placed on it."

"How could he be placed there?"

"That was the question which we had to answer. There is only one possible way. You are aware that the Underground runs clear of tunnels at some points in the West End. I had a vague memory that as I have travelled by it I have occasionally seen windows just above my head. Now, suppose that a train halted under such a window, would there be any difficulty in laying a body upon the roof?"

"It seems most improbable."

"We must fall back upon the old axiom that when all other contingencies fail, whatever remains, however improbable, must be the truth. Here all other contingencies *have* failed. When I found that the leading international agent, who had just left London, lived in a row of houses which abutted upon the Underground, I was so pleased that you were a little astonished at my sudden frivolity."

"Oh, that was it, was it?"

"Yes, that was it. Mr. Hugo Oberstein, of 13 Caulfield Gardens, had become my objective. I began my operations at Gloucester Road Station, where a very helpful official walked with me along the track and allowed me to satisfy myself not only that the back-stair windows of Caulfield Gardens open on the line but the even more essential fact that, owing to the intersection of one of the larger railways, the Underground trains are frequently held motionless for some minutes at that very spot."

"Splendid, Holmes! You have got it!"

"So far—so far, Watson. We advance, but the goal is afar. Well, having seen the back of Caulfield Gardens, I visited the front and satisfied myself that the bird was indeed flown. It is a considerable house, unfurnished, so far as I could judge, in the upper rooms. Oberstein lived there with a single valet, who was probably a confederate entirely in his confidence. We must bear in mind that Oberstein has gone to the Continent to dispose of the booty, but not with any idea of flight; for he had no reason to fear a warrant, and the idea of an amateur domiciliary visit would certainly never occur to him. Yet that is precisely what we are about to make."

"Could we not get a warrant and legalize it?"

"Hardly on the evidence."

"What can we hope to do?"

"We cannot tell what correspondence may be there."

"I don't like it, Holmes."

"My dear fellow, you shall keep watch in the street. I'll do the criminal part. It's not a time to stick at trifles. Think of Mycroft's note, of the Admiralty, the Cabinet, the exalted person who waits for news. We are bound to go."

My answer was to rise from the table.

"You are right, Holmes. We are bound to go."

He sprang up and shook me by the hand.

"I knew you would not shrink at the last," said he, and for a moment I saw something in his eyes which was nearer to tenderness than I had ever seen. The next instant he was his masterful, practical self once more.

"It is nearly half a mile, but there is no hurry. Let us walk," said he. "Don't drop the instruments, I beg. Your arrest as a suspicious character would be a most unfortunate complication."

Caulfield Gardens was one of those lines of flat-faced pillared, and porticoed houses which are so prominent a product of the middle Victorian epoch in the West End of London. Next door there appeared to be a children's party, for the merry buzz of young voices and the clatter of a piano resounded through the night. The fog still hung about and screened us with its friendly shade. Holmes had lit his lantern and flashed it upon the massive door.

"This is a serious proposition," said he. "It is certainly bolted as well as locked. We would do better in the area. There is an excellent archway down yonder in case a too zealous policeman should intrude. Give me a hand, Watson, and I'll do the same for you."

A minute later we were both in the area. Hardly had we reached the dark shadows before the step of the policeman was heard in the fog above. As its soft rhythm died away, Holmes set to work upon the lower door. I saw him stoop and strain until with a sharp crash it flew open. We sprang through into the dark passage, closing the area door behind us. Holmes led the way up the curving, uncarpeted stair. His little fan of yellow light shone upon a low window.

"Here we are, Watson—this must be the one." He threw it open, and as he did so there was a low, harsh murmur, growing steadily into a loud roar as a train dashed past us in the darkness. Holmes swept his light along the windowsill. It was thickly coated with soot from the passing engines, but the black surface was blurred and rubbed in places.

"You can see where they rested the body. Halloa,

Watson! What is this? There can be no doubt that it is a blood mark." He was pointing to faint discolourations along the woodwork of the window. "Here it is on the stone of the stair also. The demonstration is complete. Let us stay here until a train stops."

We had not long to wait. The very next train roared from the tunnel as before, but slowed in the open, and then, with a creaking of brakes, pulled up immediately beneath us. It was not four feet from the window-ledge to the roof of the carriages. Holmes softly closed the window.

"So far we are justified," said he. "What do you think of it, Watson?"

"A masterpiece. You have never risen to a greater height."

"I cannot agree with you there. From the moment that I conceived the idea of the body being upon the roof, which surely was not a very abstruse one, all the rest was inevitable. If it were not for the grave interests involved the affair up to this point would be insignificant. Our difficulties are still before us. But perhaps we may find something here which may help us."

We had ascended the kitchen stair and entered the suite of rooms upon the first floor. One was a dining-room, severely furnished and containing nothing of interest. A second was a bedroom, which also drew blank. The remaining room appeared more promising, and my companion settled down to a systematic examination. It was littered with books and papers, and was evidently used as a study. Swiftly and methodically Holmes turned over the contents of drawer after drawer and cupboard after cupboard, but no gleam of success came to brighten his austere face. At the end of an hour he was no further than when he started.

"The cunning dog has covered his tracks," said he. "He has left nothing to incriminate him. His dangerous correspondence has been destroyed or removed. This is our last chance."

It was a small tin cash-box which stood upon the writing-desk. Holmes pried it open with his chisel. Several rolls of paper were within, covered with figures and calculations, without any note to show to what they referred. The recurring words, "water pressure" and "pressure to the square inch" suggested some possible relation to a submarine. Holmes tossed them all impatiently aside. There only remained an envelope with some small newspaper slips inside it. He shook them out on the table, and at once I saw by his eager face that his hopes had been raised.

"What's this, Watson? Eh? What's this? Record of a series of messages in the advertisements of a paper. *Daily Telegraph* agony column by the print and paper. Right-hand top corner of a page. No dates—but messages arrange themselves. This must be the first:

"Hoped to hear sooner. Terms agreed to. Write fully to address given on card.
                                                    "PIERROT

"Next comes:

"Too complex for description. Must have full report. Stuff awaits you when goods delivered.
                                                    "PIERROT

"Then comes:

"Matter presses. Must withdraw offer unless contract completed. Make appointment by letter. Will confirm by advertisement.
                                                    "PIERROT

"Finally:

"Monday night after nine. Two taps. Only ourselves. Do not be so suspicious. Payment in hard cash when goods delivered.
                                                    "PIERROT

"A fairly complete record, Watson! If we could only get at the man at the other end!" He sat lost in thought, tapping his fingers on the table. Finally he sprang to his feet.

"Well, perhaps it won't be so difficult, after all. There is nothing more to be done here, Watson. I think we might drive round to the offices of the *Daily Telegraph,* and so bring a good day's work to a conclusion."

Mycroft Holmes and Lestrade had come round by appointment after breakfast next day and Sherlock Holmes had recounted to them our proceedings of the day before. The professional shook his head over our confessed burglary.

"We can't do these things in the force, Mr. Holmes," said he. "No wonder you get results that are beyond us. But some of these days you'll go too far, and you'll find yourself and your friend in trouble."

"For England, home, and beauty—eh, Watson? Martyrs on the altar of our country. But what do you think of it, Mycroft?"

"Excellent, Sherlock! Admirable! But what use will you make of it?"

Holmes picked up the *Daily Telegraph* which lay upon the table.

"Have you seen Pierrot's advertisement to-day?"

"What? Another one?"

"Yes, here it is:

"To-night. Same hour. Same place. Two taps. Most vitally important. Your own safety at stake.

"PIERROT

"By George!" cried Lestrade. "If he answers that we've got him!"

"That was my idea when I put it in. I think if you could both make it convenient to come with us about eight o'clock to Caulfield Gardens we might possibly get a little nearer to a solution."

One of the most remarkable characteristics of Sherlock Holmes was his power of throwing his brain out of action and switching all his thoughts on to lighter things whenever he had convinced himself that he could no longer work to advantage. I remember that during the whole of that memorable day he lost himself in a monograph which he had undertaken upon the Polyphonic Motets of Lassus. For my own part I had none of this power of detachment, and the day, in consequence, appeared to be interminable. The great national importance of the issue, the suspense in high quarters, the direct nature of the experiment which we were trying—all combined to work upon my nerve. It was a relief to me when at last after a light dinner, we set out upon our expedition. Lestrade and Mycroft met us by appointment at the outside of Gloucester Road Station. The area door of Oberstein's house had been left open the night before, and it was necessary for me, as Mycroft Holmes absolutely and indignantly declined to climb the railings, to pass in and open the hall door. By nine o'clock we were all seated in the study, waiting patiently for our man.

An hour passed and yet another. When eleven struck, the measured beat of the great church clock seemed to sound the dirge of our hopes. Lestrade and Mycroft were fidgeting in their seats and looking twice a minute at their watches. Holmes sat silent and composed, his eyelids half shut, but every sense on the alert. He raised his head with a sudden jerk.

"He is coming," said he.

There had been a furtive step past the door. Now it returned. We heard a shuffling sound outside, and then two sharp taps with the knocker. Holmes rose, motioning to us to remain seated. The gas in the hall was a mere point of light. He opened the outer door, and then as a dark figure slipped past him he closed and fastened it. "This way!" we heard him say, and a moment later our man stood before us. Holmes had followed him closely, and as the man turned with a cry of surprise and alarm he caught him by the collar and threw him back into the room. Before our prisoner had recovered his balance the door was shut and Holmes standing with his back against it. The man glared round him, staggered, and fell senseless upon the floor.

With the shock, his broad-brimmed hat flew from his head, his cravat slipped down from his lips, and there were the long light beard and the soft, handsome delicate features of Colonel Valentine Walter.

Holmes gave a whistle of surprise.

"You can write me down an ass this time, Watson," said he. "This was not the bird that I was looking for."

"Who is he?" asked Mycroft eagerly.

"The younger brother of the late Sir James Walter, the head of the Submarine Department. Yes, yes; I see the fall of the cards. He is coming to. I think that you had best leave his examination to me."

We had carried the prostrate body to the sofa. Now our prisoner sat up, looked round him with a horror-stricken face, and passed his hand over his forehead, like one who cannot believe his own senses.

"What is this?" he asked. "I came here to visit Mr. Oberstein."

"Everything is known, Colonel Walter," said Holmes. "How an English gentleman could behave in such a manner is beyond my comprehension. But your whole correspondence and relations with Oberstein are within our knowledge. So also are the circumstances connected with the death of young Cadogan West. Let me advise you to gain at least the small credit for repentance and confession, since there are still some details which we can only learn from your lips."

The man groaned and sank his face in his hands. We waited, but he was silent.

"I can assure you," said Holmes, "that every essential is already known. We know that you were pressed for money; that you took an impress of the keys which your brother held; and that you entered into a correspondence with Oberstein, who answered your letters through the advertisement columns of the *Daily Telegraph*. We are aware that you went down to the office in the fog on Monday night, but that you were seen and followed by young Cadogan West, who had probably some previous reason to suspect you. He saw your theft, but could not give the alarm, as it was just possible that you were taking the papers to your brother in London. Leaving all his private concerns, like the good citizen that he was, he followed you closely in the fog and kept at your heels until you reached this very house. There he intervened, and then it was, Colonel Walter, that to treason you added the more terrible crime of murder."

"I did not! I did not! Before God I swear that I did not!" cried our wretched prisoner.

"Tell us, then, how Cadogan West met his end before you laid him upon the roof of a railway carriage."

"I will. I swear to you that I will. I did the rest. I confess it. It was just as you say. A Stock Exchange debt had to be paid. I needed the money badly. Oberstein offered me five thousand. It was to save myself from ruin. But as to murder, I am as innocent as you."

"What happened, then?"

"He had his suspicions before, and he followed me as you describe. I never knew it until I was at the very door. It was thick fog, and one could not see three yards. I had given two taps and Oberstein had come to the door. The young man rushed up and demanded to know what we were about to do with the papers. Oberstein had a short life-preserver. He always carried it with him. As West forced his way after us into the house Oberstein struck him on the head. The blow was a fatal one. He was dead within five minutes. There he lay in the hall, and we were at our wit's end what to do. Then Oberstein had this idea about the trains which halted under his back window. But first he examined the papers which I had brought. He said that three of them were essential, and that he must keep them. 'You cannot keep them,' said I. 'There will be a dreadful row at Woolwich if they are not returned.' 'I must keep them,' said he, 'for they are so technical that it is impossible in the time to make copies.' 'Then they must all go back together to-night,' said I. He thought for a little, and then he cried out that he had it. 'Three I will keep,' said he. 'The others we will stuff into the pocket of this young man. When he is found the whole business will assuredly be put to his account.' I could see no other way out of it, so we did as he suggested. We waited half an hour at the window before a train stopped. It was so thick that nothing could be seen, and we had no difficulty in lowering West's body on to the train. That was the end of the matter so far as I was concerned."

"And your brother?"

"He said nothing, but he had caught me once with his keys, and I think that he suspected. I read in his eyes that he suspected. As you know, he never held up his head again."

There was silence in the room. It was broken by Mycroft Holmes.

"Can you not make reparation? It would ease your conscience, and possibly your punishment."

"What reparation can I make?"

"Where is Oberstein with the papers?"

"I do not know."

"Did he give you no address?"

"He said that letters to the Hôtel du Louvre, Paris, would eventually reach him."

"Then reparation is still within your power," said Sherlock Holmes.

"I will do anything I can. I owe this fellow no particular good-will. He has been my ruin and my downfall."

"Here are paper and pen. Sit at this desk and write to my dictation. Direct the envelope to the address given. That is right. Now the letter:

"DEAR SIR:

"With regard to our transaction, you will no doubt have observed by now that one essential detail is missing. I have a tracing which will make it complete. This has involved me in extra trouble, however, and I must ask you for a further advance of five hundred pounds. I will not trust it to the post, nor will I take anything but gold or notes. I would come to you abroad, but it would excite remark if I left the country at present. Therefore I shall expect to meet you in the smoking-room of the Charing Cross Hotel at noon on Saturday. Remember that only English notes, or gold, will be taken.

That will do very well. I shall be very much surprised if it does not fetch our man."

And it did! It is a matter of history—that secret history of a nation which is often so much more intimate and interesting than its public chronicles—that Oberstein, eager to complete the coup of his lifetime, came to the lure and was safely engulfed for fifteen years in a British prison. In his trunk were found the invaluable Bruce-Partington plans, which he had put up for auction in all the naval centres of Europe.

Colonel Walter died in prison towards the end of the second year of his sentence. As to Holmes, he returned refreshed to his monograph upon the Polyphonic Motets of Lassus, which has since been printed for private circulation, and is said by experts to be the last word upon the subject. Some weeks afterwards I learned incidentally that my friend spent a day at Windsor, whence he returned with a remarkably fine emerald tie-pin. When I asked him if he had bought it, he answered that it was a present from a certain gracious lady in whose interests he had once been fortunate enough to carry out a small commission. He said no more; but I fancy that I could guess at that lady's august name, and I have little doubt that the emerald pin will forever recall to my friend's memory the adventure of the Bruce-Partington plans.

The Adventure of the
Dying Detective

Mrs. Hudson, the landlady of Sherlock Holmes, was a long-suffering woman. Not only was her first-floor flat invaded at all hours by throngs of singular and often undesirable characters, but her remarkable lodger showed an eccentricity and irregularity in his life which must have sorely tried her patience. His incredible untidiness, his addiction to music at strange hours, his occasional revolver practice within doors, his weird and often malodorous scientific experiments, and the atmosphere of violence and danger which hung around him made him the very worst tenant in London. On the other hand, his payments were princely. I have no doubt that the house might have been purchased at the price which Holmes paid for his rooms during the years that I was with him.

The landlady stood in the deepest awe of him and never dared to interfere with him, however outrageous his proceedings might seem. She was fond of him, too, for he had a remarkable gentleness and courtesy in his dealings with women. He disliked and distrusted the sex, but he was always a chivalrous opponent. Knowing how genuine was her regard for him, I listened earnestly to her story when she came to my rooms in the second year of my married life and told me of the sad condition to which my poor friend was reduced.

"He's dying, Dr. Watson," said she. "For three days he has been sinking, and I doubt if he will last the day. He would not let me get a doctor. This morning when I saw his bones sticking out of his face and his great bright eyes looking at me I could stand no more of it. 'With your leave or without it, Mr. Holmes, I am going for a doctor this very hour,' said I. 'Let it be Watson, then,' said he. I wouldn't waste an hour in coming to him, sir, or you may not see him alive."

I was horrified for I had heard nothing of his illness. I need not say that I rushed for my coat and my hat. As we drove back I asked for the details.

"There is little I can tell you, sir. He has been working at a case down at Rotherhithe, in an alley near the river, and he has brought this illness back with him. He took to his bed on Wednesday afternoon and has never moved since. For these three days neither food nor drink has passed his lips."

"Good God! Why did you not call in a doctor?"

"He wouldn't have it, sir. You know how masterful he is. I didn't dare to disobey him. But he's not long for this world, as you'll see for yourself the moment that you set eyes on him."

He was indeed a deplorable spectacle. In the dim light of a foggy November day the sick-room was a gloomy spot, but it was that gaunt, wasted face staring at me from the bed which sent a chill to my heart. His eyes had the brightness of fever, there was a hectic flush upon either cheek, and dark crusts clung to his lips; the thin hands upon the coverlet twitched incessantly, his voice was croaking and spasmodic. He lay listlessly as I entered the room, but the sight of me brought a gleam of recognition to his eyes.

"Well, Watson, we seem to have fallen upon evil days," said he in a feeble voice, but with something of his old carelessness of manner.

"My dear fellow!" I cried, approaching him.

"Stand back! Stand right back!" said he with the sharp imperiousness which I had associated only with moments of crisis. "If you approach me, Watson, I shall order you out of the house."

"But why?"

"Because it is my desire. Is that not enough?"

Yes, Mrs. Hudson was right. He was more masterful than ever. It was pitiful, however, to see his exhaustion.

"I only wished to help," I explained.

"Exactly! You will help best by doing what you are told."

"Certainly, Holmes."

He relaxed the austerity of his manner.

"You are not angry?" he asked, gasping for breath.

Poor devil, how could I be angry when I saw him lying in such a plight before me?

"It's for your own sake, Watson," he croaked.

"For *my* sake?"

"I know what is the matter with me. It is a coolie disease from Sumatra—a thing that the Dutch know more about than we, though they have made little of it up to date. One thing only is certain. It is infallibly deadly, and it is horribly contagious."

He spoke now with a feverish energy, the long hands twitching and jerking as he motioned me away.

"Contagious by touch, Watson—that's it, by touch. Keep your distance and all is well."

"Good Heavens, Holmes! Do you suppose that such a consideration weighs with me for an instant? It would not affect me in the case of a stranger. Do you imagine it would prevent me from doing my duty to so old a friend?"

Again I advanced, but he repulsed me with a look of furious anger.

"If you will stand there I will talk. If you do not you must leave the room."

I have so deep a respect for the extraordinary qualities of Holmes that I have always deferred to his wishes, even when I least understood them. But now all my professional instincts were aroused. Let him be my master elsewhere, I at least was his in a sick-room.

"Holmes," said I, "you are not yourself. A sick man is but a child, and so I will treat you. Whether you like it or not, I will examine your symptoms and treat you for them."

He looked at me with venomous eyes.

"If I am to have a doctor whether I will or not, let me at least have someone in whom I have confidence," said he.

"Then you have none in me?"

"In your friendship, certainly. But facts are facts, Watson, and after all, you are only a general practitioner with very limited experience and mediocre qualifications. It is painful to have to say these things, but you leave me no choice."

I was bitterly hurt.

"Such a remark is unworthy of you, Holmes. It shows me very clearly the state of your own nerves. But if you have no confidence in me I would not intrude my services. Let me bring Sir Jasper Meek or Penrose Fisher, or any of the best men in London. But someone you *must* have, and that is final. If you think that I am going to stand here and see you die without either helping you myself or bringing anyone else to help you, then you have mistaken your man."

"You mean well, Watson," said the sick man with something between a sob and a groan. "Shall I demonstrate your own ignorance? What do you know, pray, of Tapanuli fever? What do you know of the black Formosa corruption?"

"I have never heard of either."

"There are many problems of disease, many strange pathological possibilities, in the East, Watson." He paused after each sentence to collect his failing strength. "I have learned so much during some recent researches which have a medico-criminal aspect. It was in the course of them that I contracted this complaint. You can do nothing."

"Possibly not. But I happen to know that Dr. Ainstree, the greatest living authority upon tropical disease, is now in London. All remonstrance is useless, Holmes, I am going this instant to fetch him." I turned resolutely to the door.

Never have I had such a shock! In an instant, with a tiger-spring, the dying man had intercepted me. I heard the sharp snap of a twisted key. The next moment he had staggered back to his bed, exhausted and panting after his one tremendous outflame of energy.

"You won't take the key from me by force, Watson, I've got you, my friend. Here you are, and here you will stay until I will otherwise. But I'll humour you." (All this in little gasps, with terrible struggles for breath between.) "You've only my own good at heart. Of course I know that very well. You shall have your way, but give me time to get my strength. Not now, Watson, not now. It's four o'clock. At six you can go."

"This is insanity, Holmes."

"Only two hours, Watson. I promise you will go at six. Are you content to wait?"

"I seem to have no choice."

"None in the world, Watson. Thank you, I need no help in arranging the clothes. You will please keep your distance. Now, Watson, there is one other condition that I would make. You will seek help, not from the man you mention, but from the one that I choose."

"By all means."

"The first three sensible words that you have uttered since you entered this room, Watson. You will find some books over there. I am somewhat exhausted; I wonder how a battery feels when it pours electricity into a non-conductor? At six, Watson, we resume our conversation."

But it was destined to be resumed long before that hour, and in circumstances which gave me a shock hardly second to that caused by his spring to the door. I had stood for some minutes looking at the silent figure in the bed. His face was almost covered by the clothes and he appeared to be asleep. Then, unable to settle down to reading, I walked slowly round the room, examining the pictures of celebrated criminals with which every wall was adorned. Finally, in my aimless perambulation, I came to the mantelpiece. A litter of pipes, tobacco-pouches, syringes, penknives, revolver-cartridges, and other débris was scattered over it. In the midst of these was a small black and white ivory box with a sliding lid. It was a neat little thing, and I had stretched out my hand to examine it more closely when—

It was a dreadful cry that he gave—a yell which might have been heard down the street. My skin went cold and my hair bristled at that horrible scream. As I turned I caught a glimpse of a convulsed face and frantic eyes. I stood paralyzed, with the little box in my hand.

"Put it down! Down, this instant, Watson—this instant, I say!" His head sank back upon the pillow and he gave a deep sigh of relief as I replaced the box upon the mantel-piece. "I hate to have my things touched, Watson. You know that I hate it. You fidget me beyond endurance. You, a doctor—you are enough to drive a patient into an asylum. Sit down, man, and let me have my rest!"

The incident left a most unpleasant impression upon my mind. The violent and causeless excitement, followed by this brutality of speech, so far removed from his usual suavity, showed me how deep was the disorganization of his mind. Of all ruins, that of a noble mind is the most deplorable. I sat in silent dejection until the stipulated time had passed. He seemed to have been watching the clock as well as I, for it was hardly six before he began to talk with the same feverish animation as before.

"Now, Watson," said he. "Have you any change in your pocket?"

"Yes."

"Any silver?"

"A good deal."

"How many half-crowns?"

"I have five."

"Ah, too few! Too few! How very unfortunate, Watson! However, such as they are you can put them in your watch pocket. And all the rest of your money in your left trouser pocket. Thank you. It will balance you so much better like that."

This was raving insanity. He shuddered and again made a sound between a cough and a sob.

"You will now light the gas, Watson, but you will be very careful that not for one instant shall it be more than half on. I implore you to be careful, Watson. Thank you, that is excellent. No, you need not draw the blind. Now you will have the kindness to place some letters and papers upon this table within my reach. Thank you. Now some of that litter from the mantelpiece. Excellent, Watson! There is a sugar-tongs there. Kindly raise that small ivory box with its assistance. Place it here among the papers. Good! You can now go and fetch Mr. Culverton Smith, of 13 Lower Burke Street."

To tell the truth, my desire to fetch a doctor had somewhat weakened, for poor Holmes was so obviously delirious that it seemed dangerous to leave him. However, he was as eager now to consult the person named as he had been obstinate in refusing.

"I never heard the name," said I.

"Possibly not, my good Watson. It may surprise you to know that the man upon earth who is best versed in this disease is not a medical man, but a planter. Mr. Culverton Smith is a well-known resident of Sumatra, now visiting London. An outbreak of the disease upon his plantation, which was distant from medical aid, caused him to study it himself, with some rather far-reaching consequences. He is a very methodical person, and I did not desire you to start before six, because I was well aware that you would not find him in his study. If you could persuade him to come here and give us the benefit of his unique experience of this disease, the investigation of which has been his dearest hobby, I cannot doubt that he could help me."

I give Holmes's remarks as a consecutive whole and will not attempt to indicate how they were interrupted by gaspings for breath and those clutchings of his hands which indicated the pain from which he was suffering. His appearance had changed for the worse during the few hours that I had been with him. Those hectic spots were more pronounced, the eyes shone more brightly out of darker hollows, and a cold sweat glimmered upon his brow. He still retained, however, the jaunty gallantry of his speech. To the last gasp he would always be the master.

"You will tell him exactly how you have left me," said he. "You will convey the very impression which is in your own mind—a dying man—a dying and delirious man. Indeed, I cannot think why the whole bed of the ocean is not one solid mass of oysters, so prolific the creatures seem. Ah, I am wandering! Strange how the brain controls the brain! What was I saying, Watson?"

"My directions for Mr. Culverton Smith."

"Ah, yes, I remember. My life depends upon it. Plead with him, Watson. There is no good feeling between us. His nephew, Watson—I had suspicions of foul play and I allowed him to see it. The boy died horribly. He has a grudge against me. You will soften him, Watson. Beg him, pray him, get him here by any means. He can save me—only he!"

"I will bring him in a cab, if I have to carry him down to it."

"You will do nothing of the sort. You will persuade him to come. And then you will return in front of him. Make any excuse so as not to come with him. Don't forget, Watson. You won't fail me. You never did fail me. No doubt there are natural enemies which limit the increase of the creatures. You and I, Watson, we have done our part. Shall the world, then, be overrun by oysters? No, no; horrible! You'll convey all that is in your mind."

I left him full of the image of this magnificent intellect babbling like a foolish child. He had handed me the key, and with a happy thought I took it with me lest he should lock himself in. Mrs. Hudson was waiting, trembling and weeping, in the passage. Behind me as I passed from the flat I heard Holmes's high, thin voice in some delirious chant. Below, as I stood whistling for a cab, a man came on me through the fog.

"How is Mr. Holmes, sir?" he asked.

It was an old acquaintance, Inspector Morton, of Scotland Yard, dressed in unofficial tweeds.

"He is very ill," I answered.

He looked at me in a most singular fashion. Had it not been too fiendish, I could have imagined that the gleam of the fanlight showed exultation in his face.

"I heard some rumour of it," said he.

The cab had driven up, and I left him.

Lower Burke Street proved to be a line of fine houses lying in the vague borderland between Notting Hill and Kensington. The particular one at which my cabman pulled up had an air of smug and demure respectability in its old-fashioned iron railings, its massive folding-door, and its shining brasswork. All was in keeping with a solemn butler who appeared framed in the pink radiance of a tinted electric light behind him.

"Yes, Mr. Culverton Smith is in. Dr. Watson! Very good, sir, I will take up your card."

My humble name and title did not appear to impress Mr. Culverton Smith. Through the half-open door I heard a high, petulant, penetrating voice.

"Who is this person? What does he want? Dear me, Staples, how often have I said that I am not to be disturbed in my hours of study?"

There came a gentle flow of soothing explanation from the butler.

"Well, I won't see him, Staples. I can't have my work interrupted like this. I am not at home. Say so. Tell him to come in the morning if he really must see me."

Again the gentle murmur.

"Well, well, give him that message. He can come in the morning, or he can stay away. My work must not be hindered."

I thought of Holmes tossing upon his bed of sickness and counting the minutes, perhaps, until I could bring help to him. It was not a time to stand upon ceremony. His life depended upon my promptness. Before the apologetic butler had delivered his message I had pushed past him and was in the room.

With a shrill cry of anger a man rose from a reclining chair beside the fire. I saw a great yellow face, coarse-grained and greasy, with heavy, double-chin, and two sullen, menacing grey eyes which glared at me from under tufted and sandy brows. A high bald head had a small velvet smoking-cap poised coquettishly upon one side of its pink curve. The skull was of enormous capacity, and yet as I looked down I saw to my amazement that the figure of the man was small and frail, twisted in the shoulders and back like one who has suffered from rickets in his childhood.

"What's this?" he cried in a high, screaming voice. "What is the meaning of this intrusion? Didn't I send you word that I would see you to-morrow morning?"

"I am sorry," said I, "but the matter cannot be delayed. Mr. Sherlock Holmes—"

The mention of my friend's name had an extraordinary effect upon the little man. The look of anger passed in an instant from his face. His features became tense and alert.

"Have you come from Holmes?" he asked.

"I have just left him."

"What about Holmes? How is he?"

"He is desperately ill. That is why I have come."

The man motioned me to a chair and turned to resume his own. As he did so I caught a glimpse of his face in the mirror over the mantelpiece. I could have sworn that it was set in a malicious and abominable smile. Yet I persuaded myself that it must have been some nervous contraction which I had surprised, for he turned to me an instant later with genuine concern upon his features.

"I am sorry to hear this," said he. "I only know Mr. Holmes through some business dealings which we have had, but I have every respect for his talents and his character. He is an amateur of crime, as I am of disease. For him the villain, for me the microbe. There are my prisons," he continued, pointing to a row of bottles and jars which stood upon a side-table. "Among those gelatine cultivations some of the very worst offenders in the world are now doing time."

"It was on account of your special knowledge that Mr. Holmes desired to see you. He has a high opinion of you and thought that you were the one man in London who could help him."

The little man started, and the jaunty smoking-cap slid to the floor.

"Why?" he asked. "Why should Mr. Holmes think that I could help him in his trouble?"

"Because of your knowledge of Eastern diseases."

"But why should he think that this disease which he has contracted is Eastern?"

"Because, in some professional inquiry, he has been working among Chinese sailors down in the docks."

Mr. Culverton Smith smiled pleasantly and picked up his smoking-cap.

"Oh, that's it—is it?" said he. "I trust the matter is not so grave as you suppose. How long has he been ill?"

"About three days."

"Is he delirious?"

"Occasionally."

"Tut, tut! This sounds serious. It would be inhuman not to answer his call. I very much resent any interruption to my work, Dr. Watson, but this case is certainly exceptional. I will come with you at once."

I remembered Holmes's injunction.

"I have another appointment," said I.

"Very good. I will go alone. I have a note of Mr. Holmes's address. You can rely upon my being there within half an hour at most."

It was with a sinking heart that I re-entered Holmes's bedroom. For all that I knew the worst might have happened in my absence. To my enormous relief, he had improved greatly in the interval. His appearance was as ghastly as ever, but all trace of delirium had left him and he spoke in a feeble voice, it is true, but with even more than his usual crispness and lucidity.

"Well, did you see him, Watson?"

"Yes; he is coming."

"Admirable, Watson! Admirable! You are the best of messengers."

"He wished to return with me."

"That would never do, Watson. That would be obviously impossible. Did he ask what ailed me?"

"I told him about the Chinese in the East End."

"Exactly! Well, Watson, you have done all that a good friend could. You can now disappear from the scene."

"I must wait and hear his opinion, Holmes."

"Of course you must. But I have reasons to suppose that this opinion would be very much more frank and valuable if he imagines that we are alone. There is just room behind the head of my bed, Watson."

"My dear Holmes!"

"I fear there is no alternative, Watson. The room does not lend itself to concealment, which is as well, as it is the less likely to arouse suspicion. But just there, Watson, I fancy that it could be done." Suddenly he sat up with a rigid intentness upon his haggard face. "There are the wheels, Watson. Quick, man, if you love me! And don't budge, whatever happens—whatever happens, do you hear? Don't speak! Don't move! Just listen with all your ears." Then in an instant his sudden access of strength departed, and his masterful, purposeful talk droned away into the low, vague murmurings of a semi-delirious man.

From the hiding-place into which I had been so swiftly hustled I heard the footfalls upon the stair, with the opening and the closing of the bedroom door. Then, to my surprise, there came a long silence, broken only by the heavy breathings and gaspings of the sick man. I could imagine that our visitor was standing by the bedside and looking down at the sufferer. At last that strange hush was broken.

"Holmes!" he cried. "Holmes!" in the insistent tone of one who awakens a sleeper. "Can't you hear me, Holmes?" There was a rustling, as if he had shaken the sick man roughly by the shoulder.

"Is that you, Mr. Smith?" Holmes whispered. "I hardly dared hope that you would come."

The other laughed.

"I should imagine not," he said. "And yet, you see, I am here. Coals of fire, Holmes—coals of fire!"

"It is very good of you—very noble of you. I appreciate your special knowledge."

Our visitor sniggered.

"You do. You are, fortunately, the only man in London who does. Do you know what is the matter with you?"

"The same," said Holmes.

"Ah! You recognize the symptoms?"

"Only too well."

"Well, I shouldn't be surprised, Holmes. I shouldn't be surprised if it *were* the same. A bad lookout for you if it is. Poor Victor was a dead man on the fourth day—a strong, hearty young fellow. It was certainly, as you said, very surprising that he should have contracted an out-of-the-way Asiatic disease in the heart of London—a disease, too, of which I had made such a very special study. Singular coincidence, Holmes. Very smart of you to notice it, but rather uncharitable to suggest that it was cause and effect."

"I knew that you did it."

"Oh, you did, did you? Well, you couldn't prove it, anyhow. But what do you think of yourself spreading reports about me like that, and then crawling to me for help the moment you are in trouble? What sort of a game is that—eh?"

I heard the rasping, laboured breathing of the sick man. "Give me the water!" he gasped.

"You're precious near your end, my friend, but I don't want you to go till I have had a word with you. That's why I give you water. There, don't slop it about! That's right. Can you understand what I say?"

Holmes groaned.

"Do what you can for me. Let bygones be bygones," he whispered. "I'll put the words out of my head—I swear I will. Only cure me, and I'll forget it."

"Forget what?"

"Well, about Victor Savage's death. You as good as admitted just now that you had done it. I'll forget it."

"You can forget it or remember it, just as you like. I don't see you in the witness-box. Quite another shaped box, my good Holmes, I assure you. It matters nothing to me that you should know how my nephew died. It's not him we are talking about. It's you."

"Yes, yes."

"The fellow who came for me—I've forgotten his name—said that you contracted it down in the East End among the sailors."

"I could only account for it so."

"You are proud of your brains, Holmes, are you not? Think yourself smart, don't you? You came across some-one who was smarter this time. Now cast your mind back, Holmes. Can you think of no other way you could have got this thing?"

"I can't think. My mind is gone. For Heaven's sake help me!"

"Yes, I will help you. I'll help you to understand just where you are and how you got there. I'd like you to know before you die."

"Give me something to ease my pain."

"Painful, is it? Yes, the coolies used to do some squealing towards the end. Takes you as cramp, I fancy."

"Yes, yes; it is cramp."

"Well, you can hear what I say, anyhow. Listen now! Can you remember any unusual incident in your life just about the time your symptoms began?"

"No, no; nothing."

"Think again."

"I'm too ill to think."

"Well, then, I'll help you. Did anything come by post?"

"By post?"

"A box by chance?"

"I'm fainting—I'm gone!"

"Listen, Holmes!" There was a sound as if he was shaking the dying man, and it was all that I could do to hold myself quiet in my hiding-place. "You must hear me. You *shall* hear me. Do you remember a box—an ivory box? It came on Wednesday. You opened it—do you re-member?"

"Yes, yes, I opened it. There was a sharp spring inside it. Some joke—"

"It was no joke, as you will find to your cost. You fool, you would have it and you have got it. Who asked you to cross my path? If you had left me alone I would not have hurt you."

"I remember," Holmes gasped. "The spring! It drew blood. This box—this on the table."

"The very one, by George! And it may as well leave the room in my pocket. There goes your last shred of evidence. But you have the truth now, Holmes, and you can die with the knowledge that I killed you. You knew too much of the fate of Victor Savage, so I have sent you to share it. You are very near your end, Holmes. I will sit here and I will watch you die."

Holmes's voice had sunk to an almost inaudible whisper.

"What is that?" said Smith. "Turn up the gas? Ah, the shadows begin to fall, do they? Yes, I will turn it up, that I may see you the better." He crossed the room and the light suddenly brightened. "Is there any other little service that I can do you, my friend?"

"A match and a cigarette."

I nearly called out in my joy and my amazement. He was speaking in his natural voice—a little weak, perhaps, but the very voice I knew. There was a long pause, and I felt that Culverton Smith was standing in silent amazement looking down at his companion.

"What's the meaning of this?" I heard him say at last in a dry, rasping tone.

"The best way of successfully acting a part is to be it," said Holmes. "I give you my word that for three days I have tasted neither food nor drink until you were good enough to pour me out that glass of water. But it is the tobacco which I find most irksome. Ah, here *are* some cigarettes." I heard the striking of a match. "That is very much better. Halloa! Halloa! Do I hear the step of a friend?"

There were footfalls outside, the door opened, and Inspector Morton appeared.

"All is in order and this is your man," said Holmes. The officer gave the usual cautions.

"I arrest you on the charge of the murder of one Victor Savage," he concluded.

"And you might add of the attempted murder of one Sherlock Holmes," remarked my friend with a chuckle. "To save an invalid trouble, Inspector, Mr. Culverton Smith was good enough to give our signal by turning up the gas. By the way, the prisoner has a small box in the right-hand pocket of his coat which it would be as well to remove. Thank you. I would handle it gingerly if I were you. Put it down here. It may play its part in the trial."

There was a sudden rush and a scuffle, followed by the clash of iron and a cry of pain.

"You'll only get yourself hurt," said the Inspector. "Stand still, will you?" There was the click of the closing handcuffs.

"A nice trap!" cried the high, snarling voice. "It will bring *you* into the dock, Holmes, not me. He asked me to come here to cure him. I was sorry for him and I came. Now he will pretend, no doubt, that I have said anything which he may invent which will corroborate his insane suspicions. You can lie as you like, Holmes. My word is always as good as yours."

"Good Heavens!" cried Holmes. "I had totally forgotten him. My dear Watson, I owe you a thousand apologies. To think that I should have overlooked you! I need not introduce you to Mr. Culverton Smith, since I understand that you met somewhat earlier in the evening. Have you the cab below? I will follow you when I am dressed, for I may be of some use at the station.

"I never needed it more," said Holmes as he refreshed himself with a glass of claret and some biscuits in the intervals of his toilet. "However, as you know, my habits are irregular, and such a feat means less to me than to most men. It was very essential that I should impress Mrs. Hudson with the reality of my condition, since she was to convey it to you, and you in turn to him. You won't be offended, Watson? You will realize that among your many talents dissimulation finds no place, and that if you had shared my secret you would never have been able to impress Smith with the urgent necessity of his presence, which was the vital point of the whole scheme. Knowing his vindictive nature, I was perfectly certain that he would come to look upon his handiwork."

"But your appearance, Holmes—your ghastly face?"

"Three days of absolute fast does not improve one's beauty, Watson. For the rest, there is nothing which a sponge may not cure. With vaseline upon one's forehead, belladonna in one's eyes, rouge over the cheek-bones, and crusts of beeswax round one's lips, a very satisfying effect can be produced. Malingering is a subject upon which I have sometimes thought of writing a monograph. A little occasional talk about half-crowns, oysters, or any other extraneous subject produces a pleasing effect of delirium."

"But why would you not let me near you, since there was in truth no infection?"

"Can you ask, my dear Watson? Do you imagine that I have no respect for your medical talents? Could I fancy that your astute judgment would pass a dying man who, however weak, had no rise of pulse or temperature? At four yards, I could deceive you. If I failed to do so, who would bring my Smith within my grasp? No, Watson, I would not touch that box. You can just see if you look at it sideways where the sharp spring like a viper's tooth emerges as you open it. I dare say it was by some such device that poor Savage, who stood between this monster and a reversion, was done to death. My correspondence, however is, as you know, a varied one, and I am somewhat upon my guard against any packages which reach me. It was clear to me, however, that by pretending that he had really succeeded in his design I might surprise a confession. That pretence I have carried out with the thoroughness of the true artist. Thank you, Watson, you must help me on with my coat. When we have finished at the police-station I think that something nutritious at Simpson's would not be out of place."

The Disappearance of
Lady Frances Carfax

"But why Turkish?" asked Mr. Sherlock Holmes, gazing fixedly at my boots. I was reclining in a cane-backed chair at the moment, and my protruded feet had attracted his ever-active attention.

"English," I answered in some surprise. "I got them at Latimer's, in Oxford Street."

Holmes smiled with an expression of weary patience.

"The bath!" he said; "the bath! Why the relaxing and expensive Turkish rather than the invigorating home-made article?"

"Because for the last few days I have been feeling rheumatic and old. A Turkish bath is what we call an alternative in medicine—a fresh starting-point, a cleanser of the system.

"By the way, Holmes," I added, "I have no doubt the connection between my boots and a Turkish bath is a perfectly self-evident one to a logical mind, and yet I should be obliged to you if you would indicate it."

"The train of reasoning is not very obscure, Watson," said Holmes with a mischievous twinkle. "It belongs to the same elementary class of deduction which I should illustrate if I were to ask you who shared your cab in your drive this morning."

"I don't admit that a fresh illustration is an explanation," said I with some asperity.

"Bravo, Watson! A very dignified and logical remonstrance. Let me see, what were the points? Take the last one first—the cab. You observe that you have some splashes on the left sleeve and shoulder of your coat. Had you sat in the centre of a hansom you would probably have had no splashes, and if you had they would certainly have been symmetrical. Therefore it is clear that you sat at the side. Therefore it is equally clear that you had a companion."

"That is very evident."

"Absurdly commonplace, is it not?"

"But the boots and the bath?"

"Equally childish. You are in the habit of doing up your boots in a certain way. I see them on this occasion fastened with an elaborate double bow, which is not your usual method of tying them. You have, therefore, had them off. Who has tied them? A bootmaker—or the boy at the bath. It is unlikely that it is the bootmaker, since your boots are nearly new. Well, what remains? The bath. Absurd, is it not? But, for all that, the Turkish bath has served a purpose."

"What is that?"

"You say that you have had it because you need a change. Let me suggest that you take one. How would Lausanne do, my dear Watson—first-class tickets and all expenses paid on a princely scale?"

"Splendid! But why?"

Holmes leaned back in his armchair and took his note-book from his pocket.

"One of the most dangerous classes in the world," said he, "is the drifting and friendless woman. She is the most harmless and often the most useful of mortals, but she is the inevitable inciter of crime in others. She is helpless. She is migratory. She has sufficient means to take her from country to country and from hotel to hotel. She is lost, as often as not, in a maze of obscure *pensions* and boarding-houses. She is a stray chicken in a world of foxes. When she is gobbled up she is hardly missed. I much fear that some evil has come to the Lady Frances Carfax."

I was relieved at this sudden descent from the general to the particular. Holmes consulted his notes.

536

"Lady Frances," he continued, "is the sole survivor of the direct family of the late Earl of Rufton. The estates went, as you may remember, in the male line. She was left with limited means, but with some very remarkable old Spanish jewellery of silver and curiously cut diamonds to which she was fondly attached—too attached, for she refused to leave them with her banker and always carried them about with her. A rather pathetic figure, the Lady Frances, a beautiful woman, still in fresh middle age, and yet, by a strange chance, the last derelict of what only twenty years ago was a goodly fleet."

"What has happened to her, then?"

"Ah, what has happened to the Lady Frances? Is she alive or dead? There is our problem. She is a lady of precise habits, and for four years it has been her invariable custom to write every second week to Miss Dobney, her old governess, who has long retired and lives in Camberwell. It is this Miss Dobney who has consulted me. Nearly five weeks have passed without a word. The last letter was from the Hôtel National at Lausanne. Lady Frances seems to have left there and given no address. The family are anxious, and as they are exceedingly wealthy no sum will be spared if we can clear the matter up."

"Is Miss Dobney the only source of information? Surely she had other correspondents?"

"There is one correspondent who is a sure draw, Watson. That is the bank. Single ladies must live, and their pass-books are compressed diaries. She banks at Silvester's. I have glanced over her account. The last check but one paid her bill at Lausanne, but it was a large one and probably left her with cash in hand. Only one check has been drawn since."

"To whom, and where?"

"To Miss Marie Devine. There is nothing to show where the check was drawn. It was cashed at the Crédit Lyonnais at Montpellier less than three weeks ago. The sum was fifty pounds."

"And who is Miss Marie Devine?"

"That also I have been able to discover. Miss Marie Devine was the maid of Lady Frances Carfax. Why she should have paid her this check we have not yet determined. I have no doubt, however, that your researches will soon clear the matter up."

"*My* researches!"

"Hence the health-giving expedition to Lausanne. You know that I cannot possibly leave London while old Abrahams is in such mortal terror of his life. Besides, on general principles it is best that I should not leave the country. Scotland Yard feels lonely without me, and it causes an unhealthy excitement among the criminal classes. Go, then, my dear Watson, and if my humble counsel can ever be valued at so extravagant a rate as two pence a word, it waits your disposal night and day at the end of the Continental wire."

Two days later found me at the Hôtel National at Lausanne, where I received every courtesy at the hands of M. Moser, the well-known manager. Lady Frances, as he informed me, had stayed there for several weeks. She had been much liked by all who met her. Her age was not more than forty. She was still handsome and bore every sign of having in her youth been a very lovely woman. M. Moser knew nothing of any valuable jewellery, but it had been remarked by the servants that the heavy trunk in the lady's bedroom was always scrupulously locked. Marie Devine, the maid, was as popular as her mistress. She was actually engaged to one of the head waiters in the hotel, and there was no difficulty in getting her address. It was 11 Rue de Trajan, Montpellier. All this I jotted down and felt that Holmes himself could not have been more adroit in collecting his facts.

Only one corner still remained in the shadow. No light which I possessed could clear up the cause for the lady's sudden departure. She was very happy at Lausanne. There was every reason to believe that she intended to remain for the season in her luxurious rooms overlooking the lake. And yet she had left at a single day's notice, which involved her in the useless payment of a week's rent. Only Jules Vibart, the lover of the maid, had any suggestion to offer. He connected the sudden departure with the visit to the hotel a day or two before of a tall, dark, bearded man. "*Un sauvage—un véritable sauvage!*" cried Jules Vibart. The man had rooms somewhere in the town. He had been seen talking earnestly to Madame on the promenade by the lake. Then he had called. She had refused to see him. He was English, but of his name there was no record. Madame had left the place immediately afterwards. Jules Vibart, and what was of more importance, Jules Vibart's sweetheart, thought that this call and this departure were cause and effect. Only one thing Jules would not discuss. That was the reason why Marie had left her mistress. Of that he could or would say nothing. If I wished to know, I must go to Montpellier and ask her.

So ended the first chapter of my inquiry. The second was devoted to the place which Lady Frances Carfax had sought when she left Lausanne. Concerning this there had been some secrecy, which confirmed the idea that she had gone with the intention of throwing someone off her track. Otherwise why should not her luggage have been openly labelled for Baden? Both she and it reached the Rhenish spa by some circuitous route. This much I gathered from the manager of Cook's local office. So to Baden I went, after dispatching to Holmes an account of all my proceedings and receiving in reply a telegram of half-humorous commendation.

At Baden the track was not difficult to follow. Lady Frances had stayed at the Englischer Hof for a fortnight. While there she had made the acquaintance of a Dr. Shlessinger and his wife, a missionary from South America. Like most lonely ladies, Lady Frances found her comfort and occupation in religion. Dr. Shlessinger's remarkable personality, his whole-hearted devotion, and the fact that he was recovering from a disease contracted in the exercise of his apostolic duties affected her deeply. She had helped Mrs. Shlessinger in the nursing of the convalescent saint. He spent his day, as the manager described it to me, upon a lounge-chair on the veranda, with an attendant lady upon either side of him. He was preparing a map of the Holy Land, with special reference to the kingdom of the Midianites, upon which he was writing a monograph. Finally, having improved much in health, he and his wife had returned to London, and Lady Frances had started thither in their company. This was just three weeks before, and the manager had heard nothing since. As to the maid, Marie, she had gone off some days beforehand in floods of tears, after informing the other maids that she was leaving service forever. Dr. Shlessinger had paid the bill of the whole party before his departure.

"By the way," said the landlord in conclusion, "you are not the only friend of Lady Frances Carfax who is inquiring after her just now. Only a week or so ago we had a man here upon the same errand."

"Did he give a name?" I asked.

"None; but he was an Englishman, though of an unusual type."

"A savage?" said I, linking my facts after the fashion of my illustrious friend.

"Exactly. That describes him very well. He is a bulky, bearded, sunburned fellow, who looks as if he would be more at home in a farmers' inn than in a fashionable hotel. A hard, fierce man, I should think, and one whom I should be sorry to offend."

Already the mystery began to define itself, as figures grow clearer with the lifting of a fog. Here was this good and pious lady pursued from place to place by a sinister and unrelenting figure. She feared him, or she would not have fled from Lausanne. He had still followed. Sooner or later he would overtake her. Had he already overtaken her? Was *that* the secret of her continued silence? Could the good people who were her companions not screen her from his violence or his blackmail? What horrible purpose, what deep design, lay behind this long pursuit? There was the problem which I had to solve.

541

To Holmes I wrote showing how rapidly and surely I had got down to the roots of the matter. In reply I had a telegram asking for a description of Dr. Shlessinger's left ear. Holmes's ideas of humour are strange and occasionally offensive, so I took no notice of his ill-timed jest—indeed, I had already reached Montpellier in my pursuit of the maid, Marie, before his message came.

I had no difficulty in finding the ex-servant and in learning all that she could tell me. She was a devoted creature, who had only left her mistress because she was sure that she was in good hands, and because her own approaching marriage made a separation inevitable in any case. Her mistress had, she confessed with distress, shown some irritability of temper towards her during their stay in Baden and had even questioned her once as if she had suspicions of her honesty, and this had made the parting easier than it would otherwise have been. Lady Frances had given her fifty pounds as a wedding-present. Like me, Marie viewed with deep distrust the stranger who had driven her mistress from Lausanne. With her own eyes she had seen him seize the lady's wrist with great violence on the public promenade by the lake. He was a fierce and terrible man. She believed that it was out of dread of him that Lady Frances had accepted the escort of the Shlessingers to London. She had never spoken to Marie about it, but many little signs had convinced the maid that her mistress lived in a state of continual nervous apprehension. So far she had got in her narrative, when suddenly she sprang from her chair and her face was convulsed with surprise and fear. "See!" she cried. "The miscreant follows still! There is the very man of whom I speak."

Through the open sitting-room window I saw a huge, swarthy man with a bristling black beard walking slowly down the centre of the street and staring eagerly at the numbers of the houses. It was clear that, like myself, he was on the track of the maid. Acting upon the impulse of the moment, I rushed out and accosted him.

"You are an Englishman," I said.

"What if I am?" he asked with a most villainous scowl.

"May I ask what your name is?"

"No, you may not," said he with decision.

The situation was awkward, but the most direct way is often the best.

"Where is the Lady Frances Carfax?" I asked.

He stared at me in amazement.

"What have you done with her? Why have you pursued her? I insist upon an answer!" said I.

The fellow gave a bellow of anger and sprang upon me like a tiger. I have held my own in many a struggle, but the man had a grip of iron and the fury of a fiend. His hand was on my throat and my senses were nearly gone before an unshaven French *ouvrier* in a blue blouse darted out from a *cabaret* opposite, with a cudgel in his hand, and struck my assailant a sharp crack over the forearm, which made him leave go his hold. He stood for an instant fuming with rage and uncertain whether he should not renew his attack. Then, with a snarl of anger, he left me and entered the cottage from which I had just come. I turned to thank my preserver, who stood beside me in the roadway.

"Well, Watson," said he, "a pretty hash you have made of it! I rather think you had better come back with me to London by the night express."

An hour afterwards, Sherlock Holmes, in his usual garb and style, was seated in my private room at the hotel. His explanation of his sudden and opportune appearance was simplicity itself, for finding that he could get away from London, he determined to head me off at the next obvious point of my travels. In the disguise of a workingman he had sat in the *cabaret* waiting for my appearance.

"And a singularly consistent investigation you have made, my dear Watson," said he. "I cannot at the moment recall any possible blunder which you have omitted. The total effect of your proceeding has been to give the alarm everywhere and yet to discover nothing."

"Perhaps you would have done no better," I answered bitterly.

"There is no 'perhaps' about it. I *have* done better. Here

is the Hon. Philip Green, who is a fellow-lodger with you in this hotel, and we may find him the starting-point for a more successful investigation."

A card had come up on a salver, and it was followed by the same bearded ruffian who had attacked me in the street. He started when he saw me.

"What is this, Mr. Holmes?" he asked. "I had your note and I have come. But what has this man to do with the matter?"

"This is my old friend and associate, Dr. Watson, who is helping us in this affair."

The stranger held out a huge, sunburned hand, with a few words of apology.

"I hope I didn't harm you. When you accused me of hurting her I lost my grip of myself. Indeed, I'm not responsible in these days. My nerves are like live wires. But this situation is beyond me. What I want to know in the first place, Mr. Holmes, is how in the world you came to hear of my existence at all."

"I am in touch with Miss Dobney, Lady Frances's governess."

"Old Susan Dobney with the mob cap! I remember her well."

"And she remembers you. It was in the days before—before you found it better to go to South Africa."

"Ah, I see you know my whole story. I need hide nothing from you. I swear to you, Mr. Holmes, that there never was in this world a man who loved a woman with a more wholehearted love than I had for Frances. I was a wild youngster, I know—not worse than others of my class. But her mind was pure as snow. She could not bear a shadow of coarseness. So, when she came to hear of things that I had done, she would have no more to say to me. And yet she loved me—that is the wonder of it!—loved me well enough to remain single all her sainted days just for my sake alone. When the years had passed and I had made my money at Barberton I thought perhaps I could seek her out and soften her. I had heard that she was still unmarried. I found her at Lausanne and tried all I knew. She weakened, I think, but her will was strong, and when next I called she had left the town. I traced her to Baden and then after a time heard that her maid was here. I'm a rough fellow, fresh from a rough life, and when Dr. Watson spoke to me as he did I lost hold of myself for a moment. But for God's sake tell me what has become of the Lady Frances."

"That is for us to find out," said Sherlock Holmes with peculiar gravity. "What is your London address, Mr. Green?"

"The Langham Hotel will find me."

"Then may I recommend that you return there and be on hand in case I should want you? I have no desire to encourage false hopes, but you may rest assured that all that can be done will be done for the safety of Lady Frances. I can say no more for the instant. I will leave you this card so that you may be able to keep in touch with us. Now, Watson, if you will pack your bag I will cable to Mrs. Hudson to make one of her best efforts for two hungry travellers at seven-thirty to-morrow."

A telegram was awaiting us when we reached our Baker Street rooms, which Holmes read with an exclamation of interest and threw across to me. "Jagged or torn," was the message, and the place of origin, Baden.

"What is this?" I asked.

"It is everything," Holmes answered. "You may remember my seemingly irrelevant question as to this clerical gentleman's left ear. You did not answer it."

"I had left Baden and could not inquire."

"Exactly. For this reason I sent a duplicate to the manager of the Englischer Hof, whose answer lies here."

"What does it show?"

"It shows, my dear Watson, that we are dealing with an exceptionally astute and dangerous man. The Rev. Dr. Shlessinger, missionary from South America, is none other than Holy Peters, one of the most unscrupulous rascals that Australia has ever evolved—and for a young country it has turned out some very finished types. His particular specialty is the beguiling of lonely ladies by playing upon their religious feelings, and his so-called wife, an English-woman named Fraser, is a worthy helpmate. The nature of his tactics suggested his identity to me, and this physical peculiarity—he was badly bitten in a saloon-fight at Adelaide in '89—confirmed my suspicion. This poor lady is in the hands of a most infernal couple, who will stick at nothing, Watson. That she is already dead is a very likely supposition. If not, she is undoubtedly in some sort of confinement and unable to write to Miss Dobney or her other friends. It is always possible that she never reached London, or that she has passed through it, but the former is improbable, as, with their system of registration, it is not easy for foreigners to play tricks with the Continental police; and the latter is also unlikely, as these rogues could not hope to find any other place where it would be as easy to keep a person under restraint. All my instincts tell me that she is in London, but as we have at present no possible means of telling where, we can only take the obvious steps, eat our dinner, and possess our souls in patience. Later in the evening I will stroll down and have a word with friend Lestrade at Scotland Yard."

But neither the official police nor Holmes's own small but very efficient organization sufficed to clear away the mystery. Amid the crowded millions of London the three persons we sought were as completely obliterated as if they had never lived. Advertisements were tried, and failed. Clues were followed, and led to nothing. Every criminal resort which Shlessinger might frequent was drawn in vain. His old associates were watched, but they kept clear of him. And then suddenly, after a week of helpless suspense there came a flash of light. A silver-and-brilliant pendant of old Spanish design had been pawned at Bovington's, in Westminster Road. The pawner was a large, clean-shaven man of clerical appearance. His name and address were demonstrably false. The ear had escaped notice, but the description was surely that of Shlessinger.

Three times had our bearded friend from the Langham called for news—the third time within an hour of this fresh development. His clothes were getting looser on his great body. He seemed to be wilting away in his anxiety. "If you will only give me something to do!" was his constant wail. At last Holmes could oblige him.

"He has begun to pawn the jewels. We should get him now."

"But does this mean that any harm has befallen the Lady Frances?"

Holmes shook his head very gravely.

"Supposing that they have held her prisoner up to now, it is clear that they cannot let her loose without their own destruction. We must prepare for the worst."

"What can I do?"

"These people do not know you by sight?"

"No."

"It is possible that he will go to some other pawnbroker in the future. In that case, we must begin again. On the other hand, he has had a fair price and no questions asked, so if he is in need of ready-money he will probably come back to Bovington's. I will give you a note to them, and they will let you wait in the shop. If the fellow comes you will follow him. But no indiscretion, and above all, no violence. I put you on your honour that you will take no step without my knowledge and consent."

For two days the Hon. Philip Green (he was, I may mention, the son of the famous admiral of that name who commanded the Sea of Azof fleet in the Crimean War) brought us no news. On the evening of the third he rushed into our sitting-room, pale, trembling, with every muscle of his powerful frame quivering with excitement.

"We have him! We have him!" he cried.

He was incoherent in his agitation. Holmes soothed him with a few words and thrust him into an armchair.

"Come, now, give us the order of events," said he.

"She came only an hour ago. It was the wife, this time,

but the pendant she brought was the fellow of the other. She is a tall, pale woman, with ferret eyes."

"That is the lady," said Holmes.

"She left the office and I followed her. She walked up the Kennington Road, and I kept behind her. Presently she went into a shop. Mr. Holmes, it was an undertaker's."

My companion started. "Well?" he asked in that vibrant voice which told of the fiery soul behind the cold, grey face.

"She was talking to the woman behind the counter. I entered as well. 'It is late,' I heard her say, or words to that effect. The woman was excusing herself. 'It should be there before now,' she answered. 'It took longer, being out of the ordinary.' They both stopped and looked at me, so I asked some question and then left the shop."

"You did excellently well. What happened next?"

"The woman came out, but I had hid myself in a doorway. Her suspicions had been aroused, I think, for she looked around her. Then she called a cab and got in. I was lucky enough to get another and so to follow her. She got down at last at No. 36, Poultney Square, Brixton. I drove past, left my cab at the corner of the square, and watched the house."

"Did you see anyone?"

"The windows were all in darkness save one on the lower floor. The blind was down, and I could not see in. I was standing there, wondering what I should do next, when a covered van drove up with two men in it. They descended, took something out of the van, and carried it up the steps to the hall door. Mr. Holmes, it was a coffin."

"Ah!"

"For an instant I was on the point of rushing in. The door had been opened to admit the men and their burden. It was the woman who had opened it. But as I stood there she caught a glimpse of me, and I think that she recognised me. I saw her start, and she hastily closed the door. I remembered my promise to you, and here I am."

"You have done excellent work," said Holmes scribbling

a few words upon a half-sheet of paper. "We can do nothing legal without a warrant, and you can serve the cause best by taking this note down to the authorities and getting one. There may be some difficulty, but I should think that the sale of the jewellery should be sufficient. Lestrade will see to all details."

"But they may murder her in the meanwhile. What could the coffin mean, and for whom could it be but for her?"

"We will do all that can be done, Mr. Green. Not a moment will be lost. Leave it in our hands. Now, Watson," he added as our client hurried away, "he will set the regular forces on the move. We are, as usual, the irregulars, and we must take our own line of action. The situation strikes me as so desperate that the most extreme measures are justified. Not a moment is to be lost in getting to Poultney Square.

"Let us try to reconstruct the situation," said he as we drove swiftly past the Houses of Parliament and over Westminster Bridge. "These villains have coaxed this unhappy lady to London, after first alienating her from her faithful maid. If she has written any letters they have been intercepted. Through some confederate they have engaged a furnished house. Once inside it, they have made her a prisoner, and they have become possessed of the valuable jewellery which has been their object from the first. Already they have begun to see part of it, which seems safe enough to them, since they have no reason to think that anyone is interested in the lady's fate. When she is released she will, of course, denounce them. Therefore, she must not be released. But they cannot keep her under lock and key forever. So murder is their only solution."

"That seems very clear."

"Now we will take another line of reasoning. When you follow two separate chains of thought, Watson, you will find some point of intersection which should approximate to the truth. We will start now, not from the lady but from the coffin and argue backward. That incident proves, I fear, beyond all doubt that the lady is dead. It points also to an orthodox burial with proper accompaniment of medical certificate and official sanction. Had the lady been obviously murdered, they would have buried her in a hole in the back garden. But here all is open and regular. What does that mean? Surely that they have done her to death in some way which has deceived the doctor and simulated a natural end—poisoning, perhaps. And yet how strange that they should ever let a doctor approach her unless he were a confederate, which is hardly a credible proposition."

"Could they have forged a medical certificate?"

"Dangerous, Watson, very dangerous. No, I hardly see them doing that. Pull up, Cabby! This is evidently the undertaker's, for we have just passed the pawnbroker's. Would you go in, Watson? Your appearance inspires confidence. Ask what hour the Poultney Square funeral takes place to-morrow."

The woman in the shop answered me without hesitation that it was to be at eight o'clock in the morning. "You see, Watson, no mystery; everything above-board! In some way the legal forms have undoubtedly been complied with, and they think that they have little to fear. Well, there's nothing for it now but a direct frontal attack. Are you armed?"

"My stick!"

"Well, well, we shall be strong enough. 'Thrice is he armed who hath his quarrel just.' We simply can't afford to wait for the police or to keep within the four corners of the law. You can drive off, Cabby. Now, Watson, we'll just take our luck together, as we have occasionally done in the past."

He had rung loudly at the door of a great dark house in the centre of Poultney Square. It was opened immediately, and the figure of a tall woman was outlined against the dim-lit hall.

"Well, what do you want?" she asked sharply, peering at us through the darkness.

"I want to speak to Dr. Shlessinger," said Holmes.

"There is no such person here," she answered, and tried to close the door, but Holmes had jammed it with his foot.

"Well, I want to see the man who lives here, whatever he may call himself," said Holmes firmly.

She hesitated. Then she threw open the door. "Well, come in!" said she. "My husband is not afraid to face any man in the world." She closed the door behind us and showed us into a sitting-room on the right side of the hall, turning up the gas as she left us. "Mr. Peters will be with you in an instant," she said.

Her words were literally true, for we had hardly time to look around the dusty and moth-eaten apartment in which we found ourselves before the door opened and a big, clean-shaven bald-headed man stepped lightly into the room. He had a large red face, with pendulous cheeks and a general air of superficial benevolence which was marred by a cruel, vicious mouth.

"There is surely some mistake here, gentlemen," he said in an unctuous, make-everything-easy voice. "I fancy that you have been misdirected. Possibly if you tried farther down the street—"

"That will do; we have no time to waste," said my companion firmly. "You are Henry Peters, of Adelaide, late the Rev. Dr. Shlessinger, of Baden and South America. I am as sure of that as that my own name is Sherlock Holmes."

Peters, as I will now call him, started and stared hard at his formidable pursuer. "I guess your name does not frighten me, Mr. Holmes," said he coolly. "When a man's conscience is easy you can't rattle him. What is your business in my house?"

"I want to know what you have done with the Lady Frances Carfax, whom you brought away with you from Baden."

"I'd be very glad if you could tell me where that lady may be," Peters answered coolly. "I've a bill against her for nearly a hundred pounds, and nothing to show for it but a couple of trumpery pendants that the dealer would hardly look at. She attached herself to Mrs. Peters and me at Baden—it is a fact that I was using another name at the time—and she stuck on to us until we came to London. I paid her bill and her ticket. Once in London, she gave us the slip, and as I say, left these out-of-date jewels to pay her bills. You find her, Mr. Holmes, and I'm your debtor."

"I *mean* to find her," said Sherlock Holmes. "I'm going through this house till I do find her."

"Where is your warrant?"

Holmes half drew a revolver from his pocket. "This will have to serve till a better one comes."

"Why, you are a common burglar."

"So you might describe me," said Holmes cheerfully. "My companion is also a dangerous ruffian. And together we are going through your house."

Our opponent opened the door.

"Fetch a policeman, Annie!" said he. There was a whisk of feminine skirts down the passage, and the hall door was opened and shut.

"Our time is limited, Watson," said Holmes. "If you try to stop us, Peters, you will most certainly get hurt. Where is that coffin which was brought into your house?"

"What do you want with the coffin? It is in use. There is a body in it."

"I must see that body."

"Never with my consent."

"Then without it." With a quick movement Holmes pushed the fellow to one side and passed into the hall. A door half opened stood immediately before us. We entered. It was the dining-room. On the table, under a half-lit chandelier, the coffin was lying. Holmes turned up the gas and raised the lid. Deep down in the recesses of the coffin lay an emaciated figure. The glare from the lights above beat down upon an aged and withered face. By no possible process of cruelty, starvation, or disease could this wornout wreck be the still beautiful Lady Frances. Holmes's face showed his amazement and also his relief.

552

"Thank God!" he muttered. "It's someone else."

"Ah, you've blundered badly for once, Mr. Sherlock Holmes," said Peters, who had followed us into the room.

"Who is this dead woman?"

"Well, if you really must know, she is an old nurse of my wife's, Rose Spender by name, whom we found in the Brixton Workhouse Infirmary. We brought her round here, called in Dr. Horsom, of 13 Firbank Villas—mind you take the address, Mr. Holmes—and had her carefully tended, as Christian folk should. On the third day she died—certificate says senile decay—but that's only the doctor's opinion, and of course you know better. We ordered her funeral to be carried out by Stimson and Co., of the Kennington Road, who will bury her at eight o'clock to-morrow morning. Can you pick any hole in that, Mr. Holmes? You've made a silly blunder, and you may as well own up to it. I'd give something for a photograph of your gaping, staring face when you pulled aside that lid expecting to see the Lady Frances Carfax and only found a poor old woman of ninety."

Holmes expression was as impassive as ever under the jeers of his antagonist, but his clenched hands betrayed his acute annoyance.

"I am going through your house," said he.

"Are you, though!" cried Peters as a woman's voice and heavy steps sounded in the passage. "We'll soon see about that. This way, Officers, if you please. These men have forced their way into my house, and I cannot get rid of them. Help me to put them out."

A sergeant and a constable stood in the doorway. Holmes drew his card from his case.

"This is my name and address. This is my friend, Dr. Watson."

"Bless you, sir, we know you very well," said the sergeant, "but you can't stay here without a warrant."

"Of course not. I quite understand that."

"Arrest him!" cried Peters.

"We know where to lay our hands on this gentleman if

he is wanted," said the sergeant majestically, "but you'll have to go, Mr. Holmes."

"Yes, Watson, we shall have to go."

A minute later we were in the street once more. Holmes was as cool as ever, but I was hot with anger and humiliation. The sergeant had followed us.

"Sorry, Mr. Holmes, but that's the law.

"Exactly, Sergeant, you could not do otherwise."

"I expect there was good reason for your presence there. If there is anything I can do—"

"It's a missing lady, Sergeant, and we think she is in that house. I expect a warrant presently."

"Then I'll keep my eye on the parties, Mr. Holmes. If anything comes along, I will surely let you know."

It was only nine o'clock, and we were off full cry upon the trail at once. First we drove to Brixton Workhouse Infirmary, where we found that it was indeed the truth that a charitable couple had called some days before, that they had claimed an imbecile old woman as a former servant, and that they had obtained permission to take her away with them. No surprise was expressed at the news that she had since died.

The doctor was our next goal. He had been called in, had found the woman dying of pure senility, had actually seen her pass away, and had signed the certificate in due form. "I assure you that everything was perfectly normal and there was no room for foul play in the matter," said he. Nothing in the house had struck him as suspicious save that for people of their class it was remarkable that they should have no servant. So far and no farther went the doctor.

Finally we found our way to Scotland Yard. There had been difficulties of procedure in regard to the warrant. Some delay was inevitable. The magistrate's signature might not be obtained until next morning. If Holmes would call about nine he could go down with Lestrade and see it acted upon. So ended the day, save that near midnight our friend, the sergeant, called to say that he had

554

seen flickering lights here and there in the windows of the great dark house, but that no one had left it and none had entered. We could but pray for patience and wait for the morrow.

Sherlock Holmes was too irritable for conversation and too restless for sleep. I left him smoking hard, with his heavy, dark brows knotted together, and his long, nervous fingers tapping upon the arms of his chair, as he turned over in his mind every possible solution of the mystery. Several times in the course of the night I heard him prowling about the house. Finally, just after I had been called in the morning, he rushed into my room. He was in his dressing-gown, but his pale, hollow-eyed face told me that his night had been a sleepless one.

"What time was the funeral? Eight, was it not?" he asked eagerly. "Well, it is seven-twenty now. Good Heavens, Watson, what has become of any brains that God has given me? Quick, man, quick! It's life or death—a hundred chances on death to one on life. I'll never forgive myself, never, if we are too late!"

Five minutes had not passed before we were flying in a hansom down Baker Street. But even so it was twenty-five to eight as we passed Big Ben, and eight struck as we tore down the Brixton Road. But others were late as well as we. Ten minutes after the hour the hearse was still standing at the door of the house, and even as our foaming horse came to a halt the coffin, supported by three men, appeared on the threshold. Holmes darted forward and barred their way.

"Take it back!" he cried, laying his hand on the breast of the foremost. "Take it back this instant!"

"What the devil do you mean? Once again I ask you, where is your warrant?" shouted the furious Peters, his big red face glaring over the farther end of the coffin.

"The warrant is on its way. This coffin shall remain in the house until it comes."

The authority in Holmes's voice had its effect upon the bearers. Peters had suddenly vanished into the house, and

they obeyed these new orders. "Quick, Watson, quick!
Here is a screw-driver!" he shouted as the coffin was replaced upon the table. "Here's one for you, my man! A
sovereign if the lid comes off in a minute! Ask no questions—work away! That's good! Another! And another!
Now pull all together! It's giving! It's giving! Ah, that
does it at last."

With a united effort we tore off the coffin-lid. As we did
so there came from the inside a stupefying and overpowering smell of chloroform. A body lay within, its head
all wreathed in cotton-wool, which had been soaked in the
narcotic. Holmes plucked it off and disclosed the statu-
esque face of a handsome and spiritual woman of middle
age. In an instant he had passed his arm around the figure
and raised her to a sitting position.

"Is she gone, Watson? Is there a spark left? Surely we are
not too late!"

For half an hour it seemed that we were. What with
actual suffocation, and what with the poisonous fumes of
the chloroform, the Lady Frances seemed to have passed
the last point of recall. And then, at last, with artificial res-
piration, with injected ether, with every device that science
could suggest, some flutter of life, some quiver of the
eyelids, some dimming of a mirror, spoke of the slowly returning life. A cab had driven up, and Holmes, parting the
blind, looked out at it. "Here is Lestrade with his warrant,"
said he. "He will find that his birds have flown. And here,"
he added as a heavy step hurried along the passage, "is
someone who has a better right to nurse this lady than we
have. Good morning, Mr. Green; I think that the sooner
we can move the Lady Frances the better. Meanwhile, the
funeral may proceed, and the poor old woman who still
lies in that coffin may go to her last resting-place alone."

"Should you care to add the case to your annals, my dear
Watson," said Holmes that evening, "it can only be as an
example of that temporary eclipse to which even the best-
balanced mind may be exposed. Such slips are common to

all mortals, and the greatest is he who can recognise and repair them. To this modified credit I may, perhaps, make some claim. My night was haunted by the thought that somewhere a clue, a strange sentence, a curious observation, had come under my notice and had been too easily dismissed. Then, suddenly, in the grey of the morning, the words came back to me. It was the remark of the undertaker's wife, as reported by Philip Green. She had said, 'It should be there before now. It took longer, being out of the ordinary.' It was the coffin of which she spoke. It had been out of the ordinary. That could mean that it had been made to some special measurement. But why? Why? Then in an instant I remembered the deep sides and the little wasted figure at the bottom. Why so large a coffin for so small a body? To leave room for another body. Both would be buried under the one certificate. It had all been so clear, if only my own sight had not been dimmed. At eight the Lady Frances would be buried. Our one chance was to stop the coffin before it left the house.

"It was a desperate chance that we might find her alive, but it *was* a chance, as the result showed. These people had never, to my knowledge, done a murder. They might shrink from actual violence at the last. They could bury her with no sign of how she met her end, and even if she were exhumed there was a chance for them. I hoped that such considerations might prevail with them. You can reconstruct the scene well enough. You saw the horrible den upstairs, where the poor lady had been kept so long. They rushed in and overpowered her with their chloroform, carried her down, poured more into the coffin to insure against her waking, and then screwed down the lid. A clever device, Watson. It is new to me in the annals of crime. If our ex-missionary friends escape the clutches of Lestrade, I shall expect to hear of some brilliant incidents in their future career."

The Adventure of the
Illustrious Client

"It can't hurt now," was Mr. Sherlock Holmes's comment when, for the tenth time in as many years, I asked his leave to reveal the following narrative. So it was that at last I obtained permission to put on record what was, in some ways, the supreme moment of my friend's career.

Both Holmes and I had a weakness for the Turkish bath. It was over a smoke in the pleasant lassitude of the drying-room that I have found him less reticent and more human than anywhere else. On the upper floor of the Northumberland Avenue establishment there is an isolated corner where two couches lie side by side, and it was on these that we lay upon September 3, 1902, the day when my narrative begins. I had asked him whether anything was stirring, and for answer he had shot his long, thin, nervous arm out of the sheets which enveloped him and had drawn an envelope from the inside pocket of the coat which hung beside him. "It may be some fussy, self-important fool; it may be a matter of life or death," said he as he handed me the note. "I know no more than this message tells me."

It was from the Carlton Club and dated the evening before. This is what I read:

Sir James Damery presents his compliments to Mr. Sherlock Holmes and will call upon him at 4:30 to-morrow. Sir James begs to say that the matter upon which he desires to consult Mr.

Holmes is very delicate and also very important. He trusts, therefore, that Mr. Holmes will make every effort to grant this interview, and that he will confirm it over the telephone to the Carlton Club.

"I need not say that I have confirmed it, Watson," said Holmes as I returned the paper. "Do you know anything of this man Damery?"

"Only that this name is a household word in society."

"Well, I can tell you a little more than that. He has rather a reputation for arranging delicate matters which are to be kept out of the papers. You may remember his negotiations with Sir George Lewis over the Hammerford Will case. He is a man of the world with a natural turn for diplomacy. I am bound, therefore, to hope that it is not a false scent and that he has some real need for our assistance."

"Our?"

"Well, if you will be so good, Watson."

"I shall be honoured."

"Then you have the hour—four-thirty. Until then we can put the matter out of our heads."

I was living in my own rooms in Queen Anne Street at the time, but I was round at Baker Street before the time named. Sharp to the half-hour, Colonel Sir James Damery was announced. It is hardly necessary to describe him, for many will remember that large, bluff, honest personality, that broad, clean-shaven face, and above all, that pleasant, mellow voice. Frankness shone from his grey Irish eyes, and good humour played round his mobile, smiling lips. His lucent top-hat, his dark frock-coat, indeed, every detail, from the pearl pin in the black satin cravat to the lavender spats over the varnished shoes, spoke of the meticulous care in dress for which he was famous. The big, masterful aristocrat dominated the little room.

"Of course, I was prepared to find Dr. Watson," he remarked with a courteous bow. "His collaboration may be very necessary, for we are dealing on this occasion, Mr.

Holmes, with a man to whom violence is familiar and who will, literally, stick at nothing. I should say that there is no more dangerous man in Europe."

"I have had several opponents to whom that flattering term has been applied," said Holmes with a smile. "Don't you smoke? Then you will excuse me if I light my pipe. If your man is more dangerous than the late Professor Moriarty, or than the living Colonel Sebastian Moran, then he is indeed worth meeting. May I ask his name?"

"Have you ever heard of Baron Gruner?"

"You mean the Austrian murderer?"

Colonel Damery threw up his kid-gloved hands with a laugh. "There is no getting past you, Mr. Holmes! Wonderful! So you have already sized him up as a murderer?"

"It is my business to follow the details of Continental crime. Who could possibly have read what happened at Prague and have any doubts as to the man's guilt! It was a purely technical legal point and the suspicious death of a witness that saved him! I am as sure that he killed his wife when the so-called 'accident' happened in the Splugen Pass as if I had seen him do it. I knew, also, that he had come to England and had a presentiment that sooner or later he would find me some work to do. Well, what has Baron Gruner been up to? I presume it is not this old tragedy which has come up again?"

"No, it is more serious than that. To revenge crime is important, but to prevent it is more so. It is a terrible thing, Mr. Holmes, to see a dreadful event, an atrocious situation, preparing itself before your eyes, to clearly understand whither it will lead and yet to be utterly unable to avert it. Can a human being be placed in a more trying position?"

"Perhaps not."

"Then you will sympathize with the client in whose interests I am acting."

"I did not understand that you were merely an intermediary. Who is the principal?"

"Mr. Holmes, I must beg you not to press that question. It is important that I should be able to assure him that his honoured name has been in no way dragged into the matter. His motives are, to the last degree, honourable and chivalrous, but he prefers to remain unknown. I need not say that your fees will be assured and that you will be given a perfectly free hand. Surely the actual name of your client is immaterial?"

"I am sorry," said Holmes. "I am accustomed to have mystery at one end of my cases, but to have it at both ends is too confusing. I fear, Sir James, that I must decline to act."

Our visitor was greatly disturbed. His large, sensitive face was darkened with emotion and disappointment.

"You hardly realize the effect of your own action, Mr. Holmes," said he. "You place me in a most serious dilemma, for I am perfectly certain that you would be proud to take over the case if I could give you the facts, and yet a promise forbids me from revealing them all. May I, at least, lay all that I can before you?"

"By all means, so long as it is understood that I commit myself to nothing."

"That is understood. In the first place, you have no doubt heard of General de Merville?"

"De Merville of Khyber fame? Yes, I have heard of him."

"He has a daughter, Violet de Merville, young, rich, beautiful, accomplished, a wonder-woman in every way. It is this daughter, this lovely, innocent girl, whom we are endeavouring to save from the clutches of a fiend."

"Baron Gruner has some hold over her, then?"

"The strongest of all holds where a woman is concerned—the hold of love. The fellow is, as you may have heard, extraordinarily handsome, with a most fascinating manner, a gentle voice, and that air of romance and mystery which means so much to a woman. He is said to have the whole sex at his mercy and to have made ample use of the fact."

"But how came such a man to meet a lady of the standing of Miss Violet de Merville?"

"It was on a Mediterranean yachting voyage. The company, though select, paid their own passages. No doubt the promoters hardly realized the Baron's true character until it was too late. The villain attached himself to the lady, and with such effect that he has completely and absolutely won her heart. To say that she loves him hardly expresses it. She dotes upon him; she is obsessed by him. Outside of him there is nothing on earth. She will not hear one word against him. Everything has been done to cure her of her madness, but in vain. To sum up, she proposes to marry him next month. As she is of age and has a will of iron, it is hard to know how to prevent her."

"Does she know about the Austrian episode?"

"The cunning devil has told her every unsavoury public scandal of his past life, but always in such a way to make himself out to be an innocent martyr. She absolutely accepts his version and will listen to no other."

"Dear me! But surely you have inadvertently let out the name of your client? It is no doubt General de Merville."

Our visitor fidgeted in his chair.

"I could deceive you by saying so, Mr. Holmes, but it would not be true. De Merville is a broken man. The strong soldier has been utterly demoralized by this incident. He has lost the nerve which never failed him on the battlefield and has become a weak, doddering old man, utterly incapable of contending with a brilliant, forceful rascal like this Austrian. My client, however, is an old friend, one who has known the General intimately for many years and taken a paternal interest in this young girl since she wore short frocks. He cannot see this tragedy consummated without some attempt to stop it. There is nothing in which Scotland Yard can act. It was his own suggestion that you should be called in, but it was as I have said, on the express stipulation that he should not be personally involved in the matter. I have no doubt, Mr. Holmes, with your great powers you could easily trace my client back through me, but I must ask you, as a point of honour, to refrain from doing so, and not to break in upon his incognito."

Holmes gave a whimsical smile.

"I think I may safely promise that," said he. "I may add

562

that your problem interests me, and that I shall be prepared to look into it. How shall I keep in touch with you?"

"The Carlton Club will find me. But in case of emergency, there is a private telephone call, 'XX.31.'"

Holmes noted it down and sat, still smiling, with the open memorandum-book upon his knee.

"The Baron's present address, please?"

"Vernon Lodge, near Kingston. It is a large house. He has been fortunate in some rather shady speculations and is a rich man, which naturally makes him a more dangerous antagonist."

"Is he at home at present?"

"Yes."

"Apart from what you have told me can you give me any further information about the man?"

"He has expensive tastes. He is a horse fancier. For a short time he played polo at Hurlingham, but then this Prague affair got noised about and he had to leave. He collects books and pictures. He is a man with a considerable artistic side to his nature. He is, I believe, a recognised authority upon Chinese pottery and has written a book upon the subject."

"A complex mind," said Holmes. "All great criminals have that. My old friend Charlie Peace was a violin virtuoso. Wainwright was no mean artist. I could quote many more. Well, Sir James, you will inform your client that I am turning my mind upon Baron Gruner. I can say no more. I have some sources of information of my own, and I dare say we may find some means of opening the matter up."

When our visitor had left us Holmes sat so long in deep thought that it seemed to me that he had forgotten my presence. At last, however, he came briskly back to earth.

"Well, Watson, any views?" he asked.

"I should think you had better see the young lady herself."

"My dear Watson, if her poor old broken father cannot move her, how shall I, a stranger, prevail? And yet there is something in the suggestion if all else fails. But I think we must begin from a different angle. I rather fancy that Shinwell Johnson might be a help."

I have not had occasion to mention Shinwell Johnson in these memoirs because I have seldom drawn my cases from the latter phases of my friend's career. During the first years of the century he became a valuable assistant. Johnson, I grieve to say, made his name first as a very dangerous villain and served two terms at Parkhurst. Finally he repented and allied himself to Holmes, acting as his agent in the huge criminal underworld of London and obtaining information which often proved to be of vital importance. Had Johnson been a "nark" of the police he would soon have been exposed, but as he dealt with cases which never came directly into the courts, his activities were never realized by his companions. With the glamour of his two convictions upon him, he had the entrée of every nightclub, doss house, and gambling-den in the town, and his quick observation and active brain made him an ideal agent for gaining information. It was to him that Sherlock Holmes now proposed to turn.

It was not possible for me to follow the immediate steps taken by my friend, for I had some pressing professional business of my own, but I met him by appointment that evening at Simpson's, where, sitting at a small table in the front window and looking down at the rushing stream of life in the Strand, he told me something of what had passed.

"Johnson is on the prowl," said he. "He may pick up some garbage in the darker recesses of the underworld, for it is down there, amid the black roots of crime, that we must hunt for this man's secrets."

"But if the lady will not accept what is already known, why should any fresh discovery of yours turn her from her purpose?"

"Who knows, Watson? Woman's heart and mind are insoluble puzzles to the male. Murder might be condoned or explained, and yet some smaller offence might rankle. Baron Gruner remarked to me—"

"He remarked to you!"

"Oh, to be sure, I had not told you of my plans. Well, Watson, I love to come to close grips with my man. I like to meet him eye to eye and read for myself the stuff that he is made of. When I had given Johnson his instructions I took a cab out to Kingston and found the Baron in a most affable mood."

"Did he recognise you?"

"There was no difficulty about that, for I simply sent in my card. He is an excellent antagonist, cool as ice, silky voiced and soothing as one of your fashionable consultants, and poisonous as a cobra. He has breeding in him—a real aristocrat of crime, with a superficial suggestion of afternoon tea and all the cruelty of the grave behind it. Yes, I am glad to have had my attention called to Baron Adelbert Gruner."

"You say he was affable?"

"A purring cat who thinks he sees prospective mice. Some people's affability is more deadly than the violence of coarser souls. His greeting was characteristic. 'I rather thought I should see you sooner or later, Mr. Holmes,' said he. 'You have been engaged, no doubt by General de Merville, to endeavour to stop my marriage with his daughter, Violet. That is so, is it not?'

"I acquiesced.

"'My dear man,' said he, 'you will only ruin your own well-deserved reputation. It is not a case in which you can possibly succeed. You will have barren work, to say nothing of incurring some danger. Let me very strongly advise you to draw off at once.'

"'It is curious,' I answered, 'but that was the very advice which I had intended to give you. I have a respect for your brains, Baron, and the little which I have seen of your personality has not lessened it. Let me put it to you as man to man. No one wants to rake up your past and make you unduly uncomfortable. It is over, and you are now in smooth waters, but if you persist in this marriage you will raise up a swarm of powerful enemies who will never leave you alone until they have made England too hot to hold you. Is the game worth it? Surely you would be wiser if you left the lady alone. It would not be pleasant for you if these facts of your past were brought to her notice.'

"The Baron has little waxed tips of hair under his nose, like the short antennæ of an insect. These quivered with amusement as he listened, and he finally broke into a gentle chuckle.

"'Excuse my amusement, Mr. Holmes,' said he, 'but it is really funny to see you trying to play a hand with no cards in it. I don't think anyone could do it better, but it is rather pathetic, all the same. Not a colour card there, Mr. Holmes, nothing but the smallest of the small.'

"'So you think.'

"'So I know. Let me make the thing clear to you, for my own hand is so strong that I can afford to show it. I have been fortunate enough to win the entire affection of this lady. This was given to me in spite of the fact that I told her very clearly of all the unhappy incidents in my past life. I also told her that certain wicked and designing persons—I hope you recognise yourself—would come to her and tell her these things, and I warned her how to treat them. You have heard of post-hypnotic suggestion, Mr. Holmes? Well, you will see how it works, for a man of personality can use hypnotism without any vulgar passes or tomfoolery. So she is ready for you and, I have no doubt, would give you an appointment, for she is quite amenable to her father's will—save only in the one little matter.'

"Well, Watson, there seemed to be no more to say, so I took my leave with as much cold dignity as I could summon, but, as I had my hand on the door-handle, he stopped me.

"'By the way, Mr. Holmes,' said he, 'did you know Le Brun, the French agent?'

"'Yes,' said I.

"'Do you know what befell him?'

"'I heard that he was beaten by some Apaches in the Montmartre district and crippled for life.'

"'Quite true, Mr. Holmes. By a curious coincidence he had been inquiring into my affairs only a week before. Don't do it, Mr. Holmes; it's not a lucky thing to do. Several have found that out. My last word to you is, go your own way and let me go mine. Good-bye!'

"So there you are, Watson. You are up to date now."

"The fellow seems dangerous."

"Mighty dangerous. I disregard the blusterer, but this is the sort of man who says rather less than he means."

"Must you interfere? Does it really matter if he marries the girl?"

"Considering that he undoubtedly murdered his last wife, I should say it mattered very much. Besides, the client! Well, well, we need not discuss that. When you have finished your coffee you had best come home with me, for the blithe Shinwell will be there with his report."

We found him sure enough, a huge, coarse, red-faced, scorbutic man, with a pair of vivid black eyes which were the only external sign of the very cunning mind within. It seems that he had dived down into what was peculiarly his kingdom, and beside him on the settee was a brand which he had brought up in the shape of a slim, flame-like young woman with a pale, intense face, youthful, and yet so worn with sin and sorrow that one read the terrible years which had left their leprous mark upon her.

"This is Miss Kitty Winter," said Shinwell Johnson, waving his fat hand as an introduction. "What she don't know—well, there, she'll speak for herself. Put my hand right on her, Mr. Holmes, within an hour of your message."

"I'm easy to find," said the young woman. "Hell, London, gets me every time. Same address for Porky Shinwell. We're old mates, Porky, you and I, but, by cripes! There is another who ought to be down in a lower hell than we if there was any justice in the world! That is the man you are after, Mr. Holmes."

Holmes smiled. "I gather we have your good wishes, Miss Winter."

"If I can help to put him where he belongs, I'm yours to

567

the rattle," said our visitor with fierce energy. There was an intensity of hatred in her white, set face and her blazing eyes such as woman seldom and man never can attain. "You needn't go into my past, Mr. Holmes. That's neither here nor there. But what I am Adelbert Gruner made me. If I could pull him down!" She clutched frantically with her hands into the air. "Oh, if I could pull him into the pit where he has pushed so many!"

"You know how the matter stands?"

"Porky Shinwell has been telling me. He's after some other poor fool and wants to marry her this time. You want to stop it. Well, you surely know enough about this devil to prevent any decent girl in her senses wanting to be in the same parish with him."

"She is not in her senses. She is madly in love. She has been told all about him. She cares nothing."

"Told about the murder?"

"Yes."

"My Lord, she must have a nerve!"

"She puts them all down as slanders."

"Couldn't you lay proofs before her silly eyes?"

"Well, can you help us do so?"

"Ain't I a proof myself? If I stood before her and told her how he used me—"

"Would you do this?"

"Would I? Would I not!"

"Well, it might be worth trying. But he has told her most of his sins and had pardon from her, and I understand she will not reopen the question."

"I'll lay he didn't tell her all," said Miss Winter. "I caught a glimpse of one or two murders besides the one that made such a fuss. He would speak of someone in his velvet way and then look at me with a steady eye and say: 'He died within a month.' It wasn't hot air, either. But I took little notice—you see, I loved him myself at that time. Whatever he did went with me, same as with this poor fool! There was just one thing that shook me. Yes, by cripes! If it had not been for his poisonous, lying tongue that explains and soothes, I'd have left him that very night. It's a book he has—a brown leather book with a lock, and his arms in gold on the outside. I think he was a bit drunk that night, or he would not have shown it to me."

"What was it, then?"

"I tell you, Mr. Holmes, this man collects women and takes a pride in his collection, as some men collect moths or butterflies. He had it all in that book. Snapshot pho- tographs, names, details, everything about them. It was a beastly book—a book no man, even if he had come from the gutter, could have put together. But it was Adelbert Gruner's book all the same. 'Souls I have ruined.' He could have put that on the outside if he had been so minded. However, that's neither here nor there, for the book would not serve you, and if it would, you can't get it."

"Where is it?"

"How can I tell you where it is now? It's more than a year since I left him. I know where he kept it then. He's a pre- cise, tidy cat of a man in many of his ways, so maybe it is still in the pigeon-hole of the old bureau in the inner study. Do you know his house?"

"I've been in the study," said Holmes.

"Have you, though? You haven't been slow on the job if you only started this morning. Maybe dear Adelbert has met his match this time. The outer study is the one with the Chinese crockery in it—big glass cuboard between the windows. Then behind his desk is the door that leads to the inner study—a small room where he keeps papers and things."

"Is he not afraid of burglars?"

"Adelbert is no coward. His worst enemy couldn't say that of him. He can look after himself. There's a bur- glar alarm at night. Besides, what is there for a burglar—unless they got away with all this fancy crockery?"

"No good," said Shinwell Johnson with the decided voice of the expert. "No fence wants stuff of that sort that you can neither melt nor sell."

"Quite so," said Holmes. "Well, now, Miss Winter, if you would call here tomorrow evening at five, I would consider in the meanwhile whether your suggestion of seeing this lady personally may not be arranged. I am exceedingly obliged to you for your co-operation. I need not say that my clients will consider liberally—"

"None of that, Mr. Holmes," cried the young woman. "I am not out for money. Let me see this man in the mud, and I've got all I've worked for—in the mud with my foot on his cursed face. That's my price. I'm with you to-morrow or any other day so long as you are on his track. Porky here can tell you always where to find me."

I did not see Holmes again until the following evening when we dined once more at our Strand restaurant. He shrugged his shoulders when I asked him what luck he had had in his interview. Then he told the story, which I would repeat in this way. His hard, dry statement needs some little editing to soften it into the terms of real life.

"There was no difficulty at all about the appointment," said Holmes, "for the girl glories in showing abject filial obedience in all secondary things in an attempt to atone for her flagrant breach of it in her engagement. The General 'phoned that all was ready, and the fiery Miss W. turned up according to schedule so that at half-past five a cab deposited us outside 104 Berkeley Square, where the old soldier resides—one of those awful grey London castles which would make a church seem frivolous. A footman showed us into a great yellow-curtained drawing-room, and there was the lady awaiting us, demure, pale, self-contained, as inflexible and remote as a snow image on a mountain.

"I don't quite know how to make her clear to you, Watson. Perhaps you may meet her before we are through, and you can use your own gift of words. She is beautiful, but with the ethereal other-world beauty of some fanatic whose thoughts are set on high. I have seen such faces in the pictures of the old masters of the Middle Ages. How a beastman could have laid his vile paws upon such a being of the beyond I cannot imagine. You may have noticed how extremes call to each other, the spiritual to the animal, the cave-man to the angel. You never saw a worse case than this.

"She knew what we had come for, of course—that villain had lost no time in poisoning her mind against us. Miss Winter's advent rather amazed her, I think, but she waved us into our respective chairs like a Reverend Abbess receiving two rather leprous mendicants. If your head is inclined to swell, my dear Watson, take a course of Miss Violet de Merville.

"'Well, sir,' said she in a voice like the wind from an iceberg, 'your name is familiar to me. You have called, as I understand, to malign my fiancé, Baron Gruner. It is only by my father's request that I see you at all, and I warn you in advance that anything you can say could not possibly have the slightest effect upon my mind.'

"I was sorry for her, Watson. I thought of her for the moment as I would have thought of a daughter of my own. I am not often eloquent. I use my head, not my heart. But I really did plead with her with all the warmth of words that I could find in my nature. I pictured to her the awful position of the woman who only wakes to a man's character after she is his wife—a woman who has to submit to be caressed by bloody hands and lecherous lips. I spared her nothing—the shame, the fear, the agony, the hopelessness of it all. All my hot words could not bring one tinge of colour to those ivory cheeks or one gleam of emotion to those abstracted eyes. I thought of what the rascal had said about a post-hypnotic influence. One could really believe that she was living above the earth in some ecstatic dream. Yet there was nothing indefinite in her replies.

"'I have listened to you with patience, Mr. Holmes,' said she. 'That effect upon my mind is exactly as predicted. I am aware that Adelbert, that my fiancé, has had a stormy life in which he has incurred bitter hatreds and most unjust aspersions. You are only the last of a series who have brought their slanders before me. Possibly you mean well, though I learn that you are a paid agent who would have been equally willing to act for the Baron as against him. But in any case I wish you to understand once for all that I love him and that he loves me, and that the opinion of all the world is no more to me than the twitter of those birds outside the window. If his noble nature has ever for an instant fallen, it may be that I have been specially sent to raise it to its true and lofty level. I am not clear'—here she turned eyes upon my companion—'who this young lady may be.'

"I was about to answer when the girl broke in like a whirlwind. If ever you saw flame and ice face to face, it was those two women.

"'I'll tell you who I am,' she cried, springing out of her chair, her mouth all twisted with passion—'I am his last mistress. I am one of a hundred that he has tempted and used and ruined and thrown into the refuse heap, as he will you also. *Your* refuse heap is more likely to be a grave, and maybe that's the best. I tell you, you foolish woman, if you marry this man he'll be the death of you. It may be a broken heart or it may be a broken neck, but he'll have you one way or the other. It's not out of love for you I'm speaking. I don't care a tinker's curse whether you live or die. It's out of hate for him and to spite him and to get back on him for what he did to me. But it's all the same, and you needn't look at me like that, my fine lady, for you may be lower than I am before you are through with it.'

"'I should prefer not to discuss such matters,' said Miss de Merville coldly. 'Let me say once for all that I am aware of three passages in my fiancé's life in which he became entangled with designing women, and that I am assured of his hearty repentance for any evil that he may have done.'

"'Three passages!' screamed my companion. 'You fool! You unutterable fool!'

"'Mr. Holmes, I beg that you will bring this interview to an end,' said the icy voice. 'I have obeyed my father's wish in seeing you, but I am not compelled to listen to the ravings of this person.'

572

"With an oath Miss Winter darted forward, and if I had not caught her wrist she would have clutched this maddening woman by the hair. I dragged her towards the door and was lucky to get her back into the cab without a public scene, for she was beside herself with rage. In a cold way I felt pretty furious myself, Watson, for there was something indescribably annoying in the calm aloofness and supreme self-complaisance of the woman whom we were trying to save. So now once again you know exactly how we stand, and it is clear that I must plan some fresh opening move, for this gambit won't work. I'll keep in touch with you, Watson, for it is more than likely that you will have your part to play, though it is just possible that the next move may lie with them rather than us."

And it did. Their blow fell—or his blow rather, for never could I believe that the lady was privy to it. I think I could show you the very paving-stone upon which I stood when my eyes fell upon the placard, and a pang of horror passed through my very soul. It was between the Grand Hotel and Charing Cross Station, where a one-legged news-vender displayed his evening papers. The date was just two days after the last conversation. There, black upon yellow, was the terrible news-sheet:

MURDEROUS ATTACK UPON
SHERLOCK HOLMES

I think I stood stunned for some moments. Then I have a confused recollection of snatching at a paper, of the remonstrance of the man, whom I had not paid, and finally, of standing in the doorway of a chemist's shop while I turned up the fateful paragraph. This was how it ran:

We learn with regret that Mr. Sherlock Holmes, the well-known private detective, was the victim this morning of a murderous assault which has left him in a precarious position. There are no exact details to hand, but the event seems to have occurred about twelve o'clock in Regent Street, outside the Café Royal. The attack was made by two men armed with sticks, and Mr. Holmes was beaten about the head and body, receiving injuries which the doctors describe as most serious. He was carried to Charing Cross Hospital and afterwards insisted upon being taken to his rooms in Baker Street. The miscreants who attacked him appear to have been respectably dressed men, who escaped from the bystanders by passing through the Café Royal and out into Glasshouse Street behind it. No doubt they belonged to that criminal fraternity which has so often had occasion to bewail the activity and ingenuity of the injured man.

I need not say that my eyes had hardly glanced over the paragraph before I had sprung into a hansom and was on my way to Baker Street. I found Sir Leslie Oakshott, the famous surgeon, in the hall and his brougham waiting at the curb.

"No immediate danger," was the report. "Two lacerated scalp wounds and some considerable bruises. Several stitches have been necessary. Morphine has been injected and quiet is essential, but an interview of a few minutes would not be absolutely forbidden."

With this permission I stole into the darkened room. The sufferer was wide awake, and I heard my name in a hoarse whisper. The blind was three-quarters down, but one ray of sunlight slanted through and struck the bandaged head of the injured man. A crimson patch had soaked through the white linen compress. I sat beside him and bent my head.

"All right, Watson. Don't look so scared," he muttered in a very weak voice. "It's not as bad as it seems."

"Thank God for that!"

"I'm a bit of a single-stick expert, as you know. I took most of them on my guard. It was the second man that was too much for me."

"What can I do, Holmes? Of course, it was that damned fellow who set them on. I'll go and thrash the hide off him if you give the word."

"Good old Watson! No, we can do nothing there unless the police lay their hands on the men. But their get-away had been well prepared. We may be sure of that. Wait a little. I have my plans. The first thing is to exaggerate my injuries. They'll come to you for news. Put it on thick, Watson. Lucky if I live the week out—concussion—delirium—what you like! You can't overdo it."

"But Sir Leslie Oakshott?"

"Oh, he's all right. He shall see the worst side of me. I'll look after that."

"Anything else?"

"Yes. Tell Shinwell Johnson to get that girl out of the way. Those beauties will be after her now. They know, of course, that she was with me in the case. If they dared to do me in it is not likely they will neglect her. That is urgent. Do it to-night."

"I'll go now. Anything more?"

"Put my pipe on the table—and the tobacco-slipper. Right! Come in each morning and we will plan our campaign."

I arranged with Johnson that evening to take Miss Winter to a quiet suburb and see that she lay low until the danger was past.

For six days the public were under the impression that Holmes was at the door of death. The bulletins were very grave and there were sinister paragraphs in the papers. My continual visits assured me that it was not so bad as that. His wiry constitution and his determined will were working wonders. He was recovering fast, and I had suspicions at times that he was really finding himself faster than he pretended even to me. There was a curious secretive streak in the man which led to many dramatic effects, but left even his closest friend guessing as to what his exact plans might be. He pushed to an extreme the axiom that the only safe plotter was he who plotted alone. I was nearer him than anyone else, and yet I was always conscious of the gap between.

On the seventh day the stitches were taken out, in spite of which there was a report of erysipelas in the evening papers. The same evening papers had an announcement which I was bound, sick or well, to carry to my friend. It was simply that among the passengers on the Cunard boat

Ruritania, starting from Liverpool on Friday, was the Baron Adelbert Gruner, who had some important financial business to settle in the States before his impending wedding to Miss Violet de Merville, only daughter of, etc., etc. Holmes listened to the news with a cold, concentrated look upon his pale face, which told me that it hit him hard.

"Friday!" he cried. "Only three clear days. I believe the rascal wants to put himself out of danger's way. But he won't, Watson! By the Lord Harry, he won't! Now, Watson, I want you to do something for me."

"I am here to be used, Holmes."

"Well, then, spend the next twenty-four hours in an intensive study of Chinese pottery."

He gave no explanations and I asked for none. By long experience I had learned the wisdom of obedience. But when I left his room I walked down Baker Street, revolving in my head how on earth I was to carry out so strange an order. Finally, I drove to the London Library in St. James's Square, put the matter to my friend Lomax, the sub-librarian, and departed to my rooms with a goodly volume under my arm.

It is said that the barrister who crams up a case with such care that he can examine an expert witness upon the Monday has forgotten all his forced knowledge before the Saturday. Certainly I should not like now to pose as an authority upon ceramics. And yet all that evening, and all that night with a short interval for rest, and all next morning, I was sucking in knowledge and committing names to memory. There I learned of the hall-marks of the great artist-decorators, of the mystery of cyclical dates, the marks of the Hung-wu and the beauties of the Yung-lo, the writings of Tang-ying, and the glories of the primitive period of the Sung and the Yuan. I was charged with all this information when I called upon Holmes next evening. He was out of bed now, though you would not have guessed it from the published reports, and he sat with his much-bandaged head resting upon his hand in the depth of his favourite armchair.

"Why, Holmes," I said, "if one believed the papers, you are dying."

"That," said he, "is the very impression which I intended to convey. And now, Watson, have you learned your lessons?"

"At least I have tried to."

"Good. You could keep up an intelligent conversation on the subject?"

"I believe I could."

"Then hand me that little box from the mantelpiece."

He opened the lid and took out a small object most carefully wrapped in some fine Eastern silk. This he unfolded and disclosed a delicate little saucer of the most beautiful deep-blue colour.

"It needs careful handling, Watson. This is the real eggshell pottery of the Ming dynasty. No finer piece ever passed through Christie's. A complete set of this would be worth a king's ransom—in fact, it is doubtful if there is a complete set outside the Imperial Palace of Peking. The sight of this would drive a real connoisseur wild."

"What am I to do with it?"

Holmes handed me a card upon which was printed: "Dr. Hill Barton, 369 Half Moon Street."

"That is your name for the evening, Watson. You will call upon Baron Gruner. I know something of his habits, and at half-past eight he would probably be disengaged. A note will tell him in advance that you are about to call, and you will say that you are bringing him a specimen of an absolutely unique set of Ming china. You may as well be a medical man, since that is a part which you can play without duplicity. You are a collector, this set has come your way, you have heard of the Baron's interest in the subject, and you are not averse to selling at a price."

"What price?"

"Well asked, Watson. You would certainly fall down badly if you did not know the value of your own wares. This saucer was got for me by Sir James and comes, I understand, from the collection of his client. You will not exaggerate if you say that it could hardly be matched in the world."

"I could perhaps suggest that the set should be valued by an expert."

"Excellent, Watson! You scintillate to-day. Suggest Christie or Sotheby. Your delicacy prevents your putting a price for yourself."

"But if he won't see me?"

"Oh, yes, he will see you. He has the collection mania in its most acute form—and especially on this subject, on which he is an acknowledged authority. Sit down, Watson, and I will dictate the letter. No answer needed. You will merely say that you are coming, and why."

It was an admirable document, short, courteous, and stimulating to the curiosity of the connoisseur. A district messenger was duly dispatched with it. On the same evening, with the precious saucer in my hand and the card of Dr. Hill Barton in my pocket, I set off on my own adventure.

The beautiful house and grounds indicated that Baron Gruner was, as Sir James had said, a man of considerable wealth. A long winding drive, with banks of rare shrubs on either side, opened out into a great gravelled square adorned with statues. The place had been built by a South African gold king in the days of the great boom, and the long, low house with the turrets at the corners, though an architectural nightmare, was imposing in its size and solidity. A butler, who would have adorned a bench of bishops, showed me in and handed me over to a plushclad footman, who ushered me into the Baron's presence.

He was standing at the open front of a great case which stood between the windows and which contained part of his Chinese collection. He turned as I entered with a small brown vase in his hand.

"Pray sit down, Doctor," said he. "I was looking over my own treasures and wondering whether I could really afford to add to them. This little Tang specimen, which dates from the seventh century, would probably interest you. I am sure you never saw finer workmanship or a richer glaze. Have you the Ming saucer with you of which you spoke?"

I carefully unpacked it and handed it to him. He seated himself at his desk, pulled over the lamp, for it was growing dark, and set himself to examine it. As he did so the yellow light beat upon his own features, and I was able to study them at my ease.

He was certainly a remarkably handsome man. His European reputation for beauty was fully deserved. In figure he was not more than of middle size, but was built upon graceful and active lines. His face was swarthy, almost Oriental, with large, dark, languorous eyes which might easily hold an irresistible fascination for women. His hair and moustache were raven black, the latter short, pointed, and carefully waxed. His features were regular and pleasing, save only his straight, thin-lipped mouth. If ever I saw a murderer's mouth it was there—a cruel, hard gash in the face, compressed, inexorable, and terrible. He was ill-advised to train his moustache away from it, for it was Nature's danger-signal, set as a warning to his victims. His voice was engaging and his manners perfect. In age I should have put him at little over thirty, though his record afterwards showed that he was forty-two.

"Very fine—very fine indeed!" he said at last. "And you say you have a set of six to correspond. What puzzles me is that I should not have heard of such magnificent specimens. I only know of one in England to match this, and it is certainly not likely to be in the market. Would it be indiscreet if I were to ask you, Dr. Hill Barton, how you obtained this?"

"Does it really matter?" I asked with as careless an air as I could muster. "You can see that the piece is genuine, and as to the value, I am content to take an expert's valuation."

"Very mysterious," said he with a quick, suspicious flash of his dark eyes. "In dealing with objects of such value, one naturally wishes to know all about the transaction. That the piece is genuine is certain. I have no doubts at all about that. But suppose—I am bound to take every possibility into account—that it should prove afterwards that you had no right to sell?"

"I would guarantee you against any claim of the sort."

"That, of course, would open up the question as to what your guarantee was worth."

"My bankers would answer that."

"Quite so. And yet the whole transaction strikes me as rather unusual."

"You can do business or not," said I with indifference. "I have given you the first offer as I understood that you were a connoisseur, but I shall have no difficulty in other quarters."

"Who told you I was a connoisseur?"

"I was aware that you had written a book upon the subject."

"Have you read the book?"

"No."

"Dear me, this becomes more and more difficult for me to understand! You are a connoisseur and collector with a very valuable piece in your collection, and yet you have never troubled to consult the one book which would have told you the real meaning and value of what you held. How do you explain that?"

"I am a very busy man. I am a doctor in practice."

"That is no answer. If a man has a hobby he follows it up, whatever his other pursuits may be. You said in your note that you were a connoisseur."

"So I am."

"Might I ask you a few questions to test you? I am obliged to tell you, Doctor—if you are indeed a doctor—that the incident becomes more and more suspicious. I would ask you what do you know of the Emperor Shomu and how do you associate him with the Shoso-in near Nara? Dear me, does that puzzle you? Tell me a little about the Northern Wei dynasty and its place in the history of ceramics."

I sprang from my chair in simulated anger.

"This is intolerable, sir," said I. "I came here to do you a favour and not to be examined as if I were a schoolboy. My knowledge on these subjects may be second only to your own, but I certainly shall not answer questions which have been put in so offensive a way."

He looked at me steadily. The languor had gone from his eyes. They suddenly glared. There was a gleam of teeth from between those cruel lips.

"What is the game? You are here as a spy. You are an emissary of Holmes. This is a trick that you are playing upon me. The fellow is dying I hear, so he sends his tools to keep watch upon me. You've made your way in here without leave, and by God, you may find it harder to get out than to get in."

He had sprung to his feet, and I stepped back, bracing myself for an attack, for the man was beside himself with rage. He may have suspected me from the first; certainly this cross-examination had shown him the truth; but it was clear I could not hope to deceive him. He dived his hand into a side-drawer and rummaged furiously. Then something struck upon his ear, for he stood listening intently.

"Ah!" he cried. "Ah!" and dashed into the room behind him.

Two steps took me to the open door, and my mind will ever carry a clear picture of the scene within. The window leading out to the garden was wide open. Beside it, looking like some terrible ghost, his head girt with bloody bandages, his face drawn and white, stood Sherlock Holmes. The next instant he was through the gap, and I heard the crash of his body among the laurel bushes outside. With a howl of rage the master of the house rushed after him to the open window.

And then! It was done in an instant, and yet I clearly saw it. An arm—a woman's arm—shot out from among the leaves. At the same instant the Baron uttered a horrible cry—a yell which will always ring in my memory. He clapped his two hands to his face and rushed round the room, beating his head horribly against the walls. Then he fell upon the carpet, rolling and writhing, while scream after scream resounded through the house.

"Water! For God's sake, water!" was his cry.

I seized a carafe from a side-table and rushed to his aid. At the same moment the butler and several footmen ran in from the hall. I remember that one of them fainted as I knelt by the injured man and turned that awful face to the light of the lamp. The vitriol was eating into it everywhere and dripping from the ears and the chin. One eye was already white and glazed. The other was red and inflamed. The features which I had admired a few minutes before were now like some beautiful painting over which the artist has passed a wet and foul sponge. They were blurred, discoloured, inhuman, terrible.

In a few words I explained exactly what had occurred, so far as the vitriol attack was concerned. Some had climbed through the window and others had rushed out on to the lawn, but it was dark and it had begun to rain. Between his screams the victim raged and raved against the avenger. "It was that hell-cat, Kitty Winter!" he cried. "Oh, the she-devil! She shall pay for it! She shall pay! Oh, God in Heaven, this pain is more that I can bear!"

I bathed his face in oil, put cotton wadding on the raw surfaces, and administered a hypodermic of morphia. All suspicion of me had passed from his mind in the presence of this shock, and he clung to my hands as if I might have the power even yet to clear those dead-fish eyes which gazed up at me. I could have wept over the ruin had I not remembered very clearly the vile life which had led up to so hideous a change. It was loathsome to feel the pawing of his burning hands, and I was relieved when his family surgeon, closely followed by a specialist, came to relieve me of my charge. An Inspector of Police had also arrived, and to him I handed my real card. It would have been useless as well as foolish to do otherwise, for I was nearly as well known by sight at the Yard as Holmes himself. Then I left that house of gloom and terror. Within an hour I was at Baker Street.

Holmes was seated in his familiar chair, looking very

pale and exhausted. Apart from his injuries, even his iron nerves had been shocked by the events of the evening, and he listened with horror to my account of the Baron's transformation.

"The wages of sin, Watson—the wages of sin!" said he. "Sooner or later it will always come. God knows, there was sin enough," he added, taking up a brown volume from the table. "Here is the book the woman talked of. If this will not break off the marriage, nothing ever could. But it will, Watson. It must. No self-respecting woman could stand it."

"It is his love diary?"

"Or his lust diary. Call it what you will. The moment the woman told us of it I realized what a tremendous weapon was there if we could but lay our hands on it. I said nothing at the time to indicate my thoughts, for this woman might have given it away. But I brooded over it. Then this assault upon me gave me the chance of letting the Baron think that no precautions need be taken against me. That was all to the good. I would have waited a little longer, but his visit to America forced my hand. He would never have left so compromising a document behind him. Therefore we had to act at once. Burglary at night is impossible. He takes precautions. But there was a chance in the evening if I could only be sure that his attention was engaged. That was where you and your blue saucer came in. But I had to be sure of the position of the book, and I knew I had only a few minutes in which to act, for my time was limited by your knowledge of Chinese pottery. Therefore I gathered the girl up at the last moment. How could I guess what the little packet was that she carried so carefully under her cloak? I thought she had come altogether on my business, but it seems she had some of her own."

"He guessed I came from you."

"I feared he would. But you held him in play just long enough for me to get the book, though not long enough for an unobserved escape. Ah, Sir James, I am very glad you have come!"

Our courtly friend had appeared in answer to a previous summons. He listened with the deepest attention to Holmes's account of what had occurred.

"You have done wonders—wonders!" he cried when he had heard the narrative. "But if these injuries are as terrible as Dr. Watson describes, then surely our purpose of thwarting the marriage is sufficiently gained without the use of this horrible book."

Holmes shook his head.

"Women of the De Merville type do not act like that. She would love him the more as a disfigured martyr. No, no. It is his moral side, not his physical, which we have to destroy. That book will bring her back to earth—and I know nothing else that could. It is in his own writing. She cannot get past it."

Sir James carried away both it and the precious saucer. As I was myself overdue, I went down with him into the street. A brougham was waiting for him. He sprang in, gave a hurried order to the cockaded coachman, and drove swiftly away. He flung his overcoat half out of the window to cover the armorial bearings upon the panel, but I had seen them in the glare of our fanlight none the less. I gasped with surprise. Then I turned back and ascended the stair to Holmes's room.

"I have found out who our client is," I cried, bursting with my great news. "Why, Holmes, it is—"

"It is a loyal friend and a chivalrous gentleman," said Holmes, holding up a restraining hand. "Let that now and forever be enough for us."

I do not know how the incriminating book was used. Sir James may have managed it. Or it is more probable that so delicate a task was entrusted to the young lady's father. The effect, at any rate, was all that could be desired. Three days later appeared a paragraph in the *Morning Post* to say that the marriage between Baron Adelbert Gruner and Miss Violet de Merville would not take place. The same paper had the first police-court hearing of the proceedings against Miss Kitty Winter on the grave charge of vitriol-throwing. Such extenuating circumstances came out in the trial that the sentence, as will be remembered, was the lowest that was possible for such an offence. Sherlock Holmes was threatened with a prosecution for burglary, but when an object is good and a client is sufficiently illustrious, even the rigid British law becomes human and elastic. My friend has not yet stood in the dock.

The Adventure of
Shoscombe Old Place

Sherlock Holmes had been bending for a long time over a low-power microscope. Now he straightened himself up and looked round at me in triumph.

"It is glue, Watson," said he. "Unquestionably it is glue. Have a look at these scattered objects in the field!"

I stooped to the eyepiece and focussed for my vision.

"Those hairs are threads from a tweed coat. The irregular grey masses are dust. There are epithelial scales on the left. Those brown blobs in the centre are undoubtedly glue."

"Well," I said, laughing, "I am prepared to take your word for it. Does anything depend upon it?"

"It is a very fine demonstration," he answered. "In the St. Pancras case you may remember that a cap was found beside the dead policeman. The accused man denies that it is his. But he is a picture-frame maker who habitually handles glue."

"Is it one of your cases?"

"No; my friend, Merivale, of the Yard, asked me to look into the case. Since I ran down that coiner by the zinc and copper filings in the seam of his cuff they have begun to realize the importance of the microscope." He looked impatiently at his watch. "I had a new client calling, but he is overdue. By the way, Watson, you know something of racing?"

"I ought to. I pay for it with about half my wound pension."

"Then I'll make you my *Handy Guide to the Turf.* What about Sir Robert Norberton? Does the name recall anything?"

"Well, I should say so. He lives at Shoscombe Old Place, and I know it well, for my summer quarters were down there once. Norberton nearly came within your province once."

"How was that?"

"It was when he horsewhipped Sam Brewer, the well-known Curzon Street money-lender, on Newmarket Heath. He nearly killed the man."

"Ah, he sounds interesting! Does he often indulge in that way?"

"Well, he has the name of being a dangerous man. He is about the most daredevil rider in England—second in the Grand National a few years back. He is one of those men who have overshot their true generation. He should have been a buck in the days of the Regency—a boxer, an athlete, a plunger on the turf, a lover of fair ladies, and by all account, so far down Queer Street that he may never find his way back again."

"Capital, Watson! A thumb-nail sketch. I seem to know the man. Now, can you give me some idea of Shoscombe Old Place?"

"Only that it is in the centre of Shoscombe Park, and that the famous Shoscombe stud and training quarters are to be found there."

"And the head trainer," said Holmes, "is John Mason. You need not look surprised at my knowledge, Watson, for this is a letter from him which I am unfolding. But let us have some more about Shoscombe. I seem to have struck a rich vein."

"There are the Shoscombe spaniels," said I. "You hear of them at every dog show. The most exclusive breed in England. They are the special pride of the lady of Shoscombe Old Place."

"Sir Robert Norberton's wife, I presume!"

"Sir Robert has never married. Just as well, I think, considering his prospects. He lives with his widowed sister, Lady Beatrice Falder."

"You mean that she lives with him?"

"No, no. The place belonged to her late husband, Sir James. Norberton has no claim on it at all. It is only a life interest and reverts to her husband's brother. Meantime, she draws the rents every year."

"And brother Robert, I suppose, spends the said rents?"

"That is about the size of it. He is a devil of a fellow and must lead her a most uneasy life. Yet I have heard that she is devoted to him. But what is amiss at Shoscombe?"

"Ah, that is just what I want to know. And here, I expect, is the man who can tell us."

The door had opened and the page had shown in a tall, clean-shaven man with the firm, austere expression which is only seen upon those who have to control horses or boys. Mr. John Mason had many of both under his sway, and he looked equal to the task. He bowed with cold self-possession and seated himself upon the chair to which Holmes had waved him.

"You had my note, Mr. Holmes?"

"Yes, but it explained nothing."

"It was too delicate a thing for me to put the details on paper. And too complicated. It was only face to face I could do it."

"Well, we are at your disposal."

"First of all, Mr. Holmes, I think that my employer, Sir Robert, has gone mad."

Holmes raised his eyebrows. "This is Baker Street, not Harley Street," said he. "But why do you say so?"

"Well, sir, when a man does one queer thing, or two queer things, there may be a meaning to it, but when everything he does is queer, then you begin to wonder. I believe Shoscombe Prince and the Derby have turned his brain."

"That is a colt you are running?"

"The best in England, Mr. Holmes. I should know, if anyone does. Now, I'll be plain with you, for I know you are gentlemen of honour and that it won't go beyond the room. Sir Robert has got to win this Derby. He's up to the neck, and it's his last chance. Everything he could raise or borrow is on the horse—and at fine odds, too! You can get forties now, but is was nearer the hundred when he began to back him."

"But how is that if the horse is so good?"

"The public don't know how good he is. Sir Robert has been too clever for the touts. He has the Prince's half-brother out for spins. You can't tell 'em apart. But there are two lengths in a furlong between them when it comes to a gallop. He thinks of nothing but the horse and the race. His whole life is on it. He's holding off the Jews till then. If the Prince fails him he is done."

"It seems a rather desperate gamble, but where does the madness come in?"

"Well, first of all, you have only to look at him. I don't believe he sleeps at night. He is down at the stables at all hours. His eyes are wild. It has all been too much for his nerves. Then there is his conduct to Lady Beatrice!"

"Ah! What is that?"

"They have always been the best of friends. They had the same tastes, the two of them, and she loved the horses as much as he did. Every day at the same hour she would drive down to see them—and, above all, she loved the Prince. He would prick up his ears when he heard the wheels on the gravel, and he would trot out each morning to the carriage to get his lump of sugar. But that's all over now."

"Why?"

"Well, she seems to have lost all interest in the horses. For a week now she has driven past the stables with never so much as 'Good-morning'!"

"You think there has been a quarrel?"

"And a bitter, savage, spiteful quarrel at that. Why else would he give away her pet spaniel that she loved as if he were her child? He gave it a few days ago to old Barnes, what keeps the Green Dragon, three miles off, at Crendall."

"That certainly did seem strange."

"Of course, with her weak heart and dropsy one couldn't expect that she could get about with him, but he spent two hours every evening in her room. He might well do what he could, for she has been a rare good friend to him. But that's all over, too. He never goes near her. And she takes it to heart. She is brooding and sulky and drinking, Mr. Holmes—drinking like a fish."

"Did she drink before this estrangement?"

"Well, she took her glass, but now it is often a whole bottle of an evening. So Stephens, the butler, told me. It's all changed, Mr. Holmes, and there is something damned rotten about it. But then again, what is Master doing down at the old church crypt at night? And who is the man that meets him there?"

Holmes rubbed his hands.

"Go on, Mr. Mason. You get more and more interesting."

"It was the butler who saw him go. Twelve o'clock at night and raining hard. So next night I was up at the house and, sure enough, Master was off again. Stephens and I went after him, but it was jumpy work, for it would have been a bad job if he had seen us. He's a terrible man with his fists if he gets started, and no respecter of persons. So we were shy of getting too near, but we marked him down all right. It was the haunted crypt that he was making for, and there was a man waiting for him there."

"What is this haunted crypt?"

"Well, sir, there is an old ruined chapel in the park. It is so old that nobody could fix its date. And under it there's a crypt which has a bad name among us. It's a dark, damp, lonely place by day, but there are few in that county that would have the nerve to go near it at night. But Master's not afraid. He never feared anything in his life. But what is he doing there in the night-time?"

"Wait a bit!" said Holmes. "You say there is another man there. It must be one of your own stablemen, or someone from the house! Surely you have only to spot who it is and question him?"

"It's no one I know."

"How can you say that?"

"Because I have seen him, Mr. Holmes. It was on that second night. Sir Robert turned and passed us—me and Stephens, quaking in the bushes like two bunny-rabbits, for there was a bit of moon that night. But we could hear the other moving about behind. We were not afraid of him. So we up when Sir Robert was gone and pretended we were just having a walk like in the moonlight, and so we came right on him as casual and innocent as you please. 'Hullo, mate! Who may you be?' says I. I guess he had not heard us coming, so he looked over his shoulder with a face as if he had seen the devil coming out of hell. He let out a yell, and away he went as hard as he could lick it in the darkness. He could run!—I'll give him that. In a minute he was out of sight and hearing, and who he was, or what he was, we never found."

"But you saw him clearly in the moonlight?"

"Yes, I would swear to his yellow face—a mean dog, I should say. What could he have in common with Sir Robert?"

Holmes sat for some time lost in thought.

"Who keeps Lady Beatrice Falder company?" he asked at last.

"There is her maid, Carrie Evans. She has been with her this five years."

"And is, no doubt, devoted?"

Mr. Mason shuffled uncomfortably.

"She's devoted enough," he answered at last. "But I won't say to whom."

"Ah!" said Holmes.

"I can't tell tales out of school."

"I quite understand, Mr. Mason. Of course, the situation is clear enough. From Dr. Watson's description of Sir

Robert I can realize that no woman is safe from him. Don't you think the quarrel between brother and sister may lie there?"

"Well, the scandal has been pretty clear for a long time."

"But she may not have seen it before. Let us suppose that she has suddenly found it out. She wants to get rid of the woman. Her brother will not permit it. The invalid, with her weak heart and inability to get about, has no means of enforcing her will. The hated maid is still tied to her. The lady refuses to speak, sulks, takes to drink. Sir Robert in his anger takes her pet spaniel away from her. Does not all this hang together?"

"Well, it might do—so far as it goes."

"Exactly! As far as it goes. How would all that bear upon the visits by night to the old crypt? We can't fit that into our plot."

"No, sir, and there is something more that I can't fit in. Why should Sir Robert want to dig up a dead body?"

Holmes sat up abruptly.

"We only found it out yesterday—after I had written to you. Yesterday Sir Robert had gone to London, so Stephens and I went down to the crypt. It was all in order, sir, except that in one corner was a bit of a human body."

"You informed the police, I suppose?"

Our visitor smiled grimly.

"Well, sir, I think it would hardly interest them. It was just the head and a few bones of a mummy. It may have been a thousand years old. But it wasn't there before. That I'll swear, and so will Stephens. It had been stowed away in a corner and covered over with a board, but that corner had always been empty before."

"What did you do with it?"

"Well, we just left it there."

"That was wise. You say Sir Robert was away yesterday. Has he returned?"

"We expect him back to-day."

"When did Sir Robert give away his sister's dog?"

"It was just a week ago to-day. The creature was howling outside the old well-house, and Sir Robert was in one of his tantrums that morning. He caught it up, and I thought he would have killed it. Then he gave it to Sandy Bain, the jockey, and told him to take the dog to old Barnes at the Green Dragon, for he never wished to see it again."

Holmes sat for some time in silent thought. He had lit the oldest and foulest of his pipes.

"I am not clear yet what you want me to do in this matter, Mr. Mason," he said at last. "Can't you make it more definite?"

"Perhaps this will make it more definite, Mr. Holmes," said our visitor.

He took a paper from his pocket, and unwrapping it carefully, he exposed a charred fragment of bone.

Holmes examined it with interest.

"Where did you get it?"

"There is a central heating furnace in the cellar under Lady Beatrice's room. It's been off for some time, but Sir Robert complained of cold and had it on again. Harvey runs it—he's one of my lads. This very morning he came to me with this which he found raking out the cinders. He didn't like the look of it."

"Nor do I," said Holmes. "What do you make of it, Watson?"

It was burned to a black cinder, but there could be no question as to its anatomical significance.

"It's the upper condyle of a human femur," said I.

"Exactly!" Holmes had become very serious. "When does this lad tend to the furnace?"

"He makes it up every evening and then leaves it."

"Then anyone could visit it during the night?"

"Yes, sir."

"Can you enter it from outside?"

"There is one door from outside. There is another which leads up by a stair to the passage in which Lady Beatrice's room is situated."

"These are deep waters, Mr. Mason; deep and rather dirty. You say that Sir Robert was not at home last night?"

"No, sir."

"Then, whoever was burning bones, it was not he."

"That's true, sir."

"What is the name of that inn you spoke of?"

"The Green Dragon."

"Is there good fishing in that part of Berkshire?" The honest trainer showed very clearly upon his face that he was convinced that yet another lunatic had come into his harassed life.

"Well, sir, I've heard there are trout in the mill-stream and pike in the Hall lake."

"That's good enough. Watson and I are famous fishermen—are we not, Watson? You may address us in future at the Green Dragon. We should reach it to-night. I need not say that we don't want to see you, Mr. Mason, but a note will reach us, and no doubt I could find you if I want you. When we have gone a little farther into the matter I will let you have a considered opinion."

Thus it was that on a bright May evening Holmes and I found ourselves alone in a first-class carriage and bound for the little "half-on-demand" station of Shoscombe. The rack above us was covered with a formidable litter of rods, reels, and baskets. On reaching our destination a short drive took us to an old-fashioned tavern, where a sporting host, Josiah Barnes, entered eagerly into our plans for the extirpation of the fish of the neighbourhood.

"What about the Hall lake and the chance of a pike?" said Holmes.

The face of the inn-keeper clouded.

"That wouldn't do, sir. You might chance to find yourself in the lake before you were through."

"How's that, then?"

"It's Sir Robert, sir. He's terrible jealous of touts. If you two strangers were as near his training quarters as that he'd be after you as sure as fate. He ain't taking no chances, Sir Robert ain't."

"I've heard he has a horse entered for the Derby."

"Yes, and a good colt, too. He carries all our money for the race, and all Sir Robert's into the bargain. By the way"—he looked at us with thoughtful eyes—"I suppose you ain't on the turf yourselves?"

"No, indeed. Just two weary Londoners who badly need some good Berkshire air."

"Well, you are in the right place for that. There is a deal of it lying about. But mind what I have told you about Sir Robert. He's the sort that strikes first and speaks afterwards. Keep clear of the park."

"Surely, Mr. Barnes! We certainly shall. By the way, that was a most beautiful spaniel that was whining in the hall."

"I should say it was. That was the real Shoscombe breed. There ain't a better in England."

"I am a dog-fancier myself," said Holmes. "Now, if it is a fair question, what would a prize dog like that cost?"

"More than I could pay, sir. It was Sir Robert himself who gave me this one. That's why I have to keep it on a lead. It would be off to the Hall in a jiffy if I gave it its head."

"We are getting some cards in our hand, Watson," said Holmes when the landlord had left us. "It's not an easy one to play, but we may see our way in a day or two. By the way, Sir Robert is still in London, I hear. We might, perhaps, enter the sacred domain to-night without fear of bodily assault. There are one or two points on which I should like reassurance."

"Have you any theory, Holmes?"

"Only this, Watson, that something happened a week or so ago which has cut deep into the life of the Shoscombe household. What is that something? We can only guess at it from its effects. They seem to be of a curiously mixed character. But that should surely help us. It is only the colourless, uneventful case which is hopeless.

"Let us consider our data. The brother no longer visits the beloved invalid sister. He gives away her favourite dog. Her dog, Watson! Does that suggest nothing to you?"

"Nothing but the brother's spite."

"Well, it might be so. Or—well, there is an alternative. Now to continue our review of the situation from the time that the quarrel, if there is a quarrel, began. The lady keeps her room, alters her habits, is not seen save when she drives out with her maid, refuses to stop at the stables to greet her favourite horse, and apparently takes to drink. That covers the case, does it not?"

"Save for the business in the crypt."

"That is another line of thought. There are two, and I beg you will not tangle them. Line A, which concerns Lady Beatrice, has a vaguely sinister flavour, has it not?"

"I can make nothing of it."

"Well, now, let us take up line B, which concerns Sir Robert. He is mad keen upon winning the Derby. He is in the hands of the Jews and may at any moment be sold up and his racing stables seized by his creditors. He is a daring and desperate man. He derives his income from his sister. His sister's maid is his willing tool. So far we seem to be on fairly safe ground, do we not?"

"But the crypt?"

"Ah, yes, the crypt! Let us suppose, Watson—it is merely a scandalous supposition, a hypothesis put forward for argument's sake—that Sir Robert has done away with his sister."

"My dear Holmes, it is out of the question."

"Very possibly, Watson. Sir Robert is a man of an honourable stock. But you do occasionally find a carrion crow among the eagles. Let us for a moment argue upon this supposition. He could not fly the country until he had realized his fortune, and that fortune could only be realized by bringing off this coup with Shoscombe Prince. Therefore, he has still to stand his ground. To do this he would have to dispose of the body of his victim, and he would also have to find a substitute who would impersonate her. With the maid as his confidante that would not be impossible. The woman's body might be conveyed to the crypt, which is a place so seldom visited, and it might be secretly destroyed at night in the furnace, leaving behind it such evidence as we have already seen. What say you to that, Watson?"

"Well, it is all possible if you grant the original monstrous supposition."

"I think that there is a small experiment which we may try to-morrow, Watson, in order to throw some light on the matter. Meanwhile, if we mean to keep up our characters, I suggest that we have our host in for a glass of his own wine and hold some high converse upon eels and dace, which seems to be the straight road to his affections. We may chance to come upon some useful local gossip in the process."

In the morning Holmes discovered that we had come without our spoon-bait for jack, which absolved us from fishing for the day. About eleven o'clock we started for a walk, and he obtained leave to take the black spaniel with us.

"This is the place," said he as we came to two high park gates with heraldic griffins towering above them. "About midday, Mr. Barnes informs me, the old lady takes a drive, and the carriage must slow down while the gates are opened. When it comes through, and before it gathers speed, I want you, Watson, to stop the coachman with some question. Never mind me. I shall stand behind this holly-bush and see what I can see."

It was not a long vigil. Within a quarter of an hour we saw the big open yellow barouche coming down the long avenue, with two splendid, high-stepping grey carriage horses in the shafts. Holmes crouched behind his bush with the dog. I stood unconcernedly swinging a cane in the roadway. A keeper ran out and the gates swung open.

The carriage had slowed to a walk, and I was able to get a good look at the occupants. A highly coloured young woman with flaxen hair and impudent eyes sat on the left. At her right was an elderly person with rounded back and a huddle of shawls about her face and shoulders which proclaimed the invalid. When the horses reached the highroad I held up my hand with an authoritative gesture, and as the coachman pulled up I inquired if Sir Robert was at Shoscombe Old Place.

At the same moment Holmes stepped out and released the spaniel. With a joyous cry it dashed forward to the carriage and sprang upon the step. Then in a moment its eager greeting changed to furious rage, and it snapped at the black skirt above it.

"Drive on! Drive on!" shrieked a harsh voice. The coachman lashed the horses, and we were left standing in the roadway.

"Well, Watson, that's done it," said Holmes as he fastened the lead to the neck of the excited spaniel. "He thought it was his mistress, and he found it was a stranger. Dogs don't make mistakes."

"But it was the voice of a man!" I cried.

"Exactly! We have added one card to our hand, Watson, but it needs careful playing, all the same."

My companion seemed to have no further plans for the day, and we did actually use our fishing tackle in the mill-stream, with the result that we had a dish of trout for our supper. It was only after that meal that Holmes showed signs of renewed activity. Once more we found ourselves upon the same road as in the morning, which led us to the park gates. A tall, dark figure was awaiting us there, who proved to be our London acquaintance, Mr. John Mason, the trainer.

"Good-evening, gentlemen," said he. "I got your note, Mr. Holmes. Sir Robert has not returned yet, but I hear that he is expected to-night."

"How far is this crypt from the house?" asked Holmes.

"A good quarter of a mile."

"Then I think we can disregard him altogether."

"I can't afford to do that, Mr. Holmes. The moment he arrives he will want to see me to get the last news of Shoscombe Prince."

"I see! In that case we must work without you, Mr. Mason. You can show us the crypt and then leave us."

It was pitch-dark and without a moon, but Mason led us over the grass-lands until a dark mass loomed up in front of us which proved to be the ancient chapel. We entered the broken gap which was once the porch, and our guide, stumbling among heaps of loose masonry, picked his way to the corner of the building, where a steep stair led down into the crypt. Striking a match, he illuminated the melancholy place—dismal and evil-smelling, with ancient crumbling walls of rough-hewn stone, and piles of coffins, some of lead and some of stone, extending upon one side right up to the arched and groined roof which lost itself in the shadows above our heads. Holmes had lit his lantern, which shot a tiny tunnel of vivid yellow light upon the mournful scene. Its rays were reflected back from the coffin-plates, many of them adorned with the griffin and coronet of this old family which carried its honours even to the gate of Death.

"You spoke of some bones, Mr. Mason. Could you show them before you go?"

"They are here in this corner." The trainer strode across and then stood in silent surprise as our light was turned upon the place. "They are gone," said he.

"So I expected," said Holmes, chuckling. "I fancy the ashes of them might even now be found in that oven which had already consumed a part."

"But why in the world would anyone want to burn the bones of a man who has been dead a thousand years?" asked John Mason.

"That is what we are here to find out," said Holmes. "It may mean a long search, and we need not detain you. I fancy that we shall get our solution before morning."

When John Mason had left us, Holmes set to work making a very careful examination of the graves, ranging from a very ancient one, which appeared to be Saxon, in the centre, through a long line of Norman Hugos and Odos, until we reached the Sir William and Sir Denis Falder of the eighteenth century. It was an hour or more before Holmes came to a leaden coffin standing on end before the entrance to the vault. I heard his little cry of satisfaction and was aware from his hurried but purposeful movements that he had reached a goal. With his lens he was eagerly examining the edges of the heavy lid. Then he drew from his pocket a short jemmy, a box-opener, which he thrust into a chink, levering back the whole front, which seemed to be secured by only a couple of clamps. There was a rending, tearing sound as it gave way, but it had hardly hinged back and partly revealed the contents before we had an unforeseen interruption.

Someone was walking in the chapel above. It was the firm, rapid step of one who came with a definite purpose and knew well the ground upon which he walked. A light streamed down the stairs, and an instant later the man who bore it was framed in the Gothic archway. He was a terrible figure, huge in stature and fierce in manner. A large stable-lantern which he held in front of him shone upward upon a strong, heavily moustached face and angry eyes, which glared round him into every recess of the vault, finally fixing themselves with a deadly stare upon my companion and myself.

"Who the devil are you?" he thundered. "And what are you doing upon my property?" Then, as Holmes returned no answer, he took a couple of steps forward and raised a heavy stick which he carried. "Do you hear me?" he cried. "Who are you? What are you doing here?" His cudgel quivered in the air.

But instead of shrinking Holmes advanced to meet him.

"I also have a question to ask you, Sir Robert," he said in his sternest tone. "Who is this? And what is it doing here?"

He turned and tore open the coffin-lid behind him. In the glare of the lantern I saw a body swathed in a sheet from head to foot, with dreadful, witch-like features, all nose and chin, projecting at one end, the dim, glazed eyes staring from a discoloured and crumbling face.

The Baronet had staggered back with a cry and supported himself against a stone sarcophagus.

"How came you to know of this?" he cried. And then, with some return of his truculent manner: "What business is it of yours?"

"My name is Sherlock Holmes," said my companion. "Possibly it is familiar to you. In any case, my business is that of every other good citizen—to uphold the law. It seems to me that you have much to answer for."

Sir Robert glared for a moment, but Holmes's quiet voice and cool, assured manner had their effect.

"'Fore God, Mr. Holmes, it's all right," said he. "Appearances are against me, I'll admit, but I could act no otherwise."

"I should be happy to think so, but I fear your explanations must be before the police."

Sir Robert shrugged his broad shoulders.

"Well, if it must be, it must. Come up to the house and you can judge for yourself how the matter stands."

A quarter of an hour later we found ourselves in what I judge, from the lines of polished barrels behind glass covers, to be the gun-room of the old house. It was comfortably furnished, and here Sir Robert left us for a few moments. When he returned he had two companions with him; the one, the florid young woman whom we had seen in the carriage; the other, a small rat-faced man with a disagreeably furtive manner. These two wore an appearance of utter bewilderment, which showed that the Baronet had not yet had time to explain to them the turn events had taken.

"There," said Sir Robert with a wave of his hand, "are Mr. and Mrs. Norlett. Mrs. Norlett, under her maiden name of Evans, has for some years been my sister's confidential maid. I have brought them here because I feel that my best course is to explain the true position to you, and they are the two people upon earth who can substantiate what I say."

"Is this necessary, Sir Robert? Have you thought what you are doing?" cried the woman.

"As to me, I entirely disclaim all responsibility," said her husband.

Sir Robert gave him a glance of contempt. "I will take all responsibility," said he. "Now, Mr. Holmes, listen to a plain statement of the facts.

"You have clearly gone pretty deeply into my affairs or I should not have found you where I did. Therefore, you know already, in all probability, that I am running a dark horse for the Derby and that everything depends upon my success. If I win, all is easy. If I lose—well, I dare not think of that!"

"I understand the position." said Holmes.

"I am dependent upon my sister, Lady Beatrice, for everything. But it is well known that her interest in the estate is for her own life only. For myself, I am deeply in the hands of the Jews. I have always known that if my sister were to die my creditors would be on to my estate like a flock of vultures. Everything would be seized—my stables, my horses—everything. Well, Mr. Holmes, my sister *did* die just a week ago."

"And you told no one!"

"What could I do? Absolute ruin faced me. If I could stave things off for three weeks all would be well. Her maid's husband—this man here—is an actor. It came into our heads—it came into my head—that he could for that short period personate my sister. It was but a case of appearing daily in the carriage, for no one need enter her room save the maid. It was not difficult to arrange. My sister died of the dropsy which had long afflicted her."

"That will be for a coroner to decide."

"Her doctor would certify that for months her symptoms have threatened such an end."

"Well, what did you do?"

"The body could not remain there. On the first night Norlett and I carried it out to the old well-house, which is now never used. We were followed, however, by her pet spaniel, which yapped continually at the door, so I felt some safer place was needed. I got rid of the spaniel, and we carried the body to the crypt of the church. There was no indignity or irreverence, Mr. Holmes. I do not feel that I have wronged the dead."

"Your conduct seems to me inexcusable, Sir Robert."

The Baronet shook his head impatiently. "It is easy to preach," said he. "Perhaps you would have felt differently if you had been in my position. One cannot see all one's hopes and all one's plans shattered at the last moment and make no effort to save them. It seemed to me that it would be no unworthy resting-place if we put her for the time in one of the coffins of her husband's ancestors lying in what is still consecrated ground. We opened such a coffin, removed the contents, and placed her as you have seen her. As to the old relics which we took out, we could not leave them on the floor of the crypt. Norlett and I removed them, and he descended at night and burned them in the central furnace. There is my story, Mr. Holmes, though how you forced my hand so that I have to tell it is more than I can say."

Holmes sat for some time lost in thought.

"There is one flaw in your narrative, Sir Robert," he said at last. "Your bets on the race, and therefore your hopes for the future, would hold good even if your creditors seized your estate."

"The horse would be part of the estate. What do they care for my bets? As likely as not they would not run him at all. My chief creditor is, unhappily, my most bitter enemy—a rascally fellow, Sam Brewer, whom I was once compelled to horsewhip on Newmarket Heath. Do you suppose that he would try to save me?"

"Well, Sir Robert," said Holmes, rising, "this matter must, of course, be referred to the police. It was my duty to bring the facts to light, and there I must leave it. As to the morality or decency of your conduct, it is not for me to express an opinion. It is nearly midnight, Watson, and I think we may make our way back to our humble abode."

It is generally known now that this singular episode ended upon a happier note than Sir Robert's actions deserved. Shoscombe Prince did win the Derby, the sporting owner did net eighty thousand pounds in bets, and the creditors did hold their hand until the race was over, when they were paid in full, and enough was left to re-establish Sir Robert in a fair position in life. Both police and coroner took a lenient view of the transaction, and beyond a mild censure for the delay in registering the lady's decease, the lucky owner got away scatheless from this strange incident in a career which has now outlived its shadows and promises to end in an honoured old age.

The Adventure of the
Lion's Mane

It is a most singular thing that a problem which was certainly as abstruse and unusual as any which I have faced in my long professional career should have come to me after my retirement, and be brought, as it were, to my very door. It occurred after my withdrawal to my little Sussex home, when I had given myself up entirely to that soothing life of Nature for which I had so often yearned during the long years spent amid the gloom of London. At this period of my life the good Watson had passed almost beyond my ken. An occasional week-end visit was the most that I ever saw of him. Thus I must act as my own chronicler. Ah! Had he but been with me, how much he might have made of so wonderful a happening and of my eventual triumph against every difficulty! As it is, however, I must needs tell my tale in my own plain way, showing by my words each step upon the difficult road which lay before me as I searched for the mystery of the Lion's Mane.

My villa is situated upon the southern slope of the downs, commanding a great view of the Channel. At this point the coast-line is entirely of chalk cliffs, which can only be descended by a single, long, tortuous path, which is steep and slippery. At the bottom of the path lie a hundred yards of pebbles and shingle, even when the tide is at full. Here and there, however, there are curves and hollows which make splendid swimming-pools filled afresh with each flow. This admirable beach extends for some miles in each direction, save only at one point where the little cove and village of Fulworth break the line.

My house is lonely. I, my old housekeeper, and my bees have the estate all to ourselves. Half a mile off, however, is Harold Stackhurst's well-known coaching establishment, The Gables, quite a large place, which contains some score of young fellows preparing for various professions, with a staff of several masters. Stackhurst himself was a well-known rowing Blue in his day, and an excellent all-round scholar. He and I were always friendly from the day I came to the coast, and he was the one man who was on such terms with me that we could drop in on each other in the evenings without an invitation.

Towards the end of July, 1907, there was a severe gale, the wind blowing up-channel, heaping the seas to the base of the cliffs and leaving a lagoon at the turn of the tide. On the morning of which I speak the wind had abated, and all Nature was newly washed and fresh. It was impossible to work upon so delightful a day, and I strolled out before breakfast to enjoy the exquisite air. I walked along the cliff path which led to the steep descent to the beach. As I walked I heard a shout behind me, and there was Harold Stackhurst waving his hand in cheery greeting.

"What a morning, Mr. Holmes! I thought I should see you out."

"Going for a swim, I see."

"At your old tricks again," he laughed, patting his bulging pocket. "Yes. McPherson started early, and I expect I may find him there."

Fitzroy McPherson was the science master, a fine up-standing young fellow whose life had been crippled by heart trouble following rheumatic fever. He was a natural athlete, however, and excelled in every game which did not throw too great a strain upon him. Summer and winter he went for his swim, and as I am a swimmer myself, I have often joined him.

At this moment we saw the man himself. His head showed above the edge of the cliff where the path ends.

Then his whole figure appeared at the top, staggering like a drunken man. The next instant he threw up his hands and with a terrible cry, fell upon his face. Stackhurst and I rushed forward—it may have been fifty yards—and turned him on his back. He was obviously dying. Those glazed sunken eyes and dreadful livid cheecks could mean nothing else. One glimmer of life came into his face for an instant, and he uttered two or three words with an eager air of warning. They were slurred and indistinct, but to my ear the last of them, which burst in a shriek from his lips, were "the Lion's Mane." It was utterly irrelevant and unintelligible, and yet I could twist the sound into no other sense. Then he half raised himself from the ground, threw his arms into the air, and fell forward on his side. He was dead.

My companion was paralyzed by the sudden horror of it, but I, as may well be imagined, had every sense on the alert. And I had need, for it was speedily evident that we were in the presence of an extraordinary case. The man was dressed only in his Burberry overcoat, his trousers, and an unlaced pair of canvas shoes. As he fell over, his Burberry, which had been simply thrown round his shoulders, slipped off, exposing his trunk. We stared at it in amazement. His back was covered with dark red lines as though he had been terribly flogged by a thin wire scourge. The instrument with which this punishment had been inflicted was clearly flexible, for the long, angry weals curved round his shoulders and ribs. There was blood dripping down his chin, for he had bitten through his lower lip in the paroxysm of his agony. His drawn and distorted face told how terrible that agony had been.

I was kneeling and Stackhurst standing by the body when a shadow fell across us, and we found that Ian Murdoch was by our side. Murdoch was the mathematical coach at the establishment, a tall, dark, thin man, so taciturn and aloof that none can be said to have been his friend. He seemed to live in some high, abstract region of surds and conic sections, with little to connect him with ordinary life. He was looked upon as an oddity by the students, and would have been their butt, but there was some strange outlandish blood in the man, which showed itself not only in his coal-black eyes and swarthy face but also in occasional outbreaks of temper, which could only be described as ferocious. On one occasion, being plagued by a little dog belonging to McPherson, he had caught the creature up and hurled it through the plate-glass window, an action for which Stackhurst would certainly have given him his dismissal had he not been a very valuable teacher. Such was the strange complex man who now appeared beside us. He seemed to be honestly shocked at the sight before him, though the incident of the dog may show that there was no great sympathy between the dead man and himself.

"Poor fellow! Poor fellow! What can I do? How can I help?"

"Were you with him? Can you tell us what has happened?"

"No, no, I was late this morning. I was not on the beach at all. I have come straight from The Gables. What can I do?"

"You can hurry to the police-station at Fulworth. Report the matter at once."

Without a word he made off at top speed, and I proceeded to take the matter in hand, while Stackhurst, dazed at this tragedy, remained by the body. My first task naturally was to note who was on the beach. From the top of the path I could see the whole sweep of it, and it was absolutely deserted save that two or three dark figures could be seen far away moving towards the village of Fulworth. Having satisfied myself upon this point, I walked slowly down the path. There was clay or soft marl mixed with the chalk, and every here and there I saw the same footstep, both ascending and descending. No one else had gone down to the beach by this track that morning. At one place I observed the print of an open hand with the fingers towards the incline. This could only mean that poor Mc-

Pherson had fallen as he ascended. There were rounded depressions, too, which suggested that he had come down upon his knees more than once. At the bottom of the path was the considerable lagoon left by the retreating tide. At the side of it McPherson had undressed, for there lay his towel on a rock. It was folded and dry, so that it would seem that, after all, he had never entered the water. Once or twice as I hunted round amid the hard shingle I came on little patches of sand where the print of his canvas shoe, and also of his naked foot, could be seen. The latter fact proved that he had made all ready to bathe, though the towel indicated that he had not actually done so.

And here was the problem clearly defined—as strange a one as had ever confronted me. The man had not been on the beach more than a quarter of an hour at the most. Stackhurst had followed him from The Gables, so there could be no doubt about that. He had gone to bathe and had stripped, as the naked footsteps showed. Then he had suddenly huddled on his clothes again—they were all dishevelled and unfastened—and he had returned without bathing, or at any rate without drying himself. And the reason for his change of purpose had been that he had been scourged in some savage, inhuman fashion, tortured until he bit his lip through in his agony, and was left with only strength enough to crawl away and to die. Who had done this barbarous deed? There were, it is true, small grottos and caves in the base of the cliffs, but the low sun shone directly into them, and there was no place for concealment. Then, again, there were those distant figures on the beach. They seemed too far away to have been connected with the crime, and the broad lagoon in which McPherson had intended to bathe lay between him and them, lapping up to the rocks. On the sea two or three fishing-boats were at no great distance. Their occupants might be examined at our leisure. There were several roads for inquiry, but none which led to any very obvious goal.

When I at last returned to the body I found that a little group of wondering folk had gathered round it. Stackhurst was, of course, still there, and Ian Murdoch had just arrived with Anderson, the village constable, a big, ginger-moustached man of the slow, solid Sussex breed—a breed which covers much good sense under a heavy, silent exterior. He listened to everything, took note of all we said, and finally drew me aside.

"I'd be glad of your advice, Mr. Holmes. This is a big thing for me to handle, and I'll hear of it from Lewes if I go wrong."

I advised him to send for his immediate superior and for a doctor; also to allow nothing to be moved, and as few fresh footmarks as possible to be made, until they came. In the meantime I searched the dead man's pockets. There were his handkerchief, a large knife, and a small folding card-case. From this projected a slip of paper, which I unfolded and handed to the constable. There was written on it in a scrawling, feminine hand:

> I will be there, you may be sure.
>
> MAUDIE

It read like a love affair, an assignation, though when and where were a blank. The constable replaced it in the card-case and returned it with the other things to the pockets of the Burberry. Then, as nothing more suggested itself, I walked back to my house for breakfast, having first arranged that the base of the cliffs should be thoroughly searched.

Stackhurst was round in an hour or two to tell me that the body had been removed to The Gables, where the inquest would be held. He brought with him some serious and definite news. As I expected, nothing had been found in the small caves below the cliff, but he had examined the papers in McPherson's desk, and there were several which showed an intimate correspondence with a certain Miss Maud Bellamy, of Fulworth. We had then established the identity of the writer of the note.

"The police have the letters," he explained. "I could not bring them. But there is no doubt that it was a serious love affair. I see no reason, however, to connect it with that horrible happening save, indeed, that the lady had made an appointment with him."

"But hardly at a bathing-pool which all of you were in the habit of using," I remarked.

"It is mere chance," said he, "that several of the students were not with McPherson."

"*Was* it mere chance?"

Stackhurst knit his brows in thought.

"Ian Murdoch held them back," said he. "He would insist upon some algebraic demonstration before breakfast. Poor chap, he is dreadfully cut up about it all."

"And yet I gather that they were not friends."

"At one time they were not. But for a year or more Murdoch has been as near to McPherson as he ever could be to anyone. He is not of a very sympathetic disposition by nature."

"So I understand. I seem to remember your telling me once about a quarrel over the ill-usage of a dog."

"That blew over all right."

"But left some vindictive feeling, perhaps."

"No, no, I am sure they were real friends."

"Well, then, we must explore the matter of the girl. Do you know her?"

"Everyone knows her. She is the beauty of the neighbourhood—a real beauty, Holmes, who would draw attention everywhere. I knew that McPherson was attracted by her, but I had no notion that it had gone so far as these letters would seem to indicate."

"But who is she?"

"She is the daughter of old Tom Bellamy, who owns all the boats and bathing-cots at Fulworth. He was a fisherman to start with, but is now a man of some substance. He and his son William run the business."

"Shall we walk into Fulworth and see them?"

"On what pretext?"

"Oh, we can easily find a pretext. After all, this poor man did not ill-use himself in this outrageous way. Some human hand was on the middle of that scourge, if indeed it was a scourge which inflicted the injuries. His circle of acquaintances in this lonely place was surely limited. Let us follow it up in every direction and we can hardly fail to come upon the motive, which in turn should lead us to the criminal."

It would have been a pleasant walk across the thyme-scented downs had our minds not been poisoned by the tragedy we had witnessed. The village of Fulworth lies in a hollow curving in a semicircle round the bay. Behind the old-fashioned hamlet several modern houses have been built upon the rising ground. It was to one of these that Stackhurst guided me.

"That's The Haven, as Bellamy called it. The one with the corner tower and slate roof. Not bad for a man who started with nothing but—By Jove, look at that!"

The garden gate of The Haven had opened and a man had emerged. There was no mistaking that tall, angular, straggling figure. It was Ian Murdoch, the mathematician. A moment later we confronted him upon the road.

"Hullo!" said Stackhurst. The man nodded, gave us a sideways glance from his curious dark eyes, and would have passed us, but his principal pulled him up.

"What were you doing there?" he asked.

Murdoch's face flushed with anger. "I am your subordinate, sir, under your roof. I am not aware that I owe you any account of my private actions."

Stackhurst's nerves were near the surface after all he had endured. Otherwise, perhaps, he would have waited. Now he lost his temper completely.

"In the circumstances your answer is pure impertinence, Mr. Murdoch."

"Your own question might perhaps come under the same heading."

"This is not the first time that I have had to overlook your insubordinate ways. It will certainly be the last. You will kindly make fresh arrangements for your future as speedily as you can."

"I had intended to do so. I have lost to-day the only person who made The Gables habitable."

He strode off upon his way, while Stackhurst, with angry eyes, stood glaring after him. "Is he not an impossible, intolerable man?" he cried.

The one thing that impressed itself forcibly upon my mind was that Mr. Ian Murdoch was taking the first chance to open a path of escape from the scene of the crime. Suspicion, vague and nebulous, was now beginning to take outline in my mind. Perhaps the visit to the Bellamys might throw some further light upon the matter. Stackhurst pulled himself together, and we went forward to the house.

Mr. Bellamy proved to be a middle-aged man with a flaming red beard. He seemed to be in a very angry mood, and his face was soon as florid as his hair.

"No, sir, I do not desire any particulars. My son here"—indicating a powerful young man, with a heavy, sullen face, in the corner of the sitting-room—"is of one mind with me that Mr. McPherson's attentions to Maud were insulting. Yes, sir, the word 'marriage' was never mentioned, and yet there were letters and meetings, and a great deal more of which neither of us could approve. She has no mother, and we are her only guardians. We are determined—"

But the words were taken from his mouth by the appearance of the lady herself. There was no gainsaying that she would have graced any assembly in the world. Who could have imagined that so rare a flower would grow from such a root and in such an atmosphere? Women have seldom been an attraction to me, for my brain has always governed my heart, but I could not look upon her perfect clear-cut face, with all the soft freshness of the downlands in her delicate colouring, without realizing that no young man would cross her path unscathed. Such was the girl who had pushed open the door and stood now, wide-eyed and intense, in front of Harold Stackhurst.

"I know already that Fitzroy is dead," she said. "Do not be afraid to tell me the particulars."

"This other gentleman of yours let us know the news," explained the father.

"There is no reason why my sister should be brought into the matter," growled the younger man.

The sister turned a sharp, fierce look upon him. "This is my business, William. Kindly leave me to manage it in my own way. By all accounts there has been a crime committed. If I can help to show who did it, it is the least I can do for him who is gone."

She listened to a short account from my companion, with a composed concentration which showed me that she possessed strong character as well as great beauty. Maud Bellamy will always remain in my memory as a most complete and remarkable woman. It seems that she already knew me by sight, for she turned to me at the end.

"Bring them to justice, Mr. Holmes. You have my sympathy and my help, whoever they may be." It seemed to me that she glanced defiantly at her father and brother as she spoke.

"Thank you," said I. "I value a woman's instinct in such matters. You use the word 'they.' You think that more than one was concerned?"

"I knew Mr. McPherson well enough to be aware that he was a brave and a strong man. No single person could ever have inflicted such an outrage upon him."

"Might I have one word with you alone?"

"I tell you, Maud, not to mix yourself up in the matter," cried her father angrily.

She looked at me helplessly. "What can I do?"

"The whole world will know the facts presently, so there can be no harm if I discuss them here," said I. "I should have preferred privacy, but if your father will not allow it he must share the deliberations." Then I spoke of the note which had been found in the dead man's pocket. "It is sure to be produced at the inquest. May I ask you to throw any light upon it that you can?"

"I see no reason for mystery," she answered. "We were

engaged to be married, and we only kept it secret because Fitzroy's uncle, who is very old and said to be dying, might have disinherited him if he had married against his wish. There was no other reason."

"You could have told us," growled Mr. Bellamy.

"So I would, Father, if you had ever shown sympathy."

"I object to my girl picking up with men outside her own station."

"It was your prejudice against him which prevented us from telling you. As to this appointment"—she fumbled in her dress and produced a crumpled note—"it was in answer to this."

DEAREST [ran the message]:
The old place on the beach just after sunset on Tuesday. It is the only time I can get away.

F. M.

"Tuesday was to-day, and I had meant to meet him to-night."

I turned over the paper. "This never came by post. How did you get it?"

"I would rather not answer that question. It has really nothing to do with the matter which you are investigating. But anything which bears upon that I will most freely answer."

She was as good as her word, but there was nothing which was helpful in our investigation. She had no reason to think that her fiancé had any hidden enemy, but she admitted that she had had several warm admirers.

"May I ask if Mr. Ian Murdoch was one of them?"

She blushed and seemed confused.

"There was a time when I thought he was. But that was all changed when he understood the relations between Fitzroy and myself."

Again the shadow round this strange man seemed to me to be taking more definite shape. His record must be examined. His rooms must be privately searched. Stackhurst was a willing collaborator, for in his mind also suspicions were forming. We returned from our visit to The Haven with the hope that one free end of this tangled skein was already in our hands.

A week passed. The inquest had thrown no light upon the matter and had been adjourned for further evidence. Stackhurst had made discreet inquiry about his subordinate, and there had been a superficial search of his room, but without result. Personally, I had gone over the whole ground again, both physically and mentally, but with no new conclusions. In all my chronicles the reader will find no case which brought me so completely to the limit of my powers. Even my imagination could conceive no solution to the mystery. And then there came the incident of the dog.

It was my old housekeeper who heard of it first by that strange wireless by which such people collect the news of the countryside.

"Sad story this, sir, about Mr. McPherson's dog," said she one evening.

I do not encourage such conversations, but the words arrested my attention.

"What of Mr. McPherson's dog?"

"Dead, sir. Died of grief for its master."

"Who told you this?"

"Why sir, everyone is talking of it. It took on terrible, and has eaten nothing for a week. Then to-day two of the young gentlemen from The Gables found it dead—down the beach, sir, at the very place where its master met his end."

"At the very place." The words stood out clear in my memory. Some dim perception that the matter was vital rose in my mind. That the dog should die was after the beautiful, faithful nature of dogs. But "in the very place"! Why should this lonely beach be fatal to it? Was it possible that it also had been sacrificed to some revengeful feud? Was it possible—? Yes, the perception was dim, but already something was building up in my mind. In a few minutes I was on my way to The Gables, where I found

Stackhurst in his study. At my request he sent for Sudbury and Blount, the two students who had found the dog.

"Yes, it lay on the very edge of the pool," said one of them. "It must have followed the trail of its dead master."

I saw the faithful little creature, an Airedale terrier, laid out upon the mat in the hall. The body was stiff and rigid, the eyes projecting, and the limbs contorted. There was agony in every line of it.

From The Gables I walked down to the bathing-pool. The sun had sunk and the shadow of the great cliff lay black across the water, which glimmered dully like a sheet of lead. The place was deserted and there was no sign of life save for two sea-birds circling and screaming over-head. In the fading light I could dimly make out the little dog's spoor upon the sand round the very rock on which his master's towel had been laid. For a long time I stood in deep meditation while the shadows grew darker around me. My mind was filled with racing thoughts. You have known what it was to be in a nightmare in which you feel that there is some all-important thing for which you search and which you know is there, though it remains forever just beyond your reach. That was how I felt that evening as I stood alone by that place of death. Then at last I turned and walked slowly homeward.

I had just reached the top of the path when it came to me. Like a flash. I remembered the thing for which I had so eagerly and vainly grasped. You will know, or Watson has written in vain, that I hold a vast store of out-of-the-way knowledge without scientific system, but very available for the needs of my work. My mind is like a crowded box-room with packets of all sorts stowed away therein—so many that I may well have but a vague perception of what was there. I had known that there was something which might bear upon this matter. It was still vague, but at least I knew how I could make it clear. It was monstrous, incredible, and yet it was always a possibility. I would test it to the full.

There is a great garret in my little house which is stuffed

with books. It was into this that I plunged and rummaged for an hour. At the end of that time I emerged with a little chocolate and silver volume. Eagerly I turned up the chapter of which I had a dim remembrance. Yes, it was indeed a far-fetched and unlikely proposition, and yet I could not be at rest until I had made sure if it might, indeed, be so. It was late when I retired, with my mind eagerly awaiting the work of the morrow.

But that work met with an annoying interruption. I had hardly swallowed my early cup of tea and was starting for the beach when I had a call from Inspector Bardle of the Sussex Constabulary—a steady, solid, bovine man with thoughtful eyes, which looked at me now with a very troubled expression.

"I know your immense experience, sir," said he. "This is quite unofficial, of course, and need go no farther. But I am fairly up against it in this McPherson case. The question is, shall I make an arrest, or shall I not?"

"Meaning Mr. Ian Murdoch?"

"Yes, sir. There is really no one else when you come to think of it. That's the advantage of this solitude. We narrow it down to a very small compass. If he did not do it, then who did?"

"What have you against him?"

He had gleaned along the same furrows as I had. There was Murdoch's character and the mystery which seemed to hang round the man. His furious bursts of temper, as shown in the incident of the dog. The fact that he had quarrelled with McPherson in the past, and that there was some reason to think that he might have resented his attentions to Miss Bellamy. He had all my points, but no fresh ones, save that Murdoch seemed to be making every preparation for departure.

"What would my position be if I let him slip away with all this evidence against him?" The burly, phlegmatic man was sorely troubled in his mind.

"Consider," I said, "all the essential gaps in your case. On the morning of the crime he can surely prove an alibi.

He had been with his scholars till the last moment, and within a few minutes of McPherson's appearance he came upon us from behind. Then bear in mind the absolute impossibility that he could single-handed have inflicted this outrage upon a man quite as strong as himself. Finally, there is this question of the instrument with which these injuries were inflicted."

"What could it be but a scourge or flexible whip of some sort?"

"Have you examined the marks?" I asked.

"I have seen them. So has the doctor."

"But I have examined them very carefully with a lens. They have peculiarities."

"What are they, Mr. Holmes?"

I stepped to my bureau and brought out an enlarged photograph. "This is my method in such cases," I explained.

"You certainly do things thoroughly, Mr. Holmes."

"I should hardly be what I am if I did not. Now let us consider this weal which extends round the right shoulder. Do you observe nothing remarkable?"

"I can't say I do."

"Surely it is evident that it is unequal in its intensity. There is a dot of extravasated blood here, and another there. There are similar indications in this other weal down here. What can that mean?"

"I have no idea. Have you?"

"Perhaps I have. Perhaps I haven't. I may be able to say more soon. Anything which will define what made that mark will bring us a long way towards the criminal."

"It is, of course, an absurd idea," said the policeman, "but if a red-hot net of wire had been laid across the back, then these better marked points would represent where the meshes crossed each other."

"A most ingenious comparison. Or shall we say a very stiff cat-o'-nine-tails with small hard knots upon it?"

"By Jove, Mr. Holmes, I think you have hit it."

"Or there may be some very different cause, Mr. Bardle.

619

But your case is far too weak for an arrest. Besides, we have those last words—the 'Lion's Mane.'"

"I have wondered whether Ian—"

"Yes, I have considered that. If the second word had borne any resemblance to Murdoch—but it did not. He gave it almost in a shriek. I am sure that it was 'Mane.'"

"Have you no alternative, Mr. Holmes?"

"Perhaps I have. But I do not care to discuss it until there is something more solid to discuss."

"And when will that be?"

"In an hour—possibly less."

The Inspector rubbed his chin and looked at me with dubious eyes.

"I wish I could see what was in your mind, Mr. Holmes. Perhaps it's those fishing-boats."

"No, no, they were too far out."

"Well, then, is it Bellamy and that big son of his? They were not too sweet upon Mr. McPherson. Could they have done him a mischief?"

"No, no, you won't draw me until I am ready," said I with a smile. "Now, Inspector, we each have our own work to do. Perhaps if you were to meet me here at midday—"

So far we had got when there came the tremendous interruption which was the beginning of the end.

My outer door was flung open, there were blundering footsteps in the passage, and Ian Murdoch staggered into the room, pallid, dishevelled, his clothes in wild disorder, clawing with his bony hands at the furniture to hold himself erect. "Brandy! Brandy!" he gasped, and fell groaning upon the sofa.

He was not alone. Behind him came Stackhurst, hatless and panting, almost as distrait as his companion.

"Yes, yes, brandy!" he cried. "The man is at his last gasp. It was all I could do to bring him here. He fainted twice upon the way."

Half a tumbler of the raw spirit brought about a wondrous change. He pushed himself up on one arm and swung his coat from his shoulders. "For God's sake, oil, opium, morphia!" he cried. "Anything to ease this infernal agony!"

The Inspector and I cried out at the sight. There, criss-crossed upon the man's naked shoulder, was the same strange reticulated pattern of red, inflamed lines which had been the death-mark of Fitzroy McPherson.

The pain was evidently terrible and was more than local, for the sufferer's breathing would stop for a time, his face would turn black, and then with loud gasps he would clap his hand to his heart, while his brow dropped beads of sweat. At any moment he might die. More and more brandy was poured down his throat, each fresh dose bringing him back to life. Pads of cotton-wool soaked in salad-oil seemed to take the agony from the strange wounds. At last his head fell heavily upon the cushion. Exhausted Nature had taken refuge in its last storehouse of vitality. It was half a sleep and half a faint, but at least it was ease from pain.

To question him had been impossible, but the moment we were assured of his condition Stackhurst turned upon me.

"My God!" he cried, "what is it, Holmes? What is it?"

"Where did you find him?"

"Down on the beach. Exactly where poor McPherson met his end. If this man's heart had been weak as McPherson's was, he would not be here now. More than once I thought he was gone as I brought him up. It was too far to The Gables, so I made for you."

"Did you see him on the beach?"

"I was walking on the cliff when I heard his cry. He was at the edge of the water, reeling about like a drunken man. I ran down, threw some clothes about him, and brought him up. For Heaven's sake, Holmes, use all the powers you have and spare no pains to lift the curse from this place, for life is becoming unendurable. Can you, with all your world-wide reputation, do nothing for us?"

"I think I can, Stackhurst. Come with me now! And you,

Inspector, come along! We will see if we cannot deliver this murderer into your hands."

Leaving the unconscious man in the charge of my housekeeper, we all three went down to the deadly lagoon. On the shingle there was piled a little heap of towels and clothes left by the stricken man. Slowly I walked round the edge of the water, my comrades in Indian file behind me. Most of the pool was quite shallow, but under the cliff where the beach was hollowed out it was four or five feet deep. It was to this part that a swimmer would naturally go, for it formed a beautiful pellucid green pool as clear as crystal. A line of rocks lay above it at the base of the cliff, and along this I led the way, peering eagerly into the depths beneath me. I had reached the deepest and stillest pool when my eyes caught that for which they were searching, and I burst into a shout of triumph.

"Cyanea!" I cried. "Cyanea! Behold the Lion's Mane!"

The strange object at which I pointed did indeed look like a tangled mass torn from the mane of a lion. It lay upon a rocky shelf some three feet under the water, a curious waving, vibrating, hairy creature with streaks of silver among its yellow tresses. It pulsated with a slow, heavy dilation and contraction.

"It has done mischief enough. Its day is over!" I cried. "Help me. Stackhurst! Let us end the murderer forever."

There was a big boulder just above the ledge, and we pushed it until it fell with a tremendous splash into the water. When the ripples had cleared we saw that it had settled upon the ledge below. One flapping edge of yellow membrane showed that our victim was beneath it. A thick oily scum oozed out from below the stone and stained the water round, rising slowly to the surface.

"Well, this gets me!" cried the Inspector. "What was it, Mr. Holmes? I'm born and bred in these parts, but I never saw such a thing. It don't belong to Sussex."

"Just as well for Sussex," I remarked. "It may have been the southwest gale that brought it up. Come back to my house, both of you, and I will give you the terrible experience of one who has good reason to remember his own meeting with the same peril of the seas."

When we reached my study we found that Murdoch was so far recovered that he could sit up. He was dazed in mind and every now and then was shaken by a paroxysm of pain. In broken words he explained that he had no notion what had occurred to him, save that terrific pangs had suddenly shot through him, and that it had taken all his fortitude to reach the bank.

"Here is a book," I said, taking up the little volume, "which first brought light into what might have been forever dark. It is *Out of Doors,* by the famous observer, J. G. Wood. Wood himself very nearly perished from contact with this vile creature, so he wrote with a very full knowledge. *Cyanea capillata* is the miscreant's full name, and he can be as dangerous to life as, and far more painful than, the bite of the cobra. Let me briefly give this extract.

"If the bather should see a loose roundish mass of tawny membranes and fibres, something like very large handfuls of lion's mane and silver paper, let him beware, for this is the fearful stinger, *Cyanea capillata.*

"Could our sinister acquaintance be more clearly described?

"He goes on to tell of his own encounter with one when swimming off the coast of Kent. He found that the creature radiated almost invisible filaments to the distance of fifty feet, and that anyone within that circumference from the deadly centre was in danger of death. Even at a distance the effect upon Wood was almost fatal.

"The multitudinous threads caused light scarlet lines upon the skin which on closer examination resolved into minute dots or pustules, each dot charged as it were with a red-hot needle making its way through the nerves.

"The local pain was, as he explains, the least part of the exquisite torment.

"Pangs shot through the chest, causing me to fall as if struck by a bullet. The pulsation would cease, and then the heart would give six or seven leaps as if it would force its way throught the chest.

"It nearly killed him, although he had only been exposed to it in the disturbed ocean and not in the narrow calm waters of a bathing-pool. He says that he could hardly recognise himself afterwards, so white, wrinkled, and shrivelled was his face. He gulped down brandy, a whole bottleful, and it seems to have saved his life. There is the book, Inspector. I leave it with you, and you cannot doubt that it contains a full explanation of the tragedy of poor McPherson."

"And incidentally exonerates me," remarked Ian Murdoch with a wry smile. "I do not blame you, Inspector, nor you, Mr. Holmes, for your suspicions were natural. I feel that on the very eve of my arrest I have only cleared myself by sharing the fate of my poor friend."

"No, Mr. Murdoch. I was already upon the track, and had I been out as early as I intended I might well have saved you from this terrific experience."

"But how did you know, Mr. Holmes?"

"I am an omnivorous reader with a strangely retentive memory for trifles. That phrase 'the Lion's Mane' haunted my mind. I knew that I had seen it somewhere in an unexpected context. You have seen that it does describe the creature. I have no doubt that it was floating on the water when McPherson saw it, and that this phrase was the only one by which he could convey to us a warning as to the creature which had been his death."

"Then I, at least, am cleared," said Murdoch, rising slowly to his feet. "There are one or two words of explanation which I should give, for I know the direction in which your inquiries have run. It is true that I loved this lady, but from the day when she chose my friend McPherson my one desire was to help her to happiness. I was well content to stand aside and act as their go-between. Often I carried their messages, and it was because I was in their confidence and because she was so dear to me that I hastened to tell her of my friend's death, lest someone should forestall me in a more sudden and heartless manner. She would not tell you, sir, of our relations lest you should disapprove and I might suffer. But with your leave I must try to get back to The Gables, for my bed will be very welcome."

Stackhurst held out his hand. "Our nerves have all been at concert-pitch," said he. "Forgive what is past, Murdoch. We shall understand each other better in the future." They passed out together with their arms linked in friendly fashion. The Inspector remained, staring at me in silence with his ox-like eyes.

"Well, you've done it!" he cried at last. "I had read of you, but I never believed it. It's wonderful!"

I was forced to shake my head. To accept such praise was to lower one's own standards.

"I was slow at the outset—culpably slow. Had the body been found in the water I could hardly have missed it. It was the towel which misled me. The poor fellow had never thought to dry himself, and so I in turn was led to believe that he had never been in the water. Why, then, should the attack of any water creature suggest itself to me? That was where I went astray. Well, well, Inspector, I often ventured to chaff you gentlemen of the police-force, but *Cyanea capillata* very nearly avenged Scotland Yard."

His Last Bow

An Epilogue of Sherlock Holmes

It was nine o'clock at night upon the second of August—the most terrible August in the history of the world. One might have thought already that God's curse hung heavy over a degenerate world, for there was an awesome hush and a feeling of vague expectancy in the sultry and stagnant air. The sun had long set, but one blood-red gash like an open wound lay low in the distant west. Above, the stars were shining brightly, and below, the lights of the shipping glimmered in the bay. The two famous Germans stood beside the stone parapet of the garden walk, with the long, low, heavily gabled house behind them, and they looked down upon the broad sweep of the beach at the foot of the great chalk cliff on which Von Bork, like some wandering eagle, had perched himself four years before. They stood with their heads close together, talking in low, confidential tones. From below the two glowing ends of their cigars might have been the smouldering eyes of some malignant fiend looking down in the darkness.

A remarkable man this Von Bork—a man who could hardly be matched among all the devoted agents of the Kaiser. It was his talents which had first recommended him for the English mission, the most important mission of all, but since he had taken it over those talents had become more and more manifest to the half-dozen people in the world who were really in touch with the truth. One of these was his present companion, Baron Von Herling, the Chief Secretary of the legation, whose huge 100-horse-power Benz car was blocking the country lane as it waited to waft its owner back to London.

"So far as I can judge the trend of events, you will probably be back in Berlin within the week," the Secretary was saying. "When you get there, my dear Von Bork, I think you will be surprised at the welcome you will receive. I happen to know what is thought in the highest quarters of your work in this country." He was a huge man, the Secretary, deep, broad, and tall, with a slow, heavy fashion of speech which had been his main asset in his political career.

Von Bork laughed.

"They are not very hard to deceive," he remarked. "A more docile, simple folk could not be imagined."

"I don't know about that," said the other thoughtfully. "They have strange limits and one must learn to observe them. It is that surface simplicity of theirs which makes a trap for the stranger. One's first impression is that they are entirely soft. Then one comes suddenly upon something very hard, and you know that you have reached the limit and must adapt yourself to the fact. They have, for example, their insular conventions which simply *must* be observed."

"Meaning, 'good form' and that sort of thing?" Von Bork sighed as one who had suffered much.

"Meaning British prejudice in all its queer manifestations. As an example I may quote one of my own worst blunders—I can afford to talk of my blunders, for you know my work well enough to be aware of my successes. It was on my first arrival. I was invited to a week-end gathering at the country house of a cabinet minister. The conversation was amazingly indiscreet."

Von Bork nodded. "I've been there," said he dryly.

"Exactly. Well, I naturally sent a résumé of the information to Berlin. Unfortunately our good Chancellor is a little heavy-handed in these matters, and he transmitted a remark which showed that he was aware of what had been said. This, of course, took the trail straight up to me.

You've no idea the harm that it did me. There was nothing soft about our British hosts on that occasion, I can assure you. I was two years living it down. Now you, with this sporting pose of yours—"

"No, no, don't call it a pose. A pose is an artificial thing. This is quite natural. I am a born sportsman. I enjoy it."

"Well, that makes it the more effective. You yacht against them, you hunt with them, you play polo, you match them in every game, your four-in-hand takes the prize at Olympia. I have even heard that you go the length of boxing with the young officers. What is the result? Nobody takes you seriously. You are a 'good old sport,' 'quite a decent fellow for a German,' a hard-drinking, night-club, knock-about-town, devil-may-care young fellow. And all the time this quiet country house of yours is the centre of half the mischief in England, and the sporting squire the most astute secret-service man in Europe. Genius, my dear Von Bork—genius!"

"You flatter me, Baron. But certainly I may claim that my four years in this country have not been unproductive. I've never shown you my little store. Would you mind stepping in for a moment?"

The door of the study opened straight on to the terrace. Von Bork pushed it back, and leading the way, he clicked the switch of the electric light. He then closed the door behind the bulky form which followed him and carefully adjusted the heavy curtain over the latticed window. Only when all these precautions had been taken and tested did he turn his sunburned aquiline face to his guest.

"Some of my papers have gone," said he. "When my wife and the household left yesterday for Flushing they took the less important with them. I must, of course, claim the protection of the Embassy for the others."

"Your name has already been filed as one of the personal suite. There will be no difficulties for you or your baggage. Of course, it is just possible that we may not have to go. England may leave France to her fate. We are sure that there is no binding treaty between them."

"And Belgium?"

"Yes, and Belgium, too."

Von Bork shook his head. "I don't see how that could be. There is a definite treaty there. She could never recover from such a humiliation."

"She would at least have peace for the moment."

"But her honour?"

"Tut, my dear sir, we live in a utilitarian age. Honour is a mediæval conception. Besides England is not ready. It is an inconceivable thing, but even our special war tax of fifty million, which one would think made our purpose as clear as if we had advertised it on the front page of the *Times,* has not roused these people from their slumbers. Here and there one hears a question. It is my business to find an answer. Here and there also there is an irritation. It is my business to soothe it. But I can assure you that so far as the essentials go—the storage of munitions, the preparation for submarine attack, the arrangements for making high explosives—nothing is prepared. How, then, can England come in, especially when we have stirred her up such a devil's brew of Irish civil war, window-breaking Furies, and God knows what to keep her thoughts at home."

"She must think of her future."

"Ah, that is another matter. I fancy that in the future we have our own very definite plans about England, and that your information will be very vital to us. It is to-day or to-morrow with Mr. John Bull. If he prefers to-day we are perfectly ready. If it is to-morrow we shall be more ready still. I should think they would be wiser to fight with allies than without them, but that is their own affair. This week is their week of destiny. But you were speaking of your papers." He sat in the armchair with the light shining upon his broad bald head, while he puffed sedately at his cigar.

The large oak-panelled, book-lined room had a curtain hung in the further corner. When this was drawn it disclosed a large, brass-bound safe. Von Bork detached a small key from his watch-chain, and after some considerable manipulation of the lock he swung open the heavy door.

SIR ARTHUR CONAN DOYLE

"Look!" said he, standing clear, with a wave of his hand.

The light shone vividly into the opened safe, and the Secretary of the Embassy gazed with an absorbed interest at the rows of stuffed pigeon-holes with which it was furnished. Each pigeon-hole had its label, and his eyes as he glanced along them read a long series of such titles as "Fords," "Harbour-defences," "Aeroplanes," "Ireland," "Egypt," "Portsmouth forts," "The Channel," "Rosythe," and a score of others. Each compartment was bristling with papers and plans.

"Colossal!" said the Secretary. Putting down his cigar he softly clapped his fat hands.

"And all in four years, Baron. Not such a bad show for the hard-drinking, hard-riding country squire. But the gem of my collection is coming and there is the setting all ready for it." He pointed to a space over which "Naval Signals" was printed.

"But you have a good dossier there already."

"Out of date and waste paper. The Admiralty in some way got the alarm and every code has been changed. It was a blow, Baron—the worst setback in my whole campaign. But thanks to my check-book and the good Altamont all will be well to-night."

The Baron looked at his watch and gave a guttural exclamation of disappointment.

"Well, I really can wait no longer. You can imagine that things are moving at present in Carlton Terrace and that we have all to be at our posts. I had hoped to be able to bring news of your great coup. Did Altamont name no hour?"

Von Bork pushed over a telegram.

Will come without fail to-night and bring new sparking plugs.

ALTAMONT.

"Sparking plugs, eh?"

"You see he poses as a motor expert and I keep a full garage. In our code everything likely to come up is named

630

after some spare part. If he talks of a radiator it is a battle-ship, of an oil pump a cruiser, and so on. Sparking plugs are naval signals."

"From Portsmouth at midday," said the Secretary, ex-amining the superscription. "By the way, what do you give him?"

"Five hundred pounds for this particular job. Of course he has a salary as well."

"The greedy rogue. They are useful, these traitors, but I grudge them their blood money."

"I grudge Altamont nothing. He is a wonderful worker. If I pay him well, at least he delivers the goods, to use his own phrase. Besides he is not a traitor. I assure you that our most pan-Germanic Junker is a sucking dove in his feelings towards England as compared with a real bitter Irish-American."

"Oh, an Irish-American?"

"If you heard him talk you would not doubt it. Some-times I assure you I can hardly understand him. He seems to have declared war on the King's English as well as on the English King. Must you really go? He may be here any moment."

"No. I'm sorry, but I have already overstayed my time. We shall expect you early to-morrow, and when you get that signal book through the little door on the Duke of York's steps you can put a triumphant finis to your record in England. What! Tokay!" He indicated a heavily sealed dust-covered bottle which stood with two high glasses upon a salver.

"May I offer you a glass before your journey?"

"No, thanks. But it looks like revelry."

"Altamont has a nice taste in wines, and he took a fancy to my Tokay. He is a touchy fellow and needs humouring in small things. I have to study him, I assure you." They had strolled out on to the terrace again, and along it to the further end where at a touch from the Baron's chauffeur the great car shivered and chuckled. "Those are the lights of Harwich, I suppose," said the Secretary, pulling on his dust coat. "How still and peaceful it all seems. There may be other lights within the week, and the English coast a less tranquil place! The Heavens, too, may not be quite so peaceful if all that the good Zeppelin promises us comes true. By the way, who is that?"

Only one window showed a light behind them; in it there stood a lamp, and beside it, seated at a table, was a dear old ruddy-faced woman in a country cap. She was bending over her knitting and stopping occasionally to stroke a large black cat upon a stool beside her.

"That is Martha, the only servant I have left."

The Secretary chuckled.

"She might almost personify Britannia," said he, "with her complete self-absorption and general air of comfortable somnolence. Well, *au revoir,* Von Bork!" With a final wave of his hand he sprang into the car, and a moment later the two golden cones from the headlights shot forward through the darkness. The Secretary lay back in the cushions of the luxurious limousine, with his thoughts so full of the impending European tragedy that he hardly observed that as his car swung round the village street it nearly passed over a little Ford coming in the opposite direction.

Von Bork walked slowly back to the study when the last gleams of the motor lamps had faded into the distance. As he passed he observed that his old housekeeper had put out her lamp and retired. It was a new experience to him, the silence and darkness of his widespread house, for his family and household had been a large one. It was a relief to him, however, to think that they were all in safety and that, but for that one old woman who had lingered in the kitchen, he had the whole place to himself. There was a good deal of tidying up to do inside his study and he set himself to do it until his keen, handsome face was flushed with the heat of the burning papers. A leather valise stood beside his table, and into this he began to pack very neatly and systematically the precious contents of his safe. He had hardly got started with the work, however, when his quick ears caught the sound of a distant car. Instantly he

632

gave an exclamation of satisfaction, strapped up the valise, shut the safe, locked it, and hurried out on to the terrace. He was just in time to see the lights of a small car come to a halt at the gate. A passenger sprang out of it and advanced swiftly towards him, while the chauffeur, a heavily built, elderly man with a grey moustache, settled down like one who resigns himself to a long vigil.

"Well?" asked Von Bork eagerly, running forward to meet his visitor.

For answer the man waved a small brown-paper parcel triumphantly above his head.

"You can give me the glad hand to-night, mister," he cried. "I'm bringing home the bacon at last."

"The signals?"

"Same as I said in my cable. Every last one of them, semaphore, lamp code, Marconi—a copy, mind you, not the original. That was too dangerous. But it's the real goods, and you can lay to that." He slapped the German upon the shoulder with a rough familiarity from which the other winced.

"Come in," he said. "I'm all alone in the house. I was only waiting for this. Of course a copy is better than the original. If an original were missing they would change the whole thing. You think it's all safe about the copy?"

The Irish-American had entered the study and stretched his long limbs from the armchair. He was a tall, gaunt man of sixty, with clear-cut features and a small goatee beard which gave him a general resemblance to the caricatures of Uncle Sam. A half-smoked, sodden cigar hung from the corner of his mouth, and as he sat down he struck a match and relit it. "Making ready for a move?" he remarked as he looked round him. "Say, mister," he added, as his eyes fell upon the safe from which the curtain was now removed, "You don't tell me you keep your papers in that?"

"Why not?"

"Gosh, in a wide-open contraption like that! And they reckon you to be some spy. Why, a Yankee crook would be into that with a can-opener. If I'd known that any letter of mine was goin' to lie loose in a thing like that I'd have been a mug to write to you at all."

"It would puzzle any crook to force that safe," Von Bork answered. "You won't cut that metal with any tool."

"But the lock?"

"No, it's a double combination lock. You know what that is?"

"Search me," said the American.

"Well, you need a word as well as a set of figures before you can get the lock to work." He rose and showed a double-radiating disc round the keyhole. "This outer one is for the letters, the inner one for the figures."

"Well, well, that's fine."

"So it's not quite as simple as you thought. It was four years ago that I had it made, and what do you think I chose for the word and figures?"

"It's beyond me."

"Well, I chose August for the word, and 1914 for the figures, and here we are."

The American's face showed his surprise and admiration.

"My, but that was smart! You had it down to a fine thing."

"Yes, a few of us even then could have guessed the date. Here it is, and I'm shutting down to-morrow morning."

"Well, I guess you'll have to fix me up also. I'm not staying in this gol-darned country all on my lonesome. In a week or less, from what I see, John Bull will be on his hind legs and fair ramping. I'd rather watch him from over the water."

"But you're an American citizen?"

"Well, so was Jack James an American citizen, but he's doing time in Portland all the same. It cuts no ice with a British copper to tell him you're an American citizen. 'It's British law and order over here,' says he. By the way, mister, talking of Jack James, it seems to me you don't do much to cover your men."

"What do you mean?" Von Bork asked sharply.

"Well, you are their employer, ain't you? It's up to you to

see that they don't fall down. But they do fall down, and when did you ever pick them up? There's James—"

"It was James's own fault. You know that yourself. He was too self-willed for the job."

"James was a bonehead—I give you that. Then there was Hollis."

"The man was mad."

"Well, he went a bit woozy towards the end. It's enough to make a man bughouse when he has to play a part from morning to night with a hundred guys all ready to set the coppers wise to him. But now there is Steiner—"

Von Bork started violently, and his ruddy face turned a shade paler.

"What about Steiner?"

"Well, they've got him, that's all. They raided his store last night, and he and his papers are all in Portsmouth jail. You'll go off and he, poor devil, will have to stand the racket, and lucky if he gets off with his life. That's why I want to get over the water as soon as you do."

Von Bork was a strong, self-contained man, but it was easy to see that the news had shaken him.

"How could they have got on to Steiner?" he muttered. "That's the worst blow yet."

"Well, you nearly had a worse one, for I believe they are not far off me."

"You don't mean that!"

"Sure thing. My landlady down Fratton way had some inquiries, and when I heard of it I guessed it was time for me to hustle. But what I want to know, mister is how the coppers know these things? Steiner is the fifth man you've lost since I signed on with you, and I know the name of the sixth if I don't get a move on. How do you explain it, and ain't you ashamed to see your men go down like this?"

Von Bork flushed crimson.

"How dare you speak in such a way!"

"If I didn't dare things, mister, I wouldn't be in your service. But I'll tell you straight what is in my mind. I've heard that with you German politicians when an agent has done his work you are not sorry to see him put away."

Von Bork sprang to his feet.

"Do you dare to suggest that I have given away my own agents!"

"I don't stand for that, mister, but there's a stool pigeon or a cross somewhere, and it's up to you to find out where it is. Anyhow I am taking no more chances. It's me for little Holland, and the sooner the better."

Von Bork had mastered his anger.

"We have been allies too long to quarrel now at the very hour of victory," he said. "You've done splendid work and taken risks, and I can't forget it. By all means go to Holland, and you can get a boat from Rotterdam to New York. No other line will be safe a week from now. I'll take that book and pack it with the rest."

The American held the small parcel in his hand, but made no motion to give it up.

"What about the dough?" he asked.

"The what?"

"The boodle. The reward. The five hundred pounds. The gunner turned damned nasty at the last, and I had to square him with an extra hundred dollars or it would have been nitsky for you and me. 'Nothin' doin'!' says he, and he meant it, too, but the last hundred did it. It's cost me two hundred pound from first to last, so it isn't likely I'd give it up without gettin' my wad."

Von Bork smiled with some bitterness. "You don't seem to have a very high opinion of my honour," said he, "you want the money before you give up the book."

"Well, mister, it is a business proposition."

"All right. Have your way." He sat down at the table and scribbled a check, which he tore from the book, but he refrained from handing it to his companion. "After all, since we are to be on such terms, Mr. Altamont," said he, "I don't see why I should trust you any more than you trust me. Do you understand?" he added, looking back over his shoulder at the American. "There's the check upon the table. I claim the right to examine that parcel before you pick the money up."

636

The American passed it over without a word. Von Bork undid a winding of string and two wrappers of paper. Then he sat gazing for a moment in silent amazement at a small blue book which lay before him. Across the cover was printed in golden letters *Practical Handbook of Bee Culture*. Only for one instant did the master spy glare at this strangely irrelevant inscription. The next he was gripped at the back of his neck by a grasp of iron, and a chloroformed sponge was held in front of his writhing face.

"Another glass, Watson!" said Mr. Sherlock Holmes as he extended the bottle of Imperial Tokay.

The thickset chauffeur, who had seated himself by the table, pushed forward his glass with some eagerness.

"It is a good wine, Holmes."

"A remarkable wine, Watson. Our friend upon the sofa has assured me that it is from Franz Josef's special cellar at the Schoenbrunn Palace. Might I trouble you to open the window, for chloroform vapour does not help the palate."

The safe was ajar, and Holmes standing in front of it was removing dossier after dossier, swiftly examining each, and then packing it neatly in Von Bork's valise. The German lay upon the sofa sleeping stertorously with a strap round his upper arms and another round his legs.

"We need not hurry ourselves, Watson. We are safe from interruption. Would you mind touching the bell? There is no one in the house except old Martha, who has played her part to admiration. I got her the situation here when first I took the matter up. Ah, Martha, you will be glad to hear that all is well."

The pleasant old lady had appeared in the doorway. She curtseyed with a smile to Mr. Holmes, but glanced with some apprehension at the figure upon the sofa.

"It is all right, Martha. He has not been hurt at all."

"I am glad of that, Mr. Holmes. According to his lights he has been a kind master. He wanted me to go with his wife to Germany yesterday, but that would hardly have suited your plans, would it, sir?"

"No, indeed, Martha. So long as you were here I was

easy in my mind. We waited some time for your signal to-night."

"It was the Secretary, sir."

"I know. His car passed ours."

"I thought he would never go. I knew that it would not suit your plans, sir, to find him here."

"No, indeed. Well, it only meant that we waited half an hour or so until I saw your lamp go out and knew that the coast was clear. You can report to me to-morrow in London, Martha, at Claridge's Hotel."

"Very good, sir."

"I suppose you have everything ready to leave."

"Yes, sir. He posted seven letters to-day. I have the addresses as usual."

"Very good, Martha. I will look into them to-morrow. Good-night. These papers," he continued as the old lady vanished, "are not of very great importance, for, of course, the information which they represent has been sent off long ago to the German government. These are the originals which could not safely be got out of the country."

"Then they are of no use."

"I should not go so far as to say that, Watson. They will at least show our people what is known and what is not. I may say that a good many of these papers have come through me, and I need not add are thoroughly untrustworthy. It would brighten my declining years to see a German cruiser navigating the Solent according to the mine-field plans which I have furnished. But you, Watson"—he stopped his work and took his old friend by the shoulders—"I've hardly seen you in the light yet. How have the years used you? You look the same blithe boy as ever."

"I feel twenty years younger, Holmes. I have seldom felt so happy as when I got your wire asking me to meet you at Harwich with the car. But you, Holmes—you have changed very little—save for that horrible goatee."

"These are the sacrifices one makes for one's country, Watson," said Holmes, pulling at his little tuft. "To-morrow it will be but a dreadful memory. With my hair cut and a few other superficial changes I shall no doubt reappear at Claridge's to-morrow as I was before this American stunt—I beg your pardon, Watson, my well of English seems to be permanently defiled—before this American job came my way."

"But you have retired, Holmes. We have heard of you as living the life of a hermit among your bees and your books in a small farm upon the South Downs."

"Exactly, Watson. Here is the fruit of my leisured ease, the *magnum opus* of my latter years!" He picked up the volume from the table and read out the whole title, *Practical Handbook of Bee Culture, with Some Observations upon the Segregation of the Queen.* "Alone I did it. Behold the fruit of pensive nights and laborious days when I watched the little working gangs as once I watched the criminal world of London."

"But how did you get to work again?"

"Ah, I have often marvelled at it myself. The Foreign Minister alone I could have withstood, but when the Premier also deigned to visit my humble roof—! The fact is, Watson, that this gentleman upon the sofa was a bit too good for our people. He was in a class by himself. Things were going wrong, and no one could understand why they were going wrong. Agents were suspected or even caught, but there was evidence of some strong and secret central force. It was absolutely necessary to expose it. Strong pressure was brought upon me to look into the matter. It has cost me two years, Watson, but they have not been devoid of excitement. When I say that I started my pilgrimage at Chicago, graduated in an Irish secret society at Buffalo, gave serious trouble to the constabulary at Skibbareen, and so eventually caught the eye of a subordinate agent of Von Bork, who recommended me as a likely man, you will realize that the matter was complex. Since then I have been honoured by his confidence, which has not prevented most of his plans going subtly wrong and five of his best agents being in prison. I watched them, Watson, and I picked them as they ripened. Well, sir, I hope that you are none the worse!"

The last remark was addressed to Von Bork himself, who after much gasping and blinking had lain quietly listening to Holmes's statement. He broke out now into a furious stream of German invective, his face convulsed with passion. Holmes continued his swift investigation of documents while his prisoner cursed and swore.

"Though unmusical, German is the most expressive of all languages," he observed when Von Bork had stopped from pure exhaustion. "Hullo! Hullo!" he added as he looked hard at the corner of a tracing before putting it in the box. "This should put another bird in the cage. I had no idea that the paymaster was such a rascal, though I have long had an eye upon him. Mister Von Bork, you have a great deal to answer for."

The prisoner had raised himself with some difficulty upon the sofa and was staring with a strange mixture of amazement and hatred at his captor.

"I shall get level with you, Altamont," he said, speaking with slow deliberation. "If it takes me all my life I shall get level with you!"

"The old sweet song," said Holmes. "How often have I heard it in days gone by. It was a favourite ditty of the late lamented Professor Moriarty. Colonel Sebastian Moran has also been known to warble it. And yet I live and keep bees upon the South Downs."

"Curse you, you double traitor!" cried the German, straining against his bonds and glaring murder from his furious eyes.

"No, no, it is not so bad as that," said Holmes, smiling. "As my speech surely shows you, Mr. Altamont of Chicago had no existence in fact. I used him and he is gone."

"Then who are you?"

"It is really immaterial who I am, but since the matter seems to interest you, Mr. Von Bork, I may say that this is not my first acquaintance with the members of your family. I have done a good deal of business in Germany in the past and my name is probably familiar to you."

"I would wish to know it," said the Prussian grimly.

"It was I who brought the separation between Irene Adler and the late King of Bohemia when your cousin Heinrich was the Imperial Envoy. It was I also who saved from murder, by the Nihilist Klopman, Count Von und Zu Grafenstein, who was your mother's elder brother. It was I—"

Von Bork sat up in amazement.

"There is only one man," he cried.

"Exactly," said Holmes.

Von Bork groaned and sank back on the sofa. "And most of that information came through you," he cried. "What is it worth? What have I done? It is my ruin forever!"

"It is certainly a little untrustworthy," said Holmes. "It will require some checking and you have little time to check it. Your Admiral may find the new guns rather larger than he expects, and the cruisers perhaps a trifle faster."

Von Bork clutched at his own throat in despair.

"There are a good many other points of detail which will, no doubt, come to light in good time. But you have one quality which is very rare in a German, Mr. Von Bork: you are a sportsman and you will bear me no ill-will when you realize that you, who have outwitted so many other people, have at last been outwitted yourself. After all, you have done your best for your country, and I have done my best for mine, and what could be more natural? Besides," he added, not unkindly, as he laid his hand upon the shoulder of the prostrate man, "it is better than to fall before some more ignoble foe. These papers are now ready, Watson. If you will help me with our prisoner, I think that we may get started for London at once."

It was no easy task to move Von Bork, for he was a strong and a desperate man. Finally, holding either arm, the two friends walked him very slowly down the garden walk which he had trod with such proud confidence when he received the congratulations of the famous diplomatist only a few hours before. After a short, final struggle he was hoisted, still bound hand and foot, into the spare seat of the little car. His precious valise was wedged in beside him.

"I trust that you are as comfortable as circumstances permit," said Holmes when the final arrangements were made. "Should I be guilty of a liberty if I lit a cigar and placed it between your lips?"

But all amenities were wasted upon the angry German.

"I suppose you realize, Mr. Sherlock Holmes," said he, "that if your government bears you out in this treatment it becomes an act of war."

"What about your government and all this treatment?" said Holmes, tapping the valise.

"You are a private individual. You have no warrant for my arrest. The whole proceeding is absolutely illegal and outrageous."

"Absolutely," said Holmes.

"Kidnapping a German subject."

"And stealing his private papers."

"Well, you realize your position, you and your accomplice here. If I were to shout for help as we pass through the village—"

"My dear sir, if you did anything so foolish you would probably enlarge the two limited titles of our village inns by giving us 'The Dangling Prussian' as a signpost. The Englishman is a patient creature, but at present his temper is a little inflamed, and it would be as well not to try him too far. No, Mr. Von Bork, you will go with us in a quiet, sensible fashion to Scotland Yard, whence you can send for your friend, Baron Von Herling, and see if even now you may not fill that place which he has reserved for you in the ambassadorial suite. As to you, Watson, you are joining us with your old service, as I understand, so London won't be out of your way. Stand with me here upon the terrace, for it may be the last quiet talk that we shall ever have."

The two friends chatted in intimate converse for a few minutes, recalling once again the days of the past, while their prisoner vainly wriggled to undo the bonds that held him. As they turned to the car Holmes pointed back to the moonlit sea and shook a thoughtful head.

"There's an east wind coming, Watson."

"I think not, Holmes. It is very warm."

"Good old Watson! You are the one fixed point in a changing age. There's an east wind coming all the same, such a wind as never blew on England yet. It will be cold and bitter, Watson, and a good many of us may wither before its blast. But it's God's own wind none the less, and a cleaner, better, stronger land will lie in the sunshine when the storm has cleared. Start her up, Watson, for it's time that we were on our way. I have a check for five hundred pounds which should be cashed early, for the drawer is quite capable of stopping it if he can."